The Mexican government was in shambles, the financial markets had collapsed, the rich had become the middle-class, and poor were now destitute. With no hope in sight, a massive wave of humanity trudged toward what they envisioned would be their salvation, America. As the border with the US buckled under the weight of humankind, with individuals seeking the freedom of US citizenship and the promise of entitlement-rich lives, confrontation was inevitable. Suddenly, American households throughout the southwest found themselves in a struggle to protect themselves as they encountered the sheer brute force of the now, starving Mexicans. With an inept and corrupt administration in Washington, the border states floundered in their attempt to defend their citizenry. Decades of American politicians using the immigration problems at the US-Mexico border as a political bargaining chip had left those federal agencies whose responsibility it was to secure the border, useless in dealing with the invasion. As the invasion progressed further and further into the United States, the Walther brothers, each living in a different border state, were severely impacted. With no hope in sight, the brothers struggled for their very existence while the emotions of love and loss consumed them.

Just When You Thought It Was Safe

The Invasion of America

Douglas Schulz

ISBN: 0-9963254-1-7

DEDICATION

This book is dedicated to my father, Colonel Robert H. Schulz, who died in 2014 at age 97. He was a highly decorated World War II hero who participated in the Normandy Invasion. The following are a few of the many distinguished awards and medals he received during his military career - Distinguished Service Cross, Distinguished Service Medal, Silver Star, two Bronze Stars, Legion of Merit, Belgium Croix De Guerre, Belgium Officer Order of the Crown, and French Croix De Guerre. He was a special guest of the country of France on the 50th anniversary of the Normandy D-Day invasion and was the representative of the United States Army at the event. He spent 30 years in the US Army and was responsible for designing the Army aviation helicopter program in Vietnam. He spent the last nine years of active duty stationed at the Pentagon on the General Staff. He was a wonderful husband to my mother and an excellent father to his four sons. He was a great inspiration to me in everything I've accomplished.

ACKNOWLEDGMENTS

This book would never have come to fruition if not for the dedicated help of my wife, Tracy Pride Stoneman, and Paul Peters, one of my best friends. Both Tracy and Paul put in countless hours editing the book and being my sounding board throughout the demanding process.

AUTHOR'S PREFACE

I spent most of my youth growing up in the Northern Virginia suburbs of Washington, D.C. In the summer of 1969 my father retired from the Pentagon and we moved to Roswell, New Mexico where my father was the Commandant of the New Mexico Military Institute. Our family moved in 1969 from an upper-middle-class, all-white neighborhood where I attended an all-white high school to a small town in New Mexico where the greatest percentage of the population was Hispanic. The transition was quite an education for a 16-year-old. My high school girlfriend was Hispanic. I returned to Washington, D.C. and graduated from American University. I returned once again to New Mexico, where I was a Special Investigator for the New Mexico State Public defender's office in Albuquerque. For the rest of my life, I have lived in the Southwest.

Over the decades, I have traveled extensively to Mexico, Central America, and Canada. I have always been intrigued by the fact that when one steps across the border from the United States into Mexico, it might as well be Kathmandu, Nepal. Yet when you cross into Canada, you never feel you left the United States.

My degree from American University was in the Administration of Justice, a combination of criminology and pre-law. The majority of my career has been in finance and white-collar crime, and I've always been fascinated by the lawlessness associated with the US-Mexico border.

In 2002 after completing my first book, *Brokerage Fraud: What Wall Street Doesn't Want You to Know*, a nonfiction on Wall Street and the investment community, I decided it was time to write a book that addressed two of my writing passions - a wonderful, intriguing fiction combined with a historical and political novel addressing the decades-long problem at the US-Mexico border.

One of the most amazing things about writing this book was that I anticipated having to manufacture stories to support why the country of Mexico and its economy were imploding. Yet in almost every incident, my extensive research found that I didn't need to make up those facts. The reality is, Mexico has been teetering on implosion for a decade. Though this is a fiction novel, 90% of the facts about Mexico and the border issues are true. For those of you who love a historical novel, I think this book is for you. For those of you who like a thriller, I think you will find this political thriller captivating and hard to put down. And for those intellectual types, who would like to know the real issues and problems confronting Mexico today and separately the entire immigration and US-Mexico border issue, you will find this book a gold mine. Enjoy.

LIST OF CHARACTERS

Craig Walther - age 59, professor at University of New Mexico, Albuquerque

David Walther - age 44, US Border Agent in San Diego and youngest of the four brothers
Wife - Anita Walther

Cliff Walther - age 48, brother, stockbroker in Houston
Wife – Debbie Walther
Son - Cliff, Jr. - age 18, High School Senior
Twin daughters - age 15, Marcie and Chelsea,
High School Sophomores

Mark Walther - age 62, oldest of 4 brothers, Executive in Phoenix based trucking company
Wife - Elizabeth Walther
Daughter - Madeleine, age 23
        Madeleine's - son Ricky, age 3

Bill and Elsie Walther - parents of four Walther brothers, retired, Phoenix

Jennifer Stiles - age 23, University of New Mexico graduate student, Girlfriend of Craig Walther

Katherine Lacey - age 58, professor University of New Mexico, Albuquerque, Girlfriend of Craig Walther

General Kurt Grayson - Chairman Joint Chiefs of Staff, US Army, Pentagon Washington, D.C.
    Major William (Bill) Pierce, top aide to general Grayson
    Lieutenant Jerome (Jerry) Roberts, aide to general Grayson

John Hardwick - Secretary of Defense

Rosemary Denton - President of the United States
    Fran Babicz - President Denton's press secretary
    Stephanie Jones - President Denton's top personal aide

Marisa Angela Lopez - US Secretary of State

Fernando Jimenez Flores - Stock Trader and PEMEX employee, Mexico City
Wife - Carla

Captain Bernard (Buck) Stewart - US Border Patrol San Diego, Dave Walther's boss

Alberto Jose Morales - Rich Industrialist, Monterey, Mexico
Wife - Maria
Son - Raul, age 17
Daughter - Gabrielle, age 16

Chapter 1

When was the last time Fernando felt the warm day's sun on his face? Normally at this time of year, he was glad that he worked in an air-conditioned office. Fernando had never imagined himself missing the sun. Growing up the son of a poor farmer, he could not remember a day that he hadn't been in the sun. Not just a day, in fact; he couldn't remember one daylight hour without the hot southern sun beating down on his entire body when he was on the farm.

Maybe seeing and feeling the sun might reassure him that his world as he knew it wasn't coming to an end. Maybe this was all just a bad dream. Maybe he was dreaming. He just couldn't remember the last time he'd been asleep.

How long had he been in this cramped basement room, surrounded by large computer monitors and terminals all flashing every color of the rainbow? Was it one day, two days? How many hours had he been staring at his computer screen? My God, just how many millions had he lost since the Bolsa Mexicana de Valores, known as the BMV or BOLSA by professionals, had opened for trading on Monday? And how many tens of millions had he lost his company?

Fernando Jimenez Flores's childhood dream had been to be a trader on the Mexican Stock Exchange in Mexico City. His dreams had come true, and in the late eighties, he had been promoted to senior trader at one of the oldest and most prestigious trading firms on the BMV. Where did those fabulous days of the early nineties go, when the BMV experienced incredible growth? Fernando himself had made millions participating in the explosive stock-market boom.

Between 1987 and 1996, the value of stocks trading had increased by over $200 billion. There was a brief correction in the market but since 1997, the Mexican Stock Market had even outdone its performance for the previous two decades.

Fernando forced himself to look up, as if looking at the chart for the BMV that he had stared at for the last twenty-something years might shake him out of his life-sucking stupor. It was unlike any other chart he had ever seen. He had studied other stock markets, especially those in the United States, and he was very familiar with their charts. But even as bullish as the US economy and stock market had been, he remembered some big dips and sharp Vs that made the US stock market chart nowhere near as pretty as his BMV chart. It was like somebody had taken a ruler and a protractor and made a perfect forty-five-degree line. For his entire career at the BMV, the line had wavered so little from year to year that it appeared you could drive a car on that line without hitting one speed bump or pothole. Now a much higher percentage of Mexicans was invested in the BOLSA. It was not quite the same level of investors as in the United States, because Mexico did not have a large middle class with huge savings in pensions and 401(k) plans. But the rate and extent of ownership had increased significantly in recent years.

Almost everyone at the firm reinvested whatever they made back into the stock market. And just like the US stock market, the trading firms and brokerage firms in Mexico were always trying to smooth talk clientele into buying more stocks. The constant bullishness created an almost continuous feeding frenzy. It was just too hard for the brokers and traders to have one story for their clients and a separate one for themselves. Sure, there were a few times that his firm would short particular stocks, but for the last twenty-five years Fernando and his fellow traders had mostly been pouring their profits right back into the market.

And it had been a profitable decade for Fernando. Fernando now owned two beautiful homes and three fully paid-for new Mercedeses. Fernando's kids had graduated from college, and he knew it was time he started thinking about retirement. He tried repeating in his mind the firm's analysts' bullish words, straining to give them credibility like never before. But those words were belied by the rapidly deteriorating economic situation. "Oil prices have pulled back dramatically, unemployment is up, inflation has picked up again, and there is civil unrest around the country," he mumbled to himself. He had worked himself into a horrible depression.

Fernando once again started to weep. Shoulders slumped, his face close to his computer monitor, as if it was listening to him, he implored, "How am I going to explain this to my wife? I've lost everything. I kept telling her I was going to get out of the market—next month, then the next month, then the next. I'm sure as hell out of the market now!" But it was not a choice that Fernando had willingly made. Most professional traders used margin to leverage their trading accounts. A 50 percent drop in the BMV in three days was unprecedented. The margin call liquidations had done more than wipe out Fernando's life savings; he had a negative balance at his firm.

Fernando somehow finally found the energy to crawl out from behind his desk and the array of computer monitors. The screens were no longer flashing. Rather, each of them emitted a horrible glare, like in the old days before cable or satellite when TV stations had displayed that constant glowing screen all night long. From the last show until the first dawn's show, all that glowed on the major network channels was a black-and-white Indian-head test pattern. He dragged himself up the stairs and down the hallway to a set of doors that led to the trading floor of the BMV.

He was somewhat stunned by what he saw. The market had been closed for over an hour, and traders are not the kind of people who stick around after hours. It was a hectic, high-strung business. Traders were up hours before sunrise to peruse the international press and the happenings in other world markets, while guzzling cup after cup of strong coffee.

Each trader set out his game plan and orders for the day. The market was only open six and a half hours in Mexico City, but when you had tens and sometimes hundreds of millions of

dollars on the line, at the end of the day everyone was mentally and physically exhausted.

So normally when the trading bell banged and the market halted, it was a quick tidying up of records and then off for martinis or tequila shots at the local bars. But today was different. It was like somehow the trading floor had been flooded with liquid nitrogen, freezing people in place. A shudder made its way from the pit of Fernando's stomach up into his throat. He felt like he was in a wax museum of stock-floor traders. As Fernando's gaze scanned the room, he noticed that everyone was either kneeling, sitting down, or leaning up against something for support. There were even a few individuals completely stretched out on the floor. Some were crying, some whispering to each other, but, for the most part, they were just frozen, their mouths wide open and their faces all directed to one specific location above the trading floor. Fernando did not need to look up to see where all of those eyes were directed. Until he had been promoted and moved into his office below the trading floor for a bit of less hectic environment, he had spent some twenty-plus years standing where these very statues stood today.

He did not need to look up to see the BOLSA's electronic trading screen, which was known to be one of the largest in the world. He had a smaller version on one of the many computer monitors in his office that he had been glued to for days now. As he sidestepped his way toward the exit, before passing through the door, he allowed himself one glance at what the many statues were all fixated on. The gigantic electronic trading screen blared the horrific news: the market had plunged 50 percent in just three days.

There was no warm sun to greet Fernando. It was too late in the day, and because of the many tall buildings, he usually had to walk a couple blocks before he could bask in the sun.

That would have to wait, however. Fernando's head jerked around to see a number of ambulances and a crowd that had formed on the west side of the BMV building.

Someone must have had a heart attack, Fernando thought to himself. He realized that he himself had felt on the verge of a heart attack almost every hour over the last three days as the market had continued its never-ending tick downward. He realized the mistake of his assumption as he approached the crowd.

"I heard he jumped from the sixth floor."

"I thought the windows in that building couldn't be opened wide enough for someone to climb out."

Two women spoke in hushed voices as they strained their necks to catch a glimpse of the body. Fernando had read about such events in a book about the 1929 stock-market crash that had precipitated widespread panic and a historic depression in America. Sure, that all seemed believable back in 1929, but not now.

Chapter 2

An old, dilapidated city transportation bus sporting an obnoxious green-and-yellow paint job screeched to an abrupt halt. Fearing the bus might disintegrate into a pile of rust before they could get off, the passengers hurriedly piled out, leaving one lonely soul behind. Fernando rose from his seat and was the last to step into the street. He didn't move as fast as he used to. What was he to do? He was down and out, his mojo gone. For Fernando, *fast moving* was about making money, trading stocks, and these days he didn't want to be reminded of anything having to do with trading stocks.

Fernando thought to himself, *Only a few months ago, I owned three new fabulous Mercedeses, and now, I am reduced to riding an old city bus.*

As the bus pulled away, adding insult to injury, it released a blue cloud of noxious exhaust fumes that engulfed him where he stood. He quickly looked up and, throwing his arms in the air, gave the departing bus and driver as nasty a look as he was capable of making. He noticed that someone had crudely painted something on the back of the bus, but he couldn't quite make it out. The pollution had gotten so bad in Mexico City that even newly painted billboards looked years old within weeks. VIVA ZAPAT was all he could make out as the bus trailed off.

Oh, well. I'm going to be late again, he thought.

Fernando had been luckier than millions of others; he had been able to find a job very quickly after being fired in the massive layoffs following the collapse of the BMV. Petróleos Mexicanos (PEMEX) was in need of an individual with currency-trading knowledge and a good head for statistics, and Fernando had both. It gnawed at him, though, that his month's salary was less than what he sometimes made in one day of good trading.

This kept the pep out of his step as he walked the two blocks to his new place of employment.

For eighteen years now, the PEMEX Tower had been the tallest skyscraper in Mexico. It housed PEMEX, Mexico's state-owned oil company. Home to the world's second-largest oil field, the Cantarell in the Gulf of Mexico, PEMEX gave Mexico the rightful claim to be one of the world's largest oil-producing countries. Mexico had nationalized all of its oil reserves in 1938, and since then its petroleum industry had generated revenues that made up fully one-third of the entire Mexican government budget. In 2012 alone, PEMEX had generated $122 billion in revenue. Fernando entered the revolving doors and left the hot morning sun behind him.

Maybe I would have had a happier life if I had stayed on the farm, he wondered, a thought that had been hounding him these last two months. He had not been sleeping well for some time, and it contributed to his recent lack of concentration.

His PEMEX Tower office was much larger than his old office at the BMV, but that was no real solace since he shared it with ten other people. Standing in the office doorway and blocking Fernando's entry was his boss, a man ten years his junior, his face heavy with a five o'clock shadow as if it was the end of the day instead of the beginning.

His boss approached him, standing too close and invading Fernando's personal space. He hissed, "You're late, and I need those statistics on my desk immediately."

"I'm sorry, sir—my car was repossessed, and I haven't figured out the bus schedule," said Fernando, with a look on his face that indicated he might break into tears at any moment. It had been so hard for him to lose his last prized possession, his silver Mercedes.

Unflinching, his boss retorted, "I don't want to hear your sob story. There are twenty million people here in Mexico City, and each and every one of them is laboring under similar hardships.

Hell, you can't pick up the paper these days without the headlines reporting that another businessman has jumped to his death out of a window." With a wicked smile, he added, "In fact, I
thought of moving our company to the first floor to make sure none of you fruitcakes gets the same idea."

"Don't worry, sir. I won't be jumping." Adding a touch of sarcasm, Fernando responded, "My wife says she'll never speak to me again if I kill myself."

"Cute, that's cute," his boss said, adjusting his tie and his attitude a bit. "I didn't know a bean counter like you had a sense of humor."

That's right. Fernando was now known as a bean counter. He found some humor in that because he had heard that in America, Mexicans are often referred to as "beaners." As he got busy with his morning's responsibilities, he amused himself by chanting out loud to himself, "I'm a beaner, bean counter." The only thing Fernando found positive about his new job was that it was a lot less stressful. However, after trading the markets for twenty-five years, Fernando found his new position, frankly, quite boring.

It turned out that PEMEX's database, which stored records on the Mexican peso and its relationship with other currencies had been corrupted. Fernando was working, sometimes around the clock with two other individuals to painstakingly log statistical information into a computer database, which then spit out various reports and charts on the past economy and oil prices.

The Mexican economy had gone to hell. The crash of the BMV only three months earlier had been the impetus for a dramatic economic downturn. The market crash was by no means the sole contributor, however. The downturn had been the effect of several events, some that had been brewing the perfect storm for many, many years and had brought Mexico's Gross Domestic Product (GDP) to a grinding halt.

PEMEX had been in debt for some time. The Mexican government had siphoned off far too high a percentage of its profits over the years, and PEMEX had borrowed massively, so much so that in 2013 it owed more than $45 billion. And since PEMEX was state run, it lacked the resources to go out and replace its dwindling reserves or build new refinery plants. That fact kept PEMEX from keeping up, much less competing with such oil exploration-companies as Exxon, Chevron, Royal Dutch, and BP (British Petroleum). Its failings forced PEMEX to export roughly 50 percent of its crude oil to the United States to be refined. The United States then eventually shipped it back to Mexico as gasoline. In fact, almost 90 percent of Mexico's crude production was shipped north to the United States. This relationship made Mexico incredibly dependent on the United States and left a sour taste toward those getting rich off of Mexico's current situation. In 2012, the large Cantarell oil field was producing a third of the barrels it had produced in 2004, only 721 thousand barrels a day from $2.2 million. The severity of the problem was masked, however, because prior to 2014 the price per barrel of oil had gone up inversely to the decline in Mexico's oil production. Mexico's political leaders argued with some support that Mexico's oil resources, at least in pesos, had not been declining.

Only in the last couple of months had Mexican government officials agreed with PEMEX that massive amounts of new exploration must take place in order to replace dwindling reserves. A report in late 2014 had estimated that Mexico's current oil reserves would last less than twenty years. Getting the commitment for the billions of dollars that would be needed for exploration would be almost impossible. The Mexican government was preoccupied with spending billions to fight the new guerrilla war that had been making great headway. Even if the money could be found, it would take almost ten years to get any serious oil production online. Mexico had entered into its worst depression in modern times.

Fernando was somewhat reluctant to complete his work on the report. The figures were depressing. The economic reports he had compiled revealed that the market crash that had taken him from wealthy to almost penniless was not just bad luck but an inevitable market correction of biblical proportions.

Due to his new position, Fernando's days were now long and grueling and came without the financial and emotional rewards he previously enjoyed. In the good old days, he had thrived during long days—but, Fernando thought, then he had been a god. Now, he worked in slavery-like conditions, his work cubicle small and claustrophobic. He was forced to create one mind-numbing and boring report after another, and it made him sick to his stomach, doing such mundane tasks. He felt as if the walls of his little cubicle were slowly collapsing inward on him. "Ah," he cried out loud as he brushed away imaginary, ant-like insects, which he could feel crawling up and down his legs. Fernando knew that at any moment he was going to explode if he didn't escape his prisonlike confinement. He jumped up and paused only long enough to drop the report on his boss's desk as he headed for the lobby and the rejuvenating sunshine that was just beyond its doors. "Oh, God, how I desperately need to find some relief to my near-penniless existence," he murmured under his breath.

Suddenly Fernando realized that he had stopped in front of the bank of elevators and mistakenly pushed the UP button. A still, small voice whispered in his ear and promised that he'd find the relief he so urgently sought if he rode the elevator to one of the upper floors. Yes, he'd go to the upper floors and look out over his once *proud* city and at the same time feel the warmth from the sunlight radiating through the windows. The elevator came to an abrupt halt, and Fernando stepped out onto the twelfth floor. He remembered that the entire floor at one time had held one of the city's premier funding groups. The company, like the vast majority of its kind, had failed during the crash. Fernando had heard that the CEO had leaped to his death rather than face his board of directors and wife with bankruptcy and financial ruin. From the moment Fernando had stepped off the elevator, he'd felt as if he had entered a trance-like state. As he walked down the deserted hallway, he stopped in front of the CEO's office. He looked up and down the hallway, half expecting to see hordes of employees racing about doing their work. Fernando shook his head to clear his now cobwebbed mind. "Of course, no one is here," Fernando chuckled out loud, calming himself and trying to break his dazed state. "The company has failed!"

Looking down, willing his feet to move, Fernando noticed that the crime-scene tape still lay on the floor of the CEO's doorway. Fernando stepped over the tape, making the sign of the cross with respect to the now departed man, and entered his unfurnished office.

Wow, thought Fernando, *the buzzards have indeed picked this office clean; not even a paperclip can be seen abandoned on the floor.*

He walked over to the window and stood there, frozen, not looking out onto the beehive of activity in the cityscape below, but at his now gaunt reflection in the window. Gray had crept into his hair, and Fernando realized that he had aged ungracefully since his fall from his revered position. His once trademarked thick, black mustache drooped on the ends and was streaked throughout with gray and badly in need of trimming. His facial features, which previously looked chiseled by skilled Mayan artisans, were now puffy from too many nights of heavy drinking and little sleep while lamenting over his meager situation.

Fernando had always prided himself on the cut and cost of his clothing. But, spying his too-thin frame in the window, he was shocked at his appearance. Fernando's daily routine had worn down his energy level to a nearly catastrophic, collapsed state. Still looking at his image in the window, he hung his head, realizing that he looked depressed and exhausted. If the saying was true, "The clothes make the man," his ill-fitting expensive suits told the world more than he wanted anyone to know. Frankly, he was near broke and could expect no real future in his present position. Tears of anguish ran down his cheeks, and he let out a wretched, soulful cry. Slowly he unconsciously reached out, his fingers finding the latch that would open the window. The still, small voice returned to whisper in his ear.

He could hear and almost feel its urging, its beckoning call to unlock the latch, push open the window, and step into the rejuvenating rays of the sun.

Chapter 3

The Acapulco Princess hotel, a resort for the truly rich and famous, sat on Revolcadero Beach, twenty minutes from downtown Acapulco. Built in the seventies, it had enjoyed a stellar five-star reputation for over forty years. Its lavish façade and grounds adorned more postcards than nearly any other site in all of Mexico. The Acapulco Princess ranked second in architectural appeal to the massive Pyramid of the Sun at Teotihuacán near Mexico City.

The hotel beach was usually a peaceful stretch of white sand and palm trees. But something was dramatically different today. It was as if Francis Ford Coppola himself was directing his epic movie *Apocalypse Now*. A trio of helicopters descended quickly onto the lawn of the famous Acapulco Princess hotel. Wagner's *Ride of the Valkyries* pulsated from the helicopters' mounted speakers as they bore down in attack formation. The guests could feel it deeply, shaking their very souls. The onset of the buffeting windstorm had the guests and staff in an all-out panic. As the helicopters drew nearer to those who watched in shock, they felt as if the air was being sucked out of their lungs. It was impossible to take a breath. The helicopters landed abruptly, like the controlled crash of an albatross rather than a gentle return to earth.

Two bellmen had left their lobby call station to step out in front of the hotel, mesmerized by the approaching choppers. When simultaneously they realized the helicopters were landing, they bolted back into the hotel's open-air lobby. Breathless, they banged on the check-in counter, shouting, "They're coming! They're coming! What're we going to do? We must warn all the guests immediately!"

The manager on duty, having heard the clatter, emerged from the short hallway that adjoined the check-in area. The Princess had been a trendsetter when constructed and was famous for its fifteen-story, open-air lobby. The reception area was flanked by charming fountains, and the entire lobby floor consisted of exquisite mosaic tiles. Large elephant-ear-blade fans blew mist that sprayed at intervals from the ceiling, cooling the air.

The manager was a small man, dark in complexion with black, shiny, slicked-back hair that was thinning on top. He wore a razor-thin mustache that curled up at the corners, in part due to his habit of constantly touching it and curling one side or the other. A perpetual frown was etched into his forehead; he was a worrier.

"What's all the yelling about? Who is coming?" cried the manager to the bellmen, who stood waving their arms in panic.

"Zapatista, that's who! We must warn all the guests immediately!" cried one of the bellmen, whose face was so contorted that the manager hardly recognized him. The other bellman was yelling incoherently.

"Quit shouting, you fools, and quit telling me to warn the guests. You, of all people, should know that ever since the depression started, we've never had more than a handful of guests in our thousand-room hotel." The manager wondered why Zapatista, the general of the guerrilla army, would want to come to Acapulco of all places, much less the Princess Hotel. He'd been watching TV, and Zapatista was, in fact, waging a war, but that was hundreds of miles away from this hotel.

"Stop yelling, you idiot, and calm down! You're driving me crazy."

From behind the bellman came a voice that turned many strong men into whimpering children: "Maybe you are crazy, my friend," boomed through the lobby.

Such a voice was not one ever to be forgotten. If the heavens were to crack open and God were to speak, it would be in such a voice—deep, confident, articulate, and of course, in Spanish.

Recognition was immediate: Zapatista himself. Zapatista and his guerrillas were wreaking havoc over much of Mexico, and the country was in such a state of financial depression that the government and the military had been able to do little to stop the rebellion. Within seconds, the immense lobby was filled with more than forty armed troops standing at the ready.

Zapatista was an imposing man. Barrel-chested, over six feet tall, he looked like a combination of Che Guevara and a young Fidel Castro. He wore camouflage-green army fatigues and a beret over thick, black hair that almost reached his shoulders. The beret and the two big flap pockets on the front his shirt displayed a striped band, the backdrop for the glistening symbol of the guerrilla movement—a rattlesnake curled and ready to strike. Two matching, expensive-looking .44-caliber automatics hung in a holster low on his hips. Zapatista was in his forties and handsome, even more so with the unshaven look so popular at the time. Zapatista, like the rattlesnake depicted on the emblem sewn to his uniform, was cold-blooded and dangerous beyond anything the manager had ever imagined. And he wore a large pair of mirrored sunglasses which, as of yet, he had not removed. Zapatista smiled with malice, looked down at the manager, and lit a fat, twisted cigar, blowing a cloud of toxic smoke toward him. Immediately, the manager felt a slight loss of bladder control, and his legs turned to jelly under the intense glare from Zapatista. It was as if Zapatista's eyes had bored two searing holes through the manager's skull; the look was death itself.

"My crazy friend, I assume you are not too busy these days. How about a room for myself and my friends?"

"Are you serious? Do you really wish to stay at the Princess?" the manager asked, the relief dripping from his words. "You wish to stay at the Prin—"

"No," Zapatista interrupted. "I just thought it would be amusing to ask you for rooms before I proceeded to take over your hotel. And that, my friend, we are doing immediately. I am leaving Colonel Hermosa here in your good hands."

With the words barely out of Zapatista's mouth, a war-worn officer in his fifties quickstepped forward, snapping to attention with Gestapo-like heel clicking. Colonel Hermosa's long face looked like an old baseball mitt—deep crevices crisscrossed his dark skin. Having worked for Zapatista for over three years, he had quickly risen to the position of colonel. He was very proud of the fact that he had never let Zapatista down.

While continuing to fix his mirrored gaze on the manager, Zapatista said to his second-in-command, "Colonel, you will be using this hotel as your base of operations for the Pacific Coast region. I will leave you thirty men and one of my choppers, with support troops coming soon."

He turned to the colonel and said, "I will expect you to have at least two hundred volunteers within the week. If these lazy capitalists here in Acapulco aren't willing to volunteer, I'm sure you can find ways to convince them to enlist. I would hate to burn down all these beautiful resorts just to find a few simple volunteers."

Returning his gaze back to the hotel manager, Zapatista said, "As a matter of fact, I have found your first recruit. What is your name?"

The manager fought to control his bowels so as not to soil himself as Zapatista's glare once again bore into his head. After managing to clear his throat, he replied, "Please, General Zapatista, I am only a lowly hotel employee. I have never carried a gun. I've never killed anything more than a defenseless chicken in my entire life!"

"I think you misunderstood me. I did not ask you if you wanted to volunteer. I asked you your name." Zapatista's voice boomed as if it were coming from a loudspeaker.

"Jesus. Ah, Jesus Gonzales, sir." He was stammering badly, and sweat was now pouring down his face. He could feel his crisp white shirt sticking to him and was sure that Zapatista and the colonel could smell his fear. He felt weak and leaned on the reception desk for support. Zapatista flashed another big smile at the manager.

"Well, Private Gonzales, welcome to the army. I know you, like millions of your fellow countrymen who have joined the cause, will serve me well in my war to return Mexico to the people."

Jesus, with newfound energy, scurried out from behind the desk and threw himself onto the tile floor, groveling and grasping at the boots of the famous general.

"No, no, you don't understand! I am a coward and afraid of guns! I can't be of any use to you. Please, please!"

Jesse James or Wyatt Earp never drew a gun so fast. Before the groveling hotel manager knew what hit him, the general had emptied the clip of his gun into the only target he was given—the manager's back. Staring down at the blood-soaked shirt, he removed the cigar that had never left his mouth and removed the mirrored shades from his eyes.

"You were right, my friend. You can't be of any use to me." Putting his glasses back on, he spat on the manager and said, "Señior, you are a disgrace to your heritage. Mexico belongs to the people, not traitors and cowards!"

Chapter 4

Most Americans who watch Mexican television have commented that all Mexicans talk too fast. The Mexico City Channel 22 news correspondent's pace today would seem frenetic even to the locals. The news was all bad, coming in hot and heavy. There was just too much news to cover.

The walls of Fernando's apartment were paper thin, and he could hear the din from other tenants' TVs like a haunting echo. The news correspondent's relentless babble added to Fernando's nausea. "Will this ever stop?" he muttered.

"In addition, we have some late-breaking news. It appears that General Zapatista has already put to use the fleet of helicopters he captured recently on a raid at one of our military bases near Mexico City. For the first time, we have reports that Zapatista's guerrillas have moved toward Acapulco. We have been unable to contact our local affiliate there, but the last word was that a number of large hotels had been set on fire.

"Now back to our earlier report. As you can see from our video footage, severe fighting in the state of San Luis Potosi has become widespread. There are heavy casualties on the part of federal troops as well as the guerrillas. It appears that General Zapatista is living up to his threats and has made new inroads into some states north of Mexico City. In his letter to Enrique Peña Nieto, which we read on the air last week, Zapatista guaranteed his followers that he will surround the capital city by the end of the year."

Fernando's reverie was broken when the door to the small apartment swung open abruptly. Fernando had been standing, eyes glued to the TV set. He turned to face his wife, Carla, entering through the doorway. His wife was short and overweight with a round, cherubic face. Her eyes opened wide as she quickly surveyed the room. It was as if a cyclone had hit. *"¡Dios mío!"* she cried. Drawers were open; boxes were turned on end. It seemed like everything in the small apartment had been searched. She was just about to ask her husband if they had been burglarized, as many of their neighbors had been since the economy collapsed, when she noticed their three matching suitcases standing side by side in the center of the room. Someone had obviously packed them in a hurry—a shirt sleeve stuck out here, a shoelace there.

"Fernando, what is going on here? Why have you packed our suitcases? Where are we going?"

"*Norte! Norte!*" he barked, as he reached forward and yanked the TV cord from the wall.

"*Norte?* Do you think we will be safe if we go and live with my sister in Guadalajara? I heard on the street that the guerrillas have moved as far north as there!"

As Fernando picked up the two heaviest suitcases, he replied, "We are not going to Guadalajara."

"But you said we were going north. My sister is the only person we know who lives north of here. Where are we going to go?"

"Where we should've gone twenty-five years ago when I left my family's farm—we're going to America!" His cheeks were flushed, and he had a fanatical look in his eyes—a look Carla had never seen before, and fear set in.

She thought she might throw up; she was going to be ill. But there wasn't time. She quickly ducked into the bedroom and then the small bathroom to ensure that Fernando had indeed packed all of the things important to her. The small crucifix that Fernando's father had given them on their wedding day was gone; a faded image of the cross could be seen where it had once hung. Carla was a poor housekeeper. After all, she wasn't a maid and refused to do the menial work of a lowly maid. Returning to face her frenzied husband, in utter frustration, she grabbed her suitcase. Tears fell, and

she stomped her feet, crushed by this new development, and tentatively asked her husband, "How will we eat? You sent me out on a fool's errand. I couldn't find anything. The stores are empty,
looted, and the streets are filled with hungry people. What will we do? What shall become of us? Fernando, I am so scared. Please hold me and tell me everything will be okay."

But Fernando had already turned to leave, shoulders hunched forward, trying to ignore his imploring wife. Halfway out the door, Fernando turned to her and out of frustration gruffly replied, "We will find something on the way. Now come!" Reluctantly, she followed him out, not even pausing to close the door.

Chapter 5

The University of New Mexico, with its Pueblo Revival architecture, sprawled unabashedly in the heart of Albuquerque. With the Sandia Mountains as a backdrop in the east, the campus projected the feel of a Pueblo Indian village updated by two hundred years. Adobe and straw construction, quaint and rustic when used in homes and small buildings, was taken to new heights in the massive classroom structures and dormitories at UNM.

As Professor Craig Walther entered the classroom on the first day of classes, most of the students had a somewhat quizzical look on their faces. Professor Walther smiled, fairly confident of the thoughts that were buzzing through their minds:

Is this the guy who wrote a book about Mexican illegal immigration that was on the New York Times *best seller list for fifty-three straight weeks?*

Is this the nationally known professor who is regularly quoted by presidents on both sides of the border?

Is this the tenured professor whose knowledge of Mexican history and Mexico's political activities is unparalleled?

Is this the author of the book considered to be the bible of Mexican-American relationships?

Of course, the answer to all these questions was a resounding yes. Professor Walther was not Mexican. There was no mistaking his heritage. He was a good ole red-blooded, dyed-in-the-wool American. Even though there were many Mexicans with Anglo names due to mixed marriages and name-altering liberalities, there was no mistaking Professor Craig Walther! However, with his reputation as a ladies' man, you'd think he had some Latin blood flowing through those veins. In addition, Professor Craig Walther was anything but nerdy, with his long, blondish-gray hair, colorful Territory Ahead corduroy shirt, black jeans, bolo tie, American Indian belt buckle, and boots. Frankly, he looked pretty damn handsome and cool.

"Good morning," Professor Walther said as he placed his papers on the large desk at the front of the lecture hall. Trim and agile, with the confidence of years of teaching, he hopped up and seated himself on the desktop. His Justin Roper boots dangling midair, he announced, "Welcome to the first day of 'Border Crossing.' Before we get underway, let me give you a couple of pieces of bad news and some ground rules. I would advise you to take copious notes and not miss any of my classes. Unlike some generous professors here at UNM, I do not grade on a bell curve. You will not pass my class just because you're slightly less stupid than the guy sitting next to you. A seventy is a passing grade. If you get a sixty-nine, you get a *F*. And let me remind you that the *F* stands for 'failed' or 'flunked.'

"The second piece of bad news is that you may experience trauma in my class." Professor Walther noticed that several of the students squirmed as if what they had already heard was enough to make them question their class selection.

"Last semester there was a fistfight in my class. It has been said that the fistfight created, let's say, a little extra interest in the usual controversy that arises in teaching a class on such a hot political topic as the US-Mexican border. Now, I know that my classes are always fully enrolled, and the dean informed me that there was a waiting list of over one hundred students eager to get into this class this semester. The chance to add or drop without penalty ends in two days, so make your decision."

Craig was taunting the class. *Am I in or am I out? Do I stay or go for a safer class?* his students wondered.

Further stirring the pot, Craig said, "Remember, there are always students requesting a change of schedule." But no one moved or said a word. Their lives were about to be changed— they just didn't know it yet!

Craig continued to challenge the students. "UNM has always had its share of racial flare-ups, and I will admit that my class can sometimes be accused of inciting such outbursts.

For that, I will not apologize. Those of you with Mexican backgrounds, please do not get *defensive*, and those of you who are non-Mexican or non-Hispanic, please do not get *offensive*.

"Oh, one more bit of housekeeping..." A boisterous exchange by some students passing the lecture hall windows could be heard within the room. However, most students by now were riveted to the professor's words, and they did not even notice the distraction.

"I tend to refer to people as 'Mexicans' if they came from Mexico or are of Mexican heritage. Those of you who find this label offensive and think this is politically incorrect can leave right now." Pausing to let his words sink in, he counted to ten and then continued, "I am not a politician, I am not running for office, and I have no interest in being the dean of this department. I grew up in Roswell, New Mexico, and my high school girlfriend was Mexican. When I drink three or four margaritas, I can guarantee you that the food I eat with them is Mexican food! It is not Latino food, it is not Tex-Mex food, and it certainly is not Hispanic food! If those in the room with Mexican backgrounds think I am picking on you, well, let me make you feel a little bit better. I call blacks 'blacks.' And, in turn, I do not ask anyone to refer to me as Anglo-Saxon. I am American!"

The professor vaulted off the desk and walked to the end of the elevated platform. "Now, let's move on to the substance of this class. What is the United States' longest border?"

A kid at the back of the room blurted out before Professor Walther had barely finished the question, "Mexico!"

"Brilliant! Just brilliant! You assumed the correctness of your answer because this course is about the US border with Mexico." With this, Professor Walther strode over to the huge blackboard and wrote in the center of it, ASSUME.

"My father used to say that to 'assume' makes an 'ass' out of 'u' and 'me.'" With dramatic flair and with as thick a stroke as the chalk permitted him, Professor Walther underlined the letters of the words on the board as he spoke.

"Do not waste your fellow students' time or mine by making such idiotic assumptions. Frankly, I don't make a habit of asking stupid questions, so don't give me stupid answers. Your parents didn't pay substantial sums for you to attend this college so that you could bear witness to the vain efforts of your classmate trying to guess the right answers. I asked the question because I wanted to see who did and didn't read the first chapter of my book before attending today's class. But before another of you blurts out 'Canada' in the hopes that it might curry some credit with me, please," he said as he held up his hands, "just sit there quietly.

"Yes, the answer is Canada. I think all of you will do well to try to read the chapters of my book prior to attending my class. I have a tendency to move very fast, and I think you will have a better chance of digesting my lecture if you've at least read the chapter that my course outline shows I will be addressing in each class. Who knows, later in the semester, we might even be able to enter into some intelligent dialogue." Craig said these last few words slowly as if talking to an infant in diapers. "That is if you've done your prep work," he added.

Then Craig shifted the class into high gear. "The United States and Mexico are joined together by 1,961 miles of border, but this is dwarfed by the US-Canadian border, at 3,145 miles. One of the most important distinguishing differences between these two borders is that the larger of the two is unmanned and unprotected." Most students by now had opened up notepads on their desk and were taking notes. Some had notebook computers, but the university had disabled Internet access within the classrooms to keep students focused. "The US-Mexican border is the fourth longest in the Americas and the nineteenth longest in the world, but it is considered one of the busiest borders in the world. In just the last two years, the economic situation in Mexico has greatly deteriorated— Mexico is in a major recession. This coupled with the recent acceleration of guerrilla activity and the decision to legalize millions of illegal Mexicans already living in America has created a hornet's-nest reaction. With fewer and fewer consequences for those illegally entering the United States, the crossings are accelerating exponentially. The president has screwed the pooch royally over immigration and is so inept that Spanish may become our national language in your children's lifetime."

Isn't that a kick in the pants? thought Craig.

"Moving on. Since this is more of an introductory course, you must first understand some background between Mexico and the United States on the immigration issue. In the past decade, Mexicans have overtaken blacks in the United States as the largest minority, comprising around 15 percent of the US population, which does not include illegals. It is predicted that by the midpoint of this century, that figure will jump to 25 percent. Those numbers will have a dramatic and demonstrative effect on the politics and economy of the United States." Craig looked out at his mesmerized class. "Now, what is driving this significant increase?" he asked but didn't wait for an answer. "Number one is the *legal* immigration of Mexicans. Number two is the *illegal* immigration of Mexicans. Finally, we find that Mexicans have a higher birth rate than other nationalities here in this country.

"The United States is the world's leader in immigration with its open-door policy. Approximately 1.2 million people a year legally cross our borders. The adage about closing the barn door after the horse left is quite applicable."

Craig paused to let that sink in before continuing. "The liberals with their 'one mind, one heart' attitude have sunk America. We need bailing out, meaning the *rescuers* have now become the victims. On the other hand, Mexico leads the world in emigration, with around five hundred thousand people leaving the country each year. Let me give you a little advice: make sure when you are answering one of my exam questions that you don't confuse immigration with emigration."

A sheepish girl in the second row raised her hand and said, "I'm confused. If Mexico is losing five hundred thousand people a year, doesn't that mean its population is going down?"

The professor could not help but notice the exceptionally long, tanned legs that were sticking out from under the desk as he turned to address the student's question. "A fair question. But no, the five hundred thousand who leave Mexico would only decrease the population if there were static population growth, meaning that the number of deaths of Mexican residents would equal the number of births. But Mexico has one of the healthier birth rates, and that is why the population is increasing. Here in the United States, we have an average birthrate of two births per woman, but in Mexico, the birthrate is running 25 percent higher, or 2.5 children per woman."

His eyes lingered a bit too long on those lovely legs, and with an enormous amount of willpower, he finally snapped back to reality, blushing a bit, and continued his lecture. "As you can imagine, it is very frustrating as a professor to not be able to provide you with actual numbers. It is axiomatic that if we knew how many illegal Mexicans came into the United States each year, as well as how many were actually here, we probably would be able to do a better job of controlling the border flow. The estimates are that somewhere around one million or more Mexicans enter the United States illegally each year and that currently there are somewhere between fifteen to twenty million illegal Mexicans residing in America. Of course, all of this has huge economic and political ramifications when you add these numbers to the earlier numbers I gave you about individuals with Mexican heritage making up the largest minority in the United States."

Chapter 6

Few on either side of the Mexican border truly appreciated the magnitude of the event as it began to unfold. Perhaps if there happened to be a small plane flying at a relatively low altitude within Mexican airspace, the occupants could have looked down and understood it. From the air, it looked like there were gigantic herds of longhorn cattle moving north. And there were hundreds, maybe thousands, of these herds as far as the eye could see.

But a closer inspection would have revealed the shocking horror—that the herds were actually people, millions of them, inching their way north toward the United States, toward the border. Most were walking, some were in vehicles, but all movement within Mexico was toward the north.

When was the last time such a vision of massive refugee movement had taken place? Was it during the American evacuation of Vietnam in 1973? Or when Cambodians ran for their lives en masse from the Khmer Rouge? Or when terrified families fled the insurrection in Syria? Or was it Africa, when one warlord hacked limbs from innocent villagers, gaining control of their lands and resources, turning men, women, and children into slaves, which is still happening to this very day?

Of course, mass exoduses were not always the result of war. The tsunami that hit Thailand in December 2004 resulted in people evacuating in droves. Even in New Orleans, tens of thousands of people fled and were evacuated when Hurricane Katrina flooded the city. Evacuation routes were quickly overwhelmed, blocked by thousands of vehicles loaded with families trying to stay one step ahead of the disaster. Though many left on buses, many more were unable to reach safety. Television sets across America broadcast the tragic results of their failed attempts. From the air, the massive throngs of evacuees had appeared like ants swarming over a Sunday picnic in the park. Only this was a swarm of humanity vying for help and rescue. It was hard to conjure, even in the mind's eye, the image of millions of people walking together over hundreds of miles across Mexico. It was the largest mass human movement history had ever known. It made Hannibal's procession of thirty-eight thousand troops along the entire northern Mediterranean coast to attack the Romans pale in comparison. It made the largest seaborne invasion in history—the Allied invasion at the beaches of Normandy with over 150 thousand troops on D-Day—seem like a trial run. This mass exodus from Mexico was larger than the mass exodus of Palestinians from Israel's occupation in 1948, which numbered over seven hundred thousand. However, the estimated 1.8 million refugees who fled from Iraq to Jordan, Syria, and Lebanon after the US invasion achieved the top spot in the history books as the greatest movement of mankind ever in recorded history.

The Mexican movement was, in many ways, like the California Gold Rush of 1848, where thousands of Americans dropped what they were doing, quit their jobs, abandoned their families, and within hours loaded up and headed west in search of gold, fame, and fortune. For millions of Mexicans, their gold lay on the other side of the Mexican border to the north. The famous Italian saying "All roads lead to Rome" would no longer be as quoted. Hundreds of thousands of Mexican families marched north, and to millions of immigrants—refugees, soon to be illegal aliens—all roads led to North America.

The pull of America's promised land was almost as great as the push from a destitute life in Mexico. Facing the long and arduous journey, many voiced their complaints. Their reasons to leave were far too many, and their causes had been ignored far too long. Fed up, facing starvation, they knew the choice to leave their beloved Mexico would be painful, but to leave was their only cure for a life filled with failed dreams and crushed ambitions.

The stories were many.

"The peso is almost worthless. If I don't exchange it for dollars soon, I will have nothing."

"I'm going to visit my sister in Tucson. She says she has a big house."

"My brother went to the Federales and offered them money if they would protect his business from the guerrillas. They shot him and took his money."

"All of my family and I had good-paying jobs at the cement company, but with the severe drop in oil prices, we all lost our jobs."

"I've heard that the doctors in America are wonderful, and it is all free."

"A Zapatista guerrilla told me I had no choice. I either fought for the guerrillas or I was an enemy of Mexico. I ran away the next day."

"My brother has his own landscaping company in Palm Springs, California. He makes $1,000 a week and does not have to pay any money to the government. I hear he can always use good workers."

A brother here, a sister there, a family of three, a truckload of strangers—they were all united in one mission—to leave the country they had known for so long and attempt to find acceptance in their new homeland.

Had virtually everyone in Mexico decided to leave? Or maybe the better question was, why would anyone stay behind? Fernando whispered out loud to himself, "God, why have you forsaken me?"

Chapter 7

Norman Rockwell may have screwed up. He never painted the all-American Friday-night high school football game in full regalia. But if he had painted such a scene, this Friday night would have been perfect for such a painting. It was not only homecoming night, but Houston's Memorial High School was also playing its cross town rival, Stratford High School. Fans packed the stands like sardines in a tin, and the fences that surrounded the field felt the pressure of bodies pushed up against them.

For Cliff Walther, being chairman of the Memorial High School Booster Club Fundraising Committee would probably have guaranteed him great seats for the big game anyway, but he had taken no chances. With his wife complaining all the way, they had shown up for the game a full two hours early. Now it was late in the fourth quarter, and if his son Cliff Jr. could just complete one more pass, he would break the Memorial High School all-time passing record that Cliff Sr. had set some twenty-plus years earlier. As Cliff Jr. dropped back, the defender slipped, which left the Mustangs' left-side tight end wide open. Cliff Jr. made a beautiful spiral pass almost forty-six yards into the hands of the waiting tight end. The young receiver sprinted just five more yards and added another touchdown for Memorial High. The crowd exploded. Despite the many pounds Cliff's wife had put on during the last few years, Cliff lifted her high into the air in celebration as if she were weightless.

"Wow! That was the greatest football game I've ever seen! I swear to you, I know he's going to get an offer! I just hope it's from Texas and not Rice," Cliff exclaimed. Almost dropping Debbie, Cliff turned quickly to the family next to them. "Hey, what do you think of *my* son? One hell of a quarterback, isn't he?"

"Yeah, yeah, Cliff, keep your shirt on. If our son, Richard, had not made that great block, Cliff Jr. wouldn't have had such a long time to make that pass."

Cliff was still so excited that he didn't even hear the rebuttal from their longtime friend. "Well, we'll see who gets the college scholarship offers, but I'm in such a great mood! Come on—grab your kids. We're heading to Ruth's Chris. I'm treating everyone to late-night steaks and some serious drinks for us well-deserving fathers."

Neither of the proud fathers noticed that nearly every Memorial student had stormed the field in celebration. In addition to tearing down the home team's goal post, they had hoisted Cliff Jr. and a number of other football players up on their shoulders and were parading around the field.

Life is good tonight, thought Cliff Sr. *Yes, sir—mighty good indeed!*

Chapter 8

"Sorry, Dad, let me turn that down," Madeleine Walther said as she reached up to adjust the volume on the TV mounted on the ceiling of the Ford Excursion. At the same time, she tickled the stomach of her three-year-old son, who was kicking his legs, eyes wide and glued to the TV set playing a SpongeBob DVD above him.

"...I was just saying that it really wasn't necessary for you and Mom to drive me to campus. I mean, after all, I am twenty-one years old, and I could have driven myself. Besides, the new car you bought me is a dream to drive and, as you noted from Consumer Reports, quite safe."

Madeleine's mother, Elizabeth, puckered her lips and blew kisses to her daughter, affirming, "No bother, dear. It's what we moms do."

Madeleine smiled, thankful she had such wonderful parents. Elizabeth carried on, "This is a big day for the Walther family, and we're proud of you. Honey, we just wanted to show our support on your first day at college—just this one day."

Smiling again at her daughter, she said, "You've put in your time raising little Ricky—I know it's been with our help—but you got shortchanged, not being able to follow in your brothers' footsteps and go to college right after high school."

Her mother's friendly manner contradicted her rather austere appearance. Elizabeth was so religious that it had been absolutely out of the question for Madeleine to have an abortion. Madeleine, when she was a high school senior, had learned that she was pregnant. She had been inclined to have an abortion, but her mother had insisted otherwise. Madeleine rued the night that her boyfriend of two months had gotten her pregnant. She and her boyfriend had broken up, and her plans for college had been dashed when her mother had convinced her to have the baby. She was lucky she had been able to finish high school.

It was a big day. The warm late August morning sun spilled into the car as they wound their way through traffic toward the University of Arizona campus in Tempe. Madeleine beamed as they approached the brick buildings of the campus, with its spacious lawns and subtropical landscaping.

"Don't you worry about Ricky," Mark said. "Your mother's going to keep him occupied at the zoo, so you can get registered and check on your schedule." Madeleine's father kept his eyes on traffic, but she caught a glimpse of him in the rearview mirror and saw that he was smiling. It was wonderful to see his smile today, after the disappointment and devastation of her pregnancy.

"I won't," Madeleine said. "Having Ricky was the right decision. I cannot imagine my life without him. You both have been wonderful to me, and I thank you." Madeleine was elated at the thought of finally being able to immerse herself in a world far removed from diapers and baby talk. She was truly grateful that her parents were going to take on the lion's share of raising Ricky, at least for a while. She was also appreciative that after classes were over for the day, she would have a comfortable home to return to with wonderful cooking smells. This was going to be the best of both worlds—going to college while living at home. Her mom was not only very religious— she was also a doting mother and a wonderful cook.

The University of Arizona served more than sixty-four thousand students throughout its four campuses. The Tempe campus sat on more than seven hundred sprawling acres. Madeleine's wide-eyed look told it all. She was excited and ready for the challenge college would provide. She'd prove herself through hard work and dedication. Yes, she was ready!

As the car rolled to a stop in front of the Palo Verde building, where registration was already underway, Madeleine hugged little Ricky good-bye, gave him a peck on his cheek for good luck, and headed to the mandatory freshman orientation. The campus was bustling with students toting brand-new backpacks, notebooks, and folders; it was all so exciting.

"I'll pick you up in a few hours, Madeleine. Just text us," her mother said cheerfully.

"Grrr, go get 'em, Tiger!" Mark said encouragingly. Madeleine waved, trying to get Ricky's attention. SpongeBob ruled Ricky's life at the moment. Mark and Elizabeth waved back and smiled. Little Ricky didn't take his eyes off the TV.

I feel like Alice when she steps through the looking glass, Madeleine thought. Madeleine had not been this excited since her first day in high school. There were students going in every direction—skateboarders juggling books, bikers carrying backpacks filled to the brim with new books, walkers, joggers—it was almost a circus scene. But the most exciting thing for Madeleine was that they were mostly all her age. She was afraid, having to start college after a three-year hiatus, that she would find herself one of the older students, but that did not seem to be the case. To her delight there seemed to be a balance of older and younger students.

The campus had so many buildings that she could just taste the lectures being taught within them. *I plan to have a class in every one of these halls of wisdom. Sitting out of college might have been the best thing that happened to me*, she thought to herself, as she was now older, more mature, and more eager to go.

Chapter 9

Professor Walther's classes were always controversial and always filled. It was said that students learned more in one of his classes than in five of their other classes combined. His classes were legendary around the campus, so much so that etched on a men's room bathroom stall was the caution, MISS ONE OF WALTHER'S CLASSES AND ALL IS LOST. He was known for presenting material that was not in the course-required text. Yes, the course-required textbook was Professor Walther's own book, *Border Crossing: An American Invasion.* Unlike most college textbooks, it had made the *New York Times* Best Seller list for fifty-three weeks and was on the short list for several awards.

Today's class was no different. The students were focused and intent, trying to absorb in one hour what normally would be covered in one week. Students regularly complained that it was unfair that they could not type or write fast enough to keep up with his lectures. Professor Walther smiled inwardly as he surveyed the room. *I can sure fill a lecture hall,* he thought.

"Now, as I said, for each of you to have a full understanding of our immigration problems with Mexico, you must first have a good grasp of our history with Mexico. We will follow that with some of the more unique arguments and insights into the immigration issue spanning nearly a hundred years.

"In 1821, Mexico gained its independence from Spain. The war between the United States and Mexico ended in 1848. With the Mexican cession, the United States took control of what we commonly refer to today as the Southwest, which included California, Nevada, and parts of Utah.

"Most of you know about the California Gold Rush in 1848, when tens of thousands of Chinese migrant workers were brought to the United States to labor on the railroads and in the mines.

This surge of Chinese immigrants continued until the late 1800s. Times were tough in the West after the Civil War, and there was resentment toward the Chinese, who were competing with Americans for jobs. So in 1892, Congress passed the Chinese Exclusion Act. The main purpose of this landmark legislation was to restrict immigration of the Chinese to America. This was important for several reasons. One such reason—it was the first time the United States had made serious inroads in an attempt to restrict immigration into our borders. Remember, at this time certain industries, specifically railroad companies, were looking for cheap labor that they had now lost.

"The first place the railroad companies turned to replace the Chinese workers was Mexico. In addition, during this same period, copper mining was a booming industry in the Southwest, mainly in Arizona, so again cheap labor was needed. They turned to Mexico to fill their workforce needs. If history has taught us anything, it is that a country's battle with immigration, both legal and illegal, rises dramatically when there is a call for a huge labor force. But historically speaking, the opposite is true during times of economic depression. As an example, in 1929, the year of our disastrous stock-market crash, the United States deported nearly a half a million Mexicans who were competing for US jobs."

As Craig quickly scanned the lecture hall, he caught the eye of a chubby Mexican student who looked as if she was just about to fall asleep. "Miss Gomez," he said, pointing at her. "Could you tell the class from your required reading what the Bracero Program was?"

He might as well have asked her to name all the past American presidents in order. To make matters worse, she had not read the chapter for this week's class.

"I forgot," the student sheepishly replied.

"No, Miss Gomez, the correct answer is, 'I don't know.' To forget something, you had to know it once, and since I am sure you did not read the chapter, you did not know it EVER!

"Initiated in 1942, the Bracero Program was a series of laws and diplomatic agreements between Mexico and the United States. The agreements were initiated because of the perceived need for cheap, temporary contract laborers in the Southwest. One of the specific needs was to harvest sugar beets in the Stockton area of California. Again, there was a need for repair work on the nationwide railroad system. The Bracero program ended in 1964, but not before there was an estimated fifty thousand Mexicans performing low-wage agricultural work and another seventy-five thousand working on the railroads."

"Professor, I have a question!"

Immediately, the hair on the back of Craig's neck stood up. He'd noticed this particular student from day one and had tried to dismiss his fear as being racially motivated. However, this tall, lanky, bearded Chicano was just too reminiscent of many of the students at UNM that he had encountered in earlier classes. Craig fought to keep the thoughts from forming in his mind, but he couldn't help it: Brown Berets. The Brown Berets were to the Mexican population in the Southwest what the Black Panthers had been to the Negroes in the South and along the east coast. They were hard-line radicals, racists, nothing but trouble. They had chips on their shoulders and were always spoiling for a fight.

"Yes? What's your question?"

"Well, Professor, it seems that you moved from 1964 to 1986, and I noticed in reading the chapters for today's class that there was a significant event in 1980."

Not missing a beat, Professor Walther replied, "I don't necessarily attempt to cover every issue in every class, but since you seem to think it's important, what is it specifically that I failed to mention?"

"Well, I think it's significant that in 1980, for the first time, the US Census Bureau used the classification of 'Hispanics' in referring to those people of Mexican origin. So why do you keep referring to us as Mexicans when the US Census Bureau refers to us as Hispanics? Seems like you've got some hang-up or bias." He paused for the class to take a collective breath, and then added slowly, "Or *something*!"

It was the way he finished his comment with the word *something* that really bothered Craig. The student had taken what seemed like a minute to say that last word, and he had overly accentuated it with a mockingly heavy accent. Like a hood might say, "Hey, you want to make *something* of it?"

The gauntlet had been tossed. The question for Craig was where he was going to take it. He was in great spirits today and not in the mood for this contest. With roughly 50 percent of the class having Mexican heritage, things could get out of hand relatively quickly. The question facing Craig at this moment was how to defuse and move on. What perturbed Craig was that he had to defuse this so early in the course. Clearly, his comments the first day of class had made this young man bitter.

Craig turned and faced his student. "Well, maybe you can help me solve this issue. Why don't you tell the class the definition of the word 'Hispanic'?"

Ah, he could see that he had caught the young man off guard. But, being young and cocky, this Mexican student was going to try not to let Craig know that he was caught off guard.

His face contorted, and he practically spat out the words, "You know what it means, man. It's us—Chicanos, Latinos, Mexicans. Those of us living in Mexico and here in United States, legally or illegally—that's what it is, and I think we should be treated with more respect. How would you like it if we referred to you as *gringo*?" The remark rippled across the hall from student to student, like heat lightning flashing across the sky from cloud to cloud on a summer's eve. Whispers could be heard, mostly from the Mexicans. A look of desperation was visible on the faces of the white students. Their collective feeling showed on their faces:

Has this student given Professor Walther a challenge he might not be able to deal with?

"That seems to be your personal definition, but since we're in a college setting, I was hoping you could give me a definition that one might find in the dictionary. Since I happen to know one, by heart, let me give it to you: 'Hispanic—Spanish: *Hispano*; Portuguese: *Hispânico*; Latin: *Hispānus*, adjective from *Hispania*, the Roman name for the Iberian Peninsula—is a term that historically denoted the relation to the ancient Hispania and its peoples.'"

The class was somewhat stunned that these words flowed so easily from Professor Walther. But he had only begun his defense; now he was going on the attack. While the words were still leaving his lips, somehow—almost magically—there was a book in his hand, and he already had his finger pointed at some paragraph, and his face was visibly reddening. It was impossible to tell where he had stopped speaking from memory and where he was now reading from his book.

"Etymologically, the term 'Hispanic' is derived from 'Hispania,' the name given by the ancient Romans to the Iberian Peninsula, present-day Spain, Portugal, Andorra, and Gibraltar. 'Hispanus' was the Latin name given to the people of Hispania, the Hispano-Romans. The Hispano-Romans were composed of people from many different origins and tribes of Hispania. Some famous Hispani, plural of 'Hispanus,' were Seneca the Elder, Seneca the Younger, Lucan, Martial, Prudentius, the Roman Emperor Trajan, the Roman Emperor Theodosius the First, and also Magnus Maximus and Maximus of Hispania."

Craig put down the book he was quoting from and turned to the student. "I will make you a deal, and, as a matter of fact, I will make this deal with every student in this room for the rest of the semester. From this point forward, for those of you who can prove to me that you have some recent direct heritage ties to any of the following countries—Portugal, Spain, or

Gibraltar—I will refer to you as Hispanics. And to show you how magnanimous I am, I will set aside my request for proof and just ask for a show of hands."

Hearing a pin drop would have been too pedestrian of a cliché for the silence that filled the room. It was as if Professor Walther had waved a magic wand, and all the tension had been immediately lifted from the room. Never in recorded history had an opponent been so easily disarmed. But Craig was not gloating in his conquest. His job was to teach, not lecture, and his teaching style was to defuse conflicts and look for solutions to ongoing problems related to the US-Mexico border situation. If he could not handle a small incident here in a single lecture hall, how was he going to help on an international level?

"*Mis amigos*, I think we've all had enough for one day. Why don't we cut our class a bit short? Class dismissed. I will see you all next week. And a reminder for all of you—try doing your required assignment and catching a catnap somewhere other than my lecture hall!"

Chapter 10

It was a middle-class house in a middle-class neighborhood. Not much more needed to be said; there was nothing bad about the house, nor was there anything great about the house. It looked like every other house on the street. It was early morning, and Dave Walther had gone outside to adjust a sprinkler that was spraying water against the kitchen window. Anita, his wife, waved at her husband from the kitchen. He looked up at her and smiled. Anita was a young, beautiful Mexican woman with thick, rich, black hair cascading down to the middle of her back. She was his angel, and at times he'd lie next to her and watch her sleep, chest rising and falling with each gentle breath. Dave knew he was one lucky hombre.

Anita buttered some toast, licked her fingers, and glanced down at her stomach—which now bulged out so much that her big sweatshirts could no longer double as maternity clothes.

Dave came into the small but nicely decorated kitchen and shook some water off the shoulder of his uniform. He grabbed some toast, put on his hat, and said, "I've got to go. I love you." He patted his wife's stomach, leaned over, and whispered, "Good-bye, David Walther Junior."

Anita smiled and said, "No, his name will be Enrico." She suddenly remembered something as Dave walked out the door. Her dark eyebrows arched upward as she shouted, "Wait! You forgot the package!"

Dave's shoulders slumped as he turned around and shuffled back to her. "Why do you do this to me?"

Not angrily but with a tinge of frustration in her voice, Anita replied, "*Why* do I do this? *Why* do you have this job? You shouldn't have taken it in the first place."

He said, "Look, we needed the money. The first time we get some money in the bank, we'll move and I'll get away from this mess, I promise!" He took the package—a heavy, large shopping bag—and got into his truck. As he exited the driveway, the side of his truck became visible. It read US CUSTOMS: BORDER PATROL.

Chapter 11

Even with the millions of dollars that had been thrown at the US Border Patrol, the San Diego office still had that drab governmental look to it. Pinkish, skin-colored paint flaked off the walls, and the floors looked like they hadn't been cleaned in weeks. A general sense of grime permeated the air. Dave grabbed a second cup of coffee in the break room and acknowledged another agent who had ambled into the room.

"Hey, Dave. I see you're taking another load of wetbacks down to Rosarito."

"No," Dave said. "Boss says this group is going to Tijuana. I just returned from picking them up. I need to grab some other things before I can leave. Oh, yeah—is the boss in? I need to talk to him before I leave."

The boss was Captain Bernard Stewart, but if anyone called him anything but "Buck," they'd catch hell. Captain Stewart was a lifer. One way or another, he had worked for the US government his entire life. He'd dropped out of high school and enlisted in the navy, then after Vietnam, he'd gone to work for the Federal Bureau of Narcotics, which in 1973 had become the Drug Enforcement Administration, the DEA. It was rumored that while he'd been in 'Nam, he had ratted on a fellow enlisted man who sold pot, so the DEA job had sort of come natural to him. He was assigned to the San Diego, California, office.

At some point, apparently, Buck had gotten himself into a little trouble with some missing drugs, again all based on rumor, but before anyone could figure out what exactly had happened, ole Buck had transferred to the US Border Patrol. After ten years, he was now running the San Diego office. The promotions had come not so much because he was well liked—because he wasn't—but rather because he seemed to get the job done when others couldn't. He was mean and ornery, and in this hostile border environment, those were good character traits. It meant he'd make it home for dinner and get to live a little longer.

Dave and Buck had been butting heads since the first day they'd met. They had absolutely nothing in common. Unlike Buck, Dave had graduated from college, just like his three brothers. Dave had never envisioned himself working for a governmental agency. His father had been a military man, and though his father spoke favorably of his life in the army, Dave had always sensed that the military had not treated his father fairly. Like their father, all of the Walther boys were headstrong and stubborn, except for maybe Mark. Likewise, it was a proven fact that Mark, Cliff, Craig, David, and their dad did not brown nose or kiss ass. That was not an acceptable way of life for a Walther. Each Walther man, at one time or another, had paid the consequence for that lifestyle choice.

Like many young students, Dave hadn't known what he wanted to do when he'd graduated from college, so his college major had ended up being history. He enjoyed history, but during his senior year, the light bulb had gone on, and he'd realized the only thing he could do with a history degree was teach. But that would require him to get at least a master's degree and probably a doctorate. Teaching sounded exciting to him; staying in school a few more years did not. Armed with a history degree, Dave's job hunting had turned out to be problematic.

While searching for a job, Dave had thought it would make sense to work in an area where he wanted to live. He'd never had the opportunity to live near a beach while he was growing up, yet on almost every vacation, he was off to one beach or another. So he'd selected San Diego as the city where he would job hunt. It was the warmest water he could find on the west coast without having to move to Mexico. The only jobs he'd found with any kind of decent pay were for one governmental agency or another. Even so, many of those doors were closed due to affirmative action—reverse discrimination, as far as Dave was concerned—plans requiring many departments to hire either women or minorities. The US Border Patrol had been looking for new agents, and since the San Diego department already employed a high percentage of Hispanics, being white didn't disqualify Dave from applying. He found the entrance exam simple, requiring only an eighth-grade level of education to get the top score. Dave had heard that law enforcement tests were dumbed down to allow Hispanic and black applicants an equal opportunity to fill the ranks of the services, but he didn't mind. He lived where he wanted to live and made a decent income. Now, here he was, twenty-plus years later, still working for the US Border Patrol. Yes, he had had promotions, but they'd been limited. It was hard to move up the ranks, and then there was ole Buck, who would have to die before he'd retire.

There was one thing that Dave really loved about being part of the border patrol and that was the bravery he witnessed of his fellow agents. Almost on a daily basis both the men and women risked their lives in the performance of their duties.

Dave knocked lightly on his boss's door and heard a response from the captain: "Come in!"

Dave opened the door and stepped into the office, his eyes resting on the bottoms of ole Buck's boots. Buck was leaning back in his chair; his lizard-skin cowboy boots propped up on his big government-issued metal desk. God, he was an ugly sight. It seemed no matter what time of day, what season of the year, or even how recently Buck had donned his green, pressed uniform, he sweated through it instantly. His face suffered from a similarly unpleasant malady. Within an hour after shaving, Buck's face sported a five o'clock shadow. Buck's big, fat, sweaty face had so many folds in it, it looked like a road map. To make matters worse, a triple chin and meaty jowels couldn't be confined by his overstarched shirt collar, and the fat mass flowed like molten lava over the top of his collar. It made Buck appear as if he had no neck at all. Dave thought to himself, *How could such a pig of a man be my superior?*

David politely asked, "Sir, can I talk to you for a moment?" Buck replied, "I thought you had a truckload to get down to Tijuana today. What're you doin' in here?"

"I had a few things I needed to fetch out of my locker, and while I was here, I wanted to speak with you for just a moment."

Buck shifted his bulking mass. "Okay, set your ass down, but keep it brief. I've got lots to do this morning and then a lunch meeting at my favorite Mexican restaurant."

Taking a deep breath, Dave began, "Well, lately I've been getting some uncomfortable feelings when I've been out on patrol."

"Indigestion or diarrhea, son?" Buck always had to add his sour humor.

"That's good!" Dave chuckled then turned sober. "I'm serious, and it's not just when I've been on patrol. In the last month, when I've been in Tijuana and Mexicali, it seemed strange. It just felt funny. Different. I can't put my finger on it, but my years as a BPO have got the hairs on my arms standing up."

"That's great, son. I can do a lot with that. Let me get on the phone with my superiors in Washington and tell them we have a serious problem down here because one of our border agents *feels funny*. Can you be a little bit more specific? *Funny* just won't cut shit with the department heads!" scoffed Buck. "Well, it's hard for me to describe. It's just a different feeling." Dave squirmed at the reaction he suspected his next sentence would provoke. "Maybe the word I'm looking for is *crowded*. It just feels *crowded*." "Crowded! Jesus Christ! Crowded! Holy hell, son, it *is* crowded. They tell me at 1.5 million Mexicans, Tijuana is bigger than San Diego. Crowded! The damn Mexicans give birth at a rate 50 percent higher than us gringos. You bet it's crowded! Get the hell out of my office. Crowded!" Buck waved Dave off, swung his feet off his desk, and began busying himself with something else, not looking up at Dave again. "Don't let the door hit you in the ass on the way out!"

Dave didn't understand why he had even ventured into Buck's office. "The jerk!" It was more than the fact that they had never gotten along. Today he felt worse than usual because he realized he had appeared foolish to his superior. Why couldn't he describe the feeling he had? Crowded. It did sound lame, even to him. Dave walked out to the parking lot and slammed the door to the border patrol transport truck and started the engine. The clatter from the slammed door woke up all ten of the Mexicans who had fallen asleep in the back.

Chapter 12

There were three US ports of entry between Mexico and the United States fairly close to San Diego—the San Ysidro station, the Otay Mesa station, and the Tecate station, which was further west. Dave drove his truckload of illegals through San Ysidro, which was just twenty miles from downtown San Diego. He then crossed over into Mexico and made his way to the major Mexican intake area just on the other side of the border in Tijuana. The entire trip was a fairly congested drive. It was often difficult, except at the border stations, to tell the difference between San Ysidro, California, and Tijuana, Mexico. The shops, the restaurants, the signs, and even the people looked the same. But in Mexico, where over 25 percent of the population had an average income of under $5,000 a year, the increase in poverty was painfully evident as Dave crossed the border.

Over the last few weeks, on his trips to Tijuana returning illegals to the intake center, Dave had observed more idle people standing around or large groups milling about than usual. Today he saw some of the same faces from his last trip. *Why would they still be here? Why are the crowds growing in size? Something is wrong, and good ole Buck called me foolish.* Buck had said, "Crowded! The damn Mexicans give birth at a rate 50 percent higher than us gringos. You bet it's crowded!"

Buck's a damn jerk! Dave thought. To be a border-patrol officer and to survive any time in the field, one developed a sixth sense. Often it is that sixth sense that made the difference between life and death. Dave's instincts were screaming at him, but he just couldn't make heads or tails of the warning. He pulled out his smartphone and scrolled to the calendar app to see what day it was. Dave's thinking leaned toward the answer being that this was some holy week observance. Because the vast majority of Mexicans were Roman Catholics, and it seemed like they were always having some kind of celebration or festival, it seemed a logical answer. Maybe that was it. As he sat at a stoplight that never seemed to turn green, he popped his head out the window and yelled in Spanish at a group of Mexicans close by.

"Excuse me, amigo, is there some celebration or fiesta today?" None of the Mexicans had the least bit of trouble understanding him. He spoke fluent Spanish, and with his Mexican wife, he even had the accents and pronunciations down perfectly.

"No, there is nothing going on special that we know about, jefe," one replied.

Dave shrugged his shoulders and thought, *What's with this crowded feeling? Maybe I'm just going crazy.* But deep down, Dave's intuition was still sounding off. Dave shook his head. He'd never ignored the warnings, but Buck's admonition continued to resonate with him. *Just forget it*, he thought, *and think about how you get to go home and eat dinner with your beautiful wife each night.*

Chapter 13

Dave had never cared much for the United States Border Patrol (USBP) office in San Diego. Its drabness only served to remind him that he worked for the government. As bad as it was, it was nowhere near as awful as its Mexican counterpart in Tijuana. Dave had been returning Mexican deportees to that office for as long as he had been stationed in San Diego. To the best of his recollection, the Tijuana office had looked as dilapidated and rundown on his first visit as it did today, twenty years later. The telephone wires were strung like Christmas lights. There was trash on the floor and blood splatter and bullet holes in the walls; broken windows covered with plywood or cardboard barely kept the blowing dust from polluting the air. It was an insult to all Mexican law-enforcement personnel. In the United States, the building would have been condemned and marked for the bulldozers.

Dave quickly parked his truck out front and opened the back door to check on his ten deportees. Once again, it seemed as if he had awakened them.

"Is it siesta time?" Dave shouted. "Wake up! You guys have your nights and days mixed up."

What is it these people do all night? he wondered as he locked the truck.

He was thankful that he never had to come down here at night. The front office that he entered was well lit, but the source of the light, he discovered, was coming in through what few windows were left intact. He had noted before that there were no lights on the ceilings, but now he noticed there wasn't even a desk lamp on any of the old dilapidated desks. It never ceased to amaze Dave how so many of the buildings in Mexico were substandard in construction. The same companies must have been awarded the contracts for the governmental buildings as well. Thank God he was here for a very short visit. He could imagine the whole detainee's office collapsing under a stiff breeze. It made the USBP office in San Diego look like the Taj Mahal.

"*¿Dónde está todo el mundo hoy?" Where is everybody today?*

That was another thing that Dave had never gotten used to— siestas. Why was it that the entire country of Mexico shut down between noon and 3:00 p.m.? It wasn't like they came to work particularly early in the morning or worked after 5:00 p.m. No wonder Mexico had never been a world power; the population seemed to be on one long siesta. It was 11:30 a.m. Where was everyone? He needed to drop off his load of wetbacks and get going. He yelled a few times but heard no response. He knew that there were cells in the back of the building but had never gone back there. But he was growing impatient. As Dave started to turn the handle of the door that led to the back, it was suddenly pulled from his hand from the other side. Standing in front of him was his Mexican counterpart, a *Federale*, a slang term for the Mexican federal government law-enforcement employees. *Thin, sweaty,* and *scarred* were the first thoughts that came to David's mind. His sixth sense was ramping up again.

"Where is everybody? I have ten deportees I need to return immediately." The Federale's nervousness and his frightened, haunted-eye look made Dave uncomfortable. "Can you just initial the paperwork and let me get out of here?" stammered Dave, feeling more nervous himself.

"Ten more? We cannot take ten more," he barked. "You will have to take them over to the Otay Mesa Station," the officer said as he wiped the sweat from his brow.

"No way in hell! In this traffic, that's over a two-hour trip. You have to take them off my hands," Dave stated with no intention of backing down.

With this, the Mexican officer for the first time allowed the door to swing open as if to invite Dave in. Immediately, the smell of rot and filth assaulted Dave's nose and stung his eyes. Something quickly rose in the back of his throat, threatening to spill out. Dave took an involuntary step back as if he had been hit with a terrific frontal blow. He forced the bile back down and stepped forward, ready to do battle with the unholy scene that lay before him.

Dave had been under the impression that the deportees were quickly rerouted back to central Mexico, but what he saw now was unlike anything he had ever envisioned. The entire back of the building was one large jail cell. The bars started immediately to the left and went straight ahead some fifty feet, turned right and ran twenty-five feet, and then returned another fifty feet back to his right. It was one large U-shaped human vault. Front to back, each part was about thirty feet deep with a hole crudely chopped into the floor for a toilet. Dave nearly vomited watching the sea of undulating, unwashed bodies and smelling the excrement-filled hole.

"My God! Just how many prisoners are in this cell?" His mind immediately flashed to one of the pirate movies he had recently seen on late-night TV. In the hold of the galleon, prisoners had been packed in like sardines. That's what they looked like, sardines, but with their heads on. There must've been a thousand of them. Even if there were not a thousand prisoners, there were still too many confined in the space behind the bars.

"Why are you retaining so many of these people? Why aren't you shipping them out?"

"There is nowhere for them to go. Everywhere is full," replied the Federale.

With this, Dave turned his back and quickly stormed across the main office and out the front door. He hastily tried to get out his keys to unlock the back of the truck. But nervousness made his hands shake, and he fumbled with the lock. Finally, he got it open.

"*¡Hacia fuera! ¡Salga! ¡Usted sale!* Out! Get out! All of you, get out!" Dave was usually very kind and courteous to the Mexicans he came in contact with, but today's trip had been unsettling, and he wanted to get back to the United States ASAP! As a group, they marched through the front door and into the office. Immediately, an argument ensued with his counterpart. Dave would hear nothing of it; he was following orders, and this place made him sick to his stomach. Besides, Buck wouldn't give a damn about the conditions here or allow him to transport the deportees to another station. Dave saw the stack of deportee-return forms sitting on a nearby desk and grabbed one. He quickly signed off, as he was required to do as the USBP officer in charge of the return. He stormed back out the front and slammed the truck door as he climbed into it, the Mexican officer still complaining that he didn't have room. Dave opened the truck's door to respond but instead slammed it shut harder than he had the first time, shaking his fist at the slack-jawed officer.

Why was this scene making him so upset? Why were his hands shaking so violently? He'd deported Mexicans on a regular basis for twenty years. What was it about seeing that retention area that made him so nervous? Was it the fact that the other officer seemed so nervous? Suddenly, a word shot back into his mind—*crowded*. That was it. *Crowded*. The word had been bothering him and getting him in hot water all day. That cell was crowded. He jerked his head around and carefully scanned the streets as he drove. The streets were crowded, very crowded. He became even more anxious as he imagined that the crowds were surrounding his truck and closing the circle even tighter. He'd soon be engulfed by the hordes of Mexicans around *him*.

Dave pulled off the road and skidded to a stop, trying to collect himself. He slumped over the steering wheel, screaming out in frustration. As he started to calm down, he saw the shopping bag his wife, Anita, had given him that morning sitting on the front seat. He'd be fine; the vision of his wife's beautiful smile snapped him out of his panic.

Oh, yes, the sandwiches. It was Anita's special thing. They had argued over them time and again, but Anita would not stop making the sandwiches. Each morning when she knew Dave had to return deportees, she'd ask him how many he anticipated; Dave hated the question. Anita prepared a sandwich, a piece of fruit, and some pieces of candy for each of the deportees, or as she called them, "my friends."

"Please make sure *my friends* get *my* food," she reminded him those mornings.

He hid it from everybody at work. He would be laughed at if anyone discovered that his wife was feeding the deportees. Frankly, he thought it was a thoughtful gesture. He certainly felt sorry for those people and didn't view them as criminals or illegals, even though that was exactly what they were. Most were only trying to find work and to feed and clothe their families. Passing out his wife's sandwiches was something he complained about but never failed to do. But not today! He wanted to get out of Mexico as fast as he could and take a shower. After what he had seen at the deportees' station, he felt dirty, filthy. Looking out the driver's-side window, he saw in his mirror a crowd suddenly appear. Dave grabbed the shopping bag and hurled it out the window. Where had they come from? What was going on? As he sped down the road hell bent for the US border, he caught a glimpse of the melee taking place behind him. The crowd had torn open the shopping bag and was eating the food. Dave noted the vehemence in their actions.

As the truck's wheels crossed the border, Dave's mind again returned to the crowds and how overwhelmed the streets had been with throngs of people milling about. It was madness.

The Mexican government gave lip service to the United States and had for decades, saying that it would assist in limiting the numbers crossing into the United States. However, the reality was quite the opposite: a game played, with America being the loser. The Mexican government couldn't give a damn about emigration from Mexico; it had more serious problems to deal with. Because of this attitude, as the US Border Patrol returned illegals to Mexican law enforcement, they just locked them up for a few days. Sometimes they would transport them further away from the border, but eventually they just let them all go free. Statistics proved that within a few short weeks, almost all of them returned to the United States. The US-Mexican border was nothing but a revolving, or worse, an *open* door!

Chapter 14

As Dave crossed the bridge into the United States, he almost jumped out of his truck and kissed the ground. Not since his disastrous trip to Peru back in college had he been so glad to be back in the States. He wondered if he had had one too many cups of coffee that morning, because it was only now that his hands stopped shaking. Then he flashed back to the nightmare he had experienced a few hours earlier. If anything, Dave was border savvy, trained to see the less obvious, and his years on the job had taught him to interpret and respect his intuition, then respond calmly. In his mind's eye, he quickly reviewed what he had observed on the streets during his trip and made up his mind. No doubt about it—he was a trained observer and that training had saved his skin on many occasions! He asked himself, *Were the* additional *numbers of Mexicans I witnessed as close to the border as I think? Yes.* He had not imagined things. His instincts were screaming at him again. They were close, pushing at the border.

And even now back in the States, Dave noticed the same thing: "more people than usual" was the best description. But Dave mumbled to himself, "Dave, you gotta get something more substantial to take back to Buck, something more than a hunch or a feeling." Remembering his brief meeting with Buck that morning, he still stung from being called foolish.

Suddenly, it struck him. Any border-patrol officer with as many years as he had under his belt should be able to tell illegal from legal. However, the issue that made identification so difficult was the millions of illegals who had been in the United States for years. It was nearly impossible to tell them apart from the legal Mexican Americans.

The USBP was not in the business of rounding up existing illegals. That was a job for ICE and local law-enforcement agencies. It was estimated that illegal Mexicans who resided in Southern California numbered in the millions. Dave and his fellow officers could fill up Qualcomm Stadium in minutes with illegals. "Crap, we could fill all of the stadiums in the north, east, south, and west and still only scratch the surface of the illegal population." So the border patrol had been mandated to stop the flow of Mexicans flooding across the border illegally. Even that was a joke. No one was stopping anything, and the flow had gotten worse and continued even with all the initiatives since 9/11 that had been enacted. In addition to slowing the flow right at the border, Dave and the other USBP officers regularly swooped down and broke up illegal businesses within two hundred miles of the border. Still, 80 percent of their work, raids, and arrests were within fifty miles of the border. The Mexicans had learned two key elements to a successful illegal crossing: disperse and assimilate.

Dave woke from his trance to car horns blaring at him from behind.

"Crap! How long has the light been green?" As he roared forward, his mind went back scanning the day's happenings. Yes, his sixth sense served him well, and his senses were now at full alert. There were the obvious telltale signs—the clothes that looked like they'd been made in Mexico and worn out from their long, hard journey. New arrivals always kept their heads down and avoided making eye contact. Dave could sense that secrecy as they were keeping a close watch on everything around them. The most telling fact, however, was their weight. In the past, many Mexicans who had snuck into the United States had traveled over a thousand miles, mostly on foot. Though their countrymen helped with handouts, the mass migration had been going on for so long there was not enough food to go around. These travelers were gaunt, just skin and bones. Clothes hung from their shoulders as if from macabre scarecrows used to frighten birds in corn fields. These new crowds Dave was witnessing looked desperate. Dave knew of ranchers who had experienced home invasions where hungry illegals emptied cupboards and refrigerators and went so far as to steal family pets. Frighteningly, it seemed that almost everyone he saw looked exceptionally lean and hungry.

Dave's calm demeanor was being pushed past its limits, and he quickly called his office.

"Is Buck in? This is Walther."

"No, he hasn't returned from lunch yet."

"Who's second-in-command today? Is it Brian? Is he in?"
"Yeah, he's here."

"Let me talk to him."

It took a few minutes for Brian to pick up the transferred call.

"Brian, this is Dave. Hey, I wanted to relay something to you. I am here in San Ysidro, and I noticed something I thought you might want to report to Buck as soon as you see him."

"This is not your *crowd theory*, is it? Man, Dave, whatever you're smoking is making you paranoid."

"Shit, how did you hear about that? Buck is such an asshole."

"As soon as you walked out, Buck told the whole office. We all had a good laugh. Man, I know you haven't been sleeping well since your wife got pregnant. But really, do you think the natives are after you?"

"Do you want to hear what I have to report or not?"

"Not if it's more about crowds—I don't want to get caught up in your paranoia."

"Assholes!" Dave yelled into the phone and threw it across the cab of his truck. Was he going mad? It was true; he hadn't been getting enough sleep lately, but those nagging suspicions told him something else was going on. He stomped the accelerator pedal trying to put the entire day behind him. His office was filled with assholes.

Chapter 15

Professor Walther stood at the front of the class with his chest puffed up. Man, he was in a great mood.

"Good morning! All right, let's see if someone read this week's chapter. Can someone please tell me the number one reason so many Mexicans emigrate to the United States?"

It was that same kid from before in the back, but now smart enough to raise his hand.

"Okay, son. I admire your bravery. What's the reason? And, please, shout it out loud enough for all of us to hear!"

"Better job opportunities," the student said, absolutely sure this time.

Making the sound of a game-show buzzer, the professor bellowed, "Good try. But the correct answer is, much better Mexican food. Those of you who have traveled beyond the border cities into Mexico are not going to try and convince me that you think the food in Mexico is better than here. Nothing anywhere competes with Baca's in Albuquerque or the Shed or Maria's in Santa Fe! Class, are you going to tell me different?" Then breaking into laughter, Craig addressed the students. "I was just in the mood for a little levity this morning. Sorry to screw with your head. By the way, son, what is your name?"

Harold, a thoroughly perplexed kid, responded, still unsure if he was the joke or if the professor was just being funny. Harold didn't have a sense of what to say or do, so he stood there looking stupid. He promised himself that never, *ever* would he volunteer an answer in Professor Walther's class again.

"Okay, Harold, you can sit down. And, yes, *job opportunities* is the number one answer! Today we will do a current, comparative analysis of the United States and Mexico mainly from an economic perspective. I will let each of you draw your own conclusions based on some of these startling facts." Craig was in the zone. This was his strength, his expertise. Starting off like a whizbang, Craig said, "If you lived in Mexico, would you stay in your homeland or would you emigrate to the United States? People, are the differences so dramatic that you might consider doing it illegally? As you recall from reading my textbook, chapter six, there is a chart on page thirty-eight showing contrasting statistics between the United States and Mexico, up to date through the end of 2013, with some of them being a bit older." His students dutifully turned in their course books to page thirty-eight and saw the following:

VARIOUS COMPARISONS
UNITED STATES VS. MEXICO 2005

Average	United States	Mexico
GDP per Capita	$43,546	$9,786
GDP	$12.7 trillion	$745.3 billion
GDP Annual Growth	3.6%	2.85%
Inflation	2.5%	5.7%

UNITED STATES VS. MEXICO 2013

	United States	Mexico
Population	312,007,212	110,090,877
Population Density	30 per sq. mile	52 per sq. mile
Television Stations	2,310	242
Internet Sites	202,455,770	1,890,444
Personal Computers (per 100)	78	14
Trade as a percent of GDP	4%	63%
GDP Per Capita	44,718	$5,010
GDP Annual Growth	3.4%	-1.3%
Inflation	2.5%	12.8%

"Now we could fill up every one of our remaining classes discussing the various distinctions between the standards of living here in the United States and beyond our border into Mexico. Some of the more glaring statistics on this chart are the TV stations and the hosted Internet sites. Other statistics not reflected here might surprise you, like the average age of a home, the below-average energy efficiency of homes, the average square footage of a single-family dwelling, the quality of the drinking water, the average square footage of retail shopping space per capita, and number of nights spent eating out. How many people in this class have traveled to Mexico? How many have traveled into Mexico other than just the border cities?" Over three-quarters of the students raised their hands.

"Can I also get a show of hands as to how many of you have traveled either to or through some of the more rural or agricultural areas of Mexico?" Now the show of hands was just under 50 percent.

"Good, I'm impressed," said Professor Walther. "It's sad that far too many Americans' perspectives of life in Mexico is defined by spring break in Acapulco, a honeymoon in Puerto Vallarta, or a drunken golf trip to Cancun. But what I would like you to concentrate on and visualize with this chart is my original question that I started with this morning. I hope some of you were alarmed by the deterioration of the economic conditions in 2013 compared to the averages of the previous years. These numbers probably come as a shock to those of you who limit your reading to *People Magazine* and your television viewing to the latest reality shows. Mexico's economy has been deteriorating significantly for the last three years. Its economy is in the toilet. Yes, Harold, your answer is correct—better job opportunities in United States are a very significant motivation for immigration to the United States. But I think that might be sugarcoating it. For millions of Mexicans today, it might be better termed *survival!*

"I think Enrique Peña Nieto, the president of Mexico, was wishing he had never been sworn into office—the guerrilla war and oil price implosion were only half of his problems. As in most world economies, everything is tied together. Mexico, for the last half a century, has had to make economic and monetary adjustments constantly to keep both its inflation rate in check and its currency from losing too much value."

Professor Walther paused and scanned the packed lecture hall; he could see the exasperated looks on the students' faces. Nothing new, the same stuff, different day. He wasn't sympathetic. He had warned the students that if they didn't read the chapter that he was going to be discussing that day in class, they would have a hard time keeping up. And as always, some in the class hadn't heeded his warning. So here they were, having a hard time keeping up. It was a combination of Craig's tendency to cram too much into one class and the rapidity with which he spoke. When Craig got on a roll, he was like a machine, staccato facts firing out at the class. He taught with intensity.

Though it was considered politically incorrect, Craig was constantly complaining to the other professors. In his opinion, he felt that the student body at UNM was somewhere between brain dead and marginally acceptable. He knew it wasn't just a problem that was singularly at UNM. The deteriorating intellect of college students everywhere was systemic. The liberals and their union buddies were responsible for the dumbing down of America.

For decades at every level of education, the quality of teachers had been weakening. When it got too bad and the schools and universities couldn't attract enough qualified teachers, they just lowered the standards, which the unions loved. Of course, the unions also set and negotiated contracts, so US academic institutions couldn't fire anyone for a lack of intelligence or incompetency. The American education system had graduated idiots for so long that those same idiots were now running the government. They were running the corporations and, worse yet, teaching at every classroom level in the American educational system. It was one horrible, vicious circle. Craig's students were missing the skill set they needed to get a degree from an institution of higher education. He found that many of them didn't even possess the most basic grammar and math skills. Garbage in, garbage out.

Craig's reverie was broken by one of his students raising her hand. "Could you slow down, Mr. Walther? I can't write that fast."

Craig wanted to respond with, "It's not just that you can't write that fast, you can't listen that fast." But the last time he'd insulted a student, he'd sat through a dressing down by the dean of his department.

"Okay, I know this is a lot to digest for one day. Let me just finish this next section, and we will call it a day. But I will remind you again to read the assigned chapter in advance, and you'll be way ahead of the game.

"In November 1991, the government eliminated all exchange controls by unifying the various peso exchange rates. The regime freed the peso, and the peso continued to appreciate in real terms. However, Mexico's inflation rate exceeded that of the United States by some eight percentage points. The government was reluctant to devalue the peso to the full extent of the inflation differential with the United States, because it feared that a large devaluation would exacerbate domestic inflation and undermine public confidence in the stability of the government's macroeconomic policy.

"By late 1994, the government was drawing heavily on international reserves to prop up the new peso. When the new peso came under heavy speculative pressure in late 1995, Mexico's monetary authorities reacted by raising interest rates sharply. Mindful of the need to restore investor confidence in Mexico's early economic recovery, the authorities allowed interest rates to fall at the end of 1995. This on-again-and-off-again tweaking continued in the same manner until 2005."

Craig paused and locked eyes with each and every student. They looked in a fog. His eyes expressed his disappointment, and they wilted in their seats.

"Class dismissed. See you all on Thursday!"

Chapter 16

General Kurt Grayson had had enough and tuned out the beehive of activity spinning around the room. Enough! He could no longer distinguish one officious comment from another.

Did these people just talk to hear themselves speak? He'd sat through meeting after meeting. The same pompous speakers piled upon one another, and he cursed the day that he had agreed to be put on the National Security Council as an aide to the secretary of defense. Thank God it required only one monthly meeting at the Department of State. He hated politics, he hated politicians, but what he hated worst was political appointees. Such arrogant, self-important asses.

The National Security Council advised the president on national security. The council consisted of the vice president, secretary of state, secretary of defense, the director of Homeland Security, the director of the CIA, and the special appointees, which was his designation.

General Grayson went back to daydreaming. *Why do I feel so unfulfilled? I've raised a wonderful family, and I'm the highest ranking officer in the military.*

This was a frequent daydream Grayson found himself escaping to when overwhelmed with minutia. Maybe that was the way with all successful men. He had graduated number one in his West Point class of '66. As he had risen in rank, he'd questioned some of the teachings of his professors from West Point, who far too often thought the military was unrelated to politics. All wars were political wars, except maybe those that were fought over religion, but ideology was a political hotbed. General Grayson had convinced himself that when he retired, he was going to study religion. Wasn't the Vatican the most political entity in the Christian world?

With his speed-reading skills and higher-than-average intellect, Grayson had found West Point a breeze. It also helped that he'd spent less time in sports than some of his fellow cadets. He'd realized early that military promotions came a lot faster to those who could prove themselves academically and who excelled in military exercises. Those who made great tackles on the football field found themselves as armchair aides to the highest ranked generals. Most Americans didn't know that the military operated like IBM or Proctor and Gamble, companies that knew that their strength lay in those who clearly could lead and hold the company line. Those who played the game by the rules were promoted quickly. The military's personnel evaluation process was second to none, and Grayson was one such individual flagged early on by his superiors for greatness.

If it hadn't been for Vietnam, Grayson would have been whisked off to the US Army's War College in Carlisle, Pennsylvania. Unlike many of his fellow graduating cadets, First Lieutenant Grayson had been ready and raring to get into combat. To him, a command leading combat forces in Vietnam was like being a white-collar criminal lawyer during the Nixon years. His West Point military history classes had taught him that the United States had been involved in some kind of war almost continually since 1776. The record showed that over the past 236 years, America had been fighting some conflict for 214 of those years or about 90 percent of the time.

However, there was a premonition at the academy that since Vietnam was going so badly, it might be the last war for the United States for a while.

Despite his unconstrained enthusiasm, Grayson had been as shocked as a Buddhist monk stepping off a bus in downtown Las Vegas when he'd first arrived in Vietnam. War did not allow people the luxury of adjustment. He was immediately immersed, and within days Grayson was on the front lines with bloodshed and bombings commonplace. Despite having his ranking officers killed, injured, or sent home in pieces or in a casket, he continued to reveal his prowess and was promoted quickly. He was a first lieutenant out the door from West Point, and after one year in

'Nam, he was a major. His fast-paced battlefield promotions were unheralded, and he refused to be sent home after his initial assignment in Vietnam had been fulfilled. By '73, with the tragic handwriting smeared on the wall in Vietnam, Grayson was already a lieutenant colonel. Though he'd loved the war for its military challenges, the political dog-and-pony show had started to wear on him.

Just as Grayson was about to slip from daydreaming to dreaming, he was jolted back to reality and the meeting at hand.

"Are we boring you, General Grayson?" Secretary of State Marisa Angela Lopez quipped with a heavy dose of disdain.

"I'm sorry. I am sorry, Madam Secretary. I clearly did not get the sleep I needed last night. Would you kindly repeat that last point?" Grayson said as quickly as he could, trying to sweep away the cobwebs and prove that he was truly not asleep. The last person he needed to piss off was Lopez.

"*Again* and especially for you, General, I was saying that the state department has looked into all of these stories and allegations coming out of Mexico and the US border states and currently feels that everyone, especially the press, is overreacting." Her statement, for the second time that morning, caused the room to explode, with everyone talking at the same time.

"I think it's totally irresponsible to ignore the fact that Zapatista's guerrilla warfare has escalated, according to the recent CIA report we have in front of us..." Bob Triden said, heard by all only because of his loud voice.

"Since when was the CIA right about anything?" retorted a sneering Madam Secretary.

"Dammit, Marisa, if our radars confirmed nuclear warheads were within minutes of hitting New York City, you'd opt for a congressional study," said John Hardwick, the secretary of defense, glaring at her. Though Hardwick had retired from active navy ten years earlier, he and Grayson were cut from the same fabric. They had relied on each other over the years and had grown to be good friends and drinking buddies.

"Well, John, putting your sarcasm aside, I think you may have something there. I think we should form a subcommittee in the House of Representatives to study these wild stories coming from the Mexican border," said Senator Lathan, the only senator on the NSC board. He was on the NSC because of his chairmanship of the Senate Security Council and Homeland Security. Hardwick and Grayson both immediately shared mutual looks of disgust. It was the nature of the beast, they thought, much like the difference between men and women. Whether good or bad, they could always count on the US military to make quick decisions. Study groups, committees, and subcommittees were for pansies and elected politicians. Basic military training taught that long battlefield discussions would only get people killed. There was no time, when the enemy was advancing, to have a latte, form a committee, and chat about how to proceed. Quick thinking and an immediate, correct response were paramount for a successful campaign and return of soldiers back home to their loved ones. Seasoned senior officers such as Hardwick and Grayson knew the score and had risen to the top ranks because of it.

"Senator Lathan, I think that is an excellent idea," said Marisa Angela Lopez. "Unless there is some objection, I would ask you to form an investigative subcommittee and get back to me with your results. Now, I would like to table this whole Mexican issue and move to the next item on our agenda for today. The recent scientific report released by China showing that its CO_2 emissions are not meeting the new international standards."

Both Grayson and Hardwick spoke up at the same time, but Grayson immediately gave way to Hardwick, who said, "I want to say on record that General Grayson and I talked about this Mexican issue before showing up today, and in our opinion there needs to be a more decisive action taken immediately. A delay today may cause serious risk to national security."

Oh, shit! thought Grayson, even though that was exactly what would've come out of his mouth if Hardwick had not beaten him to the punch. He knew Lopez was going to come unglued after Hardwick's comment. She famously loved to argue and enjoyed debating at these meetings. In reality, she was a soulless bitch who was happy only when no one disagreed with her.

"I would have expected such a comment from you, Secretary Hardwick," Lopez said, glaring at him. "It seems you flag-waving military types think you can scare the rest of us by always overstating the risk."

Grayson was watching and waiting. Lopez was way out of her league. Was Hardwick going to attack now that Lopez had made it personal? The door was now open for Hardwick to do likewise. As a matter of fact, the conversation that Hardwick had just spoken of between the two of them had been more about Secretary Lopez than about Mexico. Grayson and Hardwick often referred to people such as Lopez as "minority whores" because they were two minorities—female and Mexican—and therefore thought they received a larger dose of discrimination from those around them. To be fair, they only used this term for people who used their minority status as an inequitable tool to gain advantage over their competition or their peers. Lopez was just such a minority whore.

Frankly, for years the White House staff and cabinet had been filled with those people—underqualified, conceited political animals who got their positions because "the party needs more Mexicans, blacks, women, and Asians in office." Neither of them saw themselves as either bigots or sexists. Quite the opposite; they hated people who used their race or sex to get ahead. Both Hardwick and Grayson thought the world of Colin Powell and Condoleezza Rice. Rice could've been called a minority whore, except for one missing, vital requirement. By the time she'd reached the same position as now held by Lopez, Rice hadn't flaunted being black or female as a political tool.

Lopez, on the other hand, would use it both ways and effectively whenever it benefited her. To gain power, she'd convinced her Hispanic and female constituents that her being of the same persuasion was a political benefit. Then she'd turned around and tongue-lashed anyone who'd even hinted that she used her sex or race as a political tool, calling them sexist or racist to hammer it home for effect.

Hardwick started his reply in a controlled voice but by the end of the sentence his volume had picked up markedly.

"Since you've decided to make this personal, Madam Secretary, we might as well put all our cards on the table. Your office has been kowtowing to your Mexican constituency here in the United States since 2012 when you took office. Worse yet, you've been sucking up to the newly elected Mexican president, Enrique Peña Nieto. The entire White House has been ignoring the volatile volcano that is about to erupt in Mexico. You have single-handedly gotten your liberal Latino buddies in Congress to look the other way. Your ambition to be the first Mexican-American president of the United States has been painfully obvious since the day you took office."

"You are out of order and I—"

But before Lopez could finish her sentence, Hardwick stood up and motioned Grayson to do the same. "I will be damned if I'm going to listen to any more of this crap! I warn you, Lopez!"

Both turned and within seconds were out the door. Once outside, Hardwick spoke first.

"Kurt, I knew you wanted to butt in and give your two cents, but better for me to fight with the bitch as a fellow NSC board member. I'll still catch holy hell over this, but, dammit, we need to find out what's going on down there. This current Denton administration's got their heads up their asses, trying to push through every new liberal idea they can find—and nothing, absolutely nothing will get done. I can't even get anyone over at the CIA to return my calls.

"I've got a busy week ahead, but let's close the loop on this soon before we're all speaking Spanish. I'll want you to take the point on this investigation. You're the only one I can trust with this potential shipwreck."

Grayson finished his old friend's thought. "I'm afraid that by the time we find out exactly what the hell is going on with those Mexicans at the border, it'll be too late for sane heads to prevail. I truly believe we're doomed."

Hardwick winked and said, "Remember the Alamo!"

Chapter 17

While the average tourist in Washington, DC, would have been thrilled to be riding in a chauffeured limousine, admiring the impressive buildings and national monuments that streamed by, General Kurt Grayson found himself once again daydreaming.

Kurt's aide, Major Pierce, broke into his thoughts. "Sir, how did your monthly meeting with the security council go?"

"Well, you tell me. It's the same response I give you every time I come back from one of those meetings."

Grayson's second aide, Lieutenant Jerome Roberts, asked, "Would that be worthless, General?"

"No, that would be as worthless as tits on a bullfrog!" retorted Grayson. "I hated it when the secretary of defense asked me to sit on this council. I told him after I did those two years as special advisor to President Reagan that I wouldn't do this kind of crap again."

"Well, General, I suspect the secretary thinks that, in addition to being his top military general, you are one of the few individuals who have the political savvy to kibitz with all of the politically appointed sheep in the administration," Pierce said.

"Oh, I guess it could be worse. At least I don't have to interface with all of those political crackpots on Capitol Hill. If I ever get stuck in a room filled with senators and congressmen, I'll slit my wrists. It's the same sons of bitches who screw things up and then expect the military to come and save their asses."

Roberts knew better than to ask but did anyway. "What did they piss you off about today, sir?"

With the Capitol Building fading into the distance, the Lincoln Memorial coming up just around the bend, and the scaffolding on the Washington Monument still visible, the general leaned back and realized he had been holding his breath.

Distracted briefly by the brilliance of the setting sun as it set fire to the limo's darkened windows, Grayson counted to ten and slowly exhaled.

"They're clueless about what's going on in Mexico. It's not that I know much more than they do. That's not my job, but it *is* the job of the Department of State and the CIA. What scares me is that they don't know what they should know.

"What I *do* know is that anytime you have people killing each other, and they're just across the street, so to speak, that's cause for concern. To top it all off, we have a Mexican secretary of state who's so concerned about not alienating the Mexican vote when she runs for president that she has no concern for national security."

Pausing and staring out the darkened window, trying to gather his thoughts, Grayson came to a decision.

"Jerry, see if there is still any of that Gentleman Jack in the liquor cabinet." Grayson sunk deeper into the limo's fine leather reclining seats and sighed. "Ah, this job is a pain in the ass, but the perks are great!"

The lieutenant immediately opened the small limo bar and pulled out a bottle one-third full of the general's favorite bourbon.

"Jerry, open that up. I need my regular recipe for dealing with government types and politicos."

"Would that be a double, General? One for the bureaucrats and one for the politicos? I think that formula has worked in the past," Roberts said with a smile.

Grayson took a big gulp and leaned back; his aides knew they were in for one of their boss's philosophy lessons.

Kurt leaned back in his seat, allowing the bourbon to trickle slowly down his throat, feeling that good burn while the scent wafted up into his nostrils.

"Ah, such a heady aroma." A smile of satisfaction crept across his lips, and he began talking.

"You know, so many people think that George Washington was famous because he was the first president. Others think he was just a good president. Washington was one of the best presidents we ever had. Hit me again, Jerry. But make it a single." The general started to warm up to his subject and continued, "The real reason is that he was the president after he had been a general in the militia for eight years."

"You aren't running for office, are you sir?" Lieutenant Roberts ventured.

"The only thing I hate worse than politicians is the process by which they get elected. Lieutenant, don't you ever wonder why America's best and brightest don't run for office?"

"No, sir, I haven't."

"It's because they are unwilling to degrade themselves by asking for money from people they don't like and by making promises they can't keep. You know, we could probably debate for hours about which president has done the most to degrade the office of president, and there is quite a list. However, hands down that philandering bozo Bill Clinton takes the cake."

Grayson took a long pull on his drink and paused as he soaked in a few more of Washington's prominent buildings as they flashed by.

"I don't know if I've ever told you who my hero is."

"George Washington?" suggested Pierce.

"Good guess—but no. Ulysses S. Grant," Grayson said, turning toward the window, his haggard face reflected back at him.

"From your prior comment, I should have guessed that, General. A military general who became president," said Roberts.

Grayson replied, "I'm not quite so myopic. Andrew Jackson was one of our best generals, but he was a downright worthless president. But then again, Dwight D. Eisenhower was not only one of our country's best generals but also one of our best presidents."

"Why is Grant your favorite, General?"

Grayson continued to look out the window as the Jefferson Memorial passed by.

"Other than the fact that we both drank too much bourbon? Do you know much about the Civil War, Jerry?"

"Well, we won."

"Whoa, be careful with that 'we' word, Jerry. My wife is from Alabama," Grayson said. "We were going to lose that war, and God bless ole Abe. He was one damn fine president and was doing his best, but he had a string of bad luck with military leaders."

As the limo sped onto the Memorial Bridge heading into Virginia, Grayson sat back again; in a few minutes, he'd be at the Pentagon.

Major Pierce tapped Grayson on the knee, breaking his concentration, and said, "Are you sure you don't want Bill to take you home instead of to your office in the Pentagon, sir? It is getting late."

Grayson flashed a smile. "Are you asking me what I *want* to do or what I *need* to do? I have a couple of reports to read, and if I limit myself to those two drinks, no worries, I'll be fine.

"Yup, matter of fact, Grant was so good as a general, he scared Lincoln. But once Lincoln gave the reins to Grant..." Grayson gave a long pause; it had been a long day. "Well, let's just say that this country has fifty states today because of a combination of those two great Americans."

Major Pierce interjected, "I thought you were going to tell us why Grant is your favorite president, not your favorite general."

"Did I say that Grant was my favorite general? Hell, we wouldn't have a country if it weren't for George Patton or Douglas MacArthur."

"Well, why is Grant your favorite president?"

"Now, Jerry, don't be so impetuous. You know it takes twenty minutes to get back to the Pentagon if you convince Bill to take the long route through the National Cemetery, and that gives me just enough time to finish this drink and my story if I time it just perfect.

"Grant is my favorite president because I guess I feel so much like him. Yeah, that's right, Jerry. I've had political aspirations in the past. I don't think I would have risen so high up in the military if I weren't so ambitious. But poor Ulysses, he was one crappy politician, and frankly it's the reason I've never thought of having a political career, though it's been frustrating for me to be this high up and see the administrations come and go and screw things up, president after president after president. President Grant and I have a lot in common: we have a tendency, both before and after we have a bourbon, to say exactly what we feel, when we want to say it, and to whomever we want to say it."

Jerry interrupted, "How did Grant get elected with that attitude?"

"Well, you're right—you couldn't get elected telling the truth today. But after the Civil War and horrible administration of Andrew Johnson, there wasn't enough time to listen to what Grant was saying or not saying—the country needed somebody powerful for president, and there was no one more powerful than the general who had just saved the United States. Similar to Eisenhower after World War II. But once he was in, the lobbyists, self-interest organizations, and politicos ate Grant alive."

"I still don't understand why he was your favorite," Jerry interjected.

"Well, maybe it's because although I sound like a pessimist, I'm a born optimist. Actually, I consider myself to be a realist. Grant was one of the best individuals we've ever elected. Given a chance, he would've run that office as efficiently as he'd run his troops, and I think history would have written him an epitaph that would rival some of the greatest presidents that ever lived. So maybe you're right. Maybe I should have said Grant could have been the best president we ever had. It's that very life lesson that has kept me out of politics."

The limousine pulled into the underground entrance to the Pentagon, and the military chauffeur sidled up to the special elevator reserved for the chief of staff. Everyone loaded onto the elevator, and it quickly took them to the general's suite of offices.

Lieutenant Roberts quickly policed the general's office. A few moments later, Grayson's custom leather office chair howled in protest as he dropped unceremoniously into it. He was weary and felt as if he'd been beaten with a stick. Gathering strength, he swiveled around to look out the huge picture window behind him, where he had a fabulous view of the Potomac River, the Jefferson Memorial, and the top of the Washington Monument, which looked suspended in midair. A spotlight bathed the top third, which was still wearing its jacket-like scaffolding after being damaged by a freak earthquake that had struck northern Virginia a while ago.

Sensing that his boss was not in the mood for more work, Major Pierce opened the general's well-stocked private bar and poured another stout one.

"Well, General, you told me who your favorite president was. Who is your least favorite?"

"Years ago, they used to run a survey among grade-school kids and ask them to name their top five heroes, and the answers were interesting. But almost always, one of the top choices was the president of the United States. To me the president needs to be more than a political leader—he needs to be the moral compass and epitome of ethical conduct. The president needs to be the leading example of a true red-blooded American, not some puppet on a string, easily compromised by contributors or some pretty-legged, perky-breasted staffer."

The general paused to let his words of wisdom sink in a bit. "When you bring disrespect to the time-honored and hallowed office, I think you do more damage to the country than all the poor political decisions combined. We can both agree that we are not proud of some of the things done by a few of our earlier presidents. Nixon should have admitted his role in Watergate. The country would have forgiven him, and we could have moved on. At least he saved us the embarrassment of the impeachment process.

"But my answer is easy, Jerry." Looking directly at Jerry and swallowing his building intensity, the general closed his eyes then continued. "Bill Clinton did more harm to the reputation of 'president' than the prior forty-two that served before him. Take and add all his bad decisions and misguided acts together, and Clinton's years in the Oval Office were some of the bleakest moments in our history."

"General, I didn't think you hated anybody more than President Barack Hussein Obama," Jerry said.

"Are you trying to ruin my buzz, Jerry? That's like asking me, who was worse, Genghis Khan or Attila the Hun? Both Clinton and Obama were pathological liars. They both treated the American people like blithering idiots and got away with it. And though Obama did more harm to the country, I still feel that Clinton did more to disgrace the office of the presidency, which, up until his time in office, I had the utmost respect for." With a brief thought, he added, "Well, if you'll let me ignore Jimmy Carter.

"Respect is a very important thing in our society. Jerry, you know me pretty well, and my maxim has been that I'd rather be respected by my troops than liked. It's been tough, being a career military man. I always wished that I could have served in the glory years."

Jerry blinked, taken aback. "What years were those?"

"The years following World War II. I've only heard the stories from some of the retired officers, but they say that during the forties and fifties, if you had a uniform on and went out in public, you were treated like a hero. Civilians would even salute you. We'd not only saved the United States, we'd saved the world in both World War I and World War II. Though the Korean War was not what you'd call a success, we were still respected and loved by the American people.

"It all changed after Vietnam. That was the saddest time of my career. When I came back from Vietnam, the country had changed. Protests and an ill wind of disrespect overshadowed the returning vets. Jerry, most of the boys who served did so because the selective service draft called their numbers. They weren't warmongers and baby killers. They were fresh-faced newbies— some hadn't even started shaving. They were altogether brave men, yet they didn't get the same respect that earlier war veterans received. It made me madder than hell.

"Do you think the boys on the front lines in World War II were any more or less patriotic than the boys who served in Vietnam? No. Let's face it—I think the military is a wonderful choice for a career, but you can make a lot more money in the private workforce. We both agree that serving in the military, for the most part, is a thankless job. We ought to reinstitute the draft so that we can draft all those whiny crybabies and send 'em to Iraq or Afghanistan. You can bet your ass they would come back with more respect for a career military man and a free country."

Major Pierce, sensing the general's tiredness, said, "Sir, are you sure you want to dig into those reports this late?"

"Goddammit, we have been there for the American citizen since day one! For 250 years when America has needed us, we've been there. And all—and I mean *all*—we ask for is a little respect. We are some of the most underpaid, overworked men and women ever employed. We're like policemen and firefighters, except our life expectancy is a lot less when we're at war.

"When we enlist, ours is not a profession that reaps big rewards or a competitive salary. I am tired. I'm tired for my boys—they deserve better. The military men and women of this country have given so much, and those scum-sucking politicians take all the credit and throw us under the bus at every opportunity they get. I think I could do this country one big favor and send the next bombing strike on Capitol Hill, not the supposed enemy overseas."

Obviously, this was the end of another long day. No one in the room was in any mood to talk, much less work. Grayson had a horrible habit of talking about reality and the big picture like no one else Major Pierce and Lieutenant Roberts had ever met in their entire lives. The silence hung in the air and became so thick 80 they could cut it with a knife. The ethereal quiet was what must have prompted the Korean cleaning crew to push open the door, ready to scrub and vacuum the entire suite. It was anyone's guess who was more surprised to see the other. Grayson waved them in, a gesture gratefully accepted by the somewhat shocked crew.

As the sound of vacuum cleaners filled the room, the general and his staff shuffled out as if the entire two-hour dialogue had never taken place.

Chapter 18

Inwardly, Dave groaned. He'd seen it all before. Many of the younger recruits hurried to slide out from behind their desks to stand at attention as he entered the small classroom. A couple of the border-patrol officers embarrassed themselves in their attempt to rise to attention because the desks in which they were seated were hand-me-downs from a local high school.

They were the standard, hard-to-get-into type, familiar to all students across America. The shellac, worn off the tops down to bare particle board with chips and chunks missing, made it difficult to take notes. Just about every high school boy who had piloted these relics had carved his initials or some men's-room-stall philosophy across the face. It was best not to touch the undersides of these relics lest you come away with some disease. And like stalactites in an underground cave, enough old chewing gum hung from the desk bottoms to plug a hole made by a .50-caliber round.

Covering his mouth, Dave smiled to himself, thinking, *Collectively the amount of chewing gum plastered to the underside of these artifacts could repair a major break in the Hoover dam. Crap! Such sad equipment for the new inductees.*

It appeared that the US government was not properly funding the US Border Patrol. *Au contraire*, Dave corrected himself. Since 9/11 the US government had increased funding by the hundreds of millions of dollars. No, the dilapidated desks and the small, antiquated surroundings were merely the results of the fast buildup of events. The San Diego office had ordered fifty new desks, which had been approved over five months ago. But when this order had been added to the orders of other numerous new USBP offices that had opened in the last two years, the Lincoln Desk Company in Ohio had been swamped. These antiquated public-school rejects would just have to do for a while longer.

"Good morning, gentlemen. I hope you found the accommodations in our local Motel 8 up to your usual, demanding standards."

"Yes, sir!" was the reply from the forty energetic new recruits.

How pathetic, thought Dave. *This is the cream of the crop?*

But outwardly he said, "No need to call me 'sir.' I'm just a border-patrol officer like the rest of you. But you're lucky. I just happen to be the one BP officer in this area who's been on the front lines longer than anyone else assigned to this shit hole.

"So our superiors think that qualifies me to teach you new recruits, so let me start by wishing each and every one of you *Buena suerte,* or as we BP officers say, 'good luck.'

"Protecting the border between the United States and Mexico is no cakewalk. If you were looking for an easy assignment, you should have been assigned to the Canadian border, where the biggest threat is being gored by an elk or bored to death by every single Canadian sentence finishing with, 'eh?'" Dave's sarcasm was starting to reach its peak. "Oh, life's so rich down here! Just you wait and see!

"I know most of you thought your assignment here was going to be relegated to chasing Mexicans through mesquite bushes and rattlesnake shit. Though our compadres in the DEA are predominantly responsible for NARCO-related issues in this part of the country, it's an issue that we border-patrol officers are forced to deal with on a regular basis."

He held up his laptop for all to see before opening a page he had previously marked.

"I want you to have some background information on the drug trafficking across the US-Mexican border, so I'm going to read a little bit from the DEA's resource bible, a website called DrugWarFacts.org, because it says it better than I could."

He started reading: "'Due to economic disparities between these two nations, the US-Mexico border has become a breeding ground for illegal activity. The trafficking of illegal drugs is a

multibillion-dollar industry for the Mexican drug cartels, who utilize their geographic proximity to cater to the lucrative, money-flush US market.

"'Mexico has now replaced Colombia as the largest exporter of illegal drugs to the United States. All of this has brought an upsurge in violence that is currently plaguing Mexico and particularly the border region. Crimes connected to the NARCO cartels have reached unprecedented levels: in just the last two years in the Nuevo Laredo Area alone, there have been over three hundred people killed, including more than thirty government employees and police officers. Most of these were drug-related. Some US agents were killed with weapons purchased through a failed US ATF Operation Fast and Furious, where known dealers were allowed to purchase illegal guns.'

"Hey," Dave said, "some bang-up program, *eh*? 'Despite our heightened border control, narcotic traffickers have successfully increased the drug trade in recent years, exposing a dangerously intricate, unperceivable, and impenetrable web of court corruption. Due to the thriving nature of the business, money abounds for bribery and coercion. In order to complete and sustain illegal transactions, payoffs are made at every level, from politicians to police officers to border patrol and control officials'...Mainly on the Mexican side of the border," Dave quickly added.

He quit reading and said, "I tell you this because I know it's natural for many new recruits to wonder why the Mexican government is not doing a better job of simply controlling the border from its own side. The Mexican government has left far too much of its own responsibility in the hands of the US states that border Mexico. Unfortunately in Mexico, hundreds of millions of dollars are available to bribe border officials, and the money comes from not only narcotics trafficking but from the lucrative business of transporting illegal aliens. This has all but halted any intervention by the Mexican government.

"I've worked here almost twenty years, and the changes since 9/11 have been dramatic. Frankly, that's why you're here today. We have hired more individuals in this department to be *boots on the ground* in the last three years than we've hired in the previous ten years. 9/11 also changed the traditional border-crossing points. Prior to 9/11, the majority of illegal crossings were within a few miles of urban areas. After 9/11, the US government allocated millions of dollars to strengthen these traditional illegal-entry points. This has forced the Mexicans to now cross in more rural areas. The average border patrol officer now covers five to ten times more miles in an average week than he did just a few years ago."

"Sir, I mean, ah, Mr. Walther, some of us have been hearing about this group called No More Deaths. Are they making our job harder or easier?"

"An excellent question, recruit! But the word 'easier' isn't used around here very often. There is no easier, only less grueling. I was going to address this issue later today, but since you asked the question, I will address it now."

As Dave directed the class's attention to a map of the southwestern United States and northern Mexico, with the border between the two highlighted, he said, "Here are some basic statistics. Each of you has received study materials prior to today, so let me highlight some of the key points. The entire border with Mexico is 1,951 miles long.

Modes of Entry for the Unauthorized Migrant Population		
Entered Legally with Inspection	Nonimmigrant Visa Overstayers	4 to 5.5 Million
	Border-Crossing Card Violators	250,000 to 500,000
	Subtotal Legal Entries	*4.5 to 6 Million*
Entered Illegally without Inspection	Immigration-Inspector and Border-Patrol Evaders	6 to 7 million
Estimated Total Unauthorized Population in 2006		11.5 to 12 Million

There are forty-seven legal border crossings along these 1,951 miles, and there are three more that are either proposed or are currently under construction."

"One correction to the chart—it is now believed that, as of 2015, there are between fifteen and twenty million illegal Mexicans living in the United States.

Unfortunately, the most recent hard data I could obtain was this chart from the Pew Hispanic Center which you will note is from 2006. That just goes to show how reluctant the US government is to disclose even the range numbers of illegal aliens living in this country.

"The majority of those crossings, as you would suspect, are concentrated in tightly packed urban areas. As you can see from the map here on the wall, the highest concentration of these border crossings is at the southern tip of Texas, near the Gulf of Mexico in the city of Brownsville, the sister city to Matamoros in Mexico. The line of crossings also runs through the Texas city of Laredo and its Mexican sister city of Nuevo Laredo.

"Along this stretch are other Texas towns that you might recognize, such as Brownsville, Harlingen, and McAllen. Going west on the map, the next town we come across with such a large concentration of crossings is El Paso. For geography majors, you know that El Paso is on the extreme western tip of Texas and the southern tip of New Mexico. El Paso has more border crossings than any other city or area on the border—nine of them. Can anyone tell me why there are so many crossings here?"

A hand was thrust into the air. "Is it because El Paso is such a large city?" asked a young Hispanic recruit.

"You're correct—or actually, half correct," replied Dave. "Though El Paso is not in our jurisdiction, it is important for you to understand its situation.

There are approximately seven hundred thousand people living in El Paso, which makes it the fourth-most-populous city in Texas and the twenty-second-largest city in the United States.

"It's also the third-fastest-growing metropolitan area in the entire United States. Why? Just on the other side of the border is Juarez, which has over 1.5 million people, thus making the US-Mexican metropolis a combined population of over 2.2 million people. Note that in Juarez, one of the more amazing statistics is the average age which, as you can see, is only twenty-seven years old."

To Dave, statistics never lied. To the recruits, these numbers were mind numbing and difficult to grasp. But Dave, ever the big dog, pointed back at the map and continued.

"Until you get here in San Diego, most of the crossings are limited to one or two at most in any area. Here in San Diego proper we have two crossings with two more on the way, and then we have two more outside the city. Anyone want to take a guess which specific US ports of entry have either the most pedestrian crossings or individual automotive crossings?"

There was a unanimous shout of, "El Paso!" Dave paused and slowly smiled.

"Wrong. It is our very own, only a few miles from here—the San Ysidro, California, crossing. In 2007, there were just over ten million personal vehicles crossing this entry point alone, and, in addition, there were over 4.3 million individuals crossing on foot, or as we generally refer to this crossing, pedestrian traffic. Your answer of El Paso, Texas, was not too far off though. It's second, with roughly 9.5 million personal vehicles crossing and 4.1 million pedestrians crossing. In your study materials, you'll find each and every US port of entry listed with statistics, in addition to some other important information that will put this huge flow of Mexicans in perspective. Up on the board, I have only highlighted those ports that ranked the highest as for crossings."

"Sir, how many of those people crossing here in the San Diego area are legal, and how many of those are illegal?"

To Dave, it was the worst question a new recruit could ask. It seemed like there was one in every class he had taught over the last ten years. Some greenhorn always asked this ridiculous question. He remembered how, the first time it'd happened, he had made the new recruit feel foolish. But now he was older and wiser. Sadly, it reminded him that even though someone might have volunteered to be a US Border Patrol officer, it didn't necessarily mean they had a better working knowledge of border problems. No, they were clueless, just like the rest of the country, including the politicians in Washington. Dave liked to say it this way: "If you aren't in the trenches or have boots on the ground, you don't have a clue."

"Well, young man, I will make you a deal. You take all the time you want, and if you can answer that question for me by the end of this week, I'll guarantee you'll be promoted to my job of teaching this course. Let me give you the kindest possible answer I can. These numbers only include the US entry ports we know of, the *legal* crossings."

With that statement, David pulled down a chart that represented information on the border crossings he had been discussing.

"If we knew the *illegal* crossings, by definition, we would have caught them."

Dave continued, "This chart is for the top ten most active border-entry points. The list is ranked by the highest pedestrian entries at the top." All the recruits stopped writing and looked up at Dave. "What's most alarming to us in the department is that, over the last year, we've seen a significant increase in illegal crossings in remote areas. All largely pedestrian, but curiously, it seems to be getting worse in some of the most remote areas of Arizona."

US-MEXICO BORDER CROSSING

2014

Top Ten Ports of Entry

Border Crossing	Non-Commercial Personal Vehicles	Pedestrians
San Ysidro, California (San Diego Region)	21,116,089	7,925,371
El Paso, Texas	19,134,740	6,572,313
Calexico, California (South-Central California)	7,221,481	4,567,333
Laredo, Texas (Southwest Texas)	10,335,481	3,447,437
Otay Mesa, California (San Diego Region)	12,040,318	3,415,957
Nogales, Arizona (Southeastern Arizona)	6,798,080	2,886,022
Hidalgo, Texas (Southern Gulf Coast)	9,252,030	2,290,469
San Luis, Arizona (Yuma Region)	5,536,747	2,287,955
Brownsville, Texas (Southern Gulf Coast)	8,527,359	2,232,400
Douglas, Arizona (Southeastern Arizona)	2,821,853	1,011,564
Total for top 10 ports	**102,784,225**	**36,636,821**
Total for top 25 ports	**129,242,838**	**41.233,292**

It seemed the greenness of the recruits never changed, with the same questions and the same bravado. Each class's students boasted how they were going to be the one class to make a difference, put their fingers in the dike, stemming the flow of illegal immigrants.

Yeah, right, thought Dave. After his years in the trenches he knew the chances of that happening were slim.

"Winding up," said Dave, nearing the end of the class, "let me amuse you with a few Power Point slides of some Mexicans', let's say, creative ways to cross over into the United States."

Dave allowed the tension to drain a bit through some well-needed laughter. The slides progressed through photos of fancy slingshots, catapults, and pneumatic cannons, all employed to launch fresh immigrants into their new country. Unfortunately, it was more like launching fresh meat into the air with bad landings. One grim photo was of a crushed man who had used a "pumpkin-chucker" trebuchet to launch himself well over the fence and had landed some two hundred yards away. Unfortunately he had missed the soft landing zone—hence the crushed body. Then there were slides of technical tunnels collapsing and cars and trucks attempting to drive through the fence. *Is there ever an end to the desperate acts from those who cross borders illegally?* Dave wondered.

"It's time to look at the harsh statistics. We have almost twenty million illegal aliens presently residing in the United States, with up to twelve thousand additional illegal aliens entering every day!"

Dave pulled a sheet out of his briefcase and continued on about the illegals. The statistics also focused on the ratio of border apprehensions to "getaways." He clicked the next Power Point slide, and the methodology used in this analysis was as follows:

1.

   Estimate the gross number of illegals entering the United States, as well as the number of those that evade apprehension by the border patrol.

A "getaway" ratio is applied to the numbers of illegals entering, resulting in a gross estimate of illegals entering and evading apprehension.

2.

Factor in repeat apprehensions of the same individuals and legalizations out of the overall estimate. Many illegal aliens who are apprehended and are returned home try to enter the United States again and are subsequently apprehended. Others are legalized and are allowed to stay in the United States.

3.

Factor short-term stays from the overall estimate. Some illegal aliens voluntarily return home in less than year.

4.

Estimate the total number of illegal aliens living in the United States, based upon the estimate of illegals entering and evading apprehension each year.

Dave repeated the statistic to get everyone's attention: "Up to twelve thousand additional illegal aliens entering every day!"

A question came from the class. "With that sobering statistic, don't you feel useless and impotent?"

Dave grew grave faced as he concluded his thought. "Using the latest conservative Census Bureau data from 2012 and 2013, the Center for Immigration Studies reports that more than sixty million immigrants—legal and illegal—live in the United States, and that 'Absent a change in policy, between twelve and fifteen million new immigrants—legal and illegal—will likely settle in the United States in the next decade.'

"What if thirty million new immigrants arrive in the next twenty years? The magnitude of the number of illegal aliens in the United States represents a serious crisis and an urgent need to return to *the rule of law* and secure borders, which the United States Constitution demands."

If it weren't for the droning noise of mosquitoes, he could have heard a pin drop in the room. No one moved, no one spoke, no one dared make eye contact with Dave. This was the call to arms they'd heard so much about in the academy. They were now in the trenches, boots on the ground, and *they alone* were entrusted to do the impossible.

Without another word, Dave dismissed the recruits. Tomorrow was another day, and it was going to be hot and sticky out in the field. Hopefully, the bodies weren't piling up overnight out on the ranches where the illegals took shortcuts to avoid the ground sensors. Yes, boots on the ground began tomorrow for these recruits! After tomorrow, there wouldn't be a naive man or woman in the whole bunch, God help them.

Dave's mind drifted back to his first day and the pile of dead bodies he'd found only a half a mile from one of the watering holes of a sympathetic organization, one like No More Death.

Yes, Dave thought, *life turns ugly tomorrow for these recruits.*

Chapter 19

As Professor Walther entered the lecture hall, he began with, "Good morning. I know I won't hear any protest, but I've made a major decision and the dean has approved it. We're going to deviate a bit from the original outline for this course.

"If you recall, we still have a number of classes taking us through Mexico's history, and last class, I think we left off somewhere around 1996. Of course, with this class called 'An American Invasion,' that part would be in the last half of this course. But you have to have been living in a cave not to have noticed the numerous, perplexing reports that are surfacing about the situation on the US-Mexican border.

"So what I'm going to do is speed things up a bit. I'm going to jump to some of the more current topics, before we take the issue of the border dispute head-on in the next couple of weeks. That being said, we're going to jump to 2012."

"Presidente Enrique Peña Nieto was elected to a six-year term in 2012. As a member of the Institutional Revolutionary Party, the IRP, he succeeded Felipe Calderón. No one was surprised by the defeat of Calderón. The corruption and the economy in Mexico suffered severely under his administration. In addition, the IRP, prior to Calderón, had ruled Mexico for seventy-one consecutive years. There is a strong argument that in Mexico there is really only one party.

"One of Nieto's campaign promises was to take swift action to fight the organized crime and drug trade that had proliferated under the Calderón administration. Fifty-five thousand people supposedly died due to the organized crime and drug trafficking industry in the six years prior to the 2012 election. Additionally, he promised to open up PEMEX, the nationalized oil company, to get more competitive bidding. Next week we're going to concentrate at least one and potentially two classes just on the issue of the deteriorating oil prices and its effect on Mexico's economy.

"It's hard for me to criticize the corruption of politics in Mexico, when in the last few elections here in America...let's just say that would be the pot calling the kettle black. But somewhat like in some of our previous elections, in the last presidential election in Mexico, Peña Nieto obtained only 38.21 percent of the votes.

"The security policy of Peña Nieto prioritizes the reduction of violence rather than attacking Mexico's drug trafficking organizations head-on, marking a departure from the strategy of the past six years during the Calderón administration. Peña Nieto has set up a number of conceptual and organizational changes from the past regime policy, and one of the biggest contrasts is the focus on lowering murders, kidnappings, and extortions, as opposed to arresting or killing the country's most-wanted drug lords and intercepting their drug shipments.

"The government of Calderón, however, justified their position by stating that the violence in the country is a necessary stage in Mexico's drug war, as weakening criminal groups fight for territorial control against one another and the government.

"Moreover, part of Peña Nieto's strategy also consisted of the creation of a national police made up of forty thousand members, known as a gendarmerie, though in November 2013 it was announced that this force would be reduced to five thousand members and would not be operational until, let's just say, only God knows when."

Craig took a drink of water and continued. "While campaigning, Peña Nieto appointed a former general of the National Police of Colombia as his external advisor for public security and boldly promised to reduce Mexico's murder rate by 50 percent by the end of his six-year term. Critics of Peña Nieto's security strategy, however, say that he has offered little sense of exactly *how* he will reduce the violence. Peña Nieto was not explicit on his anticrime strategy, and many analysts wonder whether Peña Nieto is holding back politically sensitive details in his security strategy or
simply does not yet know how he will squelch the violence and carry out the next stage in Mexico's drug war. Moreover, US

officials are worried that the return of the IRP after previously ruling Mexico for seventy-one years may mean returning to the old IRP tactics of corruption and backroom deals, with the cartels exchanging bribes for relative peace.

"Let me finish today on the issue of political corruption, which we're going to spend the entire class on next time. I'm just going to touch on one aspect. It's called the Televisa controversy. Again, I know many of you will agree with me when I say I don't think the United States can any longer criticize other countries for corruption in their television and other media. In the last couple of decades, the liberal press in America has taken ineptness and biased reporting to new lows—Allah, Dan Rather, Chris Matthews, Rachel Maddow, and Keith Olbermann as examples."

"The Televisa controversy refers to a series of allegations published by the British newspaper *The Guardian* in June 2012 that claimed Mexico's largest television network, Televisa, sold favorable coverage to top politicians in its news and entertainment shows. Three documents presented by the newspaper allege that a secretive circle within Televisa manipulated its coverage to favor the IRP presidential candidate, Peña Nieto, the candidate who was poised as the favorite to win the 2012 Mexican presidential election.

"Televisa supposedly commissioned videos promoting Peña Nieto and lashing out at his political rivals in 2009. Protests in Mexico have broken out over this more than once. Televisa, the largest media network in the Spanish-speaking world, owns around two-thirds of the programming on TV channels in Mexico. The newspaper coverage is small, and research on the Internet and cable TV is largely limited to the middle classes; consequently, the country's two major television networks— Televisa and TV Azteca—exert a significant influence on national politics. For the remainder of the class, Craig talked about corruption of the Mexican government and the press.

Chapter 20

"Craig Walther," said Craig into the phone with a half-dozing, half-boozed voice, which is what one got, phoning him at home late most nights of the week. Though he loved his job and his classes, and to some degree his students, Craig was really a loner. Stretched out on the sofa, he held Don Julio 1942 in one hand and that week's edition of *The Economist*, rather crumpled, in the other. The TV volume was turned down low but loud enough so that if one of the nationally known pundits said something of interest, Craig could grab his remote and quickly hit REPLAY.

Keeping up on everything was easy. He had all of his favorite shows recorded—mostly news, of course, especially Fox News. His favorite was the panelist segment from the evening news, Bret Baier's *Special Report*, consisting of Charles Krauthammer, Steve Hayes, George Will and A.B. Stoddard. He hated commercials and hadn't had to watch one in ten years, thanks to modern technology.

"Craig, it's Dave. Are you awake and sober enough to talk to me—or rather, should I ask, are you alone and able to talk?"

Dave knew that ever since his brother's last disastrous divorce, Craig had made up for lost time and spent many nights with various new visitors to his mountain home outside Albuquerque.

"No, it's fine. Let me turn down the TV," he said "What's on your mind, little brother?"

"Sorry to bother you so late, but I had some recent incidents when I was visiting the border area, and I wanted to run some of my concerns by you. I know this whole border issue is your passion, though I have to admit, I never finished your latest textbook on the subject. You know, I've always been a little scared being down here so close to the border."

Dave paused. "I really think that the Mexicans, all in all, aren't a violent people, but I just have always felt the border area was a boiling pot—or maybe the term is 'tea kettle.' I

96

don't know what I'm trying to say. That's why you're the famous college professor making big bucks, and I'm a lowly border-patrol cop, but...Well, my fear has gotten the better of me in the last few months."

"Calm down. I've never heard you so worked up. Is everything okay at home with Anita and the baby? Are you getting enough sleep?"

"Yes, yes, things are great at home, and Anita is well. She's built for babies and I know...well, I don't know for sure, but I'm convinced she's going to have a boy."

"That's great," Craig said and really meant it. "So what's got you all frantic?"

Dave spent the next hour telling his dozing brother his observations of the last month and the intimate details of his recent border crossing. Craig, fully reclined on a sofa that had far too often functioned as a bed due to the lateness of the hour or the volume of tequila he'd consumed, was the dutiful listener.

Dave continued, "Most people don't realize that a high percentage of illegal Mexicans residing in the United States didn't enter the country illegally by jumping a fence, climbing through a tunnel, or a performing any of the myriad of perfected methods. Instead they just legally entered through one of the many US customs border stations with a day pass or work visa and then just never returned. Ever since Obama announced the plan to legalize millions of Mexicans living in the country...well, I think that is where this increase in numbers is coming from."

As Dave paused, Craig asked, "Remember you are talking to an expert on the subject, but I will have to admit that even though I have warned Washington that this was going to be a ramification of the president's announcement, I did not know for sure that it was actually taking place. Are you sure these are newcomers?"

Craig's interruption caught Dave unprepared. Dave had assumed up until this point that his brother had been merely listening to his ranting out of pity and couldn't care less. Dave had resigned himself to total dismissal by his professorial brother before he had even called him.

"I swear, Craig, I know the difference—and these crowds are not locals or residents, they're fresh illegals. I would guesstimate that most of them have crossed the border in the last sixty days," Dave said. "I think you should call Cliff and Mark and warn them." He realized his mistake as soon as the words left his mouth, but it was too late to retract them.

"Whoaaaaaa...Hey little brother, I'm the one who's had too much tequila this evening, not you. Warn them about what? Calm down! Okay, let's take your observations at worst-case face value. There's a large influx of illegal Mexicans in California—if your story holds water. For now that's all we know. Let's even assume it's not just localized in your region but is happening all along the US-Mexican border. That doesn't mean we cry out like Chicken Little that the sky's falling. With the increased guerrilla activities and the economic disasters of the last two years, I've been predicting a major insurgence for some time. Warning our brothers is going too far out on a limb, even for me. Are you implying that President Denton's affirmation that she is going to follow through with Obama's plans to legalize five to ten million illegal Mexicans is creating this surge of illegal border crossings? If so, what would you say to our brothers? What will warning them do?"

Dave needed this. Craig had such a way of putting things in perspective. Craig was the rational one, and once again he was right. Dave had freaked out. He knew that Craig was right and that he had let his emotions run away with him again. He was just too close to the situation to see the bigger picture!

He took a big breath and said, "Well, as always, you're right, but could you at least call them, to, well, you know, tell them to be on the lookout?"

"No, you call. I haven't talked to them in months."

"You need to call Mark."

"Right," Craig said. "I'm going to call my older brother and tell him what to do?"

"There're more years between the two of us than there are between the two of you. Craig, he's more likely to take advice from you than he is from me," Dave insisted.

"No, I don't think you get it. It's easier when you're ten years younger because there's no competitiveness. But I'm only four years younger, and he has a harder time taking advice from someone who's just slightly younger."

"I don't know—I can't talk to Mark. You know, praise the Lord and God bless Jesus. I know Anita has me going to church now regularly—it was part of the deal when we got married—but it's just not my bag. Mark and I have just never been that close. Every time I talk to him, he puts me down because I stay on here at the border patrol. Okay, it's not where I intended to be for my career, but I wish he would get off my case."

This wasn't a conversation that Craig wanted to have, much less after a buzz from a couple of tequilas. "Well, I guess I take it from your comments that you haven't talked to our two brothers any more than I have over the last few months."

Dave realized that, as much as he cared for all of his older brothers, Craig was really the only one he had been able to relate to, even going back as far as grade school.

"I guess I'm not being fair. I'm the one who's paranoid, yet I'm asking you to call our brothers, but...never mind. Craig, hey, just forget I called."

"Now hold on, little brother. I'm very glad you called. I've been suspecting the very same problem you're seeing at the border, and I want to stay in close contact about this issue, but let's just hold off a bit before either of us starts getting the rest of the family all worked up." Craig added, "I'd better get some sleep. I have an early class, and you need to go take care of that beautiful,
young pregnant wife of yours." After saying their good-byes, they hung up. However, there was no way that Craig was

going to sleep after that phone call. His mind was on fire. He couldn't get

Dave's story out of his head. This was the very essence of his theory, the reason for his intensity in his class. His mind ignited. Were his fears on the subject of the Mexican migration about to come true? Would his life's work be validated? If so, how would the United States respond to this potential invasion? But then he thought, *How could brothers be so different?* As he finally drifted to sleep, he dreamed of his three brothers.

Chapter 21

A perfect package of a college girl strode quickly down the hall in the Montoya Center for Social Sciences, which housed the School of Political Science at UNM. Her long, thick blond hair seemed to have twice its usual body as the air filtered through it. To go along with her gorgeous hair, she was also one curvaceous young lady. She knew it and intentionally accentuated her physical gifts by wearing tight jeans and short, tight blouses. Today she had made doubly sure both were extra tight.

Jennifer Stiles opened the door to Professor Craig Walther's office with no knock and caught him leaning back in his cushy office chair, papers strewn from the end of his deck, across his lap, and most of the way up to his neck.

"You haven't called me in a week!"

"Sorry," he said. "I've had a lot on my mind, and I'm way behind on grading these term papers. I warned you not to take our relationship seriously. I'm old enough to be your father, and besides, I said it would just have to be an off-and-on-again kind of thing."

Her face lit up, and she cocked her head in such a sexy way that she must have learned it from some movie star from the fifties. "Yes, that's the part I like—the on-and-off part."

Craig realized he was losing the battle. "Now, don't get cute with me," he said, affecting a more stern expression.

"Now, Professor, isn't the fact that I'm so cute why you can't resist me?"

"I think that is a little unfair," Craig countered. "Yes, I admit it—I can't resist you, but I am trying. That night at my house was, well, a bit out of control." That night, that infamous night. No fewer than a hundred times had he questioned whether opening the door that night had been the stupidest or most glorious thing he had ever done. Craig almost never had visitors, and never unannounced, so when the doorbell had rung at 10:15 that evening months ago, he had answered the intercom only to find a student's voice at the other end.

"Professor Walther," the coed had started. "I'm so sorry, I know this term paper was due today, but I had some family issues to deal with and since technically it's still Friday, I thought I would deliver my paper to you personally. I've heard you're a stickler on deadlines, so I wanted to see if it wasn't too late for you to take it."

She had been right on all counts. The paper was due that day, and technically it was still Friday night. Yes, he was a stickler for deadlines, and if the paper had been delivered on Monday, he would have docked her for being late. But how in the hell had this student gotten his home address? In his less-than-sober state, he was not going to pull any technicalities. It was 10:15 p.m. on a Friday night, and if some energetic student had been willing to drive an hour into the mountains to make sure her term paper wasn't late—well, maybe it was time for him to not be such a hard-ass.

"Ms....what did you say your name was?" Craig had said into the intercom, trying to sound totally sober.

"It's Jennifer Stiles, Professor Walther."

"Okay, Ms. Stiles, give me a minute." He quickly zipped up his pants, which he rarely did when at home, and glanced in the mirror on the way to the door. After all, he *was* a tenured professor, so he should look the part; he fuzzed up his hair and wiped any lime bits off his face. But when he swung open the door, a flock of geese could have flown through the opening that was his mouth.

Just exactly how long had he stood there before he'd been able to force his lips to form words? It must have seemed like an eternity. In the dark of the mountain night stood a gift from the Greek gods: Aphrodite of Milos, better known as the Venus de Milo, an ancient statue that depicted the goddess of love and beauty. This student would have been the perfect model for that ancient Greek sculptor.

She was tall but not too tall, with blond hair that looked as thick and golden as Kansas wheat in the fall. Her eyes were the size of saucers and as piercing as any of the arrows of Achilles.

And that was just the start. From what he could see, she also had a body that hourglasses were clearly modeled after.

For the next few months, when Craig had looked back on that evening, he had fantasized about the thought processes the young lady had gone through as she'd selected the outfit that she would wear to innocently deliver the "late" term paper. Whatever time she'd spent, it'd been time well spent. She must have done her research well. Seducing Professor Walther was almost a UNM letter sport. The *Albuquerque Journal* had selected him as the number one eligible bachelor of the year, and he was occasionally invited onto local talk shows and often quoted by the press. Yet he turned down 90 percent of the invitations to speak.

How had she known exactly what to wear? Anything too overplayed, and Craig would have taken the term paper, thanked the ambitious student, and closed the door quickly to retreat back to the safety of his sofa. Instead, she'd worn jeans, tight but not too tight, and a UNM sweatshirt that fit perfectly, if a little snuggly, and that looked worn but not worn out. The eyes of the UNM mascot, the lobo, on the front of her sweatshirt seemed to bulge to life because of their positioning on her chest. And just to make sure nothing went overlooked, she had cut and sewn a very sharp *V* in the neckline to reveal more of God's handiwork.

Craig was no novice. He had been around the block and back again. His two previous wives had been quite established women, and his work and popularity had forced him to mingle often with the muckety-mucks of high-end society. Having women flirt with him was such a regular occurrence that, in fact, it had become more of an annoyance than a compliment to him. Movies were made, books were written, and relationships were born on split-second interludes, right-time-right-place happenstances. Such was the case that night, with the hour late and the tequila drunk.

"Thank you, Ms., ahhh, Stiles. I have to compliment you on your fortitude and willingness to drive out so far and so late to make sure you made the deadline. I'm not easily impressed, but you have gained my, let's say, respect. Won't you step in for a minute and warm yourself by the fire before your downhill trek back to town?"

Playing her cards perfectly, she took a calculated risk. "Oh, no, Professor, I couldn't impose. I apologize for the intrusion, but I just couldn't take the risk of waiting until Monday."

"I respect your ambition. I wish more of my students were as forthright. It's cold—let me offer you some refreshment, warm your bones by the fire, and then send you on your way," he offered again.

And the rest was history. The refreshment was a tequila shot, as was the second, third, and fourth.

"Craig. Craig! *Craig!* Are you listening to me?"

She snapped him back from his daydream—not an unpleasant one, just one with complications.

"Unfair? Wait, how can it be unfair? I'm twenty-three and you are fifty-nine, so it's unfair of me to take advantage of you? What's the excuse for the twenty times you've seen me since that night?" She was boxing Craig into a corner. She was smart, or he wouldn't have liked her so much, but she was on the attack, and he had lost ground while daydreaming.

Trying to recoup, Craig said, "Now, you listen."

"The incredible Professor Walther is being outsmarted by a twenty-three-year-old psychology grad student. You can build up your ego all you want, but let me just give you the facts. You aren't the first boyfriend I've ever had, and if you want out of this relationship, just say so."

She'd caught him. Craig cleared his throat and then said, "I'm not sure you'd call what we have a relationship. It might be better called an affair."

Her face tightened up. "I thought that was a term used when someone is married, and you haven't been married for years."

"Young lady, are you going to start correcting my grammar now?"

"Don't you call me 'young lady'—only my father gets away with that."

"I apologize, but let me get back to my point. It's not that I want out of this affair—it's that I shouldn't be in this affair in the first place."

She jumped at the chance to interrupt. "I'm not in this relationship for the sex. If you haven't noticed, with my looks and body, I don't have any problem attracting men. One of the main reasons I was attracted to you was that you're one of the few men I've ever met who thinks outside the box. I didn't come out to your house that night just to get laid. When I was taking your classes, I found you fascinating, worldly, and intoxicating, and don't try to fabricate some bullshit story just to get me to fall out of love with you."

Craig's head snapped back. He was taken aback, and he spilled the term papers that had remained on his lap throughout the conversation onto the floor. He didn't know it had gone that far.

Jennifer was no dummy. She saw that she had thrown the famous professor for a loop. "What? Did I strike a nerve?" Jennifer asked, and then quickly added before Craig could catch his composure, "That's a look I don't see often from you. What's the matter, Professor? Does it make you a little nervous to have someone twenty-six years your junior—and the best lay you've ever had—tell you she loves you? Does that just complicate your life a bit too much?"

With all the confidence of a well-orchestrated military maneuver, Jennifer stormed out of Craig's office. The best part about it was that it wasn't orchestrated at all. Jennifer had shot from the hip and the heart from the minute she'd entered his office.

Chapter 22

Since Thomas Jefferson moved into the White House just after it was completed in 1801, Americans have considered it our greatest American symbol and a bastion of freedom. Rarely did either an American or foreign tourist get within 100 miles of Washington, D.C. without a drive by the White House. Often they took the tour, parting with an awe-inspiring story of their visit. Similarly, there wasn't any room more famous in the United States than the Oval Office. For 200 years, some of the most important decisions ever made in this country were formed and made in that very room.

However, in the last couple of decades, both the White House and the Oval Office had been tarnished by scandal and political posturing. From being the unceremonious location of an extra-marital affair with an intern, to the start of a war based on weak and unsubstantiated intel, to an administration whose entire background and policies were in constant question by the public. The Oval Office was now considered by millions of Americans in the same vein as the crooked evangelists who bilked billions from Christians worldwide.

No one had more ruthlessly dreamed, conspired, and clawed her way to the presidency than Rosemary Denton. Although there may have never been more talented liars than some of her predecessors, President Denton took this art form to new levels— but with an added twist. She didn't give a damn. She had never given a damn, because it was just a political game. As long as she kept winning—which she always had—it didn't matter whose career she destroyed or whose life she stepped on to gain ground against her opponents. Denton didn't care if she eliminated the very essence of what America stood for, or if she appeared to sell out the American people who'd voted her into office.

Much like her predecessor Obama, President Denton thought it wasn't her job to serve the American people but instead to decide what was best for them, and be damned with opinion polls and Congress. She was in charge!

Like that of her predecessor, Rosemary Denton's checkered past had been kept from the voting public, and so her rise to power was not questionable. Though her political opponents had tried to bring forth the facts, Rosemary had suppressed most of them with the unwitting help of the media. One such damning circumstance included the mysterious deaths of twelve Americans with whom she had come into contact during her political career, many of whom had been viewed as blocking the path of Rosemary's political ambitions.

President Rosemary Denton turned to her secretary of state, Marisa Angela Lopez, and said, "So how did your meeting last week with the National Security Council go? Before we get into other matters, I'd like to know if there's anything I need to address in my press conference later this week."

"I can't think of anything really significant. Of course, those male chauvinist pigs from the Pentagon, Secretary Hardwick and General Grayson, both have their heads up their asses. All they can talk about is what's going on at the Mexican border. As I've told you before, I think they, as well as all those journalists over at Fox News, have blown these events way out of proportion. I know that the CIA director has, to some degree, parroted the concerns of Grayson and Hardwick, but he has admitted they really don't have a full understanding of what's going on and what any guerrilla activity has meant."

"What do our friends over at NBC, CBS, and MNSBC think about the situation?"

"I've been in close contact with them all week, and they agree with my feelings that the conservatives are just trying to stir up a bit of political trouble and public panic. They're still upset that your predecessor sidestepped Congress to give amnesty to millions of illegals. I think we can follow in those footsteps with our protocol today and just ignore them. The tide is turning back in our favor. Sure, the Republicans did well back in 2014, but with your succession to the presidency,

I think the trend is now firmly back in the hands of our party," Lopez concluded smartly. She knew who buttered her bread.

The president's personal advisor, Stephanie Jones, had been sitting quietly by, listening while filing her nails. Stephanie was no timid political animal herself, which had facilitated her rise up through the political ranks on weak credentials and little experience. She had become one of the former administration's most trusted aides, and she'd found that being a minority female gave her incredible political power in a changing America. She had even thought of admitting she was a lesbian, and then she would, in fact, be the perfect presidential candidate.

Rarely did a top presidential advisor pass from one administration to the other. Almost every president came in with their own top people and conducted housecleaning from the previous administration. But like her predecessor, President Denton was having a serious problem attracting qualified individuals to serve in her cabinet. Even the staunchest liberal and socialist followers were reluctant to sign on to the Denton administration. They had seen what the previous administration had done, destroying so many promising and powerful people's careers.

For eight years, they had flip-flopped on so many key internal and international issues that aides and cabinet members had found it difficult to keep the proper spin. It usually created career-ending debacles to continually explain or defend their actions. Because Rosemary Denton had a checkered political past and was known to throw people under the bus to save herself, even the most avid liberal defenders were petrified to sign on with her.

So she had kept on Stephanie Jones. It was a marriage made in heaven, since she was as much a political animal as Denton— and just as ruthless. If she couldn't be president, Stephanie was happy as long as she constantly had the president's ear.

Blowing off the dust created by her nail filing, Stephanie said, "I think Marisa's right. To prepare for today, I called Clarissa Martinez-De Castro of the National Council of La

Raza. As you know, Rosemary, La Raza is one of the strongest and most influential Mexican-American advocacy groups. They feel very strongly that both the Pentagon and the Republicans in Congress are gunning for them and making a huge political mistake, and I concur.

"Though neither of us is a big fan of your predecessor, he did give us the Hispanic vote on a silver platter by introducing the directive to legalize all of those Mexican illegals living here in the United States. Ms. De Castro feels we are in a position to permanently lock up the Hispanic vote in this country. We're golden if we handle the situation favorably for both the legal and illegal Mexicans in America and, to some degree, the Mexicans on the other side of the border. La Raza is willing to support us 110 percent. Be aware, they have a couple of bargaining chips on the table."

"Why am I not surprised by that?" chided the president.

Stephanie shrugged. "No big deal. You still have a couple unfilled federal judge seats and ambassadorships to award, and they just want you to make sure all those appointments are Hispanic."

President Denton spun her chair slowly to look out the window at the Washington Monument, and then let out a big laugh. "You know, ladies, the last administration started this trend, and we've taken it to a new level. At the rate we're going, there won't be a white male in any position of power within our administration, or even as a department head in any federal court in the country."

Stephanie Jones smirked. "It's just payback for decades of suppression. I don't think the Republicans will win another major election in our lifetime. We have sewn up the minority and female vote for the next fifty years."

The president swung her chair back around. "Okay, I'm going to put you two in charge of figuring out how to get the most political mileage out of this whole Mexican thing. Stephanie, can you leak some additional information to our friends over at the networks about Senator Boone? He's been threatening to start a Congressional investigation into the incident in Algeria, and I just can't afford that heat right now."

Stephanie smiled. "Of course—they're always at our beck and call." Especially Chris Mathews, who tended to be a lap dog for Stephanie. She smiled, wiggled a bit, and then jumped up, adding, "Men—such pathetic little boys and so eager to please."

Chapter 23

Downtown Houston had some of Texas's largest office buildings, each housing at least one high-end brokerage firm. These firms were cutthroat businesses, trying to outdo each other by having their branch offices on the highest floor in the newest building with the snazziest client accommodations. Cliff Walther's Morgan Stanley office was just such a place, and since Cliff was a heavy hitter, he had one of the premier corner offices, with a million-dollar view. His office looked more like that of a sports agent than a stockbroker—the walls were plastered with sport shots, each one starring Cliff: Cliff fishing in Mexico, Cliff skiing in Colorado, Cliff tarpon fishing in Florida, and Cliff golfing at different courses all over the world. What room was left by the brazen display was taken up with football awards, photos, and memorabilia of his son, Cliff Jr.

Cliff was in his office when his wife, Debbie, called to say that she was swinging by to pick him up for the volleyball game. She would be there in thirty minutes.

Cliff responded, "I forgot to call you. An important meeting has come up with clients, and I can't make the game."

"This means a lot to the girls," Debbie pleaded. "You haven't made one of their matches all year. If their team wins this tournament in Galveston, they could go to the state volleyball invitational."

"Sorry, honey. These new clients could generate a lot of commission dollars." After an uncomfortable pause, he softly added, "I promise I'll go next time."

Cliff and Debbie had identical twins, fifteen-year-old girls. Considering himself a man's man, Cliff just didn't care for women's sports, even if they involved his own daughters.

As Debbie hung up the phone, Chelsea, usually the less brash of the daughters, was the first to speak. "So, let me guess: Dad can't make the game, but he promises to make the next one?"

Her sister, Marcie, rolled her eyes. "Yeah, right! And a buffalo is going to fly out my ass!"

Debbie took a halfhearted swing at her. "Young lady, you watch your mouth, or I will turn this car around right now, and the two of you can just miss this game."

Marcie shot back, "It's bullshit and it's totally unfair. He hasn't missed one of Cliff Jr.'s stupid football games ever. It's total bullshit."

Debbie reached for the radio to drown out her daughters. "Just one more word, just one more, and I will do a 360 so fast it will make your head spin! I am not putting up with the two of you cussing."

Chelsea always came out on top in these arguments between her sister and Mom. She was just as mad about her dad's no-shows as her twin, but she had learned years ago to let her sister do the fighting and cussing for her.

Chelsea was a mirror image of her mother. They wore their hair the same—long, bleached blond, and nearly always pulled back into a ponytail with a big bow. They both wore too much makeup, and their clothes were almost always perfect. Perfectly perky, dressed in lots of pastels and short shorts to combat Houston's warm weather, Chelsea and her mother looked like they were always off to some polo or tennis match.

Marcie wanted no part of this, calling them the Barbie Doll twins. Marcie had multiple piercings in her ears and one in her nose, which she always had to remember to remove before her dad saw it. The same held true for her beautiful butterfly tattoo perfectly centered just above her butt crack. She just had to keep her shirt tucked in, lest her father see it and physically throw her out of the house.

It seemed like Marcie and Chelsea were twins in looks only, because they were polar opposites on just about every issue. Because Chelsea was Little Miss Popular, she couldn't imagine a world without a cell phone. She seemed to be constantly either receiving a text or an e-mail or a phone call from what seemed like an unlimited supply of friends. It wasn't that Marcie didn't have friends, but her friends were a lot less clingy, more independent, more go-your-own-way-and-do-your-own-thing friends. To Marcie, her smartphone just gave her greater access to movies, games, and music.

Chelsea turned in the front seat and stuck her tongue out at Marcie, quickly enough so that Debbie didn't see. Marcie responded with her usual middle-finger salute and mouthed *Fuck you* three times, careful to keep it quiet so that her mother wouldn't make good on her threat to turn the car around.

Back at Morgan Stanley, Cliff talked heatedly with a client on the phone. He leaned back in his imported leather armchair and loosened his tie. He wasn't sure what was making him feel a bit flushed. It was either the annoying client or the two martinis he'd had at lunch. His door was ajar, which allowed his sales assistant to overhear the unsettling conversation.

As she was about to close his door, Cliff slammed the phone down and said, "Goddamn Mexican!"

He didn't realize that his sales assistant stood there in the doorway, but it wouldn't have mattered to him anyway. He viewed his sales assistant as an overpaid secretary who answered his phone and took stock brokerage orders. Lately she'd seemed to think she had the right to talk back to him and was doing so more and more often.

"Shame on you!" she admonished him. "You shouldn't speak to clients like that. Or about them to others either!" She stood in the doorway with her hands on her hips.

"Well, for one, all that guy wanted to do was buy flimsy Mexican stocks, which is idiotic. And second, I harbor a grudge. If it weren't for all of these goddamn Mexicans and Cubans who came in and displaced good baseball players like me, I probably would have been the next Nolan Ryan."

Ever since Cliff had been cut from his semipro baseball team when it drafted a slew of Latino players, Cliff had hated all Mexicans and all Spanish-speaking people. The only consolation for Cliff for being cheated out of the Baseball Hall of Fame was the boatload of money he'd made working as a stockbroker.

"Who's Nol—?"

The telephone rang, and Cliff snapped, "I'll get it. Go back to your desk and get some work done."

His assistant flounced out, and Cliff answered the phone, "This is Walther."

"Hey, Cliff, were you able to ditch the bitch and kids so we can play golf?"

"Yeah, Johnny, it went smooth as silk. Debbie's a bowhead. Are you picking me up, or am I meeting you at the country club?"

It was true. His wife was a bowhead, which was a slang term for a woman from Texas who sacrificed her true self to fit in. The classic bowhead had bleached-blond hair pulled back into a ponytail with a big bow. The stereotypical bowhead was superficial and shallow, spending 90 percent of her day shopping, lunching, or getting beautified at the salon or spa. They often had that sickeningly heavy Texas accent, which Debbie did. When it came to shopping, no one could out shop a Texas bowhead. People from New York liked to claim that New York City was the shopping Mecca of the United States. Not so, as there was more square footage of shopping per capita in Dallas, Texas, than in any other city in the United States.

Whenever Cliff complained about his wife's spending, she would come back with, "Those people who say you can't buy happiness don't know where to shop."

But Cliff didn't complain much; Debbie and the girls always looked great and dressed to perfection. Their home was always immaculate and decorated to the nines. Of course, all the credit didn't go to Debbie since they had a full-time maid and a high-paid decorator. All in all, the relationship worked well; Cliff made a lot of money pushing stocks and bonds, and Debbie spent it.

Debbie had grown up in Kilgore, Texas, a town of eleven thousand residents, small by Texas standards. The summer before her first year at the University of Texas in Austin, she'd bleached her dark-brown hair shockingly blond and gotten a boob job, going from a AA to a CC. Debbie believed it was these two steps alone that allowed her to snag the handsome Cliff Walther while in their junior year of college.

Cliff had become enamored with Debbie at a fraternity party and married her shortly after graduation. Debbie had been thrilled when Cliff was drafted and offered a position pitching for a semipro baseball team in Houston. Ever since she had been a little girl, Debbie had dreamed of living in the big city, far away from Kilgore.

Cliff had accepted a position with Morgan Stanley after being released from the team. As a young stockbroker, he'd quickly become successful, bringing in such a hefty salary that he'd encouraged Debbie to quit her job at the fabric store where she worked. When Cliff Jr. was born, they bought a nice-sized house in the well-respected River Oaks area of Houston.

Three years later, the twin girls had arrived. Debbie had become a sports-oriented taxi mom as the three children got older. With the kids about to get driver's licenses, Debbie's free time would soon be spent lunching with friends and discussing mostly unimportant, mindless drivel that they had read in *People Magazine* that week.

Cliff had had brief liaisons with many different women, but they'd all had something in common: they were all blondes with large breasts. None of the affairs had been serious, and fortunately none of them had been with *Fatal Attraction* personalities. However, Cliff was rather careless in trying to conceal his philandering behavior, giving inconsistent stories and arriving home much later than a lengthy client meeting would have taken him.

Debbie believed they had a healthy, strong marriage. It wasn't that she did not suspect Cliff of cheating on her. Frankly, she just didn't want to know.

Chapter 24

"Whadja do for lunch today?" Cliff asked his sales assistant as he stepped outside his office and put on his coat.

"Went with Sheila and Kathy to Subway. Where are you going?" She correctly detected that Cliff was being extra friendly to her, probably because he needed her as an accomplice.

"I have an *important* meeting out of the office."

"Oh, one of those—I see. I'll be sure to tell anyone who calls looking for you, particularly *your family*," she said, smiling. Cliff snapped his fingers, said, "You got it, babe. See ya' tomorrow," and strutted out the front door like a peacock in full plumage.

The Royal Oaks Golf Club was one of the oldest private clubs in Houston. There was a waiting list to get in, and no one could do so without the sponsorship of at least three members of the club, plus an approval vote from all the other members. Cliff got in not long after he joined Morgan Stanley, through several coworkers who were members. Nobody voiced any opposition, basically because Cliff was unknown at the club. His firm was pleased with his membership; it was partly through the contacts he met on the golf course that he quickly rose to one of the top hundred producers in the firm.

On that day, however, Cliff wasn't playing golf with a client. He had arranged a game with three of his broker buddies and, not for the first time, was glad he always kept a change of golf clothes in his locker at the club. The foursome met on the first hole of the Fred Couples Signature Course, and Cliff bent down to tee up his ball. "Yeah, I had to give Debbie the ole 'important client meeting' story."

"That's right. I did the same thing," said Johnny, one of his golfing buddies, as he rummaged in his golf bag. Cliff's friends were a lot like him—jock-like in appearance, successful, and extremely cocky. Cliff hit a wallop of a drive, sending the ball easily three hundred yards down the middle of the fairway. He didn't pick up his tee; he just kicked it away instead.

"Glad to see I haven't lost it," Cliff said, twirling his square-faced Callaway FT1 driver for effect, and then added, "It's been two days since I last got to play. I was getting rusty." He let out a big laugh and the others joined in.

Cliff suddenly grabbed his pocket, where his phone had just vibrated. Cliff motioned to his friends to go on playing as he stepped behind some bushes to talk. When he walked back out a few moments later, he had a big smile on his face.

"Well, I just sold that bozo client of mine $50,000 of our new Morgan Stanley Venture Fund, which will not only generate a hefty commission for me, but it'll put me in line for that trip to Hawaii! Hey, Debbie and the girls are driving down to Galveston for a volleyball game and won't be back until late. How about we get some cocktails and steaks at Morton's? Then let's head over to The Men's Club for some pleasant viewing. My treat."

Johnny said, "Sounds like a plan! I just gotta call my wife, but I'll tell her we're working on your venture sale..." He paused to control his laughter "...together!"

This almost brought them to their knees in guffawing.

One of the other golfers joined the conversation. "Hey, I was afraid that might have been your wife on the phone. Wouldn't that have shot your cover if you had answered and it was her?"

"Hell, no," Cliff said. "My wife is so clueless. If she heard a flock of birds squawking in the background, it wouldn't occur to her to say, 'I thought you were in a business meeting.' I knew marrying a woman who was good in bed and stupid in the head would be a smart move in the long term."

They all laughed and nodded their heads in unison. None of them was the sharpest knife in the drawer, but these boys could sell ice cubes to Eskimos, and in the stock-brokerage business, that was all that mattered.

Chapter 25

Cliff rubbed three fresh twenty-dollar bills between the fat fingers of his left hand while holding a Manhattan in his right.

"Well, thank you, *suckers*—I mean clients! You know how I hate to take your money." He laughed, but he couldn't see the three buddies he was talking to because there was a voluptuous, twenty-four-year-old mostly nude dancer blocking his view.

"Keep rubbing on me, baby, and shortly these twenties will end up in your G-string!"

Ever since the Million Dollar Saloon had closed, The Men's Club on Sage Road in Houston was, to Cliff and the boys, their home away from home. On a good night—and this would be a good night—with a big commission and the wives placated, they might make the rounds: The Ritz, The Cabaret, Baby Dolls, The Trophy Club, and finish the evening at Glamour Girls. Both Dallas and Houston were known nationwide as titty-bar capitals of the world. From 5:00 p.m. until 2:00 a.m., each club had a steady stream of beautiful young girls. Bodies like Natalie Portman and Kate Beckinsale combined, silky smooth and perfectly tanned with no tan lines. They sported white-capped teeth, bleached platinum hair, and, of course, the best boob jobs money could buy, courtesy of the tips they brought in each night. The boobs were an investment—an investment because these babes could make $15,000 a month if they had the right appeal. The successful girls had their regulars like Cliff and his buddies, but then there were always the out-of-towners. Conventioneers were the best, especially from the Midwest, where titty bars were either nonexistent, or the girls were so ugly the men would rather stay home.

The song was winding, down and that was always the signal to put more cash in the 'music box,' strip-club slang for the girls'

G-strings. Cliff pulled to the side the thin string from his current babe's buttocks. The G-string wound around to the front where it was barely held in place with a small Band-Aid-like adhesive strip. He carefully slipped in one of the twenties he had been waving around and let the G-string snap back with a whack. Cliff was drunk, hot, and horny. The sound of the G-string snapping really set him off.

"Honey, you're a lot more of what I was in the mood for than some stupid volleyball game!" he declared to the girl, and with that, Cliff and his buddies broke out into uncontrollable laughter.

Chapter 26

It looked like every other kitchen in America. Like many older Americans, Elsie and Bill Walther spent most of their day at the kitchen table. Bill's morning routine since he'd retired from the Air Force started by picking up the *Phoenix Sun* and *Los Angeles Times* from the front porch, throwing them down on the kitchen table, and in one swift movement clicking the TV remote to turn on Fox News. He grabbed the coffee pot off the kitchen counter and got to work reading the papers and ingesting Fox.

An hour later, Elsie slid in next to him in the kitchen nook and poured herself a big cup of coffee.

"The papers are as bad as the stuff on TV. Boy, if I could find something else to fill my mornings, I would cancel these papers and sell the TV," groused Bill.

Oh, God. Here he goes again, thought Elsie. It had become a regular occurrence, listening to her husband rant and rave about the press or TV.

"I thought you were going to replace the *Phoenix Sun* with the *Wall Street Journal*."

"Elsie, they're all bad, and I'll give you an example. You know when we're traveling through airports and we go to the newsstands, have you ever actually looked at all those magazines? They cover what seems like every subject in the world. But what's in those magazines isn't news, and it isn't *new*, either. It's all just reprinted and regurgitated. There's only so much stuff you can write about. It's no better in the newspapers. They don't have a choice—they have to fill the newspapers from cover to cover, and if there's no news, they make up stuff, and if they can't think of something, they'll just print garbage. Ever notice how no one reads last week's newspaper? It was pretty worthless the day it was printed, so it's really worthless a week later."

His ranting was interrupted by the female Fox newscaster telling a story about an Arizona border incident. Two USBP agents had been missing for days, but Bill had already missed most of the story.

"Shit, I wanted to hear that. I'm going to call Mark—he usually has the news on, on Saturday mornings."

Elizabeth, Mark's wife, answered the phone.

"Mark's kind of busy right now."

"I promise I won't keep him long," Bill said.

Elizabeth walked over to the window and stuck her head out to say, "Mark, your dad's on the phone."

Mark hated heights and tall ladders, but once a year he had to clean the outsides of the upstairs windows. They were fixed windows and couldn't be washed from the inside. Last year, he had paid a service to do it, but they had charged him an arm and leg, so this year he was doing it himself.

"What?" he yelled back at his wife at the top of his lungs. "I don't care who's on the phone—I'm not coming down off this ladder! I just got up here!"

"It's your dad, honey!" she yelled again so Mark could hear her.

"Tell him I'm busy, and I'll have to call him back."
When no response came from Elizabeth, Mark was relieved. He thought, *Maybe I can get this job finished and get down off this darn ladder.*

But it wasn't to be. After only a few seconds, his wife yelled to him again. "Honey, he says it's important. He missed something on the news, and he wants to ask you about it."

It was times like this that Mark hated being a religious man, because he would feel a whole lot better if he could just tell Elizabeth to tell his dad to go to hell.

Mark mumbled to himself, "Why does he call me with that kind of question?" Then, yelling so loud everyone within a square block could hear him, he said, "Tell him to call Craig! Craig's the political guy, the professor, the Mr. Know-It-All in this family."

Chapter 27

"Now if you'll recall from an earlier class, I said we were skipping forward a bit in our textbook. Today we're going to be talking about the civil unrest that has plagued Mexico for the last decade. Mexico always had a fairly significant amount of civil unrest, but Americans were not that critical, because when compared to the rest of Central and South America, Mexico looked downright peaceful. That was, however, up until the massive murders and unrest directly related to the drug trafficking.

"Today we'll ignore the lawlessness relating to the drug wars and just concentrate on the political unrest. I'm not picking on Mexico, and I want those of you in the class with Hispanic descent to not think I'm doing so. But I don't think you can evaluate what's going on currently without understanding the conflicts and pressure on the government because of the political upheaval."

Professor Walther had decided before this week's class that he was going to change his original position on not using the word "Hispanic." There had already been a couple of demonstrations on campus, and he had already noticed that his full lecture hall had grown to standing room only with students who were just "interested" in this hot subject.

"Yo Soy is an ongoing Mexican protest movement centered on the democratization of the country and its media. It began in opposition to the Institutional Revolutionary Party, or IRP, candidate Peña Nieto. The Mexican media's allegedly biased coverage of the 2012 general election was haunting Nieto's administration. In May 2012, at a campaign event at the Ibero-American University, Peña Nieto was criticized by most of the attendees, who expressed their strong opposition to his candidature and called him a murderer. Their protest was centered on the 2006 San Salvador Atenco incident, in which then-governor of the State of Mexico called in the state police to break up a protest by local residents. Two protesters were killed, and human-rights groups charged the police with numerous violations of civil rights during that raid.

"Can anyone in the room remind the rest of us from your earlier reading what the 2006 San Salvador Atenco incident was all about?" Craig was glad that it was one of the Mexican students who raised his hand. "Thank you, what do you recall?"

"I have a brother who was involved in the incident, and he told me all about it when it happened. I think it was when Vicente Fox was president, somewhere around 2002. In San Salvador Atenco, some locals resisted the government's attempt to claim eminent domain and take their land to build an airport. Because of the resistance, I think it was in 2006, state and federal police forces raided San Salvador Atenco and violently took many of its citizens into custody, unleashing civil unrest in the area. Three hundred unarmed civilians and three thousand police officers clashed. A bunch of law-enforcement officials retaliated, and one of the leaders of the movement, a retired general named Zapatista, was sentenced to 150 years in prison. The rest of the members were accused of alleged 'organized kidnapping' of police officers and sentenced to maximum-security prisons. In February 2009, the civil unrest raised its ugly head again over the same incident, and the Federales shot about forty-three people."

The student sat down with a proud smile on his face.

Excelente, excelente, thought Craig to himself, and he said out loud, "Excellent, excellent, I'm very impressed. Now do you recall what happened to Zapatista?"

The Mexican kid stood back up and said, "Yeah, that was totally awesome—he broke out of jail. He escaped and now he's leading a major revolution."

"Thank you," Craig said. "I'm impressed, whether you got that information firsthand or from reading."

Craig continued his lecture. "In Chilpancingo, Mexico, just recently thousands of demonstrators descended on the state capital to once again protest the massacre of those forty-three individuals. Protesters then seized dozens of governmental buildings and briefly shut down airports and blocked all forms of transportation and utilities. What your fellow classmate didn't mention was that the leader of the initial uprising, General Zapatista, has been very busy amassing a small army of loyalists since escaping from jail. Compared to the original defense of their land, the last six months have been eye opening. The general's now massive fighting forces have made heavy inroads and have been raiding and capturing caches of weapons and vehicles.

"Ladies and gentlemen, of course the Nieto government has labeled them *terrorists*. As is often true in any country when there is civil turmoil, the definitions of 'terrorist,' 'revolutionary,' and 'patriot' are up for debate. But the Mexican press has done an excellent job of keeping the successes of Zapatista out of the eyes of the international press."

One student, without even raising his hand, blurted out, "My cousin in Mexico City tells me that Zapatista is the second coming of Che Guevara."

Craig chuckled. "Well, I don't want to insult your cousin, but I think you should suggest that he come up and take my course. Che Guevara was not from Mexico—he was from Cuba. Your cousin should have compared Zapatista to two of the most famous Mexican revolutionaries, Emiliano Zapata and the legendary Poncho Villa, who is often referred to as the 'Mexican Robin Hood.'"

Craig spent the rest of the class talking about the issues relating to the revolutionaries. "Let me conclude with our main point today. We've established since the beginning of this course that Mexico is basically imploding: the drug trafficking, drug cartels—the utter devastation of the economy, including the Mexican stock-market collapse and complete devaluation of the peso—the continuing corruption in the new government of Nieto, and the continuing civil unrest and protest. Add to that the ever-popular revolutionary Zapatista, and you've got a recipe for a perfect storm. The imploding of a country.

"Class, that's all for today. We're going to concentrate on just one issue in our next session, and that's the drastic drop in oil prices over the last year and the incredible pressure that has put on the Mexican economy."

Chapter 28

It was a good thing that Fernando and his wife had left Mexico City when they did. The very foundation of the city was collapsing.

Mexico City was not only large, at 573 square miles, but was the sixth-largest metropolitan city in the world, at just under twenty-two million people. Because the vast majority of its inhabitants were Catholic and didn't believe in birth control, it had one of the fastest growth rates of any city of similar size in the world, only to be outdone by San Pablo. For almost half a century, Mexico City had been considered one of the most polluted cities in the world, and its residents had had the highest incidence of lung-related diseases. The traffic jams in Mexico City had made those on the local Los Angeles news channels look like a Sunday drive to the park for a picnic. Horror stories of individuals being stuck in traffic jams for eight to ten hours were not unusual.

To make matters worse, over half the people in Mexico City lived below the poverty level.

All of these statistics were in place before the depression that started in 2014. Life in Mexico was bleak. Hope for a better life was attached to the idea of going to America. America was the promised land for many; for others it was salvation incarnate. Life was always greener on the other side of the fence. However, for most, the passage to the promised land, the better life, and the other side of the fence was beyond their abilities. They felt doomed to a life without promise and without hope—and with starvation on their horizon. The final nail was driven into the proverbial coffin when the value of the Mexican peso started plummeting. Though the country's prediction of inflation was at 13 percent, most academics predicted an inflation rate closer to 25 percent. The most significant reason was that Mexico imported so much from the United States; the devaluation of its currency had caused the country's purchasing power to be devastated.

Even prior to the horrendous currency numbers, the roughly 22.5 million people living in Mexico at poverty level faced a daily challenge to feed their families. That had always been a problem in Mexico because there were so many mouths to feed. The average number of people per family household, at 3.9, was the highest in all of Central and North America, but since the depression had started, putting enough food on the table had gone from a difficult task to an almost impossible one.

In the previous three months, federal troops had to be called out at least once a day to food outlets and vendors throughout Mexico City. Most food-related disturbances had been minor skirmishes, but they had been escalating such that each incident had become more of a mini riot. There had been one protest by the hungry and poor in just the last month where over one million people marched on the capital. Sadly, instead of the president and his administration meeting with the protesters, the Federales had been called in. Thirteen people had been killed and another 160 injured.

It became a daily occurrence for a few more grocery stores, restaurants, and street vendors to permanently close their doors. Some closed because they were scared of the hostilities breaking out in businesses like theirs throughout the city, and others closed because they simply didn't have any food.

These days, there was only one bright spot for those living in Mexico City: Zapatista and his revolutionary guerrilla army had not yet ventured inside Mexico City.

But even that had a negative side. Millions of Mexicans might have considered deserting the city to escape to the smaller communities, where the scarcity of food was not quite as acute. They didn't, however, because of the atrocities carried out by Zapatista's guerrilla army in the surrounding countryside.

Chapter 29

After Craig's second divorce, he hadn't seen any reason why he still needed to live in the city. He'd always had a love-hate relationship with America's big cities. Sure, he found them exciting, almost pulsating, and because he was a man of the arts, he loved having access to the symphony, chamber music, and the theater. But he hated feeling like an ant in a large colony.

So years later, after he had moved to Albuquerque and found himself single again, he'd decided to take his promise to himself more seriously.

The Sandia Mountains made up one of the southernmost ranges in the Rocky Mountain system. The Sangre de Cristo Mountains comprised one of the longest chains in the Rocky Mountain system, but they petered out in Santa Fe, New Mexico. The Sandia Mountains were not nearly as tall and in fact constituted one of the shortest ranges in all the Rockies. They almost seemed like just a backstop on the east side of Albuquerque. The Cibola National Forest encompassed the Sandia Mountains and a few other, smaller ranges in northern New Mexico. Craig knew that finding thirty acres in the Sandia Mountains would be a very difficult task. It wasn't as if Albuquerque and the surrounding areas were newly developed. Santa Fe, the capital of New Mexico, less than an hour away, was the second-oldest city in the United States, founded in 1607 by the Spanish. Albuquerque, also founded by the Spanish as a fort, had been established almost one hundred years later in 1706. As a state, New Mexico was one of the least populated in America, with just over two million people spread out in the fifth-largest state. However, Albuquerque and the surrounding suburbs had almost 1.3 million inhabitants.

So when Craig had set out to find land, he had known that it would be impossible to find that much acreage that had not already been developed. Fortunately, he had been in luck: a house with thirty-five acres had just come on the market.

The property was everything that Craig had been looking for: heavily treed with some incredible rock formations and wildlife everywhere. The house, on the other hand, was a different story. It was a small adobe home that had been added onto with every changing season. It looked like a smorgasbord of designs, but that was no problem for Craig. Craig's high-society first wife was so glad to get out of the marriage and Albuquerque that she had gladly left him with millions in exchange for an incredibly swift and uncontested divorce. So, after buying the property, Craig had had the house razed.

Big, roomy, and rustic. He loved the fact that, from the very first day he'd moved in, the house had felt warm, comfy, and inviting. It had cost him almost $2 million, but he didn't regret one penny of it. It wasn't that Craig had a lot of friends. Frankly, he had very few friends, so he did very little entertaining, other than girlfriends. He just loved how the house made him feel.

There were three different buildings. The main house had four bedrooms, all oversized. Next to it was a two-car garage, and lastly was a combination workshop, storage shed, and greenhouse. Instead of hiring a decorator, Craig had spent two years, while he supervised the construction of the house, shopping for southwestern furniture and accessories. He had found a wonderful store in Albuquerque that made custom-made, hand-carved southwestern furniture. In addition, he'd taken numerous trips to El Paso and into Mexico itself to find some of the more unique pieces. His one main criterion was comfort.

The second, most important criterion was that the furniture be easy to keep clean and not show dirt easily. It wasn't that Craig was a neatnik, but he had two large Alaskan malamute dogs that lived much of the time indoors. He thought it was unfair to try to keep them from getting up on the furniture; they were his family.

Craig's southwestern compound had become the love of his life. He usually got up early, drove down to the college, and put in fairly long hours, especially on days that he had classes. Then he drove directly home every night and did it all over again. He didn't tend to go much of anywhere else, except to the occasional theater or symphony. Craig was an excellent cook, and since he'd decided he could eat Italian or Mexican food alternately every other night, he had perfected cooking both cuisines. He just couldn't see any reason to go out to noisy restaurants.

When he had a date, the date was required to drive up to his house and possibly stop to pick up dinner, but the majority of the time Craig enjoyed showing off his culinary skills. Craig's only other pastimes were hiking or cross-country skiing – skijoring - with his dogs. Fortunately, his property was situated just a mile from one of the best hiking, biking, and skiing trails in northern New Mexico. Life was good, and Craig was thoroughly enjoying himself.

Chapter 30

The doorbell rang, and Craig Walther grunted, "Why does my doorbell always seem to ring at night?"

He immediately saw the foolishness of his comment, and he chuckled. *You idiot!* he thought to himself. *You're always at work during the day, so of course you only hear it ring at night.*

Craig had been staring at a catalog on his computer screen for a southwestern art auction that was going to take place in Santa Fe in a few weeks.

"Damn that Jennifer," he said as he scowled at his watch. Putting down his margarita on a side table, he went over to the intercom and hit the talk button. "Jennifer, what are you doing here? This is finals week."

A sexy, mature female voice came back to him over the intercom. "Well, that's an interesting comment, Professor, since I'm the one giving the test, not taking it."

Craig grabbed his forehead with both hands and let out a big sigh, carefully making sure he made no sound.

The female voice on the intercom continued, "And who might this Jennifer be? Is this my rival? I didn't know that a late-night, unannounced visit would get me called by somebody else's name."

Craig quickly regained his composure, tried to sound sober, and responded, "I'm sorry, Professor Lacey, I—I..."

Professor Lacey laughed. "Well, now you've made me even madder—some other woman gets called by her first name, and I'm demoted to Professor Lacey."

"I'm sorry, Katherine. I'm clearly batting zero here." He hit the buzzer to open the latch on the front door, and then he added, "Please come up."

Craig jumped off the sofa and immediately regretted that he buzzed Katherine in so quickly: Jennifer had spent the night before with him, and unfortunately, she had a horrible habit of always leaving something. He scrambled around the living room, searching. From his years of dating, Craig had learned that women usually left some feminine item behind, sort of like how a dog marks its territory. Bingo! A pair of earrings, which he quickly deposited in an antique Navajo ceramic bowl.

As he did so, Craig's mind flashed with thoughts of Katherine.

Professor Katherine Lacey—wow! What a woman! And this from a man who had just spent the night before with a girl he thought close to perfect. He never liked to allow himself to compare Katherine with Jennifer, but the thought did creep into his mind. It seemed that in many ways Katherine was a grown-up version of Jennifer.

Katherine had all the beauty that Jennifer possessed, but being thirty years her senior, she was more refined, like a great red wine. Her makeup was more professionally done, but of course, she'd had thirty years to perfect it. Craig often suspected that, since Katherine was fairly well off, things like her makeup and hair were professionally done. When it came to comparing his lovers' bodies, Craig found that Katherine held her own even for a woman in her late fifties. She played tennis, ran often, and never missed a day in the gym. But Craig was a fair man; not once did he fault any part of Katherine's physique because it was just a little less tight or supple than Jennifer's. He was no fool, and although he himself tried to keep in shape, he knew there was only so much a person could do to fight the effects of age and gravity.

The love of everything southwestern was one of the things that had attracted the two of them to each other. They had met two years ago at an Indian jewelry store in Santa Fe; they both had a serious interest in southwestern art and jewelry and liked to highlight their collections by wearing what they could and displaying the rest in their homes.

Katherine was an anthropologist at UNM, although she'd received her doctorate in anthropology from MIT. She'd been married for almost twenty years but had no children. Her husband, who was also a nationally known anthropologist, had died twelve years earlier from a brain aneurysm.

After meeting, Craig and Katherine had dated off and on for two years before the relationship had grown somewhat serious. Though no one would describe Katherine as "lonely," she had been deeply in love with her husband, and she didn't like living alone, much less not having a serious, warm, and loving relationship. She had worked hard at developing such a relationship with Craig, but just when she had thought things were going well, Craig had put on the big skids. Katherine had been devastated. She knew a relationship that was not growing was going nowhere, and it was pretty obvious to her that their relationship was going sideways at best.

Craig had been her first serious relationship since her husband's death, and she had taken the disappointment well. At first, she'd tried to end the relationship completely, but she just couldn't do it. She was clearly in love with Craig. They were seeing each other a lot less frequently now, and Katherine was pretty sure that Craig was cheating on her. But 'cheating,' she knew, was somewhat of an unfair term, since there was no official commitment.

Craig was fluffing up the pillows on the sofa when he heard Katherine behind him.

"Your teaching skills are slipping, Professor Walther, or maybe it's that one of your students just refuses to be taught."

Craig turned to find Katherine standing there holding a hairbrush in her hand.

"Oh, Katherine, I'm glad you brought your hairbrush. Does that mean I'm going to be able to convince you to stay the night?"

"Cute, very cute! But I can't say I'm impressed with whoever your new lucky student of the month is, considering that I found the hairbrush on the front porch by the door. I don't mind the obvious clues planted by your girlfriends, but this is incredibly unimaginative."

"Look, I can understand why you'd be upset that I called you by somebody else's name on the intercom, but I've had a few drinks. Can I pour you a stiff one and allow you to catch up with me?"

From behind her back, she revealed a bottle of tequila and said, "I thought you'd never ask."

Craig suspected he was out of the doghouse for the moment and quickly slipped over to the bar to grab a set of custom-made shot glasses that Katherine had given him the previous Christmas. He took the bottle from Katherine and remarked playfully, "Still drinking that Patrón? I thought I converted you to Don Julio."

"I'm not easily converted."

He grinned. "Halt. It's too late, and I'm too drunk. Let's not do our quid pro quo tonight. You'll only kick my butt."

She returned his grin and said, "I knew this Mexican thing would have you up in arms. I saw you quoted in the press last month about President Denton following in Obama's footsteps in continuing to grant amnesty to all those illegal Mexicans. I understand that it might cause a surge in illegal border crossings. Do you need someone to talk to about it?"

With tequila in hand, Craig flopped down on the sofa and gestured Katherine to join him. Once settled, he said, "No, I'm tired of talking about it—anything but Mexico."

"Works fine for me. Let's talk about us!"

He suddenly felt like he was in quicksand, so he grabbed for the papers he had just thrown away. "The problem with the Mexican situation is—"

Still standing, Katherine held up her hand like a traffic cop. "Now you halt!" She took off her gloves and coat and tossed them on an overstuffed leather chair next to the sofa. He could now see she was wearing a beautiful custom-made denim shirt with Indian beading, unbuttoned far enough to reveal some of her better attributes. She filled both shot glasses with tequila, immediately downed one, and then refilled it. She handed the other one to Craig and then sank into the plush sofa a few feet away from him.

"Last time we had this conversation," she said, "I was sober and I didn't see you for a month. Let's see if I can be a little bit more successful if we're both drunk. Worst case, instead of storming out of here mad like I did last time, maybe I can get laid, which God knows I need more than anything else right now."

"I have a better idea," Craig interjected. "Why don't we just go upstairs and jump in bed now and forget about another one of our marathon 'commitment' conversations?"

"You're not getting off that easy." She gulped down more tequila. "I'm better armed than I was the last time, and I'm not referring to the tequila. I've done a lot of thinking about myself, about you, and about our relationship. I don't think I have it completely figured out because we both know no one in this world ever gets it completely figured out. Let's just say I'm getting closer."

"You know, Katherine, when we have these discussions, I never know if you're complaining or trying to help me."

"I'm doing both—I'm complaining because I'm so hooked on you, and that makes me want to help you. But before I do any helping, though, I've got to use the little girl's room. Don't you pass out on me!"

Craig sank back into the soft sofa cushions and started thinking about the conversation that he knew was coming. After receiving his doctorate, Craig had worked for twenty years in Washington, DC, for a government think tank. That's where he'd met a wealthy political socialite and, after dating for almost a year, married her. Hobnobbing in Washington was a lot of fun, but Craig had quickly grown tired of all the snootiness, backbiting, and politics. He'd wanted to do what he'd always dreamed of doing, which was teach.

When he'd gotten the offer to teach at the University of New Mexico in Albuquerque, it had satisfied both of his needs: an excellent teaching position and a job far away from the craziness of the East Coast. He and his wife had had a wonderful relationship, or at least he'd thought so, but Albuquerque, and for that matter, the entire state of New Mexico, was just not her cup of tea. She'd never understood the southwestern culture, much less the heavy Mexican influence. As hard as she had tried, she just couldn't make it work, and after five years of marriage, she had just up and left. But she was fair; she left Craig with millions of dollars in his bank account.

Craig had been crushed; he'd never seen it coming. Of course, he had been putting in a lot of hours at the university, but what was there to go wrong? They were in love, they had lots of money, and he'd thought they were happy.

As so often happens, after the divorce Craig succumbed to the rebound theory. He met another woman about a year later and immediately remarried. Again, Craig thought he had a wonderful marriage, but after three years he caught his wife having an affair. If he had been crushed by the first divorce, the second divorce totally devastated him.

It was now five years since his second divorce, and Craig very much enjoyed being single. Though he thought he had liked being married, the two experiences had completely soured him on the entire institution. He now considered himself a confirmed bachelor.

He awoke from a somewhat drunken stupor to find Katherine laying a big wet one on him.

"Wake up, lover boy. My tequila is starting to kick in, and I'm ready to talk."

"Well, my drinks kicked in a couple of hours ago, and I will guarantee you we'll accomplish a lot more up in the bedroom than we will down here debating on the sofa."

Katherine's speech wasn't nearly as slurred as Craig's because she was still early in her tequila high. If anything, it was giving her a burst of energy.

"There's plenty of time for that, and as drunk as I've seen you, I've never seen you unable to perform in the rack room. But would you at least sit up straight, so I know you're listening?"

Craig tried to right himself on the sofa, but to Katherine he still looked far too comfortable.

"Aren't you tired of trying to get back at women?" she asked. "Look, I know you were totally hosed by your two wives, but that doesn't mean you have to spend the rest of your life treating all women as if they were evil."

"All I'm trying to do is protect myself. I've had enough pain for one lifetime."

"Fair, a fair comment," Katherine said. "But come on, you're a big boy. It's been five years since your most recent divorce. Are you going to live the rest of your life alone because of the pain you endured so long ago? And you talk about pain. I haven't brought you any pain, except maybe these occasional conversations where I'm just trying to get some kind of more serious commitment from you. Is that pain all that bad, considering all the wonderful times we've had together? How long do you expect me to stay around while you get over this— protecting yourself from potential pain?"

Craig let out a big laugh. "I will have to admit, I feel absolutely no pain at this very moment."

"Funny, very funny." Katherine hated it when she was trying to have a serious conversation with Craig, and he deflected the conversation by trying to interject humor. "You won't think it's so funny when you find yourself having to have sex with yourself."

"Don't knock it if you haven't tried it. You know what they say—stay with your first love, your left hand." Craig barley managed to get that out, as he started to laugh uncontrollably. However, this wasn't a smart move, and even though Katherine was starting to feel a bit tipsy, this was not where she wanted the conversation to go. She had driven all the way up here for a serious conversation, and now all Craig could do was crack crass jokes.

"I can see I've wasted my time and maybe some very good tequila. Are we going to be able to get this conversation back on track, or are you going to continue to do everything you can to keep from being serious with me?"

"I apologize, but remember I told you I was drunk when I answered the doorbell. Those two additional tequilas you've pumped into me are really inhibiting my ability to be too serious. And isn't that really what it's all about, my lack of being serious? You hate that I'm so serious about my research, writing, and teaching, yet I'm not willing to be serious about our relationship. Isn't that what's really bugging you?"

Katherine filled both glasses one more time. "No, you couldn't be farther from the mark. You know I'm every bit as serious as you about my position at UNM. If it were just your work that I had to compete with, you wouldn't hear a peep out of me. But it's all the other women that you can't seem to do without. It's bad enough you're catting around, but it's very embarrassing for me, among my colleagues who know that we've been seeing each other, that my competition for your attention is not only women thirty years my junior but many of them your students."

"Well, I don't know where you're getting your information, but you're wrong. Some of the girls *are* my students, but some of the other girls are just attending UNM."

"One more smart-aleck remark like that and I'm not only leaving, I'm taking the Patron."

"Okay, you know my weakness. I'll do anything to keep the Patron, but once again I want it on the record that I much prefer the Don Julio, especially the 1942."

Katherine still didn't like the sarcasm, but it was just too close to the mark. She had purposely brought the tequila to use as a bargaining chip, and Craig was starting to enjoy both the conversation and the tequila buzz he had on.

Craig said, "I think the fact that I date both professors and students at UNM is just an excellent way to broaden my academic relationships with various campus groups. I'm sure you remember that the dean, in our faculty meeting at the beginning of the semester, stressed the need for all of us to broaden our interaction with professors outside our department and with the students themselves. I've just taken his advice to heart."

Craig allowed himself a small chuckle but realized that if he burst into laughter again, Katherine and the Patron would go out the door.

"Bullshit! I know why you date those college girls. First of all, they aren't looking for a commitment. They aren't looking for marriage. You aren't forced to have the kind of conversations with them that you have with me. And second, you do it for safety. For your protection. I'm not sure you're able to fall in love with somebody thirty years your junior, but even if you were, I know you well enough to know that you sure wouldn't marry anybody with that age difference. And so you get exactly what you want—fun with no fear. And that's what I've been thinking about. That's what I came up here to discuss."

Finally, Katherine had hit a nerve, a nerve that even a tequila buzz couldn't dull. Craig knew she was absolutely right, but he didn't need her to come up to his house to tell him that. It had become clear to him in his conversations with Jennifer. It was the reason he kept telling Jennifer to stay away. Sure, he wasn't willing to make a commitment, much less fall in love, with somebody that much younger, though he had to admit to himself that his feelings for Jennifer were getting serious and starting to make him uncomfortable. Katherine was absolutely right. He never wanted to go through the pain of marriage and divorce again. He'd even considered giving up women completely, but he enjoyed their company too damn much, not to mention that sex was something he could never fathom doing without.

"You're right. Ultimately, you're always right. That's why you graduated summa cum laude, and I only graduated magna cum laude. Okay, I give in. You have me figured out. I'll save you the breath. So where do we go from here, Professor?"

Katherine slugged down the last of her shot glass, stood up, and ripped off her blouse, causing sterling silver buttons to fly everywhere. She leaped onto Craig, knocking him flat onto the cushy leather sofa, and, with the sexiest voice she could muster, said, "Who needs the bedroom? How about I fuck your brains out right here? I'll show you some tricks your little sorority girls haven't even dreamed of."

Chapter 31

Craig Walther was sitting in his office at UNM grading term papers when his cell phone rang. It was his dad.

"Hey, pop, what's up? How's Mom?

"Fine, but she's going to have that bunion on her left foot operated on. Look, I'm sorry to bother you at work, but I tried calling your brother, and once again he ducked my call. Did you know that Mark calls you Mr. Know-It-All and says that I should call you if I had any questions that need an answer? You know, it gets tiring, hearing the same old thing repeated from him. He just loves to get that dig in about you, Mr. Know-It-All! Really, Mark should have grown up by now."

"That's fine, Dad. When it comes to Mark, I do know it all. His head has been caught in that religious fog, and it has rotted his brain. You know, he'd be smarter and we'd get along better without all that religion."

Bill realized that he shouldn't have told Craig about Mark's disparaging comment. No reason to make things worse than they already were between the two brothers. Nothing had changed in fifty years—having four boys was like being a permanent referee. He was either breaking up a nasty verbal battle or, worse, a serious fistfight. Bill still couldn't believe that one of his boys hadn't gotten seriously hurt from one of those teenage brother-versus-brother boxing matches. The rivalry and animosity between his sons certainly provided enough angst to sink a ship.

"I'm sorry to get into all that. Let's start over, and I'll tell you why I'm calling. As crappy and wrong as these talking heads in the media are, I do think there's really something to this border problem Dave's been preaching about for a while now. Your mom and me living in Phoenix, close to the trouble, is probably why I'm panicky. The feeling in my stomach would be less if we lived farther away. The damn liberal press has hidden from the American people that Phoenix is now one of the top three cities in the world for kidnapping. Kidnapping?

Can you fucking *believe it*—Phoenix, Arizona? It's related to those damn drug traffickers in Mexico! Craig, of course everyone knows it, but no one gives a crap!"

Craig impatiently broke in. "Dad, Dad—you read that in my last book. I hope you didn't call me just to read to me what I wrote."

"Oh, I forgot. I thought I'd heard that on the news. Okay, okay, okay, but the main reason I'm calling is that one of the newscasts said that there are a couple of US border agents missing, and I didn't catch their names. I think it was in that district that David works out of in San Diego. Since you're the expert, I thought you might have more of the details."

Craig sat back in his seat and said in a high-pitched voice, "Dad, give me a break. Sure, I do have my finger on the pulse, and I am trying to stay on top of all this, but the timeline is moving so fast that it is near impossible to collect all the input and make heads or tails of it. Dad, remember there are thousands of US Border Patrol agents. I'm connected, but I'm not so connected that I know who's doing what. Frankly, both the department heads at Homeland Security and Immigration have ripped my name out of their Rolodexes and burned my card. They've told me—and I'll use polite terms—to take a hike since my last book pretty much called them totally inept. Man, the truth always hurts! But, Dad, seriously, I wouldn't worry about it. David may be the youngest, but I think he's the toughest of all of us brothers. If anyone could survive in that dangerous environment, it's him. However, I do worry about his wife. But that hard-headed Dave won't listen to me."

"Okay, you're probably right." Like a pit bull, Bill couldn't let it go. "Craig, how serious do you think this is? Your mother was thinking of going down to the grocery store and stocking up on some provisions. She wants to put together a seventy-two-hour survival kit. I have thought of swinging by Wal-Mart to pick up a couple extra boxes of ammunition before there's a run on ammunition. Your mother agrees. Do you think I'm overreacting? If I could only trust the news, I wouldn't be so worried. But I remember how all the major networks downplayed or totally ignored such serious national issues as Fast and Furious, Obama's missing birth certificate, Benghazi and the ISIS initial surges. And you being the expert, I know you know the press has always ignored the entire issue of illegals crossing the border. The fact that there is so little in the news about this border blowup might make most viewers comfortable, not me."

"Dad, I think you're overreacting. Look, if you lived in Nogales, you should be scared. But you don't live in Nogales. If you did, I would've made you move a decade ago. Sure, the crime rate in Phoenix has gone up tenfold in the last decade, and the fear of being kidnapped has risen to a ridiculous level. When it comes to small border towns, it isn't even safe to walk the streets. You never know when a gang shootout is going to take place. Hell, you know I used to go down to Acapulco almost every winter to stay at the Princess Hotel, but after that shootout last year at the Mexico City Airport, I figured nowhere in Mexico is safe anymore. Besides, Dad, I thought you stocked up your gun safe with ammunition after Obama got elected. With the stockpile you've got, how could you need more ammunition? You're not out at night again, taking potshots at shadows, are you, Dad? You nearly killed the neighbor's cat last year."

Bill let his son's allegations pass without comment. After all, it was true. Bill's wife, Elsie, had threatened to call the police if Bill didn't stop his nightly habit of patrolling the yard, loaded rifle in hand. She'd fussed at him, saying, "At your age, you should be ashamed of yourself, acting like Sergeant York. With your eyesight, you couldn't tell an illegal Mexican from one of our neighbors!"

Returning to Craig's question, he responded, "Son, you can never have enough ammunition these days. What with all those crazy liberals getting elected, I'm surprised I'm even allowed to own a gun. You remember that I had to wait an entire year to buy all that ammo because after Obama got elected, literally every store in the country was completely sold out, except for the odd calibers. Now doesn't that say something about his administration?"

"Whoa. Look, Dad, I apologize, but I don't have time for this. I have conferences set up with some key people this week to see if I can get a better handle on exactly what is going on. I promise, and you can tell Mom, if I hear *anything* that I think is alarming relating to Dave's situation in San Diego, you'll be the first to know."

Chapter 32

Most of Professor Walther's students were used to having him stride into the lecture hall after everyone was in place. But that wasn't the case today. As the students poured into the lecture hall, they found Professor Walther hunched over the desk at the front of the room, with no fewer than twelve books and other research papers opened and marked with numerous yellow stickies. There was something else interesting about today's class—there were guests.

Even though New Mexico was not a big oil-producing state and Albuquerque was anything but an oil hub, the fact that oil prices had plummeted even further in just the last few weeks had been on everybody's mind. Word had gotten around campus that this week's lecture by Professor Walther was going to be on the oil industry as it pertained to Mexico. Some curious fellow faculty members had decided to attend Craig's class. Craig was so involved with the stack of books surrounding him, he had hardly noticed that not only was the lecture hall full, but the occupants had also been waiting for a couple of minutes for class to start. It was only when one of the faculty members went up to say hello that he lifted his head and, embarrassed, noticed his delinquency. Craig stood and faced the room. He addressed the class as his eyes scanned the occupants. "I am honored that a number of my distinguished colleagues have graced our lecture hall today. I feel the need to enter into the record a bit of a qualifier. I am anything but an oil expert. I'm lucky enough to get the gasoline into the right part of my car. And as you can see from my desk, I felt the need to put in a little overtime to make sure I was totally on top of the issue for today's discussion.

"With that being said, let's start with a little history, and I hope all of you will impress our guests by showing them you have read the required chapters for this week's discussion. Before we get into the history, I'd like to know everyone's knowledge or at least understanding level from the reading assignment for today.

"Hold on, there's one more caveat. We can overcomplicate this if we focus too much on the minute details when we discuss oil production and sales. Rather than getting too technical, let's just say that we are talking about barrels of crude oil. Okay, who's the largest producer of oil today?"

"Saudi Arabia," a student blurted out.

"Wrong, it is Russia. Who is the largest exporter of oil today?"

"Russia," another student proffered.

"Wrong, it is Saudi Arabia. Where does the United States import most of its oil products from and in which order?"

"Russia, Saudi Arabia?" a small voice from the back of the room squeaked.

"You're getting closer. Canada is number one and Mexico number two. Okay, let's delve into the history of the oil market in Mexico. Mexico has been a major player and producer in the oil market for over half a century. Though the United States has always been a larger producer than Mexico, in Mexico the oil industry is much more venerated than here in America. The reason is simple—in the United States we have a laundry list of some of the most successful companies and industries in the world. That's not true in Mexico, where it's all about the oil industry. Every other industry in Mexico pales in comparison.

"Mexico's GDP over the last few decades has been comprised of three items—the oil industry, tourism and the remittance or repatriation of American dollars. I don't want to get into the third item today, but I want you to keep it fresh in your mind because I think it's going to be very important in future lectures. Millions of Mexicans living in the United States either legally or illegally send a large portion of their income back to their families in Mexico. This practice is called remittance or repatriation. A November 18, 2013, study done in conjunction with the Pew Research Center found that remittances from Mexicans living in the United States back to their families in Mexico peaked in 2007 at about $25 billion. It has been suspected for decades that one of the main reasons the Mexican government has been quite lax in policing the illegal immigration into the United States is because this flow of American dollars back into Mexico is such a boon for the Mexican economy. There is even speculation that the Mexican government encourages it."

A short pause and Craig's observations told him that he was in charge. The class was hanging on his every word.

"Let's get back to oil. There are five items crippling the Mexican oil industry today: a) the drop in production, b) the drop in oil prices, c) the lack of modern technology to improve production in the oil fields, d) the slowdown in drilling in the Gulf of Mexico due to the Deep Horizon oil platform disaster, and e) the corruption and politicking surrounding fixing Mexico's state-owned oil industry, PEMEX.

"As you all should know from your reading, Mexico nationalized its oil industry in 1939. Despite its troubles, PEMEX is still a giant. It is the largest corporation in Mexico and the fifth-largest oil firm in the world, with average daily production in 2013 of about 3.3 million barrels of oil, 4.8 million cubic feet of natural gas, and 435 thousand barrels of natural-gas liquids. It is the second-largest source for US-imported oil, after Canada, at a daily average of 1.9 million barrels.

"It is estimated today that oil income accounts for somewhere between forty and sixty percent of the Mexican federal government's annual revenues. As you can see, the recent decline in the price of oil is having a disastrous effect on Mexico's budget.

"Though the Mexican government has had a stranglehold on PEMEX, it has attempted to slow the decline in its reserves in oil production." Craig reached down and read a quote from an article in *The Economist* that described the dire economic situation with PEMEX.[1]

One of the other professors asked a question as Craig paused. "How did the Gulf oil spill affect all this?"

"Thanks, Bob. That was my next topic. As you all know from the newspapers and your reading, the BP Deepwater Horizon oil platform that caught fire and sank deposited thousands of barrels of oil into the Gulf of Mexico. Forgetting for the moment the devastating environmental impacts, just about every country and more importantly the major oil companies put an immediate halt to any deepwater drilling in the Gulf of Mexico. That has had a disastrous effect on Mexico and PEMEX's attempts to expand and improve its production and reserves. Only recently have countries and companies been willing to take a risk once again in the Gulf, but the current plunge in oil prices has put all of that on the back burner for now. These deep-water drilling rigs have some of the most expensive exploratory drilling costs that an oil-exploration company can experience. Any questions thus far?"

As usual, Craig could see the frustration on the faces of his students, trying to keep up with his fact-intensive lecture. Or maybe they were grimaces caused by writer's cramp.

"Now, let's quickly shift to the technological challenges of Mexico and PEMEX. Even with Mexico's attempts to revamp its oil production and return it to pre-2005 production levels, success has proven difficult given PEMEX's technological deficiencies on the production side. Even if the Gulf of Mexico completely opens up again to drilling, PEMEX also lacks the necessary capabilities to do deep-water drilling, thus preventing it from tapping resources in the deep Gulf of Mexico. In addition, PEMEX lacks the necessary refining capabilities to process the majority of its heavy oil, which constitutes more than half of its total production.

"In order to satisfy its domestic demand for refined fuels, Mexico has has had to export most of its heavy oil to the United States, one of the few countries with the necessary technology to process the Mexican oil mix and import it back as a processed product. Put simply, the Mexican federal government has been siphoning off such a high percentage of PEMEX's annual revenues that it just doesn't have the money to spend on modern technology to attract some of the better oil geologist and executives in a competitive world market. And now to conclude today's lecture, let's move to the political challenges of Mexico's oil industry.

"In one of the articles I read here..." Craig fumbled through the papers on his desk. "This indicates that at PEMEX, there is no transparency. Nobody watches over the contracts. For starters, they ask for a 10 percent bribe off the top of the price. When anyone complains, they are repressed. That is the way business is done down there."

Craig continued, "Even now, despite the free-market rules adopted by Mexico under the North American Free Trade Agreement, or NAFTA, the oil sector is a bastion of old-style socialism, with tighter restrictions on foreign investment than in any other major petroleum-producing nation. The problem is that the constitution of Mexico gives the state oil company, PEMEX, exclusive rights over oil production, and the Mexican government treats PEMEX as a major source of revenue. As a result, PEMEX has insufficient capital to develop new and more expensive resources on its own, and it cannot take on foreign partners to supply money and technology it lacks.

"Because of these vested interests, overcoming the constitutional barrier to reform the country's energy sector, which is already difficult, seems impossible. According to the Mexican Constitution, oil is the property of the nation, which has granted legitimate monopolistic production rights to PEMEX.

"In addition, any event within the oil industry has immediate public-opinion effects. Mexicans have traditionally reacted negatively to any action considered a 'foreign intervention.'

Interest groups and politicians have taken advantage of this, politicizing any possible oil issue, shielding themselves in the constitution, and preventing the advancement of necessary reforms in the sector. Hence, it will be very difficult to open the oil market to much-needed foreign investment.

"Mexican president Enrique Peña Nieto has given lip service to overhauling the country's energy sector as a top priority for his administration. Reforms under consideration include letting national oil companies partner with their foreign counterparts to open the country to new investments. Despite having been favored with considerable hydrocarbon resources, Mexico's energy security is in a dire state. Years of a corporatist and a clandestine regime under the Institutional Revolutionary Party's consolidated structural flaws have prevented the state-owned PEMEX from being able to adapt to changes in the energy market and the difficulties in upstream activities."

Luckily, Craig was coming to the conclusion of this week's lecture; he had noticed that most students had put down their pens, and that even included the three faculty members who had been scribbling some notes. It was always impossible to keep up with a Professor Walther's lecture.

"If the dire situation of Mexico's oil industry isn't enough on its own to drive Mexico into a major depression, let me add one more set of statistics. Mexico is currently the largest borrower from the International Bank for Reconstruction and Development in terms of exposure, with $15.2 billion in US dollars in outstanding debt as of the end of September 2014. The economy appears on track to register its third consecutive year of dramatically below-estimated growth, which has been held back by a sputtering recovery in the global economy and by sluggish domestic consumption and investment. As we showed in an earlier chart in an earlier class, the Statistics Institute's revised 2017 GDP estimated growth is down to negative 1.3 percent, from the previously reported negative 0.8 percent. Mexican authorities expect the decline in oil production to continue in the future and are pessimistic that it can be raised back to previous levels even with foreign investments.

"Perhaps the biggest challenge that Mexico faces regarding its energy security is its blind belief in oil as the center of economic development. Even with the current significant dive in crude oil products, it seems as if Mexico treats oil as a mythical product that will solve all of its problems."

As Craig started to stack up the papers and books on his desk, evidencing to the class that today's lecture was to be quickly concluded, he made a final comment.

"Interestingly, and a subject we will discuss in later classes here, the current administration in Washington, DC, seems to be oblivious to the meltdown of the Mexican economy. I find that surprising because even as far back as June 2007, former US Federal Reserve Chairman Alan Greenspan warned that declining oil production in Mexico could cause a major fiscal crisis there, which could have dangerous repercussions for the United States. And that wasn't even taking into consideration the recent drop in oil prices by almost two-thirds. Class dismissed."

1. From an August 10, 2013, article in The Economist, titled 'Unfixable PEMEX.' 'Its first problem is structural; it has never been treated as a profit-making company. Astonishingly for a monopoly that drills every barrel of oil in Mexico at an average cost of less than $7, and sells that for around $100, it lost an accumulated 360 billion pesos, or $29 billion, in the five years to 2012. This is partly because although its oil and gas production side makes a fat profit, it's refining business loses a fortune, and its petrochemicals division is also loss-making. Worse, the government sucks out cash to compensate for the lack of tax revenues it collects in the rest of the economy. Last year 55 percent of Pemex's revenues went to royalties and taxes. This perpetual drain on its cash flow means its debt has soared to $60 billion.'

Chapter 33

It was a small, dilapidated church, built at least one hundred years before of adobe brick and stucco walls, yet today much of the stucco had fallen off, exposing the ancient handmade adobe bricks. It was located on the outskirts of Bisbee, Arizona, a small border town halfway between Douglas and Nogales. Bisbee, the county seat of Cochise County, contained residents mostly of Mexican descent. As was true in the outskirts of any border city, this area and the practitioners of this church were 100 percent Mexican. No one, not even the local sheriff, knew exactly what percentage was legal versus illegal.

It was a Catholic Church. It was no surprise some ninety-five percent of the Mexican population living in the border states was Catholic. Earlier that afternoon, some of the parishioners had come by to take confession, but it was growing late, and the padre was locking up the doors for the evening. As opposed to residing in the church, as so many Catholic priests did to save costs in these small communities, this padre lived in a very modest rectory behind the church, the funds for which had been raised by the parishioners in this community.

As the padre stood outside and locked the last door, he thought he heard something inside the church. He unlocked the door, stepped in, and listened very intensely. It sounded like the usual scurrying mice, but nothing more. Once again, he left the church and locked the door behind him.

It was not mice. As the massive wooden doors closed and the old worn lock mechanism engaged with a loud clank, one hundred brown faces popped up. As one, they rose and peered out over the ancient hand-hewn pews. Since the padre had been in the confessional booth all afternoon, he had not noticed the flood of individuals that had snuck into his church and hidden under the pews. Each had found whatever small crannies he or she could and hid.

The next morning, the padre returned for services at 8:00 a.m. As he unlocked the door, the ancient mechanism groaned and flew open. He was knocked to the ground, and in one swift tide, the previous night's residents rushed past him. His pride was injured more than his body by the Mexicans flooding past him.

At the fear of being trampled the padre started yelling in an attempt to stop the onslaught. One raggedly dressed man leaned over and prepared to punch the padre in the face. His arm was immediately grabbed by two short, plump Mexican women, who said, "He is a man of God. He has done us no harm. Leave him, and *vámanos*!"

By the time the padre steadied himself and was able to stand once again, no one was in sight. Was this a test from God? Was it a bad dream? The padre made the sign of the cross, knelt, and asked God for an answer.

Chapter 34

"Good morning." Craig said this with a little more gusto because he found today's subject one of his favorites. "Before I get started, I will warn you that today's lecture is not in your course textbook, so you need to take copious notes.

"As you will recall, one of the reasons Mexico is imploding is due to revolutionary activity, or what some people prefer to call 'guerrilla' actions. The guerrilla base has been increasing over the last decade. Most Americans aren't paying attention to nor do they care about these actions and cannot relate to the Mexicans' plight. Of course, the United States of America was founded by and through revolutionary acts. Our US revolution went up against a foreign power hell bent on enslaving our nation through unregulated taxation and heavy-handed rule by royalty and parliament across the ocean. The closest thing we've had to any internal strife that pitted countrymen against countrymen was the Civil War, which was one of the bloodiest wars in American history.

"I won't get into the reasons today, but Mexico and much of Central and South America have a history of revolutions. The current revolution in Mexico is being conducted by a group calling themselves *Ejército Zapatista de Liberación Nacional* or Zapatista Army of National Liberation, which also goes by the acronym EZLN.

"Currently, EZLN has conducted one successful raid after another. One of the most recent raids was at Acapulco's Princess Resort. It went very well and conscripted many new 'volunteer' recruits." Craig made air quotes around the word "volunteer."

Craig took a deep breath and continued, "The EZLN's leader, Zapatista, is a Mayan, and although it is known that he has taken on the name of Zapatista, no one actually knows his real name. It is believed that he took his name from Emiliano Zapata, a supporter of the 1910-to-1920 Mexican Revolution.

Zapatistas see themselves as his ideological heirs, and in 1994, they declared war against the Mexican state.

"The Zapatistas are against the North American Free Trade Agreement as an example of neoliberal policy that negatively impacts the indigenous Mexican agricultural market. The cheap, mass-produced US agricultural product drastically reduced the incomes and standard of living of many southern Mexican farms. That was because they weren't able to compete with the subsidized, mechanically harvested, and genetically modified imports from the United States."

Craig paused and scanned the room to make sure he wasn't putting all the students to sleep. This was a lot of information to jam down their young minds in one class period. He thought, *It is college, not high school.*

"Up until 2013, the Zapatistas had been gradually forming several autonomous municipalities, more or less independent of the Mexican government."

Craig asked his students, "Have you heard the quotation, 'Power corrupts, and absolute power corrupts absolutely'? In the beginning most leaders are magnanimous. Later in the lives of their administrations, they become selfish and destroy their good work.

"Starting in early 2014, everything started to unravel as the EZLNs attempted to gain power with as little violence as possible. As the Mexican economy started to deteriorate rapidly and the revenues from oil production shrank dramatically, reparations and payments that the Mexican government had promised Zapatista, the EZLN, Yo Soy were cut off, discontinued! In June 2013, the combined entities of EZLN and Yo Soy declared war once again on the Mexican government. Their forces and supporters had gone up a hundredfold in less than a year. At first, their successes were small and costly.

However, EZLN had found sympathetic, wealthy, and willing donors in the Middle East. Those unnamed donors were actually terrorist organizations who were more than willing to contribute billions to do anything to disrupt the United States' border country, Mexico. The EZLN has forced the Mexican government to spend billions defending scattered areas throughout the country, which exacerbated the huge recession that was already plaguing the country."

Professor Walther stopped his pacing and asked, "Are you up to speed with notes from today's class? Let me offer some last comments for the day. Are there additional consequences resulting from terrorist and revolutionary activity in Mexico? Remember, Zapatista and his military henchmen are not the most sympathetic leaders. They see everything in black and white: People are either with the revolutionaries or against them. Those with them either join their forces voluntarily, or they are forced to join. Although the actual number of Zapatista forces is unknown, it has become apparent that thousands of Mexicans have died. They've been killed by EZLN's forces when they've resisted joining. Millions of Mexicans have flooded north, not only to avoid bloodshed or being forced to join Zapatista, but also because EZLN has not yet moved any forces into northern Mexico.

"Okay, next week were going to have a short exam, covering the last two weeks of material we've covered. Any questions?" Without waiting a beat, Craig said, "Class dismissed."

Chapter 35

Mark hung up the phone. Over the past many months, he and his brother Craig had rarely spoken to each other by phone; however over the last few days, they had spent considerable time discussing Mark's unsettling feelings stemming from the throngs of roving crowds that his brother Dave had observed in Tijuana when delivering his load of illegals.

Listening to his brothers and watching the news, Mark thought, *Due to Mexico's collapsing economy, the number of those unable to afford life's basics—food, shelter, and clothing— has increased exponentially. Life as a poor or middle-class citizen living in Mexico sucks!*

From where Mark Walther sat this Saturday morning, staring out the kitchen window, drinking his second cup of strong, dark, rich coffee, the world looked normal. Nothing out of place, no great storm clouds looming overhead, the sun shining. Getting deeper in thought by the moment, he wondered why even *more* Mexicans hadn't tried for decades to move to the United States. It was a frustrating thought. He wasn't an expert on Mexico. He'd left that kind of reasoning to Craig. But living there in Arizona, one of the hotbeds of the Mexican movement, he felt he had a pretty good feel for the Mexican people. Additionally, he and his wife Elizabeth almost annually took a trip to one of the more popular tourist towns or beaches in Mexico.

It almost seemed impossible that there had not been a mass exodus to America decades ago. Even the poorest and most ignorant Mexican had heard that the United States, in one way or another, was the land of golden opportunity. If a Mexican family had gone to one of their own beach resorts, they would find multimillion-dollar homes, the vast majority of them built by Americans. If they had traveled to one of the US border cities, they'd find that the cars driven by Americans were always newer and much more luxurious. When they turned on their TV sets, Mexicans found both Mexican and American programming available. When compared, the content and quality of the shows were like the difference between night and day.

And though Mark had never thought of himself as an art snob, and he was fully aware of the cliché 'beauty is in the eye of the beholder,' he could just never bring himself to appreciate Mexican art and music. When it came to Mexican art, it seemed to him that there were only two choices: those horrible paintings on black velvet that were always of Elvis Pressley or Marilyn Monroe, or the huge murals plastering the sides of buildings and walls, which always seemed to depict some supposedly famous Mexican battle.

And then there was the music. Could anyone actually tell the difference between one song and another? Maybe it was the fact that 90 percent of the time when he was traveling in Mexico, the local music was always turned up to the highest volume. Bugles and horns blasted through cheap speakers was anything but pleasant.

Even if it wasn't completely true, it seemed like the majority of Mexicans believed that Americans had it one hundred times better than any one of them. It appeared that Americans lived in the promised land, to the exclusion of the rest of the world.

Whenever Mark traveled to Mexico, the land and its people seemed more like the Eastern-Bloc, Iron-Curtain countries before the Berlin wall came down. For forty-something years under a communist stranglehold, progress had ground to a halt. Full employment, such as it was, meant ten people assigned to do a job that took only one. There was no incentive to be efficient, and no one was rewarded for efficiency.

That was the impression Mark had of Mexico. Besides, Mexico was dirty, with little to no opportunity for the poor or even middle class to provide for themselves. He knew that if he had traveled to Mexico City or other large Mexican cities back in the '50s and '60s and then leaped forward to today, he would have discovered that very little had changed. The architecture, roadways, signage, and overall feeling of filthiness still existed. It seemed like Mexico would always be trapped in its past.

Yet, when one traveled throughout America and drove through a business district or residential neighborhood, one could discern, even with an untrained eye, the age of an office building or home simply by its material and style. Americans were always moving forward. Their structures were built more efficiently and were more pleasing to the eye. Mark did not include in his critique the opulent homes built by Americans in Mexico City, Monterrey, Guadalajara, and the Pacific beaches. Those homes were nearly always designed by American architects and designers.

No, Mark thought, *you could describe Mexican architecture in one word: 'cement.'*

CEMEX was not only the largest cement company in Mexico, it was the largest company of its kind in the world, second only to PEMEX as the largest company in Mexico. Whenever Mark visited Mexico, he always thought it was fascinating to drive around and see residential homes or commercial offices being built. No plywood, no drywall, and very little steel could be found on the job site. Rather, he'd see concrete pillars, flooring, walls, and ceiling. It was all done by hand, at a cost of around 74 pesos, or $5 US, an hour.

Mark's rumination continued. Why wouldn't Mexicans think all Americans are rich? Most Mexicans who came into contact with Americans did so with a visiting tourist. Even the goofiest hick from Arkansas appeared rich while on his honeymoon at a fancy beach resort, throwing down piña coladas and margaritas like there was no tomorrow. Meanwhile, most Mexicans were barely able to put beans and tortillas on their tables. No wonder America appeared to be the promised land!

Mark snickered. "Yeah, the grass *is* greener on the other side of the fence."

But he had recently learned a fact about Mexico that he thought was most telling. On his last trip to Cancun with his wife, he'd noticed something he hadn't noticed before. First, the cars were almost all made in America. Second, they all looked at least twenty years old. It turned out that a very significant percentage of the older used cars in America eventually find their way into Mexico. Most Americans had no interest in buying a twenty-year-old used car with several hundred thousand miles showing on the odometer. In Mexico, that same car was considered a real find.

Mark realized if he didn't get to his wife's "honey-do" list, he was going to find himself in trouble. However, he had one more item to contemplate before putting his thoughts on the back burner. He had always wondered why so many Mexicans that moved to the United States, both legally and illegally, settled within the border states. Yeah, he knew the percentages were in their favor if, after crossing, they quickly got settled and blended in with the rest of the Mexicans.

Once on a college break Mark had taken a train from El Paso to Mexico City. The trip, Mark remembered, had been a real eye opener. He had been living in Ann Arbor, Michigan, so never in his life had he seen so many hundreds of miles, actually 1,200 miles, of barren land. He never saw one blade of grass, and it even appeared that the cacti were dying from lack of moisture. So why, when these people came from such a desolate land, would they be content to relocate in Arizona, New Mexico, or Southwest Texas—dry, hot, and dusty locations? Frankly, it was substituting one hell for another. Hell was hell, so why move?

If you decided to change countries, why not go someplace where there was lush vegetation and a change of seasons?

Mark caught himself being hypocritical and said to himself, "I moved from much greener parts and ended up here in the desert of Arizona. Who am I to criticize?"

But then Mark had green grass and a large garden at his Arizona home.

Chapter 36

It's not that Fernando had thought that emigrating to the United States was going to be easy, but he was having second thoughts—perhaps he had not thought this out as well as he should have.

From the very day he and his wife had stormed out of their apartment, leaving their front door wide open, it had been one continuous nightmare. Fernando had found himself swimming in a current of his fellow countrymen trying to flee Mexico and get into the United States as quickly as humanly possible. There must have been millions, and what he now thought might even be tens of millions, attempting the same feat. Fernando had decided that it had to be now or never. He was sure that at any moment the border patrol would bring in reinforcements to plug the dike, and no one would cross over, legal or otherwise.

Fernando had not heard about Obama's presidential amnesty program, during which President Obama had announced his intention to grant citizenship to ten-million-plus illegal Mexicans living in the United States. But he learned it on the road from the continual grapevine of underground communication. Embarrassingly enough, he learned that he must have been the only Mexican citizen who had not heard the US president's proclamation. Before his career had bottomed out, he had always kept abreast of current affairs. In fact, before his financial ruin, Fernando would pore over several newspapers each morning, devouring anything that seemed to gain him an edge over his competitors.

Fernando thought, *It was all everyone was talking about. How could I have missed such an important proclamation?*

At first, the understanding was that this new, lenient policy was only going to be granted to Mexicans already living in the United States for a limited period, so no one thought it could benefit them. Even so, they all spoke of having relatives who were already in the United States, both legally and illegally, who had told them, "No way would the US government be able to figure out the length of time anyone had been here."

They said the Americans might have some records existing for those who were living there legally, but even that was now questionable. But the new amnesty program was for those living in the United States illegally. And by definition, since all the illegals had been living in America under the radar, the US government couldn't prove one way or another when they had arrived.

Consequently, millions of Mexicans had decided to cross the Mexico-US border as fast as possible so they could become bonafide, legalized US citizens under the new program.

Then the benefits of being an American would start. Being a poor citizen in the United States meant they would be eligible for free medical care and medicine from the free medical clinics. Mothers with infants up to age of two got WIC benefits, eggs, milk, cheese, and postnatal care for free. Social Services would award families arriving in their new homeland with the SNAP program, placing money on an EBT card so they could buy food. The elderly would immediately be eligible for Social Security payments. The United States was wonderful; it even gave families a cell phone with 240 free talk minutes and unlimited text messaging a month.

Food pantries, clothing outlets, and free meals served at churches balanced out their so-called 'benefits package' into citizenship. All in all, a single person could live like a king, and a family had a dramatically better life than its meager circumstances in Mexico. Fernando made the sign of the cross, looked toward heaven, and blessed the good ole US of A, smiling all the while.

But Fernando still felt a little uneasy and stopped and questioned some of the smarter individuals as he came across them. They, like him, were doing everything in their power to get to the border in a hurry. Of course, the answer didn't matter to him because Fernando had decided he was going to the United States regardless. He was dumbfounded that so many other Mexicans had come to the same conclusion.

Fernando was pleased to come across a college professor on the trail and took the opportunity to pick the college professor's brain. He asked, "If the United States is going to legalize the ten to twenty million Mexicans living in the country illegally, there's no way that it will also legalize so many of us, is there? How can the US federal government grant citizenship to so many more people than it thinks are there?"

The professor looked unfazed by Fernando's question. "As part of my teaching assignment at the Mexican University, I teach US history. Don't worry my friend. I can assure you that before this mass migration is over, the number of Mexicans that will be granted US citizenship will be in the tens of millions. Mark my words: The American people will become the *minority population*! We will become the *new majority*!"

"But how can that be so?" inquired Fernando. "Why would they do that?"

"Politics, *mi amigo*, politics. Though our Mexican government has been plagued with corruption for decades, the Americans can compete in corruption and power mongering on the international level. America is no longer a country of prominent, entrepreneurial, successful white businessmen. My friend, in today's America, the moral majority have become dinosaurs. It's true at almost every level of political leadership— in business and in higher institutions of learning—the white, educated male is becoming a thing of the past. When I attended a lecture thirty-three years ago at American University in Washington, DC, 85 percent of the professors in attendance were up there in years, and were all white males. Just a year and a half ago, I attended a similar conference at Georgetown University, in Washington, DC. The majority of the professors in attendance were female and young. But, my smart friend, two-thirds were minorities."

But now, Fernando was more confused than ever. "What does this have to do with the legalization of millions of more illegal Mexicans?"

"The current president of the United States is a female and almost 90 percent of her administration consists of minorities and women. Even the US Congress and Senate have much higher percentages of minorities and women in office now. America has been heading down the path to a more liberal and socialist country, but in the past two administrations it has moved to the left exponentially.

"There's one more key factor involved. Americans in the last decade gave the presidency to a black man for two terms. Currently, Americans now have the first female sitting behind the desk in the Oval Office. A woman American president was unheard of only a few years back. Now, the odds are incredibly high that the next president of the United States will be of Hispanic descent. The Latino vote in America is becoming sacrosanct. It is the very reason that the American Democratic Party was so thankful when President Obama went around Congress and issued an executive order proposing to turn so many Mexican illegals into American citizens. First of all, no one doubts that every single one of those individuals will vote for the party that gave them their citizenship, the Democrats. Add to their numbers another ten million Mexicans, now the largest voting minority in America, and within the next decade, every Mexican man, woman, and child living in the United States will be a legalized American citizen. And that includes you and me if we can get there in time."

Fernando continued speaking to the college professor, savoring his conversation with someone intelligent rather than the usual, less-than-educated man on the trail.

Fernando was quickly learning that getting there in time might be the most difficult task. When Fernando had left Mexico City with his wife in tow, it had been 1,300 miles to El Paso. Fernando was willing to go to one of the closer border cities but had heard that El Paso's sister city, Juarez, had the largest number of entry points along the US-Mexico border. He thought that going there should make things easier. His original plan had been to board the train with his wife and ride one of the oldest train routes in all of Mexico. But thousands, maybe millions, of other Mexico City residents had had the same idea. Not to mention that, besides the Mexico City inhabitants trying to gain access to the train, it seemed as if every Mexican who had flooded into Mexico City was competing to find transportation out of the country. Every single train ticket was sold three months in advance. If there were tickets available, they were going at exorbitant premiums. He had heard of people paying the equivalent of $1,500 for a single ticket that normally went for under $100. One enterprising ticket agent had sold tickets to ride on top of the train cars.

Next he had gone to all the airports in and around Mexico City. It was not his first choice because of the cost. Though Fernando had grabbed every single peso he could put his hands on, two airline tickets would have taken more money than he wanted to spend at that point. But again it didn't matter. All the flights either direct or via every conceivable connection were sold out, even farther out than the train tickets. Again, the prices had gone through the roof. As he had entered the main flight terminal in Mexico City, Aeropuerto International de la Ciudad de México, he had seen a well-dressed businessman standing on the curb holding a sign. It read in Spanish, WILL PAY $2,500 US FOR FLIGHT TO ANYWHERE IN CANADA OR UNITED STATES.

Fernando had cursed himself. He had been forced to sell off the last of his cars to pay their rent. He'd finally decided that they would try to go toward Laredo. It was closer than El Paso, and it appeared now as many of his countrymen were going in that same direction.

As he talked to more and more of his fellow travelers, it appeared that the route to America by car was not necessarily a breeze. He heard some incredible stories. Many of Mexico's highways going north had become big parking lots. Mexico had never had the interstate highway system that America was so proud of, but still if one were going north from one of the larger cities, such as Mexico City, Guadalajara or Monterrey, the roads were modern. However, even in normal times, Mexico's internal highway system and even its interstate highways were always a bumper-to-bumper experience. Since the US-Mexican NAFTA trade agreement of '94, the number of commercial trucks traveling north from Mexico to the United States had gone up a hundredfold.

Many Americans assumed California to be the largest provider of fruits and vegetables to the US market because of the consistent warmer weather and growing climate. However, Mexico had surpassed California over the last decade. The fruit was all transported by truck, further overloading an already overcrowded highway.

Now add to these already jam-packed highways thousands of Mexicans who had decided to jump in their cars and drive to the border. To complicate matters, thousands of vehicles were out of gas and abandoned where they came to a stop. PEMEX had no way to anticipate such a sudden, massive increase in vehicle traffic, nor the corresponding huge increase in gasoline and diesel consumption. When PEMEX had finally noticed the increase in consumption, it had put all its refineries to work 24-7. Despite these extra man hours and production, PEMEX couldn't make a dent in the increased demand.

Grocers in Mexico City began seeing fights in their stores over the limited food supplies; it was the same story for the nation's gas stations. The number of gas stations shutting down for lack of fuel increased daily.

Some ingenious desperate travelers had taken matters into their own hands. It was easy to notice that the southbound traffic had little congestion, and the more venturesome had decided to drive north on the southbound lanes. At first they were only using the southbound shoulders, but as the numbers increased, they had taken over the entire southbound lanes. It had been only a matter of time before traffic the accidents had started, with each one causing additional accidents. There were stories of fifty-car pileups blocking the entire southbound lanes.

What was the net result? Millions and millions of northbound travelers were on foot. And of course, depending where one started and how fast one could hike, the journey could take weeks or months. But what nobody knew was just how many Mexicans had embarked on this pilgrimage, where they had all begun, and more importantly when they had all set out. Because to the millions of Mexicans who were on the road, it was pretty obvious that there was going to be a wave of people hitting the US border like nothing that had ever been witnessed in the world. It was apparent to those millions traveling north, but what was more important and more deadly, is that it wasn't fully apparent but to only a handful of people living in the United States.

Chapter 37

Hacienda del Largo was one of the most beautiful estates in all of Monterrey, Mexico, which is saying quite a bit because some of the richest families in all of Mexico have incredible mansions in and around Monterrey. Traveling through Monterrey, however, one might never know the mansions exist. Unlike in the United States, in Mexico the wealthy did not flaunt their wealth. They hid it. Almost a century of kidnapping wealthy individuals for ransom had instilled in the wealthy a secretive way of life. There was hardly a wealthy family that had not had some family member kidnapped or had not at least suffered an attempt.

Mexico had always been somewhat of a lawless country, and kidnappings for ransom were popular because much of the country's wealth was concentrated in just a few families' hands. In fact, for generations, much of Mexico's wealth had been held by just ten families.[1]

Alberto Jose Morales was by no means one of the top ten, but owning some of the largest beer distributors in northern Mexico had given him a wealth estimated to be at least $100 million.

One of the reasons Mexico, like many of the other Central and South American countries, always had such upheavals and revolutions was because there was hardly any middle class. There were the wealthy and there were the poor and never much of anybody in between. That kind of dichotomy was always a formula for social unrest. It was only in the last decade that Mexico had started to build a middle class, but with the onset of the depression, that transition had come to a screeching halt.

Alberto screamed at his wife and kids, "Hurry, hurry!" Their limousine had arrived, and he wanted to get to the airport as soon as possible. Maria, his wife, was frantic. Alberto had announced that morning that they needed to pack for a trip: "Pack only your essentials and valuables!"

They were leaving Mexico that day, by plane. Maria did not know where to start, considering that her husband had limited her to only two large suitcases. She had enough clothes and shoes to fill ten footlockers. Should she take mostly clothes? Should she only take her jewelry? Her jewelry would take up less space, and the pieces were certainly the most valuable items she owned. But she kept thinking that maybe her clothes were her most valuable possession because her outfits were all custom made.

"I might never be able to replace them," she mumbled to herself in disgust. She decided to try a happy compromise; she started throwing things into her suitcases. "Damn Alberto!" As she started to cry, she moaned, "Why is this happening?"

The children were allowed only one suitcase, which wasn't working since their most prized possessions were pairs of boots and shoes which took up far too much space. One of the children said aloud, not even knowing if anyone was listening, "If I could just wear a couple pairs of shoes at one time, I might be able to make this work."

The driver packed the suitcases into the limousine while the family got in. Maria said to her husband, "That was awful. Now why was I forced to pack all my treasures so quickly and uproot the family? Alberto, where are you taking us?"

Maria was not stupid; quite the opposite, actually. Raising a family of two and managing the estate, Maria did not have time to keep track of the economy, politics, or anything that had anything to do with current events. One of her passions was movies, and even that had been set aside to manage the family. It was Alberto's job to keep current with the business world and politics. Alberto had been fairly rich when she had married him and had done an excellent job of increasing their wealth substantially. She had never questioned his decisions, and it had worked out wonderfully. But now she was concerned.

Alberto made a couple of calls on his cell, confirming the private jet that was awaiting their arrival at a small, private airport used primarily by the wealthy, as well as tending to a few other of his business matters. When he'd finished his business calls, he turned his attention toward his wife. It was time he answered her questions, and for the next forty-five minutes on their drive to the airport, he gave his wife and children a history lesson. Alberto was patient and told them about the immediate problems that were facing Mexico: the recession, the devaluation of the peso, the crash of the Mexican stock market, and the ever-increasing terrorist activities of the revolutionary, General Zapatista.

"But what I don't understand," Maria interrupted, "is, please, why now is there an urgency? From what you tell me, most of these problems have been with us for over a year. I don't understand this sudden panic and the need to leave this morning, giving me and our children little time to pack properly?"

Alberto tried to explain. "I'm sorry. I owe an apology to both you and the kids. I was so consumed with my work that frankly I was not paying close enough attention to a lot of the negatives that are currently overtaking our country. Ever since the depression hit, I've been putting in double and triple time trying to keep up our sales. I was aware of the economic downturns we were experiencing. You know, of course, since we export a few of our brands, that I was aware of the devaluation of the peso. But it was only yesterday afternoon at the conference I attended at the Hilton that I learned the extent of the problem. A number of the most prominent businessmen and politicians that I respect addressed the group. It was then that I learned about the total breakdown of the very fabric of Mexico. But what gave me this sudden urgency was when I found out that many of our closest friends have already left the country."

"Our friends? Alberto, where have they gone?"

"It appears that most went to the United States. Both the United States and Canada have attempted to tighten the borders since 9/11, but it appears that Canada has done a much better job at closing its borders to mass immigration. So emigrating to Canada has become much more difficult, nearly impossible. Americans, though they give lip service to the problem of Mexicans emigrating to their country, have never been serious about fixing the problem, and everyone knows it.

"One of our company's vice presidents pointed out to me that many wealthy Mexicans are flying private jets into America. Even as stupid as they are, someone in the United States government was going to finally catch on and close that incredibly easy entry point.

"You know the Romeros from the club? I found out that he and his family flew to America two weeks ago. I called him on his cell phone—they settled in New York. He said it was unbelievably easy. He told customs that he and his family were on a combination business-pleasure vacation and would be in the United States for three months. He said as far as he can tell, the immigration system in the United States is so screwed up and bogged down with red tape that it will take years for them to notice they are residing there permanently, if they ever do. And with the proclamation by that buffoon of a president, Obama, that he was going to legalize between five and ten million Mexicans living in the country, Romero figured that the last thing the United States was going to do was throw out rich people like himself, who already own a number of homes and employ Americans in their businesses."

Their son, Raul, broke in. "Cool, Dad, let's go to Chicago. They've got the Bears, the White Sox, the Cubs, and the Blackhawks."

His father chuckled. "Well, frankly, I have some good news for all of you. Your mother has put up with me being too dedicated to my work while she raised you kids. That's about to change. We finally have enough money put away so I don't have to work again, even with the horrible conversion rates of pesos to US dollars. I'm going to let the three of you decide our destination."

As he finished his announcement, the limousine pulled up alongside a sleek Gulfstream G650. Alberto's brewing company had purchased the impressive private jet for $65 million in 2012.

"We can continue this conversation in a few minutes. Let's get on the plane."

Alberto lingered at the top of the gangway to take one last deep breath of his beloved but dying Mexico. This was not his Mexico anymore. With that, he stepped into the cabin, squared his shoulders, and put forth his best father face.

Their unknown future held promise only because they were rich. What ill wind would befall the millions of his countrymen who had never had a chance from their beginnings for a better life? How would they manage in a new land with a new language and a different culture? Many would fail. Some would end up back in Mexico, a broken mess with no future.

"Thank God we have money," Alberto murmured, smiling at his family as they pored over a map of the United States, their new home.

1. 1. Carlos Slim—US$ 74 billion—Telmex, INBURSA, América Móvil, CompUSA, WorldCom, Telcel

    2.Ricardo Salinas Pliego—US$ 17.4 billion—TV Azteca,Iusacell, Unefon

    3.Alberto Baillères—US$ 16.5 billion—Peñoles

    4.Germán Larrea Mota-Velasco—US$ 14.2 billion—GrupoMexico

    5.Jerónimo Arango—US$ 4 billion—Founder of Aurrerá(currently part of Walmart Mexico)

    6.Emilio Azcárraga Jean—US$ 2 billion—Televisa, Univision,Club América, Necaxa, Club San Luis

    7.Roberto González Barrera—US$ 1.9 billion—Maseca,Banorte

    8.Carlos Hank Rhon—US$ 1.4 billion—Bank

    9.Roberto Hernandez Ramirez—US$ 1.3 billion—BancoNacional de México (Banamex)

10.Alfredo Harp Helú—US$ 1 billion—Banamex, Red Devilsbaseball team

back

Chapter 38

Of the three border watch shifts, Dave disliked the graveyard shift the most. They always worked in teams of at least two officers, but this night his shift partner had called in sick, and there wasn't an agent at that hour to replace him. As a result, at 2:40 a.m., David found himself forty miles from nowhere. The only thing that reminded him that he was not on the moon was his USPB truck parked alongside the metal observation tower that he was sitting in. Thank God the moon had finally come out. Sitting there with only starlight was gorgeous, but it also gave Dave the creeps. Of course, his pair of the latest high-tech infrared field glasses could spot any movement at almost a half mile, but that gave him little comfort when for hours he had just been staring into mesquite bushes. It was so quiet that Dave knew he probably would hear anyone before he could see them.

The illegal-entry corridor that Dave was watching was one of the favorites of illegals in this area. It was far enough from the bigger cities that there was less scrutiny, and once a crossing was made, it was just a hop, skip, and jump to Chula Vista, San Diego, or Escondido. For years, there had been rarely two nights in a row without an attempted crossing.

But the last couple of months, activity had picked up dramatically—and not just in California but along the entire US-Mexican border. It wasn't just the number of attempted crossings but also the number of individuals. Larger groups of individuals traveling on foot were also crossing the border. In the past, most illegal crossings by foot had been groups of only five to fifteen people. Larger groups were usually trucked almost the entire way to the border, where the people would be let loose to cross individually, or where the truck would try to cross carrying the whole group. The last couple of months, it had seemed that the number of large groups traveling on foot had increased exponentially.

Dave was more diligent than some of his fellow officers, and in twenty years he had only once fallen asleep on the graveyard shift. Except, he *had* let his mind wander, as it often did, to a different career. He had convinced himself that if he made a change it would be to a career in the field of teaching. He had found himself the happiest in a classroom setting, working with the new recruits. A master's in history would be...

Wait! What was that?

Dave sprang to his feet so fast he almost fell off the observation platform. The infrared field glasses were at his eyes before he had even fully regained his balance. Nothing. Another 360-degree turn and still nothing.

Dave slowly returned to musing over his future. He'd always enjoyed history; the main question for him was whether he wanted to teach at the high school or college level.

There it was again! But it wasn't a sound he was used to. The sound of a jackrabbit jumping into a bush he could identify, or, in this vast nothingness, sometimes officers swore they could hear a mouse scamper across the sand. This sounded more like the wind, but very far off.

Again, nothing in the field glasses.

He did something he had never done before. The platform's major support beam extended beyond the eight-foot-wide platform up another six feet. Dave shinnied himself up the beam to get a better view.

The mesquite bushes were well below him, but when he tried to look much beyond a mile, they pretty much blocked the view of the ground around them.

Shinnying up another six feet might extend my field of view.

He did so. Holding on with one arm at his new vantage point, he struggled to get the field glasses up to his eyes, but when he did, he saw movement. The mesquite bushes were moving.

"It's got to be the wind," he said quietly. "It's got to be the wind—because it looks like *all* the bushes are moving."

He was about to lose his grip on the pole, but he mustered all his strength for one last look. Stunned, he fell from the pole, to hit the deck with a painful groan.

It wasn't the wind. It was a wave—a wave of people.

Chapter 39

President Denton's fist came down like a sledgehammer on her desk in the Oval Office. She leveled her famous laser-like look, a look that was so intense that most people looked away, afraid to make eye contact lest they become blinded. Man, if looks could kill, Secretary of State Marisa Angela Lopez and Stephanie Jones, Denton's closest advisor, would have been dead meat. Denton had lost her self-control.

"Ladies, I put the two of you in charge of being my *spin doctors* on the political fallout from whatever is going on at the US-Mexico border. What happens? I'll tell you! Senator Boone from Texas is having a heyday. Even our friends over at the major networks are starting to ask uncomfortable questions."

Stephanie was the first to speak. "Rosemary, I wouldn't give a damn what Senator Ted Boone is doing. Even his own Republican Party threw him under the bus during his bid for this office in the last presidential election. And that was a real boon for us." She paused to chuckle at her own pun. "He's probably the most articulate voice of the conservative cause. But the three of us know this country is not going to vote in a *real* conservative presidential candidate in our lifetime or two of our lifetimes! Madam President, also don't worry about our *friends* at NBC, CBS, ABC, CNN, or MSNBC—they're still 100 percent on our team. Rosemary, they adore you and are tightly wrapped around your little finger. So forget it—don't be concerned. They have to give lip service to Boone occasionally to keep Fox News off their butt."

President Denton turned to Marisa and said, "Okay, all right, now what about all this shit over our border with Mexico?"

Behind closed doors and then only in front of her innermost circle Rosemary Denton allowed herself to speak coarsely. She enjoyed the shocked expressions on the faces of those who came under her tongue lashing. She was anything but ladylike at times.

Marisa responded to President Denton. "Presidente Enrique Nieto is going to help us with the situation. I talked to him again just yesterday per your request. He assured me that the situation is well under control. His administration has proposed legislation that he feels, when ratified, will put the Mexican economy back on track and put a cork in the illegal immigration issue. He acknowledged that a few extra of his countrymen have bailed and decided to emigrate to the United States. In fact, he emphatically denied that a mass exodus from his country to ours was underway. He called it ludicrous and wanted to promise you that it is not a plan to destabilize the United States. He further said that some of his staff had watched Fox News, which they get in Mexico City, and he categorically denies their accusations and statistics. I told him to ignore Fox News just like the rest of us. He said we should have them arrested and jailed. I told them Obama had tried to do that but failed due to our constitutional freedoms."

Rosemary Denton's eyes flashed with the mention of Fox News. Fox News had continued to be a burr under her saddle. *Shit,* she thought, *why couldn't they get on the bandwagon like everyone else?*

She'd need her team to keep applying pressure on them. They'd get on board with her, or she'd find a way to crush them. She allowed herself a cruel smile. That was a promise she made to herself. There would be hell to pay.

No one screws with Rosemary Denton, the president of the United States, the most powerful person in the world, she thought.

She leaned back and settled deeper into her soft, pink-dyed, high-backed leather chair. *Being president is better than sex*, she thought, which she had never liked in the first place. It was orgasmic being so powerful, and she felt a wave of pleasurable sensation flow through her body.

Finally, President Denton got out of her chair and paced back and forth a few times before she said, "Maybe this will be our opportunity to put Fox News finally out of business for good. God knows we've tried, and if what you're telling me is correct and they blow this whole Mexico border situation way out of proportion, just like they did with my problem in Algeria, we can hang them out to dry." She paused a moment and continued. "So do we have any updated information on exactly what is happening at the border?"

It was quite obvious to Rosemary Denton that both ladies were reluctant to speak.

"All right, dammit, what aren't you telling me?"

Stephanie stared at Marisa and with a mean look said, "Go ahead, you're the secretary of state."

Marisa glared back. "Don't try to dump all this shit on me. You were just as sure as I was that none of this border issue was going to escalate."

Wow, a real catfight breaking out in the Oval Office, thought Rosemary. *The good ole boys that worked this office before didn't have anything on us ladies. In fact, we'd have had Obama on his knees licking our boots, the little bugger.*

Rosemary broke in, "Okay, ladies, I don't have time for this little catfight. Give it to me straight."

Marisa took a deep breath and began, "Well it's worse than the CIA told us. It appears that there's been a breakdown at most of the US border entry points, and, yes, a significant number of Mexicans have crossed into the United States illegally. There have been a few minor instances of hostilities. For the most part, the Mexicans have been behaving themselves. I can't seem to get any verification of their intentions, though. The border patrol seems to have a finger up its butt. I don't see any reason for concern, much less alarm."

The president nearly smiled. "Okay, let's put the destruction and any serious breaches at border portals on the back burner for a moment. It doesn't sound too bad. Hell, we've had thousands of Mexicans illegally crossing our borders for decades. I don't understand why everyone's getting their panties all in a bunch— seems to me that it's just business as usual." Chuckling to herself, she said, "All those illegals crossing are just more Democrats that will assure my next term in office!"

Both the secretary of state and the president's closest advisor found themselves chuckling likewise. A shared glance told them that they were out of the president's doghouse. As the president turned, preparing to leave the Oval Office, she said, "Anyway, who gives a shit about some dumb illegal Mexicans anyway? What difference does it make if there's a few more illegal Mexicans in America?" Glancing in the mirror by the door, she said loud enough for all ears, "If my reproductive organs were on the outside, I'd be a king."

Laughing at that thought, she looked at her well-coiffed hairstyle in the mirror and said to herself, *Rosemary, there's no man or woman on God's green earth more feared or more powerful than you are and no one willing to piss you off.* She smiled and said aloud, "That's right world, show me some respect. This bitch could start World War III just for chipping a nail." Now that was orgasmic indeed!

Chapter 40

"Senator Ted Boone's office. Can I help you?"

"This is Craig Walther from Albuquerque, New Mexico. I'm somewhat of a friend of Senator Boone. Do you know if he has time to talk with me for a few moments?"

The receptionist was not impressed. By definition, everyone who voted for her boss considered him or herself a friend, and this caller was not even from Ohio. "Well, I don't think he has time. What did you say your name was, again?"

The next thing Craig heard on the other end of the line was the booming voice of Ted Boone. "Craig, remind me to give you my direct line. I pay my receptionist big dollars to keep out every yahoo outside of Ohio. My God, it's bad enough that I have to rerun for office every two years, but the way people call here, you'd think I was up for election every other month. Where've you been, stranger? Ever since your last divorce you sort of fell off the map. I hope you're calling to tell me that you're finally sick and tired of that backward state of New Mexico and willing to move back here to DC. I need a man like you in my office. Fighting eight years of Obama and now that crazy liberal Rosemary Denton has about got me convinced that being in Congress isn't worth it anymore."

Craig chuckled. "If you want to try and get me to move back to Washington, I suggest you don't start by telling me how bad the liberals are these days. I couldn't stand them when I was last in Washington, and they weren't even in power. But save your breath. As much as I love and miss Washington, a team of wild horses couldn't drag me back there. I just wish my job didn't force me to keep such day-to-day tabs on the political situation in the nation's capital, because just about every news story coming out of there is depressing."

"You're not trying to blame me, old buddy. You know I've been fighting those bastards going on twenty-five years. So if you're not calling me to have one of my assistants help you house hunt, what's on your mind?"

"I was hoping as the chairman of the House Committee on Foreign Affairs, you might give me some insights into some rumors I'm hearing about problems down at the US-Mexican border."

Now it was the senator who was chuckling. "Craig, that's a strange comment coming from you, an expert and author on that entire border problem. What rumors? What the hell do you mean 'rumors'? The Mexican border situation has been an embarrassment to this country for decades. That ain't no rumor, and it ain't new!"

Craig realized he'd started the conversation off on the wrong foot. "Okay, okay, maybe I didn't preface this correctly. As you know, I've got a brother on the US Border Patrol in San Diego. He's been telling me stories. It's hard to describe, but the best way I can put it is that there seems to be a significant increase in his district in illegal Mexican residents. He hasn't confirmed that they're all recent crossings, but he's just very cognizant that on both sides of the border there are massive numbers of Mexicans that weren't there just six months ago. And before you interrupt, as you know, I did a massive amount of research on this whole subject for my last book. And since I'm constantly getting inquiries from the press, I have felt obligated continually to update my statistics about what is going on in Mexico. Now, I know it seems out of place for some professor in some no-name college out of New Mexico to be calling the Senate to tell you what's going on in Mexico, but..."

"Go ahead, Craig, you're among friends. You can't insult me. Hell, the popularity ranking of everybody in Washington these days is so low, it's almost impossible to insult any of us these days. Spit it out."

"I just want to know if the intelligence reports you're getting as chairman of Foreign Affairs show statistics that jive with my research. We're both aware that Mexico has entered into one of the worst depressions that it's seen in the last half century. What I'm not sure you're aware of is that the downward spiral has gone into hyperdrive in the last few months."

"Oh, we are well aware," Senator Boone said. "Since I know where you're going, yes, I have been warning the White House that the entire economic situation in Mexico could have devastating effects on our continuing problems at the border."

Craig let out a big sigh. "Well, that's good news. I was worried that no one in Washington was paying attention. I feel very relieved that you and the White House are on top of this."

"Whoaaaaaa, I never said that the White House was on top of this. Frankly, it's the opposite. As far as I can tell, the Mexican economy, not to mention the continuing problem at the border, doesn't even make the top forty priority list for President Denton and her administration. And let me tell you something I think you don't know. My buddies over at the CIA have said that this revolutionary or guerrilla—between the two of us I never really understood the difference in definitions—Zapatista is gaining ground very quickly. The CIA told me just the other day that they have indications that the top military muckety-mucks in the Mexican government are so afraid that Zapatista might topple Nieto's government in the near future that many of them have joined forces with Zapatista."

This time Craig let out a big moan. "Shit, just what this country needs—a country of over one hundred million that shares a two-thousand-mile border with us imploding, and we have an administration that's playing Nero's fiddle."

"Come on, Craig. You were in Washington for almost twenty years. You know nothing's changed here. Hell, between the Obama administration and Denton's current administration, I think they have single-handedly screwed up about every major foreign-policy issue for the past ten years. But let's try to end this conversation on a positive note, because I've got a committee meeting coming up in less than an hour. Now I know I'm supposed to know a lot more than you with all my connections here in Washington, but I'd like you to keep a regular, open line of communication between the two of us. Other than our military bases near the border, I don't have anybody on the civilian side down in the southwest that I trust to keep me apprised. Is that a deal?"

Craig reassured Congressman Boone that he could count on Craig. They said their good-byes and Craig hung up, not feeling particularly reassured himself.

Chapter 41

David stormed into Buck's office. In his hand was the most recent USBP monthly statistics on both arrests and suspected illegal crossings for not only their district but the entire US-Mexican border. It was bad enough that the government was so sloppy and inept, but these reports were almost worthless because they came out so late that the information was useless. This particular set of reports for some reason hadn't hit David's desk until later than usual. He wondered if somebody had purposely delayed it, because the numbers had shot up so dramatically. The numbers had not just gone up 10 or 20 percent—which often could happen based on seasonality and other short-term factors— but almost 100 percent. Dave's other reason for being so mad was that, as head of the district, Buck had access to these numbers way before everyone else did, yet as alarming as the numbers were, Buck hadn't said anything to anybody.

"What the hell is going on here?" Dave demanded. "How come you didn't let the senior officers know how alarming these numbers were when you first saw them?"

Just another reason that Buck hated Dave so much. Buck thought to himself, *Who the fuck does Dave think he is, yelling at me anyway, much less questioning why I do or don't do something?*

"Fuck you, Dave! When you're sitting on this side of the desk, you can question how things are done in this district. But as long as I'm in charge, I'll do it my way! I'll fucking do it when I goddamn feel like it. You don't like the way I do business, then request a transfer, Mr. Smarty-Pants College Boy."

Though the USBP had been trying over the last decade to only hire new recruits with college degrees, they couldn't fill the ranks. But what pissed Dave off so much was that the district director was so stupid, everyone questioned if he had even graduated from high school.

"You're so full of shit, Buck. You know for the last month, I've reported significant increases in all the numbers. As a matter of fact, I even checked the files. You fat fuck, you must have purposely deep-sixed some of my reports—I couldn't find any of them in the file."

With speed that defied his whale-like size, Buck leaped from his sad, well-worn chair and, as fast as his fat ass could move, circled his desk and got into Dave's face. Sure David was twenty years his junior, but at six feet four inches and 280 pounds, Buck didn't fear anything or anyone. Ever since he and Dave had met, Buck had been looking for an excuse to beat the shit out of this uppity college graduate.

"Look, son, I'm only a year away from retiring, and after forty years working for our illustrious federal government, I am not rocking the frigging boat. I've got twenty years with the DEA and twenty years in this shithole. The last thing I'm going to do is allow some little mama's boy to start issuing reports panicking the boys in the home office. It'll just cause a lot of questions I don't intend to waste time answering.

"Now those hotheaded Washington boys have thrown hundreds of millions of dollars at our department to placate the complaining conservatives that say the current administration is soft on immigration. Now, we've all greatly benefited from that money, and the last thing our department can afford is to be sending up reports to Washington that say we aren't doing our job. The last thing those asshole politicians want to hear is that there are more illegal crossings now than ever before. They don't mind wasting taxpayers' money, but you can damn well bet that Fox News would plaster it on the TV screen day and night, telling listeners that every dollar and every program to slow down the border crossings have been complete a waste of time and money.

So go ahead and write your reports. I've got the round file right here waiting to deep-six them.

"And let me give you one last piece of advice. In my *uneducated* opinion, one of the reasons Washington has never done anything serious in the forty years I've been working on the border is

because they know that the average American voter gives even less shit than the politicians do about the border issue. I'd be willing to wager your college buddies feel the same way I do. You know what? It's higher wages, fancier cars, more vacations, and legalized drugs—that's what matters! Other than that, it's who's going to win the next frigging Super Bowl!"

Buck was on a roll, and his cruel side was baring its ugly face. He had worked himself into such a lather laughing so hard that his cheeks had turned red, and he'd started to choke. Dave hoped that Buck would fall to the floor, his windpipe blocked, and choke to death.

But Buck only continued laughing in his face, spittle flying everywhere. White froth was forming around Buck's mouth. Dave was so disgusted that he bolted out of Buck's office and stormed toward his truck. He got in and slammed the door. He immediately started pounding the steering wheel, so enraged, so out of control that he hit it so hard he thought he'd broken his wrist. He sank his head into his hands and nearly broke into tears. He hated that bastard, Buck, but what he hated most now was that the fat fuck was probably right. No one, but no one, gave a shit.

Chapter 42

The routine! Day after day the same boring routine. Anyone who'd ever held a line job in a factory or been a security guard in an office building knew what that daily grind felt like. The reality was that even some of the most exciting jobs, after one had worked them day after day, year after year, for what seemed like an eternity, could likewise become boringly routine.

Such was the life, each day, for the men and women of US Customs and Border Protection who manned the many official government entry points between Mexico and United States. The numbers of individuals both crossing on foot and entering by either car or truck was mind boggling. There was no more active entry point than the one at Paso Del Norte in El Paso. Ten million individuals a day traversed the border with just over six million walking and roughly four million driving. They crossed over on the Paso Del Norte Bridge, which was approximately 250 years old. This US-Mexico entry point had been manned and open 24-7 since 1898.

For the hundred-plus US customs officers that worked on the Paso Del Norte crossing, it was expected to be another boring day. Sure, on a daily basis they would discover and sometimes arrest as many as a hundred Mexicans trying to enter the country illegally, most being discovered hiding in some unique fashion. The game of searching for these stowaways was the high point of any shift. Of course, there were the daily drug busts, which now were so routine that they, too, had become boring. Then, almost hourly, there was some college kid trying to sneak more than the one quart of liquor that he was allowed to bring back home without taxes. Boring, goddamn boring.

Things were about to change. Over the last month, the predictable daily activity had been changing exponentially. It seemed in the last month, almost on a daily basis, that the volume of people had been greater than the day before. Arrest statistics had also been creeping higher. No customs officer had taken any note, other than the fact that the lines on the Mexican side of the border seemed to be much longer than normal.

But the shift supervisors had started to take note when they'd filed their weekly number reports. Every week their reports had shown a significant increase in the numbers from the prior week. But, as usual, they'd forwarded them to Washington, per protocol. When they had received no inquiry or question on the increased numbers, they had figured it wasn't their job to question them. But the shift leaders could not help asking himself what was driving these great migrating herds of Mexicans forward in ever-increasing numbers and why the activity had increased so much.

Things had become much more intense these past couple of weeks for all the shifts. The lines had become more difficult to manage, and the amount of time required for both pedestrians and drivers had tripled, at a minimum. The Mexicans were now constantly complaining to the US customs officers about it taking too long to make the crossing. No one paid any attention to the complaining Mexicans. In fact, the agents thought it was somewhat comical that they were complaining while trying to enter the country. The customs department followed a very rigid checklist for every single vehicle or individual crossing into the United States. The regimentation and routine of the procedure were not going to change. The mere fact that the line on the Mexican side of the border had increased to as much as a mile long was of no concern to anyone on the US side of the border. It took time to process a thousand individuals properly, and that was not going to change just because somebody waited a little longer in line.

But not today. It started at the gate that controlled the individuals who walked across the Paso Del Norte Bridge over the Rio Grande River. As in a rock concert or sporting event, it was the people at the back of the line who became impatient and pushed forward into those who were in front of them. In turn, those pushed got frustrated at being crowded and pushed forward themselves, and in a domino-like, cascading effect, everyone started their own push forward just to keep ahead of the pressing weight of humanity. Before they knew it, the poor individuals at the front of the line were being crushed—not pressed forward, crushed—and the birth of panic was visible in their eyes.

The estimate of the line was close to one hundred thousand people. The official immigration gates for pedestrian entrances into the United States were fast becoming bottlenecks, bulging like overstressed levees holding back floodwaters.

Like a cork popping from a shaken champagne bottle, one of the pedestrian gates finally burst open, spewing forth the pent-up mass of humanity. This was a customs officer's nightmare. The push was too much to be contained any longer, and the first few through the gate were trampled underfoot, crushed to death on the very day they were going to be set free of what had felt like bondage. Tomorrow would have found them looking for a job or a relative to help them on their way to a new life in the United States. Not today.

"Stop pushing—I will get to you when I'm through with the individual in front of you," said a chubby female agent at another gate.

"We are not pushing. Everyone from behind is pushing us."

Just about this time, it became much more than a push—it became a battering ram, a human battering ram. The tens of thousands of people in this line focused their energy and pushed as hard as they could. Forward, ever pressing forward, forward into the United States. It was almost like shaking a warm can of Coca-Cola, popping the top, and then thinking there was any chance in hell of slowing the copious amount of spitting, flowing foam.

The chubby US customs agent was knocked to the concrete, and within a matter of seconds, she too was trampled to death by the inflow of panicked Mexicans. The crowd moved as a tsunami, flowing in an unbreakable mass forward, unable to stop or control its own direction.

Unfortunately, twelve agents chose that very moment to address the crowd. Their pleas of "stay and stop where you are" fell upon deaf ears. Due to the wave's kinetic energy the agents were swept first up, then down to earth, then underneath the stampeding feet. Not one shot was fired, not one gun drawn, but now, thirteen agents lay crumpled and dead on the pavement of the border station.

It was like a scene from a John Wayne western. The bad guys had caused a herd of cattle to stampede into the good guys' camp, trampling many fine cowboys to death. The cattle were not motivated by mean intent in their panicked stampede. But some poor cowboy standing in the pathway of the stampede was killed by the panicked cattle. Such a scene was playing out at the Paso Del Norte entry station.

The wave of humanity flooding through the entry point had started a station-wide panic. All hell was breaking loose in the vehicle lanes. There was no way to tell how it had started. Not unlike the deadly consequences that had left thirteen agents lying dead on the concrete floor, the drivers crept their vehicles forward, blowing their horns and tapping the vehicles ahead.

"No one move your vehicle!" shouted one of the agents.

Out of sheer frustration, one driver jammed his gear shift into reverse and stomped violently on the accelerator. The vehicle responded and raced in reverse, first knocking over a border agent checking for drugs and then running him over, dragging the agent to his death.

A perfect storm had arrived, consisting of border-patrol agents and Mexican immigrants in full-blown panic. The noise and confusion created the remaining two ingredients for the perfect storm. There was no doubt that the storm was finding its own life and stretching its wings. The crowds were starting to swell and throb, enthralled with the deaths and suddenly feeling empowered. Like predators smelling fear in their intended victims, the people, having tasted strength in numbers, were not going to be contained behind a wire fence or commanded to go home. The agents felt the electricity jump from one person to another, and with each jump, confidences were made stronger and commitments bolder.

Agents lined up and drew an imaginary line that was to be protected at all cost. The agents' guns blazed, bodies fell, and yet the agents could not see the magnitude of the enemy crossing illegally into the United States. There was no end to the advancing army of immigrants.

Lives were instantly cut short. Vehicles pushed vehicles that pushed trucks that pushed forward, over the border agents and into the United States. The masses surged forward with a rallying cry.

A trail of broken dreams, dead agents, and lost sanity was left at the border.

Chapter 43

A large, thirty-year-old cargo truck was next in line at the US Border Patrol station in San Ysidro, California. US customs agents were different from other government employees. Most government workers were overpaid and underworked, but things were different for the US customs agents, especially those who manned the most dangerous border-patrol station at the busiest entry point on the US-Mexican border. They were underpaid and overworked, putting their lives on the line every minute that they were on station. Each agent harbored an individual hatred or resentment for his or her job, but they all shared one particular hate: they all hated large produce trucks.

Because produce was second only to petroleum as the number one export from Mexico to the United States, hundreds of these produce trucks rolled through the US entry points daily. The drug cartels were fond of using these trucks as smuggling platforms. There were probably a hundred different ways that these imaginative smugglers had found to hide their contraband in and around these lumbering trucks. Another advantage the drug cartels had was that the average US Border Patrol agent was lazy. The last thing an agent wanted to do, especially on an incredibly hot day, was to trudge through thousands of pounds of fruit, vegetables, and crates filled with everything under the sun. This was exactly the tactic the smugglers employed to make life as difficult and annoying as possible for the agents. The odds were high that the agent manning the gate would just wave the driver through the point of entry.

On occasion, a young or new recruit would take his job seriously. Today, one such agent barked out, "Okay, pull that truck to the last kiosk on the right for inspection." Even though a high percentage of trucks went through without the most cursory of reviews or inspections, today this agent was going to be hell on these trucks. Thanks to an overzealous agent, this lucky truck was going to get the full Monty.

The driver gave a friendly wave to the border agent who had given him his instructions. That was the last friendly thing this man would do for months to come. Instead, he floored the gas pedal on the thirty-year-old truck and begged God with all his might that his truck, all twenty tons, would escape the border-patrol agents and their resources.

Not one of the agents could believe his eyes. A couple of the agents were veterans and couldn't remember the last time somebody had attempted to bolt through the gates. It seemed to take almost a minute for them to react, since they were frozen in disbelief. That was their first mistake. By the time they came to their senses and drew their guns, the truck had already ripped through two barricades and demolished the front end of a government vehicle. Shots were fired in total hopelessness. They did manage to put about fifty holes in the watermelons stacked at the back of the truck.

That was the least of the border agents' worries. The truck driver's brazen tactic seemed to be a well-orchestrated call to arms. Immediately, every single motorized vehicle—regardless of make, shape, or model—likewise gunned its engines and fought to keep up with the lumbering truck. It was an amazing sight, like being at the Indianapolis 500 when the green flag was waved to release the supercharged race cars.

Amazingly, no one was killed. Not one of the agents on duty had ever killed anyone in his or her life. As a matter of fact, none of the agents had ever shot at a person before. Though there were at least twenty-eight agents standing around, all with handguns drawn, not one attempted to shoot at any of the drivers. They shot car doors, truck tires; they shot up tons of fruits and vegetables and fifty-five-gallon drums that were now spewing a mysterious fluid every which way. Some agents even fired fruitlessly into the air. Though a few tires were shot out, this did nothing to impede the progress of one single vehicle.

The fleeing Mexican drivers were just as courteous. Not a single one of them swerved in an attempt to run down any of the border agents. Matter of fact, it appeared they did everything possible to avoid hitting anybody.

But an incredible roar filled the air as the convoy of trucks and cars was unleashed, racing hell bent into America. Illegally.

Chapter 44

"This is Sergeant Wilcox of the El Paso, Texas, District Seventeen police station. How may I help you? What...what...can you repeat that? Thank you, I will look into it immediately."

Wilcox hung up and walked into his superior's office.

"Lieutenant, I just got a call from our 911 call center. It appears they received a phone call a few minutes ago from someone who they think was a US border agent at the customs border crossing at the Paso Del Norte Bridge. It appears he was trying to report something about a disturbance, but he was cut off. What do you want me to do about it?"

"Radio the closest patrol car we have to that border crossing, and have him get over there and check it out immediately."

Sergeant Wilcox did as instructed. The two patrol officers who responded to the call dumped their coffee out the window, revved up the engine, kicked on the siren, and sped off toward the location.

One officer said to the other, "What exactly are we investigating?"

"The sergeant wasn't particularly sure about it himself. Supposedly 911 got a call from one of the US border agents at the bridge about some disturbance or something. Could be another one of their drug busts that didn't go so well."

His partner responded, "Maybe it's something more. You know, I was talking to a bunch of the guys in the locker room this morning, and just about everyone has sensed a significant increase in the number of Mexicans milling around on our side of the border in the last couple weeks."

"Legal or illegals?"

"Hell, how would they know? How would I know? How does anybody know? That's what so fucking wrong with this whole thing. There are just as many illegals living in El Paso as there are legals. How the hell are we ever supposed to figure out who the hell is who?"

They had just turned onto the street that would take them to the border crossing in question, when the driver slammed on the brakes, screeching to a halt in the middle of the street.

"Wow," the officer said. "We almost plowed right into these...What the hell is going on? Where did all these people come from? Holy Christ, call the sergeant! Get someone out—" He did not get to finish his sentence.

The wave was all encompassing. In less than a minute, the patrol car was completely surrounded by Mexicans. But they didn't seem to pay any attention to the patrol car. It was like it didn't exist, as if the mass of people were a swarm of ants that sensed a box of sugar at the other end of the street.

Both officers were fully armed, and they feared for their lives and readied themselves to start firing their weapons through the windows if necessary. They both tried opening their doors, but the swarm of people was so dense they couldn't budge the doors an inch.

Just as they were starting to radio for help, their patrol car started to move, to tilt. The agents screamed as their car was turned over, and within seconds was rolled again.

But none of this affected the wave of Mexicans. They were zombie-like, overtaking everything in their path. The destruction they left was beyond comprehension. It looked like some biblical plague, like locusts had descended from the heavens and left nothing whole.

Chapter 45

While heading toward his work assignment at the Rio Grande border-crossing station, Juan, a two-year veteran of the CBP, started to think, *There are only forty-three points of entry to the United States spanning the US-Mexican border. Texas, whose border with Mexico is 1,254 miles long, has twenty-nine entry points. But 1,254 miles divided by ten equals a lot of space between legal crossings. We don't have the manpower or the resources to cover the gaps! There are simply too few agents to oversee the entire length of the border, leaving the underbelly of the United States exposed in what must seem like an open-door invitation to cross without proper documentation. Man, I feel like an insignificant flea.*

Then Juan thought better of his concerns. After all, as a CBP officer he did have job security. Well, at the moment he had job security, but he'd heard that the bitch serving as president might decide to rubber-stamp every damn illegal and legal Mexican crossing the border, making them US citizens immediately. Boy, that'd be a kick in the pocketbook; Juan might lose his job because everyone who crossed over into the United States would be a red-blooded American. It sure made Juan question why they even had border entry points if they were going to just make everyone legal. This president was a national embarrassment for Juan and his fellow agents. As CBP officers, they were constantly putting their lives on the line, though there was little consequence for breaking the US immigration laws. All their work the last few decades had been totally in vain.

Juan's wife was pregnant with their fifth child, and what he needed most at this time was this job and the health benefits. Thankfully, he was earning more than ten times what he had at his previous job as a car mechanic. Reaching over he pushed the button to turn on his radio.

"Damn! What a crappy mechanic. I can't even get this radio to work!" He pounded the steering wheel in frustration. "Now I'm left spouting geography lessons to myself to pass the time."

Actually, Juan wanted a raise, but that would mean a grade increase, which in turn meant that he had to pass another useless exam proving he knew his stuff. So he ground out the details and statistics out loud sounding like a Trivial Pursuit master in geography.

"Rio Grande City, Texas, one of the smaller, less active entry points of the ten in the Texas system. On an average day it might get less than a thousand total crossings, including individuals and vehicles."

A pittance, he thought, recalling that some of the more active stations, such as El Paso and San Ysidro, combined, could get millions a day.

Protocol almost always required a backup agent, but today she had called in sick and the department had not sent a replacement. Juan was a bit nervous because in the last couple of weeks the activity at his entry point had picked up significantly. He had even requested that his superiors assign one additional agent, because the lines for both individuals and vehicles were, for the first time in his memory, getting backed up on the Mexican side. Unlike agents in the larger entry points, Juan was not a stickler for procedure and anytime the line started to grow in length, he'd speed up the process to the point where he would wave through 90 percent of the individuals. It wasn't that far out of the norm. Anyone who had ever crossed the border either way had experienced that 90 percent of the time, most agents just waved people through. To keep things moving along speedily, Juan had just increased that to nearly 100 percent.

Whereas most of the border crossings in the larger cities were open 24-7, these smaller, less-active stations closed down for the evening.

But what Juan found this morning when he drove into the border-crossing station was well beyond his wildest dreams.

Man, he thought, *I must have missed the memo telling us that today everyone in Mexico was moving to America.*

As far as he could see in almost every direction, there were Mexicans. Bodies were being pressed against the station entry, which wasn't altogether unusual, but they were pressed up against the fencing that sprawled both east and west from the station as well.

Wow, they look and act like little cockroaches crawling out from every crack and crevice. Where did all these people come from? And why this morning?

Sure, things had been incredibly busy the last few weeks, and for the first time, he'd had to turn some people away when he'd closed the station for the evening. But this morning at only 7:30 a.m., he was staring at thousands. Thousands.

He just stood slack jawed, tongue flopping about, as he tried to say what he was thinking: *What am I supposed to do?*

He needed to make a decision and make it fast. He was supposed to open the station and start processing individuals by 8:00 a.m. He quickly called his supervisor, who was located in Laredo.

After he explained the situation, his supervisor merely replied, "Why don't you open the station a little early, and when the other agent arrives, why don't both of you do double duty and process these individuals as quickly as possible?"

"I don't know, there are so many. I don't think that, with both of us working all day and not taking a lunch break, we'd even make a dent. I'm not even sure how many people are on the other side of the fence. I bet there are thousands, and I mean thousands and thousands," Juan said pleadingly into the phone.

Juan's supervisor was staying calm and cool. "Do the best you can. That's all you're expected to do. And if you can't get them all processed by the end of the day, just use the megaphone to apologize and tell them you will open a bit earlier tomorrow. I am positive everything will be fine."

It was just about then that everything became unfine. Juan noticed that everything seemed to be leaning. There were just too many people; there was just too much weight. Juan was scared to death. Should he run, should he jump in his truck and leave immediately? He was afraid he would be fired if it was discovered that he had abandoned his post. But he feared for his life. He decided on a compromise. He'd open the gates, but he was not going to make an attempt to process the people. He felt better; he'd made a decision. He was going to open the gates, the floodgates holding back masses of humanity.

Juan tried addressing the crowd. "Move back, I need you to move back. Please move back or someone is going to get hurt."

Juan realized that he'd missed one simple fact. But it was too late. He had already set the gate mechanism to open.

As he heard the click of the gate's latch, the full force that had been applied burst the gate up with enormous pressure. Too close, Juan was caught in the gate's outburst, thrown back to land on the concrete pavement. Within seconds, the massive horde with it mob-like energy pounded across the border.

Juan had realized his error just as he had seen a Mexican trampled to death near the fence, sacrificed by his cohorts. Juan realized the same would be his fate, and at that very moment the full weight, mass, and movement of thousands trampled Juan. He'd never see his wife again or witness the birth of his fifth child.

As life drained out of Juan, he saw the highway sign that confronted the people as they streamed forward into their new country: Corpus Christi 162, San Antonio 228, and Houston 355.

Chapter 46

Craig slammed his palm down on the OFF button on his shrieking alarm clock, trying to focus. As he groped about for his glasses on the nightstand, there was a rustling in the bed behind him. The most delicate, most seductive scent of perfume rose from the sheets. Craig's nostrils flared, and he was instantly spellbound. His eyes flashed intensely, then slowly closed. Craig imagined being embraced in the arms of the Greek goddess Aphrodite. Craig moved slightly as Jennifer did a bit of her own groping.

"Stop that! Get your hands out of my underwear. I don't have time for that this morning!" Craig jumped out of bed, turned back to Jennifer and, said, "You know I've got an 8:00 a.m. class to teach, and if my memory serves me correctly, you are enrolled in that class, so you better get your ass out of bed as well." He took a few more steps toward the bathroom and said, "Hey, while I'm showering, would you mind making me a cup of coffee? You remember how I like it, don't you, kiddo?"

"You know, Dr. Walther, you're a real hypocrite. You go on and on about not wanting to make a commitment. Remember, you told me how you were screwed over in your first two marriages, and you took an oath never to do it again? Well, Doc, you sure want all the benefits and creature comforts that come from having a wife, without the commitment."

Jennifer was still lounging in the gorgeous, hand-carved, southwestern-style bed and had pulled off the sheets to offer a glance at her perfect body. Jennifer had a unique way of making sure that when she made a statement, she incorporated a bit of nudity to be sure the message was sent with extra emphasis. Pulling off the sheets, she lay, perfectly tanned, her long flowing hair cascading around her perfectly shaped, perky breasts, and wearing the skimpiest Victoria's Secret panties, leaving the right amount covered to tweak his imagination.

"I'm *not* sure these occasional one-night stands justify my donning the apron of domesticity and running downstairs to fetch your coffee. Next thing you know, you'll be asking for other domestic duties, such as cleaning up the kitchen or picking up your laundry at the dry cleaners."

Craig was slowly making his way to the bathroom. He hated it when Jennifer called him 'Doctor.' As a matter of fact, he hated it when anybody called him that. Sure, he'd gotten his doctorate; he couldn't teach at most universities without a PhD. But he hated the habit, practiced by 90 percent of his colleagues, of teachers referring to themselves as doctors and insisting that everyone else do the same. *Doctors*? Craig hadn't gone to medical school and didn't treat patients or prescribe medicine. Craig felt that was one of the biggest hypocritical games in the academic world. It didn't surprise him, however. He found the entire college and university system in America one big fat pretense. Even when Craig had been in undergraduate school at twenty-two years of age, he'd quickly subscribed to the adage "Those who can, do. Those who can't, teach."

He'd run into the same idiots during his master's program and again when he was pursuing his doctorate. The teachers and professors spent all their time fluffing themselves up and little time instructing their students. It was no wonder kids were coming out of college behind the eight ball. They were being taught by egotistical morons. But every single one of these morons had a PhD in some subject. It was one big circle jerk.

Maybe 7-11 awards PhDs with every ten Slurpees sold!

Academia's finest wanted a system that guaranteed that they were the royalty of education, tenured from the beginning. They kept themselves at the highest pay levels, placed on glorified pedestals and free to teach from their own life experiences, not bogged down by outdated, boring textbooks.

Being a staunch conservative in a system run by liberals and soft-on-society mollycoddlers, Craig was amazed that he'd gotten in at all. It was hard for Craig because every single professor he came into contact with was a bleeding-heart liberal, and he had to swallow his own principles in order to move ahead—paying his dues, as required in the academic world. When working on his master's, he'd received some excellent advice from one of his professors at Georgetown.

"A) keep your political beliefs to yourself, b) don't pick too controversial—or worse, conservative—a topic for your master's thesis, c) be willing to suck up to your liberal professors and avoid a discussion on politics as if it were the plague, and finally, d) wait until you've gained tenure as a professor before *come out of the closet.*"

Although the bearer of this great advice had considered himself a liberal, he had been so impressed with Craig that he'd felt it would be a loss to the academic world if Craig had been blackballed and kept out.

As Craig was climbing out of the shower, Jennifer swept in with his steaming cup of coffee. Craig took a sip.

"Wow, thank you—you always make it perfect." Closing his eyes, Craig took a moment and savored the custom-prepared brew. Boy, Jennifer had hit a home run—lots of sugar, lots of cream, and just the right amount of coffee for color. Craig was type A+; the last thing he needed in his life was a lot of caffeine, and a strong cup would send him into a tizzy of biblical proportion.

Craig opened his eyes and noticed that Jennifer had made some adjustments to her morning attire. She was a sly fox and had done just enough to look casual but not enough to look like she would discourage Craig's sexual advance if he should make one. Her thigh-length silk robe, was left strategically open, exposing her tight, firm, and tanned tummy. Craig said under his breath, "Mm, that's the right term, 'tummy.' Taut and tanned."

"You sure I can't entice you to one last round between the sheets?" With mock innocence, she said, "I'm not sure you got your full money's worth last night—after all, you were a tad bit drunk."

Craig gave her a loving kiss on the cheek and then artfully slid his face down and gave a corresponding kiss to each of her breasts.

"That's the closest thing to sex I have time for this morning. And as for your comment about last night, I can assure you, young lady, that I am fully capable of enjoying sex to the nth degree even when I am totally shit faced."

Just then the phone rang, and Jennifer quickly volunteered to get it, suggesting that Craig should get dressed. Jennifer always tried to answer Craig's phone, a game she played to be sure everyone knew they were sleeping together. It was the exact ploy she used by leaving something feminine in the house after each visit.

But Craig wasn't fooled by her feigned innocence. He had forbidden her from answering his phone, but he was in a rush this morning, not to mention that it was a bit cold and he was still standing in the bathroom naked, water dripping off of him. "Okay, you can answer the phone, but no pranks."

It was almost like Craig had told Jennifer he was taking her on a trip to Paris. She bounced into the bedroom, flung herself onto the bed, and then paused for a moment, making sure she was completely composed before answering the phone with the sexiest of voice she could conjure: "Professor Walther's residence. Can I help you?"

Jennifer had hit pay dirt. "Yes, if he has time I would like to speak to Professor Walther. You must be his maid," Katherine Stiles said, with a tone one might use to speak to the hired help. "Yes, as a matter of fact this is Professor Walther's maid, housekeeper, and personal assistant, and I'm even known to, on occasion such as today, serve the illustrious professor a cup of specially brewed coffee in bed. Can I tell him who would like to speak with him?"

Jennifer wasn't exactly sure, but she thought she heard "Bitch!" just before the line went dead.

Jennifer rolled onto her back, enjoying the huge ornate bed, and let the phone conversation drift back through her mind. She allowed herself a smile of satisfaction and wiggled deeper into the bed linens. Yes, her ploy was working, and she hugged herself in congratulations.

Chapter 47

Chula Vista, California, was a beautiful city located only 7.5 miles from the US border with Mexico. It was the first large city that anyone entering United States from the San Ysidro border entry point would come across. It was roughly ten miles south of downtown San Diego, located on the San Diego Bay.

The Chula Vista Police Department received word about the disaster at the San Ysidro border point, and updated information was pouring in that huge, determined mobs had already overrun many small communities. The reports were horrifying, describing an immense inflow of Mexicans encompassing everything in its path and moving at 3.5 miles an hour.

Getting out a map of the area and drawing a line from the mob's starting point, the Chula Vista police chief and his emergency-response leader extrapolated where they should allocate their forces and designate, if needed, a fallback position. The chief looked up at the clock to gauge how long he had until the leading edge of the mob arrived. A large banner hung below the clock that reminded everyone who entered the building the mission of the Chula Vista PD.

Boy, thought the chief, *We're going to be tested today.*

He gathered his team members and read the statement out loud to buoy what surely must be mixed emotions. These were not battle-ready troops. They all had families, coached Little League, went to church on Sundays—and no one in the room had ever drawn his or her weapon except at the range. Today would be the finest or worst day of their lives. He really needed to give them the pep talk of his life.

"This is not going to be your average protect-and-serve kind of day. People will die today. Of that I am certain. Remember," he said reading the banner, "The mission of the Chula Vista PD is to enhance the quality of life in the city by treating all persons with respect, dignity, and fairness and to provide professional and proactive police service.

"I have a feeling," he continued, "that today will test our mettle. We've never had to defend our way of life on our own soil, so, boys, make me proud."

An hour later, three cop cars lined up in a typical roadblock formation. Two stationary cars faced in toward the center of the road, with the middle car set slightly back. In this formation, the middle car was able to move left or right, allowing open passage to support personnel or emergency-response vehicles. The police had managed to block one of the major southern routes into town; they were prepared for the onslaught. The officers gathered behind the middle vehicle shook hands and started sharing their speculations about their assigned roadblock post and the presumed threat.

"Explain to us exactly what's going on," said one of the younger officers.

They all turned toward the most senior officer in their group. Thinking *Shit, these guys think I have all the answers and are depending on me*, he responded, "Supposedly thousands of Mexicans busted through the San Ysidro border crossing, and they are coming this way."

The younger officer responded, "No way! No fucking way!" But as the words left his lips, a loud buzzing noise could be heard in the near distance. Coming toward them was a sight that loosened bladders: an incredible mass of humanity undulating toward them, still too distant for the officers to pick out any individuals or potential spokesman within the group. At that point, it didn't matter since the mass would be upon their roadblock very quickly.

"Shit, shit, what are we going to do?" This came from the senior officer, who only moments ago had sounded in charge and on point as their leader.

The senior office blubbered out, "Did anyone tell us what we're supposed to do? Should we shoot tear gas?"

"It's too late for tear gas—they are too close," replied one of the other officers.

Trying to regain control of himself, the senior officer reached into his car and grabbed the megaphone he had checked out earlier from headquarters. Failing to control his shaking hands, he addressed the oncoming wave of humanity.

"Halt! Stop where you are!" And as fast as he could, he repeated the commands, alternating between English and Spanish.

Another officer radioed headquarters to get further direction.

"Yes, we've tried that, No, they still won't stop. Yes, they're Mexicans. How the hell do I know if they're here illegally? No, it doesn't appear they're armed. Should we start shooting? No, we can't use the tear gas—they're too close!" Then nothing but static took over the frequency. That was the last thing the Chula Vista PD dispatcher heard.

Chapter 48

Dave hadn't had a day off in almost a week. Everything seemed to be falling apart all around him, and at the same time no one could exactly figure out what was going on. Feet propped up on the coffee table Dave consumed his third beer and prepared himself for the local news. The Channel 6 theme started, the news-desk reporters put on their canned smiles, and the usual dog-and-pony show began.

A young, perky Mexican news correspondent began talking very quickly. "We have further information on the story we brought you this morning. It is not yet verified, but it appears that the city of Chula Vista has been overrun by a mob of some kind. We cannot confirm this because all means of communication— radio, landlines, and cell phone towers—are down. Governor Harry Black is currently in Northern California on a fund-raising campaign but said that he will try to look into the matters by late tomorrow. This so-called mob has left a path of destruction in its wake. We are not aware of their final destination, but for some reason they've chosen to avoid San Diego, despite the fact that San Diego is in their direct path. San Diego's chief of police made a statement earlier that if, in fact, these invaders change their path, San Diego is prepared. Helicopter photographs taken of the advancing mob and their path have been classified, so we don't have anything to show you at this time. However, we've been told that there are indications that the bulk of the movement has swung east of San Diego toward the communities of Jamul, El Cajon, and Lakeside.

"Police Chief Rogers of San Diego told us he's still not exactly sure what's going on because there are so many unverified stories. But he said he wasn't surprised that these people avoided San Diego, saying, 'With two US naval bases and two marine bases, I think anyone would be stupid to try to invade San Diego.'"

The perky reporter continued her report, but her canned smile was starting to wither, and her makeup couldn't hide her now pale face. "One of our correspondents interviewed a number of roving mob members, and, in fact, they have verified Police Chief Rogers's suspicions. They said that friends in Tijuana spread the word that San Diego is a city to be avoided because of all the military." All perkiness gone, the reporter suddenly blurted out, "We now move to a commercial break!" Fifteen seconds of dead air time commenced.

The smell of disaster now permeated the area surrounding San Diego. The events were unfolding too fast, and no one was willing to put his or her career or life in harm's way by making a poor decision.

Dave cracked open his fourth beer and slammed it down onto the coffee table. "Shit," he said, "the country is falling apart, and our worthless president is probably on a fundraising junket, like our illustrious governor."

Chapter 49

It had always been a source of frustration to Dave when his wife, Anita, had forced him to take her homemade sandwiches with him when he returned illegals to Mexico. But had he known what she had been up to lately, he would have been furious.

Anita was in close communication with many of the Mexican families that lived in and around them and knew what was going on with the breach at the border crossing at Rio Grande. She had learned that thousands of Mexicans were crossing the border, overwhelming communities, and collapsing the infrastructure just outside San Diego. Many of Anita's friends, both legal and illegal Mexicans living in San Diego, were organizing a secret food drive to help those who were now on American soil. Anita and her friends had just learned that many of the Mexican illegals had gone at least a week without proper food and that some were close to dying from starvation.

Anita and her friends were collecting as much food as they could, not only from Mexican families with whom they were in contact, but also from many sympathizers. Three times already Anita and her group had driven to the outskirts of San Diego and distributed the food. Sadly, there was never enough for everyone, and a few skirmishes had broken out when the provisions had run out too quickly. But Anita was not discouraged by these reactions and continued to do what she could to keep her involvement secret from Dave. Dave would not only be furious, but he would also have to respond in an official capacity, perhaps charging her with aiding and abetting fugitives from justice.

Oh, God, she thought, *Dave's boss, Buck, would make his life a living hell if Dave ever got wind of my involvement!*

Chapter 50

Dave turned off the TV and answered the phone. "What? How quickly? How long? Okay, I'll pack and be there in about two hours."

As Dave hung up the phone, Anita walked through the garage door and into the living room.

"Where've you been?" Dave asked. "I thought we agreed you were not going to go driving around during this stage of your pregnancy. Anita, what the hell are you doing going out at all? Haven't you seen the news reports about what has happened in Chula Vista?"

"No!" said Anita. "That's not what we agreed to. That's what you ordered me to do. The doctor said it's just fine for me to drive wherever I need to go. I'm just supposed to be extra careful about getting in and out of the car, and I'm not to lift any heavy packages.

"And we both know that nothing has been confirmed yet about Chula Vista. Aren't you the one who is always complaining about the media and press always blowing things out of proportion?"

Dave waited an appropriate moment while trying to regain his composure before responding.

"I'm sorry," he responded. "It's just this whole mess with the border. I wish we could get a better handle on exactly what's going on. I don't believe the news stories. I know there was a bust out at the Rio Grande's customs station, and ever since I witnessed that mass of people just inside the border the other night...well, I guess it doesn't matter.

"Listen, I just got a call from Buck. There has been an additional breakout at the San Ysidro station. Every customs and border-patrol agent has been called in for active, full-time duty.

It's all hands on deck, and until further notice I'm going to be eating and sleeping in some makeshift barracks. I don't even know when I'll be home."

Anita asked, "What is active, full-time duty?"

"I've never heard of it before either. I guess I never realized working for the US Border Patrol is sort of like being in the military. Buck explained to me that it's in my contract. I was told to pack whatever I could get into a midsize duffle, and then report for duty at the main station. Buck said that we should inform our families that there is no telling when we might be coming back home. But, with everything that has been going on and with your pregnancy, I hate to leave you." Lowering his head, Dave opened his heart and said, "Anita, frankly, I am just afraid to leave you."

Anita rewarded her husband's response with a kiss to his cheek and a big hug. Well, as big of a hug as she could muster, considering her stomach was the size of a beach ball, and she couldn't get her arms around him.

"Don't worry about me. I can take care of myself, and the baby is just fine. Don't get yourself hurt. We need you back home as soon as Buck will let you."

All the time Anita was secretly thinking that this was going to work out for the best, because Dave wouldn't discover her helping to feed her starving fellow countrymen. With Dave gone and out of the picture, she could double her efforts and truly make a difference.

Chapter 51

If Bill Walther had squeezed his hand any tighter on his morning newspaper, the *Arizona Republic*, the ink would have run down his fingers and flowed onto the floor. "Dammit all to hell!" he barked from his seat at the kitchen table.

"Bill, please don't cuss," Elsie said. "Especially so early in the morning. You'll raise your blood pressure and spoil the whole day."

"How come these fricking politicians promise us they're going to solve this immigration problem when they're all running for office? They cheat us by telling us what they think we want to hear, and then when they get to Washington, they all fall asleep. How the hell is that representing us?"

"Okay, honey, what did you read in the paper that has got you upset this morning?"

"What I just read is a continuation of the stupidest, most screwed up immigration policy I could ever imagine. I really could do without the current situation we now have in America."

Elsie was readying herself for what was fast becoming a daily routine of shouting and cursing. The government's immigration policy was a real problem for her husband and others that they knew.

"Those damn illegal aliens." Bill bowed as if addressing royalty, "Okay, Missy President, what's your new plan today, eh? Are you going to send them all back by truck, train—or have you moved to buses? How about making them walk back? They walked here so, let 'em walk back. Or are you going to continue with the Obama plan to just make them all legal?

"Doing anything would be better than what we're doing now. For heaven's sake, it's the worst of all worlds. We've got twenty-plus million illegal Mexicans in this country. They get free education, free medical attention, they overcrowd our parks and overburden public transportation. They get to use all the same city, county, and state services just like you and me. Except there's one big difference between them and us—they don't pay taxes."

Bill grabbed the newspaper and, with a tremendous amount of effort, shredded it and sent the confetti flying throughout the kitchen.

Elsie jerked her head around from her sink duties. "What did you say?"

Bill smiled. "Oh, for once, did I get your attention?"

Elsie sputtered, "They pay some tax, don't they?"

"Not a fucking red dime, not one!" Bill said in his loudest bark of the morning. "Okay, okay! I'll correct myself. They do pay consumption taxes. You know, like sales tax, cigarette tax, and gasoline tax. But consider all the taxes they don't pay." As he ticked off each one, he physically trembled with anger. "Federal income tax, state income tax, federal unemployment, state unemployment, self-employment tax, Social Security, FICA, Medicare, school taxes, city taxes, county taxes, real estate taxes, and inheritance tax." Bill's list would fill a notebook. "Most of these illegals get paid in cash, under the table, and they send home a huge percentage of what they make here in the United States to family members in Mexico."

Bill tried to take another drink from his coffee cup, not realizing or caring that he had finished his coffee an hour ago. "I can't imagine myself saying that we ought to make them all US citizens, but I hate the current system worse. Since they're getting all the benefits of living here in the United States, we ought to at least make 'em pay for it, like the rest of us who do pay their taxes."

Elsie chimed in, "Do you know what Mrs. Crocker said to me yesterday? You know Mrs. Crocker? Her son's serving in Afghanistan. He wrote her a letter and told her that they had the perfect solution to this whole immigration problem. If the Mexicans want all the benefits of living in

America, then sign them up and ship them off to Afghanistan. He said that they could use the help. But he also said that most of his friends wouldn't trust them as far as they could throw them."

Bill smiled for the first time that morning. "Hell, that is the best damn idea I've heard yet. Why hasn't some dumb politician suggested that? Never mind, I guess it is just too damn logical. Seems like a win-win situation to me. I'd be the first person to welcome them to America if they were willing to fight to be Americans. We don't need to build a fence—let's just put up big billboards: 'Come to America! Be a citizen! Serve two years in Afghanistan!' By God, that'd stop them sons of bitches in their tracks!"

Chapter 52

"Hello, David Walther speaking."

"Dammit, Dave, how come you haven't returned any of my phone messages?" barked Craig into the phone. "I've been trying to reach you for days."

"Sorry, Craig, I got your phone messages. All of the southern agents have been drawn into 24-7 duty. All leave has been canceled, and those on leave have been recalled. Craig, this is an all-hands-on-deck cry to action. Didn't you get my e-mails?"

"Dave, we're on the verge of a crisis, and everybody wants to rely on e-mails and text messages. Did I e-mail or text you? Hell no, I called you! That's why we're going to hell in a hand basket. No one knows how to use a frickin' phone! When I call you, I expect you to return my call, and that means on the damn phone. I don't think walking around staring at a cell phone or PDA is any way to communicate. I don't care how damn fast you and your friends think you can text message, speaking with another human being is the proper way for adults to communicate."

"Whoa, hang on big brother. What are you so frickin' ticked off about? Okay, okay, maybe I should've returned the call, but really things are not going well down here. You big college professors with your collective fingers up your butts probably haven't heard anything up there in your silver towers of academia, but down here in this part of the country, things are falling apart. Saving lives seems a little bit more important right now than returning my professor brother's phone calls."

Craig took a deep breath and realized he had been grossly unfair, especially since his calls were on the very subject that Dave was talking about. He felt like a real ass.

"You're right, little brother—this isn't the time. So the border patrol is going to an all-hands-on-deck position? What the hell is going on down there? I've made a dozen calls to

Washington, but as usual they have their heads so far up their asses, they're going to have to unbutton their shirt collars to take a drink of water. Hey, come on, little brother, give me the scoop."

Dave accepted his brother's apology and responded, "You know, we've been sworn to secrecy. The word from on high is not to tell anybody about what's going on around here. They've even banned use of our cell phones unless we're calling in a report or calling home to check on our wives and families. Craig, I think they have cell-phone-signal-blocking software in use. Our personal cell phones only work in certain areas of the building and during specific times. It's pretty damn obvious that no one here, in any department or at any level, knows the whole picture. They won't give us a fucking clue as to what is really going on. Craig, since you worked in DC for years, you'll understand when I tell you that everyone's scrambling to cover their asses. It seems that any superiors within the DEA, Homeland Security, US Customs and Border Protection, and others who, at one time or another, worked with illegal immigrants are quaking in their boots. They're scared to death that their department is going to be blamed for not anticipating this invasion. Oh, man, Craig, don't let anyone know that I said 'invasion.'"

Regaining a bit of self-control, Dave continued on, "It's comical to watch the finger-pointing and backstabbing. I'm not in charge down here, but my boss, Buck, who you've heard me talk about for years, has been using me as *his* sounding board. His superiors are looking for scapegoats, and since he's so close to retirement, he is doing everything he can to dodge blame, but his head is on the chopping block. As far as I can tell, everyone is trying to keep a lid on the volumes of information flowing between various law enforcement departments. Craig, here it is, in a nutshell—the entire two-thousand-mile border with Mexico has completely dissolved!"

It seemed to Dave that the phone had gone dead. There was only hollow, empty air between the two brothers. Then Craig burst out, "Holy shit, you're not serious, are you? Dave, speak to me—tell me that my predictions haven't come to life. Mexicans are invading!"

"Well, I can't actually prove what I've told you because, like I said, everybody in administration has gone into a state of CYA. No one wants to admit that this has happened and is continuing to happen. I'm getting my information from a few of my fellow agents that went to the academy with me. We've grown up in the patrol, our families are friends, and together we've put a lot of good years under our belts. We trust each other but still have to be careful. We've been threatened over any nonofficial communication. Not only could we lose our jobs and pensions but we could be arrested and jailed for breach of orders. Listen, Craig, I've got friends at US Customs and Border Protection, and we have been trying to piece together the puzzle for the last two days."

Craig couldn't stand it any longer. Sometimes his brother carried on like an old woman, a trait he'd picked up from their father.

"Dave! What have you all pieced together? Please, Dave, I just need the facts. Remember, I wrote the book on this, so just tell me what you know!"

If he had been given his whole life to prepare for this moment, this earth-shattering announcement, it would not have been sufficient. Craig was not ready, nor could he ever have prepared for his brother's answer.

"Remember, Craig, this is off the record. I cannot prove or disprove what I'm about to tell you due an information blackout. Are you sitting down? The fucking numbers are off the charts. I think we are talking about swarms of thousands, maybe millions of illegal aliens crossing a now nonexistent US border! It's unbelievable, like a movie. Only it's live. They're raiding houses for food. I'm worried about my wife and our unborn child being pulled into this invasion. Craig, I'm afraid we may face a total collapse of our state-wide infrastructure and become a third-world country before this is over."

Craig could feel his brother's grasp on reality slipping. Dave was becoming unglued by the minute.

Then, in a voice that Craig had never heard his brother use before, almost prayer-like, Dave said, "Dear God, it's like a plague, a literal black cloud has descended over us, and there's no stopping it." Then, nothing but dead air. Their connection had been severed.

Chapter 53

Craig looked up from his notes and realized his phone was ringing. He wondered how long he'd been ignoring the ringing sound. The thought of his recent bout with his brother Dave and the diatribe about answering the phone and returning messages hit him like a ton of bricks. "Enough of the recriminations," he said to himself. "Hello?"

"Professor Walther, my name is General Kurt Grayson. I work at the Pentagon. I was wondering if I could grab a few minutes of your time. I wouldn't bother you except that it's of the utmost urgency. A national crisis, if you will."

Craig was tired of the research he was currently conducting and was actually happy to be interrupted. "Go ahead, General, I'm always happy to help my friends in the Pentagon."

"You have friends at the Pentagon?"

"Sorry, General, I was trying to be a bit colorful. Though I did work and live in DC for a decade, I will have to admit I didn't develop any friends in the Pentagon. That doesn't mean I don't have anything but the utmost respect for those of you who serve our country in the military. I just was never popular, nor was my work welcomed by those in power back then. But I wasn't hired to win a popularity contest. And being one of the few conservatives in academia today, I still find myself often bucking the trend."

"You know, Professor, I graduated magna cum laude from West Point and even taught there for a number of years. But without a PhD, you're dirt to those who have them—you're not even good enough to shine their shoes. Look, Professor, being honest, I can tell you this: if the United States had to rely on those dainty pricks in the academic world to defend this country, we'd all be speaking German or Russian. Ha! For that matter Japanese or maybe even Korean! Sorry, I've been kicked around by the best of the academic world and have a no-love-lost attitude for it."

Craig chuckled. "General, sir, what's on your mind? I know you didn't find me just to tell me that my peers don't like me. It doesn't take a rocket scientist to know how the axe falls in this university. So enough foreplay—let's get to your point. I'm not a mind reader, but I bet I can tell you why you've called."

General Grayson leaned back in his custom desk chair and prepared for a serious conversation. One he thought he'd never need to have. "Professor, my aides tell me that you're one of the best experts in this country when it comes to the issues surrounding the US-Mexican border and the United States's relationship with the country of Mexico."

A pause followed that went on far too long for the general's liking.

"Professor, am I correct?"

"While I appreciate your presumption, let's just say I try my best to be kept totally abreast of the issues."

"That works for me. So just how currently abreast are you? But before you answer, the Pentagon is getting all kinds of phone calls coming out of the southwest, but no one seems to be able to put their finger exactly on what's going on. I was hoping that with your being the expert in the field and living in Albuquerque, with eyes on the prize, so to speak, you might be able to clarify the situation for me."

Craig couldn't think fast enough to respond without sounding insulting. "I don't know if I should be honored or afraid, General. I had this very conversation with one of my friends in the Senate this past week. He covered your concerns, and his request for information was the same request you are making now. How the hell do you expect me to sleep at night when I find out that both our Senate and our Pentagon don't have a clue as to what is going on with our two-thousand-mile border with Mexico?"

General Grayson paused for a moment. He didn't know if he was mad or just plain embarrassed.

"Touché, Professor, touché. You win the first round. But I don't have time to spar with you, and I would hope the both of us can put our egos aside. I'm afraid that there's some truth to what I'm hearing, and if so I think thousands of American lives are at stake. Frankly, I don't give a shit about anything else. A lot of Americans and a lot of people in Congress don't have a fucking clue about what the American military is all about. And though my teaching at West Point was on the issue of military tactics, ultimately all battles and all wars boil down to politics. Over 250 years ago the militia of our original thirteen colonies had only one goal: protecting American lives and the sacred land we live in, the United States. Now cut the shit and tell me what the hell is going on!"

Craig took a big deep breath. "Well, as I've been predicting..."

"Stop, stop, stop!" Grayson shouted into the phone. "'I'm not one of your students and I'm not interested in a history lesson. I read your book and need your help, or I wouldn't have called you. Now, goddammit, give me the facts without the academic lecturing!'"

Craig had an ego larger than most and the fact that one of the most powerful generals in US history had read his book was intoxicating.

"General, I'm sorry to say that I think that what I've predicted is exactly what is happening. I think Mexico is at this very moment imploding, and we're experiencing the first waves of a major citizen cast-off. Since you've read my book, I won't repeat all the reasons why, but the situations causing the instability within Mexico's borders have come to a head with predictable results. Look, the Mexicans have been using our border as a revolving door for decades with basically little or no resistance.

What little resistance there's been has been nothing more than a political Band-Aid to appease the conservatives."

Craig took a deep breath and continued, "The Democratic Party loves Mexicans because they almost always vote democratic. The Mexican government loves shipping their less productive Mexicans to the United States who send billions back to Mexico. Imagine what a boon to the Mexican economy American dollars makes. But when President Obama announced that he was going to grant citizenship to upward of ten million illegal Mexicans living in the United States—that was the straw that broke the camel's back. Millions of Mexicans who were thinking or planning to migrate to the United States woke up and saw a pot of gold at the end of the rainbow, the United States. Now, all of a sudden there was a time clock, and the countdown was ticking. If you wanted to enter the United States and be immediately made an American citizen, there was not a minute to waste. The time was now."

Craig waited a beat for the dramatic *coup de gras*. "General if you're looking for a scapegoat, there isn't one. If you are looking for responsibility, it's closer to home than you know. We are responsible for opening the floodgates."

"Well, that was valuable information, Professor, and thank you for being so dramatic. But a more pressing question is, do you know what's actually going on today at the border?"

Craig sensed an almost unmilitary-like, up-the-creek-without-a-paddle pleading in the voice of General Grayson. He now realized how compartmentalized this president's administration had become, leaving generals impotent and scrambling for their own information. Somehow, they'd been removed from the need-to-know list. That left Craig more nervous than the recent conversations with Dave about the border-patrol issues. If the powers that be in Congress and now the Pentagon didn't have a clue as to what was going on, the country was in serious trouble.

"The only firsthand, boots-on-the-ground knowledge I have, General, is from my brother, who's a twenty-plus-year veteran of the US Border Patrol in San Diego. I'm sad to say that he tells me that the agencies trying to deal with the problem seem to be more concerned about covering their asses. They're pointing fingers at who's to blame for the border breakdown. General, there's no doubt that heads will roll after the dust settles. At this point, it appears to be somewhere between a mini and massive invasion."

Craig could almost sense the frustration on the other end of the phone line. Finally General Grayson spoke.

"Man, I need your help. Your country needs your help. I need someone outside of the federal government to be my inside man. I agree with your brother's bluntness, and he's right. It appears right now that almost every department at the federal level is much more worried about finger-pointing and avoiding blame than saving American lives. It's CYA first, then everything else second. Listen, you seem like a straight shooter. In your book, what you wrote spoke volumes on topics no one else was willing to address because they were afraid of not being politically correct. Frankly, I do everything I can to keep from being politically correct. The world was fine with our forefathers on down to my generation speaking from our hearts without the fear of offending some lightweight liberal pansies. Professor, if you'll be my eyes and ears, I'd be grateful. Actually, the nation would be grateful if they weren't sheep."

"Anytime, General. I've got nothing to lose. I'm a tenured professor, and my previous wives have left me with plenty of cash. I didn't write my books for self-gratification. I knew our country needed waking up. So now I guess we're paying the price for decades of being asleep at the wheel. General, I am at your beck and call. Please call me whenever you want, and I'll do everything I can to help."

Grayson paused. "On behalf of a grateful nation, let me thank you for the service you are about to provide. Let me give you my direct line that you can call 24-7."

After their proper good-byes, Craig went to the refrigerator to grab a beer. His conversation with General Grayson haunted his every thought. That was a historical phone call, but the public would probably never know of its existence. Craig smiled while twisting the cap off his bottle of Santa Fe Brewery American Pale Ale. This border fiasco had all the earmarks and drama of a Watergate-rated clusterfuck.

"Man, Craig, what have you signed on for?"

Chapter 54

Belmont Park on Mission Beach Boulevard in San Diego was one of America's premier beachfront amusement parks. It had everything you would expect: a gravity- and death-defying roller coaster, a huge Ferris wheel, acres of arcades, and unlimited, nonstop junk food. One could easily eat his or her way through the park, finding everything from corn dogs to deep-fried Twinkies. For the California health nut, the park boasted its Pilates and yoga classes and sported themed weekends, such as its famous Sweetheart Salsa night.

That Sunday was just another typical, gorgeous Southern California day, with thousands of thrill-seeking Californians enjoying the amusement park, while others were picnicking at the nearby public beach. With the water temperature being sixty-two degrees, none but the brave or foolish even dipped their toes into the light surf.

Little did these carefree souls know that their lives were about to be changed forever.

Within a matter of minutes, the already crowded amusement park and beach area became intolerable with more bodies, then more. The free flow of bodies continued to pack in, and the over crowdedness blossomed to an uncontrollable degree. Although these newcomers weren't distinguishable in appearance from the other Mexican-Americans enjoying the park and beach that day, their clothes told a different story. Their clothes were well worn, made from a coarser cloth. Many of the newcomers were carrying backpacks, duffel bags, or small rope-tied suitcases.

The park officials began noticing that the temperament of the crowd had dramatically changed, becoming more mob-like. Small scuffles broke out, and from somewhere in the crowd there came a scream, then another.

A little girl and her brother were just about to take their first bites of their ice cream cones from the Sweet Shoppe & Beach Treats store in the heart of the Midway. Suddenly, they were pushed to the ground, cones yanked from their hands by two of the newcomers. Injured by the fall but more so from the loss of their monster ice cream cones, both children broke into loud, wailing cries. Adding to the noise and confusion, their father grabbed one of the thieves, a Mexican, and punched him in the face. Then three of the newcomer Mexicans jumped him and started beating the father mercilessly. The mother added her screams to those of her children and started a full-fledged riot.

A long day and night lay ahead for the park security and the San Diego Police Department.

Like in the scene from the 1978 movie *Animal House* when someone yelled "Food fight," a full-blown riot broke out. The new park intruders started grabbing every piece of food in sight. Monster ice cream cones, cotton candy, bags of popcorn, fudge of all types, soft drinks, and even the fried Twinkies were grabbed out of the hands of the park visitors. One of the workers cried out, "Oh, my God, they're everywhere!

Things quickly escalated. Roughly twenty Mexicans broke into one of the vendors' food trailers and began tossing anything that looked like food out the service window and the back door. As the intruders scrambled to grab for the free food, additional fights broke out. Within a matter of minutes, every food facility in the park had been ransacked and picked clean of anything edible. The feeding frenzy was like a pack of hyenas descending on a recent kill.

Panic had truly broken out, and thousands of fun-seeking amusement park goers were streaming toward the gates of Belmont Park as if Satan was chasing them. As the crowds, moving in a panic-like stampede, flowed through the exit gates, the slow movers and those frozen by fright were trampled underfoot.

However, the onslaught was not confined to the park itself. As the food ran out at the park, the starving Mexicans moved toward the hundreds of families on the beach who were picnicking out of their large coolers. By the thousands, the

Mexicans swarmed over the beach crowd and devoured anything edible in a matter of minutes.

Belmont Amusement Park also had a fishing pier that ventured out a hundred yards into Mission Bay. It was a favorite spot for fishing and picnicking, and the invading Mexicans soon discovered the entrance and continued their technique of knocking down people and grabbing whatever food was available. Food stands were ransacked, and one fisherman, who was in the process of taking the hook out of his catch, was knocked down and the fish yanked from of his hands. The attacker managed to fend off his comrades as he voraciously ate the fish, scales, organs, and bones.

The California state government was liberal; in its administration were Democrats who ran on platforms against handguns and firearms, in general. But this was San Diego, where many active-duty military and retired military families lived. One such family of five was near the end of the pier, where the husband had his fishing line out while the family picnicked. The husband had witnessed the Mexicans move down the pier toward his family. As usual, he had packed a revolver with his fishing gear; this he now removed from his tackle box and pointed at the approaching Mexicans.

He held back twenty or so individuals from advancing on him and his family. However, the number advancing kept climbing, up to well over fifty within minutes.

His wife and children started to panic as the crowd advanced, and his youngest started to whimper then cry. The father was normally a patient man, but he knew he'd lose it shortly if relief didn't arrive. The group kept advancing; his children and wife were now hysterical, and he had had all he could take. It was time to prove he meant business.

He shot and killed the three closest Mexicans. But by that time it was a fruitless act. The ever-advancing group didn't even hesitate as they stepped over their fallen comrades. The man gave a determined look at the group and waved his gun, hoping beyond measure that they'd stop. But the group continued forward, pressing the family into a tighter shell. The revolver held six shells and was quickly emptied.

One Mexican grabbed a fish gaffe that sat in the tackle box and in one swift move thrust it through the man's chest. Death came quickly, and his wife started screaming for help, knowing she and her children were facing certain death if she didn't come up with a solution quickly.

She gathered her children together, and they turned and jumped fifty feet into the ocean. The young boy, who had recently taken Red Cross swimming classes, was the only one in his family who was able to swim. He tried the best he could to help his mother and sister stay above the waves and move toward shore, but they were driven into the pier's pilings. They soon tired and sank toward the ocean floor.

Finally, with his energy level drained, the young boy headed toward shore. He found it a struggle to get up onto the beach. Finding his life shattered, he buried his head in his hands and started crying.

Chapter 55

Fort Bliss is on the northern outskirts of El Paso, Texas. Located at the extreme western tip of Texas, El Paso is nearly surrounded by New Mexico. It's the second largest US Army base in the US Interestingly, the *largest* Army base is in New Mexico, just two hours north of El Paso at the White Sands Missile Range.

Fort Bliss is home to the Army's 1st Armored Division, as well as the 32nd Army Air and Missile Defense Command. Biggs Army Airfield is also located within Fort Bliss. Approximately 8,700 people reside at Fort Bliss, the majority being US Army personnel. Including civilians, the base employs over 35,000 people. Major General Tillman, commander of the Fort Bliss base just outside El Paso, slammed the phone down, hit the intercom button on his desk, and barked, "Captain, get your ass in here STAT!"

The young army captain was standing in front of Major General Tillman before he had even moved his finger from the intercom button. Without even looking up, the general started talking.

"Captain, one of the last communications we had with the El Paso PD told us that the US border with Mexico had collapsed, and estimates are that thousands of Mexicans are streaming into the state. Remind me of the current number of military personnel that are living off base in civilian housing?"

"Sir, at present there are roughly 2,622 military personnel living off base."

"Captain, get as much assistance as you need, but within one hour I want every one of those individuals and their families on my base. I don't mean ASAP, I mean now! When you get that accomplished, then we'll powwow about housing and feeding them. Lastly, tell them they have no time to pack anything other than bare essentials. Be emphatic, and tell them nothing more."

Tillman once again hit his intercom and said, "Get me Colonel Ramirez in here now."

About fifteen minutes later, Colonel Ramirez stood in front of the general, awaiting orders.

"Colonel, have you heard about the problem at the border?" the general queried. Colonel Ramirez responded in the affirmative.

"Well, I have some concerns. Is there going to be any conflict with our Mexican-American military personnel? Let me be more direct—am I going to have any problems with *you*, Colonel?"

Ramirez bristled. "Sir, I was born in San Antonio, not in Guadalajara. What are you insinuating?"

Under normal circumstances, Tillman might have apologized for what he had clearly insinuated, but time wasn't a luxury he had. "Look, Ramirez, I just need to know that you're on board with my decisions. What I fear is that, for the first time, the Mexicans in this country are thinking of going down the same path as blacks have in the past with race riots. A stupid path, I might add.

"Look, Colonel, you know me. I couldn't give a rat's ass about the color of someone's skin. Shit, now that we have women and gays in the military, I had to change a lot of my outdated ideas. You're one of my finest officers, and I have the utmost respect for you. Our country will likely have its first Mexican president within the next few elections. But we don't have time for that shit now. My question to you today is simple: can you assure me that if we get into a military confrontation with the illegal Mexicans who've recently flooded into this country, that every one of our Mexican-American soldiers will do their duty? I expect them to uphold the Constitution and, if need be, shoot to kill anyone who threatens the safety of this base."

"I beg your pardon, sir, but what makes you think that just because my parents were Mexican that I somehow know what every Mexican-American soldier might or might not do? As you're aware, we're always having some confrontation with some of the more outspoken blacks in our division, but to my recollection, we've never had a single issue relating to our Mexican-American soldiers. Why this sudden fear that this will change?"

"You've got a good point. With the border collapse and the break in communications, I haven't been able to get any answers out of Washington about how to proceed. Let me ask you a question, Colonel. If you were to guess what percentage of our soldiers has relatives living in Mexico, what would you say?"

"Well, that's a difficult question. Mexicans tend to have a larger extended family than Americans have, so when you say 'relatives,' it could include aunts, uncles, cousins, and even some who aren't related to them by blood. Given that, then I'd have to say that probably 100 percent of them have relatives in Mexico."

Ramirez continued, "I think I know where you are going. Let me see if this helps. I think most of the Mexican-American soldiers on this base, like myself, were born in America, and many of us are second-, third-, and fourth-generation Americans. I can only speak for myself, but my ties to the country of Mexico don't go much beyond the fact that I drink Dos Equis beer."

"Perhaps I'm a little paranoid," General Tillman added, "but I think in times like this I'd like to err on the side of being a little too cautious. Should this get down to fighting, I want to make sure that the enlisted men see that all my officers— regardless of their heritage—are 100 percent behind their country and willing to do what needs to be done."

As Colonel Ramirez was leaving, another officer grabbed the door from him and entered the office. He asked, "You wanted to see me, General?"

"Yes, Major. Have you been able to find out anything more about the breakdown at the border? It appears that a lot of our normal communications aren't working, and nobody can figure out what's going on with the El Paso Police Department."

"No, sir. It seems to be total mayhem, and the lack of communication is making things that much worse. It may be causing more panic than is justified."

"Have you been interviewing everyone that I ordered to move onto the base?" the general asked.

"Yes, General, per your orders we are asking everyone coming on base what they know. The problem is that almost all of our off-base residents live relatively close to the base, which means they all live too far from where the disturbances are happening to know much more than rumor."

"Do we know what the disturbance is?"

"The only thing that seems to be clear is that the border crossing at El Norte has been completely breached, and thousands of Mexicans are flooding into El Paso."

"Does anybody have any idea exactly how many illegals we're talking about?"

"No, but from the rumors I'm hearing, it appears that it's a continual wave of Mexicans flooding across the border, but we have no way of knowing how many are crossing."

"Any word on the level of violence so far?

"You've got to understand, General, that most of what I'm getting is more rumor than fact, but it appears thus far there hasn't been a lot of violence. But there's been quite a bit of looting, especially of food stores. Do you want me to send out a reconnaissance patrol?"

"Hell, no! We're still trying to get everyone on base. The last thing I want to do is send a patrol out. And frankly, I don't know if I even have the authority since Washington has not only failed to issue any orders, they seem to be somewhere between disbelief and denial. So, for now, I think our best strategy is for us to play this like the US Cavalry."

"What exactly did you have in mind, General?"

"Well, we'll just assume we're about to be surrounded by Indians and, at this point, we'll just hold the fort. Keep trying to get hold of someone over at the El Paso Police Department who can give us more details about what's going on. You're dismissed."

He quickly hit his intercom and said, "Get me Sergeant Curtis on the phone," then picked up the phone.

"Sergeant Curtis."

"Sergeant, what is the current status of our provisions at the base commissary?"

"Excellent, sir. We just had in all the major truck lines in the last two days."

"Excellent. What is our status of MREs?"

"I would have to say more than excellent, sir."

"Why is that?"

"Well, if you remember, General, last month we were supposed to have that two-week-long joint-training exercise with Alamogordo, and it got canceled. We had stocked enough provisions for a two-week exercise that never got used. So that's still on hand, in addition to our normal provisions."

"Sergeant, I'm not sure you're aware of this, but in the next two days we'll be moving onto base all military personnel who were living off base in civilian housing. In addition to having to find quarters for these people and their families, I'm concerned if we can properly feed them."

"General, I'd like to say that we've got plenty of food, but I guess it depends on how long you're talking about."

"I'm not really sure. I don't want to create any panic, but I want you to get together immediately with all food staff on the base. We've got to go immediately into a rationing system. There's a possibility that we may not be able to get additional food shipments onto the base in the foreseeable future. I don't have a clue how long we might be isolated from the outside world, and the last thing I want to do is run out of food or water.

"Which brings me to the next subject. I know we have our own well, and I think the chance of us running out of water is probably impossible, and with the base generators, I can't even conceive of how that could happen. But I'd like to make sure that every piece of equipment on this base that can hold water is filled to the limit within forty-eight hours."

"Yes, sir, General."

"I expect to hear back from you pronto. That's all." He hung up and punched the intercom again.

"Get me who's in charge of base housing these days."

Moments later, the intercom buzzed, and his secretary announced that Lieutenant Murphy was on the line.

"Lieutenant, they tell me you're in charge of base housing. Is that correct?"

"Yes, sir."

"Have you been told that we need to find housing for approximately 2,600 soldiers and their families who have been ordered back to the base for an unspecified amount of time?"

"Yes, sir."

"Are you going to have any problems finding housing for these people?"

"No, General, I don't think that's going to be a problem. How long are you talking about?"

"Plan for a month until you hear differently from me."

"Yes, sir," he said and hung up.

On the intercom, the general barked, "Judy, get me Ramirez back in here."

Ramirez came in, saluted, and waited for the general to speak.

The general slowly turned to look out the window that gave him a panoramic view of the front entrance of the base. He stood at parade rest, with his hands clasped behind his back, and addressed Ramirez. "At this point, Colonel, I don't know what to expect, but I know that as base commander it's my job to anticipate the worst-case scenario. I don't know if Washington is going to order us to hold tight and keep the base secure or go on the offensive. Colonel, in your opinion, do we need to concern ourselves with the possibility of local citizens joining forces with the illegal Mexicans if it comes down to hostilities?

"I've heard that there are groups helping feed those crossing the border, but, General, that's a far cry from aiding them in physical aggression."

"Good point. I think the chance of the base being attacked is close to zero, considering the amount of weapons and trained personnel we have. It seems that anyone who would try that would have to be either stupid or suicidal. However, it also seems like the violence we're hearing about is where the illegals are going after food, and they might figure out that we have stockpiled provisions here. As stupid as it might be to attack a military base, our food supply could still make us a target."

Chapter 56

Located at Nogales Airport, Bob's Aviation Services, an FAA-approved flight-training school, had one of its instructors and a student up at about 1,500 feet. They were seventy-five miles from the outermost marker in a Piper Matrix, cruising at a speed of 213 knots. Mrs. Wilson, one of the students, was flight testing a speedy little number that seated four, and she looked quite comfortable in the left seat.

Into the headset her instructor said, "You're doing fine, Mrs. Wilson. You'll have your license in no time at all. Wait, hold on, I've got the stick, Mrs. Wilson."

"You have control of the aircraft, sir," Mrs. Wilson replied, leaning back and looking toward him for further information. She feared that she'd done something wrong, and it would be a black mark on her flight-training certification.

Instead of critiquing her on a technique error, however, the instructor pointed down toward the ground. He saw what at first glance appeared to be the largest gathering and concentration of livestock in one place that he'd seen in decades.

"The local ranchers must have combined their livestock and are herding them en masse to one of the railroad junctures," he said.

The instructor checked his air space, radioed the tower that he was observing an unusual phenomenon, and requested permission to break his pre-filed flight plan to investigate. After gaining permission to descend, he pointed the nose over and headed toward the livestock for a closer view. As he completed his descent and began his pass toward the livestock, he quickly realized it wasn't livestock at all—it was thousands, maybe tens of thousands, of people on the move. The instructor quickly lost his nerve and started a rapid ascent, sending Mrs. Wilson into a tizzy of panic and befuddling the regional air-traffic controller following his flight path.

"It's a goddamn wave of people," he said to no one in particular. "And they're moving in a northerly direction. Holy crap! What in the world is going on?"

Chapter 57

H-E-B was a superstore of gargantuan size, a Texas-based store that had a reputation greater than Costco's. However, unlike the other big-box stores, H-E-B had in recent years opened stores in Mexico.

In the suburbs of Corpus Christi, Texas, H-E-B had built one of its flagship superstores, and on any given day the store was packed with shoppers. Like most grocery stores, H-E-B stocked their shelves based on the purchases from the local population. Demographics showed that the majority of the shoppers were Mexican-Americans. Even though those from the highest income level in the area were Caucasian, as minority shoppers, they often did not find their favorites on the shelves, which infuriated more than a few customers. Having the most buying power, the Caucasians felt like they were being treated like second-rate citizens. H-E-B tried to balance the wants and needs, but products moving rapidly from their shelves was their number one goal.

Since this particular H-E-B had such a large Hispanic following, its product line matched that of their sister store just over the border. Since this H-E-B was always crowded with Hispanic shoppers, no one seemed to take notice of the increase of shoppers that had filled the store within a span of minutes.

Short lines were one of H-E-B's marketing strategies, and managers were schooled about opening new lines to keep the customers happy. The assistant manager couldn't believe his eyes when he scanned the dairy section to be sure the refrigerated product shelves were well stocked. Shoppers were ripping open packages and wolfing down everything in reach. Some were filling their pockets to overflowing. A man downed an entire half-gallon of milk without pausing for a breath. Another opened up a carton of sour cream and scooped the white, creamy goo into his mouth with his hands. A chubby woman grabbed an armload of cheddar cheese blocks and stuffed them into her backpack while eating Slim Jims without removing the wrappers.

Disgusted, the assistant manager stormed off to find their one security guard. Then he realized it would be fruitless to get the guard; the same event was transpiring in every single department. He slowly walked to his office, sat down at his desk, picked up the receiver on his phone, and dialed 911.

After a few rings, an automated voice came on the line and explained that all resources were stretched beyond capacity and that if he still needed help he should select from the following choices. The announcement was repeated, but this time in Spanish. He selected *one*, indicating an immediate need for assistance, and a voice said that due to an unusually large call volume, he would need to leave his name and number at the beep, or if there was a more urgent need, an Internet link would send an e-mail to the dispatcher.

The store manager hung up, beyond incredulous. He laid his weary head down on his desk, covering it with his hands. Succumbing to the pressure of the riot and the major loss to the daily till, all he wanted to do was scream. But first, out came a bottle of the store's most expensive wine from his bottom desk drawer. He realized that today was a career-ending day. Like the marauders who vandalized his store, he too had stolen from his own bottom line. But he deserved it, he convinced himself. His only regret? He was drinking alone.

The riot continued until the store was almost stripped bare, and like a herd of wild buffalo, the mob turned as one and stampeded toward its next objective.

Just when the employees thought things couldn't get any worse, a couple of the rougher-looking Mexican men realized they had forgotten one last valuable: the cash in the registers. Brandishing the baseball bats and various poles and rods they had picked up at the store, they one by one confronted each of the cashiers and demanded all the money.

Up until that point, the lone security guard had decided it was best to keep out of the way. He felt there really wasn't much he could do with so many people partaking in the stealing, and at least thus far no one had threatened violence. But when he saw one of the young Mexican men waving his baseball bats at one of the cashiers, threatening to hit him if he didn't open the cash register, he pulled his revolver and confronted the young man.

A stupid mistake.

Before he even realized what had hit him, a gang of Mexicans pounced on him and quickly beat him to death with the various odd weapons. One proud Mexican held up the guard's revolver as he ran from the store.

Chapter 58

Satiated from his high-calorie lunch at one of the better joints downtown and still basking in his own glory from a very successful morning, Cliff was laid out supine with his feet propped up on his desk. His rotund, overweight body stressed his fancy, high-dollar office chair practically to its breaking point. Cliff had a flair for casualness and had raised it to an art form that irritated his bosses to no end, but because his production rate was so phenomenal, they gave him a long leash.

Cliff employed all the tools of his trade and enjoyed being on the cutting edge of technology. His junk-drawer collection would be the wet dream of most techies if he ever shared. Cliff brazenly sported the most expensive Bluetooth headset, which he wore every second of his office hours. At $999.99, his new top-of-the-line AKG in-ear Bluetooth had a range that put its competitors to shame. Since he was on the phone nonstop when the market was open, he considered his Bluetooth a tool of the trade that separated the big boys from the mice that ate his crumbs.

Man, he thought. *I am alive today!*

Speaking to a client, Cliff said, "Yes sir, another record day for Morgan Stanley, so say a prayer to thank God and the Fed Chairman for keeping interest rates ridiculously low. Bless our friends at the US Bureau of Engraving and Printing in DC for having the American dollar rolling off of the presses nonstop." He chuckled. "My God, I love America!"

Cliff stroked his client a bit more but never took his eyes off the lights on his monitors indicating stock activity. The twinkling lights on his twin monitors looked like miniature Christmas lights dancing their merry little hearts out, just for him. For Cliff, every day was Christmas, and he was good ole Saint Nick giving goodies to all the boys and girls. However, he had another side that his clients never saw; he was Grinch-like and a spoiler for a fight.

The lights on his monitors spoke to Cliff like a beautiful mistress cooing in his ear. Cliff was the master to her slave and was both brutal and brilliant, causing pain as well as pleasure; he was in control. This combination made Cliff feared by his cohorts but a very rich man. After all, in this business, he was a god.

"What? No, I haven't heard much more than you about the Mexican-border problem. Yeah, it can't be that serious. The stock market hasn't fluctuated in response. Yeah, yeah, yeah. I've heard those rumors, too. But hell, it's roughly 350 miles from Houston to the closest border crossing, so I'm not too worried. Shit, I assume that Mexico may try to annex a few of the border cities like Harlingen and Brownsville. Shit, it's nothing but fucking Mexicans anyway, but they'll be unsuccessful. What's that? Right, now that you mention it, I guess we stole the whole state of Texas from them back in the Mexican-American War. But this is America, and you don't annex or overrun America. Man, John, the military is liable to nuke the shit out of Mexico if it blinks. Hey, John, I got to go take a piss. Call me back tomorrow, and we'll see how those trades worked out."

Cliff hightailed it to his favorite downtown Houston bar, Grand Prize, for cocktails with his other broker buddies. Happy-hour drink prices and the catfish and spicy slaw with queso fresco drove Cliff crazy. Hands down, Cliff was the biggest lush among the group, and after winning the competition to see who could eat and drink the most, he rose unsteadily to his feet and headed toward the front door and home.

Cliff was way past tipsy, and his normally outlandish personality had succumbed to all the alcohol. He clapped his hands, getting everyone's attention in the room, and shouted, "Yippee ki-yay...motherfuckers." He turned, nearly losing his balance, and stumbled through the front door on his way out.

One of his buddies said to no one in particular, "Man, old Cliff's gone from obnoxious to way out of control. Someday it's going to bite him in the ass."

As Cliff's car rolled up the driveway and into the garage, his mind was on the next two nights with his buddies. He couldn't wait. On Thursday and Friday nights, the usual suspects gathered at The Men's Club for a little drinking and a lot of debauchery. Cliff thought The Men's Club was Houston's best titty bar, and he always spent too much money there. But luckily for him, The Men's Club had an ATM filled with one-dollar bills so he could flirt and tease the girls.

The words drooled out of Cliff's mouth as he wobbled through the garage after parking his car at a crazy angle in the garage. Skipping through the garage like a little elementary kid, he sang, "Oh, I'm so lucky, oh, so lucky. Cha, cha, cha! Cha, cha, cha-ching! Oh, man, am I funny or what?"

He banged through the connecting door from the garage.

"Debbie, I'm home, where is everyone, what's for dinner? Man, I could eat a forty-eight-ounce cowboy rib eye with all the fixings. Hey, I'm starved. What does the breadwinner need to do to get some service around his own home?"

Just about then, Cliff's two daughters, Marcie and Chelsea, came bounding into the entryway from one of the back bedrooms. Being twins they often spoke at the same time in unison. "Daddy, Daddy—you *won't* believe what happened at school today. There was a big fight. It was really cool."

"Okay, okay, you two, let me get a beer and then you can tell me the whole story. Debbie! Debbie! Hey, girls, where the hell is your mother?" He popped the top on his favorite Teas Shiner Bock brewed beer and flopped into a lounge chair.

Allowing her dad to take a long pull on his beer, Marcie started, "It was like super cool. All anybody could talk about in school today was about how a bunch of Mexicans broke through the border down near Harlingen, Brownsville, and McAllen. I heard they ransacked a bunch of stores and destroyed a small strip mall. Wow, I hope something like that happens here. Wouldn't it be cool?"

Chelsea gave her sister a dirty look and said, "You and your crazy punk-ass friends are sickos. I don't know how you can find it anything but disgusting. Dad, can you imagine how disgusting it would be if a bunch of Mexicans ransacked stores near us?"

"Fuck you!" Marcie retorted.

"God dammit, Marcie, you're not allowed to use that kind of language in the house," Cliff barked. "You'd be in deep shit if your mother heard you talking that way."

Chelsea shot Marcie a middle finger salute. "My sister's a loser. She only cares about, clothes, sports, cheerleading, shopping, and boys! What a frickin' loser—she and her bowhead friends get squeamish at the thought of a little lawbreaking. Personally, I think it's totally awesome!"

Cliff had had enough and reached for the TV remote, hoping to find something on his 255-plus channels that would short circuit the battle of the twins.

"Hold on, ladies, I thought you said there was a fight at school today. What was the fight about? Why did you say it was cool?

This time it was Chelsea who beat Marcie to the punch. "Some of the Mexicans at school made a few posters, nailed them to broom handles, and paraded around the school building. They said stuff like 'Viva Zapatista' and 'Viva de Revolution,' and there were two that made the football players madder than a hornet's nest on fire: 'Return Texas to Mexico!,' and 'Don't Mess with Texas,' but with 'Texas' crossed out and replaced with 'Mexico.'

"There was even a rumor that one of our Mexican students was going to borrow his father's pickup truck, fill it with food, and drive down to McAllen to feed illegals that had crossed our borders. When he marched, sign in hand, by a few of the football players, they taught him not to mess with Texas. It took most of the PE teachers to rescue the Mexican student. I don't think he'll be protesting anytime soon."

Marcie had been not so patiently cooling her jets, pacing back and forth, and Cliff could almost see steam rising from her ears. "Yeah, Dad, it was awesome. A huge fight broke out, and it went from name calling to pushing to rock throwing. Then one of the Mexicans pulled a knife on Ted. Boy, that was a mistake. You know Ted, Dad—he's a linebacker or something on the football team and he's a giant. Before the Mexican with the knife knew what hit him, Ted had picked him up and threw him against the lockers. From there, the riot began, and they moved outside. Someone yelled 'They're going to take down the flag.' OMG, Dad, I thought the world was—"

At that moment, Debbie walked into the living room. She could almost taste the tension in the room. "What's all the commotion? Girls, can't you carry on a conversation without shouting?" She turned to Cliff, who had escaped to his wet bar and was rummaging around in the mini fridge for another Shiner Bock beer but only finding crap he wouldn't serve to a dead dog. Debbie gave him a laser-beam stare that would have cut through eight inches of steel plate. "When did you get home?"

"Dammit, Debbie, I thought I told you to quit buying that crap light beer. You know I hate that shit. Light beer is for women, homos, and metrosexual types. If you're going to buy that crap, keep it in the refrigerator in the garage. Don't mess up my wet bar with that pansy, tasteless crap."

Still feeling a bit groggy from his earlier drinking session with his buddies, Cliff turned to Debbie and, using his best operatic voice, sang out, "Fewer calories, less filling, fewer calories, less filling," quickly changing his voice from a deep bass to a high-pitched falsetto.

Then he started doing his best imitation of an old male ballet dancer, Mikhail Baryshnikov. Cliff, at 250 pounds of pure beer belly and fat, was an ugly sight at best. Debbie could only thank God the curtains were drawn, sparing the neighbors a view of Cliff's most embarrassing moments. Debbie realized that Cliff was once again drunk, shot him another look to kill, and out of complete disgust turned and headed for the kitchen.

"Pops, you're weird," Chelsea said. "What if one of my friends had looked in the window and seen you dancing around? I would've been mortified." With that, she stomped out of the room.

However, it was Marcie who seemed to be the most upset. Being an outcast, Marcie hung around with all the other outcasts, weirdoes, punk rockers, and cult-seeking students at Memorial High. Marcie had friends that were homosexuals and some that were transvestites.

"Dad, why do you always have to make fun of homosexuals? They're just people like you and me. They just have different preferences and are harmless."

Cliff's fun had come to a screeching halt, and he resented that his nightly buzz was being spoiled. "Don't give me that liberal, everything's-acceptable crap. Remember, I pay the bills around here, and like I've told you before, don't you dare bring any tattooed, body-pierced fruitcake pieces of crap or one of those fudge packers into my house! If I find one here, you'll be living in a trailer park paying your own expenses. Act like trash, and you'll live like trash. Remember that, girly!"

Marcie felt like she'd been slapped. She couldn't even raise her eyes to meet her father's glare. Her father was out of control, and she was not going to cry or show any weakness. To do so would send her Dad into a roaring tear. Marcie lowered her head, mumbled something about homework, and slunk away.

Ah, Cliff felt powerful. He knew Debbie was in for a rough night in the bedroom.

Chapter 59

Alfred had screwed up, and to get back into his wife's good graces, he decided to mow the lawn before she could give him another round of sarcastic comments. She'd been nagging him for days to mow the lawn, so he decided to get up at the crack of dawn and mow the lawn before most of his family was up. He decided to start in the backyard since it was the longest. *Crap,* he thought, *first I need to move a couple of the kids' toys out of the way.* The plastic playhouse from Toys"R"Us had to be moved, for one thing. Though it looked heavy, it was made of hollow panels, so it was easy for him to push it around. It weighed about forty pounds, and Alfred, being a big guy, went up to it and gave it the good old college try. But instead of the playhouse moving, he bounced off it and fell to the lawn with a large thump. Shaking his head, he tried to figure out why he'd failed to budge the plastic structure. Suddenly, six Mexicans, three men and three women, crawled out of the tiny playhouse entrance. Apparently, they had been sleeping in there, and he had awakened them. They appeared to be illegals, from their threadbare clothing and thin, emaciated faces. They had found refuge from the cold desert night air in his children's playhouse.

The Mexicans looked startled to see Alfred. Quickly they gathered their wits and started to rush toward the back gate. But Alfred wasn't going to let these trespassers get away without a tongue lashing and then some. Alfred spied an old garden rake and grabbed it as he lurched after them.

At that very moment, Alfred's wife, Gloria, opened the window facing the back of their house to see what all the hubbub was about. Gloria's timing couldn't have been worse. Alfred had cornered one of the Mexicans and was preparing to whack him with the garden rake. But the much younger Mexican man had pulled a pocketknife that Alfred hadn't seen. As Alfred reared back to gain momentum on his swing, the Mexican lunged forward and planted the knife directly into

Alfred's plump neck. Gloria saw the blood spurt from her husband's neck and started screaming hysterically. Panic set in as Alfred fell limply to the ground. Gloria never saw the intruders exit through the gate.

Chapter 60

Fran Babicz, President Denton's press secretary, was perfect for the job. She had been *the* press secretary at the state department for years, where she had perfected the art of saying a lot of nothing while doing and saying whatever it took to protect the secretary of state and the state department.

Fran Babicz had been groomed and for bigger and better postings since proving herself a team player. Fran had kept the press at arm's length during a particularly embarrassing moment for the state department concerning Israel during the Obama administration. Her spin on the truth had short-circuited what would have been called "Sanction-Gate." Obama had once again shown his dislike for Benjamin Netanyahu and Israel and leveled sanctions on Israel for some minor infraction.

Fran had been asked to stay on by President Denton and serve as her press secretary because of her phenomenal talent for shit slinging. She had been a godsend, too, and one of the reasons President Obama had been one of the liberal media's favorite presidents. She could sling shit and spin it with the best. She had a plaque on her desk, facing away from anyone who entered her domain, that read: SHIT IN, SHIT OUT. That was the standing order for any press secretary. Hers was the face of the presidency. Without a doubt, she took *all* the flak from an angry, mean press and in response disseminated false rumors to misdirect bad attention from the presidency. As the press secretary, it wasn't Fran's job to like the man or woman in office. The press secretary was the whipping boy and ultimate scapegoat for anything the president said that was off topic, stupid, or nonfactual. Also, like her predecessors, she knew where all the political bodies were buried. The White House employed a staff of spin doctors who would voluntarily throw themselves under the bus, ultimately taking full blame for any misspeak, and all were well paid.

However, after the herculean effort it had taken to cover, sanitize, or apologize for all the lies from Obama's administration, and now President Denton's administration, Fran did her best to keep the desks filled with qualified lapdogs. Dancing with the devil the way she did was very stressful, and not many had the cojones to keep the razzle-dazzle going.

Fran entered the White House pressroom and immediately went to the podium. Without missing a beat, she began to speak. During her years in office, she'd spent hours in front of the mirror practicing and perfecting the official neutral-but-intelligent look. The look was somewhere between an intense, honest expression and a poker player's bullshitters' face. Today, she needed the look more than ever because once again, she'd been hung out to dry by the president.

"Before I open this up to questions, President Denton would like me to assure the American public that the situation in our southern border states is not as alarming as many in the media would have you believe. There is evidence, though it's not been confirmed, that there have been some breaches at some of the US-Mexican border entry points. But let me repeat that you can rest assured that we have taken immediate steps to close those breaches and return the entry points to their original effective status.

"Yes, the president won't deny that a few Mexicans took advantage and crossed illegally into the United States without being adequately screened when a few border crossings stations were not functioning at maximum capacity. We are still unsure, at this point, how many were undocumented, but the numbers are very manageable.

"There are accusations and rumors flying around, but, as you know, President Denton deals only in fact, not accusation or rumor.

"In just the last few days the president has spoken personally with the president of Mexico several times, and he has assured our president that on his side of the border all is well and under control. In addition, he has offered to take whatever steps necessary to help us secure our borders.

"Also, I'm pleased to report that even as we speak the Mexican economy is on the path to substantial improvement and is reestablishing itself as a world player.

"The Denton administration is working very closely with each of the border states' governors and has promised full cooperation in whatever they feel is needed for the protection of the Mexican-American border. We have assured the governors that the federal government will do whatever is necessary to buoy up and secure their state's borders."

Surveying the room, Fran saw the smiling faces of a sycophantic press. "Once again, the president would like me to assure every American citizen that there is no reason to panic. The situation is in hand. In conclusion, thank you, and I only have time for a few questions."

For the next fifteen minutes, Fran worked her perfected art. Rapunzel in her tower couldn't have spun a more golden weave. She called on one reporter after another, always making sure it was a *friendly reporter,* soft on the president's administration. The secret was not to allow any outside, controversial questions. The White House press corps had already handed to the major networks an outline of Fran's speech. As usual, they provided the reporters the same, as well as suggested questions. Everything was going as scripted. Fran had learned this tactic while working in the Obama administration and the state department. It had worked well and was going even better today.

Fran was doing an excellent job of avoiding the reporter that was assigned to the White House from Fox News. Ed Henry had been a thorn in the White House's side under the Obama administration, and being an up-and-coming reporter for Fox News, he would need to make his bones. There was even talk that he one day might replace Bret Baer as anchor of Fox's evening news show *Special Report with Bret Baer.*

Hopefully Ed wasn't holding his breath. Bret Baer had no intention of retiring soon, and his lucrative contract kept him in the good-life.

Unfortunately for Fran, one can only avoid Fox News so long. Ed Henry had now built up a reputation as such a good, hardworking, honest reporter and even the liberal station reporters were starting to notice that Fran was avoiding him.

"Yes, Ed," Fran said as she pointed at him and took an unnoticeable deep breath while smiling.

"Fran, Fox News has received a written document from Arizona's Maricopa County sheriff, Joe Arpaio, indicating that Tucson is within a day of being completely overrun by hordes of illegals who have entered en masse and in force.

"Now, using your words, 'A few Mexicans took advantage and crossed illegally, without being adequately screened,' into the United States. Fran, how do you compare Sheriff Joe's communication and the Oval Office's shameful whitewashing of the real situation?"

"I'm sorry, Ed, I'm running out of time, but I will try to address your question the best I can. Our administration, and previously the Obama administration, has never agreed with the racist opinions of Sheriff Joe Arpaio and to some degree of the Arizona governor, Jacqueline Brewmeister. Neither the president nor I are going to respond to individuals who are just trying to inflame racial tensions and scare communities into panicking. Thank you for coming. Check the schedule for the next scheduled briefing."

Chapter 61

"Shit!" Willie exclaimed as another big bug splattered against the windshield of his Peterbilt 386 cab. Reminded of his favorite joke, he reached for his old, faithful CB radio microphone so he could share it with someone on the road. "Breaker, breaker, this is Little Willie on the I-10 headed for the Dome." The Dome was trucker lingo for Houston, Texas.

Willie continued, "Have I got some humor for you tonight, come back." Willie waited until a trucker replied.

"You've got Daddy Longlegs here. Headed for the Alamo." This was trucker speak for San Antonio, Texas. "Go ahead, good buddy. I'm headed down the way in a cow wagon on your six, back atcha."

Willie's heart warmed at the use of truckers' slang; it fit well with his personality.

'*Cow wagon.*' *Now there's a name that says it with simple grace,* thought Willie. His CB friend was hauling a cattle trailer. "Ten-four, copy," replied Willie. "Okay, friend, here goes—my all-time favorite joke.

"What is the last thing that goes through a bug's mind as it hits the windshield of a truck at seventy-five miles an hour? Come back and give me a holler." A few seconds of dead air turned into a minute plus, so Willie picked up the mic and said, "Hey, you got peanut butter in your ears, friend?"

Daddy Longlegs replied, "No, I had to pass a stagecoach being a road hog. Okay, I give, what's the last thing that goes through a bug's mind as it hits your windshield at seventy-five miles an hour? Come back."

Willie savored the few seconds of superiority, knowing the answer before replying. "His ass!" he replied and broke into heavy laughter.

Willie could hear the hacking laugh of a lifelong smoker over his CB's speaker. "Well, good buddy, you got me there," said Daddy Longlegs. "Thanks for sharing the humor. I'm down." Daddy Longlegs signed off, and only dead air remained. The exchange had lasted a mere three or four minutes but put Willie in a good mood. He returned to his previous thoughts about his rig. It sported the latest Paccar MX-13 engine. She was a beauty and William "Willie" Crawford was a fanatic about keeping his new eighteen wheeler clean. It was his pride and joy, his home away from home. Actually, his rig had cost more than his home and his beat-up F-150 combined.

He had just filled up at Love's Truck City and spent twenty minutes spraying off all the bug juice from his all-night travels in the self-serve truck wash. Willie had driven the I-10 from Los Angeles to Houston so many times that he wished he could set his rig on autopilot to drive itself while he snoozed. It was a monotonous and boring route. Each trip he hoped to find something interesting along the way. Even a new roadside billboard would be preferable to the same old, same old. He had dissected, analyzed, questioned, and cursed each mile along the route.

Willie noticed it was getting dark, and he flipped on his running lights, virtually turning his truck into a "rooster cruiser." That was Willie's other passion, lights. He'd put so many running lights all over his cab and trailer that it looked like an amusement park on wheels, all lit up. His truck had so many lights that people riding in the next lane could read a book while driving alongside.

A few hours earlier, on the other side of El Paso, a fruit company had loaded Willie's truck to the brim with cantaloupes and watermelons. Willie had pushed the speed limit because he wanted to be on the other side of El Paso before dark. He was now going into the graveyard shift, as he called it, which meant he would be making the ten-hour drive from El Paso to Houston in the dark. The good news was that meant fewer cars and cops.

But he hated going through the big interchanges around major cities when it was dark. Doing so hadn't bothered him so much when he was younger, but he found now, as he got older, the glare from approaching vehicles give him a bit of night blindness.

Willie thought his eyes were failing him; he could've sworn he saw on the interstate some distance ahead of him a bunch of people rushing across the highway. He thought, *Am I hallucinating? Shit, I can't be that tired. I just got started.*

But he saw nothing else strange and figured it must be his eyes playing tricks on him.

"Hey, what's that?"

Once again, somewhere in the distance at the end of his bright lights' reach, he saw what looked like something crossing the road. He couldn't tell if it was people or cattle or debris. Willie couldn't imagine what reason would cause people to be running across a major interstate in the dark. Maybe somebody's cattle fence had busted, and the cattle had gotten out and were wandering on the highway. In Willie's years of long-haul trucking, he had seen cattle on the highway a time or two.

A convoy of trucks came barreling down I-10 going in the other direction, and their lights illuminated the superhighway.

"Holy shit!" Willie yelled, at the same time almost losing his grip on the steering wheel. The lights of the approaching trucks had illuminated a sight beyond belief. People, hundreds of them, swarming. They seemed to be everywhere, on both sides of the highway. Some had managed to get onto the median and were encouraging others to join them. Willie had been distracted by the movements on the roadway and had failed to notice that the highway had suddenly turned into a parking lot. Standing on the brake pedal to stop his truck, shouting, "Holy Fuck!" Willie nearly rear-ended the stopped minivan in front of him.

Without warning, as if floodgates somewhere had opened up, there were people everywhere, milling about. In a tsunami-like wave, they kept coming, advancing. Willie felt butterflies in his stomach. Never had he, or anyone else for that matter, witnessed such a swelling of people. Within minutes, the entire interstate was blocked in both directions. Everything had come to a screeching halt, and crowds had formed around his truck and the other vehicles as well. Willie heard a sound like breaking metal, but it was too dark, even with his fancy running lights, to see anything of reason.

Even though Willie weighed upward of three hundred pounds and had never feared anyone or anything in his entire life, he was positively at a loss. *Who are these people? Why are they blocking the highway? Where are the frickin' police?* He reached for his CB to call for help. Depressing the button, he got nothing but static. Then it struck him—the breaking-metal noise had been the antenna being broken off his rig. He couldn't communicate with anyone, and his cell phone was in a no-service area. *Holy crap,* he thought, *What's next?*

But Willie remembered one of the nice features of his Peterbilt 386. The bottom of his cab door was taller than most people, so he was above the hordes of wandering people. Still, he needed to get underway and away from this ticking time bomb of humanity. He opened the door and climbed up a rung of the ladder to his electronics package on the cab roof.

"Get the fuck away from my truck!" he yelled, but it was such a madhouse that no one noticed.

He quickly climbed on top of his cab to get a better view of what was going on. Willie couldn't see more than a few feet ahead, due to the dark, but luckily none of the cars or trucks that had stopped had turned off their headlights. He did a 360-degree look around and cried out, "Oh, my God, there ain't hundreds out here—there's thousands." Willie even thought there could be more out beyond the reach of the lights.

About then, a ruckus at the back end of his trailer reached his ears. People were opening the back door. He climbed back down into his cab and pulled out the Taurus 608. It was a stainless steel .357 Magnum. At 8.375 inches with a ported barrel, it was an intimidating revolver. He had been stashing the gun under his seat for decades, waiting for just such an emergency. He sure hoped it worked; he hadn't shot the damn thing since the last time he'd visited his cousin's place in the country eleven years ago. The same cartridges that he'd loaded eleven years ago were still in the chamber.

Willie hitched up his britches, climbed back on top of the cab, and unloaded two shells into the night air. He might as well have shot off a cap pistol; the only ones who heard the explosive shells go off were clinging to the front of his cab. Willie swirled around in time to see people running away from his truck, not in fear for their lives but because they had emptied his load.

Every one of those suckers is carrying at least two or three melons, my melons.

He thought about shooting a couple of them, but then he noticed that every truck within view had been busted into, and the masses were hauling away all their goods too. As he focused on the receding crowds, Willie realized something he hadn't noticed before. Every goddamn single one of these thousands of people was Mexican. The second thing he noticed was that they were only stealing from trucks carrying food.

My God, the rumors are true.

Chapter 62

Elizabeth Walther was listening to her favorite gospel show on the radio while cleaning house. At the top of the hour, there was some news, something about problems in southern Arizona and the movement of illegal Mexicans heading north toward Tucson. She couldn't quite hear all of the details because she was in the other room running the vacuum cleaner, but she remembered that her husband, Mark, had said something that morning about border problems.

The phone rang. It was Barbara, one of her neighbors and her best friend from church. "Oh, Elizabeth, have you heard the news about what's going on in the southern part of the state?"

Elizabeth told her what Mark had said about the problem that morning and what she had heard on the radio.

Barbara shared her own news after Elizabeth had finished. "What I've heard is that a lot of people are getting scared and rushing to the grocery stores to stock up. I thought I'd go, but I wanted to see if you wanted to go with me. I'm a little frightened to go out by myself."

Elizabeth agreed that it was a good idea, and they made plans to go. Barbara volunteered to pick her up in a few minutes.

As the two of them got closer to the neighborhood Safeway, they couldn't help but notice that there was somewhat of a traffic jam ahead. After a few minutes without making any progress, they realized that all the traffic was stalled, waiting to get into the Safeway's parking lot. It seemed everyone in the neighborhood had had the same idea at the same time. The two women decided it was best to park on the street and not even try to get into the parking lot.

But if they thought the traffic jam was unusual, what they saw inside the store was bizarre. It looked like a game show where the contestants were given thirty seconds to grab off the shelves as much as they could. It was mostly women running frantically around, grabbing anything and everything edible. It was sheer pandemonium. No one paid any attention to what they were grabbing, throwing items into their carts and going back for more.

The shelves had been decimated, some fallen to the floor, others bent from being stood on to reach items on higher shelves. What products were left weren't edible.

Barbara turned to Elizabeth and said, "Go see what you can grab in the dairy department, I'll see if there's anything left in the meat department, and then let's meet in the bakery aisle."

There was only one cart left, and as Elizabeth and Barbara reached for it, a heavyset woman knocked Elizabeth aside and said, "Oh, no you don't, honey pot!" and jerked the cart from her hands. She flipped Elizabeth the bird and said, "Tough luck, chickies! Find another one!" She turned to leave, but she didn't get far.

Barbara, pushed past her limit, suddenly caught up with the rude woman, spun her around, and punched her in the nose. As the shrieking women grabbed her face, Elizabeth grabbed the cart with one hand and Barbara with the other and said, "Come on, Barbara, let's go!"

Horrified at her violent reaction, Barbara broke into tears as she trotted to keep up with Elizabeth.

"Oh, God, forgive me," said Barbara. "I can't believe it. I hit that woman in anger. I've never hit someone so hard. My goodness, is her nose is still bleeding?"

"I don't know, but it doesn't matter. She deserved it," Elizabeth responded. "We've gotta hurry—there's hardly anything left on the shelves."

Ten minutes later, the two women rendezvoused in the bakery aisle. Barbara had been unsuccessful in the meat department, except that she had managed to grab about eight packages of cold cuts including salami and bologna.

"There was no meat," she said to Elizabeth.

Shocked, Elizabeth said, "If there was no meat, how did you get this salami and bologna?"

"I stole it out of somebody else's cart."

"First you go Muhammad Ali on that obnoxious lady, and now you've stolen food out of somebody else's cart. That's not very Christian."

"Elizabeth, this is not the time to go all Holy Roller on me. I'm not the Bible scholar you are, but I've read enough to know that God helps those who help themselves. It's pretty obvious that if we're going to get out of here with any food, it's going to be a dog-eat-dog battle." Barbara smiled darkly. "Dog is what we might be eating if we can't get any more food."

They both turned their attention to the bread department but found that hot dog buns were all that remained. Barbara grabbed them and threw them into the cart.

"We don't have any hot dogs. Why are you grabbing those buns?" Elizabeth asked.

"Elizabeth, we don't have the luxury of being picky. What do you think a hot dog is made of anyway? It's made of the same pig snouts as that bologna in the cart."

Just then, a woman with a blond ponytail grabbed Elizabeth's right arm and yanked her away from the cart, while a woman with short red hair tried to knock Barbara to the side. Barbara, however, regained her balance, shoved the redhead hard to the floor, grabbed the cart, and rammed it into the blonde, who was still struggling with Elizabeth. Miss Ponytail yelped in surprise and pain as she landed squarely into the remaining hot dog buns, crashing the picnic display to the floor. Barbara and Elizabeth wasted no time in racing the cart out of the store to their car, never stopping to pay. It wasn't until the food was in the trunk and the car doors locked that the two women were finally able to catch their breath. Now it was Elizabeth who started crying while Barbara couldn't stop laughing.

"That was the most fun I've had in years," Barbara said. "Want to go again?"

"Oh, no you don't," pleaded Elizabeth. "We need to get home as fast as we can." Still crying, she told Barbara more bad news. "I ran into one of the Safeway store managers when we were separated and asked him when they'd stock the shelves again. He said that trucks coming from the south were no longer running. They've been rerouted to come in from the north, but it will take a week before they'll arrive."

"What are we going to do if we run out of food?"

Elizabeth couldn't quit shaking. "Mark's in the trucking business. I'll call him as soon as we get home and see what he thinks."

The two women sped off with their ill-gotten treasures, heading for the safety of home. Seeing all those people at the store in such a frenzy had been very unsettling.

"Yea, though I walk through the valley of the Safeway of death," Elizabeth said, "I will fear no overweight or aggressive woman: for thou art with me. Thy pretzel rod and thy foodstuff, they comfort me and deliver me a twenty-pound ham. Amen."

Barbara looked over at her. "Elizabeth! Isn't that blasphemous?"

Elizabeth smiled, and despite their harried experience, they both broke out in laughter, releasing the tension of the past hour. Shopping at Safeway would never be the same again.

Chapter 63

"Elizabeth—Elizabeth, honey, please calm down. Honey, you're talking too fast. I can't understand anything you're saying. Tell me again what happened at the grocery store?"

Elizabeth, half crying, half laughing, relayed the entire story to Mark once again, including the manager's comment about the delay in food deliveries, but this time more calmly and slowly.

"Well, I'm not surprised. Safeway has its own truckers' union, and they carry a lot of clout. They've been calling here repeatedly, asking us if we could be of help. There are rumors circulating that some trucking unions are going to refuse to drive into Texas, New Mexico, and Arizona, and that may include parts of Southern California, as well."

Mark's comments were not calming Elizabeth down. "What does all this mean? What's going to happen to us? Mark, what's happening?"

"Honey, get a hold of yourself. At this point, it's the wild rumors that are panicking the public. It's not like hordes of Mexicans have broken into the grocery stores and stolen all the food. Honey, it's exactly the opposite. Look, Elizabeth, all it took was one person thinking they should stock up on food, and now there's a panic run on grocery stores in the border states. Trust me, if everyone had stayed calm and rational, this would've never happened."

"But I've heard that it's more than rumors now. Barbara heard that Governor Brewmeister was talking to Washington about calling out the National Guard to protect Tucson. Why isn't the governor sending the National Guard here? There's a lot more people in Phoenix than Tucson. I would think she'd want to save her largest city!" Elizabeth's voice broke. "I think you should come home immediately, and let's take Madeleine and little Ricky and drive north as fast as we can. At least until everything settles back down."

"Please, Elizabeth, you have to calm down. Try to put this in perspective. You just ran into a very bad situation at the Safeway. Honey, I can assure you everything is fine. So far, we've had a limited number of our truckers call in with any problems. Though I don't have a lot of confidence in Washington, I have a lot of confidence in our governor, and I'm sure she's going to be on top of this. Now look. Before I tell you what I want you to do, are Madeleine and Ricky at home?"

"Yes."

"Great, don't let them leave. Now, you know all the milk jugs you've been saving for the greenhouse that you keeping pestering me to build? Fill every one of them up with water. As a matter of fact, fill every bottle, bucket, and container you can find to the brim with water."

"But I don't understand," she implored. "We have plenty of water. It's food that we may run out of sooner than later."

Mark tried to slow his voice down, hoping it would have a soothing effect on his wife, who was sounding like she was going to have a nervous breakdown. "Look, honey, I want to congratulate you for your initiative at the grocery store. You were really using your head. But let's, for a minute, assume that things do get worse. I remember the three basics rules I was taught in Scouts: food, water, and shelter. It seems impossible that somehow Phoenix's water resources could get contaminated or cut off, but grab Madeleine to help fill up all of those containers! I've spent my entire day resolving issues with this person and that person, this company and that company. There's one more thing I must resolve before I can leave. Oh, and something else—close all the blinds and lock all the doors."

Mark hated himself for the last words he'd said, knowing that they would just add fuel to the fire. Mark had lied to his wife about his knowledge of the situation and the danger that may arrive at their doorstep soon. He rarely even stretched the truth unless it was an emergency. This was such an emergency; his wife was clearly panicked and he did not want to exacerbate the situation for her.

"Believe me," Mark said to himself. "This is one big lie compounded by other lies on top of lies." He couldn't tell Elizabeth the truth, that the governor's office had already put out an emergency request to all Arizona trucking companies earlier in the day. The request had been simple:

- Avoid all routes south of Interstate 10

- Ask all drivers to arm themselves

- Accelerate all deliveries that include foodstuffs

- Reassign all trucks from nonessentials to medical and food supplies

- Report all highway problems to the governor's office immediately.

Chapter 64

Later that same day, Mark found time to call his brother Craig, who spoke with a voice barely concealing his irritation.

"Well, I haven't heard from you in quite a while. How is the trucking business with all that is going on at the border?"

"It's not like your phone's broken. Couldn't you pick up the phone and call? I haven't heard from you, either. You're so damn oversensitive about everything."

"I'm oversensitive? You're the one with the damn chip on your shoulder, being the older brother and everything."

"I could care less about being your brother. It's always about you, Mr. Know-It-All, Mr. College Professor. You think you're superior to us flunkies who don't have a PhD. You know what 'PhD' stands for? Well, think! It stands for 'piled higher and deeper!'"

There was dead air on the phone for a few seconds, and Craig thought that it would probably be better to hang up. Instead he said, "I'm going to assume that you didn't call to mend the differences that we never seem to mend. Look, Mark, I'm busy these days, so if you have something to say, say it. If you don't, just hang up."

Mark was not willing to back down so quickly. "Oh, you think you're the only one who's busy. I can tell you that being in the trucking business right now is a madhouse. I've got to tell you, the drivers are spooked and probably with reasonable cause."

"Mark, that's something I'd like to talk to you about—if we can bury the hatchet and call it a truce," Craig responded.

"Sorry, I guess I started this call all wrong. I apologize. Man, I've just been under a lot of stress lately. Elizabeth went to Safeway to stock up on supplies and wouldn't you know it? Every woman in the neighborhood had the same idea. With the combination of panicking women and a mob mentality, it turned into quite a brawl. You know Elizabeth often takes things to the extreme. So listen, one thing that she has done has been to create a seventy-two-hour emergency kit for each of us. In a backpack, each of us has enough supplies for shelter, food, and water for three days. Extra prescriptions for a week, first aid kit, and solar-powered radio. She also hoards food. I think we have enough brown sugar and flour to bake two hundred cakes. Her goal was to store a year's supply of the basics. It was the Mormons who started this whole thing, but the federal government, ever since Katrina, put it on its preparedness website. Craig, don't repeat this to Elizabeth, but I might finally have to appreciate her hoarding.

"But that's not why I called. Since you're an expert on the Mexican border problem, I thought you might be able to enlighten me. I need to know what I'm sending my guys into if they go south."

"I wish I could, big brother, but I recently talked to both a US senator and one of the more senior generals in the Pentagon. Like you, they were calling me for information. As best as I can tell you, there are hundreds if not thousands of Mexicans streaming across the border as we speak. All ports of entry are completely disabled, and all barriers or fencing have been torn down. The invaders are now just waltzing into the country."

"Have you talked to Dave at his office at the US Border Patrol? He should be able to give us all the updated information."

"Yes, I've talked to Dave, and he has more knowledge than anybody about the situation along the border, but it appears that every federal department is scrambling to do the CYA routine rather than dealing with the problem. The word went out about keeping a tight lid on communication, so everyone is afraid to talk. The last I heard from Dave was that his division was abandoning its headquarters and getting on the road to reestablishing their office in Los Angeles."

"They've pulled out of San Diego?" Mark sat back in his chair and pounded his fist on the table.

"I spoke with Dave the other day during one of his few breaks, and he didn't know why the information was on a need-to-know basis. He did indicate that, because of the large military presence in San Diego, most of the illegal Mexican invaders were avoiding there and moving to points north from there. I understand that El Paso has been completely overrun, and that also includes other border cities such as Brownsville, Harlingen. and McAllen. And I've heard that an incredibly large mass may overtake Corpus Christi."

"Craig, what has happened in New Mexico?" Mark asked.

"First, let me give you a scenario of how the situation will be if this situation isn't remedied. Right now, one plus one-half equals two—meaning that one tax-paying citizen's real estate, personal property, sales, and gas tax pays for his city services plus half of an illegal's services. Why, you ask, is a taxpayer paying to cover one-half of an illegal? Mark, most have been qualified for government subsidies or don't work, don't own real property, or are paid under the table. The system can only balance and absorb so much before the entirety crashes into bankruptcy. Soon the math won't add up correctly, and it will be a total collapse. You see, at this moment, with the border gates down and the United States being flooded with illegals, the ratio of illegal to legal will quickly tip the scale, and the entire infrastructure—police, government agencies, and hospitals—will fail. The illegals will overload existing resources, and businesses will move away or simply close. Jobs will disappear. Like in other third-world countries, the area will just be a dead zone, not able to support its population. And if, under the Obama-Denton plan, they are all legalized, they will still just go on welfare. It's a march into Dante's *Inferno*. That, my friend, is the dire news, in a nutshell."

"But, Craig, why are so many hell-bent on getting to America? Is Mexico that bad off? Is its economy really imploding?" Mark blurted out, not able to listen to his brother's lecturing any longer.

"Now don't tell me you didn't read my recent book? I sent you a signed copy."

"Yes—well, most of it. The way you write is the perfect sleeping pill. I can't stay awake reading it. Is there a way to tell me in a down-to-earth way why this is happening now?" Mark asked, knowing full well the longwinded answers his brother always spouted in professorial style.

"Okay, so combine what I've already said with the fact that our past nutcase president Obama pulled an end around by issuing a presidential order to legalize between five and ten million illegal Mexicans living in the United States. That was an open invitation to every Mexican who had ever thought of emigrating to America to come on in. You know the saying 'The grass is greener on the other side of the fence'? Well, for Mexicans, the grass is not only greener—it's golden with opportunity."

Mark pondered for a minute. "Well, I guess you're feeling safe, living outside Albuquerque in the wilderness. Elizabeth is panicking, and to some degree I can't blame her. I hear that Tucson is in dire straits, and Phoenix is just two hours away from Tucson. I suspect we're next in their path. I don't feel very comfortable being stuck in the city, which seems to be where these attackers are concentrating their efforts. I think it has to do with food."

Now Craig sat up straight, and his tone became much more serious. "Why did you say that? Why did you say a lot of this has to do with food?"

"Well, you know that half of our trucking business is transporting foodstuffs, and because of that we are in constant contact with hundreds of grocers and distributors in Arizona, New Mexico, and Southern California. Now, of course, the statistics are a bit distorted..."

Craig tuned out his brother's explanation and started forming a theory that had been an abstract until now.

Mark droned on for several minutes. "...Separately from that, our grocer contacts have said that these Mexican invaders are concentrating their attacks on any store or facility that's carrying food and ignoring every other merchant. I've thought about it a little bit, and the only conclusion I can come up with is that these Mexicans must be starving."

Smiling to himself, Craig muttered, "Holy shit." The answer had been there all along. Craig thanked his big brother and congratulated him for providing the most valuable information anybody had given him to date.

"One last question. Have you talked to Dad?" Craig asked.

"No, I didn't want to alarm him even more. But you know he watches Fox News almost nonstop, and I suspect he's on top of this as much as anyone. I was going to give him a call because if it's true that Tucson has fallen, maybe I should round up him and Mom and my family and get out of Phoenix as fast as I can. I'm just hoping it's not too late."

"Too late? I thought you said that the invaders were still south of Tucson."

"Our trucks have reported that bumper-to-bumper traffic has already blocked Interstate 17 north out of Phoenix toward Flagstaff. I'm not the only one who thought of getting out of town. One of our drivers took six hours getting to Flagstaff, which normally takes two, and he said it was getting worse by the minute." Mark groaned and continued. "If we lived in the Midwest or Northeast, we probably wouldn't even know there was anything going on down here."

"I think that's part of what's exacerbating the problem. Washington doesn't seem to be taking this seriously. Have you talked to Cliff in Houston? Do you know if he's aware of the problem or if he has any information about what's going on in southern Texas?" Craig asked and for the first time thought about his other brother and his family.

"No," Mark said, indifferently. "Cliff's the last guy I am worried about. Knowing him, he's probably grabbed all his hunting rifles, and he and his buddies and are off to defend the state."

"Do me a favor, big brother, give him a call and make sure he knows about the severity of the situation. And I'll try to get back in touch with Dave as soon as I can. I think the four of us should stay in close contact. Living in separate border states...well, it would be beneficial to keep each other informed.

"Mark, one last favor. You might consider asking Mom and Dad to come over and stay with you for a while or at least until this is all over. I know Dad will tell you no, that he has all the guns and ammo to protect his home. But he and Mom are too old to play a game of egos with you."

Again, the two brothers found dead air space as each waited for the other to be the first to give a bit of brotherly love. Finally, Mark said, "Sure thing. And hey, I'm sorry I started out busting your chops, little brother."

Craig hung up his phone and immediately regretted not sharing a bit of sentiment with Mark. But after Mark's comment regarding possible starvation within the marauding groups of illegals, his head was spinning.

Chapter 65

Bubba's Gun Store was proudly situated in the 300 block of E. Corpus Christi Road, catty-corner from the McClanahan House, the oldest business structure in Beeville, and a few doors down from the court house. Bubba's had been the meeting place for the townsfolk for as long as anyone could remember. The sign used to read, BEEVILLE'S RIFLES AND PISTOLS, but after watching the movie *Forest Gump*, Bubba renamed his store Bubba's Gun Store because he liked the character's name, Benjamin Buford *"Bubba"* Blue.

Bubba was a bear of a man and the salt of the earth. He loved to give bear hugs to all his lady customers, and he had many of those. After all, this was Texas, and any woman worth her spit could shoot and ride as well as any man. In return for his hugs and pampering, they'd reward Bubba with a traditional peck on the cheek—that was, if they could find any bare skin to kiss. Bubba had a beard that rivaled Dusty's from ZZ Top. Bubba tipped the scales at a staggering 315 pounds, and at six feet five, he was bigger than his fresh-bait refrigerator in the store.

Bubba's Gun Store always had a fresh pot of coffee and a set of checkerboards set up on old whiskey barrels for his customers. It was a fact that old Bubba would challenge anyone to a game at the drop of a hat. He had a hundred-pound wheel of fresh cheddar cheese and sleeves of crackers on top of one of the glass display cases, which he offered old or new friends, as well as loyal customers who dropped in to visit or buy. Bubba let customers slice off their own chunks of cheese, grab a handful of crackers, and sit down to play a game of checkers, watch the latest hunting or fishing video, or just shoot the breeze.

Bubba's Guns was the first place a wife would call if her husband went missing; Bubba had straightened out many a misguided husband over the years.

At high noon on the last Saturday of each month, Bubba would hold a drawing to guess the weight remaining on the hundred-pound wheel of cheese. One would think he was giving away a new AK instead of cheese, judging by the number of customers, coffee in hand, waiting for Bubba's announcement of the winning weight. It was a monthly excuse for friends to gather informally, share some coffee, and jawbone.

Bubba always had cracker crumbs in his beard and a spittoon by the register for those who indulged. To the townsfolk of Beeville, Texas, Bubba was a combination of Santa Claus and Paul Bunyan. The only difference was that Bubba would have eaten the legendary Babe, the blue ox. That's how big his appetite was.

Despite the reverence shown to Bubba, he still had his run-ins with the occasional drunk or unruly customer, along with a few break-ins over the years. However, no one ever dared rob him. If Bubba caught a robber, he would gladly give him the money, express his sympathy for him, and asked him his life story—while sitting on his chest waiting for the sheriff to arrive. Bubba was that kind of a man—friendly, churchgoing when he felt like it, long suffering and loving to his family. It was only after the local sheriff requested that Bubba conceded to have retractable steel grates and heavy-duty, reinforced front and back doors installed to help deter Beeville's nighttime crime.

As weeks went, it had been a profitable one at Bubba's. As more southern Texans heard about the invading and approaching Mexicans, Bubba had sold more guns and ammunition in a few days than he usually sold in two months. When the townsfolk had started pulling up stakes and heading north, though, business had totally dried up.

Bubba's spirits were still high, but then things took a turn for the worse. Mexicans had started to break into businesses in the downtown neighborhood. At first it had been only the food store chain and local mom-and-pop markets that catered to the local Hispanic families. However, when the gas stations and nonfood businesses were looted, Bubba started to get concerned. Bubba had no idea if all the Mexicans he saw wandering the street outside his store were the illegal border crossers that he'd heard about on the local news. Poor Bubba, a man without a prejudiced bone in his body—to him they all looked alike.

It was obvious that no one was going to be successful at breaking in during the nighttime hours because of the metal grates and reinforced doors. Bubba was concerned that an overwhelming force during regular business hours could pose a problem. He was thinking of keeping the grates in the windows closed and locked during this turbulent time—after all, people could still see the guns but not touch them. He had also toyed with the idea of installing an electronic door lock and vestibule-gate system that would allow him to admit one customer at a time through the door. He'd then buzz the customer through the vestibule gate, keeping the threat contained. Hogue's Jewelry on N. Washington Street had installed such a system recently. Hogue's was three blocks down and one block north and had been in continuous operation since 1976.

Bubba had heard that the shop had been spared any serious damage during a midnight raid by the Mexicans two nights ago. Hogue was the president of the local chamber of commerce and at eighty years old was finally thinking of handing the reins of his office over to Bubba. Old Man Hogue would rather fish than conduct meetings, and he hated collecting dues and was tired of Robert's Rules. Bubba, on the other hand, could call a quorum vote most any time of day since chamber of commerce members packed Bubba's Guns, playing checkers and shooting the breeze.

Bubba's thoughts of upgrading his entrance security were shattered by the sight of an unruly crowd at his windows. Suddenly breaking the glass were bottles and rocks. Bubba grimaced at the thought that he was too late: he had purchased the manual steel grates for the windows, which needed his attention to close. Plus, he'd never hooked up the panic button, which went directly to the sheriff's office. Unfortunately, the norm for most small-town businesses was to never expect the unexpected.

Bubba and his son, Jeb, were nervous but not scared. They immediately took defensive positions behind the gun counter in case someone tried to shoot up the store. Both Bubba and Jeb kept the cream of their gun inventory for themselves, and both sported AR-15s with sixty-round magazines and dual-burst triggers. In Bubba's other hand, he held a Glock 41 Gen4, tactical .45 auto— which had a custom-made, double-round, extended magazine. Jeb held a sawed-off twelve-gauge Remington 1100 semiautomatic with double-aught buckshot loads and an extended tube that held ten cartridges. Both had scrambled into full tactical gear with bulletproof vests and SWAT helmets outfitted with GoPro cameras to record the upcoming confrontation.

They were quite a sight, primed and pumped up for the attack. "Goddammit," Bubba swore. "I sure wish I had purchased those *black market* hand grenades last year!"

The rock and bottle tossing slackened once the assailants realized that all they had accomplished was to break the glass storefront. The heavy-duty metal grating was holding firm.

"Dad, I think we're okay. I think they're leaving," Jeb said.

Cautiously, they both emerged from their barricaded locations to inspect the damage from the barrage of rocks and junk hurled at their storefront. Carefully they peered through the grating to see what direction the mob was heading. There was still a lot of Mexicans milling around, but no one seemed to be concentrating on his store, and Bubba hoped that this was the total of the mob's effort. As Bubba and Jeb peered down the front of the building, feeling good about the outcome, there was an incredibly loud crash at the back of the store.

Bubba's Guns was a one-level freestanding cinderblock building. When Bubba had accepted the sheriff's request to beef up the windows and doors, he had had his flat roof converted, at considerable expense, to a steep gabled roof. He had paid to have concrete tiles installed that were nearly impenetrable and slick— both ideal to ward off the "bad guys," as Bubba had playfully called them.

Boom! By this time, both Bubba and Jeb were at the back of the store and the repeated sound was deafening. Father and son looked at each other and in unison said, "Shit!"

"Someone's ramming the door with something very powerful by the sound of it," said Jeb.

Again the deafening blow came, accompanied by a resonating echo. Then again and again, each time louder. With each blow came the metal-on-metal sound that frayed Jeb's nerves, but the heavy metal door and its metal frame were, for the moment, holding firm.

Kaboom! This time the door only shook slightly. Jeb put his ear to the back door to try to hear what the plan was.

"Dad, I can hear a truck! They're using a truck to ram our door. Do you think it will hold?"

Bubba wasn't listening. Instead, he was trying to reach 911 on his cell phone. What was happening to this town? He couldn't believe what was happening! *There was no answer!*

"Dad, Dad! Do you think the door will hold?" pleaded Jeb.

"Shit, son, that door was built to last until the cops arrive, but no one answered my 911 call." Bubba made eye contact with his son, gently clapped him on the right shoulder, and with gentle care, said, "Jeb, we're totally on our own. If those Mexican sons of bitches have a big enough truck to somehow bring down the door, we'll have to do something to protect our store." Again, as gently as the big bear could deliver bad news, he said, "I don't think the door will hold much longer."

A whimper escaped Jeb's lips, his eyes glistened, and tears silently rolled down his pudgy cheeks. He had not cried in front of his father since the fourth grade. At that time, his dad had told him that he was not rearing a crybaby and to not cry in his presence again. But now Jeb was scared to death.

"Dad, what are we going to do?"

With all their equipment and heavy armor, trying to give a father's hug was at best fruitless, so instead he gave his son a high five.

"First thing first! Jeb, stop crying. Be a man. Second, I love you. And lastly, let's pray, because if we ever needed God, it's now."

Just as they eased down onto their knees to pray, the door was crushed inward, coming off its hinges and crumpling to the floor with a loud crash.

The sights and sounds of the imploding doorway, the smoke and confusion, were too much for Jeb, and he froze on the spot. The last things he heard and felt as shock set in were the concussive booms as his dad fired blindly into the opening that only a few seconds earlier had been a double-reinforced back door. Jeb's world became overloaded even more as two of the invaders fell from Bubba's barrage and another was crushed by the stampede of his fellow countrymen trying to get out of the line of fire.

Bubba repeatedly called Jeb's name, hoping to bring him out of his stupor and into the present, to save his life.

Snapping to attention, Jeb let loose a volley from his Remington 1100 semiautomatic shotgun, staving off a shot from a Mexican sighting a bead on his dad. Jeb was impressed by the violent impact of the double-aught buckshot as it impaled, pierced, and drove the Mexican out the door.

They both reloaded; the air was thick with the acrid smell of spent gunpowder mixed with blood and sweat.

Once again, the Mexicans attempted to breach the doorway, and an errant round struck Bubba's bulletproof vest. Bubba went down on one knee, took a deep breath, felt broken ribs where the round had impacted—but then rose to meet the incoming tide of attackers. Bubba feared that his right lung was on the verge of collapsing but recognized beyond a shadow of a doubt that if he succumbed to his injury, his loving son, Jeb, would die, never reaching his potential.

But Bubba's thought was cut short as he witnessed Jeb take a shot to the head and drop face first to the floor.

There was no telling that day how many invaders Bubba and Jeb stopped in their tracks. The battle was fierce, and it robbed the town of Beeville of its gentle giant.

Before Bubba's last breath, he thanked God above for his life and family. He prayed for relief from his pain and anguish and told God how proud he was of his son and how honored he was to die alongside him protecting their store, their property, their American dream. His heart swelled as the vision of his youth, his wonderful marriage, and the birth of his children flashed across his consciousness. He was contented with his life and what he stood for. The memories of his father and grandfather, both volunteering to serve overseas in the military, defending freedom on the killing fields of World War II and Vietnam, came to mind as his oxygen-deprived brain began to fail.

He wondered, as his eyesight experienced the final tunnel vision toward death, what they would have thought of Bubba fighting the good fight, protecting American freedoms not as they did, overseas, but here on American soil. Bubba glanced at his son one final time, and tears silently rolled down his cheeks and into his thick beard, something he'd never let his son see.

Chapter 66

"Man, Paco makes a mean Mexican omelet," said the newbie border-patrol officer named Jackson with egg dripping from his mouth. His companion, Ryan, another recent graduate of the fifty-eight-day "Basic Academy" in Artesia, New Mexico, could only smile and nod in agreement, since his mouth, too, was filled a with a fire-roasted-pepper-and-egg concoction. Both were in heaven. It was 2:00 a.m., and the officers were seated at Paco's 24 Diner, a popular haunt of the late-night gang in Alamogordo, New Mexico.

The two agents had worked in the Otero County Sheriff's Department for the last few years and had decided together to join the US Border Patrol. That's where the action was—they were tired of the same old routine of drunken domestic-violence calls and shoplifting arrests. There was the occasional drug bust, but those cases were handed over to the detectives. The BP—their abbreviation for the border patrol—was perfect for them; they were young and fluent in Spanish, and for them, completing the application process and their training had been a breeze. The fifty-eight-day academy had been a walk in the park, and their assignment to the 11:00 p.m. to 7:00 a.m. shift was accepted eagerly. After all, being young and turned on by the constant blur of calls was sexy to them.

"Alamogordo," translated as "fat cottonwood," described the trees that grew along US Route 54, which connected Holloman Air Force Base in Alamogordo to Fort Bliss in El Paso, Texas. Alamogordo was the closest town to the White Sands National Park and the White Sands Missile Range and was always hopping with border patrol work.

The Alamogordo Border Patrol Station's responsibility consisted of 16,285 square miles and was characterized by mountain ranges and a large valley. The valley extended one hundred miles north and was thirty to forty miles in width. It was also one of the preferred routes of drug smugglers and human traffickers alike.

Pushing back from his plate of eggs and peppers, Ryan asked Jackson what time he had.

"It's 2:00 a.m.," replied Jackson as he loosened his belt. "I ate too much."

Ryan paused, looked out the big bay window, and addressed his companion. "You know, something's weird. The streets always have at least some traffic, even at this hour, but I haven't noticed any cars since we sat down for our breakfast break. It just feels weird. Aw, it's probably nothing. Just my omelet coming back to haunt me."

As the two agents headed toward their border-patrol truck, they became mystified. There wasn't another vehicle on the road heading in either direction. Jackson, now behind the wheel and driving ahead, told Ryan to call into the station to see if a curfew had been enacted.

"This is something right out of *The Twilight Zone*." With a nervous snicker, Jackson continued. "Really, it's like aliens have beamed up all the cars. What the hell is going on?"

Ryan placed the radio call, but it went unanswered. Both agents felt the small hairs on the backs of their necks stand straight up as the creepiness of the situation deepened. Rolling down his window to get some air, Jackson slammed on the brakes. The usual night sounds from the resident animals had been replaced by a cacophony of panicked cries and an unusual din.

As the agents sat in the middle of the highway, their imaginations ran wild. There were fleeing shadows just beyond the scope of their vehicle's headlights. It was a moonless night, and Jackson's and Ryan's nighttime vision had been reduced to the level of a blind man attempting to read the paper—useless.

"What's that?" Ryan asked. "Over there. No, over there." His eyes had once again fooled him into seeing what he thought was movement.

"There! No, there!" shouted Jackson.

In that same split second both agents recognized that there really was movement. Ryan grabbed his flashlight and stabbed at the ON button. Finally, with the flashlight blazing, Ryan lit up the area surrounding the truck. The newbie border agent could not comprehend the sight within the beam of light. There, approaching the vehicle was what looked like a stampede of people that stretched far beyond his meager light. He turned on the headlights. Now totally visible was a wave. A human wave. A tidal wave.

The earth shook with the pounding of thousands of running feet. It felt like the oxygen had been sucked from his lungs, and Ryan's bladder involuntarily released, soiling his uniform.

"It's the end of the world," shouted Ryan. But before the words were out of his mouth, the wave of humanity had passed, leaving both agents questioning if it had really happened. In the ensuing void, Jackson and Ryan came to the stark realization that they were lucky to have survived.

Chapter 67

Looking up at an eager-to-please soldier, his focus broken once again, Tillman barked, "Corporal, apparently none of the phone lines in El Paso are working. We are going to have to switch over to our tactical field communication systems, and if that fails and worse comes to worst, we'll use our goddamn cell phones if need be. But, Corporal, do not misunderstand me. I am holding you personally responsible for keeping us in constant communication with Washington. That's your number one priority. If you have to get two tin cans and stretch four thousand miles of string to the Pentagon, I don't care. Just do it and don't bother me with the how. Now, I have other fires to put out, so if you don't mind, let me get back to work. Dismissed."

The sharp rap of knuckles on his office door continued the interruptions, and Tillman cursed under his breath. "These boys need a swift kick in the ass. They can't do anything without me holding their hand. What kind of army am I running down here? Come in."

One of his aides entered. "Sorry to disturb you, sir. General Grayson is on the phone for you."

"Holy shit." He picked up the receiver. "General Grayson, am I glad to hear from you."

"Charlie, what in God's green acres is going on down there?" barked Grayson.

"All hell's broken loose, sir!"

"How in the blazing hell have I not heard more about this from you until now!"

Familiar with the well-known wrath of General Grayson, Tillman hesitantly responded, "Well, sir, I've been talking to General Harris."

Bellowing so loud Tillman could have heard him from his desk in the Pentagon without the aid of a phone, General Grayson shouted, "Dammit man, Harris has shit for brains.

From now on, *you deal with me* and *only me* on this issue. Now I want an immediate SITREP on your command."

"Sir, I apologize. I assumed you would want me to follow the chain of command. And so I assumed that General Harris was keeping you and the other top brass fully informed."

"Hell, Charlie, not only does General Harris have shit for brains, he's scared to death of his own shadow. These days the only thing he gives a damn about is his fucking golf game. When Obama was president, all the two of them ever did was play golf. Now, give me the lowdown, general!"

"I've moved all off-base personnel back to the base, canceled leave, instituted a curfew, checked all supplies, and placed the PX on lockdown. Sir, we've doubled the watch and have a continuous rolling checkpoint routing the perimeter. We are now operating at all hands on deck, 24-7. General, I have personally looked into any military personnel with Hispanic heritage and vetted all staff. Our water will last a long time. We're standing and ready at full alert."

"Great job, General," Grayson said. "Have you had any casualties?"

"Sir, we've had the usual bumps and bruises associated with relocation and troop deployment, a few pregnant wives complaining about their new base-side accommodations. We have a hell of a lot of frightened people but no, General, no casualties."

"Charlie, what information can you give me about the situation in El Paso and outside the base?"

"We've lost contact with the El Paso Police Department, and I think every other agency I've contacted has gone on vacation because no one is answering their phone."

"You're the closest thing I have to the front lines," said Grayson.

Stunned at the lack of information flow, Major General Tillman stuttered, "You're asking me, General, what I've been asking everyone else. I asked General Harris if I can get an order allowing me to send troops out on an expeditionary patrol. But I could never get him to make a decision. Most of what we're getting in the way of information is from local TV and radio, and they stopped all broadcasts the other day. I was going to send out helicopters or a fixed-wing drone, but General Harris told me he didn't think that was a good idea. He thought they might get shot down."

"Shot down? This is America. We're talking about flying within American airspace. What does that idiot think—that these poor Mexicans crossed the borders with shoulder-mounted SAM missiles? My God, that man should retire and work on his golf game. He's no good as a general. Sorry sack of shit has the ego the size of the moon but the brain of a pea!"

Grayson was nearing the end of his patience. The top brass at the Pentagon were mostly brilliant soldiers, but all it took was one high-ranking nimrod officer to totally fuck things up, and that's apparently what General Harris had done.

"Now Charlie, if I haven't made it clear to you already, from now on you answer directly to me and only me, so don't make one more call to that shit-for-brains Harris. And if he calls you, you tell him I told you to have him call me. I know he will never do that. I'd give him a tongue lashing so hard he'd have to open his zipper to see the sunrise. End of discussion!"

General Grayson let out an exhalation of disgust and frustration, gave it a ten count, and continued. "Now, send out the choppers for reconnaissance STAT, and I don't want any damn paper report. You call me immediately with the results! Got it, General?"

"Yes, sir. General, may I ask you one question before you hang up?"

"What's that, Charlie?" said Grayson.

"What are your orders, sir, if the base goes under attack?"

Grayson was knocked back in his chair, shocked by the question. "Charlie, you are one of my best generals. We go back to the Point together, so you don't need me to tell you what to do. You're in command of one our best bases in the country. On top of that, you're the home of 1st Armored Division, the 15th Sustainment Brigade, the 32nd Army Air and Missile Defense Command, as well as the 402nd Field

Artillery Brigade. General that's not even fucking all you've got, so I don't have any doubt that you can fully protect your men, their families, and the base."

"Sir, there's an additional problem and I think one that's more imminent. What am I supposed to do if they don't attack but simply surround the base? General, this is going to make me awfully uncomfortable. Personally, in all my years, I've never been in a situation where I've let the enemy surround me on purpose."

Grayson hesitated for a moment to contemplate what Major General Tillman had said. "Dammit, Charlie, the base is 1,700 square miles. You command 1,500 square miles of restricted airspace. I don't think that's an issue. However, I feel that is the problem with the border states. It appears that the incidents of attack by the invading Mexicans are limited. Except for a few Mexican military and police deserters, most crossed the border unarmed. The expat military and police and the civilians are starved and to someone's thinking might be considered refugees. To date, General, we have not been shooting illegal immigrants who've crossed our borders, and it doesn't look like we're going to start shooting them now, at least not yet."

General Grayson recognized that Major General Tillman was stuck in an untenable position, between his duty and his heart. But that's why people like Tillman were promoted to general in the first place. No war was fought, won, or settled without US military people making incredibly challenging judgments. That's what their country asked of them.

"Look, Charlie, I know you're in a very tough spot, and from the best estimate I can tell, the largest number went through Juarez, Mexico, and up through El Paso. Based on everything you've said, I'm surprised you haven't been surrounded by now."

"Sir, it's not only hard for me. It's hard for me to give the command to sit and let the enemy surround us without firing a shot. Sir, these are trained, skilled soldiers with experience under their belts."

"General, you said 'enemy.' Herein lies the problem, Charlie. No one in Washington has called them the *enemy* yet. For now, your country is asking you to sit tight and not engage lethal force unless fired upon or provoked by fear of lost personnel."

General Grayson heard the anguish on the other end of the phone line.

"Yes, sir. I read you loud and clear. I'm starting to feel a little like Colonel Travis at the Alamo or General Custer at Little Bighorn. I don't care how well armed we are, sir. I'm not sure eight thousand soldiers can hold back an invasion of starving people."

Chapter 68

There are a lot of things that Professor Craig Walther liked about his life, but there was one in particular at the top of his list. His favorite was waking up next to a beautiful woman after a night of starry-eyed sex. Their intimate night of exploration and pleasing, giving in to each other's appetites, had been so passionate that they passed out immediately.

"What is there about the scent of a freshly showered woman that inspires me to act like a teenage boy?" was Craig's question to the ceiling above his bed. He slid over to wrap his bed mate with his strong arms, hugging her close. The scent of her shampoo from her late-night shower was an aphrodisiac of biblical proportion.

At that moment, Professor Katherine Lacey opened her pale-blue eyes, smiled up at Craig's passive schoolboy look, and said, "Neither of us has the luxury of sleeping the day away." Craig looked down and was struck speechless. Katherine, looking refreshed, oozed sex appeal and desire while lying next to him nonchalantly.

Finding his voice, Craig asked, "Young lady, do you know how desirable you look at this moment?"

Katherine broke his embrace and rolled over to face Craig. "Young lady?" she replied. "Don't you have me confused with one of your little college chickies?" She knew that her remarks hit home. Craig was a good catch yet carried a lot of baggage from past relationship that made him fear a one-woman lifestyle.

Craig tried to roll Katherine gently over, facing away from him so he could enjoy the fullness of her hips and buttocks. Shutting her words out of his mind was difficult, and it only served to deflate his ego. They both knew it was true. He was a hound dog, but at this moment all he had on his mind was sharing a little warm intimacy with the goddess in his bed.

"I was just trying to pay you a little compliment. You know I think you have a great body. Katherine, I truly enjoyed our evening and *la réunion de Deux Amoureux,"* Craig purred, testing the limits of his French language skills.

Katherine laid a warm, passionate kiss on Craig and said, "You'll get no argument from me. I thought it was a glorious evening. I really love watching movies on your big-screen TV. I laid here thinking about it before I went to sleep last night. I think *My Fair Lady* might be my favorite musical. Audrey Hepburn was such a fabulous actress. She had one quote, in particular, that exposes an essential element in my life: 'The best thing to hold onto in life is each other.' Now you know a secret about me," whispered Katherine into Craig's ear.

Knowing her secret and how much Katherine cared about him brought about a bonding intimacy between them. Of course, Craig was cursed to be guided by his sexual desires, not his heart. It had proven to be his downfall many times over. His wandering eye and fast-responding libido haunted him when it came to good, solid relationships. Wandering through life having multiple sexual relationships was not the way to a woman's heart. But it sure made him feel young, virile in spirit, and appreciative of the female form.

"They don't make musicals like they used to," Craig said. "I guess for that matter they don't make anything like they used to. But my favorite character was Harry Higgins. What a great character."

"Oh, you just like him because everyone refers to him as Professor Higgins. You love being addressed as 'Professor,' so you relate well to him."

"Well, I worked long and hard to deserve the title. Only I detest being called 'Dr. Walther.'"

The conversation was a buzzkill, and Katherine slid her sleek body out from under the sheets and immediately grabbed a thick, luxurious bathrobe that Craig had placed at the foot of the bed for her.

Slipping it on and hugging herself as she moved toward the bathroom, she stopped and said, "It really was a fabulous evening, and I enjoyed talking politics with you before we started the movie. It was a fun diversion bantering back and forth. But, I fear our ideals will never be in the forefront of voters' minds again. That time has sadly passed. I can't believe I'm using this analogy, but I feel like we are the Flintstones in a Jetsons age!"

The happy, content look on Craig's face quickly left, and a look of grave concern replaced it. "Speaking of politics, I have a very serious concern that is far too important to ignore in this blowup at the Mexican border."

Katherine came back, lay next to Craig, and gently took his hand in hers, and said, "How do you mean?"

For Craig, his second-most-favorite thing in life was to have a stimulating conversation with someone of equal intelligence. However, finding that person was difficult. Katherine was a close second to his intellect, and he found the conversations with her to be nearly orgasmic. But not this time. This time the conversation centered on his fear of America losing its border with Mexico and the deaths of too many innocent people.

Craig squeezed Katherine's hand and gently put it to his lips before he could finally get out the words he feared most. "I'm very concerned that Americans are not taking adequate steps to protect themselves from this blitzkrieg movement of illegal Mexicans moving across our border."

Releasing Katherine's hand and gesturing emphatically, he continued. "I can't blame them. The media and press have completely downplayed this entire debacle. If it wasn't for Fox News, I'm not sure Washington wouldn't even know anything about it. It's the same old problem we've been having with the weak-chinned liberal politicians and the sold-out media for decades. Some of the better minds like that of Charles Krauthammer have postulated that these media types pick up their liberal bias in college."

Katherine chuckled. "Craig, we've had this same discussion a dozen times. We'll never change the status quo. We both know the system is flawed and that most college professors, teachers, and plain ole educators have gone over to the dark side of being liberal and that they spout off during every class about the dangers of conservatism. The void between liberals and conservatives has never been so great. Naturally, the vast majority of kids fresh out of college come out with a liberal bias. Besides, their student loans emanate from the government, as do other subsidies and handouts. Why should they bite the hand that feeds them?"

Craig got out of bed, put on his bathrobe, and lay back down. "I think that's the problem right there. Liberals are blind to reality far too often."

Katherine gave Craig big hug and said, "I think we need to get dressed, considering we have classes that start at nine. By the way, you mind if I change the subject for a moment?" Katherine opened her cosmetic bag and stood in front of a small mirror on the wall, since Craig didn't own a vanity. "How come you always invite me over for the evening on the days that you know I have to teach class the next morning? Is it so you can be sure I will leave the next morning and not linger? Is that the same reason you refuse to allow me to keep some of my personal items in your bathroom?" She paused. "Is it that you don't want one of your little college girls to know that their competition is a college professor? Or is it just pure unwillingness or fear of commitment?"

Craig didn't stop dressing. He'd hoped that if he could get dressed fast enough, he'd be able to get out of the house without having to face Katherine and deal with the issue at hand. But it was too late. Katherine had positioned herself so he'd have to pass her to leave, which meant he needed to deal with it.

Craig took a breath, exhaled, and confessed, "Katherine, I've done a wretched job in my life with full-time relationships. As you know, I've been married twice, and I've been divorced twice. They broke my heart, and I don't think I can go through that again."

"I see. So once again I end up paying for the mistakes you made in your two previous marriages. Are you ever going to get over the pain of what those two women did to you? Can we ever have a meaningful relationship without you comparing everything in our relationship to your previous two wives?"

Craig turned to face Katherine. "Isn't that what life's all about? Aren't we told to learn from our mistakes? After my first marriage, I promised myself I would not make that mistake again, but then I did. You keep reminding me that you're different than my two previous wives. My second wife promised me the same thing! Twice at the altar I've said 'till death do us part.' I'm not sure why Americans still go through that entire delusion. The divorce rate has been running near 50 percent in this country for decades. My dear Katherine, don't you see? Too many couples disregard their oath of marriage. To them, it is a piece of paper, just a document like so many others in our lives that we sign and accept on a superficial level. If we treated marriage as a sacred covenant rather than a document with an exit strategy in the guise of divorce, marriage would be a grand institution instead of a joke."

He sat on a chair while putting on his shoes. "Look, we are all human. We all make mistakes. And I don't think anybody should stay in a bad marriage. God knows there's nothing worse than waking up every day with somebody you either hate or you have nothing in common with. So I'm not saying we should dissolve the divorce process. What I am saying is that far too many people get married for the wrong reasons."

Katherine walked across Craig's bedroom, put her arms around him, and gave him an incredibly warm and loving embrace.

"You know, that's what I love about you most and why I keep coming back. You've got such depth and a wonderful conscience that keeps you honest. I want to spend the rest of my life with a man like you. Craig, I'll pray that given time you'll someday see how boundless our love could be if you'd drop the wall that you've erected to protect yourself. I'm a patient woman, Professor Walther, and your little indiscretions won't break my indomitable spirit. Professor, I love you."

A long, silent pause ensued between the two lovers, who were consumed by the moment's honesty.

Then reality hit. The hallway clock chimed, announcing with each mean strike of the gong just how late they were.

"Come on," Craig said. "I'll race you to our cars."

Chapter 69

Sheriff Joe Arpaio was intimidating. Even at eighty-two years old, Sheriff Joe cast a huge shadow. The son of Italian immigrants, he'd joined the army at age eighteen. After serving his country for four years, he joined the Las Vegas police department and was appointed to the Federal Bureau of Narcotics, which later became the Drug Enforcement Agency (the DEA). His career with the DEA had lasted twenty-five years, and at age fifty he had become the sheriff of Maricopa County, Arizona.

Sheriff Arpaio's work ethic came from his father, the owner of a small grocery store in Springfield, Massachusetts, and he had always been fiercely patriotic. His huge shadow had put him in harm's way, but he had never shied away from doing what he felt was right. He was a true crime fighter who faced his opponents and liberal naysayers head-on, not backing down from a righteous debate or fight. There had never been, in modern times, a more famous or more controversial sheriff in the United States.

Wearing his traditional blue suit, Sheriff Arpaio cut across the political ruff and did things his way. His tent city, volunteer chain gangs, and inmates wearing pink underwear endeared him to the voters who had placed him in his sixth term as sheriff.

Sheriff Arpaio had been a thorn in the side of past president Barack Obama, even going so far as to sue him over his immigration policy. He had often been the target of US Attorney General Eric Holder and his office, which, on many occasions, tried to have Joe removed from office for upholding unconstitutional jail conditions and closing cases without arrest or proper investigation. As much as the liberal government disliked Sheriff Joe, his voters loved him.

Sheriff Arpaio has always been tough on crime, but his illegal-immigration policy was even tougher. Joe was a major supporter of Arizona Governor Janice Brewmeister's attempt to solve the Mexican illegal immigration problem, despite the obstacles thrown in her face by the Obama administration and the US attorney general's office.

In 2005, Joe Arpaio began focusing on illegal-immigration enforcement after Maricopa County Attorney Andrew Thomas was elected using the campaign slogan "Stop illegal immigration." Arpaio admitted that prior to 2005, he didn't view illegal immigration as "a serious legal issue."

But starting in 2005, Sheriff Arpaio regularly conducted saturation patrols and immigration sweeps, targeting Latino neighborhoods. He ran a large number of operations targeting businesses that employed Latinos and arrested illegal alien employees for identity theft. According to Sheriff Arpaio, 100 percent of the people arrested for using stolen IDs in fifty-seven raids conducted until March 2012 were illegal immigrants. Until 2011, Sheriff Arpaio employed an immigrant-smuggling squad that stopped cars with Latino drivers or passengers to check their immigration statuses.

At present, Sheriff Joe Arpaio had an entirely new problem. He was getting reports from Maricopa County and Phoenix and from the sheriffs in the southern part of Arizona around Tucson that there were possibly several hundred thousand new illegal Mexicans coming his way.

Sheriff Arpaio stepped into the offices of Bill Montgomery, the Maricopa County attorney general, and walked directly into his private office without waiting for an invitation. Banging open the door, Sheriff Arpaio got directly to the point.

He dropped his traditional cowboy hat onto a chair and slammed his hand down on Bill's desk. "Bill, I think it's time to get the governor on the line. From what I hear, the shit is just getting ready to hit the fan here."

Montgomery smiled patiently at the sheriff, which caused Sheriff Arpaio's heart to sink a bit. The sheriff knew that when an attorney smiled, that meant he had something up his sleeve. Bill had always been one of his tried-and-true supporters, so Sheriff Joe just stared at Bill with a questioning look.

Chuckling, Bill said, "Joe I was wondering what was taking you so long to get your ass in my office. I called the governor about this two days ago. Hey, old man, you're slipping."

"Shit, Bill, you had me worried." Returning the chuckle, he said, "Hey, even at my advanced age, I could take you down with both arms tied behind my back and never break a sweat. Now! What did Fran say? Has she turned out the National Guard?"

Bill Montgomery and Sheriff Arpaio were at opposite ends of the career pole and looked at things in a different light. Montgomery was young and methodical and looked forward to a very successful political career, including thoughts of a future governorship. Sheriff Arpaio was nearing the end of a long career in crime fighting, had no political aspirations, and reacted instantly to all situations.

"Now, Joe, we agree on most things, but we go about them in different ways. Don't repeat what I'm about to say, but I think we should've called out the National Guard last week as soon as the border was breached. Frankly, I will vehemently deny I said that if you repeat it. Governor Brewmeister agreed with me, but we've been fighting the feds ever since Obama and his liberal cronies came into office. And again I will deny it if you say I said it, but there was a call from one of the president's top aides, a Stephanie somebody, who called the governor when this thing first broke. She warned that if we took any action without direct approval from the president and Congress, we were going to be held in contempt."

Montgomery could see the steam coming out of Sheriff Arpaio's ears and his face turning beet red. "What the fuck are we supposed to do, sit on our thumbs and accept these invasive hordes of illegal Mexicans? Come on, Bill, our budget, not to mention the state's budget, has been busting at the seams for the last decade because we've been forced to feed, house, educate, and provide every public service that we offer American citizens to all these illegals that have taken up residency here. Bill, I haven't mentioned the increase in my jail population. We should serve tortillas instead of bread, and now we need bilingual guards. We've sunk to third-world-refugee status."

Bill Montgomery was a great negotiator, and that's how he had gotten to where he was today. But Sheriff Arpaio was his own man, and Montgomery thought that Sheriff Arpaio was just the kind of man that America was in need of.

"Work with me on this, Joe. I'm as sick about this as you are. I still have young kids, and I'm scared to death. Hell, I'd jump in a car or plane and take my family to North Dakota tonight, but I'd never be able to run for office in the state again. I need you. Now work with me on this. We've got to be patient a little longer. I'm praying that those weak-lipped idiots in Washington will come to their senses and catch on to the impending national disaster. The problem is that Washington doesn't see us as important, and what they can't see is out of sight, out of mind. This disaster in the four border states will spread like a plague if not nipped in the bud. I hope those assholes in DC aren't planning on throwing Texas, New Mexico, Arizona, and California under the bus. It's all politics as usual, and I think the current administration is just too stupid to consider the ramifications of allowing this pestilence to move throughout the country unabated."

Joe calmed himself down a bit and leaned forward. "I might trust you, Bill, but on my last dying breath, I will never trust those bozos in Washington. This isn't over. I've never been one to sit on the sidelines and let someone else run the game. If I have to deputize inmates to repel the illegals, I'll do so. It may be my last hurrah, and they'll send me off to prison, but I'll go knowing that the country is safe from the impending infestation."

Chapter 70

The two F/A-18 Hornets were flying maneuvers when they received a call from MCAS Miramar.

"Major, we've had contact with the top brass at the Pentagon, and they want you reassigned to do a little reconnaissance for them today. They'd like to know what's going on as it relates to vehicle traffic on the major highways between San Diego and Los Angeles and north out of Los Angeles."

"Copy that, sir," replied one of the navy pilots. "But if you don't mind me asking, since when are navy jets slaved to do traffic reporting? Isn't that stuff left to the San Diego and Los Angeles TV station copters?"

"Sorry, fellas," came the response. "Just orders. But if you'd like me to get you that general's phone number at the Pentagon, I am happy to do so."

"That's a big negative. We'll do a flyover and report in by 1300 hours. May I inquire if this has anything to do with the rumors that we've heard about the suburbs of San Diego being swarmed by thousands of Mexicans who recently breached the border?"

"No, Major, you may not ask any questions, and I'd suggest that you keep any thoughts of speaking with anyone outside of command to yourself!"

Less than two hours later, the pilots reported in with their sightings. "This is Major Thornton reporting relating to vehicular movements on the major interstate traffic in the areas requested."

"Go ahead, Major."

"First, I know I wasn't supposed to ask, but it does appear that on the outskirts of San Diego, there is an unusually large mass of people in transit. As best as we can determine, they are circumventing San Diego and moving in a northerly direction.

"As to the requested traffic report, I've never seen anything quite like it. Sir, there doesn't appear to be any vehicular traffic in or around San Diego at all. The streets are empty of any movement, and as we get closer to Los Angeles, it's the same observation. There is no movement on the highways at all. However, as soon as we cross over to the north side of the city, every single access road, highway, and intersection is backed up. Sir, the roadways are blocked, bumper to bumper, an absolute traffic jam. I've seen situations like this on occasions prior to a major storm moving into the area.

"I've flown over a lot of Los Angeles's historic rush-hour traffic jams, but this makes that look like a joke. There's got to be millions of vehicles on the roadways. Again, it's only the north-and northeast-bound traffic lanes that have any vehicles on the roadways."

The second pilot piped in. "Sir, I dropped down a bit to take a closer look. You won't believe what I saw. I'm still having trouble comprehending it. Sir, there's so much traffic northbound out of LA proper and the outlying suburbs that vehicles have crossed over into the southbound lanes and are driving north on them. I didn't see any major accidents, but sir, that is inevitable. It's crazy. Frankly, it's such a mass movement, it's as if the devil himself is chasing these folks."

Chapter 71

For Alberto Morales and his family, their private jet flight from Monterrey, Mexico, to Chicago had been a combination of exhilaration and sadness. For Alberto, the flight to freedom had been wrought with glad memories of his parents and grandparents, his youth, and his beloved homeland. Mexico had changed and was now foreign to him; it was not his Mexico any longer.

Alberto knew his decision was correct for his family and he had accepted that his grief-stricken heart would always weigh upon him due to leaving Mexico. But to stay would have meant the ruination of their lives. The country was imploding, and the rise of the guerrilla forces threatened to ensnare him, even at his age, to fight against his countrymen. No, to save his family had been the right decision, but it was a decision accompanied by guilt and shame. Guilt for leaving behind family and friends and shame for abandoning his homeland when it needed him the most. However, it was the one chance for his family to be together and live free, protected by American laws and self-determination.

Alberto was shocked that both of his children were totally ecstatic about the announcement that they were going to live in the United States. The fact that they would never see their high school friends didn't seem to faze them. During the entire three-hour-and-forty-minute flight, all they could talk about was shopping in the cool American malls. Up to this point, they had only read about them or seen them on TV. Once they found a place to live, they wanted their dad to take them to the Mall of America in a place called Minnesota. It looked as big as the town where their grandparents had lived. There was so much to do in America for two teenagers. Alberto had never realized how Mexican kids so idolized America. The decision to settle in Chicago, Illinois, had been unanimous.

But it was the opposite for his wife, Maria. She had cried the entire trip. Maria's parents had died early during their marriage, but she had left behind two brothers, three sisters, and a boatload of cousins, nephews, nieces, uncles, and aunts, not to mention all her childhood friends. Her life for the last decade had been one of luxury and leisure, and she had wanted for nothing. They'd lived in luxury, in a lifestyle nothing like the way American cinema portrayed Mexicans. Alberto always watched American westerns, such as *Butch Cassidy and the Sundance Kid* or *The Wild Bunch* with William Holden and Ernest Borgnine. Maria despised how her country looked in the cowboy movies and resented the bleak representation. True, there were many impoverished and starving families but not hers. No, they lived in the gem of Mexico— Monterrey, where the richest of the richest lived in Mexico. No, her family was not the usual depicted Mexican eating beans and rice. Maria and her family were the privileged, and she hated that Alberto had uprooted their lives to go to America. Maria had heard that Chicago was one of the largest and more famous US cities, but it was not her home. She was unhappy and bitter about the forced move.

As Alberto had suspected, US customs was a breeze. Yes, there was a tense moment because his suitcases contained five million US dollars, but since they'd arrived in a private jet and off-loaded at the VIP terminal, the agents rubber-stamped their entrance. They even bid them welcome to the United States.

However, even if the customs agents had confiscated the entire amount, there would have been no real harm. Alberto had managed over the last few days to wire transfer ten times that amount to a few of the larger US banks. It turned out that though the United States thought it had finally resolved the issue of illegal money entering the country, every year billions entered legally due to a loophole covering wire transfers.

The family quickly negotiated a year's lease in a beautiful penthouse apartment at the Gold Coast in the northern part of downtown. The hotel was in the neighborhood of Streeterville and was second only to New York's Upper East Side as the most exclusive neighborhood in all of America. The papers were drawn and signed with never a batted eye or inquiry made into Alberto's affairs. Wealthy foreigners were already the majority owners and tenants of Chicago's more prestigious properties, as they were in New York, Miami, and Washington, DC.

Alberto was a smart man and knew how to alleviate his wife's funk. He arranged to send her on a spending spree to totally furnish their new penthouse. If anything made Maria happy, it was shopping, so Alberto said the magic words— "unlimited budget." He hired a bilingual personal shopper to accompany her. They became fast friends and within their first week, Maria had furnished and decorated their luxury high-rise apartment tastefully—and, of course, expensively—in American décor. Alberto smiled the smile of a happy man. Even Ivana Trump would have been impressed.

It was Sunday and the Chicago Cubs, down two games already, were hosting a three-game series with the Washington Nationals. Alberto had not been able to buy seats for the family for any of the sold-out home games, and everyone was disappointed.

Feeling disappointed himself, he announced that the following Saturday, there was a home game against the Cardinals that they would watch at The Cubby Bear Sports Bar on West Addison. The bar was legendary in Chicago and sported some of the biggest big-screen TVs. He explained to the family that Americans considered going to a sports bar, in many ways, better than seeing the game live. Maria had concerns about taking the children to a bar for an entire afternoon, but Alberto quickly convinced her that in America, sports bars are not the seedy hangouts that were the norm in Mexico.

The Cubby Bear was packed as the Cubs game got underway. But Alberto tipped the hostess $100, and amazingly a table was immediately available. There were screens and games spread all over the walls. It was a cornucopia of events playing all at once. Nothing like this had existed where they had lived, and the kids couldn't believe their eyes. The family didn't feel out of place, as everyone was united cheering on the Cubs. The beer flowed freely. As a matter of fact, in the two weeks they had been in Chicago, they had grown to feel at home and not like recent transplants. Chicago was not like Monterrey, but their wealth softened the impact and opened doors that regular city dwellers missed. In fact, Alberto was surprised just how few white Anglos he'd seen in downtown Chicago. Yes, Monday through Friday the streets were filled with white office workers, but after sundown, the streets reverted back to mostly blacks, Hispanics, and Asians. He had learned from a new friend that in many, if not most, of the US cities, the whites were distinct minorities due in part to something called "white flight." This friend had then told Alberto a story about Detroit, which had been, at one time, the-auto manufacturing hub of the United States. The city had been taken over by liberal blacks decades ago, and they had bankrupted the city. He continued the story by concluding that most whites would not venture into the city and that it was forever doomed as a slum.

The Cubby Bear Sports Bar had a healthy mix of every nationality imaginable, and Alberto was impressed at how so many different cultures could blend so easily. Alberto asked the waitress what the specialty of the bar was and asked what he saw her constantly serving the tables around them.

"Wings," she responded, smiling.

Maria choked on her drink. "Wings?" She winced. "People actually order chicken wings? In Mexico, only poor people eat wings, along with necks, feet, and gizzards."

But the waitress did not back down and insisted that The Cubby Bear was world famous for its chicken wings. She told them that if they didn't like them, she wouldn't charge them.

When she brought the big platter of wings, Maria was even more horrified. They were smothered in some glow-in-the-dark, bright-red goo. When Maria tried to cut into one, the waitress stopped her and said, "Honey, you eat them with your fingers."

By this time, the kids had gotten the hang of it and were quickly devouring wing after wing. Maria grabbed one but quickly dropped it back on the platter. This grossly colored thing stuck to her fingers, and all she could do was shudder. Alberto had watched his wife and had wondered how she'd react to the messy wing. He half laughed at her repulsed reaction but of course he'd do whatever it took to make sure Maria was happy in their new home. It had been his idea to go to the sports bar, and the last thing he was going to do was criticize this supposed American delicacy.

Finally, Maria got her nerve back and picked up another glowing, gooey wing and rushed it to her mouth before her discriminating eyes could stop her once again. But Maria had a discerning nose, and it acted as a sensory guard. Just as she was about to bite into the scary-looking, once-live tidbit, she exclaimed, "Egad, what's that horrid smell?"

Maria had grown up eating spicy food, but she had never experienced a smell so pungent. It smelled like a combination of barbecue sauce, tobacco, Cajun-Creole seasoning, and toilet bowl cleaner. Once again, she dropped—no, actually threw—the winged thing back on the platter.

Alberto was becoming concerned. His plans for their first time out as a family doing traditional American things did not please his wife. He thought of abandoning the entire sports-bar experience and heading over to Morton's of Chicago, which his new friend had said served some of the best steaks in the city. He would have, except his kids were having the time of their lives. They had already devoured the first platter of wings and were on their second. Cherry Coke with an actual cherry, which they said they could not get in Mexico, was the drink of the day for them.

Additionally, they were conversing with some Asian kids sitting next to them about the game, which was now in the fifth inning.

To encourage his wife, Alberto picked up a wing for the first time, smiling, and took a bite. It wasn't a good experience. If he could forget the horrible aroma and the sticky feel, he couldn't forget biting into bone. He hid his disappointment, hoping to encourage his wife to dig in.

Decades ago, he had heard an American burger-chain ad that used the slogan "Where's the beef?" Other than a foul-smelling and sickening red mess, the only substances to chew in this wing were chicken fat and skin. Alberto wondered out loud, "Where's the chicken?"

Finally, Maria broke into a laugh and said, "Thank you."

Alberto had not made his millions by being stupid. He knew that despite Maria's efforts, no chicken wing was going into her mouth. When they had first arrived, Alberto had scanned the menu and seen two of his wife's favorite American foods: cheeseburgers and onion rings. Alberto, joining Maria in laughter, corralled the waitress and loudly said, "My wife would like a big, juicy cheeseburger and a large order of onion rings!"

Maria leaned forward gave her husband a big kiss while she simultaneously shoved the remaining platter of scary objects in the direction of the kids, who once again dove into them.

Just about this time, during a commercial break in the game, the local Chicago news channel had a special news alert. "The situation at the US-Mexico border has grown worse, and it appears that what was once thought to be contained has gotten out of control. An expanded story on the situation will be broadcast following the game."

A few tables away sat a couple of ugly Americans. They were loud, obviously drunk, and obnoxious. Shouting curses at the umpires on the TV, playing grab ass with the waitresses, these were just typical, overweight, slovenly, beer-guzzling fools out for a good time at the expense of others. The loudest-mouthed drunk stood up, hoisted his Budweiser in the air, and shouted, "Those fucking Mexicans. We should have closed that damn border years ago and shipped the rest of those damn illegal bastards back home. Goddammit, those wetbacks have been stealing our jobs for years!"

Before Mr. Big Mouth redneck could sit down, a giant of a Mexican grabbed him and lifted him in the air. At 250 pounds of fat and stink, this American wasn't the kind of guy most men would confront. But here he was held in the air by the

Hispanic Hulk, a man who was no stranger to hefting free weights in the gym daily. In a voice that sounded like The Terminator, he said, "Hey, gringo, I am a fucking Mexican. How about you try to send me back to Mexico."

That was all it took. The customers inside The Cubby Bear were frustrated at the Cubs and another losing season, and as if it were an orchestrated event, the entire bar exploded into a huge brawl. The overabundance of libations had rid the fighters of any inhibitions, and within seconds, the place was knee deep in broken chairs and tables. Glasses were thrown, and the fighting was fierce. Not since the great bar brawl seen in the movie *Cat Ballou* had there been such an epic bar battle. It was as if Elliot Silverstein, the director of *Cat Ballou* himself, was in his director's chair giving direction to his actors. The employees could only stare at the insanity.

Alberto quickly slipped $100 under the plate of chicken wings, grabbed his family, and slid out the side door. Once everyone was safely in their taxi, Alberto gave the family a little speech that he had been preparing for days.

"I have something to say, and I want everybody's undivided attention. One of the main reasons I considered the northern cities for our move was because I thought it was as important to get away from the hate and prejudices against Hispanic people. Conflicts like the one we just witnessed in the bar are going to be very common in the US border states. Maria, I know in your heart that you are dreaming that someday we'll return to Monterrey or Mexico. You can forget that. I am not going to live a life of bifurcation. I'm not going to live in America with my heart in Mexico. I love my native country every bit as much as you. But Maria, it is time to move on, and that day is today. We are no longer Mexicans. I've already filled out the paperwork and have applied for US citizenship for all of us. I'm not sure it will be necessary under Obama's amnesty plan, but I do not want to take any chances. I know that the Mexicans coming to America by the thousands are going to try to become US citizens, and I want us to be at the head of that line."

Alberto smiled and with a confident look said, "The American people will become the minority population! We will become the new majority!"

Their son and daughter seemed to be taking this all in stride, but Maria's mouth had not closed since he had started the speech. No comments and no sounds. She knew better than to speak up and protest. When Alberto spoke in that tone of voice, she knew there was no argument.

"There are new rules in our house," he continued. "We are no longer Mexicans, and we are not going to be Mexican-Americans. We are going to be Americans, and that is the only way we will ever refer to ourselves. I have read countless treatises and books about how the blacks in America made a major mistake when they demanded that they be called 'African-Americans.' After almost a hundred years of blacks in America fighting racism and bigotry, just when the tide was turning, they made that horrible mistake. They said they didn't want just to be Americans—they wanted to be different. And, of course, then came along President Obama, who set the issue of racism back a hundred years.

"This family is not going to make that mistake, and I pray to Almighty God that all Mexicans moving to this country do not go down the same horrific path the blacks went down. I know US history, and the majority of the black population arrived in America a few hundred years ago. Today's black population has got as much connection to Africa as I've got to Spain. The last of the Morales family left Spain to move to Mexico four hundred years ago, when some of the first blacks were being brought to America.

"Recently, I was shopping in a butcher shop where the butcher was Hungarian. We had a friendly conversation while he was packaging the sausages I had bought. He never once intimated or said that he was a 'Hungarian-American.' The same day I was buying wine for dinner, and the man waiting on me was clearly Italian. He told me that he had moved with his family to Chicago from Italy in the last ten years, but he did not call himself an 'Italian-American.' I don't get it. This guy who's clearly Italian, who was born in Italy, who grew up in Italy and has lived in United States only ten years, doesn't call himself an 'Italian-American.' I'll never understand why the blacks in America demanded that they be called African-Americans.'

"We are not going to make that stupid mistake! We are Americans, we live in America, and we are proud of our adopted country and grateful for its freedom. From this day forward, no one in this car will speak Spanish again. Maria, the same goes for the Mexican maid you hired last week.

"Maria, I know you might think I'm going a bit overboard, and I recognize that most product labels are in both English and Spanish. We will be US citizens, and we will speak English."

His son, Raul, knew better than to interrupt his father, but he just had to add something. "Dad, can I say something that I think's important?"

"Sure, son."

"Did you see those Chinese kids I was talking to during the game? One of the boys brought it up, not me. I think he suspected that we were recently from Mexico. I think that's why he brought it up."

"Go ahead, son, spit it out. What did he say?"

"He said that his family had just recently applied for citizenship, but his father was explaining to him that the immigration system in America is backward. Instead of the United States favoring citizenship among the wealthy and educated, it favors the opposite. He said that poor, uneducated people have a better likelihood of being granted citizenship than the affluent and educated. His father was a doctor in China. Why would they do that, Father? Why would any country not want to attract people of higher wealth and education? Wouldn't that be better in the long run for the country?"

Alberto was glad that his son was already thinking like a man. But now he had to explain why their new country acted so poorly toward the wealthy and educated.

"I am convinced that coming to America in the long run was the best choice I could have made for our family. But remember, this is not a country without problems. Just like our country, the United States has inept, egotistical, corrupt politicians. It has something called 'liberalism,' which is what we know as 'socialism.' It has been an infection that has been growing in America for decades and has warped its perspective of right and wrong and what's best for the country. I don't think any of you know this, but our country's immigration policies are ten times stricter than they are here in America. Life in America has its promise, but at the same time, it can lead one down the path of ruination and poverty with its entitlement programs. It can steal one's self-worth and morals and destroy ethics. This once proud nation is twisted by those who have become enslaved, dependent on government handouts and subsidies, unable to take care of themselves. This, my family, is the greatest lesson of all. Don't let anyone rob you of the pride we brought with us. America is our dream. Don't let it become your nightmare."

Chapter 72

Major General Tillman ordered his aide to get General Grayson on the special line they had set up after the phone system went down. "This is Major General Tillman calling for General Grayson. Is he in?"

"Yes, sir, Major General Tillman. This is his aide, Major William Pierce. The general told me to put you through as soon as you called."

There was a short pause, and then Grayson came on the line. "Charlie, I hope to hell you're calling me with that report I asked for after the flyover. I feel impotent, sitting here in Washington without more information."

"Yes, sir. First, they seem to be more intelligent than we might have given them credit for. Also, my concern about the force attacking the base is a nonissue. They're like an army of ants avoiding a chemical spill. My helicopter pilots tell me that what they saw was the strangest thing they've ever seen. There is a massive wave moving aggressively north, but it's like Fort Bliss has a moat surrounding it. There is a quarter-mile buffer that the invaders have created. I would estimate that within a of couple days, they might be as far north as White Sands. But if I were to guess, they'll avoid that like a plague, just like they have Fort Bliss."

"What did your boys spot over El Paso?"

"It doesn't appear that there are too many deaths yet, but there have been some major injuries thus far. No doubt the entire metropolis of El Paso has been overrun. Between you and me, General, due to the population demographics, we've considered El Paso an unofficial suburb of Juarez, Mexico. Frankly, when my chopper boys flew in for a ground-level view, they couldn't tell the difference between the illegal invaders and the residents. They all seemed to have blended together."

"I know, it's the same issue I'm hearing everywhere. In the border states, especially those counties closest to the border, the Mexican population is at such a high percentage that no one can differentiate between the two. I think it's going to be problematic," Grayson said. "Okay, we haven't experienced much in the way of fatalities, but we have some injuries. Now, what about property damage?

Major General Tillman interjected his findings. "There is quite a bit of looting, but it's very selective. In addition to our aerial surveillance, we've had some additional nonmilitary who have sought refuge here at the base. We've allowed a few to enter, but we've used them for intelligence gathering. General, without them we're virtually blind to the outside world."

"Good thinking, Charlie. What have you learned?"

"Sir, as I was saying, the looting is selective: grocery stores, basically any facilities selling food. In that vein, a couple of the more interesting stories were about the massive warehouse stores and big-box stores being raided and stripped bare of foodstuffs. Trucks carrying food deliveries, sodas, and alcohol have been commandeered, leaving the drivers stranded at the side of the road. Additionally, we've heard back that liquor stores, convenience stores, and businesses selling firearms have been targeted as well."

"That's a very disturbing trend, Charlie. I was afraid of that," replied Grayson. "At least when they crossed the border they weren't armed. I know Texas well enough to know that there's a gun store at every milepost along the highway, all stocked and ready for bear! Hell, I thought that was going to turn out to be an advantage for us, but now its sounds like it might be a detriment. What else have you got for me?"

"Sir, I command one of the top fighting forces in the army with enough firepower to level half of Europe, yet we sit here with our thumbs up our asses. General, my men want to engage the *enemy* and close the border. Any idea, General, when Washington will pull the trigger and unleash our troops? No disrespect meant, sir, but this is crazy."

"Charlie, the powers to be are not deserving of your disrespect—nor mine either. The secretary of defense and I are about ready to blow a gasket. But I can't get those liberal, pansy-ass people in the White House to pull their heads out of their asses and make a decision. You want to hear the worst news? Now the president has asked Homeland Security to work with FEMA to see if they can come up with a reasonable working solution to the issue of our broken border and the illegals that are making a mockery of our country. Charlie, I nearly busted a gut when I heard that one. After FEMA completely fucked up the Hurricane Katrina disaster in New Orleans, I was praying that just once in our American history a US government agency would be disbanded. Instead, its budget was increased."

"I'm sorry, sir," Tillman couldn't help but butt in. "I don't understand their goddamn reasoning."

"It's complicated, Charlie. Or maybe I should just say it's more liberal politics from our friends in the nation's capital. Everyone is pointing fingers, and now it's down to that age old issue: the feds versus states' rights. As you well know, in some of the more progressive states like Texas and Arizona, the governors have been trying to fight the illegal immigration issue for the past decade. But that past president asshole Obama and his left-wing communist buddy Eric Holder took each of the states into federal court to keep them from accomplishing a damn thing. Nothing ever got resolved, and now that same damn issue is slowing down any decision."

Major General Tillman paused before he said more. He and Grayson went way back, and he didn't want to risk pissing off an old friend. But with his base surrounded by maybe a million Mexicans, the last thing he wanted to do was cut his ties to Washington.

"What's it going to take, General? What's it going to take for Washington to put its military to use to stop this damn thing?"

Grayson could feel the frustration in Tillman oozing through the phone. "I'm going to give it to you straight. And I know you've got a lot of fine officers who would like to know the story, but I'm sorry, this is got to stay just between the two of us. The White House and its liberal congressmen and senators aren't willing to admit that we are being invaded. And since they won't own up to those facts, they're not willing to unleash the military on what they see as nothing more than just a slight increase in illegal border crossings. To them, it's business as usual. After all, it's been happening for decades.

"Those liberal Democrats have had us by the short hairs and are planning on converting most of these invaders into new citizens to keep them in office. They'll provide them with entitlements, and who'd bite the hand that feeds them? So the liberals have in essence guaranteed their place in the White House and the Senate and Congress for decades."

Grayson knew that he'd already become a liability to the current administration, and if he continued talking like he was, he'd be relieved of duty and asked to resign. But he, like Tillman and the other true patriots who had come before him, had spent his entire life in honorable service to his country, even to the degree of sacrificing his family life to maintain watch over the democracy.

Grayson knew he'd crossed the line but continued his explanation to his old friend. After all, if his friend was going to be forced to make a decision that had a major impact on his career, he should know all the facts.

"But dammit," said Grayson. "They don't realize the fault in their thinking. Why participate in keeping an American in office if you are the new majority? Like the blacks who elected Obama—they were the majority, and they put a black man in the White House. Yes, yes, we both know how that turned out. It was the tipping point of our country's ruination. Of course, there were other presidents who helped bring down the ethics and moral structure of our way of life. But an incompetent black president was too much, and he broke this country's backbone. His treatment of the military at its highest echelon—his forced resignations and removals from position have compromised our once superpower status. We're now just a joke to the rest of the world."

Grayson, on a roll now, took a much-needed breath but continued, knowing that he had surely signed his fate. He'd be asked to resign, and he'd do so rather than break the oath he'd sworn on his first day in the military. Remembering his enlistment day, the proudest moment in his life, he paused to repeat the words he'd memorized for that day:

I, Kurt Grayson, do solemnly swear that I will support and defend the Constitution of the United States against all enemies, foreign and domestic; that I will bear true faith and allegiance to the same; and that I will obey the orders of the president of the United States and the orders of the officers appointed...

He, like Tillman and millions of other military personnel, had sworn to uphold the decisions of their commander in chief, but sadly he knew he was becoming a hypocrite, unfaithful to his oath and embarrassed at the path the country was on. But the die was cast, and he'd finish with a flourish.

"Charlie, I'd bet my pension, if I get one after this mess is over, that as soon as that liberal bitch Rosemary Denton gets her fat ass out of the White House, we're going to have our first American-born Mexican president in the Oval Office. Even some of our more conservative Republicans have rolled, too comfortable in power to lift a finger and risk alienating the Mexican vote."

"Shit!" moaned Tillman.

"I know you know as much as I do about American political and military history. You little shit, I suspect you copied my answers on the finals at the Point, so I'm not going to tell you something you already know. But nothing's changed in a hundred years. The politicians get us into wars that Americans don't want, and then they keep their fingers stirring the pot to keep the fighting going until it becomes a political hot potato, and then they blame it on a less-than-adequate military. Shit, they tie our hands and don't let us win the war. Charlie, it's no different this time. It's all fucking politics!"

"Hell, sir, the way you're talking, I'd feel safer if I was surrounded by Mexicans than surrounded by a bunch of nutcase liberal politicians. So honestly, Kurt, I understand your position. Hey, maybe you should call out the troops from Fort Belvoir and Fort Myer and surround the White House. Wouldn't Denton just wet her pants?"

For the first time in days, General Grayson allowed himself a chuckle. "Shit, Charlie, don't think I haven't thought about that a hundred times."

Now Tillman allowed himself to also chuckle for the first time in days. "Oh, man, General, aren't we a bunch of dinosaurs? Oh, and about your accusation—I never had to cheat on the exams! I was always smarter than you. So fuck you...sir, and God bless America!"

As their receivers fell into their cradles, they each broke out in laughter that was reserved for those under the utmost stress. Both needed the heartfelt relief of two old friends who didn't get enough time to enjoy humor like the rest of the world. These men carried the weight and honor of the country on their shoulders and took their jobs seriously. They were survivors who had lost friends under hostile conditions and felt lucky to be alive and still in service to their country.

Chapter 73

Dave Walther and his fellow border-patrol officers, along with the border-patrol officers of Operation Gatekeeper, were responsible for protecting the United States from those who would cross the US-Mexico border illegally. Their mission had been expanded in the last few years to include the buffer zone— the desert—and certain cities in an attempt to stop the flow of narcotics, human traffickers, and simple border crossers. It was an immense job that had Dave on a regular basis returning illegals to the detention center in Tijuana, Mexico.

During this current situation with the border breach, Dave's squad had been merged with the DEA Special Operations Division. Since the onslaught of the massive wave of illegals, the joint task force had been brought into active, 24-7 duty, with people working twelve hours on and twelve off, seven days a week. Dave had requested emergency leave since his wife, Anita, was pregnant with their first child and needed his help. But Buck, good old Buck, had denied his request and had done so with a chuckle.

"No fucking way. If I've got to be here, so do you!" Buck, always the diplomat.

The phone restriction was still in effect, and Dave could only speak to his wife once a day. The censorship regarding the situation with the border was still in effect. To break the rule meant time in prison and the loss of any pension. Good old Buck was the senior officer in charge, and as usual, he was an asshole to Dave. Buck relished his command, and he let everyone know he was the big man who made all the decisions.

Dave was worried about Anita, especially since he knew she was sympathetic to the great wave of illegal immigrants. If he wasn't around to keep her from doing something stupid or illegal, there might be trouble.

If Dave had known that Anita and her friends were providing food to the illegals, he would have gone AWOL to put a stop to her misguided effort. He knew that when you fed *wild animals*, and that's how the illegals had been acting, they would stay, begin to feel entitled and emboldened, and go farther into the neighborhoods. Next would come looting and bullying of US citizens. He also knew that if they were turned away, they would get violent and act without reason. Anita was playing with fire and didn't know it.

Anita and her friends felt that it was their responsibility to feed and care for their own people, and her kind, naïve heart was simply crushed because of their circumstances. Being pregnant and wearing her heart on her sleeve, she organized a group of women to adopt these immigrants as extended family temporarily and provide for their needs.

However, this particular group seemed to be especially shy and mistrusting. Anita and her friends vowed to do their best to acclimate them to the American culture. Anita especially had taken them under her wing. Due to her personal situation, she felt in a nesting mood, fussing about and spending a lot of time each day offering whatever help she could. Anita and her friends prayed for the blessed Mother to intercede in the illegals' lowly situation and allow them to trust their rescuers. Anita knew that they were the poorest of the poor from her country, probably uneducated, and that they were just hungry. She knew humble people like these had no intention of hurting anyone.

In fact, to help break the ice, she encouraged the women and young children to put their hands on her stomach and feel her unborn baby kick. This act of motherly love melted the immigrant women's and children's hearts. It was a great bonding moment for the group, and that, above all, pleased Anita. The group, to Anita, was fast becoming her extended family, and it had been a long time since she had had any real family, at least family from her homeland. Anita was so engrossed in them that she ignored the alarm bells going off in her head.

It had seemed to Anita that every time they went out with food, there was never enough. So she and some of her closest Mexican friends had quadrupled their efforts. They had enlisted four other Mexican women who lived in the neighborhood to help to prepare sandwiches. A few neighbors only kicked in money to purchase bread and meat for sandwiches because their husbands disapproved of their association with the illegals.

This time they had prepared nearly two hundred sandwiches, along with chips and approximately one hundred apples, and they were determined to not run short.

They had pulled the pickup truck belonging to Bernadette, or "Bernie," a neighbor, into Anita's garage to load the food. Anita's group had decided to load their supplies under the cover of her garage so nosy neighbors wouldn't see what they were doing.

Bernie's pickup truck had a shell over the bed area that kept the food covered for the twenty-mile drive. They were going a little west of San Diego, where they had been handing out food for the last few days.

It was a small green-scaped area surrounded by fairly barren landscape. It was not easily visible from far up the road because the road was winding and blocked by small, sandy mounds. The two friends excitedly chatted that there was no way they were going to run out of food. As they rounded the last twist, they were totally shocked at what they saw. Up until that day, they'd never encountered more than two hundred Mexicans. But today there were upward of a thousand waiting for her and Bernie to arrive.

Bernadette, nearly choking at the sight, exclaimed, "Anita, how are we going to manage to feed that many people? Where have they come from?"

"They must've heard about the free food from the others!" Anita excitedly answered, then crossed herself that she and her unborn child had the strength to make it through the day.

As they drove in and parked near a set of abandoned picnic tables, the hordes quickly started moving in their direction.

Both Anita and Bernie got out of the truck and opened the back.

They felt that if they could start distributing the sandwiches, chips, and apples as quickly as possible, it might keep the swarm under control. Bernie suggested that they cut the sandwiches in half, and that way they could satisfy a lot more people.

Anita removed a large kitchen knife out of her utensil bag.

Anita found and wiped off a board that was lying in the back of the pickup. She immediately started cutting the sandwiches and passing them on to Bernie, who would then distribute them to the masses of arms and hands that were waving in front of her.

"*Mueva hacia atrás, movimiento detrás, allí es abundancia para todos!*" *Move back, move back, there's plenty for everyone!* they both shouted at the crowd.

The group was swelling, getting more aggressive, and the two women had a harder time distributing the food. It seemed everyone just wanted to grab for themselves. And what made everything so difficult to control was that the smaller, weaker people were being forced to the back. No one paid attention to their pleas. They were equally hungry, but in a pack frenzy, the larger, more aggressive fed first, leaving almost nothing for those in the back of the pack.

The mass of hungry immigrants surged forward, pinning Bernie and Anita's backs against the pickup truck.

"Oh," cried Anita. The baby was kicking wildly due to her being shoved back hard in the stomach. Oh, how she wished Dave was here. He could control the crowd or at least rescue her from being injured. She never thought her act of loving kindness would come back to hurt her. Would Dave find it in his heart to forgive her?

Just then, a man known as George, one of the large, aggressive illegals in the crowd, reached between Bernie and Anita while laughing cruelly at the two ladies and grabbed a handful of sandwiches that Anita was getting ready to cut in half for the hungry crowd. Anita nearly sliced the man's hand as he reached for them. Hurting from the blow to her pregnant stomach and upset due to the aggressiveness of the huge crowd, Anita spun to face the buffoon.

Anita called, "Hey, caballero," and grabbed his shirt to spin him in her direction. She was not going to let him bully his way to the front of the line and grab what he wanted in spite of the others who were hungry but waiting patiently. How dare he show such disrespect to those who were trying to feed and help his own kind. Her anger was fueled by his rudeness and her pregnancy hormones; she came unglued. She wouldn't stand for his or anyone's bad treatment.

Little Anita reared up and spun George about, still holding her best kitchen knife in her cutting hand, exposing the gleaming knife blade to the crowd.

At that very moment, George's best friend saw the big blade in Anita's hand. He quickly advanced to where Anita was holding his best friend by the shirt and screaming at him. Anita was waving her hand holding the knife in George's face.

Bernie shouted her name again and again, and Anita stopped, suddenly realizing she was still holding and waving the knife, ashamed at being so aggressive. She started to apologize to George, whom she still held at bay. But it was too late.

George's friend seized Anita and drove his knife into her chest, his adrenaline flowing with such intensity that he buried the knife to its hilt. Anita collapsed, reeling with pain.

Anita's body lay quite still, the spark of life having fled her now empty shell. Bernie, unable to focus through her tears, loosed the tormented cry of a torn soul.

Sounding like a wounded animal, Bernie reached down, pausing for a moment of reverence, and removed the knife from Anita's ruined body. She turned and drove the knife into Anita's assailant so forcefully that she broke the wooden handle off of Anita's best knife.

Within a matter of seconds, the Mexicans, using clubs and rocks, dealt Bernadette the same fate as Anita. Then they quickly grabbed every morsel of food and melded into the surrounding area as if they'd never existed.

Chapter 74

If a reporter had been a fly on the wall, he would have seen that it was another all-girl meeting in the Oval Office. It was the holy trinity in the guise of President Denton, Secretary of State Marisa Angela Lopez, and the president's closest personal advisor, Stephanie Jones.

For the country as a whole, it was about to get worse. President Denton started in. "Okay, ladies, I have Secretary of Defense Hardwick scheduled to be here by 10:00 a.m., but I want to make sure the three of us have our script well polished before I call him in. I have a little announcement for you this morning that I know will brighten your day considerably. I decided last night who I'm going to replace Secretary Hardwick with. The new secretary of defense is going to be Virginia Wade."

"That's an excellent choice, Rosemary. She was at the top of my list," said Marisa.

However, it was quite obvious from her face that Stephanie was anything but enthusiastic. "Rosemary, I knew you were considering Virginia, but I didn't voice my opposition to her because I didn't really think you were serious. I believe you will have an incredibly hard time getting her confirmed. You are going to have a hard enough time with Congress once we announce you're firing Hardwick, but I think with what's going on at the border, it's a political hot potato to put in a controversial secretary, plus someone the Republicans are going to try to block with a huge fight during her confirmation."

Though President Denton rarely made such a key decision without the approval of Stephanie Jones, in this instance, she merely waved her hand and cooed to Stephanie, "I knew you wouldn't approve. But I have a bigger agenda now. The United States has never had a secretary of defense who was a woman, and though President Obama did everything he could to rid

Washington of all those old dinosaur white men, in my election campaign, I promised our female liberal supporters that I would take what Obama started to a whole new level."

Stephanie injected, "I completely understand and agree with you. It tickles every female organ in my body to replace one more *man* in our administration..." Stephanie sneered and continued, "...with one of us. But it's the timing I am questioning.

"Look, I know Obama set quite a precedent. He changed secretaries of defense more often than I change my underwear." They shared a laugh among lady friends. "Of course, he fired them when he needed to blame someone for either his foreign-affairs incompetence or administration's failures, or for botching every military issue confronting America. Still, Rosemary, this problem at the Mexican border is getting more serious by the day, and you might find yourself needing an exit strategy or scapegoat. Blaming a man for the situation and bringing in Virginia at that point would be a feather in your bonnet."

President Denton was still dead set on Virginia now instead of later. "We'll talk more about the Mexican-border problem later.

"Ladies, let's stay focused on this replacement issue, and we need to hurry. Hardwick's due here in a few minutes."

"Let Hardwick wait," Stephanie continued snidely. "It'll do his male ego some good. Look, Virginia Wade would not only be the first female secretary of defense, she'd probably be the least militarily experienced in our history. And let me repeat emphatically, I'm all for it. But the conservative Republicans are going to have a field day with her confirmation hearings."

President Denton shook her head. "I'm not worried about the Republicans. We've got the press in our breast pocket. As always, they'll help us convince the American public that it was the Republicans that are responsible for the problems at the border. We'll show that their unwillingness to bring in a fresh face to fix the problem...Well...come on, we don't need to worry about the details. The press will fix that for us. And on that note, Stephanie, while I'm meeting with Hardwick, I want you to get on the phone and contact all our key people at NBC, CBS, ABC, CNN, and MSNBC and give them the spin on Hardwick's forced resignation and his replacement. I want them to have advance notice so they can put out as much positive coverage before Fox News has a chance to go on the attack."

Marisa spoke up. "This is a red-letter day for *all* women in America. However, I am a little disappointed at your selection of a white woman. I think there were plenty of Mexican or even black females that you could've chosen over Virginia."

"I know," said Rosemary. "But come on, gals, between Obama's and my administrations, 90 percent are black, Mexican, or some other minority, and the vast majority of those are women. At the rate we're going with my first term, I'll be the only white woman in office." They giggled, rose, and gave a three-way high five. "Yes, ladies, we're an ole girls' network. Hey, ya gotta wear heels to be in this club!"

Marisa asked, "What is Virginia's opinion about the situation at the border? As a Mexican-American, I have grave concern about how these innocent individuals are going to be treated in the United States."

Rosemary gave a dismissive, arrogant shrug of her shoulders. "Why the hell would I care? Virginia will do exactly what I tell her to. She's so thankful to have a job after she lost her position as the Democratic National Committee chairman—she'll fall in line. Compared to Hardwick, and I've hated that bastard ever since I inherited him, she will be a godsend. Not so much for the country, but for us."

Clapping her hands to dismiss the holy trinity, Rosemary spoke in a perky tone, "All right, ladies, you've got a lot of spinning to do. Someone, on your way out, ask my secretary to send in Hardwick."

None of what was going to take place in the next few moments would be any surprise to Hardwick. He knew when Rosemary Denton was elected president that his job security had gone down the tubes. That was the way it had been in Washington since Obama's time in office. The last time a secretary of defense had held his position for any serious length of time was the six years Donald Rumsfeld served in the Bush administration. Of course, sadly, that had been the last Republican administration. He had gotten word last night that he would be summoned to the White House for an important meeting with President Denton the next afternoon. Reading the handwriting on the wall, he had already started to clean out his desk and had told his wife the realities of his position that night. She had been elated. For roughly the last two years, she had had to sit and listen to her husband's nightly rants about the president and how her administration was following the business-as-usual trend started by Obama. The president was seeing that the military was being dismantled piece by piece and that the US military presence and its strength in the world were being raped, their readiness destroyed. Because of that, the stability in the world today was reaching proportions not seen since the Cold War days. Hardwick hoped the meeting would be brief and painless. If not, he knew that he would say something he would regret. No, on second thought he realized there wasn't a damn thing he could say to Rosemary Denton that he would ever regret.

"Sit down, Secretary Hardwick. I have an issue or two to discuss with you today. Let me be blunt, because I know you are a man who appreciates getting to the point. I am getting daily stories from all over town that you and some of your compatriots over at the Pentagon have been criticizing me and my administration's position over what's happening at the Mexican border. I cannot afford that disrespect and dissension in my administration. I've warned you before about keeping your mouth shut."

So much blood rushed to Hardwick's eyes that he thought his eyeballs might explode. He wasn't even sure that he could get the words out. "Mouth shut..."

President Denton was a woman, and behind closed doors there was not a man in a country that could get a word in edgewise when she was on one of her bitch rolls.

"I'm not going to put up with you talking behind my back, and frankly I'm not in the mood for anything you have to say today! This is my Oval Office, and you will sit there until I'm through. You're fired. Clean out your drawers and get out! I'll give you a little heads up. Tell those conservative friends of yours at the Pentagon that they can start cleaning their drawers out too."

There was no response needed. Secretary Hardwick's blood pressure had returned to normal, and in a matter of seconds he realized the president had maybe just saved him from a heart attack. He knew beyond a shadow of a doubt that in the coming weeks, the matter at the border was going to get totally out of control, and the president would blame the new secretary of defense for mismanagement of the situation. He had just been handed a get-out-of-jail-free card, and though he loved his country more than anyone in the Denton administration, he was relieved in more ways than one to be released from the living hell serving this president had become.

He reached for the door of the Oval Office, paused for a moment, and turned back to address President Denton. "You know, Madam President, there's one huge difference between the two of us. I took this job because I care about the country. You became president because all you care about is power, reelection, and your legacy. You don't give a damn about our country!" With that, he stormed out.

Chapter 75

Rocky slammed down the TV remote and turned to his wife, Kathy. "Take one suitcase, and I mean only one suitcase, and pack the bare essentials that we absolutely need for a two-week trip. Absolutely the essentials, and not your usual 10 pairs of shoes. Kathy, I need you to do this immediately."

"Honey, don't you think you're overreacting? You know how you've said that the press always blows everything out of proportion just to get people to watch their show. You're always reminding me that we can't believe 90 percent of what we see on TV, so why are you taking this so seriously?"

"Maybe I didn't say it loud enough or stern enough. Start packing! You've got two minutes to start, and when you're finished, grab my three largest hunting coolers and pack them with as much food as you can find. That means nutritious stuff only, not Klondike Bars. Then take the two empty boxes I've saved out of the garage and pack the most nutritional food you can find from the pantry."

Their kids were grown and out of college, and Rocky and Kathy shared a good marriage lasting thirty years. Rocky didn't often speak to his wife in such a stern manner. In Rocky's eyes, a state of emergency should have been called by the governor's office days ago, based on everything he had seen on the news. But doing so would be political suicide for the governor because it would halt the economic wellbeing now being enjoyed by many private firms for the first time in ten years. The tourist industry was just gearing up for the winter season when the snowbirds from the North were making plans to winter here. Yes, it would be political suicide, and the governor enjoyed his position and rank.

As Rocky continued to order around Kathy, a very successful real estate executive, she reminded him of the pact that they had made early on in their relationship. She was going to be treated as his equal. But Kathy was smart enough to know that both couldn't wear the pants in the family at the same time, and someone was going to be in charge when it came to their physical well-being. Hands down the physical welfare of the family was Rocky's forte.

Putting it lightly, Rocky had had a "rocky" start in life. His parents had constantly fought and were divorced when he was in junior high school. Rocky had been interested in just about everything in life but school. His main interests were getting girls and hanging out with his friends. Far from stupid, Rocky had realized after he'd graduated from high school that he needed to do something more than just chase women, so he joined the army. Enlisting in the army in 1970 had guaranteed a tour in Vietnam. For thousands of Americans, Vietnam had been anything but a pleasant experience, but for Private Rocky Canfield, it had fit him to a *T*. His time in Vietnam had been almost as good as Forest Gump's stint in the army. *Forest Gump* was Rocky's favorite movie after *Apocalypse Now*.

Rocky had grown up in a community where all the working residents were active duty or worked for the military. Even the male high school teachers were ex-military. Rocky and his classmates had to address them by their military titles. There were no plain old Mr. Teachers at the school, except for the short, fat, and balding principal, who acted like Napoleon reincarnated. Rocky had been fascinated with the military and had already decided if he couldn't get into college, he would enter the ROTC program at the local community college.

Rocky was fascinated with guns, and he and his father, even though their relationship wasn't close, had spent time shopping for guns, going to the indoor shooting range, shooting skeet, and hunting together. Rocky fondly remembered some great philosophical jawing while cleaning their guns, though their relationship had often been characterized at the end of a leather strap.

Rocky had received his first gun at age ten, a family heirloom handed down from father to son for several generations. The handgun was a Smith & Wesson 48 single-action revolver. Boy, could Rocky fan the hammer action like his favorite TV cowboy, Sugarfoot, played by Will Hutchins.

Today's model 48 was essentially the same weapon he had had but the cost for this historical, recreational weapon topped the charts at $949, far more than it had cost when his dad had received it on his tenth birthday from his father. His father thought it was a perfect gun for a young man. The Smith & Wesson single-action was one of the most popular guns. Today, Rocky's handgun collection included revolvers like a .38 Special and the movie studio's favorites—the .357 and .44 Magnums.

Rocky did well in the United States Army, and after his four years, he left with the rank of Sergeant Canfield. Rocky came from a long line of military men but had the distinction of becoming the highest-ranked Canfield in the family. Like 72 percent of Vietnam veterans, he took advantage of the army's GI bill and entered college, graduating four years later with honors in petroleum engineering. After a successful career in the business of oil and petroleum engineering, he and his wife had decided to retire and moved into one of the most exclusive gated golf-course developments outside San Antonio.

Unfortunately for Kathy, Rocky was a bit uncouth and acted like the proverbial bull in a china closet. Rocky didn't dress or act to impress his wealthy neighbors. He still drank beer from a can, chewed and spit tobacco into a soda bottle, and drove an old, beat-up F-150 in constant need of washing. Rocky told Kathy one day as she was complaining about his dirty, derelict F-150, "If I wash that truck, it'll fall apart! It's the dirt that's holding it together." From then on, Kathy knew not to chastise her husband on any subject because he always had a biting comeback.

Kathy could tell that Rocky had his military game face on, and she knew there were to be no further discussions. As she was climbing up the attic stairs to fetch a suitcase, she turned, knowing the answer before she asked: "Am I allowed to ask where we're going?"

"You can ask, but at this point I don't know the answer," he replied. "All I do know is that we need to leave and leave here fast. I'm going to start making phone calls to some of my friends around the state to see if I can get a handle on what is happening with this border thing. After that, I'll be in a better position to make plans."

Kathy knew that Rocky was usually right, but he wasn't always right, and she was going to make one last attempt at questioning his decision. "Can't I wait to pack until you've made your calls? You could be wrong, you know, and jumping the gun." Rocky turned in disbelief. Kathy had broken his first rule. Never question or doubt his decision once it was made. Rocky bristled. Clasping his hands behind his back like he was General MacArthur addressing his troops, Rocky faced his wife and, in his best drill-sergeant tone, made her sorry that she had opened her mouth.

"The single most important thing taught in the army was 'be prepared'! It is not only the most important thing they taught, it was the very first thing they taught me. I remember to this day when a corporal spelled out the six Ps to us grunts—Prior Planning Prevents Piss-Poor Performance! These six words were an inspiration, and it was like a lightbulb went on in my head. The six Ps not only helped me move up fairly quickly in the army, they're what allowed me to graduate at the top of my class in college. I was always prepared for every course, every class, and every exam. These words are etched forever in my mind, and they're words to live by.

"If what the press has reported about the infiltration of Mexicans in southern Texas is correct, the old military adage will keep us one step ahead of everyone else. There's going to be a lot of Texans who are going to be caught off guard, and we aren't going to be a part of that group. Now get your ass packing!"

Within minutes Rocky was working the phone and talking with his friends from college, guys from his military unit, and his oil buddies still in the fields to see if he could get a better handle on the situation. The stories were mixed with a little good news, but the stories that were bad, were very bad. There had been shootings and lootings, and everyone seemed to be utterly confused and unclear about the true situation. Worse yet, not one person had an idea what direction to take to offset the invading illegals and their advancing movement.

But what chilled Rocky's blood the most was the fear in the voices of everyone he spoke with. Rocky's friends were all die-hards, men who had seen it all and returned for more. Not one of his friends was a wimp; each was a hard-working, self-made conservative. Rocky described these men as the last-standing, pure-hearted backbone of a once great nation. They were the way men once were. The TV news programs were shy of the truth, as usual; something serious, very serious, was taking place, and the country needed to know that it wasn't just serious, it was downright dangerous. The essence of America was at stake.

Chapter 76

"Ladies and gentlemen, the GoToMeeting conferencing session has been activated, and all participants are logged on. Please take a moment to check your connections. If you have any difficulties with the audio or video, please press *zero* on your phone. Thank you again for using GoToMeeting services."

Governor Brewmeister's chief of staff immediately followed with, "At this time I'd like you to introduce yourselves."

"Hello, everybody, this is Judy Rodriguez from New Mexico."

"Likewise, this is Governor Berry from the great state of Texas."

"Richard, don't give me that 'great state of Texas' crap. With the way oil prices have been plummeting, I'm not sure you guys are going to survive," said Governor Harry Black from California.

"Gentlemen, I don't think we have time for that today, and if you don't mind, since I'm the one who proposed this conference call of the governors from the states that border Mexico, I'd like to chair this conference call unless anyone has an objection," said Jacqueline Brewmeister, the governor of Arizona.

Governor Berry went first. "Have at it, Jaqueline. It seems like you women have just about taken over the country. Hold on, hold on, before you bite my head off, I'm more than comfortable with that fact. I just have one question before you start: does anybody on this call feel that they have a good handle on this situation? I mean with the facts on how we're positioned today?"

Governor Rodriguez jumped in. "Well I can only speak for the state of New Mexico, and excuse my French, but we're in deep shit! As you're aware, the federal government is doing nothing to help. It like we're the black sheep of the family, sitting at the children's table at Thanksgiving dinner. They're ignoring us. The border-patrol and customs agents are nowhere to be seen.

I've called every US military base in the state and demanded that they take action. They told me that their hands are tied by Washington. Speaking of Washington, I saw the news conference the other day by the president's press secretary, where she said that the president has been working closely with the governors concerning the situation. Boy, at the rate the lies are coming out of that office, it's a good thing our president isn't Pinocchio."

"Thanks for that picture and update, governor," said Jacqueline. "I am sure that my office is not the only one that is getting tons of calls from people simply with questions or outright panicking. I guess every day more and more tweets and streams are being shared, especially by those witnessing some of the happenings firsthand. We can thank the Denton Administration and the liberal press for either ignoring this or at best downplaying it all. I keep hearing from some of my friends that if Washington, the military and the press don't think this is a big deal, why should I? Now, Richard, you've got the biggest exposure with the border. Can you give us any update as to your status?"

"Not good, but I would like to bump up this issue to include all of us. I think we should call out our individual National Guard components collectively. The only reason I haven't done it yet is that I received a phone call from both President Denton and the US attorney general threatening to immediately cut our funding for every government project in the state. Now I don't want to brag about who gets more money from the federal government, Texas or California, but we all know Texas gets in the tens of billions. Before I commit political hari-kari, I want to know if we can agree on a unified course of action. Have the rest of you had the same threatening call?"

Harry Black piped up first. "Sure thing. President Denton said in no uncertain terms that she would personally make it her mission in life to have the Department of Transportation immediately cut off funding for the new bridge between San Francisco and Oakland. It's put eight thousand workers on the job, and I can't afford that politically."

"I got the same call," chimed in Governor Rodriguez. "If the rest of you don't mind, I'd like to bring up El Paso to Richard. We lost communications there almost immediately after the border's collapse. I have family there, and as of today, I have been unable to establish the well-being of my family. This is impossible to imagine in our day and age, but believe me when I say this: our vulnerability and exposure are very real. We're at the mercy of these invaders! Yes, we all share the same threat. The common denominator is the very high percentage of Mexicans already living within our states, legal or illegal. Let me remind you that New Mexico has the highest percentage of Mexicans and a great many first-generation Mexican-Americans. I'd like to share a little secret with you: just yesterday, highway patrol officers brought in a group that'd just crossed the border and were picked up near Las Cruces. When the officers interrogated them, they told my patrol officers that they learned from others crossing the border that it was safer for them to cross into the United States in either New Mexico or California."

Richard Berry let out a big, "Ha! I wish somebody would have told that to the thousands that have already crossed into the state of Texas. We're like Disneyland to the hordes who have eaten, ransacked, and trashed their way across our great state with every mile they've traveled."

Governor Black smirked. "Well, Richard, that's what you get when you announce to the world on a nationally televised debate that you thought any American that disapproved of Texas providing free medical aid and education to illegal Mexicans was heartless. Hey, what a great presidential platform, governor! What's next, a big fat chicken in every pot and a year's subscription to *People Magazine*?"

Governor Berry's blood pressure was almost audibly rising, and his ears seemed to be billowing steam. "Oh, that may be true, but last year California started issuing driver's licenses to all illegal aliens. Say, I understand that there are lines circling the blocks and that all the DMVs have had to stay open 24-7 for the last six months. How's your budget now, Governor?"

Jacqueline Brewmeister broke in. "Governors, I don't think this is the time or place to argue which of our states is more or less liberal to the illegal Mexicans living within our country, but let me add my two cents. As you all know, I butted heads on the illegal-alien issue with Obama, and I've been butting heads with our illustrious President Denton. She called the other day, and I refused to take her call, so I had the call forwarded to my attorney general. We are having major problems with the wave of illegals working through and around Tucson. But I think at this point Arizona doesn't have the numbers the rest of you are experiencing, at least not yet. My advisory team thinks it's because we don't have any major interstates connecting with Mexico and because we have been aggressively halting illegal entries and deporting any illegals caught since I've been governor. I think the fact that we have been very vocal about that issue has probably reached the people of Mexico and forewarned them of our no-nonsense policy. And of course, we have our famous sheriff, Joe Arpaio, here in Maricopa County. I'm not saying he's as famous in Mexico as he is here in the states, but I suspect a lot of invading Mexicans are going to stay away from Phoenix just because he's here."

"Well, I guess it's futile," said Governor Rodriguez. "We certainly don't have the time or luxury to collectively file a class-action lawsuit in federal court to block President Denton from enforcing her threats if we call out our National Guard, do we?"

"I'm afraid not," agreed Jacqueline. "Here in Arizona, we've never agreed with anything that came out of Washington since Obama was president, and it continues today with Rosemary Denton's administration. We've had a hell of a lot of experience fighting the White House in federal court, and my attorney general said that ultimately we would be victorious, but it would take years. Denton would be out of office by then, and our children would be speaking Spanish as their first language!" The last statement sucked the life out of Jacqueline. With bitter rancor, she let loose her pent-up frustration and said what no one had the nerve to express. "We're up shit's creek without a paddle. Governors, we're screwed!"

Pausing to let the words sink in, Governor Rodriguez broke the silence. "I'm curious and haven't figured out why those Mexicans we picked up said that they were told they should avoid Texas."

"I can answer that," Richard said quickly. "The commercialized picture of a typical Texan is a big cowboy carrying an even bigger gun. Mexico TV still shows our old, wild, shoot-'em-up westerns with gunfights in the streets. What a great deterrent. We may not have the greatest per capita of households with firearms, but I can assure you that Texans know how to use their guns, and they won't hesitate to do so. Hey, Mr. Liberal California Governor, did you know that Reuters reported that ninety out of one hundred red-blooded, taxpaying US citizens exercise their right to bear arms? Furthermore, only 12 percent of civilian weapons are thought to be registered. Just in 2011 alone, California gun dealers sold over 601 thousand guns. Those were the ones that were purchased and registered. So put that in your liberal peace pipe and smoke it."

Harry Black had tried to keep a relatively low profile and not attract attention to himself since his earlier stab at Governor Berry. He felt he had failed miserably, especially after the whipping he'd just received from Richard. Being the only Democrat on the phone, he didn't have much in common with the other three governors, and frankly, he probably was the one governor on the phone who wasn't really all that concerned with the invasion. Sure, there had been accidents involving the illegal migration north that had resulted in death and property destruction, but it was nothing that much worse than one of his state's incredibly destructive storms. He was now in his fourth term as California governor, and the liberal Democrats had had the run of the state for the last couple of decades. With the help of the Mexican vote, the Democrats had been able to get into office some of the most liberal, socialist-leaning politicians now serving in Washington: Barbara Boxer, Dianne Feinstein, and the queen of liberalism, Nancy Pelosi, all of whom owed their election success to the thriving Mexican population. The last thing Governor Black was going to do was alienate the Mexican vote for himself or his fellow liberals.

After the last diatribe, dead air ensued. No one spoke.

Finally, Jacqueline Brewmeister broke the uncomfortable silence. "Well maybe I was a little too optimistic about what we might be able to accomplish during this session. Let me put this out on the table and see if I can get a vote. My proposal is this: I propose the four of us jointly send a statement to the president stating that we think the threats to withhold federal funds are unconstitutional and a breach of states' rights. Furthermore, that we collectively intend to activate and call on our states' National Guards within forty-eight hours. In my opinion, if we do it collectively, we might call President Denton's bluff. Can I get any agreement?"

"I'm in, if we can get around the cut off of federal funds," said Richard Berry.

"I'm out," said Harry Black.

The New Mexico governor said, "Though I know under our state's Constitution I have the right to activate the National Guard as governor, with a Mexican controlled state House and Senate, I might face impeachment if I make that decision on my own. But I'm on the record that I support your efforts, 100 percent. I will immediately try to address the New Mexico State Congress and petition for approval. I am, however, not optimistic."

Jacqueline Brewmeister was furious. Once again, her fellow governors had caved to the federal government's threat of withholding the purse strings. Much worse, however, was Governor Harry Black.

He didn't give a damn about his citizens. He only placated them to keep himself in office, the self-serving bastard! she thought to herself.

Jacqueline feared what she might say and later regret, so she cut her losses. In a tone that left no doubt in her fellow governors' minds how she felt about their devotion to the hand that fed them, she said, "Thank you for your time today. I fear that I have wasted my effort, and I, for one, clearly have more pressing matters at hand!"

The line went dead, and so did Jacqueline's attempt to save the border states.

Chapter 77

Bill and Elsie Walther didn't watch the news as much as they used to; it was too depressing. It wasn't the same as the good old days with Chet Huntley and David Brinkley. Back then, people got the news and only the news. Today, the news was so filtered that people only got the news that the liberal executives at NBC, CBS, and ABC wanted them to know about. Luckily, Bill turned on the news early enough to catch *Your World w/ Cavuto*. Bill and Elsie's favorite news programs were *Special Report* with Bret Baier, followed by Sean Hannity and Megyn Kelly. Bill also liked that he had a backup to Fox News. There was the Patriot radio station on Sirius radio, where he could access his favorites— Glenn Beck, Andrew Wilkow, Sean Hannity, and Mark Levin. And of course, there was always Rush Limbaugh. Bill was looking for any news about the Mexican situation and especially what was going on at the border. The news reported that Jacqueline Brewmeister, the governor of Arizona, was thinking of calling out the National Guard—something about disturbances at one of the Arizona border entries.

When compared with Texas's border, Arizona's 378-mile border with Mexico seemed small. What made it seem even smaller was the fact that, unlike the other three bordering states, Texas, New Mexico, and California, there were no major highways that connected any of the Arizona-Mexico entry points. Despite this, Arizona had more than its share of illegals crossing into its state.

Arizona had a history of being tough on illegal immigration, unlike the other three border states. Bill thought New Mexico had never been tough enough. Hell, 90 percent of the state's population was already Mexican, and only God knew how many were legal. California, or as Bill referred to it, "the most screwed up state in the country," was nothing more than one big contradiction. Bill thought it probably had the biggest concentration of liberals outside of Massachusetts, yet at the same time, its legislature had enacted stricter regulations than the other forty-nine states. As liberals, Californians had always been soft on immigration, providing programs to support them until they could provide for themselves, a joke that many shared.

Then there was Texas, another big contradiction. Bill had many great memories of and much love for the state of Texas; he had been stationed there in the army. But Texas Governor Richard Berry, who once ran for president, changed his position on immigration more often than Bill changed TV channels. During one of the presidential debates, Berry had said that one was not a red-blooded, compassionate American if they didn't think every Mexican in America, including all the illegal ones, should be given free food, clothing, and shelter, along with free medical care and a free college education. After he got his butt kicked in the 2012 presidential election, he reversed and tried to portray himself as tough on immigration. Luckily for the majority of Texans, they didn't give a hoot what Berry thought. He was a true politician and could flip-flop his position at the drop of a hat.

Or at the drop of a Mexican sombrero, thought Bill.

Then there was Arizona. Bill savored the thought, *By God, Barry Goldwater's rule of law during the early 1960s sure got stuff done. It was a great and honorable state back then.*

To Bill, John McCain had been such a big disappointment. McCain was just another one of those Republicans who wasn't really a conservative. But the governor, Janice Brewmeister, was a godsend. She was one of the few governors in the entire nation who was sick and tired of *waiting* for the federal government to get serious about illegal immigration. She had attempted to take steps to handle the illegal situation herself. Bill hated the fact that he had to say 'attempted.' Brewmeister and the Arizona legislators had passed some of the most rigid policies concerning illegal immigration and, in addition, had passed legislation to *rid* the state of the millions of illegal

Mexicans that were residing within its borders. When President Obama had been in office, he'd directed the US Attorney General Eric Holder as if he were a sheep. Like President Obama, Eric Holder was a *racist socialist*. Holder had had the US Department of Justice file a lawsuit against the state of Arizona to block its attempt to fix its immigration problem.

It had been the first time in his entire life that Bill had thought of moving to another country.

Bill refocused his attention back to the TV. Cavuto didn't seem to have much to add to the story, and it seemed that both the White House and the state department were releasing little to nothing about the border situation. So Bill turned off the TV.

Just about then, Elsie came back in the living room. "I thought you were watching the news to see if you could get an update on the border situation. Doesn't anyone have any news at all about the situation?"

Bill took a deep breath and said, "After eight years of Obama, I would have bet $1 million that there couldn't be another administration as inept and corrupt as his. But Rosemary Denton and her cronies over at the state department are trying to give Obama a good run for his money. This is adding fuel to the fire for conspiracy theorists. There cannot be any other reason for so little communication and information flow."

Chapter 78

"Kathy, can you get me the phone directory for all the members of the club?" Rocky was still in his military mode and almost every conversation came in the tone of a military order. "Great, call every single member, and tell them I've called an emergency meeting at the clubhouse's main dining room for 7:00 p.m. this evening. Let them know it's a matter of life and death. If anyone asks what it's about, tell them you don't know."

The last time anyone had seen the Cordillera Golf Club dining room this full was for the annual member-guest golf tournament. But tonight, instead of the usual happy-go-lucky drunk crowd, not a soul was in a festive mood. Hours prior to Kathy's call to round everyone up for tonight's meeting, more and more stories had circulated about the illegal Mexicans that had crashed the US border and were now roving around San Antonio in pockets.

At the portable podium normally used to introduce the winners of the golf matches, Rocky stood, hands clasped behind his back, as he addressed the members. "Quiet down, quiet down, please give me your attention." Rocky raised his voice. "If I can get everybody to quiet down and take a seat, we'll start this emergency meeting."

Amazingly, everybody did what Rocky wanted. Rocky was amazed because he didn't hold any of the club's leadership positions, he wasn't a board member, and he and Kathy had only become members in the last few years. But everyone knew them because he and Kathy had recently won the husband-wife golf tournament. Living in an exclusive, gated golf community like Cordillera was, to many, the closest one could get to godliness.

"I don't think I need to explain why I called this meeting nor describe the importance of the situation at hand. It's obvious that everyone in the room has heard the news stories or rumors about the impending assault by a large band of illegal Mexicans, or you wouldn't be here. I'm sorry to tell you that on my drive over here I learned there is a fairly large group, or maybe I should say a massive wave, of illegals who just overran and ransacked the businesses and homes in Lytle. So it's confirmed. We now know that this massive wave of illegal immigrants is only a few miles from here. I'm in the same boat as the rest of you. None of us knows exactly what's happening or why it's happening, but what I do know is this— the time for talking and wringing our hands is over. No one is coming to our aid, and from what I've heard from friends throughout the state, the National Guard will not be activated, and law enforcement is completely overwhelmed and impotent to help regular citizens like us. From what I can see, there is no one but no one, including our local county sheriff's department, that can be counted on to come to our defense." Rocky paused, looked each member in their eyes, took a well needed breath to calm his nerves, and with emotion told the members as kindly as he could, "Friends, fellow members, it is time that we take matters into our own hands."

A woman in the back shouted to Rocky, "Just what in tarnation are you proposing we do? We're a bunch of old retirees!"

Rocky shook his head in disgust but calmed himself down before he responded. It was obvious that the group was already agitated and was now bordering on panic. "Before I respond to your question, Collette, let me ask a question of all of you. How many of you in the room own a gun and reasonably fresh ammunition? Please raise your hand if you own a weapon."

The response literally brought tears to Rocky's eyes. As far as he could tell, every single damn person out of the four hundred there raised his or her hand. "Thank you. We may need to fight for our homes and our very way of life."

Later that night, Rocky and Kathy lay in bed; they hadn't yet slept a wink. Both were awake and energized, ready to face the unknown. Rocky had had less than an hour to strategize a game plan, organizing the other club members for the fight to come. The 100 percent gun ownership was reassuring. Even more so was that every single member immediately volunteered to do whatever Rocky suggested. Luckily, he wasn't the only ex-military in the room, and five retired military officers—four men and one woman, who had been a colonel in the Army Medical Corps—had formed a management team. Their plan was crude but relatively easy and could be quickly implemented for the nonmilitary. Every single member was to return to his or her home and bring supplies on the list that Kathy had prepared prior to the meeting. Everyone was to bring the items back to the clubhouse no later than noon the next day.

The golf course itself was a par seventy-two, and it spread out over roughly two hundred acres, including a three-acre centralized pond and fountain. But as part of the gated community, the homes and the clubhouse added an additional 2,300 acres. An eight-foot fence bordered almost the entire property. They weren't fooling themselves into thinking that an eight-foot fence would keep anybody out. Worse, because everyone was so spread out by their two-to-five-acre properties, there would be no way to defend against a focused, major onslaught.

Rocky was a fan of old westerns and got his strategic inspiration from the cowboy-and-Indian battles where the wagon train circled the wagons in a defensive stand against unknown odds. This was an entirely different way to fight from that used in Vietnam. The last item on the list was the family vehicle or vehicles. The plan was to "circle the wagons" and keep the massive onslaught of illegals at bay, hoping that they'd lose enough of their group to make them want to move on.

Wow, this was going to be one expensive wagon train. His wagon defense was made up of Jaguars, Range Rovers, Mercedeses and full-sized pickup trucks, instead of the Conestoga covered wagons seen on the big screen. At Rocky's direction, they had created a tight circle of cars surrounding the clubhouse. Of course, not everything went smoothly with this many people involved. When Rocky told one of his neighbors that she needed to drive her new $120,000 Mercedes into a culvert, she refused. Rocky politely but very, very sternly repeated that he had not asked her to drive her car to that particular location; he had told her to. Shocked, she drove the car right into the ditch, at which point both Rocky and the woman realized that the vehicle would probably never be retrievable.

The woman got out of the car, walked up to where Rocky was standing, and said, "I never really did like that color."

Rocky was becoming more and more proud with every interaction with his fellow club members. It almost brought tears to his eyes that from the very first meeting, not one member even brought up the option of leaving. But he wasn't surprised, considering the vast majority of them were Texans.

Like any good military wives, the club women took over all the responsibilities concerning the bathrooms, food, water, sleeping arrangements, and so forth. They had already cranked up all the large commercial coffee urns. Coffee was being served at the rate of half a gallon a minute.

The club had six hundred family memberships, but only three hundred families were in residence at this time of year, including children. In total, there were 526 people now staying together in the clubhouse. It appeared that all but one family had moved to the clubhouse. The one holdout family was a couple in their late eighties. Both had acknowledged the importance of a unified front but said that if they were going to die, they'd prefer to do so in their home. No one questioned their decision, but Rocky drove down to visit them and made sure that each of them had a pistol to use with plenty of ammunition.

The men's locker room had been converted into a munitions storage. Every single gun and round of ammunition was now being organized by type and caliber, and their actions were being cleaned and oiled. When the final inventory was calculated, Rocky was in shock. Combined, the tally of firearms consisted of 618 rifles, 280 shotguns, 850 pistols, three illegal machine guns, and a wild, crazy assortment of other weapons that included a few slingshots donated by the children. The amount of ammunition was so huge they finally gave up counting it and just made stacks of the weaponry.

When Rocky and the other members of the management team reviewed the incredible collection, Rocky had only one response: "If Jim Bowie and Davy Crockett had this arsenal at the Alamo, they would've, hands down, defeated General Santa Anna."

It was time to settle down and rest the troops. The real battle hadn't begun, yet the hours of preparation and stress showed heavily on the newly assembled army of the Cordillera Golf and Country Club. Lying down while others took the first watch, Rocky rolled over to meet Kathy's eyes. She was quietly lying in tears, hoping that she'd hold up under pressure when she was needed. Rocky took his wife's delicate hands in his large, rough, working man's hands and with great care massaged them. Comforted by his steady confidence, Kathy slowly relaxed and drifted off into a well-earned, deep sleep. Rocky kept sharp vigilance over his wife as she slept. With a deep sigh, Rocky recognized and fully accepted his responsibility to protect so many people. He thought of his father; though they didn't see eye to eye on most things in life, Rocky hoped that his father would be proud of him now.

Chapter 79

On the other side of Phoenix, Bill and Elsie's granddaughter Madeleine was enjoying her first few days at Arizona State University. Her parents had been wonderful by offering to take care of her son, Ricky, while she got her feet planted in college. Madeleine enjoyed the challenge of getting back into the academic world after so many years away, and life was looking rosy.

As class started that day, Madeleine noticed a good-looking Mexican boy, probably a year or two younger than she was, watching her every move. In a crowd, she would have never noticed him, but because they shared two classes it was hard for her not to. It seemed like every time she looked around the classroom, there he was, staring at her. She was both flattered and worried. On the one hand, she thought nothing was ever going to come from his flirtatious glances, and on the other hand, she was thankful that he had not approached her. Dating was not on her agenda.

Then one afternoon, he approached her after class. "Hey, my name is Angelo. Did you know we share two classes together?"

Madeleine didn't want to get into a conversation, but at the same time she didn't want to be rude.

"I hadn't really noticed." Being a bit coy, she said, "How coincidental."

"Yeah, like, wow. Like, ah, totally awesome. Maybe we can share notes or something. Something like that. I mean like, that's really cool that we're in two of the same classes. That must mean we have the same interests. What's your major?"

Madeleine inwardly groaned. *Great, what do I do now?* Since her pregnancy, Madeleine had not had a single date and didn't miss it for one minute. She thought that she had been in love with that high school senior, the now nonexistent father of her baby who had gotten her pregnant. But as time passed, she'd realized that the best that her memory could invoke was that she had thought she was in love. Having sex was what everybody did in high school. They experimented with drugs, they listened to too much loud music, they fell in love, and they had sex. Getting an education was way down the list for going to high school.

For Madeleine, getting pregnant and having a son were maybe the best things that ever happened to her. In her short time as a mother, she felt like she had aged tenfold. Madeleine always thought that she had the best parents God could ever give someone. When she had announced that she was pregnant, her parents never skipped a beat and rallied behind her 100 percent.

Though her parents never criticized or condemned her for getting pregnant, she knew that she had let them down. Sure, she had siblings, two older brothers, but as the only daughter in the family, she'd always been doted on by both of her parents. As loving as they were toward her brothers, her brothers couldn't hold a candle to the lavishness and attention her mother and father had shown her. Being devout Christians, neither of her parents believed in premarital sex, but Madeleine had always suspected that they too had been sexually active at the same age she was when she got pregnant. But she and her parents had openly talked about premarital sex and the risk of getting pregnant, and she had let them down, big time! But they had been there when she'd needed them the most. She was going to try to be as wonderful a parent to her child as her parents had been and were being to her.

In the back of Madeleine's mind she would on occasion ask herself, *If I could, would I roll back the calendar and start over without my son?* Her answer was always the same. She loved Ricky and the joy he brought into her life. She'd never give him up for the freedom of not being a single parent, even if it meant not marrying in the future.

Bouncing back to her present situation, Madeleine said curtly, "Yes, it's neat that we share two classes, but I've really got to go." She was trying her best to be nice, but all she wanted at that moment was to escape the conversation.

But Angelo wasn't going to be dissuaded so easily.

"Yea, that's way cool, I can dig that. But...I don't know if you know it, but the band Zapblood is going to be playing at Freddie's this Friday night. How about we go together?"

Madeleine had tried to be nice. She had tried to be kind. She had tried to be polite. Those were all of the things she also tried with her old high school boyfriend, and what had that gotten her? Pregnant!

"Okay, okay, so we go to the concert," she said. "So we have lots of drinks and get really drunk. And then you tell me how I'm really super cool, and you really dig my mojo. You'll tell me that I'm the best girl you've ever met. Then what? I'll tell you what. It's the same old story: boy meets girl and then boy wants to get into girl's pants. So, either that night or the next night, you try to get into my pants. Why? Because you want to get laid! Because that's all you really care about, getting your rocks off! To put it in your terms, you think that's *way cool*. Do you want to know what I think? Seriously? Do you really want to know what I think? Or, Angelo, we could just end this conversation now and go our separate ways. Come on, speak up. What's the matter? Cat got your tongue? Do you want to know what I think?"

Angelo didn't know what he'd gotten himself into, but he'd gone this far, so he figured he might as well go all the way.

"Sure, sure, I want to know."

"Okay, sport! I'll give it to you straight. All I've thought about since I got pregnant more than three years ago—that's 24-7, 365—is that there is more to life than drugs and sex. Sure, they feel good, and doing them at the same time feels really great. But where does it get you? Where do you go with it? What about next week, next month, next year, and for the rest of your life? I was stupid, yes. Of course, I was stupid, and I was only eighteen. My parents tried to warn me. Did I listen? Does anyone ever listen to their parents? Hell, no! We think we're adults! We think we have our shit together. Am I right? Well, am I right?"

Angelo could hardly keep up. Madeleine had been wanting to vent her pent-up frustrations for more than three years. Her parents would listen and understand, but they didn't deserve a tongue lashing like she wanted to give and she surely couldn't lean on Ricky with her anger. Angelo was getting it with both barrels.

"My parents talked about sex between two people being a loving experience. A sharing of a special bond between two people in love, an experience of intimacy. No way, José! The first time I had sex was when I was fourteen. Shocked? A lot of my friends started sooner than that. Now looking back, I wonder if I was getting more pressure to have sex from the boys I dated or from my girlfriends. Having sex and experimenting seemed to be all we ever talked about. Frankly, I thought it sounded weird and a bit perverted. But if I opened my mouth, I was called a loser. As I see it now, I really was a loser. So I went along for the ride."

Madeleine was working up a lather. "When I became pregnant, I thought of committing suicide. Here I was, eighteen years old, wonderful home, wonderful parents, great grades in school with lots of friends—and I was fucking pregnant.

"But I wised up. The credit is mostly due to my parents and their support. The rest of the credit goes to my baby. He needs me. But he needs more than just a mother—he needs a mother who is responsible. He needs a mother that's logical. He needs a mother who has cleared her head of the mess of cobwebs from doing drugs and alcohol. So, Angelo, I'm tired and refuse to do what everybody thinks I should do. So where does that leave us? Nowhere! Absolutely frickin' nowhere! Nowhere now, not going anywhere. No interest in dating, no way. I lost three years of my schooling being pregnant and raising a baby, and I plan on getting those three years back. Will I fall in love someday? Probably. Will I get married someday? Probably. Will I have more children? It's very likely. Are any of those options on the table today? No way! Now if you'll excuse me, I have a term paper that's due, and I have a child who is missing his mother, and he needs me a lot more than you. Have a nice life!"

And with that Madeleine spun on her heels and without a backward glance strode away, feeling better about herself than she could ever remember. She felt electrified, she felt empowered, and she felt alive! For the first time in her twenty-three years of existence, she knew what she wanted, what she was going to do. She was her own woman, and her destiny awaited.

Chapter 80

As President Rosemary Denton entered the Oval Office, Secretary of State Marisa Angela Lopez was already seated and waiting for her.

"Good morning, Madam President. How are things with you today?"

"Fine, Lopez, and how was your meeting with the NSC yesterday?"

"Excellent, Rosemary. I think we are making excellent progress with more to look forward to. I've set up a personal call this morning with Presidente Nieto. I'm optimistic that the *presidente* is anxious to resolve the border issue without involving any law enforcement, much less our military forces."

"That's great news, Marisa. I know that Presidente Nieto and you have always had an excellent working relationship. I was confident that you'd be successful in working behind the scenes in breaking the stalemate. Your negotiations with Nieto's people in the past were productive. However, I want to sit down with you to get an in-depth briefing on Nieto's position regarding his country's breach of our border. Also, I'll need a fast lesson on diplomacy about threatening Nieto's administration with military action. This border joyride has cost the American people a shitload of cash and property losses. The people are going to demand some sort of retribution to resolve the situation. We've lost Americans during this melee, and we'll need a strong defensive appearance in order to keep me from possible impeachment hearings."

Rosemary was shooting wildly from the hip and needed help in finding the correct direction her administration should go. Frankly, she couldn't give a flying fuck about Nieto. What she needed were warm bodies that could vote her into a second term in office.

"What type of speechmaking will I need to endure to placate Nieto's sensitivities? Again, not that I care about Nieto or his internal problems—or if Mexico is nuked and becomes a glow-in-the-dark desert landscape. My only concern is my reelection, and if I have to endure his mumbo jumbo to keep world opinion polls high, I'll do so."

Stopping to look at her nails and smooth down her freshly coiffed hair, Denton said, "Marisa, you're aware that the hawks on both sides of the aisle are pressuring me to take immediate military action. Even a few of our closest allies and supporters in the press are having a hard time continuing to support our inaction to date. I don't know if you've seen this morning's poll, but now 90 percent of Americans think we are making a mistake not taking immediate military strikes against the invaders and Mexico itself. I'm not sure the press can hold out much longer. Our friends in the press have bent over backward to support anything my administration has done and have whitewashed over any miscalculations, as well. However, at some point they're not going to be willing to jeopardize their careers. They might be willing to ignore their ethics, but they're not willing to go down with the ship. You'll recall, after supporting every initiative coming from President Obama's administration, that when his ratings tanked, even his most valiant supporters gave up the ghost and finally went to the dogs. We've got to be careful. We're walking a fine line, and I am planning on being reelected. Without having the press in my breast pocket, we couldn't win an election as a dog catcher."

"I wouldn't worry, Rosemary," Marisa responded. "The president of Mexico has great respect for me, and I'm sure you and I can convince him that it is in his best political interest to take steps to stop the intruders." Glancing at her watch, Marisa said, "It's ten. Time for the call to Presidente Nieto. Would you mind if I ask your secretary to patch him through?"

Within minutes, President Denton was speaking to the president of Mexico, and after the long introductions and obligatory praises and compliments, they finally got down to the brass tacks of the call.

"Thank you, Presidente Nieto," Denton said. "I agree and as soon as we've cleared up this matter, I think it would be a prudent political move for both Secretary Lopez and me to come to Mexico City. Let's let the world see that we have resolved our differences. Since we both have reelections coming up next year, it wouldn't hurt either one of us politically to be seen in a friendlier light."

Clearing his throat, Nieto said, "Madam President, of course I know why you're calling, and I must assure you that my administration is doing everything we are capable of to try to dissuade our countrymen and women from entering your country illegally. My administration has always worked with the United States to secure the common border and to keep the cartels from smuggling drugs across, as well. We have just passed new legislation that, when fully enacted, will bring new vitality to our nationally owned petroleum industry. We've taken other economic measures to return our country to positive growth. I am most assured that these steps will turn our economy around and will demonstrate a strong message to all of our citizens. Madam President, Mexico is a great country with a great future indeed. We need to educate our citizens that there is no need to emigrate to the United States. We will return pride to our flag and instill patriotism where it is now lacking."

"Thank you, Presidente Nieto. Angela Lopez is a major supporter of yours, and she has been assuring me that you have been doing everything you can to address your financial difficulties. I agree that, following the steps you've outlined, you should return your country once again to positive growth.

"But wouldn't you agree, Mr. Presidente, that all of these steps are going to take some time? I'm sure you can appreciate my position. I'm getting a lot of pressure to take steps immediately to resolve the ruined border and the loss of life and property. I think I'm going to need something more substantial if I'm going to present your plan and dissuade the hawks in Congress and the Pentagon to stand down and be patient. What guarantees can you offer, Mr. Presidente?"

Nieto spoke so rapidly that President Denton nearly missed his words. "You need not worry. Of course, I know that these measures will not turn around our dreadful financial situation immediately. But despite what Americans might think, Mexicans are not stupid. The PRI party has almost complete control over and support in the press. My staff and I are convinced that we will be able to get the word out that, though things won't be turned around tomorrow, within a few years, our growth will far outpace that of your country. I am confident in my fellow Mexicans. These positive steps will be enough to slow down and stop the mass exodus from our country."

"Yes, that is excellent news, Mr. Presidente. Would you be sure to get all of these measures to Secretary Lopez in writing as soon as possible? I will distribute them to our press. I think with your media push and our media blitz, we can quickly resolve this unpleasant matter. Thank you for your time. I will let you and Secretary Lopez iron out the details."

Chapter 81

The crowd at the NRG stadium in Houston jumped to its feet when Ryan Fitzpatrick connected on a sixty-yard Hail Mary pass to his wide receiver for the go-ahead touchdown against the St. Louis Rams. That left everyone going into the halftime show in a good mood.

Cliff turned to the other families sharing the Morgan Stanley skybox and declared, "I told you Ryan still has it! I'm sure glad O'Brien didn't trade him."

Just then, two Mexican service employees opened the door to bring in more food for the buffet. They spread out enough snacks to feed a small army and then quietly left.

Cliff and one of his friends got up to grab more beers out of the refrigerator, and then they piled their plates to overflowing from the buffet. Cliff, returning to his seat with a mouthful of food, said, "I'm surprised they're allowing Mexicans to keep working here considering what's happening at the border."

One man responded, "Cliff, your brother works for the border patrol. Have you talked to him? What does he say about all this?"

Cliff let out a big belch. "Yeah, I've talked to him, but I don't know that he knows much more than we do."

The women, standing a little apart from the men, were having their own conversation about the border problem. One of the ladies commented to Debbie, Cliff's wife, "I don't understand what this is all about, but it can't be that important. I haven't seen anything about it in any of the magazines I read."

Cliff overheard her. "Amy, that's because the only shit you read is *People Magazine*, *Good Housekeeping*, *Cosmopolitan*, and all that other garbage."

Amy's husband laughed "Yup, Amy couldn't tell you who the president of the United States is, but she has at her fingertips the current statistics on Oprah's weight and if it's going up or down."

He grabbed another chicken wing off his plate, gave his wife a wink, and said, "That's okay, honey. I think it's important for our family to keep up with who's sleeping with who in Hollywood. *Not!*" He immediately high fived the other guys amid loud, male laughter.

Debbie came to Amy's defense. "Go ahead, make fun of us, but we girls learn a lot more in our magazines than you guys will ever learn from reading all that sports crap." Now it was the ladies' turn to laugh and high five each other, just to outdo the men.

Cliff decided he needed to change the subject while their manly egos were still intact. "My brother, Craig, is an expert on the US-Mexican border issue, and if he was concerned about what was going on at the border, he would have called me."

"I don't think we need to worry, living here in Houston," Debbie said. "I don't know exactly how far it is, but it's got to be at least three hundred miles between us and the Mexican border."

"Well, I'm concerned," said another woman. "I was surprised that the stadium was so full today because I've heard that a lot of people in Houston are starting to head north. If so many Mexicans have already crossed the border, couldn't some of them be close to Houston by now?"

Her husband, ignoring her question, said, "Well, hell! I can explain the full stadium. No loyal Texan football fan would miss a home game, losing season or not, even if the Mexicans had the stadium surrounded!"

Chapter 82

Jennifer and Craig rarely went out in public on their dates; Craig just didn't like the whole dating scene. For Craig, a great evening meant a wonderfully prepared dinner, a good buzz, a lovely lady to entertain, and, above all, stimulating conversation. His Albuquerque home was the perfect venue with a gourmet kitchen, a media room with all the trappings a bachelor would desire, and a formal library. He had a game room, too, with an A. E. Schmidt pool table, a ping-pong table, and an antique jukebox filled with classic forty-fives for entertainment. Long ago, Craig had decided that he was a homebody and made his home his castle. Frankly, once he finished his long days at UNM, he usually wanted to go home. He loved to cook and entertain; his home dates were perfect.

Craig was an excellent cook, but on occasion he liked to eat at one of his favorite Albuquerque Mexican restaurants, Perea's Tijuana Bar. Tonight was one of those rare occasions.

As he drove to pick Jennifer up, Craig closed his eyes for a brief moment to imagine his date. Jennifer was always well dressed. She wore the minimum amount of makeup, as well as just a hint of Obsession, strategically placed as only a woman practiced at ensnaring a male's libido could do. At twenty-three, Jennifer had the body of a goddess and the face of Helen of Troy. Craig wasn't the jealous type, but when Jennifer walked into a room, men that fell within her purview instantly fell for her charms. He knew it well; since day one, he had had that experience. But tonight, she was reserved for him and him alone. Letting out a lion's roar and pounding the steering wheel, Craig smiled with exuberance. He felt virile tonight!

Craig arrived at Jennifer's apartment, where she was waiting out front. She gracefully climbed into the Range Rover, handed Craig a neatly wrapped gift box, and leaned across the middle console and planted a kiss on his right cheek. She was wearing a bow in her hair that matched the one she'd put on the gift box, and while playfully twirling her ponytail in her fingers, she cooed, "You can undo both bows later tonight if you play your cards right. But don't think you're getting off easy. I'm starved, and since you're tonight's designated driver, I plan on drowning myself in top-shelf margaritas."

Craig set the box down and with a big smile on his face replied, "Thanks for the gift. But I thought the deal was if I take you out, you'd be the designated driver. You know I love tequila when eating Mexican food." Craig, feigning injury at being named the designated driver, pouted for a few seconds, then out of his coat pocket popped a small silver flask.

Jennifer narrowed her eyes as if thinking hard, smiled at Craig, and answered his inquisitive look. "Let me see if I can guess what's in the flask. A) We are going out for Mexican food, b) you only drink tequila or beer with Mexican food, and b) you only drink the best tequila. So...it's Don Julio 1942? But I better take a taste to make sure." Jennifer took the flask and with her perfect lips took a ladylike sip, smiled at the taste, and took another.

"Hold on, darling, the contents are for two, so don't drink my share."

Jennifer took one last sip and handed the flask back to Craig. "I thought you were the designated driver. You can't drink this and then have margaritas with dinner."

Craig used his authoritative voice. "I don't need some graduate student telling me what I can and can't drink. However, I would appreciate it if you hold me to two margaritas at the restaurant."

By now Jennifer had gotten the flask back and taken another sip. "So what's that devious mind up to, Professor Walther? Are you trying to get me drunk so you can get lucky later?"

"No, young lady, it's a thirty-minute drive to the restaurant, and I'm trying to get lucky now.

Jennifer batted her eyes.

"You're trying to get me drunk so we can have what Bill Clinton had in the Oval Office with Monica Lewinsky!"

Craig looked over at Jennifer and couldn't help himself. He broke into a cat-who-ate-the- canary smile because Washington political misconduct was one of his favorite subjects. Since his time working in Washington, he jumped at any opportunity to share his knowledge of the DC rumor mill and tell anyone who'd listen in which closets the juiciest skeletons were hidden.

"Did you know that good old Bill in the '80s said to an Arkansas state trooper that oral sex wasn't sex? Oral sex is the favorite of politicians everywhere. Just ask Newt Gingrich and Senator Robb from Virginia. They preferred oral sex in their extramarital affairs because they could deny sleeping with the women. Now, isn't that a hoot?"

Jennifer winked at Craig. "Do you want that while you're driving, or would you prefer to pull over, Professor?" Jennifer had said the words in such a suggestive manner that Craig could hardly control the car. By the time they reached the restaurant parking lot, both were bursting with grins.

Craig remembered Jennifer's gift box and started to open it but stopped. He looked at Jennifer for her nod of approval before he opened the package. She nodded with a smile on her lips as she reapplied her makeup, looking at herself in the passenger side's vanity mirror.

Craig was nearly impossible to buy for because if he wanted something he just bought it. Craig was addicted to Internet shopping and loved Amazon.com. But now, Craig beamed because Jennifer had bought the perfect gift—a bolo tie. Craig was a huge fan of Native American jewelry and wore it often. His collection of bolo ties topped seventy, and over the last few years he'd had them custom-made by a Native American jeweler in Albuquerque. The stone that Jennifer had chosen was called picture jasper, a rare semiprecious stone. What made picture jasper more valuable than green jasper was the way its minerals were formed. When the stone was cut and buffed out, it had the appearance of vegetative growth, like a landscape.

Jennifer could immediately tell that Craig loved it. "I wanted you to open it before dinner so you could wear it into the restaurant."

Craig took off the bolo tie he was wearing and replaced it with Jennifer's gift. "I feel like I'm cheating. You gave me two great gifts tonight, and I'm not sure dinner and margaritas will properly repay you."

As Craig opened her car door, Jennifer said, "I'm sure I can think of something, Professor."

Since Craig and the owner of Perea's Tijuana Bar had grown to be good friends over the years, Craig and Jennifer were seated in one of the best tables in the restaurant. It was essentially private and boasted candlelight and fresh-cut, fragrant flowers. The volume of the Hispanic-themed music was perfect for conversations. As Jennifer held a fresh margarita glass to her lips, Craig's smile disappeared and his demeanor shifted slightly.

Jennifer set her glass down on the coaster and turned serious. "What is it? What's bothering you? Is it something I've done?"

"It's this border issue. I should perhaps not have invited you out tonight. The illegals could be getting closer to this city, and I have a feeling that between their desperation and the vigilantes who will no doubt try to protect every inch of American soil, remaining out at night could become a very poor choice."

"You sure know how to show a girl a good time." Jennifer raised her glass in toast to Craig's news, and he looked totally perplexed.

"Oh, come on, Professor, I know you're in love with me. Is warning me about the approaching Mexican border invaders just your way of asking me to come live with you? Oh, Professor, would you be my knight in shining armor and protect my feminine virtues from the attacking Mexican hordes by having me move into your castle?"

She delivered the line with such a damsel-in-distress attitude that Craig was caught completely off guard. To complicate matters, Craig had allowed himself to drink too much, and his buzz had morphed into drunkenness. He suspected that Jennifer might have had a hand in having his double tequila margaritas spiked as triples, perhaps to trick him into asking her to move in with him.

After paying the bill and leaving a hefty tip, the two swayed to and fro, arm in arm. Finally, they made it back to Craig's car. Climbing up into the Range Rover their bodies felt as if they had climbed the 897 steps to the top of the Washington Monument.

"I'm drunk," stated Craig simply.

As they drove down the road going well under the speed limit, Craig confessed, "My head is spinning like a schoolboy after his first real beer. I think maybe I should pull over and let you drive."

After an elongated and clumsy exchange, Jennifer had them back on the road.

"I haven't gotten an answer and just because you're drunk and your big head is spinning, don't think for a second that I'm going to let you slide. Look, we've been dating off and on for quite a while. I know that you see other women on occasion, plus we've beaten the subject about your ex-wives to death. I know that you are scared to fall in love with another woman and commit yourself. I know the one thing you're more afraid of, other than love itself, is that it might lead to some kind of serious commitment, like marriage, which you've learned to hate."

At the mention of the word 'marriage,' Craig finally forced himself to make a statement, knowing that the evening would be ruined.

"Twenty-five years, Jennifer, there it is—twenty-five years' difference in age between the two of us. I've known a number of people that have wonderful relationships and marriages with big age differences, but I'm not sure I know anybody with that big of a gap."

Jennifer's light, airy banter cooled down. "So is that it, Professor? Was I just another college fling? Was I just another admiring, young, naïve college student, falling in love with her professor?"

Craig was becoming dizzy and didn't want to have this conversation now, if ever.

Jennifer navigated up her street and parked the big SUV expertly in front of her apartment. She turned off the engine and turned to face Craig, her warm and charming self returning.

"I know this is a lot all at once, but I've been thinking about this for the last week. So let me take this to its logical conclusion—you've been married twice, and they were both failures. And though we've never talked about it—"

Craig sat up straight in his seat. "It's late. I've really enjoyed this, and you've given me a lot to think about, but I had better go."

Jennifer, stretched across the console, grabbed Craig by his new bolo tie and gave him a passionate kiss that lasted too long. Out of desperation, Craig pulled back from the kiss. He thought for a second he would pass out from being robbed of oxygen for so long.

Jennifer frowned. "I'm not letting you drive home as drunk as you are. Craig, are you trying to get out of staying with me this evening because of our conversation?"

His poor head felt like a spinning top again, but he managed to get the words finally out of his mouth. "The thought did enter my mind."

Jennifer ignored Craig's last statement and replied, "I had as many margaritas as you, and now I'm horny for some of Professor Walther's best sex ever...but Craig..." She faltered and let a long pause fall between them, almost to the point of discomfort. Her head hung dramatically, she slowly raised her eyes to look at Craig's handsome, chiseled features and took a deep breath.

"More importantly," she said, "I'm madly in love with you." The seriousness of the moment had passed, and Jennifer giggled.

"Now, get your drunk ass out of the car and into my apartment. Oh, professor, even if I have to drag you by your brand-new bolo tie, you're going to sleep in my bed tonight."

Chapter 83

All the predictions had been wrong. The two large groups of Mexicans that had crashed the border and proceeded through El Paso and Laredo numbered close to several hundred thousand, maybe even a million. The original estimate of a few thousand was not just off; it was criminally off. At the same time, a group that had crossed the previous week and had been milling about the border station was now moving toward Houston. They had already advanced through McAllen, Harlingen, Brownsville, Beeville, and Corpus Christi, Texas.

For Jess Bellows, it had been just another day on his cattle ranch, one-hundred-plus miles southwest of Houston. He was driving Betty, his forty-eight-year-old prized possession, a Dodge pickup that, though it was down to primer gray, he refused to repaint. He was searching for a stray calf that had separated from the herd and wandered off.

Jess knew better to than to drive as fast as he was going in the arroyo, but it was his land, and he was in the mood to give old Betty a good time this warm Texas afternoon. He rounded a bend in the arroyo and literally ran into a wall of Mexicans.

"My God," he cried as the vehicle slammed into a wall of bodies, flinging bodies, dead and injured, to the side and pinning and dragging others under his beloved Dodge pickup. The truck's momentum slowed with the crush of bodies, and the engine stalled under the stress. Jess fumbled for the door handle and finally got it open. He climbed out of the truck and immediately dropped to his knees, frozen in place and unable to respond to the cries all around him.

Jess wouldn't hurt a flea, and never in his life had he seen such carnage, even during his service in Korea. The realization that he had caused the deaths and injuries of so many was more than his heart could handle. His old ticker started to seize—it would, he knew, shortly become fatal. He lay there unable to move, but even amid the shortness of breath and the crushing pain against his rib cage, he was not saved from the outcome of his involuntary action. His field of vision narrowed, and his mind screamed at the horrific sight as he started to lose consciousness.

In a matter of seconds, two Mexicans had dragged Jess's now limp body away from his truck, tossed it onto the pile of carnage, and jumped into the cab of old Betty. They restarted the engine and sped away down the arroyo. Anyone that could leaped into the bed of the truck as it raced from the scene. A few missed their mark and, falling short, were crushed under the rear wheels.

But the truck thieves would not get far. As almost all of the Mexicans who were trying to get to Houston or other more northern cities were finding out, there was no gasoline anywhere to be had.

The remaining mass of Mexicans moved on, shuffling down the arroyo and toward Houston. In a matter of minutes, the deadly section of arroyo quieted.

Chapter 84

Craig tapped in the ten digits and listened while the phone rang. It seemed to Craig that the phone rang twenty times before Dave finally answered.

"Hey, Dave, I've tried your home phone, but the system is down, so I'm glad I had your cell number with me." Craig had been worried about his brother, since he and Anita lived in the area that was now supposedly surrounded by the illegal Mexicans. Craig didn't have much patience, and his concern had gotten the better of him. "Dave, what's going on? Why did it take you so long to answer the phone? What's wrong, Dave? Answer me."

There was a long silence, and then Dave said in the saddest of voices, "Our country's being overrun, and San Diego is under siege, and you're asking me what's wrong?"

"Hey, brother, I know when you're in pain and these marauders wouldn't affect your character like this. What's going on? I know we haven't seen eye to eye on nearly any issue, but I am trying to be a good brother, and I'm concerned. What aren't you telling me?"

Another long pause. Craig thought the call had been disconnected, but finally Dave cleared his throat. "Anita was killed."

It was time for Craig to let dead air preempt his words. "Dave, I'm sorry, I didn't know. Do Mom and Dad know? How did it happen? Why didn't you call? What about the baby? Were they able to save the baby?"

Dave didn't answer.

"Dave, I wish there was something I could say to ease your pain. I know how much you loved Anita and looked forward to being a father. Can you give me some idea of what happened?"

Slowly Dave began. "She was found two days ago about twenty miles from home. I had suspected that she and a friend had been feeding groups of illegals, but I guess I just didn't know how far she had taken it. Our unit had been placed on active duty, serving twelve on and twelve off but unable to go home on the off hours. We were assigned to makeshift bunkhouses, and with the added phone restrictions, none of us had spoken to our spouses or families.

"Craig, it's all so sketchy. Because the police are stretched so thin, no one's been able to do any kind of serious investigation. I had hoped that the investigators would give it priority since Anita was my wife and maybe the killing was a revenge killing as punishment for my border-patrol service. But there isn't any evidence that that was the reason for her murder. Craig, I blame myself for her death. I suspected she was involved with others in humanitarian relief, but never did I consider that they would be so bold in their efforts. I should have realized that blood was thicker than water, and being Mexican, she would offer aid and food no matter the risk to her from the border jumpers."

"Oh, my God," cried Craig. "How awful."

"What I cannot live with is the fact that Anita lay on the ground dead for two days before anyone found her. Craig, I had to identify her in the morgue. The destruction from the knife wounds was terrible, but the vultures and other animals had gotten to her."

Craig felt terrible for putting his brother through the tortuous ordeal of reliving the horrific series of events. He felt his skin crawl at the thought of Anita lying on the ground for forty-eight hours until being discovered. Craig could hear an almost animal screeching coming through his receiver. Dave's mind had come apart and couldn't take the pain anymore.

In a frantic tone, Dave related how he had not been able to reach Anita by phone for a few days and had become worried. He had called the hospital, thinking that the stress of the situation had started premature labor. But no, the hospital hadn't admitted anyone with premature labor or anyone named Anita.

Dave continued the story in a low monotone; his self-preservation mode had taken over to protect what was left of his sanity. Dave had received a call from the desk sergeant at the San Diego Police Department with some updates. Dave had asked, "Sergeant, have there been any traffic fatalities or any Jane Doe reports in the last few days?" Since Dave was in law enforcement, the sergeant had related their discovery of two women who had been feeding groups of illegals. He described the women, and at that point, Dave's world had imploded.

It took Craig a moment to realize that the line had gone dead. He couldn't bring himself to reestablish the connection. Instinct told him to allow Dave some space to mourn. The time was too raw for any discussion, but there'd be time soon enough. Craig would see to it.

Chapter 85

"I wish I could tell you I know how you feel when it comes to Anita," Craig said the next day, when he called Dave back. "But I can't. I've never lost a loved one. But I can sure relate to your second comment. It is sad to see our country so incredibly vulnerable."

With a fire lit under him, Dave responded, "The states need to call out the National Guard, and Congress and the president need to call out the military. Now!

"Ten years ago, I would not have thought, much less said, such a thing as I'm about to say. But I'm beginning to believe that one of the biggest problems here is that we don't have any white men with any seniority at the head of one single government agency! It's mostly women, blacks, Mexicans, and gays, who, of course, are all bleeding-heart liberals. No wonder none of them are willing to do the manly thing and pull the trigger on this invasion!"

"Right," Craig said. "A decade of a politically divided country is now showing its ugly underside. Obama's agenda in dividing the country worked perfectly. Poor versus rich, blacks versus whites, liberals versus conservatives—our country has never been so divided. And now Washington is both divided and frozen. And that's why I am calling. The unlucky thing for the Walther family is that we are all living in the path of the invaders. It's time for us to stop hoping and praying that our government will do something to slow down or stop the advance. I want all of you to come here and hole up in my mountain home until this is resolved."

"I can't even think of that," said Dave. "We are already stretched so thin here in the department, there is just too much for me to do here. I can't run out on my fellow agents at a time like this."

369

"Look, you guys have been left high and dry by the administration for years. It's time you worry about yourself for once. Get out of there!"

Dave paused. "You're right. Craig, you are always right. And I'm so mad at Govenor Black, I could gag. But I just feel funny. Anita died trying to help these people. And now I'm somewhat responsible for helping fight against them. I will admit it's completely fucking up my priorities. But again, I don't think I can leave. And even if I wanted to, the airports are closed. And even if they were open, there are no planes. No commercial airlines have been willing to land in the southern part of California for a week. And all the rich fat cats took their private jets and left here almost two weeks ago. To make matters worse, driving out of Southern California is now an impossibility. Though the reports are sketchy, it appears just about every major road going north is so congested that I understand people are abandoning their cars as they run out of gas and just trudging northward on foot."

"Dave, have more faith in your big brother. I didn't call to suggest you escape without having a game plan. And you're not going to believe what it is. You know that rich bitch of a wife that dropped me like a hot potato? Well, I guess she has a conscience after all. I got a call from her yesterday, though I won't say it was the friendliest phone call I ever got. It was pretty obvious she was just trying to buy off her feelings of guilt. She has a friend with a good-sized jet parked up in Aspen, Colorado. I guess he's some kind of rich daredevil, but she's offered to pay him whatever he wants if he would pick up each of my brothers and their families and bring them here to Albuquerque."

"Wow, maybe you were better in bed than you thought you were," Dave said. "But wait a minute—you admitted that in New Mexico the Mexicans have gotten halfway through the state. Wouldn't that mean that Albuquerque is in their path, just like Houston and Phoenix? If we're going to fly somewhere, let's go to Fairbanks, Alaska."

"Well, that's not exactly the offer we were given. The guy who owns the jet is willing to fly to the southern part of the country, for whatever reason, and land in Albuquerque. I don't think he's willing to fly too far away from Colorado and the southwest. I get the feeling the guy is getting a lot of offers and wants to stay in this part of the country.

"But you've never been to my place. It's pretty damn remote. We understand that the Mexicans tend to be concentrating their efforts on the bigger cities and more concentrated neighborhoods where they can be most effective in getting food. Hiking an hour up to the top of the Sandia Peaks over rocky terrain and through dense forest to rob a limited number of homes doesn't seem like a smart game plan for starving Mexicans. And I will admit that I do have a selfish motive, other than trying to save my brothers. If for some reason some small contingency of these Mexicans were to find themselves somehow at my doorstep, I'd feel a lot safer with four brothers who are excellent shots—at least last time I remember."

"I don't want to brag, but for six years running I've won the Western Regional shooting competition among both DEA and border agents. Have you saved all those guns we grew up with? Would everybody need to bring their own guns?"

Craig was glad he'd gotten his brother's mind off his wife's death. He chuckled. "Let's just say I'm well stocked. Yesterday I made the rounds, pun intended, to see if I could obtain some additional ammunition, but no such luck. Walmart and every single gun store in Bernalillo County is not only completely sold out of ammunition, the only guns that are available are such small caliber, they're not worth having. So if I send a plane, are you willing to come?"

"No, I would feel like a deserter. I now hate our federal government. I've always hated the morons in Washington, DC, and I'm hoping the one good thing that comes out of this is that someone banishes our governor to Ecuador. The only problem is, living here in California, they always seem to replace one liberal moron with another. Hell, we're so screwed up out here—they might take that plastic-faced imbecile

Nancy Pelosi and make her governor. But no, you take care of the other brothers. I can fend for myself."

Chapter 86

Craig hadn't realized just how far he and his brothers had drifted apart. Anita was dead, and Dave hadn't called him or Mark. With the thought of being the family coordinator, Craig dialed his parents' phone to fill them in about Anita's death. After a few rings, their voice mail came on, and he left a message to call him back ASAP. Feeling frustrated Craig decided to try his brother Mark in Phoenix.

"Mark, hey, this is Craig. I just called the folks and no one's home. Any idea where they are?"

"Yeah, they're here with me. I got a little nervous two days ago and made them move in with us. It was a knock-down, drag-out fight to get Dad here. He swore the only way he'd ever leave his home was feet first on a gurney and that he'd shoot every damn Mexican that got within ten feet of his property. Mom interceded and gave him no choice, so he did what she said."

Craig quickly interrupted. "So what's the latest word in Phoenix?"

Mark described the same scene that his brother Dave had described less than an hour ago. "I can't figure out to be madder at—the invading Mexicans or the powers to be in DC."

"Sorry, Mark, I just got off the phone with Dave, and I haven't told you that Anita was killed a few days ago. Dave is having a terrible time with his loss. I'll call back and fill in the blanks, but first let me tell you why I'm calling. I've made arrangements to have a private jet fly to Phoenix to pick up Elizabeth, Madeleine, little Ricky, Mom, Dad, and you. I want all of you to come up here and stay at my mountain home until this whole thing has blown over. I know I'm not that far north, but the Mexicans are concentrating their efforts on the bigger cities, where they think there is more food." Craig was more concerned than he could remember being in recent years.

373

"Mark, could you all be ready to go within forty-eight hours? I have arranged for a private plane to come pick you up."

Mark paused for a minute, and Craig sensed that he was having a hard time and might even be crying. Sibling rivalry had plagued the two brothers for their entire lives, and they had fought like cats and dogs.

"I know you're not big on the God thing, but may Jesus bless you." An uncomfortable pause ensued and then finally, Mark resumed. "Sorry, Craig, I had to sneak into the bathroom for privacy. I didn't want anybody to overhear what I have to say. I've been scared to death for the last few days. And though Dad is hanging tough, both Mom and Elizabeth have been nervous wrecks. I couldn't let them know how scared I was. Being in the trucking business, I am more aware of the blocked and stalled highway situations. Craig, there hasn't been a truckload of food delivered into Phoenix for nearly a week. Every single grocery store, mom-and-pop convenience store, fast-food joint, and restaurant has been wiped out of everything edible. Pure panic has erupted here in Phoenix, and the illegals are still days away. I've heard of home invasions, neighbor on neighbor. And more seriously, raiding parties have been holding neighbors at gunpoint demanding their food storage."

Craig gasped. "Holy moly, I didn't anticipate that happening already. You've got the best governor in the entire border state region. I would've expected her and Sheriff Joe to be on the front lines, duking it out with the Mexicans."

"Because of my drivers out on the highways, I know that every highway outbound from Phoenix, save for those going south, is completely jammed, and I mean both lanes."

"Okay, Mark, you're in. But I do have a huge favor—you know the pair of post–Vietnam Era Browning automatic rifles that Dad purchased under the table from that guy, Bubba Something-or-Other, in Beeville? Does he still have them? Also, if I know Dad, he negotiated for a big box of ammunition for them. Mark, please grab them and bring them along."

For the first time, there was a bit of relief in Mark's voice. "Don't worry, Brother. When Dad walked in the house two days ago, he was carrying his whole arsenal.

"Craig, tell your pilot the closest airport to our house is in Scottsdale, and I'll figure out some way to get some aviation fuel ready to refuel as soon as he lands."

"Dave isn't going to come. I wish he wasn't so damn loyal to the border patrol, but we can deal with that later. I'm going to call Cliff next and see if I can get him and his family picked up as well."

Before Craig could hang up, Mark, sounding emotional, asked, "Hey, bro, can I tell you something that I've never said to you ever? Craig, this is awkward for me but..."

The silence grew as Craig waited for Mark's final remark. "Craig, I love you."

Chapter 87

Cliff's secretary stepped into his office. "Cliff, your brother Craig is on the line. I don't know if you've noticed, but you and I are the only two people left in the office. Most people didn't even come into work today, and those that did come left hours ago after the news of the illegals heading our way. I'd like to leave now and get home. Do you mind?"

"Everyone's acting like a bunch of sissies. I think this story is blown way out of proportion. I'm not leaving until I see the whites of their eyes. Sure, go ahead, abandon me. When I'm the only one left in Houston and nothing happens, ya'll will feel foolish."

He put his feet back up on his desk and picked up the phone. "Hey, brother, don't tell me—you're calling to warn me that the Mexicans are coming, the Mexicans are coming! My God, I never thought my fellow Texans would turn into a bunch of lightweights, afraid of their own shadows."

"Well, Cliff, that is not exactly why am calling. But I was hoping that you wouldn't answer the phone because you'd gotten out of the city. I hope you're aware that you've got one of the largest groups of Mexicans moving toward Houston."

"Shitfire, me and seventy-one thousand of my fellow Texans were at NRG Stadium watching the Houston Texans football game last week. Man, the place was packed, standing room only. So I guess the city must have panicked in the last few days, or they're using it as an excuse for a few days off. So if you're not calling me about leaving, why are you calling?

Craig knew that if he called Cliff and told him he was sending down a jet to pick him and his family up, Cliff would laugh it off. Cliff was not the smartest of the boys, but he was the toughest.

When they were kids, they had all teased Cliff about being the milkman's child. All the Walther men stood at five feet eleven and weighed between 160 and 170 pounds—not exactly skinny but no extra pounds. All had blond hair and blue eyes.

Not Cliff. No, Cliff stood six feet two inches, weighed over two hundred pounds, and had dark hair and dark eyes. And Cliff was the only jock in the family. Cliff and Craig had only one thing in common—they had been skirt chasers when they were in school.

However, all the Walther men were die-hard conservatives, especially fiscal conservatives, though they didn't necessarily agree with every single platform of the Republican Party. But as a family, they'd rather cut off their left arms than vote for the liberal socialist Democrats that had been running the country for over a decade.

Cliff was different from Craig in that he believed in every single conservative cause and was a major contributor to the Tea Party. Cliff's office wall space included photos of him at fundraising events with George Bush Sr., George Bush Jr., and many Republican governors, all with shit-eating grins and pumping handshakes.

No, Craig had already decided. If he was going to try to convince Cliff to join the rest of them up in Albuquerque, he was going to have to take a softer approach in selling the whole idea. "Well, that's not the reason I'm calling. It seems everyone in Washington has noticed that I am not only the top expert on the border issue, but I happen to live in one of the states that has been invaded. Other than a few contacts at Fort Bliss, I thought you might be able to help me out, since you're in Houston. Can you give me any update on what the press is reporting, or have you heard if the governor is going to call out the National Guard?"

Cliff paused then spoke to his brother in earnest. "Everything appears to be coming apart at the seams, and I can tell you that if the people in my office are a barometer for panic, the world is coming to an end. I've heard that there haven't been any food shipments into the city for a couple of days and that every single food outlet in the city is empty. Our building is like a ghost town, no one is working, and the streets are empty. But, Mr. Expert, if the federal government and our illustrious governor don't think it's a serious enough situation to call out the military or the National Guard, why has everyone got their panties in a bunch?

Craig replied with a chuckle, "I'll give you credit for that one, Cliff. Well, the liberals in Washington, including that fat-assed President Denton, are so scared of alienating the Mexican vote that they're unwilling to unleash the troops on them."

"That's brilliant," said Cliff. "If this is true and Houston is invaded, do the Democrats think they'll ever get a vote out of Houston, much less Corpus Christi, which I understand has already been overrun?"

Craig smiled, enjoying the banter, and said, "Hell, Cliff, when was the last time anyone in Texas was stupid enough to vote Democrat. But I'm sorry to say I think that is part of the problem. The past and current presidential administration is so corrupt. They know they're going to lose the Texas vote anyway, so they're more than happy to throw Texas to the dogs."

"I told the governor of Texas the last time I saw him at a fundraiser," Cliff said, "that we should secede from the nation. I'll tell you this—I think this is the last time Texas is going to let Washington get away with hanging us out to dry or anything akin to it. Craig, you'll see that when this is over, there will be a serious attempt by Texas to withdraw from the country. We all thought seriously about it when they jammed stupid Obamacare down our throats.

"But explain this to me, big brother. If you're correct that this is political wrangling, why doesn't Governor Berry just say to hell with waiting for the US military and call out the Texas National Guard? Also, since New Mexico has voted for the Democrats in the last ten presidential elections, why wouldn't Washington at least jump to its aid?"

Craig knew that if he was going to try to save his brother and his family, he would have to convince him that it was to his advantage to get away from Houston. But, because Cliff lived and breathed politics, he would debate until the cows came home and never budge from his opinion, right or wrong. "Cliff, I don't have all the answers. I left Washington ten years ago when I became a professor at UNM. I couldn't figure out what those idiots were doing then, and I have no idea now. Frankly, they're vote happy and will do anything to maintain their places in the sun. My guess is that Washington has threatened the governors of the border states that if they call out the National Guard, they will cut or suspend federal funds to them. As for New Mexico, I don't think a presidential candidate has visited the state in twenty years because we're nobodies. We only have five presidential electoral votes. We couldn't sway an election on a good day. And I don't need to remind you that both the past and the current presidents despise the governor of Arizona. Now, for California, that's easy. Harry Black got himself into the governorship by sucking up to the bleeding-heart liberals and the Mexican-American voters for decades. I'd bet he personally called the president to encourage her to not do a damn thing. But regardless of how this turns out, California will probably add a few more of the Mexican-American voters who'll thank him by voting Democrat. They'd do anything for allowing their family members to move in and adopt into California's welfare program. They might as well change the governorship title to 'king,' since he'll be in office until he dies."

Cliff gave a grunt. "As far as I'm concerned, that liberal bastard has been mentally dead for decades. Morgan Stanley has had a negative rating on California municipal bonds since he was voted back into office. It's just a matter of time before California completely implodes from its liberal spending."

Craig paused for a minute. "Well, I did actually have another reason for calling. Considering all the family is living in the path of invaders, I'd like to suggest that everyone fly up to my home until the dust settles down. Do you know if you can still get out of the Houston airport?"

"That's a kind thought, big brother, but no, I heard the last plane took out of both Houston Hobby and George Bush International two days ago. Plus, I heard all the major airlines have refused to fly into Houston or any of the southern border states. The assholes! One of our brokers called this morning and tried to charter a private jet. They told him that the prices have gone up ten times their normal rate."

"Look, I may be able to get a private plane to pick you and the family up. Would you do that?"

The phone line was quiet for several seconds. Finally, Cliff in an uncharacteristically quiet voice asked his brother, "Do you really think I should get out of town?"

With a deep sigh, Craig responded, "Yeah, I really do. The reports of the situation getting completely out of hand are finally breaking through to a few, but it's not like the Mexicans are an invading army. Hell, they don't even have any weapons other than the ones they've stolen. But I am now hearing that they are breaking into homes and stealing food. They have gotten more desperate and are now stealing weapons and ammunition. I think things could escalate and get more violent very quickly, even if that wasn't their original intention. If you've got two million Mexicans coming into Houston to find food, water, and shelter and the shelves are stripped bare, I don't think you want to be the last guy in town facing starved, pissed-off Mexicans."

Cliff was stubborn but not stupid. "Okay, you win. Craig, you've convinced me. I'll do something. I'll call you later when I know exactly what I'm doing, but I'm going to get my ass outta here."

The line went dead, leaving Craig unsure of what to do. Cliff had always danced to a different drummer and done what he wanted to do. Even if he didn't want a flight out on a private jet to join the rest of the family, he'd at least do something to save himself and his family. That, ultimately, was the best Craig could have hoped for. Now the rest was up to Cliff.

Chapter 88

Food was becoming harder for the illegals to find. Grocery stores and other convenience stores were out of food long before the Mexicans got close. As it became more and more apparent to Americans in the border states that they were under a state of emergency, grocery store shelves were emptied in a matter of hours. Although the Mexicans had thought they would be able to get food from the many grocery outlets, they found that they had to resort to stealing food from homes in order to survive.

A gated community like the Cordillera Golf Club seemed like a windfall for one group of illegals. They anticipated that the homes would be well stocked with food and other things that they would find useful. However, when the illegals climbed the fence around the Cordillera Country Club and broke into homes, they had a rude awakening. There was no food, not even staples. All the cars were gone, and there were no people around. The illegals suspected there would be plenty of food in the main clubhouse, and they headed in that direction en masse.

It had been roughly seventy-two hours since the first emergency meeting at the clubhouse. All three of the San Antonio radio stations had stopped broadcasting, and no one was sure if they had been overrun or if the staff had just refused to go into the broadcasting studios. The closest station that was still broadcasting was in Houston, but they had little information about the locations of the bands of illegals.

There was, however, something more worrisome on Rocky's mind. If the clubhouse was attacked, how would the residents react? Only a few of them were Vietnam veterans. The people barricaded inside the Cordillera clubhouse had some experience shooting at paper targets, and quite a few had been hunting. Rocky wasn't fooling himself: he knew that shooting a defenseless woodland creature wasn't the same as pulling the trigger on a human being. If they were attacked, would the residents be capable of pulling their triggers and actually killing people?

Vietnam hadn't been quite like the battles of old, when everybody had just lined up close together and then fired at will. More times than not, soldiers in the old wars had actually shot at somebody and seen them fall or stumble. That wasn't how it worked in Vietnam. As opposed to the open fields and plains of Europe, where both World War I and World War II were fought, Vietnam had densely vegetated jungles. Ninety-five percent of the time, when American GIs were fired upon in Vietnam, the US military had a hard time telling where the shooting was coming from. And when they returned fire, they were unloading their M-16s into dense vegetation, hopefully hitting whoever had shot at them. But they never saw anybody fall. They weren't shooting at a person; they were shooting in a direction. No one really knew if they had killed anyone or how successful the battle had been until all the shooting stopped and the battlefield, or better put, the jungle, could be investigated. Usually, if they did, in fact, find a dead Vietcong, no individual US soldier could take claim for killing that person.

Rocky and the others in charge had assigned rotating guard duty to the residents. Everyone was involved, except for the children and a few of the elderly. There were ten people equally spaced on the interior of the circle of automobiles, each with a pair of binoculars, with orders to report any suspicious movement.

The sentries had had only one challenge so far, which had provided a bit of comic relief to the stress of being on guard duty. A member who had returned from a trip to Houston to find his house had been broken into and his food stolen, raced up to the clubhouse when his calls to the police went unanswered. After a brief explanation, he had been ushered into the safety of the clubhouse.

Now things turned more serious.

"Rocky, Rocky, come quick! Susan and Melissa have spotted a small group of people coming up Scrub Oak Lane toward the clubhouse."

Rocky and two others grabbed AR-15s and joined the women sentries. By the time they arrived, about fifty people could be seen milling around about a quarter of a mile from the clubhouse.

Rocky immediately returned to the clubhouse and set off the prearranged alarm using the old-fashioned triangle dinner bell on the dining patio. Since it was midmorning, most people were already up, and the dining hall filled quickly. Everyone came fully dressed and prepared for a confrontation. After a quick announcement about the approaching mob, Rocky sent the residents to their preassigned posts. Two people had been assigned to each of the cars encircling the clubhouse as an outer line of defense. Fifty people were purposely not assigned to any post. These were the residents whom Rocky had decided were the less able bodied, and he wanted to use them to ferry ammunition to any area that was running short and to act as replacements for anyone who was injured. Also, these people could be rushed to a hot spot if pressure was put on any particular part of the circle of cars.

Besides this group of fifty, there was another set of residents that Rocky felt especially thankful for: the ten retirees who had been in the medical profession in their professional lives. They had already set up a makeshift hospital—just in case.

Everyone rushed to their positions. Rocky and the others immediately started monitoring and supervising the setup. Rocky was amazed to find that one woman could find humor at such a time like this. As Rocky coached her on where behind a car she should stand to get a clear shot while retaining as much cover as possible, she said, "This reminds me of a scene from the TV show *Wagon Train* that I saw last week."

The funny thing was that Rocky had seen the same rerun of the old show himself, and it reminded him, too, of their present situation. On the show, when the Indians attacked the wagon train, the men formed a circle with their wagons so they could have cover while defending their families against the attacking Indians.

Just then, four Mexicans breached the car barrier. Apparently, the Mexicans not only had spotted the barriers, but they had also seen what Rocky knew was one of their weaker areas of defense. There was a very thick grove of scrub oaks that went right up to the clubhouse, and it had been difficult to get the cars close enough together to complete the circle. Making the situation even worse, the scrub oak was fairly thick, making it hard to see any attackers until they were almost upon the residents.

Sure enough, the four attackers were inside the circle before anyone even noticed them. One had a large stick, two had large knives, and one had a gun. They confronted three residents, whose shock and fear turned into natural self-preservation; with little hesitation, they shot the Mexicans.

The shots started an all-out war. Both inside and outside the barricade, it was like everyone had been waiting for a signal to start shooting. Within seconds, from almost every direction, the attackers charged the clubhouse. Yelling, screaming, and waving everything from clubs and pitchforks to guns and knives, they ran toward the barrier of cars.

The gunshots that had spurred on the attackers also spurred on the defenders. Shots from all the cars rang out simultaneously. Almost immediately, several dozen Mexicans fell to the ground, many mortally wounded.

The results shocked both sides. The attackers stopped running forward, but instead of retreating, they just paused as if a whistle had been blown. The defenders also froze.

For Rocky, the question now became what to do next. The Mexicans hadn't dropped their weapons nor raised their hands in surrender. They had just stopped moving. Should he order everyone to keep shooting?

Before he could do anything, the decision was made for him. On the main road to the clubhouse, a small group of men who seemed to be better trained charged toward the front of the clubhouse. Rocky considered that a serious tactical mistake. He and three of the other men, all of whom had taken the machine guns from the arsenal, now braced themselves and unloaded their clips into the surging Mexicans. Jolted out of their stupor, the other defenders opened fire as well until they ran out of ammunition and had to reload. The message finally got through to the Mexicans: not only were they outgunned, but also these Americans wouldn't be easy prey. The invaders turned and ran, abandoning their dead and wounded.

Chapter 89

Interstate I-10 a little over 150 miles west of Houston was a stream of slow-moving cars and trucks all headed east. To an observer from the air, the stream of vehicles looked normal; however, when seen from the roadside, the impression was anything but. Each vehicle was packed with Mexicans. The vehicles had been commandeered by Mexican illegals who were headed to Houston. Being the largest city in the Southwest, Houston was the illegals' destination. There they would hopefully find food. It seemed that food became scarcer at each stop they made. The old saying that an army travels on their stomach certainly held true for the Mexicans. The massive groups had broken into smaller groups due to the food crisis, and they couldn't or wouldn't hold on for much longer without something to eat.

None of the vehicles were going the speed limit of seventy-five miles an hour. The shoulder of the highway was lined with Mexicans walking toward Houston, as well. The pedestrians were forced to walk so close to the travel lanes that it affected traffic speed. Many of the Mexicans were waving at the passing vehicles and trying to encourage them to stop and pick them up. The highway was littered with cars and trucks that had run out of gas. And it seemed that thousands of fleeing Texans had strewn nails and screws on many of the highways, which was having a devastating effect on the Mexicans' progress.

One of the many stolen pickup trucks was driven by a middle-aged Mexican man who had his wife and three children in the front and two others riding in the truck bed. The wife continued to ask her husband to stop and pick up a few of the walkers because they had extra room in the bed of their pickup. But he would have none of it. Earlier in the day, he had seen what happened when a vehicle stopped to pick up fellow countrymen. When that vehicle had come to a stop, four Mexicans had yanked open the driver's side door, pulled the driver out, and stolen the vehicle. It mattered not that they had stolen a vehicle that hours earlier had been stolen.

No, he wasn't going to tempt fate nor put his family's safety at risk by stopping for a stranger, even if it was a countryman in need.

His wife saw a pregnant woman with two young children, dragging their belongings and barely able to walk, up ahead. She shouted at her husband to stop and pick them up, but he shook his head. Out of frustration, to help her fellow countrymen, she grabbed the steering wheel and twisted it toward the shoulder of the road. Even though they were not going very fast, the abrupt jerk of the steering wheel caused the truck to go sideways. It flipped end over end before landing in the middle of a group of unfortunate souls, including the pregnant woman and her children.

The accident was off of the roadway. However, the horrific scene could be seen by the people traveling on I-10 and created the beginnings of a massive traffic backup. At first the rubberneckers caused a slowdown; then, in the blink of an eye, a car tapped the rear end of the car in front of it. Suddenly, car after car slammed into the cars in front of them, creating a pileup of over thirty cars. The carnage continued to grow as more vehicles slammed into the pile.

It was an epic pileup, not only because of the number of vehicles involved but because each vehicle had been filled to capacity and beyond. Each pickup truck's bed had been loaded with passengers, now ejected and lying crumpled in the road.

Before anyone could get out of a vehicle, a stolen semi loaded with illegals jackknifed and slammed broadside into the pile of twisted metal and humanity.

Chapter 90

Marcie and Chelsea decided they needed to get gas on the way home from school. But as they approached the Shell station, they found that there was a double line of cars a quarter mile long.

Marcie, who was driving, said, "Screw this. We can go to the Exxon near home."

But as they got closer to the Exxon, instead of a line of cars, they found that the station was closed. A large sign hanging on the gas pumps read, OUT OF GAS. Both girls found that going from station to station was a waste of their time, so they headed home.

Anxious to tell their mom about the incidents at the gas stations, they rushed into the kitchen and found their mom intensely watching TV.

"Mom, Mom, you won't believe what just happened when we tried to buy gas!" they said, simultaneously as usual.

"Quiet, girls, I am trying to hear the special news alert," Debbie said as she turned up the volume on the TV.

"We urge all citizens to remain calm and not panic. At this time, we are attempting to verify the stories coming out of southwest Texas concerning two groups of illegal Mexicans that successfully crashed the border, as reported on earlier this week. It appears that they may be getting closer to Houston, but reports are a bit sketchy. We're attempting to send out our two helicopter crews, but the station has been unsuccessful in obtaining the fuel necessary for the helicopter's flight time."

His co-anchor began her report, and Debbie commented to the girls, "I hate how these news shows use two co-anchors, usually a man and a woman, who then bounce the reporting back and forth. They've even gone so far as to finish each other's sentences." To Debbie it was annoying and distracting. "I just want to hear the damn news."

"That's right, Jamie," the original anchor was saying. "Our reporter on the scene has reported that there has been a run on gasoline and that only 10 percent or less of our local gas stations still have gas supplies."

Jamie turned toward her co-anchor. "Yes, Bob, and before our copters were grounded they reported that all highways leading north and northeast out of the city are bumper-to-bumper traffic jams everywhere."

"Jamie, it seems that many of our citizens aren't waiting to see if the rumors of approaching illegals are true or not."

Cliff and Cliff Jr. burst into the room.

"Ladies, it's time to pack up. We're heading out of town immediately."

Chelsea quickly asked, "How long are we going to be gone?"

Cliff was already halfway out the kitchen door and had to come back to answer. "How the hell do I know? I guess until the governor pulls his head out of his ass and calls in the National Guard, or those bigger morons in Washington call out the military to defend us against these border-crashing, sons-of-bitch Mexicans! We've already waited too long. Uncle Craig called and finally got me to wise up. Everyone at the office left hours ago, and I heard on the car radio that all roads north and east are blocked. It seems the entire city is on the road and fleeing. We have neither the time nor the space for you ladies to pack your usual wardrobes. You get to take what you're wearing and one change of clothes."

"But, Daddy, I can't wear the same thing two days in a row. I just can't," moaned Chelsea.

Marcie beat her father to the punch. "Sorry, Little Miss Prissy, maybe it will do you good to learn there is something else in life other than your clothes and how you look in the mirror."

"Shut up, the both of you!" Debbie turned her attention to Cliff. "So if all the highways are jammed, where are we going?"

Cliff yelled down the hall to Cliff Jr. to start rounding up all the guns and ammo, and then he answered his wife. "We're heading to our beach house in Galveston. From the news reports it seems relatively clear that even though the invading Mexicans traveled on the coast for a while and ransacked Corpus Christi, they are now collectively moving toward Houston. No one knows exactly what they're after, other than food."

"Well, they are to be in for a rude awakening," retorted Debbie. "The news channels have been reporting that not only are all the gas stations running low on gas, but the grocery stores have been completely out of food for days with no hope in sight for the trucks to arrive with fresh stock. That's the main reason everybody's been abandoning the city and driving north. CBS had a special on the 'emptying of our grocery stores' and said it was a combination of people panicking and the food-delivery trucks either being attacked by the Mexicans in the South and West or refusing to drive toward Houston. It's a nightmare!"

Cliff ran back into the hallway and yelled to Cliff Jr. "Cliff, stop what you're doing and go into the garage and make sure those gas cans that I use for hunting are completely filled."

"Yes, Dad, all four of them are filled with gas, and I turned on the caddy, and it has a full tank. I have an empty five-gallon gas can in my Jeep. Do you want me to siphon gas out of Mom's Mercedes to fill it up?"

"Smart thinking, son. You take care of the gas, and I'll take over collecting the guns and ammunition."

With Cliff off to take care of the guns, Debbie and the girls were left in the kitchen to pack the food from the refrigerator and pantry and start collecting supplies to carry down to their beach house.

While frantically packing, Marcie related a story. "Mom, one of the girls at school today was telling a story about her grandparents who live in Corpus Christi. She said that the Mexicans overran the city and the first thing they did was ransack all the grocery stores. After the food was gone from the stores, they started to break into people's homes looking for food."

Without looking up from packing a box full of food, Debbie said, "Did they invade her grandparents' home? Were her grandparents injured?"

Marcie looked concerned. "She said no one knows exactly what happened in Corpus Christi. All the phone lines, cell phones, and the Internet didn't work. It seemed that the only people who were injured by the illegals were those who stood in their way of getting food. Also, she said the police were scarce and there was no answer if you dialed 911."

Cliff had done an excellent job of pushing everyone to get packed and to load the Cadillac Escalade. Each sat quietly in the Escalade, their minds reeling with memories of happier times. Cliff's mind swirled with regrets of leaving behind his prized possessions and a few recriminations for having missed family activities when the kids were young. As the car backed out of the garage, not knowing if they would ever see their home again, the twins cried freely.

Chapter 91

Dave was slumped over in the corner of their makeshift barracks. He had tried all night to catch some sleep, but it had been impossible. Two thoughts kept spinning in his head—Anita's death and Craig's invitation to join the rest of the family in Albuquerque.

He was quickly shaken from his semisleep as Buck stormed into the room where Dave and five other US Border Patrol agents were bunking.

"Okay, boys, it's about time you earned your pay."

What a joke, thought Dave. For the last week and a half, he'd been putting in twenty-plus-hour days trying to put out one crisis after another.

"The big bosses want me to head up a patrol and go down to the San Ysidro border station and report back what condition it's in," Buck said. "I guess somebody's trying to figure out how to close down the borders again and feel they can't make decisions until they know just how bad a condition the stations are currently in.

"This is going to be a fairly dangerous mission, considering the scant reports we've been getting. The reports are telling us that thousands of Mexicans are still flooding through the abandoned entry stations along the entire border each day."

Buck made eye contact with each man and acted like the pompous ass he was by reviewing his men as if they were soldiers in the military. "Chins up, stomachs in, tuck in that shirt, what a sorry sack of shit you are!"

The men in his unit hated his guts and could hardly wait for his retirement.

"I only need two men!" Buck shouted. "Can you fucking believe it? *My* boss has demanded that I go too. Frank, you don't have a wife and kids, so you're coming."

Then Buck stopped in front of Dave and said in as mean a voice as he could muster, "Hey, Dave, you don't have a wife anymore. Or a kid anymore. So you're my number two m—"

Before Buck could finish his sentence, Dave punched Buck in the stomach with all his might. However, with Buck's enormous girth, Dave barely made him grunt from his effort.

"You'll pay for that, you little Mexican loving-bastard. I guarantee it," Buck shouted at Dave, spittle flying in all directions. Buck's face was so red from anger that Dave pictured him keeling over with a massive coronary any second. But Buck disappointed Dave by pushing him out of the way and proceeding to collect his gear for the mission.

The three of them loaded into Buck's patrol wagon and headed down toward the San Ysidro border station. Buck didn't think they'd get as far as the station after hearing the reports about pockets of Mexicans still hugging the border stations looking for food or an opportunity to work. The local citizens that resided in the area surrounding the immigration station, for the most part, had fled north hoping to stay with relatives or friends until they could return to whatever was left of their homes. The vehicles left behind had been commandeered by the invading Mexicans, and those had been driven north.

Buck had learned that almost every gas station south of Los Angeles had run dry, plumb out of gas, in the last week. He double-checked his patrol vehicle before they left, and luckily it was full. There was a gas station on a small knoll about a quarter mile from the San Ysidro border station, and Buck pulled into its lot and parked where he had full view of the border station.

Buck got down to the business at hand. "Okay, boys, sneak down to the station and see how much damage has been done to the buildings, the barriers, and the fencing. I'll need you to write out a fully detailed report. Meanwhile, I'll wait here to keep an eye on things."

Dave looked over at the other agent, who was obviously scared, to see if he was ready to go. Dave was sure the agent had pissed in his pants; he hoped Buck wouldn't find out. The reported incidents of illegal Mexicans attacking Americans unprovoked had been limited. However, sneaking down to the entry point where the illegals were flooding in, appearing in uniform, and carrying guns might provoke these Mexicans toward violence.

Looking through the patrol car's windows, Dave could see at least a few hundred Mexicans milling about. Being the senior of the two officers, Dave figured it was his job to speak up and let Buck know how he felt about this assignment.

"Fuck you, Buck. We aren't going on a suicide mission just to let your boss know the conditions I can see from here. We don't need to get close to the station to see that the destruction is pretty extensive."

Buck, wearing one of his disgusting shit-eating grins, said, "Go ahead, college boy, refuse. I'll make sure you're not only fired but that you never get your twenty-year pension."

Dave knew that Buck had him by the short hairs. Though the US Border Patrol wasn't quite like the military, refusing a direct order from a superior would be more than enough grounds for dismissal and pension revocation. Hell, he had hated every year of the last twenty and was already planning on getting out as soon as his twentieth anniversary arrived in a couple months. He was stuck, and Buck, the bastard, knew it. Buck had planned the whole thing.

Dave told the other agent to strip off his border-patrol shirt and take off his cap and gun belt. They both stuck their standard-issue Heckler & Koch P2000, .40-caliber semiautomatics in their pants, and grabbed shotguns, and left the safety of the patrol car.

They got about one hundred yards from the patrol car when they looked back and saw that a band of Mexicans had surrounded it.

Bullheaded Buck, always acting the part of the ugly American, rolled down his window and started to yell at the Mexicans, shooing them away from the car. The ever-increasing crowd did nothing, not even backing up slightly. As usual, Buck acted without thinking; he pulled his automatic and shot two of the Mexicans. Immediately, the Mexicans surrounding the vehicle moved to one side of the patrol car and started rocking it from side to side. Rocking more and more, the vehicle finally rolled over onto its side then fully upside down. Buck was held upside down by his lap belt and, due to his bulk, was unable to reach and release the seat belt latch that would allow him to right himself.

The car was sitting on a knoll and with another push the car would roll side over side down the steep hill. It would take one more flip and the car would roll down the hill, looking like an odd shaped log. That's what happened. The patrol car finally came to a stop at the bottom of the hill upside down and with Buck trapped inside.

Dave and the other agent rushed toward the rolling car, but by the time they reached the patrol car it had come to rest, upside down at the bottom of the hill, its top crushed in. Neither could tell if Buck was still alive, but as they rushed toward the car, Dave's partner for the day toppled over from a shot fired by one of the many Mexicans who had come down the knoll toward the crushed car.

Dave drew his weapon and returned fire, wounding the Mexican that had fired upon them. Dave faced the crowd, found his next threat, and fired a second time. The round found its mark.

The rest of the Mexicans backed away from the patrol car but remained close, keeping an eye on Dave. Dave was alone and at odds with himself. He was outnumbered, and the threat of injury or death for him was real. Yes, the mob was guilty of Buck's death. Buck had surely felt intimidated when the crowd surrounded him, but he had discharged his weapon, killing two Mexicans, unprovoked by an unarmed group of men.

Dave's thoughts turned to Anita's killers. Even though it had been Mexicans that killed her, these were not the killers, and he was not prepared to kill indiscriminately for revenge.

The situation had not changed, and he was unable to call for backup and needed to rely on his training and experience to save his life. Dave pumped the action on his shot gun. The sound of the pump action chambering a round made the short hairs on the back of his neck stand up. The model 870 shotgun was nicknamed "scatter gun," meaning exactly that. The round scattered little metal pellets out in a spreading cone and could tear flesh from bone and bone from limb easily.

Dave fired a round into the side of the knoll and pumped another round into the chamber. One blast from the model 870 was all it had taken; he didn't know Mexicans could move so fast.

After the crowd dissipated he was able to investigate Buck's death. Sure enough, what he had suspected was correct; Buck's skull had been crushed by the roof of the car. Dave then checked on his fellow agent and found that he too lay dead. Dave didn't regret the loss of Buck, but his fellow agent's death was purely the result of poor leadership by Buck. He solely felt his loss on a personal level. *Goddamn you, Buck, you fucked up royally this time.* Dave knew there'd be paperwork coming out his ass for the next two weeks.

Dave determined that the patrol car was a total loss. He found an old pickup truck parked by a nearby building. He attempted to start the truck. It turned over but wouldn't start. It was apparent that it was out of gas. Luckily Dave found a length of hose in the truck bed and an old metal bucket lying next to the gas station's restroom door. Quickly he siphoned the gas out of the patrol car and into the old metal bucket. Reversing the process, Dave filled the truck with what he hoped was enough fuel to get him a safe distance from the killing field.

The truck cranked and cranked but was reluctant to turn over. Finally the fuel fed into and through the fuel rail, and the truck's engine leaped to life as if it had had an adrenaline boost.

Dave had one more thing he had to do before he left. He left the pickup truck running and went back over to the patrol car. Both of the doors were too crushed in to open, but he was able to crawl in one of the windows, which had been completely broken out. And he was happy to find that the satellite phone had not been crushed.

He placed a call to central dispatch, asked for immediate air support, and then was transferred to Buck's immediate supervisor, to whom he reported the loss of two agents and his observations of the San Ysidro station. Dave was told to wait for the shooting team investigators, to maintain the crime scene until agents could arrive to take over the investigation. He was then ordered to report to the US Border Patrol's Critical Incident Team's facility to be debriefed.

Dave decided that after he was cleared from today's incident that this would be his last duty day. He'd retire early and try to forget the tragedies he'd experienced in recent weeks. But no matter how far he removed himself from that day, it would forever be etched in his mind. Losing Anita, Buck, and a new partner was too much for any sane man to endure. Every time he closed his eyes, Buck's death replayed over and over.

Dave picked up the satellite phone, having come to another life-altering decision.

"Operator, yes, for Albuquerque, New Mexico. The number for Professor Craig Walther, please." He was fed up with his life at the border patrol. Once he got his brother on the line, he was going to ask him, if the offer still stood, if he could get that private jet to pick him up as fast as possible.

Chapter 92

With the coming of the new age of technology, the Internet had fast become America's workhorse and the most dynamic enhancement to individuals, researchers, and the success of the financial and business world in the last decade. Americans' premier newspapers didn't carry the same weight in shaping public opinion anymore. The public was fast becoming dependent on digital sources for their opinions and daily news. Not only was it easier to carry a newspaper or book on a digital device, but that option allowed greater choices, and since most had at least two devices, access at both work and play was simple. No more folding a newspaper in half then into quarters to be able to read on a bus or commuter train. The *Wall Street Journal*, first published in July 1889, succumbed to its readers' opinion and started its electronic version. It was able to carry on its fine tradition: if one was a successful businessman, entrepreneur, politician or involved in the world of finance, one subscribed.

The one problem with the new digital age of opinion? Everyone had one and could publish it. So how did the common man discern a good opinion from bad? That question would haunt Americans forever. In the last decade, once Rupert Murdoch purchased the *Journal*, the *Wall Street Journal* had tried to become something more than the best financial publication in the world. One could now find such metrosexual topics as which wine goes best with sushi and how to deal with stress in the workplace. But even with the dumbing down of the great *Wall Street Journal*, those in power still relied on the *Journal* or the *Washington Post* to be fully informed.

The once powerhouse *New York Times* came in a distant third. No one other than local New Yorkers relied on it for any serious news reporting due to its far left liberal attitude. A conservative Republican in good standing wouldn't even line the bottom of a birdcage with the *Times*.

This morning's *Wall Street Journal* headline was as big as ever—MEXICAN INVADERS ATTACK SAN ANTONIO.

What Rocky and the others at the Cordillera Golf Club outside San Antonio didn't realize was that one of their fellow club members had been photographing and videotaping the entire attack and had forwarded them to a friend who had passed them on to the *Journal*. There it was—a huge photograph of the large surge of Mexicans against the defenders at the clubhouse. It was a scary photograph that showed a large group of Mexicans wielding pitchforks, hatchets, and guns charging directly at the photographer.

The accompanying story was nowhere near as dramatic as the photograph. It was limited because what the *Journal* had received was fairly sketchy, and the *Journal*, not known for sensationalism, took some liberties in trying to create a story that matched the photograph. But they left enough gaps in the story that even the most astute reader couldn't figure out what had taken place at the clubhouse.

The national papers had carried a multitude of stories over the last few weeks about the problems at the border. None had been anywhere near as alarming as the one splashed across the *Wall Street Journal* that day. All the previous accounts had been watered down for a combination of reasons. First, almost all of the communication from the border states had collapsed as soon as the illegals had entered. The second reason was that most newspapers and media outlets were owned and operated by liberals who supported President Denton and her administration. The liberals by definition always sided with minorities—the blacks, Mexicans, and Asians. Women were the next big item that the liberals championed. It worked for President Rosemary Denton. Though the vast majority of women couldn't stand her, it had been time for a woman president and President Denton was the best they could put forward.

So the last thing the liberal media in America wanted to do was to write negative stories about Mexicans crossing the border. As far as the liberal press was concerned, it was antiquated to have closed borders; why not let people go where they wanted to go? It was an incredibly myopic and destructive attitude. But the media had been successful in propagating it. One of the reasons that every politician running for national office gave lip service to doing something about the border problem was because every politician knew that the liberal press would give a pass card for ignoring the subject once elected. So that's what many politicians did.

But today was going to be different. The US stock markets had been on one of the longest bull runs in history. The Federal Reserve had artificially kept interest rates low for so long that Americans and investors worldwide had no other option than to invest in US stocks. Equity markets had been driven to incredible new heights and multiples. Yes, there had been a number of corrections over years, but each and every time the market had recovered and gone to new highs. There still persisted significant anxiety over the fact that in addition to the stock market being at historically high multiples and prices, the country had been struggling economically after eight years of a liberal administration by Obama. And what followed with the election of President Rosemary Denton was yet another term of liberal administration and stagnant job growth.

The headline was all it took. Even though the New York Stock Exchange (NYSE) had put in mechanisms designed to halt when the stock market dropped over a certain percentage, nothing went right that morning. In the first hour of trading, the stock market had the worst percentage drop in an opening in over its hundred-year existence. The NYSE dropped 1,200 points, and the other exchanges, like the NASDAQ, suffered equally dramatic drops. By the close of the day, the NYSE closed down 2,633 points, the second-largest single-day drop in percentages since the stock market crash in 1929. Finally, at least someone in America was taking notice of what was happening at the border. Yet, most of the liberal media and press were still downplaying the entire border issue.

Chapter 93

"General Tillman, this is Corporal Blake at the airstrip. We've got an inbound military transport that's asked permission to land."

"That's fine," barked Tillman into the phone. "Why the hell are you calling me, Sergeant?"

Corporal Blake had been a bit nervous since his recent reassignment to the Biggs Aviation Tower at Fort Bliss. He didn't have a reason or opportunity to talk to the base commanding officer, General Tillman. When he placed the call, he had been patched directly through to the general's office.

"Well, General, I just thought you might want to know the plane flew directly here from Davidson Army Airfield from Fort Belvoir in Fairfax County, Virginia."

"Thank you, Sergeant. Excellent job. Keep up the great work. Would you do me a favor? As soon as you identify who's on that plane, will you buzz me?"

"Yes, sir!"

Who the hell is flying from Washington, DC? Why didn't anybody call to alert me in advance? Someone is going to pay for this lack of communication!

Punching the intercom, the general bellowed, "Find Colonel Rodriguez and get him in here immediately."

These days, Colonel Rodriguez was trying to stay as close to General Tillman's office as possible. It was quite clear the general wasn't going to put up with any delay, even a few seconds, responding to any order or request. Rodriguez entered the general's office and at salute said, "Yes, sir, General."

"Do you know anything about a plane that's landing out at the airstrip? I've been told from the tower that the plane has been identified only as being from Davidson Army Airfield at Fort Belvoir."

"No, sir, General. I didn't know we had incoming."

"Hell, son! We've only got a few minutes to prepare for the unknown. Alert my staff immediately and clean up your damn office. The last time I walked by your desk, it looked like a grenade had exploded. Get the cleaning staff in here immediately. It looks like my office hasn't been cleaned in four days."

Colonel Rodriguez reluctantly said, "General, don't you remember? You ordered the cleaning staff to stay out of your office a few days ago. You said the files on your desk needed organization and that you were going to that yourself. You told me that the last thing you wanted was some cleaning crew doing your organization."

"Shit. Okay, get the hell out of here. Colonel, I'd like to know who the hell is on that damn plane."

As if Corporal Blake had heard the general's question from the aviation tower, Sergeant Blake buzzed the general again. "General, I've got more information for you. The pilot radioed a request—he's asking if there is any civilian press on the base. If so, I was to ask you to isolate them or eject them from the base."

"Dammit! What the hell is going on? Did they identify who was on the plane?

"No, sir. I asked, and the pilot said that was confidential information."

"Crap, just what I needed today. Well, contact the press office and see if we have any media types on base. If so, have them entertained away from any windows and keep them distracted. Son, just keep me informed."

The Gulfstream V, C-37A taxied so close to the terminal that one of its wings nearly clipped the roof. Communication between pilot and tower had been suspended. The engines were shut down and the aircraft made secure. A small contingent of military police and a sergeant at arms secured the space surrounding the aircraft. The gate crew moved the portable air stairs into position. The MPs had their weapons at the ready since it was highly unusual for an executive aircraft to arrive unannounced. When the stairwell was in place, the door swung open, and two military police stepped out onto the platform from within the cabin. They were fully armed and seemed to be agitated and looking for something. They scanned the individuals manning the stairwell and then the terminal's entrance. They had com sets and Heckler & Koch MP5s. After what seemed like a small lifetime, they both stepped aside and came to attention.

Four-star General Grayson deplaned immediately, and as he jogged down the steps, ex–Secretary of Defense John Hardwick exited the cabin and followed. Both men were vital to America's military strength; however they ducked into the terminal without any fanfare. A long line of general staff members, including another four-star general, followed the fast-moving line into the terminal as quickly as they could. Within seconds, the top brass had disappeared. If the flight-line sergeant hadn't been there to see the deplaning brass, no one could have ever convinced him that anyone important had arrived.

Immediately everybody sprang to attention and saluted the top brass. The flight-line sergeant stepped forward, saluted, and stuttered as he tried to say, "General Grayson, welcome to Fort Bliss. We weren't expecting—"

Grayson cut him off in an instant "Thank you, Sergeant. You weren't supposed to be expecting us. Let's just say we are traveling incognito. Sergeant, I don't want anyone else to know that we're here. Can you get us a transport immediately? Instruct everyone here and our driver that they're not to speak to anyone, not even General Tillman, about us. We need to move immediately to General Tillman's office!"

The sergeant decided that using a base limousine would announce to the base that someone important had arrived. If the general didn't want anyone to know about them, then he'd drive the transport to General Tillman's office.

As the top brass climbed into the back of the military transport, Grayson winked at the sergeant. "Smart thinking, son. I think you've got the idea."

As they sped off, one of the remaining staff turned to ask, "Wasn't that General Grayson—the General Grayson?"

This time it was Corporal Blake's phone that rang. "Tillman here! I hear our guests have landed. Did you identify the passengers?"

Corporal Blake didn't know what to do. He knew that General Tillman was relying on him to find out who these mystery passengers were, but General Grayson had requested him to not divulge their identity. "Sir! I'm sorry, sir, it happened too fast. I know there were three individuals, two in uniform. They climbed into a transport driven by our flight-line sergeant, but I don't know their destination."

"Well, son, where in the hell did that transport go? This is my goddamn military base, and I can't have planes landing and people being ferried around my base when I don't know what the hell is going on! You get your ass out of the terminal, and find out who the fuck just got off that plane. And I mean now, Mister!"

General Tillman didn't have to wait long for his answer. He wasn't off the phone but three minutes when his door burst open and in walked General Grayson, ex–Secretary of Defense Hardwick, and the chief of staff of the United States Air Force, four-star General Andrew Williams.

Tillman had gotten out of the habit since he had left the Pentagon of having to snap to attention in front of superior officers, but hadn't forgotten how to do it. He flew out of his chair and at full attention gave a crisp salute before he fully focused on the entourage.

Grayson spoke first. "At ease, Bill. You're among friends. But do me one big favor."

"Anything, General." Tillman hadn't experienced nervousness in front of a superior in many years and was as shaky as a private meeting a general for the first time.

He had no idea why three of the most powerful military people in the country were now standing in his office secretly, but he imagined it was about the border situation.

"I've been on that damn plane for almost four hours, and the coffee tasted like the crap you get at 7-11. General, can you get me a proper cup of java?"

Both Hardwick and General Andrews requested the same. Tillman picked up his phone, pushed a button, and told the corpsman at the other end of the line to bring an urn to his office immediately with some sandwiches.

General Williams stepped forward to shake Tillman's hand. "Your reputation precedes you, and I must tell you that there are not many people in the army that can run both an army base and an army airfield at the same time."

"Thank you, sir. I had some excellent training at the *Air War College* at Maxwell Air Force Base in Alabama. If I had it all to do over again, who knows? I might have been a flyboy."

Tillman, remembering his manners, asked everyone to sit before he took his own seat.

"Okay, gentlemen, you've got my attention. It's obvious that you're here over the Mexican border situation. So why do I have the honor of hosting three of the top six military commanders in Washington in my dumpy office in El Paso, Texas?

"Oh, and excuse me, sir," Tillman continued as he looked toward General Hardwick. "By way of the grapevine, I understand that you and our *favorite* president had a falling out." This was said with a large dose of sarcasm. "Forgive me if I am behind in the news arena, sir. Our local stations have been down for a few weeks, and we are behind on our news quota. But aren't you off the government tit, with all due respect, sir?"

The coffee urn had arrived, and the men were finally enjoying a good cup of grade-A military coffee. In other words, it was strong and as thick as paste.

Hardwick donned a big smile and responded, "General, let's just say the president finally couldn't stand the fact that we couldn't even agree on the time of day. I sit in front of you today for the first time in decades as a private citizen."

Grayson interjected, "I had already planned on the flight down here to see you when I heard that that bitch of a president fired John. Actually, it worked out perfectly. I would've had a hard time sneaking him out of Washington if he was still in office. But between the..." Grayson was about to speak frankly, then realized the corpsman who had brought the coffee and Colonel Rodriguez were still in the office.

Tillman noticed the hesitation and addressed Colonel Rodriguez and the corpsman. "That's all, gentlemen. Please wait outside until I need you. As you were saying, sir?"

Grayson continued, "First of all, let's drop the formalities, Charlie. As I was saying, keeping this between the four of us, John is here as a consultant to me." Grayson looked over at Hardwick and started to laugh, slapped Hardwick on the knee, and said, "Now isn't that a fucking turn of events."

Grayson put a serious look on his face and focused on General Tillman. "Look, from our conversation the other day you know how mad I am, but let me say how mad all of us are that the president and, to some degree, Congress and the Senate are just unwilling at this point to face up to the facts of what's going on at the border. But John, Andrew, and I agree that we don't have the luxury of waiting until the president pulls her head out of her ass to start forming a game plan. That's why we're here. John has asked me to put together a proposal that he can take to the president. I suggested we come down here to get a firsthand look at the situation and talk to you, because we're going to need you. We're going to need your airfield."

"Thank God!" Tillman said, maybe a bit too loud. "But you're not moving forward without the permission of our 'commander in skirt,' are you? If I recall my military history correctly, that hasn't been done since Teddy Roosevelt and the Rough Riders stormed Kettle Hill and San Juan Hill, ultimately disobeying an order from President McKinley to hold the line during the Spanish-American War."

Grayson turned to Williams. "See, didn't I tell you that Charlie always thought he was smarter than me?" Grayson turned his attention back to Tillman. "That's not what's on our minds. You could never pass up an opportunity to show off. No, at least at this point we are not planning on circumventing the president. But I can assure you she's going to break a nail when she finds out the plan. We're down here to work out the details and prep for when we get the presidential order."

Tillman let out a big, exasperated sigh. "Damn her! Damn her to hell and her socialist liberal cronies. It hasn't sunk into her thick skull that every hour she delays, the country is drowning in Mexicans."

Hardwick scanned the room; he needed to reassure himself that it was just the four of them. "It's worse, Charlie. There are some in Washington who suspect that this invasion was part conspiracy and was agreed to by people high up in Denton's administration. No proof yet. However, we believe it goes all the way up to Secretary of State Lopez."

"Holy shit!" Tillman said and whistled.

"Obama's announcement to legalize between five and ten million illegal Mexicans already living in our country was a scam. You know as well as I do that the estimates range between ten and twenty million. Now here's where it gets worse. We now know that Secretary Lopez, who has her eyes on being the first US president of Hispanic heritage, has been in cahoots with Mexico's Presidente Enrique Peña Nieto.

"Look, Mexico has never hidden the fact that it has prospered over the last couple of decades from our lack of shutting down the border, allowing illegals to simply mosey across. It's like when Castro emptied the jails and the asylums and sent the prisoners to suck dry our resources while we attempted to care for them. Not only are the impoverished crossing the border but the uneducated and unskilled."

Laughing he said, "Mexico was thrilled to have them leave. What's worse, when they come to America and find employment, they are taking jobs from Americans. Since they don't pay taxes, they send upward of 50 percent of their untaxed cash back to their families in Mexico. One of the largest industries in Mexico is its version of a Western Union cash transfer. The third-largest industry in Mexico is the repatriation of US dollars, which are then converted into Mexican currency.

"If that's not bad enough, the jobs they take from Americans leave US families needing handouts. That creates the perfect opportunity for liberals to be reelected. My God, voters receiving food stamps, Medicaid, TANIF, WIC, and SNAP certainly wouldn't bite the hand that feeds them. It's perfectly understandable. Why vote the person out of office who controls the purse strings that feed and clothe your family, that provide your shelter, healthcare, and even gives you a cell phone?

"Today, I'd say that too many Americans have become complacent. In pioneer days, families lived off the land, and they worked hard to provide for themselves. Today, families live off the teat of the government. Say, I myself would vote that way if I was in their shoes. Actually, no! I have too much pride and dignity to lower myself into being addicted and lazy, being cared for by others."

Hardwick stopped when the corpsman knocked and entered the office to replace the coffee urn and add more sandwiches. The tray was void of cream and sugar; these were soldiers, not Starbucks groupies. They drank their coffee hot, black, and strong enough to dissolve paint.

Tillman couldn't believe his ears. No, actually—he considered what had come out of Washington over the last nine years and held his head in his hands for a moment.

Grayson took a manila folder out of his briefcase. It was sealed and stamped on the front, TOP SECRET, LIMITED DISSEMINATION.

Grayson turned to Tillman. "You're going to learn why we traveled here in secrecy, but before I hand you this, I'll give you an opportunity to show off your military-history acumen, since in our last conversation you implied you got better grades than me at the Point. Charlie, do you remember the Zimmermann Letter and what part it played in World War I?"

"Wow, you are trying to test me. Let me see..." Tillman stood up, turned to face the window for a minute, and then sat back down and addressed the group. "How could anybody forget? First, let me start by correcting you. It's historically referred to as the Zimmermann Telegram." Tillman was in his element. "World War I had dragged on for years and even though the British and French had pleaded with the United States to join, we stayed out other than military aid. In 1917, the British intercepted and decoded a message from the German High Command."

Here Tillman stopped to think for a minute. "The German that sent the message was a high-ranking muckety-muck in the German Empire named Arthur Zimmermann. The message was sent to Germany's ambassador in Mexico. The plan was simple— the Germans wanted to convince Mexico to declare war against United States and take back Texas and other land they had lost in the Mexican-American War. The Germans promised troops, money, and equipment to support Mexico in its war against the United States. Once the American people learned about the message, Woodrow Wilson didn't have much choice but to declare war against Germany." Tillman smiled and looked over at his West Point classmate.

Grayson calmly said, "General Tillman, you don't have the clearance to read what is inside this envelope, but since we are basically at war, I'll take full responsibility for the breach. Open the envelope!"

As Tillman began reading the document, Hardwick broke the silence. "General, we had to call in a lot of markers and cut some pretty serious deals to get our hands on this document. But before we get into the details, I've been told that you have in your brig an inmate by the name of Romero Gonzalez. Is my information correct?"

"Yes, sir. He was in La Tuna Correctional Facility in El Paso when the first breakthrough at the border took place. The El Paso Police Department thought that the border situation was a distraction, part of an attempt by the Sinaloa drug cartel to break out Gonzales and return him to safety of Mexico. We have him locked in isolation and in chains. Why do you ask?"

Hardwick reluctantly said, "I'm now a citizen, so I can't give orders," and looked over at Grayson, so he could continue the conversation.

"Sorry to lay so much on you so quickly, Charlie, but you need to double, no triple the guards on Gonzalez, because we're going to need him. I can't go into the details now, but we traded him to get the information in your hands right now. Frankly, we're trying to save American lives. So if we have to trade some punk drug lord back to Mexico, that's the least of our concerns."

Tillman had been trying to listen as he was perusing the document. Tillman dropped the letter onto his desk and ran his hands across his head, smoothing down what was left of his hair. Shock was evident across his face. He'd been in "this man's army" for many years and thought he'd seen and experienced it all, but this...this was beyond his imagination. Everyone in the room shared Tillman's shock as if they were reacting to the document for the first time.

Quietly Tillman asked, "Has this been corroborated?"

Hardwick responded, "General, at the highest levels. As you can see from the report of the transmission, it is a coordinated effort by a Muslim radical cell and several combined terrorist camps that are working within a faction set up in Mexico. Based on this and other correspondence, we have reason to believe that they've already been successful in transporting a dirty bomb into Mexico. We don't believe that anyone in the Mexican government knows anything about this, and we have not shared any information with them. More importantly, we have no reason to believe that they have any involvement whatsoever in this plot. The Mexicans currently flooding into the country don't have any knowledge of it, either. The illegal border crashers are just pawns within the plot. World sanctions have limited the Iranians from completing their nefarious plot to detonate a nuke, but believe me when I say that they have nuclear capabilities and are online with a reactor. Luckily, neither Iran nor North Korea has the bomb or a vehicle capable of delivery anywhere close to the United States.

"As best as can be determined, the breakthrough at the borders turned out to be an unbelievable opportunity for the Muslim terrorists. We've known about the human smuggling of ISIS terrorists through the porous border area between Acala and Fort Hancock, Texas. Hell, we learned in the spring of 2015 that ISIS is operating a camp a few miles from El Paso! Now that our borders have been breached, a smuggled nuke could be a piece of cake for these guys."

Tillman interjected, "Does the president or anyone in Congress know this document exists?"

Hardwick shook his head. "No. Fate acts in strange ways. I just received word of this document only a few hours before I was summoned to the White House and summarily fired. I actually had the document in my coat pocket when I arrived for my meeting with Denton and had every intention of giving it to her. But when she deep-sixed me, I realized she would do nothing with the document, just bury her head in the sand. I was concerned that she, like the previous administration, would not take the Muslim threat seriously. I was stripped of my command and clout, so I immediately phoned Grayson, and we met in private with the Joint Chiefs of Staff. So, General, you're up to speed—and you're one of only nine people in the entire country to know what's going on, other than our people at the CIA, who got their hands on this document first."

Hardwick's voice became sullen. "There's one more piece to this story, and it isn't good news. We have every reason to believe that once the terrorists have gotten the bomb into the United States, they are going to try to detonate it in one of the largest cities along the border states. Being in El Paso, you could possibly be at ground zero. San Diego is also a natural target with its military bases. But we feel, after hours of discussion and reams of reports, that we may have determined the bomb's ultimate location.

"At first the illegals wended their way through the border states without a destination or pattern. Now, as if they have suddenly been given direction, they've turned their attention on Houston. We now think Houston is the terrorists' target."

Chapter 94

Cliff didn't know what to expect. There were so many stories and different versions of those stories of what was taking place in Houston. The only thing that was common among all the stories was that accidents and abandoned vehicles blocked all roads leading north. There were thousands of pedestrians attempting to walk out of the impending danger zone. Cliff's decision was to go south since the family owned a well-stocked beach house on Galveston Beach in Galveston, Texas. That would be their perfect destination. He announced to the family that they were going to hide out and allow the Mexican situation to blow over. He was hoping that the stories he'd heard were correct—that the Mexicans, after they had overrun Corpus Christi, had veered away and were heading toward Houston. He and his family would travel in the opposite direction of the Mexicans.

As they sped down the I-45 south corridor out of Houston, about fifty miles past Highway 610, things started to change. With each mile, the family saw more and more Mexicans along the highway but all were heading north toward Houston. Cliff wasn't overly alarmed because the numbers were not what he had heard. There were, perhaps, a few thousand, not the tens of thousands that some forecasters had predicted were heading toward Houston.

But as they traveled farther along, things got worse. Not so much the number of Mexicans, but the destruction to property. Every gas station and convenience store looked as if a small bomb had hit it. Abandoned cars and trucks were everywhere. The most upsetting sights were the occasional bodies splayed out on the shoulder. Cliff had ordered the twins and Cliff Jr. to cover their eyes with their hoodies and not to take them off until he gave the word. They did so without the usual arguments. Looking back at his wife, he noticed that Debbie had turned pale. At the speed the Escalade was traveling, Cliff couldn't tell if the bodies were fellow Texans or Mexican illegals.

Coming out of her stupor, Debbie tried to speak with her husband. "Cliff! Cliff! Are you seeing what I'm seeing? Cliff, answer me!"

But Cliff didn't answer. For once in his adult life, Cliff's larger-than-life ego failed him. He was dumbfounded and confused. He was afraid, an emotion he wasn't prepared for. He didn't know what to say. Had he screwed up and put his family in greater danger than they might have been in by staying home in Houston?

"Cliff, I think we should turn around and head home," Debbie said. "I'm seeing more and more that's making me nervous. Cliff, have you noticed that we haven't seen another car going south? Dammit, Cliff, answer me." Her shrill voice was somewhere between pure panic and crying. In any case, Debbie was reaching full hysteria.

"Daddy, Daddy, we're scared," Marcie and Chelsea cried out in unison.

Cliff Jr. was riding up front with his dad while the three ladies were huddled in the back. Cliff Jr. had never seen his father so quiet; it wasn't his style. If his dad was anything, it was confident and fearless.

Quietly he said, "Dad, what do you think we should do? I mean, we'll do whatever you say, but do you think we should continue on or turn back like Mom said? The girls might be right. We may be driving into a mess."

Cliff Sr. finally spoke, frustration and fear evident in his voice. "Don't you think I've got eyes? I can see the same things you can. Now, dammit, leave me alone. I'm trying to figure out what to do, and I can't do it with everyone screaming at me!" Panic and fear now coming to the surface, he shouted, "Shut the hell up, everyone, just shut the hell up!"

For the next five minutes, they drove in silence, each experiencing a private hell. At least there was something positive. Though the destruction seemed to get worse with each mile, the number of Mexicans that they could see became fewer and fewer.

Finally, Cliff spoke again. "Okay, here's what I've decided— we're going to drive as far as the causeway to Galveston Island, and if the view stays the same or gets worse, we'll turn around. But returning to Houston could be a mistake. From what I heard before we left, the entire mass of illegals may be advancing onto Houston, and I don't think that's where we want to be."

Trying to calm everyone down, Cliff Sr. turned on the car's radio. But instead of music he found what most people had discovered when they'd turned on their radios lately—dead air or static. Finally, he found a distant station that came in with a bit of static but at least had some conversation broadcasting. What he heard wasn't what he needed at this time in his life: news that the stock market had had its second-worst day in history. Cliff, being a stockbroker for Morgan Stanley, had 80 percent of his clients' money invested in US stocks.

Fuck! Fuck and double fuck! Shit! he thought. *Maybe instead of going to Galveston, we should just drive to Mexico. My career is going to be ruined when my clients see what Morgan Stanley and I have done to their portfolios.*

Oddly, that one good thing that he could always count on from Wall Street—that when it screwed its clients, it screwed them all in unison—eased his fears a bit.

All eyes were open and watching intently as they approached the causeway. "Hey, guys, I think we might finally have some good news. I've hardly seen a Mexican in the last few miles, so I think we made the right decision. Let's take the causeway over to the beach house."

Their beach house was one of those zero-lot-line configurations: all wood, three stories, with the first story up on stilts to protect the house from extreme high tides or the destructive wave action of offshore storms. The lower area was where families stored their gear and parked their cars.

Cliff's positive thinking was dashed as they approached the neighborhood and got closer to their house. The look of horror was on everyone's faces.

Marcie spoke first. "Dad, the neighborhood has been destroyed."

For once in her life, Debbie didn't have the energy to respond. It was all she could do to take in the carnage. Though there wasn't a Mexican in sight, it was obvious that they had been here. Every home had been ransacked. Windows were broken, and doors had been left wide open or had been torn off their hinges or kicked in. A few of the houses had had all the furniture thrown out into the street or burned in the driveways. It was evident that the invading force had been angry and out of control. Obviously, the actions of the invaders had not been opposed, and they had moved freely, at will. Their beach home hadn't been spared, but it wasn't much worse than many they had seen. The neighborhood was void of any movement, except for a few stray dogs roaming about, looking bewildered and lost.

Cliff Sr. quickly reacted. "Okay, everyone, let's go see how much damage has been done. Remember, just because we haven't seen any Mexicans for a while doesn't mean we don't need to be vigilant and careful. He grabbed the shotgun and one of the nine-millimeter semiautomatics lying on the front passenger floor and told his son to do the same. As they got out of the car, Cliff Sr. said to the girls, "Stay in the car while we go in first. I'll holler at you when we've checked the house for any remaining intruders." "We'll lock the doors as soon as you get out. But don't yell for us. Come and get us when you're sure it's safe." Debbie turned her attention to Chelsea, who was crying.

As Cliff and son went from room to room, they were surprised that the majority of the household was intact, even the brand-new stereo equipment Cliff had installed a month ago. It was clear that the invaders had come for food. The kitchen and the pantry were totally ransacked, salt and spices dumped on the floor and anything edible gone. *My God, they even consumed the jars of condiments.* When Cliff Sr. was confident that there was no one in the home, he sent Cliff Jr. out to get the girls. Immediately, everyone started bringing in the provisions, and Debbie set about straightening the household as best she could.

The good news was that the electricity worked, which was a relief because they had a lot of food that needed refrigeration. The bad news was that the water wasn't working.

"Well, ladies," Cliff announced, "I have some bad news. The water's out, so we'll need to use the great outdoors for toilets."

"Dad, what am I supposed to use for toilet paper?" Chelsea said.

"Say, how about using that stupid scarf you've had on all day to wipe your pretty little butt?" Marcie said, using every opportunity to stick it to her sister with sarcasm.

Debbie was in no mood for her daughters' squabbles. "That's enough. Both of you give it a rest. We're all hungry, and it's starting to get dark. You two work on putting together a salad, and I'll cook some hamburgers." She reached into the cooler, pulling out two beers, and opened them, handing one to her husband and one to her son. Never in her life had she handed her son a beer, but she'd never in her life been so happy to have two men with loaded guns at her side. "Drink up, men. You deserve it."

After they had finished their dinner, Chelsea said, "Okay, Mother Nature's calling. I guess I'll be the first to use the outdoor facilities!"

"You'd better take a gun with you," Marcie said. "There's no telling who might grab you with your pants down. But that would be nothing new for you. I hear at school, you've pulled your pants down for every boy on the football team."

With toilet paper in hand, Chelsea turned to her sister and said, "Dream on, loser breath. The only boy in the entire school stupid enough to try to get into *your* pants is the janitor." She stormed out of the house with a smile at having had the last word. Chelsea didn't take a gun with her, but as she pulled down her pants behind a row of short hedges near the house, she wished she had. The neighborhood had never been particularly well lit, but with the invasion almost every post light had been broken out. As she stood up and buttoned her jeans, someone grabbed her from behind.

If Chelsea was anything, she was a great screamer, and the bloodcurdling scream that came out of her would've woken the dead.

In an instant, both Cliffs were out the front door with guns into the darkening night. Lucky for Chelsea, Cliff Sr. had brought his rifle instead of his pistol. As the Mexican was dragging Chelsea toward the next house, Cliff took careful aim and pulled the trigger. Cliff's years on the gun range and his lifetime of hunting in all weather and conditions rewarded him.

As the Mexican fell and Chelsea started running and screaming toward the house, two more Mexicans came out from around the house and grabbed her. Before Cliff could react, a third Mexican appeared out of nowhere and stabbed her repeatedly in the stomach in revenge for their companion's death.

"Dad, look out!" his son yelled. Three Mexicans appeared on the stairs, heading to the landing where Cliff Sr. stood. Cliff Jr.'s years of hunting with his father also paid off. He had a twelve-gauge pump shotgun and emptied three rounds into the advancing trio. It was overkill, since his shotgun had an open choke that sent a wide burst pattern and killed all three in the first shot. The adrenaline was flowing through his veins, and his emotional reaction as he witnessed his sister's murder was beyond reasonable control. He gave each of the dead Mexicans on the stairs his own judgment—an individual, triple-aught buckshot as they lay.

But he did not have time to recover from his revenge before a shot rang out from a distance. Cliff Jr. was hit in the left shoulder and fell. His dad grabbed him by the collar, pulled him into the house, and barricaded the door behind them. Cliff was winded— being overweight, he'd spent most of his reserve energy to drag his son inside. He fell to the floor in an attempt to get his heartbeat and breathing under control. In his condition, he wouldn't last another round of fighting. He knew he had to get himself together. His family was depending on him.

Debbie had seen her daughter brutally murdered and was lying on the ground sobbing uncontrollably. Marcie was trying her best to console her, but shock was starting to take hold of both of them. Neither had ever thought that a nightmare like this could ever find them. This scene was reserved for the latest action flick.

Cliff Jr. was partly lucid and lay bleeding where his father had dropped him. "Holy crap, Dad, what are we going to do? I thought they'd ransacked this area and moved on. Why have they come back?"

Cliff Sr., still trying to overcome his years of over-the-top living, had already thought of the answer. He figured that some Mexicans had never left for Houston. Like insects drawn to a porch light at night, the starving Mexicans had no doubt been drawn to the smell of the cooking hamburgers. They might as well have raised a flag with the words, VENGA CONSÍGUELO, CENA SE SIRVE—"come and get it, dinner is served."

But he didn't have time to dwell on their naivety. Just then, the window that Debbie was lying under shattered from a gunshot.

Trying to sound less-than-totally panicked, Cliff Sr. said, "Ladies, I'm sorry, we don't have time to cry over Chelsea. But if we don't get our act together, and I mean now, none of us will live to see the sunrise." He loaded two revolvers using the speed loaders he had brought along and handed one to Debbie. Making eye contact and nodding in reassurance, he handed one to Marcie.

Marcie couldn't help it. She said, "God, this is like the movies. I don't believe this is happening."

Only then did Cliff realize the mistake he had made with his children. He and Cliff Jr. had been shooting and hunting together for over a decade, but he'd failed to teach his wife or daughters how to hold a firearm, much less fire one. How could he have been so stupid? At this moment, to save his family, he needed both Debbie and Marcie to help in the fight.

"Marcie, do you know how to use that?" he asked his daughter.

Marcie gave him the look—the look that all kids gave their parents when they'd asked a stupid question "Dad, please! I have the second-highest score of any of my girlfriends in Hitman: Absolution. Let's see. I assume all I do is pull the trigger." She quickly unloaded two rounds out the broken window, followed by a third. "That's cool. Wow, that has a lot more kick than the fake one at the bowling alley."

"Great, here's a box of shells for both of you. Now, I want both of you to go upstairs and lock yourselves in the bedroom and don't open the door unless you are absolutely sure that it's me or Cliff Jr. If anyone but us opens the door, don't hesitate—blast away, no warning, no talking, just start shooting."

After pausing for a hug, Marcie and her mom scrambled up the stairs.

Cliff turned to his son "The best we can hope for is that there's only a few of them. My plan is straightforward. There are two stairwells to the second floor. They'll either come up the front stairwell, or they'll come up the inside stairs from the garage by the kitchen door. If there is a lot of them, they'll come up both. I'll take the front stairwell, and you cover the inside one. We have plenty of ammunition, so don't feel like you need to budget your shooting. However, we'll be lucky if they give us enough time to reload. Look, if there's a lull, load up the empty clips. Using them will definitely cut down on our reload time."

He paused quickly and looked out the broken window. "Man if we only knew how many were out there. Since you'll be covering the indoor entrance, I'll take the rifle as well. That leaves each of us a shotgun and our semiautomatics. My God, I'm glad Texas didn't pass that stupid law like they passed in Colorado restricting magazine capacities. It was worth the extra money so that both of our Beretta nine millimeters have thirty-round, factory-original extended clips—plus one in the chamber! Son, do you have those extra clips?"

"Yes, sir," Cliff Jr. responded.

"Listen, if one of us gets shot, the other should go upstairs and stay with the ladies. Good luck, son. You know I love you. After I saw what you did to those Mexicans on the stairs, I have all the confidence in the world in you."

And with that, Cliff Sr. stepped out onto the porch landing, prepared to defend his family.

He was never more thankful that he had added tactical laser sights to his protection guns. That was how he defined them. He believed that any gun used for self-defense and not for hunting was a protection gun. With the street and porch lights broken out, the night was now very dark. He was going to have a hard enough time spotting anyone moving but an even harder time sighting in to get a shot off. However, even in the darkest of conditions, the red laser beam emitted from the sight extended farther than the eye could see. He knew if he got the beam on his target, all he needed to do was squeeze the trigger. He could shoot from the hip if he needed to because the barrel was in line with the beam. Whatever the beam touched was where the bullet landed.

However, it wasn't like a laser-guided missile or bomb that followed the beam. It was still possible to aim and fire but miss the target. If he didn't hold the gun still or if he allowed a recoil, the round would not be accurate. The tactical laser sight was a great advantage to a decent shooter, but it wasn't helpful to a shooter who couldn't hit the side of a barn standing ten feet away. In that case, they'd be safer if they had a shotgun or hand grenade.

What Cliff Sr. needed right now was a little more confidence, something he hadn't needed in years. He admitted to himself that he was scared; he was damn scared. At that very moment, he was appalled at just how scared he was.

Why am I so afraid? I've been hunting for almost forty years. I've had a wild boar jump out of the bushes and charge me. I've had a pronghorn that I had only grazed awaken as I grabbed his antlers and throw me down. I've got two fully loaded guns with lasers, and I'm one of the best shots in the state. Even though I am exposed, I have great visibility being up here on the landing.

Suddenly he realized why the situation so shook him. Not one of the animals he'd hunted had had a gun and could shoot back. He'd never paid attention to the animal rights people who criticized hunters for killing innocent, defenseless animals. He considered them a bunch of pansies. Now, for the first time in his life, he understood that he and his hunting buddies weren't as tough and macho as they thought they were. With their fancy guns, battery-powered coolers, portable TVs, compact stereos, and miniature espresso maker, never was a single shot fired in return. Cliff Sr. even had a night-vision scope that allowed him to use starlight to enhance his vision. The scopes were so accurate that Cliff could shoot the eye out of a chipmunk fifty yards away and bag a whitetail at the distance of half a mile.

Were those animals he killed as scared as he was tonight? No, they had no idea that they were the target. The high-velocity guns and great scopes Cliff Sr. and his buddies used made a one-shot, one-kill hunt a blessing to the animal. That was Cliff's redeeming thought—the animals weren't afraid because they never knew what hit them.

That was the last thought that Cliff Sr. would ever have because he didn't know what hit him. A bullet traveled right through the front of his skull and out the other side in less time than it took to blink. He slumped to the porch and rolled down the stairs.

Cliff Jr. heard the single report, and even though he was still weak from the earlier shot to his shoulder, he ran through the house, threw open the door to the porch, and was surprised to find his father gone. Quickly his eyes found a trail of blood leading down the stairs. As he focused on the trail, he realized that clumped with the Mexicans he'd shot earlier was his father, face down. The damage to his father's skull was massive.

Instinctively, Cliff ran back into the house, but now he couldn't figure out which staircase was more important to protect.

Just then, the door leading up from the basement burst open, and a Mexican ran in and rushed him. The enormous force from Cliff Jr.'s shotgun fired nearly point blank flattened the assailant against the wall.

Cliff Jr. snapped to his senses, and he remembered his dad's order that if either one was shot, the other should join the girls and protect them. He bolted up the stairs to the bedroom door, but he found the door locked.

He turned, thinking he'd heard someone downstairs. He didn't want to be caught there in the hallway without any defendable position. He knew he wouldn't be any good to himself or to his mom and Marcie. In a panic, he turned and kicked the bedroom door in.

He was immediately shot. One shot hit him in the arm, and the other shot him in the chest. He collapsed on the floor.

Debbie lowered the smoking firearm, her face frozen in shock. She had done exactly what her husband had told her to do. But there was only one problem. When she and Marcie had heard the shooting downstairs, they had gone into the bathroom to consider going out the window if both her husband and son were killed. That was the exact same time that Cliff Jr. had been yelling at them to open the door. They hadn't heard him.

She and Marcie had just returned to the bedroom when Cliff kicked in the door, but she had remembered the last instructions of her husband: don't ask questions, just start blazing away.

Just as she was about to rush to the side of her fallen son, three Mexicans burst through the open door. They stepped over Cliff and came toward her. Debbie held the pistol pointed at the three of them, quickly moving from one to the other, in her attempt to keep them at bay. She noticed that none of them had a gun. One was carrying a shovel, one had an axe, and the other one had a long knife.

"Stay back—stay back or I will shoot."

The three of them were yelling at her in Spanish. She couldn't understand a word, but she suspected they were saying something not much different than what she was saying.

But she didn't have to wait long to make a decision. Cliff Jr. had regained consciousness behind the backs of the Mexicans. When he'd fallen, he'd still had his revolver in one hand, and with perfect accuracy, he dropped two of the Mexicans. He was then motionless. But in that instant before Cliff could shoot the third, the man lunged at Debbie and caught her directly in the throat with his knife. Blood gushed out instantly.

After that he too fell to the ground. Debbie had had time to get off one shot, and she had killed her assailant at the same time he had killed her. Now five lay dead on the bedroom floor.

Marcie had witnessed it all—her mother and brother, both dead. She wasted no time. She just wanted to sit down and cry but she knew she didn't have that luxury. She turned and ran once again back to the bathroom. She and her mother had earlier noticed that the window would be easy to climb out of. And Marcie had spotted what she thought was maybe a way of escaping along a ledge.

Once she was out the window, she was convinced the only way to safety was to somehow get on the roof of the house. It was dark, but there was just enough light from a somewhat distant streetlight. She groped her way along the ledge, came upon a section of roof without much of an overhang, and finding strength she never thought she had, pulled herself up onto the asphalt-shingled roof. There was a large dormer on this side of the house, and she crouched herself in a shadow that was so dark, she knew no one could see her from the ground.

Luckily for Marcie, she always tended to wear too many clothes; it was the style. It was not unlike all of her friends wearing stocking caps in the heat of a Houston summer. Even she thought that was a bit crazy. But after being up on the roof for, she figured, something close to six hours, she was glad to be fully clothed.

After so long, her legs ached from being crouched in such a tight position. She was pretty sure that no one was around.

But that hadn't been the case for the first couple hours after the shooting. She hadn't heard exactly what was going on in the house below, but after all the shooting had stopped, it was pretty apparent that a fairly large number of Mexicans had entered the house. She had either heard or sensed them going from room to room. But it was obvious they had concentrated all their efforts in stealing the provisions that the family had just loaded in the house that very afternoon. Marcie had started to cry, but as quietly as she could. She had been thinking how mad her dad would be if he'd been here to witness all the guns and food that he had trucked down here for their survival, now in the hands of the various Mexicans who had killed him.

She waited another hour or so until there was just enough of the sunrise for her to safely climb down. She wasn't surprised to find the Escalade was gone. But there were still a couple of those abandoned cars that had been there when they had arrived. Her brother had checked them out and told everybody that they were out of gas.

Just then Marcie remembered that her dad and brother had brought all those cans of gasoline. She ran into the garage and flipped on a light and was saddened but not surprised to see that they were gone. She wished someone had thought of hiding them. But then she thought, *My dad is smarter than that*.

There was a storage area where they usually kept all their rafts and kneeboards for the beach. She opened the latch and voila! There they were, four gas cans filled to the brim. But all it did was force her to start crying again. How could she have so much pleasure and pain at the same time? Her father was smart enough to hide the gas, but he wasn't smart enough to save himself.

"Oh, shit!" But as the words were leaving her lips, she once again had a weird thought—a thought so bizarre she couldn't even believe it had crept into her mind: *Now I can cuss all I want, and no one will give a damn.* She immediately berated herself for even letting such a thought creep into her mind.

But then it was back to why she had cussed in the first place: *How the hell am I going to get the gas from those cans into one of those cars?*

When they had been packing, she had witnessed her brother siphoning the gas out of her mom's Mercedes. She figured it must be just as easy to do the same but go in the opposite direction.

She never realized that a five-gallon can could weigh so much, but she had to hoist it up on the hood of the car. And she had luck once again because, for some reason, her brother had decided to throw the siphon hose he had used in Houston into the back of the Escalade, and when they'd unpacked, it had been left on the garage floor. She had never done this before, but Marcie never shied from trying things she'd never done before.

Matter of fact, that was one of her favorite games after school between some of her best friends. They called it Dare. Once, she had drunk half a bottle of Tabasco sauce after enough of her friends dared her. She'd thought she was going to die. But she was glad she had remembered that. If she could drink a half a bottle of Tabasco sauce, what was a little gasoline?

And that's exactly what she got. It took her a couple of tries, since she learned she had to suck really hard to get the gas going through the hose. But once it started, it gushed. On the first can, not only did gas fill her mouth, but as she yanked the hose out and started to gag, the hose sprayed gas all over her face. She was partially blinded and barely got the hose into the car's gas-tank opening.

She threw up. She threw up three times. As horrible as it was, she actually felt better after puking. She had wanted to throw up when she'd seen her sister killed. She had wanted to throw up when she'd witnessed her mother shoot her brother. And when she'd seen the Mexican stab her mother in the throat and the blood spurt out, she thought she actually had thrown up. But she realized now that she was having a hard time remembering any of it.

As she was siphoning the other cans into the car, now having it down to a science and barely spilling a drop, she could only think of one thing: *If I could just find something to eat.* It wasn't so much that she was hungry; she just needed to get that taste of gasoline out of her mouth and throat. After she emptied the last gas can, she went back into the house, something she was reluctant to do. But she had to find something to get that taste of gas out of her mouth. But it forced her to experience all last night's horrors all over again.

Since she had climbed down the back of the house, she had actually never seen her father since he had been killed. She almost missed him completely. She climbed up the stairs having to step over the dead Mexicans her brother had killed, and when she thought she was about to step over the very last one, she recognized her father's shirt. It was being worn by a man who'd had the back of his head shot off.

Marcie just didn't have enough left in her stomach to throw up again. She plopped down on the stairs not more than three feet from her father and cried. Not like she had ever cried before. She thought she had cried the hardest she could when her boyfriend had broken up with her, her freshman year at Memorial. But she had outdone that a year later when their family cocker spaniel had died of cancer.

Nothing compared to the cry she was having now. She was shaking, shaking violently. It got so bad she started to cough and felt like she was going to suffocate from lack of air.

Now all of her energy was gone. She didn't think she could climb the rest of the stairs, even though there were only five left. Somehow she made it work. She just wanted something to drink. But things only got worse. As she approached the sink, she remembered that there was no water. The very thing that had forced her sister to go outside to go to the bathroom, the very thing that had killed her. And as she turned away from the sink, there was the dead Mexican that Cliff Jr. had shot. His insides were coming out, and it was the grossest thing she'd ever seen.

She looked everywhere. There wasn't a Coke, a soda, nothing. She immediately went to the refrigerator, even though she knew it would be empty. She remembered there had been a bottle of ketchup that they'd used on the hamburgers last night. It might not quench her thirst, but it would get the taste of vomit and gasoline out of her mouth. But it was gone; there wasn't even a jar of mustard. But she was not going to go upstairs; she had witnessed as much death in the last twelve hours as she wanted to witness. She'd rather drink more gasoline than to go up in that bedroom, that bedroom of death.

Luckily, her things were still sitting where she had left them the night before. The Mexicans had missed them because she had thrown them behind the sofa. She grabbed her coat, baseball cap, cell phone, and iPod, even though she had no idea how or when she'd ever be able to charge it.

It took a while to get the Honda Acura started because even though she'd filled up the tank with almost seventeen gallons of gas, the engine had been run dry. But after pumping the accelerator for about five minutes, she got it to kick in. For the first time in twelve hours, there wasn't exactly a smile on Marcie's face—just relief and maybe a little bit of hope.

She sped out of the neighborhood and was just about to connect to the main highway to get back off Galveston Island. But as she slowed down to make a turn, a Mexican jumped out in front of her from behind a small billboard. Marcie didn't hit the brakes, and she didn't swerve to miss the Mexican. Instead, she slammed her foot on the accelerator and took dead aim. At impact, the man was thrown up on the hood. And for a split second Marcie was scared that maybe she'd made a mistake because now there was a wounded man on the hood of her car.

But Marcie was now madder than she was sad. This Mexican now sprawled out on the hood of her car and his fellow Mexicans had brutally slaughtered her sister, brother, and parents. That is why she did not swerve to miss him.

And Marcie wasn't finished. She slammed on the brakes, and the man slid forward and off the hood of the car. Marcie did not look to see if he was alive or dead. She had already decided her next move. While she had been up on the roof of their beachhouse, she'd realized she had never taken even one shot with the gun her father had given her to help defend the family. All of her family lay dead, and she had never made a move to help. She put the car back into drive, slammed on the accelerator, and made sure that she had at least some revenge for the death of her family.

Chapter 95

Texas A&M University's ROTC, based at College Station about an hour northwest of Houston, was one of America's premier military schools. The ROTC program at A&M was three-thousand-plus cadets strong. The current corps structure was divided into the army, navy and marines, air force, and joint services and carried on a long tradition of pride and service with 42 percent of the corps receiving commissions in the armed forces since 1876.

So when the news that the illegal border crossers were slowly approaching Houston, the Sergeant Major of Cadet Corps Tom Evans, the ranking officer in the ROTC program, immediately moved into action. He had already heard rumblings and felt that it was just a matter of days before the government unleashed its military might and Governor Berry sent in the National Guard. But he would be damned if he was going to sit there with over three thousand cadets without coming to the aid of Houston, where so many of the cadets' parents resided.

He called in his top cadet officers, and together they formed an action plan. The cadets would move southeast to defend access to Houston. He knew without a doubt that his forces would be overwhelmed by the advancing Mexican onslaught. But he also knew that with his three thousand cadets, he could at least delay the forces' forward movement into Houston. Hopefully, the country's leaders would come to their senses very quickly and dispatch active duty forces to fortify his stand and push back the wave of illegals hell-bent on capturing Houston.

He'd heard estimates that the Mexicans were somewhere between 150 to 170 miles west and southwest of Houston. Traveling on foot, supposedly half starved, they could, he believed, reach Houston in three to four days at best. Coordination was going to be somewhat difficult; all the cadets whose families lived in Houston told him that the landlines were down. Cell phone use was bogged down due to high usage.

Sergeant Major Evans's plan of attack was to position his cadets on I-10 a few miles before it connected with the circumferential highway, Route 610, that surrounded most of Houston. His cadets filled every military-transport vehicle available and packed themselves into personal vehicles. They had loaded up every single piece of weaponry at their means and inventoried as much ammunition as possible for each man to carry. The column began to roll out.

Unfortunately, the cadet weapons were nicely polished but old. The cadets had the old M1 carbines. Still used by fighting forces, they were certainly not modern or normal frontline weapons for today's army. But they'd been the meat and potatoes of the army for years, and, by God, they'd do to keep the Mexican invaders at bay until the unit was relieved.

Each cadet had his or her own thoughts on this new assignment. It didn't matter what the cadets' personal feelings or thoughts were; these were well-trained cadets that thought and moved as a unit. God help the Mexicans if they challenged this young and eager force of cadets.

Chapter 96

Stephanie Jones walked past the secretary and stormed into the Oval Office without knocking. Because of her intimate working relationship with Rosemary Denton, she was one of a few who could enter the president's inner sanctum without an appointment. Frankly, her comings and goings were as she pleased.

"Rosemary, I hope you're on your medication because what I'm going to tell you will send your blood pressure through the roof. I just got word that General Grayson flew out to Fort Bliss, Texas, to have a secret powwow with General Tillman."

Unfazed, the president said, "So...I may be the commander in chief, but I don't think that requires me to know, or frankly to give a damn, where all the frickin' generals are."

Stephanie leaned over the president's desk and placed her palms flat on it. "Right, but how about the fact that John Hardwick was on the plane with Grayson?"

Stephanie's prediction that her boss's blood pressure would reach a new height was right on the money. Behind closed doors, Rosemary's reputation of demonstrative anger and uncontrolled responses were well known to her girls' club. She swept her forearm across the huge presidential desk, knocking everything within reach to the carpet. Rosemary's face turned crimson, and she leaped to her feet.

"What is that fucking asshole up to? Is that legal? I fired him. He's no longer the secretary of defense. Can he just board a military plane and jaunt about the country as he pleases? He's a civilian and doesn't work for the government anymore! Can he be arrested and lose his pension?"

"Frankly, Rosemary, I don't think there's a damn thing we can do. I'm positive that he went on the invitation of General Grayson. I'm sure that technically it's legal. The chairman of the Joint Chiefs of Staff could probably invite a plane full of high school cheerleaders to travel with him, and there is not a damn thing we can do about it."

"Get Secretary Wade over here immediately. I don't know if she can do anything about this, but I think we need to know what those two bastards are up to. Also, be sure that an order goes out to Grayson that he is to meet with her when he returns from Fort Bliss. We may not be able to rein in Hardwick, but I will tell that bastard Grayson what he can and can't do."

"Yes, Madam President, I'll get right on it." She turned and fled for the door. She wanted to get away from Denton as fast as humanly possible. They may have an intimate relationship, but "Madam President" was well known to cut off her nose to spite her face. Stephanie didn't want to be another notch on her long list of past-tense appointees. Having unlimited access to the president and being in the girls' club was heady; however, having the ear of the free world's most powerful person was simply orgasmic.

Chapter 97

Dave had arrived at Montgomery Field, located a little over six miles outside downtown San Diego, a full hour before Craig's private jet would fly in and pick him up. It was an hour he needed, and thankfully the airport was completely deserted because he needed some space to come to grips with everything that had transpired in the last few weeks. But it was hard to think clearly. He'd slept less than...Well, he couldn't remember the last time he'd had three uninterrupted hours of sleep since...

Just then his thoughts were interrupted—and what a beautiful sight to have them interrupted by.

It appeared that the colorful jet that had just filled the sky had come from the middle of nowhere. It was a relatively clear day, and Dave thought he would've spotted the inbound jet as it slowed on its approach to one of the three runways. Instead, the jet seemed to drop out of the sky more like a rock than a plane. Dave knew his planes well, and this was a beautiful number, a Bombardier Learjet 75, one of the most advanced business jets on the market. The Learjet was custom painted in the Denver Broncos football colors of orange and dark blue. The tail section was painted with the Broncos logo, a feisty Bronco named Thunder. The plane's paint design was, unusual to say the least, but the owner of the plane was a close friend of the Denver Broncos' owner, Pat Bolen. He was only too pleased to have his team's logo displayed on his friend's plane.

After the jet landed, it taxied up to where Dave was standing, and within seconds the door opened. A good-looking man in his late thirties jumped out and greeted Dave at the bottom of the stairs. He was wearing the classic private-jet uniform—black dress shoes shined to a military gloss, black slacks with a silk stripe along the outer seam, and a short-sleeved, starched white shirt with captain loops in the epaulets on each shoulder.

"Good morning, sir. You must be Mr. Walther? Is that all the luggage you have?'

"Yes, my brother didn't give me much time to pack, and he told me not to worry about it. He said all my Southern California clothes and Hawaiian shirts wouldn't do me any good in the Rocky Mountains. I've never flown on a private jet, and I kept a lookout for your approach, but it appeared you just dropped out of the sky and touched down in an instant. How did you do that?"

As the young copilot was about to answer, a man stepped out of the cockpit door and bellowed down to Dave, "Hellfire, son, I didn't buy this here Learjet to fly it like a lumbering cow." With a wink, he said, "That wouldn't be any fun, now would it? For its size, this baby will fly at the altitude of them big boys, and at a fifty-one-thousand-foot ceiling, we can go higher than some.

"I didn't want to take a chance of being on the FAA's scope too long with a particularly shallow glide path, so we did that little maneuver to avoid too much conversation. I'm not sure exactly what the FAA is afraid of, but they're hot to trot scrutinizing all flight and passenger manifests. I suspect they're afraid that some illegal Mexicans might be trying to fly into the United States, in addition to what's been entering here down on the ground. So I decided not to take any chances and figured they wouldn't be looking for anybody at about fifty-one thousand feet. Now pop your ass on board, and let's beat feet before someone discovers that I dropped in."

Dave quickly climbed the stairs and reached out to shake the hand of his savior.

"Nice to meet you, young man. You're lucky to get your ass out of here, frankly, being a border-patrol agent. At least that's what your brother told me you are. You're damn lucky to be alive, son. You can call me Tex."

"I can't thank you enough, sir. But I can't help but ask—from the plane's markings I thought you were from Colorado, a Denver Broncos fan."

Tex turned to his copilot and said, "Secure the door and fire up the turbines and let's get the hell out of Dodge. Set our flight plan for Phoenix. I want to be there in about an hour. Strap yourself in, little fella—the pilot's about to light the candles."

Tex turned back to Dave and his pending question. "Hell, today Colorado is like Southern California back in the 1970s. Everyone's been moving to Colorado in droves over the last few decades. People from Kansas and Oklahoma come over to go skiing just once, and that's all it takes. I can't argue with them. Why would you go back to Kansas or Oklahoma once you've visited Colorado, even if it's just for the weekend? That's what happened to me, but I came from Dallas, Texas. And with my accent, which I'm proud of, I couldn't pass as a native Coloradan. I'm honored by my roots and can't hide my bigger-than-life personality, so I figured I'd let everyone call me Tex."

Equal to the steep glide path in, their takeoff felt more like a rocket lifting off then a gentle ascent. Dave had never witnessed a plane leave the ground so quickly; the vertical inclination and the force of the plane were unnerving.

"Wow," he said. The power of the g-force had Dave's head flat against the headrest, and he was pushed deep into the custom high-backed swivel seat.

Chapter 98

The Walther boys had been raised with proper manners and respect, and as part of that training they were taught never to be late. The family's policy had been if they weren't fifteen minutes early, they were late, and there was hell to pay! So Mark, Elizabeth, Madeleine, little Ricky, and Mark's parents, Bill and Elsie, arrived an hour before Craig had told them the plane would be there to pick them up.

Elizabeth had something on her mind. She left everyone in the private aviation airport terminal as she motioned Mark to follow her outside.

"Mark, I still don't understand why we're leaving Phoenix. I don't understand why you accepted your brother's invitation to fly to Albuquerque. Are you sucking up to your brother again? Why are you letting him tell you what to do?"

"Elizabeth, this is neither the time nor place for this! My brother is trying to save our lives. Even the Bible teaches us to not bite the hand that feeds us!" Mark wasn't in the best of moods.

But Elizabeth just could not control herself. She wouldn't turn loose of the third degree line of questions. "You're the older brother, but I've never been able to understand why you are jealous of Craig. We have a good life and things that he doesn't have. You make more money than he does, and we have a wonderful daughter and grandchild living with us, two grown boys with fine careers, and all he has to show for himself is two horrible divorces. Mark, worse, Jesus is part of our lives, and as far as I can tell your brother might be an atheist."

It was obvious to Mark that he was not going to be able to avoid this conversation. Fed up and tired of Elizabeth's complaining, he'd rather have it out here and now as opposed to on the plane or in front of Craig. "Why are you so sure that I'm jealous of Craig?"

Elizabeth sneered. "Don't play that 'I'm so innocent' game with me. You know you're jealous of Craig. We've been together thirty years, and I know what I'm talking about. Every time you either talk about him or after you've been on the phone with him, you're depressed or angry. I can tell. I'm your wife, remember?"

"Okay, okay, I'll admit it! Is that what you want? You're right. I'm jealous of my younger brother. Now! Does that make you happy? Sure my brother is not the Bible thumpers we are." Mark paused, letting Elizabeth absorb what he had just said, then asked, "Can we have a little religious tolerance here? My brother has never criticized either of us for our strong religious beliefs, so I think we're being a bit hypocritical to criticize him for his beliefs or lack thereof."

"I just don't think I can trust a person who doesn't believe in God and Jesus Christ. And now we're flying off to move in with him for God knows how long."

Mark calmed down a bit. "Again, I hope your intolerant insensitivity is not on your agenda while we're with my brother. Let me remind you of something, dear. I urge you not to go down that path with my brother. You can like or dislike whatever you want, but I would not get into a philosophical conversation with him, one especially over religion or about how you do or don't trust him because of his lack of religious beliefs. My brother will not enter into a debate or an argument he's liable to lose. I can tell you where he would quickly go. He'd list every single religious leader worldwide that has been proven to be nothing but a con artist or pedophile, and he'd make your distrust or disgust over nonbelievers look hypocritical and silly. He doesn't play fair. With Craig, all bets are off."

Realizing this was a losing argument, Elizabeth fell back on her earlier accusation. "Then, why are you so jealous? What is it about your brother? What does he have that you don't have?"

Mark had been under a lot of pressure during the last week, with the trucking company that he managed imploding and

437

truckers refusing to enter any of the southern border states. Plus, the governor's office and other officials were threatening to sue him for failing to deliver goods and foods to the cities that had run out. Overwhelmingly, the fear for his family had overtaken him. His nerves were shot. The last thing he needed in his life was for his wife to go on the attack wearing her religious righteousness on her sleeve. Life had not been a bowl of cherries these last few weeks. Mark had developed a short fuse and a weak constitution. God help the person who set off Mark's powder keg, as it would not be a pretty sight. Unless Elizabeth wanted to feel his wrath and ranting, she'd better pull back a bit.

Mark and Elizabeth had a good marriage, and they didn't fight too much. But when they did fight, it was not healthy. Elizabeth had a bad habit, when she got mad, of blurting things out that she shouldn't have said. She felt that because they were husband and wife, she could say darn well whatever she wanted to say. Mark thought the opposite. If there was anyone in the world she should hold his tongue for, it should be with those she loved. He couldn't believe how TV talk shows derogated families and the gift of life as a whole. A sane person would never voluntarily divulge or expose any individual or family dysfunction for all to see. But, sad as it was, that was the world that they lived in.

Mark admitted to himself that he was becoming nervous about taking the family to Craig's. Flying to Albuquerque might not be the total resolution to the situation. However, the Mexicans were moving toward Phoenix and being away at this time *was* the best thing for his family. His wife had never gotten along with Craig, because for Elizabeth, religion was black and white.

Moreover, Mark thought he was doing the right thing if for no other reason than that he had grown up with all three brothers, all lifetime members of the NRA, and he knew that they could, if called upon, make a stand. No, they were taking refuge in his brother's mountaintop compound. It was the correct decision for his family, and it sounded a lot safer than Phoenix.

Mark thought that maybe it was best for the two of them to clear the air right here and now before the plane arrived.

"Do you really want to know? Do you really want me to tell you right here and now why I've been so jealous of my brother for all these years? Elizabeth, can you really handle the truth?"

Elizabeth didn't like Mark's tone. Maybe she'd opened a Pandora's box that she'd live to regret. She was nervous and afraid for some reason.

"Yes, Mark, as God is my witness, please tell me."

Mark was also a bit nervous about going forward. He hadn't prepared for this conversation or to bare himself in front Elizabeth. But he decided to forge ahead and see where it went.

"When Mark and I were young, we overheard a conversation that Dad had with our mom. He questioned why, after his service in the Korean War, he didn't leave the military and return to the family business back in Iowa. He had been a colonel in the army longer than anyone he knew. Yet, his closest military friends, with whom he had served for decades, had been promoted to general. Not a one of them was anywhere near as qualified or as dedicated as Dad was. Even though Dad wanted more than anything else in the world to make general, there was one thing he was not willing to do for that promotion. He refused to suck up to his superiors, especially if they were not as smart as he was. You've been around my father a long time. You know that my dad would rather slit his wrist than ingratiate himself to anyone, especially someone he thought was less dedicated or qualified or someone who had his nose up the decision board's ass just to be promoted. It was obvious to us while we listened to him talk to Mom why Dad was depressed. We'd never seen our father like that before.

"I remember to this day, as clear as a bell, what Craig said to me after we overheard Dad's conversation with Mom. He said, 'I'm never going to let that happen to me. I'm not going to get into my senior years and wonder if I wasted my life. That's not going to happen to me.'"

Elizabeth looked a bit befuddled, but she'd lost the look of anger. "What did that statement have to do with your being jealous of Craig?"

A glow of anger flashed across Mark's face. "Because Craig kept that promise to himself. Throughout Craig's schooling and career, he walked away from opportunities, promotions, and higher pay so that he would never regret one single moment of his life. Elizabeth, I feel like I've done the opposite.

Mark's words hit Elizabeth like the swing of a baseball bat striking a fast pitch. She actually recoiled a bit from his last statement. "What do you mean, you've done the opposite? You've had a wonderful life."

"Have I? Maybe, if you define having a wonderful life by doing everything you're supposed to do. I will agree to that. On a comparative basis, this is one place that Craig and I are opposites. He does everything he can do to keep from doing what everyone thinks he should do. I have done the opposite. And before you ask the question, yes—not to a huge degree, but to a degree, I regret it. And luckily, due to my own self-esteem, in our marriage and our relationship, this regret has rarely raised its ugly head. It's only when I think or talk to my brother that I get this feeling of regret. But isn't that really what so much of our happiness is all about? Isn't it all about life on a comparative basis? If you are the only person in the world, how could you complain about your life? You would have nothing to compare it to. You couldn't be envious or jealous if there would be no one for you to be envious or jealous of."

"But, Mark, through the Bible, Jesus has taught us—"

Mark did not let Elizabeth finish her sentence. "If we're going to complete this conversation before the plane arrives, the last thing I want you to do is start quoting Jesus or the Bible. And frankly, I want to get an agreement with you that until we return to Phoenix, if you feel the need to pray or talk about religion, you will do that in the privacy of our bedroom.

Yes, I believed in Jesus and God before we met, but you knew it was not a major part of my life. And you made me promise before we got married, you even made me promise before you would sleep with me, that I would make religion a major part of my life.

"And I have fulfilled that promise. And I'm not regretting that decision, and I'm not going to renege on that decision, but you need to know something. It has been a crutch that I'm tired of using. I'm tired of every time something goes good or bad in our lives that it has to be tied to Jesus or God. It has blinded you, and it has caused me to go down paths I should've never gone down."

Elizabeth was in shock, so much so that she sat or somewhat crumpled to the ground. But before she could talk, Mark said, "I don't know why you are in such a state of shock. It's not like this is the first time I've let you know that I've had some concerns about the direction of our marriage. I'm not a complaining man. But I've told you in the past I was not happy in my work but more importantly, I've indicated to you that I didn't feel like I was getting the love and attention I deserved as a husband."

Mark continued. "I hate the trucking business. I've always hated the trucking business. I hate being stuck behind a desk all day. I feel like a caged animal. And just when I was going to do something like Craig would do and announce to you that I was going to quit and that we were going to move out of that godforsaken desert, maybe somewhere where things grow without having to pour gallons of water on them 365 days a year, it didn't happen because you announced you were pregnant. And once again I had to do *the right thing*. I had to do *the right thing* for you, and I had to do *the right thing* for our unborn child. So I suppressed my hate for my work.

"I thought I was only biding my time. I figured if I could just work that much harder and put aside that much more money, that maybe within a few years, we could take our new child and for once in my life, I could finally have a career in something that brought me pleasure, not just money. But you never gave me that option. You just kept getting pregnant because your religion prevented us from using birth control.

"And of course, you wanted only the best for our kids. I'm not saying I didn't want the same, but at what cost? At the cost of my dreams? So with each new child, I worked harder and harder, hoping I could still pay for the private schools, the best clothes, the great vacations, the summer camps, the colleges and advanced degrees. All the while, I hoped I could get out of the job I disliked while I was still young enough to enjoy myself."

Elizabeth stood back up. She heard the plane approaching and pointed to this incredibly shiny blue-and-orange missile coming down out of the air. But Mark was on a roll, and for some reason he was actually starting to enjoy himself. Or maybe the first time in his life, he was able to tell someone why he was so jealous of his brother.

"And now for the worst part of the story. It was bad enough that I wasn't getting to do what I wanted to do. Worse was the fact that I had to work in a job that I hated. It was unbearable that I had to put in sixty to seventy hours a week, but what was the most intolerable was is that I lost you! That's right, I lost you the day you became pregnant with our first child. The love of my life. A woman with whom I was even willing to spend countless hours in this charade of religious zealousness because you meant so much to me.

"But you threw me under the bus. Other than your God, before you were pregnant, you treated me as if I was the most important person in the world, and I think you thought that. But that all changed the day you got pregnant. From that moment forward, all I heard the next thirty years was 'But it's for our child.' And then it was, 'But it's for the children.' As if not only our love and marriage had moved down to the bottom of the totem pole, but I too had become a second-rate citizen, a prisoner to the desires and needs of my children, some of whom were even unborn.

"Consider this: if every parent in the world sets their personal lives aside for the sake of their children, do adults ever get an opportunity to fulfill their dreams? Do any adults who have children ever get to live in the now, as opposed to the future, the future of their children?"

Elizabeth still looked like she'd been hit with a baseball bat, but now she was having to concentrate on both this incredible outpouring from her husband of thirty years and the sleek jet that was taxiing in their direction.

Mark too couldn't help but notice the incredibly colorful jet that was closing the distance between them, and so he picked up his pace. "This issue of a spouse becoming secondary when the children are born I have since learned is not unique to our relationship. Over the decades, I've had this conversation with some of the guys at work and at the gym. It turns out to be a universal problem, and sadly it's just not any spouse that gets thrown under the bus, it's always the man. I guess even though women can't get pregnant without us, the fact that the children come from their wombs—that builds a relationship that we men will just never understand.

"But I can tell you this: not a single one of the men I've talked to has understood why we have to become such second-rate citizens in houses that we have often built. So before the plane gets here, let me conclude. It's clear that since this is a universal problem, it's not something you and I are going to solve in any one conversation, no matter how long we talk about it.

"But you need to hear one more thing. What I am most jealous of when it comes to Craig is his sex life! Don't think for a minute in the rare conversations that Craig and I have had that either of us have ever shared anything about our private sex lives. I don't have to ask Craig to know about his sex life. Every single time we talk, I can sense he's got some new girlfriend with him. And I haven't shared anything with Craig, since I don't have anything to discuss! You want to add up every time we had sex before the birth of our first child compared to afterward? As in the last twenty-five years. I have! I don't know what happened to your sex drive, but I can assure you of this: *mine's been alive and healthy the last frustrating twenty-five years!*"

Elizabeth wasn't sure that that's where Mark planned on ending this conversation, but it didn't matter. The entire family had now joined them, as the plane was within one hundred yards of where they were all now standing. Elizabeth grabbed Mark's hand as they started to board the plane. Though she hadn't thought it possible, she had gained a new understanding of and respect for her husband.

Chapter 99

Of the hundreds of trucks that carried illegal Mexicans across the border through San Ysidro, one stood out from all the others. The Peterbilt semi had been modified and readied in advance of the border collapse by Señior Roberto, who was driving the truck. Señior Roberto had attended the University of Guadalajara and had been a supervisor at an automobile-parts-manufacturing plant in Merida, Mexico, before it had closed. The manufacturing plant had been the main employer in the town and the family's only source of income. The main facility in the United States had lost its contract and shut down and in turn closed the Mexico facility.

Roberto, unlike many of his fellow Mexicans who had illegally crashed the border, had a game plan to get revenge for the plant's closure and the family's now poverty-level existence. However, the truck he'd stolen from the factory had needed modifications for his plan. With his knowledge of the truck's systems, he and his family members had added three additional fifty-five-gallon inline fuel tanks, bringing the fuel capacity to 220 gallons of diesel. Roberto's math told him that at 6.7 miles per gallon, he would be able to travel approximately 1,474 miles without refueling.

Roberto realized that the best thing for his younger brother and the eleven other Mexicans who had joined them was to head north but in a different direction than the others. He wanted to stay as far away from the column that the other vehicles had formed as he could. Roberto knew that if he could get out of the border states quickly, he and the others would meld into the general population and not be discovered.

His strategy had worked perfectly. He'd completely bypassed San Diego, and instead of going toward Los Angeles, he'd gone on Route I-15 heading straight for Las Vegas. They had been on the road for twenty-four hours straight, taking turns driving.

They'd slept or helped navigate when not driving and badly needed to stretch.

Roberto felt helpless in the United States without a weapon, but here he was, illegal, having driven through the border without papers, knowing that they'd be treated as criminals. On their trip north, Roberto and his group had witnessed bloodshed, and they were afraid of being blamed. Roberto and his group had not harmed a soul after crossing the border, but they knew that the Americans, feeling under siege, might take out their frustrations on them, backed up by their love of guns. After all, he was driving a stolen truck, and everything in it was stolen. He would just feel a bit safer if they all had guns.

Roberto pulled the truck off I-15 in Barstow, California, and turned left onto L Street then right onto Main. It looked like a town big enough to have a gun store, and it didn't take long for him to spot one. It was less than two blocks away.

Main Street Guns & Ammo was their target, and it looked like a mom-and-pop store. With thirteen of them, it should be easy to overpower the store employees and then smash and grab whatever was available. Roberto, who spoke excellent English, entered the store with his brother, who spoke English haltingly. As the salesman showed Roberto how properly to load the semiautomatic he was pretending to be interested in, Roberto grabbed the gun from the salesman's hands and pointed it at his head. The other salesman had just started to reach for his holstered gun when Roberto's brother hit him in his head with the butt of a rifle that he had picked up. Luckily, the store was empty, and the rest of Roberto's group quickly jumped from the truck and barged into the store. It was like a candy store for grown-ups. The hardest decision was just how many guns and how much ammunition to steal.

As they loaded the truck, they finished placing gags and tying the salesmen's wrists and feet. Before going back onto the I-15, they found a QMart less than two blocks from the gun store, where they topped off their tanks. But as the group headed inside the "Q" to buy food, a police car pulled into the station.

Roberto knew a sustained gunfight with the police would be a losing battle for them, so he ordered the group back to the truck and paid the fuel bill. Roberto and his men left as quickly as they could without attracting any unwanted attention.

As they entered the outskirts of Las Vegas, Roberto and his group had still not eaten that day, and as they exited the highway, they were in search of a neighborhood convenient store that they could rob. They had only a few pesos between them after their long travels, and they were nervous about trying to convert them to US dollars.

The smell of food in the air overwhelmed the group, but there wasn't a restaurant or fast-food place anywhere to be seen. Keeping their eyes open as they drove ever deeper into a residential neighborhood, they found that the smell of cooking meat became even stronger, almost intoxicating.

Rounding a bend in the road, Roberto spotted a primary school with about one hundred children, some racing about and others lining up for a hamburger, beans already on their plates. The aroma coming from the charcoal smoke was enough to drive a hungry person beyond desire. The grills were going full tilt, with hamburgers laid out from one side to the other. From the truck, Roberto and his group could swear that they heard the sizzling of fat popping. Between the sound and the smell, their saliva glands began to fill their mouths with fluid, and they began to drool.

Instead of parking the truck out front, Roberto drove the truck around back of the school, out of sight from the prying eyes of nosy neighbors and bossy school staff. It also allowed them direct access to the kitchen next to the school's cafeteria. On the loading platform outside the school's kitchen were the telltale crates and boxes of food and dairy containers. He parked the truck, and with caution the thirteen of them approached the back door. So far so good, but the next part would be the tricky part.

Roberto's group was unaware that there had been several recent incidents of racial unrest at the school and that that day's barbeque was being heralded as a "day of healing and coming together." Without realizing it, Roberto had chosen the wrong day and place for his food raid. Even though this was an elementary school, tensions between the blacks and the Mexicans had festered into a full-blown tragedy, with the death of a Mexican student by a black student seeking revenge. KLAS-TV and station KTNV had reported the incident.

However, the kids knew the correct version: A fat, loud-mouthed, black bully who rained down fear on every kid in his path had enraged twin Mexican brothers and their best friend. The adage "Sticks and stones will break my bones, but words will never hurt me" had never been farther from the truth. When the taunting had become too much to bear, the three Mexicans had dragged the bully from the playground during recess, held him down, and beaten him until he passed out. That night, the black kid's father had beaten him with a leather strap for letting three Mexicans get the best of him.

The bully then stole a gun from his father's drawer, returned the next day to school, and shot to death one of the Mexicans who had beat him. The police had been called in, and since then the Las Vegas Police Department had left three armed police officers at the school. They would remain until things settled down.

Roberto and his comrades showed up on the day that the news stations had been given access to the students and teachers to interview them about the shooting earlier in the week and to cover the barbeque, a media event showing how the children could mend fences and move on.

Roberto's plan was to sneak into the back of the kitchen while everyone was distracted and steal whatever food was inside. But his plans were dashed when he and the others realized that they had arrived too late; there were only morsels and crumbs left. The kitchen had been emptied to feed the students outside. The students who had been in line for the burgers had carried their plates to their tables inside the cafeteria.

Roberto and his men were too hungry to leave empty handed. They decided that stealing food from young children would be easy, and they could be on their way in no time.

They rushed the cafeteria, and panic immediately set in. As the gang ran around the tables, scooping up anything and everything on the kids' plates, stopping momentarily to shove burgers into their mouths and pocket rolls, the combination of surprise and shock wore off the kids, and as a group they started screaming and wailing. Ignoring the cries, Roberto's group even scooped up succotash out of the plastic trays and shoved it into bags they had commandeered from the kitchen.

Suddenly, three Las Vegas police officers entered the cafeteria and drew their guns. Everyone froze. The Mexicans couldn't believe their eyes. What the hell were three armed policemen doing in a grade school? The three officers were even more surprised when they faced the thirteen poorly dressed, dirty Mexican men. They didn't know what to make of them stealing food off of the cafeteria trays. This isn't supposed to happen; this was a nightmarish situation. Roberto and his men were carrying the guns from the gun store they had earlier robbed. Each of the Mexicans had a revolver stuck in their pants or pocket. Roberto was the first to awake from the nightmare and went for his gun. The rest of his men followed suit.

The police didn't have time to think or react. The armed intruders had pulled their weapons and were prepared to defend themselves; the police now drew their firearms.

Without thinking, Roberto discharged his weapon in the direction of the officers. His shot went wide and barely grazed the left shoulder of one of the police officers. In the blink of an eye, the Mexicans and the three officers engaged in what would be viewed as the worst school shooting to date in America. Three police officers emptied their weapons, leaving three Mexicans dead on the cafeteria floor. Two police officers were severely wounded, and the third was killed.

But the worst travesty was that five children had been killed, and nine others had been seriously wounded. A KTNT cameraman had entered the cafeteria just in time to catch it all on film.

The crew was able to transmit the gruesome images by satellite to the station. Within minutes, every TV station across the United States had the feed and was repeatedly playing the scene of carnage into every household in America. It only took an hour for the footage to upload onto YouTube. It went viral in less than a day.

Chapter 100

President Denton and Stephanie Jones were in the limo returning to the White House from a particularly boring rubber-chicken-and-white-glue-mashed-potatoes fundraiser.

Stephanie said to her boss after her stomach made some very unpleasant sounds, "Wow, for a $500-a-plate dinner, you'd think there'd be something redeeming about the function."

"Hey, what am I, chopped liver?" asked Denton in her humorless manner. "Just hearing me talk was worth every penny those people paid to my reelection campaign's coffers. Those yahoos were lucky that I showed up for such meager pickings. Plus, I don't support their cause. Really, the Animal Care and Use Committee? Imagine me without my makeup. I don't care if they use animals to test cosmetics. I'll damn straight wear what I want to wear. Some of those old hags should try using some makeup. They look revolting. I could barely look down from the podium and look at their sagging faces. I'd kill myself rather than look like—"

The presidential limousine's mobile phone rang out. Stephanie answered. "Oh, my God. What? Repeat that again. Okay, okay got it. Yes, I'll tell the president immediately."

"What is it, Stephanie? You look like you've seen old Abe Lincoln sleeping in his bed." President Denton enjoyed her well-deserved reputation for inappropriate humor that the *Washington Post* had bestowed upon her. President Denton could never be mistaken for a caring individual.

"Rosemary, we're in big trouble. I think we called this Mexican thing all wrong. We're in big trouble."

"Okay, dammit, Stephanie, what the fuck is going on?"

"A group of Mexicans, illegal Mexicans who recently crashed the border, got into a shootout with the police in the cafeteria at an elementary school in Las Vegas. The shootout was over food.

Five grade-school children were killed, and a yet-undetermined number were wounded or severely wounded."

So much blood rushed to President Denton's face that she looked as dark as her black aide. She again let her anger get the best of her and cried out, "Just how the fuck did those goddamn Mexicans get as far as Las Vegas? I thought Marisa promised me this would all be contained in the border states. How the hell did they get into Nevada?"

"Rosemary, it's worse than that. The children's deaths were caught on film. Several news teams were on site for the school's activity—'a day of healing and coming together,' they said—and for the last hour, every TV station in the country has been playing it on a continuous loop. Someone uploaded it to YouTube and it's already gone international."

That was all it took. Rosemary Denton was infamous worldwide for having one of the worst tempers of any American political leader. She was ruthless and, at times, downright evil. In fact, she made Disney's Cruella de Vil, the evil character who made coats out of Dalmatian puppies, look like Mary Poppins. She'd been on the political rise in power for decades, and no one dared get in her path—or today, her warpath.

Those who had discovered her evil side found themselves suddenly missing from the cadre of political appointees or a cushy agency job. In the next ten minutes, President Denton used every curse word in the book, many Stephanie Jones had never heard before. Stephanie seriously considered having the limousine go directly to Bethesda Naval Hospital for a check of Rosemary's off-the-chart blood pressure, since she thought Rosemary was well on her way to having a heart attack.

"Get me my goddamn new secretary of defense, Virginia Wade, on the phone immediately. No! Get on the phone and tell her to get her fucking ass over to the White House immediately. Tell her I will be there in fifteen minutes. Stephanie, tell her if she arrives in sixteen minutes not to bother stopping by the Oval Office. I absolutely mean it. If she's not there on time, she better get her fucking résumé polished and in the mail because her name will be off the office door. I'll order the Marine Guard to eject her ass right through the Pentagon's front door."

Stephanie hung up the phone from doing her boss's bidding and turned to face her.

President Denton said. "You're right. We are fucked! I should've never listened to that sack of shit Mexican, Marisa. If I didn't know better, I'd swear she had a hand in this. I think we're out of options. If we don't play our cards right, I'll never win another election, even if it's for the county's dog catcher."

Chapter 101

Craig was hoping to get to the airport at least an hour early, a family tradition, but he had underestimated the amount of traffic. The roadways were filled with citizens who were fleeing from Albuquerque looking to find refuge in the approaching storm of Mexicans desperately seeking food or worse.

Craig's home was located in the wilderness at the top of Sandia Peak, and the fastest route to Albuquerque was to slide down the back roads and connect to I-40, which ran due west into Albuquerque proper. As Craig had found in the past, there were no cars on the hilly, mountain road from his home, but as he merged onto I-40 he came to a screeching halt. The highway was completely jammed with both the eastbound and westbound lanes moving as slow as molasses in the winter. Some drivers had become so frustrated that they had crossed the median and were going head-on into oncoming traffic, making the I-40's flow unpredictable and extremely deadly.

"Holy crap! Why did everyone decide to leave Albuquerque at the same time?" To make it on time, Craig joined a line of cars winding its way in and out of traffic and on the shoulders, often dodging oncoming cars. For Craig, it was a harrowing experience. He was quite relieved when he made it.

Even though he'd been driving to the airport for many years, Craig still laughed every time he passed under the entry underpass and saw the sign, ALBUQUERQUE INTERNATIONAL AIRPORT.

What a hoax! he thought. *The only foreign country with flights into Albuquerque is Mexico, and most of those are smuggling drugs.*

Craig entered the tarmac area through the private air terminal gate. Craig waited a moment to see on which runway the plane was going to land and then drove out to wait where he thought the plane would roll to a stop.

Tex's Denver Bronco–painted beauty dropped out of the sky and landed. When the plane finally came to a stop a short distance away from him, Craig opened all the doors and the back hatch of the Range Rover and then approached the plane as the stairs were being lowered. First out of the door was Elizabeth, followed closely by Madeleine holding Ricky by the hand. As they reached the bottom of the stairs, Ricky broke free from his mother and ran toward his uncle. Craig picked him up and swirled him around. Craig had never wanted kids, but for short periods of time he'd thought they could be a lot of fun. He loved the energy and enthusiasm in little kids and dogs.

Next came Madeleine, who gave Craig a big hug and said, "Ricky has heard so much about the uncle he's never met. It looks like the two of you are going to hit it off just fine."

Craig had a big smile on his face. There hadn't been a lot of reason to smile the last couple weeks. He was so relieved that his family was here. "We'll get along just great as long as he can shoot a gun." Madeleine shot him a glare. "Come on, niece, I was just kidding," Craig added.

Next came Elizabeth. Craig could feel himself tense up as she approached him. Though their meetings had been limited, they hadn't always been friendly ones. Elizabeth, however, surprised Craig by almost leaping off the ground and catching him in a big bear hug. She tightened her grip so that she almost squeezed the air out of him. Before Craig could react, she kissed him on both cheeks. Craig finally regained his senses and hugged his sister-in-law back, finishing with a little spin like he did with Ricky.

When he set her back to the ground, she let go but didn't back off. Although she tried to whisper in his ear, she was still loud enough that Mark, who was now standing next to them, could hear. "As a mother, I can't thank you enough for saving my family. God bless you!"

Craig, normally not a hugger, was not a mushy kind of guy. He couldn't remember the last time he'd cried, and he sure wasn't going to cry here in front of his brothers. But the emotion shown by Elizabeth had gotten to him, and something was welling up inside him which he had no power to stop. Quickly calculating a deflection, he grabbed his brother Mark and hugged him just as Elizabeth had done to him.

None of the Walther boys were known for their affection. It just wasn't their style. So Mark, too, was caught completely off guard. Frankly, he couldn't remember a time when his brother had hugged him. Now it was okay for Craig to cry, because Mark had beaten him to it. For almost a minute, the two brothers held a tight embrace, while letting tears stain each other's shoulders.

It took Dave to break up the affair. "Hey, what do I look like—chopped liver?" Mark and Craig broke their embrace just long enough for Dave to squeeze in, and the three of them returned to hugging and back slapping.

Now it was Tex's job to break up the warm reunion. "My God, boys, maybe ya'll need to see each other more often. I hate to be the one to break up this mushy affair, but the last thing I want to experience is gun holes in the side of my new Learjet. As I was taxiing over here I saw—well, let's just say the folks I saw didn't look too friendly."

With that, everyone scattered and started unloading the luggage. As they loaded up the Range Rover, Mark said to Craig, "I see your packing Dad's old .45 automatic." Mark opened his coat and showed off the nine-millimeter Beretta he was wearing in a side holster.

Craig then turned to Dave. "I assume you brought some of our illustrious government's hardware?"

Dave took off his coat to reveal three guns, one on each hip and one in his shoulder holster. "I don't want you to think I'm scared, but this is what I've been wearing for the last two weeks. San Diego has been under siege to some degree for a matter of weeks. If you get hit here in Albuquerque with what we were hit with, I don't think you can have enough guns."

Their parents, Bill and Elsie, had grabbed the lighter items and had already gotten themselves quietly into the car. Craig announced to everyone, "This is going to be a packed ride. Most of the time, I wonder what I'm doing driving around in this big Range Rover, but for once, we're going to have to pack in like sardines. All you ladies and Ricky are going to have to sit on laps."

With everyone finally squeezed into the car, Craig approached Tex. "You know, Tex, most New Mexicans don't speak favorably of Texans, but you and I both know they're just jealous. This is one New Mexican who's thankful as hell that a Texan came to our rescue." Craig pulled out a box he had hidden under his coat and handed it to Tex. "My ex said if I tried to offer you money, you would refuse. I don't know much about private jets, but I know this little jaunt has cost you a small fortune."

Tex took the box and opened it to discover a beautiful, intricately inlaid bolo tie. He looked up and for the first time noticed that Craig was wearing a bolo tie.

"Damn! I've always wanted to wear one of these. No one in Dallas ever wears one except to those fancy charity Western balls, but a lot of my friends over in Fort Worth wear 'em. I guess I could just never get up the nerve."

He slipped off his cowboy hat and slid the bolo around his neck. Tex spun around for everyone to see and asked, "How do I look?"

"Studly, very studly," Craig answered for all of them. "You're now an official Southwest cowboy. I don't want you to think that this is full payment. When this crap is all over, fly on down, and I'll give you a deluxe tour of New Mexico you'll never forget."

They gave each other a quick handshake, and as Tex turned to leave, he said, "I'll see you again. Somehow I just know we're destined to be friends."

Craig got into the Range Rover and started it up, but before he drove off he gave one last look over toward the most beautiful jet he'd ever seen. But it was already gone.

"Okay, everyone, buckle up as good as you can, and make sure someone's got a good hold on little Ricky. The highways are pretty treacherous." He turned to Dave, who was in the front seat with Madeleine on his lap. "Hey Dave, what—no uniform?"

"I've hated that job for twenty years. After the last couple weeks, I hate the thought of going back. When this thing is all over, I'd like to talk to you about some ideas I have." Dave changed his tone in an attempt at being a little more jovial. "So how about Mexican food? You've been bragging to me for years that San Diego doesn't know a damn thing about Mexican food when compared Albuquerque."

Before Craig could respond, they found they already had problems. As they approached the exit out of the Albuquerque airport, there were two Mexicans with rifles pointed at the oncoming Range Rover. Dave was in the passenger front seat, and Mark was in the back seat on the driver side of the car. Even though both were laden with family on their laps, within seconds both had pulled out their automatics.

Dave, although the youngest of the brothers, immediately took over. "Mark, can you take out the guy on the left? I'll concentrate on the guy on the right."

Mark had already rolled down his window. "Sure thing, little brother. You just worry about your guy."

Dave then said to Craig, "Step on it, Craig, but if you think this loaded-down SUV can handle it, swerve around as much as you can."

Craig had experience swerving his bulky Range Rover to keep from hitting his furry friends on the winding mountain roads, so he was familiar with what his car could do. He started jerking the steering wheel back and forth while maintaining his speed, jostling his occupants uncomfortably.

Two shots hit the car. The first hit one of the headlights and the other one ricocheted off the corner of the roof. They were rapidly approaching the two Mexicans. Craig opened his mouth to ask if he should quit swerving so they could take a bead on the two individuals, but before he had time to speak, Dave's automatic rang out, and the man on the right dropped to the ground. Before Mark could take aim, Dave pushed Madeleine off his lap and pulled himself halfway out the window. He let off four more shots, dropping the Mexican on the left.

Craig immediately stopped swerving, and they zoomed through the front gate approaching sixty miles an hour. Mark yelled at Dave as he slid back into the car, "My God, Dave! I guess I had forgotten how good you were with a gun. But it wasn't really necessary. I had my guy."

Dave slammed home a fresh clip. "I know, Mark. I know you had him but, I guess it's just my training. It's something I try to instill into every new agent—never count on the other guy. Take down the assailant as fast as you can. If your fellow agents take him down at the same time, so much the better. Never assume another agent is going to be as good a shot or as confident as you."

The women in the car were somewhat shell shocked, literally. Even though David had discharged his automatic outside the car, their ears were still ringing. The women couldn't decide if the shooting made them feel more scared or more comfortable, but Craig's words quickly resolved the issue.

"Honestly, a couple times I wondered if begging both of you to come up here was the right decision. With shooting like that, there's no doubt I made the right decision." He reached across and slapped Dave on the knee. "Before things get any more hectic, the three of us should do a little boning up on shooting skills, like we did back in grade school. I can see at least one of us hasn't lost his edge. Frankly, I've never been that good."

Mark bit back his ego and spoke up. "Thanks, Dave. Since we're both being honest, with Craig swerving the car like that, I didn't think I had a chance in hell of hitting my man. I probably could use some shooting pointers myself."

Now it was Elizabeth's turn. "Let me use Dave's words: what do we ladies look like, chopped liver? Mark taught me to use a gun. We'd only been married a few months when he told me that it's stupid to have guns in the house and not know how to shoot them. Plus, it may be necessary for self-defense. I think it's time that Madeleine learned as well, especially if we're going to experience more of what just happened at the gate."

"I want to learn, Dad. You've been promising me for the past year to teach me," Madeleine said, pleadingly.

Craig let out a sigh. "Well, Dave, you've accomplished quite a lot in just a few minutes. You saved us from those attackers, and now you've got everyone in the car wanting to shoot like you. Maybe there's a future there."

They drove along in silence for a while, and then Madeleine said, "Uncle Craig, can I talk to you about your college courses? You know I returned to college and I'm really enjoying it, but of course, with the Mexicans invading us, it got cut short. How are you going to teach while holing up in your house?"

Bill joined in. "Yes, Son, your classes should be awfully exciting these days, considering what's going on at the border right now is your topic."

"That's a great question, Madeleine, but before I answer, let me tell you how proud I am that you've gone back to school. If you're having any problems, let me know. I've got a couple good contacts at ASU if you need help getting into a class. To answer your question, my two courses relating to Mexico and the issues at the Mexican-US border were suspended. As the problems at the border worsened and the invasion expanded, I shifted gears in my two classes, and that's all I was talking about. In the last class, there were so many other professors who were attending, it was standing room only. There was even a reporter from the *Albuquerque Journal* there. Things really got tense in the lecture hall when everyone started to realize that within a week or so Albuquerque was going to get pressure from the attackers from the south. I tried to be as diplomatic as I could, but as you can imagine, three-quarters of my students have Mexican heritage, and I already knew from earlier classes that I had some Mexican radicals in the class. I never called them 'invaders,' and I never called them 'attackers.' I called them 'recent entrants' and 'illegal aliens.' I knew it was just a matter of time."

Craig checked his rearview mirror before he continued. "In my last class, before the university suspended my classes, I was talking about an incident in Las Cruces where a police officer was forced to shoot one of the invading Mexicans who was beating up some kid over his lunchbox. One of the Chicanos, for lack of a better term, stood up and yelled, 'Power to my people! They should've killed the cop!' and then he raised his fist in the air like he was Che Guevara. That was all it took.

"The white student sitting next to him happened to be a linebacker for the UNM Lobo football team. He took him out with one punch, and that was when the fight broke out. There were as many girls in the fight as there were boys. Luckily for everyone, two of the school's security guards, who had been posted outside the lecture hall by the dean for precautionary measures, heard the yelling and came running in. When yelling at the fighting students didn't accomplish anything, one of the officers tasered the closest Mexican student, and that was the end of it. The next day the university suspended both of my classes. It didn't really matter. I had already decided on my own that it was best to shut down my classes for the rest the semester."

After exiting onto I-40 east, Craig ran into the same quagmire of blocked roadways that he had on the way in. However, he joined the ever-increasing amount of people driving east on the westbound lanes and forcing the oncoming traffic to shift over one lane and use the shoulder as a traffic lane. At first it scared his mother to death, but when she realized that that was the only way they were to make any progress, she held her tongue.

"Son, where in the hell did you learn to drive like this?" Bill asked. "You've been watching too many James Bond movies."

"That's right, Dad. I do own every Bond film, and in many, Bond drove Range Rovers, including in one of my favorite movies, "*Octopussy*."

"Where is Cliff? How come you didn't arrange for the plane to pick up his family? Now, I hope you didn't exclude your brother and his family just because you two don't get along," Craig's mother said.

"No, Mom, I didn't. But you know Cliff, and frankly, we're all as stubborn as mules. I didn't think I'd be able to convince anyone to come. Dave refused the first time I called, and I was actually quite surprised how quickly Mark agreed."

Mark said, "As I earlier conveyed to you on the phone, I was scared to death of what was going to happen in Phoenix. I'd been talking to my truckers, and it was getting completely out of hand. I can't tell you how glad I am that we're all here."

Elsie broke in. "Craig, you didn't answer my question. If Cliff refused to come, what's he doing?

"I did convince him that he needed to do something. He's so damn stubborn, he'd convinced himself that this was all blown out of proportion by the press and that he was going to stay in Houston regardless of what he heard. But I promise you, I convinced him that he was wrong, and he swore to me he'd get the hell out of Houston."

Finally, they arrived at Craig's house and quickly unloaded. This was the first time any of them had seen Craig's home, and none of them had seen anything like it; it truly was a mountaintop compound. It looked like an Indian adobe pueblo from southwestern travel magazines. The main house was two stories, and the other two buildings were one story. It was hard to take in all the beauty with one glance. The ponderosa pine trees were interwoven with the buildings, and there wasn't any pavement; in fact, they hadn't seen pavement for miles. There was no grass in the yard, just trees, native bushes, and shrubs, with pine needles everywhere.

Craig immediately went into his office and turned on his answering machine, but there weren't any messages from either Jennifer or Katherine. He'd been planning to pick up both of them when he picked up his family at the airport. He'd realized, though, that he was barely going to be able to squeeze in everyone in his Range Rover as it was.

He had left messages for both of them the evening before and had been hoping they'd been returned. Instead, his machine held only one garbled message: something about "call as soon as you can," and although he couldn't quite make out the name or the phone number, it was definitely a young, female voice. He was afraid it was Jennifer and that she was in trouble. Luckily the phone had caller ID; it wasn't Jennifer's phone or a number he recognized, but it was a 713 area code.

Good news, he thought. The 713 area code was Houston and had to be a message from Cliff, but why would it be a young girl's voice?

He left his office to make sure everyone was finding a bedroom and a drink and that they knew they were welcome to anything in the refrigerator. With that chore out of the way, he grabbed himself a glass of water, went into his office, and closed the door.

Sitting down, he punched in the phone number from the message and set the receiver on speakerphone. At first the call didn't seem to go through, and he tried once more. On the third try there was an answer, a voice he didn't recognize, but it sounded like the person on the other end of the line was crying.

"Hello, hello?" he said. There were a couple of sniffs and sniffles. It was now clear to Cliff that the voice was that of a young girl, who was clearly crying. "Hello, can you hear me? This is Craig Walther. Who is this?"

"Craig? Is this Uncle Craig? Oh, my God! Please, please God, is this my Uncle Craig?"

"Chelsea? Marcie? Is that you? It's me, it's your Uncle Craig! Where are you? Where is your father? Where are you calling me from? What's happened? You sound horrible!"

Marcie took a couple of seconds to regain her composure. It was hard enough driving the stolen car while she had been crying for the last five hours, but now she had to drive and try to explain to her uncle what had happened. She stopped crying long enough to get out three words: "THEY'RE ALL DEAD!"

Then she was crying so hard that she almost lost control of the car. She pulled off onto the shoulder to get herself under control. "It's Marcie, Uncle Craig. They're all dead. Daddy thought it was best if we all went down to our beach house in Galveston. At first we thought all the Mexicans were gone, but we were attacked. They first killed Chelsea, and then they killed everyone else. I only escaped by climbing up on the roof." Marcie could hardly tell the story between her sobs.

"Oh, my God! I can't believe it! I'm sorry. I'm just so sorry! Where are you now? Are you safe?" Craig was afraid for his niece, but he knew the last thing she needed was someone else sounding afraid, so he was trying to sound as confident and calm as possible.

"When they left, I climbed down and stole a neighbor's car. I just kept driving. I don't know much about what's going on, but from what I heard Daddy saying, it sounded like the best place I could go was east. I sure wasn't going to go to Houston because that's where we had just left. And for some reason Dad thought Houston was in big trouble."

Craig tried to be as reassuring as he could. "You're a smart girl, Marcie. Your dad would be proud of you. He always told me you were the smartest of his kids. You're doing the right thing. Do you know where you are now?"

"I think I just passed through Beaumont, Texas, and the last sign said that I'm about to enter Louisiana. But I have a big problem. I'm on empty, and the Mexicans stole my wallet. I don't have any money at all, and the only thing I have of value is my cell phone. That's when I thought I could call you. What am I my going to do?"

Luckily Craig had turned on his computer. "Hold on a minute. Wait, is your cell phone charged?"

"Yeah, I guess that's the only good news."

Craig pulled up Google maps and found eastern Texas and western Louisiana. "Listen to me, Marcie. I've got a plan for you. It looks like the next city you'll come to is Lake Charles, Louisiana. Have you seen any signs for that?"

"Hold on a minute, I think I see a sign coming up now." There was a pause. "Yeah, I mean yes, it says 'Lake Charles ten miles.' I think I might have enough gas to just get there."

"Okay, Marcie. Pull into the biggest gas station you can find, preferably a big-name company like Exxon or Shell. Find the manager. Dial my number and hand him the phone, and I'll make arrangements for him to fill up your car. Do you understand me?" He waited for her affirmative response and then continued. "Okay, good. Have them call me as soon as you get to the gas station. You'll be fine. We'll talk later about your dad and the family. Be safe."

The fifteen minutes seemed to go by in an instant. Craig could not get his head around the fact that his brother and family were dead.

"Hello? Hello?" came a voice that had such a strong southern accent that Craig was wondering if his plan was going to work. "This is Bobby, at the I-10 Lake Charles Conoco. Anybody thar?"

"Sir, my name is Craig Walther. That's my niece who just handed you her cell phone. Some people have stolen her purse, and she needs to get to Baton Rouge, but she's out of gas. Can we work out a deal that I can pay you by credit card on the phone?"

"I don't rightly know about that. I may be the manager, but I don't know if the owner would approve of me doing some'un lak tha-a-at."

"Listen, what did you say your name was—Bobby? Listen, Bobby, if you're willing to help out my niece I will make it worth your while. There's an extra $100 in this for you."

"I sure in could use a hundred bucks. You know my alternator just went out on my pickup—"

Craig didn't have time for this. "Bobby, I'm sorry to interrupt you, but I've got to get my niece back on the road. Now I'm going to ask that you fill up her car, but I have a couple other favors. When you charge my credit card I want you to put another $100 on it for you. I don't have time to tell you the whole story, but I assume that you've heard about the Mexicans overrunning the border stations?"

"Oh, man, you're not that famous guy who wrote them books...Ah, what was the name of that last one? Ah, *Mexican Invasion* or some'um like that?"

Craig couldn't believe his luck. He was talking to some hillbilly in Lake Charles, Louisiana, who was the manager of a dumpy gas station—and he knew about his books. "That's right, Bobby. That's me, Professor Craig Walther, the Mexican expert," Craig said, not meaning to sound pompous but hoping to move along the conversation."

Bobby was beside himself. "Gertrude, Gertrude get on up here! You'll never guess who I have on the phone! You know that professor fella, something or other, that wrote that book I loved about the Mexican invasion? Guess what? He's on the other end of the phone and wants me to do 'im a favor for this here girly!"

Craig could hear a woman's voice in the background, so garbled it sounded like she'd lost most of her teeth. "I wouldn't trust nobady, nobady at all. How ya know he's who he sayin' he is?"

"I'm sorry, Mr. Craig, but my wife don't trust nobody. You know these days you just can't—"

Craig cut him off again. "Bobby, in addition to the $100 I promised you, how about a whole box of my latest book, all signed and made out to you?"

"Sheeit! You got yourself a deal, old buddy! I mean, Professor Craig. You just tell me what ya need."

Craig gave Bobby a long list. He knew there wouldn't be much in the way of healthy food in a gas station, but he tried anyway. He asked Bobby to fill a box with as much healthy food as he could find. His greatest challenge was to first educate Bobby on what constituted healthy food. It turned out in the end to be a huge waste of time trying to explain healthy food, especially when Bobby considered fruit punch to be fruit. Craig moved on and made sure Bobby put bottles of both water and soda in a cooler. Lastly, after finding out that the

Conoco had gas cans for sale, he instructed Bobby to fill two of them and put them in the trunk of Marcie's car.

"I'll be glad to do all that for y'all. Now you're sure you're okay with me puttin' that hundred dollar on your card? I mean, you bein' a famous professor an' all, I'd be glad just to get them thar books."

Craig finally felt a bit of relief. "No, that's the deal, Bobby. Just get it all together and then call me back to tell me the total including your $100, and we'll put on my credit card. And give me your address, so I can mail you the books."

For Craig, the time with Bobby on the phone seemed interminable but it actually only took a few minutes. After the credit card was run and a few more "hot damns" were given from Bobby, Craig requested one last favor: for Bobby to tell Marcie to give him a call once she was back on the road. The last thing he heard as he was hanging up was, "Hot damn! Wait till I tell the boys at bingo tonight that I know a celebrity, and I done read both his books!"

The phone rang within thirty seconds, and Craig moaned a bit. He still had not had an opportunity to mourn the loss of his brother, nor the time to break the news to the rest of the family. However, Marcie's predicament took precedence over anything else.

"What do you want me to do now? I'm scared and don't know where to go," Marcie said.

"Okay, Marcie. Did Bobby take good care of you?"

He listened for a moment as she ran through a few of the things Bobby had given to her. Then he asked, "Can you hold on for a little longer? I'm working things out for you." Marcie wasn't totally in control of her emotions, but at least she had stopped crying. She told her uncle that after what she'd just been through that she felt like she could handle almost anything.

"Good girl, sweetheart," Craig told her. "I had time while the gas station attendant was loading your car to make a phone call. It turns out that one of my old college buddies from graduate school teaches history at LSU. That's only the next city away from where you are now. You're not going to need all that food and gasoline, but I wasn't sure if I was going to be able to get in touch with him or not. He's got two kids your age, and when I told him the story, I didn't even need to ask. He demanded that I send you his way. So I think the best thing I can do now is put you directly in touch with him. I don't want you to write while you're driving, so if you can, pull over and I'll give you his phone number."

After giving her the friend's name and phone number, Craig said a tearful goodbye and promised to stay in close contact. Finally, something had gone right, and Marcie was on the road to safety.

What a day. What an incredible day. Craig broke into tears immediately after he hung up the phone. He wasn't sure if the tears were the result of his emotional day, Cliff's death, or the fact that he'd been right all along about the Mexicans and their border crash. He felt little relief in having predicted the situation, and all he wanted now was to get life back on track. He was worried about the two women in his life and knew he'd need to find a resolution to the distractive tug on his heartstrings.

Craig was determined not to panic his family over how Cliff and his family had been killed so brutally. He sat at his desk trying to regain his composure and attempted to find some meaning in all that had happened. His mind, however, continued to play out the possible scenarios and the many directions those scenarios could go. He couldn't turn off his mind, one of the curses of being so intelligent. On the one hand, his family was safe, but on the other, his bitterness toward the Mexican illegals for killing his brother and family would stay foremost on his mind for years to come.

He was happy that he had helped get his niece to safety, but now how was he going to break the news to everyone else?

Chapter 102

As President Rosemary Denton and her aide Stephanie Jones stormed through the reception area just outside the Oval Office, new Secretary of Defense Virginia Wade sat there waiting, per the request by Jones just a few minutes earlier.

"Let's go, Virginia!" President Denton said. The three of them quickly disappeared into the Oval Office.

As they all got situated, the president launched in. "I am going to assume that you are fully apprised of the shooting incident involving some Mexicans in that grade school in Las Vegas. Am I correct?"

Though Virginia Wade was probably the most inexperienced and unknowledgeable secretary of defense the United States had ever had, she had been around the block a few times. But she was nervous, mostly from the tone the president was using to address her. "Yes, Madam President, I can assure you I am fully apprised of the situation."

"Well, it's a whole new ball game with this shooting in Las Vegas. Even with all our loyal friends in the press, this is one issue they've already shown they're not going to kowtow to us any longer on. That televised shooting at that school cafeteria is playing 24-7, even at MSNBC, who never goes against our policies and demands."

Finally sitting down, she continued. "Now I don't have the time to explain why this administration and the previous Obama administration have been soft on the entire border issue. Frankly, my personal opinions on this whole matter now have to be set aside. This could be a political nightmare. And behind closed doors, I'll admit, some combination of getting bad advice from my advisors," at which point the president gave a glaring look of disgust at Stephanie, "and refusing to acknowledge the warning signs may be to blame. But we are in deep shit. Of course, the people over at Fox are saying this is a total repeat of Algeria, only one thousand times more serious.

"I was shocked that President Obama didn't get impeached for half the crap he pulled, but if we don't take immediate steps, Ted Boone and a few other Republicans, whose butts I kicked in the last election, might just make a motion for *my* impeachment."

Wade spoke up for the first time. "What's your game plan? What do you want me to do?"

President Denton yelled so loud even the heavy doors to the Oval Office rattled. "What's *my* game plan? You're the secretary of defense! What the hell have you been doing since I hired you? Are you going to tell me, like everyone else in this administration, you too have been ignoring every damn thing that's been going on at the border?"

Wade nervously started, "I've had three or four meetings in just the last week with Secretary of State Lopez and National Security Advisor Nancy Wheat. They both assured me that these problems are completely blown out of proportion. I took the liberty of calling Marisa on my way over here. She was aware of the incident at the school, and she assured me that this is a lone incident and that we should not overreact."

Steam was now starting to come out of the president's ears. "Look, Virginia, some pieces of the puzzle are starting to fit together for me. And the only reason I haven't fired Lopez is because my administration's already coming under enough heat from what's going on at the border, plus my recent firing of Hardwick and replacing him with you. But I can assure you of this: as soon as I get this all under control, Marisa is going to be in Mexico eating tacos, permanently!"

Virginia nervously spoke up. "I don't mean to question your opinion, Madam President, but I think you've misjudged Marisa's loyalties. She assures me that she only has the best concern for the American people. And I was just thinking that—"

Denton waved her arms in the air. "Yeah, right, and an elephant's going to fly out my ass. Look, Virginia, you're new to this administration, and you've got a lot to learn. I run this office the same as Obama did—my way or the highway. Even if Marisa doesn't have a serious conflict of interest because of her close relationship with Mexico's Presidente Nieto, she has been completely wrong about this whole border situation, and now I'm having to pay for it. But I don't have time for this anymore. I want you to take immediate action, and since you've told me you don't have a game plan, you better come up with one pronto! I need a proposal on my desk by tomorrow morning!"

Virginia looked a bit befuddled. "What are you suggesting that I propose?"

For a minute, it looked like Denton might slap Virginia in the face. "Why the hell do you keep asking me questions? This is your job, remember, Secretary of *Defense*? Hello? Anybody home? *Defense*! We need to *defend* our country. It's under attack. Jesus Christ, Virginia, you're acting like a fucking housewife. You've got four branches of the military under your command. I'll give the order, but I'm no military person. I don't know what plan you should come up with. That is your fucking job!"

"With all due respect, I have to disagree. I don't think this incident in Vegas merits us coming unglued. Sure, there are some other lone incidences of aggression. But this is not a military, much less an armed group of Mexicans who are crossing the border. Other than stealing some food and breaking into some homes and businesses, in my opinion, it's relatively peaceful. Frankly, it's nothing new. Mexican illegals have been responsible for a high percentage of the criminal activity in the Southwest for decades. I don't know why everybody is so alarmed."

President Denton was getting madder by the moment. "You don't get it, Virginia. You just don't get it. Even if I were to ignore the deaths so far, we are talking about political suicide here. We've all been sitting on our asses since the first report of these problems and ignoring the entire thing. There is going to be a Senate investigation, and I don't think I can survive one more of those. I barely got through the last one. And you're not going to be enjoying your cushy new job if I'm thrown out of office. I need you to come up with a plan ASAP and get the military into action now! I've got enough of my own problems trying to calm down the press and the conservatives in Congress."

Amazingly, Virginia was still holding her ground. She wasn't buying into the president's argument at all. "Well, first of all, it would be impossible for me to even contemplate putting together any kind of logical plan in anything short of a couple weeks. Per your request, I will call a meeting of both the NSC and the Joint Chiefs of Staff, and we will set up subcommittees to study the situation, and they'll come up with some recommendations for me. Once that takes place, I will form a plan that I will present to you. But I must repeat, I think it's premature to take military action against these innocent Mexicans who, from what I understand, have merely entered the country to take advantage of both your and President Obama's legalization program. Honestly, I don't see how you can blame them. That's what I would do if I was a poor Mexican."

Denton now flopped back into her large Oval Office desk chair, and for a minute, it looked like she was going to pass out. She had felt on the verge of a heart attack from the very minute she had heard about the Vegas incident in the limo, and she was getting no relief. She leaned forward on her desk, her hands pressed against her temples, and shook her head.

"This is what I get for surrounding myself with nincompoops. I should've known that something was wrong when Marisa was so enthusiastic about my selecting you to replace Hardwick. The two of you are sniffing the same gasoline fumes. I am not going to take the blame for all of this, not again! And what do you mean 'innocent'? I might've bought into that a couple of weeks ago, but now, I think the conservative's argument is more accurate, and it's evident now more than ever. There's nothing 'innocent' about foreigners who break down our borders, enter this country illegally, stay here illegally, and break into people's homes and businesses. I don't care if they're hungry or not—it is anything but 'innocent'! Now, are you or are you not capable of getting something on my desk in twenty-four hours? Or, fine, take forty-eight hours, but don't take one minute longer."

Virginia was holding up rather well, considering that the president had been yelling at her ever since she entered the room. "Honestly—" she started.

President Denton snapped back, "No, Virginia, lie to me. Why does every moron I know begin a sentence with, 'Honestly'? Am I supposed to think the rest of the time you're lying to me?"

Virginia had never been spoken to like this. "Well," she said. "I think this is no reason for you to get insulting with me. You know I graduated—"

"Cut the shit, Virginia. I don't give a crap when or where you graduated or what the fuck you did before you got here. Just answer my question and then get out of here and get it done."

"Well! My family warned me about coming to work for you. I heard you could be a bitch, but I had no idea. You're sure not the friendly, cordial woman you display yourself as on TV. But I just want to warn you, just because you're the president and we're behind closed doors, that you can't talk to me this way."

Now President Denton stood up, and as the normal color returned to her face, she actually smiled. "Oh, really, I can't talk to you the way I want to? She continued with the most sarcastic voice she could conjure up, "I'm sorry, Virginia. I forgot. You're a lady, and I need to speak with you in a respectable, ladylike manner like you were talked to at your sorority in college. I really do owe you an apology. Let me start over: *You're fired. Get the fuck out of my office!"* And with that, the president stormed out the side door.

The now defunct Secretary of Defense Virginia Wade was so shocked that she could've been knocked over with a feather. She had been a political science major at William and Mary and by no means felt like she deserved being fired. Setting aside the temporary "acting" secretaries of defense, since 1949 the shortest-serving secretary of defense had been Clark

Clifford, who served under Lyndon B. Johnson. He only lasted 326 days. George C. Marshall lasted exactly one year, or 365 days. Virginia Wade was now making history, with her esteemed position lasting just under two weeks.

She looked over to Stephanie Jones, hoping to get some sympathy, but she got quite the opposite. Stephanie was biting her lower lip hard to keep from laughing. "Sorry, Virginia. You couldn't have played that any worse. I think Rosemary hit the nail on the head. You have a total misconception of what life in the Oval Office is all about. We just don't have time for that sorority bullshit. Rosemary is right—if this thing isn't handled correctly, her political career is gonzo."

Virginia Wade was still in shock. "But...but...but what is she going to do now?"

Stephanie was laughing. "I don't know. She's the president. She will think of something. All I know is that you're not going to be a part of it."

And Stephanie walked out, leaving Virginia Wade still stunned and paralyzed, sitting in the now vacant Oval Office.

Chapter 103

Craig sat through dinner eating hardly a thing. Everyone was under such a strain that he just couldn't bring himself to tell the family what Marcie had relayed to him just a couple of hours earlier. But there was even more weighing on Craig's mind.

For the first time since his second divorce, he realized just how much in love he really was, not just with one woman but with two women at the same time. And even though he'd left countless messages for each, he hadn't been able to get through to either of them in the last couple of days. With things starting to fall apart in Albuquerque, in combination with learning about the brutal murder of Cliff and his family, he was worried even more about the safety of Jennifer and Katherine.

Elsie broke the silence. "Son, it was you who told us we needed to be judicious in our eating. The food we have may have to last four weeks or longer. Don't you think you should practice what you preach and at least eat the food on your plate?"

His mom's words broke Craig out of his spell. "Sorry—sorry, Mom. What did you say?"

She repeated what she had said.

"You're right, I'm sorry. If everybody's finished I have a little something I'd like to say."

Bill Walther spoke up first. "Son, what's bothering you? I've never seen you look so down."

Craig first let out a big sigh. "That was Marcie on the phone earlier this evening. It seems...Well, it seems...Well, I told you that Cliff refused to come up here with us. I guess he decided it was safer for him to take the family and go to their beach house in Galveston. I didn't want to press Marcie for all the details."

Craig's mother threw her hands up to her face, started crying, and almost fell face first into her empty plate. "No, dear God, say it isn't so!"

Bill put his arms around his wife. "Craig, I think you best stop beating around the bush and tell us what happened."

"I don't know all the details, Dad. But the entire family was attacked. And they're all dead. Only Marcie escaped. She's safe. She's on her way to Baton Rouge, Louisiana, and I've arranged for her to stay with a friend of mine, a professor at LSU. As best as I could piece together from Marcie, they thought all the Mexican invaders had already cleared out of Galveston, but they were wrong, and they were attacked. I'm sorry, Mom. You must know I begged him to come up here with us."

While the three Walther men just stared at each other in disbelief, Madeleine and little Ricky joined in with Elsie in a long cry. The three men cleared the table and proceeded to clean up and load the dishwasher. But Craig couldn't contain himself any longer. He turned to his father, threw his arms around him, and buried his head into his shoulder and started to cry.

"I know that Cliff and I were never very close. None of us boys were ever very close, but that didn't mean I didn't love him."

"I know, son. I watched the four of you do everything you could when you were kids to rip each other's throats out. And when you became adults, you replaced your physical confrontations with verbal arguments. I always wondered if maybe I put too much pressure on you boys. Too much pressure to succeed, too much pressure to do the right thing. But then I look around at some of our friend's kids who haven't amounted to a hill of beans. I'm proud of you." They broke their embrace, and his father turned to Mark and Dave. "I'm proud of all of you."

They were interrupted by the sound of a car pulling into the front of the house. Dave immediately, almost instinctively, reached for the shotgun that was by the kitchen door. Craig pulled back the curtain and looked out the window. It was

Katherine's Volvo. He realized he couldn't show his excitement, not in front of his grieving family. Instead, he rushed out the door and met Katherine just as she was getting out of her car.

Before Katherine knew what hit her, Craig had swept her up in his arms and was kissing her face. He set her back down on the ground and gave her the same embrace he had just given his father, letting out a couple sobs into her shoulder.

She returned his embrace and said, "What's wrong, Craig? What has happened? Why are you crying?"

Craig pulled back, but still holding her arms and stared into her face, and said, "All of us just found out a few hours ago that my brother Cliff and almost all of his family was just brutally killed south of Houston."

Katherine drew Craig back into her arms, and now she was giving him warm, tender kisses.

Craig said, "I've been trying to reach you for a couple days. How come you haven't answered my phone call?"

"I'm sorry. You know I got rid of my landline, and something's wrong with the cell phone towers in Albuquerque. Every person in the country is calling every single person in Albuquerque to see if they're okay. I didn't know you could overload the cellular system, but I guess that's what's happening." Craig grabbed her suitcase, and then she said to him, "I have a big cooler in the back. I emptied my refrigerator of everything in it."

"We may need to leave it in the cooler for now. I've jammed both refrigerators and the deep freezer to the top. With everyone here and not knowing how long we're going to need to hide out, the last thing I wanted to do was run out of food. Thanks for thinking of bringing more." They went into the house and Craig introduced her to everybody as a fellow professor at UNM and a very close friend.

When they were alone again, Katherine said to Craig, "I know your parents are here, but we are grown-ups. Can I put my suitcase in your bedroom?"

Craig didn't know how to react. Jennifer might show up at any minute. But he needed to think, perhaps the fastest in his life. Katherine was one sharp cookie. He needed to not only give her the correct answer; he needed to make sure that his face didn't reveal his panic. "Ahhhhhhhh, why don't you set it here in the hallway for a moment? We may need to adjust who is sleeping with who based on who all is going to show up."

Katherine was not happy with the answer but decided this was not the time. "Are you expecting more people?"

Craig was caught once again. He had invited both Katherine and Jennifer up to his house to wait out the pending invasion of Albuquerque. What he hadn't worked out was what he was going to do when Katherine and Jennifer met. Should he tell Katherine now?

But he was saved by the bell. "Craig, Craig! You have a phone call," his father yelled. "Someone who said he is a dean at UNM."

Craig gave Katherine a quick kiss and rushed into his office to take the phone call.

Several hours later, it was getting late, and at the other end of the house, something kept waking up little Ricky. There was a strange noise in the bedroom adjacent to his.

Madeleine asked, "What's wrong, honey? Why aren't you asleep?"

Ricky tried to pull a pillow over his head and said, "Scary sound... screaming."

And he buried his head even farther into the pillows and covers. Madeleine sat up. Little Ricky was right. There was a strange sound coming from the next bedroom. It was the bedroom where her parents were sleeping. And he was right, it did sound like someone screaming. Madeleine tried her hardest to hear what was going on. It was her mother. But why would her mother be screaming? Was she having a nightmare?

In the next bedroom, Mark whispered to his wife, "Shh, you're going to wake the whole house!"

"Come on, Mark, now you're starting to sound like me. You complained we haven't had sex all those years because I was too concerned about the kids. And we've just had the best

478

sex in decades, and now you're complaining I'm too loud. I've got news for you, honey. Madeleine and little Ricky are just going to have to get used to it. When we get back to Phoenix, we have a lot of lost time to make up."

Elizabeth grabbed Mark and yanked him back on top of her for round three.

Chapter 104

Craig didn't sleep a wink that night. The death of Cliff and his family plus his worries about Jennifer were just too much for him. But, he figured, it worked out for the best because if he was bunked down with Katherine and then Jennifer showed up, that would create a situation that he just didn't need right now. He asked Katherine if she would sleep with Madeleine and little Ricky because they needed an adult nearby in a situation like this. Katherine had been completely understanding. Craig loved that about her.

But now, he had to figure what to do about Jennifer. It was going on three days without any contact from her. He had been a little relieved to learn that the cell phones were down and that maybe that was the only reason she hadn't responded to his messages. But where was she, and why had she not called on her own?

It was 4:30 a.m., and he was in the kitchen making a large pot of coffee when in walked Dave. "You couldn't sleep either?" Craig said to his brother.

"No, I never sleep past 4:30 a.m. Plus, I could smell the coffee from my room, which was all the motivation I needed to get out of bed."

Craig needed to confide in somebody, so he proceeded to tell Dave the entire story about his love affairs with both Katherine and Jennifer. He concluded about how worried he was about Jennifer and her safety. "Dave, could you help watch over everything? I think the only option I have now is to drive into Albuquerque and see if I can find her. I can't just sit up here and wait any longer."

"I don't think that's a good idea," Dave said. "The family is distraught over Cliff's death. And I think there's just too much to be done here. I don't know where everything is, and I don't actually know what your game plan is. Why don't you stay here and console everyone and try to get things set up as you want? I'll take your Range Rover and go into town. But you're going to have to tell me where I can maybe find her."

Cliff poured his brother a cup of coffee and then grabbed the cup and repoured it into the to-go coffee cup he took to school every day. "Here you go." Craig pulled out a map of Albuquerque and a yellow highlighter. Craig imagined that Jennifer could only be in two places—either in her apartment or at the school library, where she tended to spend 90 percent of her time. He highlighted those for Dave and gave him the best routes. "I tried to fill up the Range Rover before I picked up everyone at the airport, but the gas station was rationing gas. I only was able to fill it up halfway. But no problem, I have a five-hundred-gallon tank over behind the shed. We'll gas it up before you go."

Dave looked shocked. "Why do you have a five-hundred-gallon tank? It's not like you're *that far* from civilization."

"I don't really have time to tell you the whole story now. Let's just say with all the research and writing I've been doing on Mexico for the last decade, I was starting to get a little nervous, especially with Albuquerque only 380 miles from El Paso and the Mexican border. I just thought I would start to take a little precaution. Let me make you a quick egg sandwich, and why don't you get on your way? I'd like you to be gone before Mom gets up, or in her state, she might refuse to let you go."

They ate a quick egg sandwich together and fueled up the Range Rover, and Dave was on his way. Dave was wide awake from the coffee, but his alertness was accentuated by some red sauce that Craig had slathered all over his egg sandwich. He thought his lips might burn off, and he wished he had a cold glass of orange juice instead of hot coffee.

When he hit I-40, it was twice as bad as they had just experienced the day before. Of course, since Dave was going west toward Albuquerque, he ran into all those escaping Albuquerque residents who were driving east on the wrong side of the highway, scrambling to get out of town. But Dave was a pretty adept driver, since the last couple decades he had regularly driven the agency's pickup truck down a lot of rough dirt roads, chasing down Mexicans in the pitch dark. Not to mention that Cliff's luxury, off-road Range Rover made his pickup truck feel like a go-kart. He was actually having fun dodging the oncoming cars.

Craig had suggested Dave go to Jennifer's apartment first. Craig had given Dave excellent directions, and he found the apartment complex and her unit fairly quickly once he got into town. He buzzed her apartment number on the intercom and waited for a response. There was no response, and he buzzed again.

"Who's there?"

"David Walther. I'm Professor Craig Walther's brother from San Diego. Craig sent me to find you. Can you let me in?"

Jennifer's fear was clear in her voice. "You can't be Craig's brother. He lives in San Diego."

"It's a long story. I don't think we have that much time." Dave had to think quickly. How could he convince her that he was Craig's brother? "My brother doesn't have any hair on his chest. He has seventy-two bolo ties and one of them is a whale's tooth." There was a short pause, after which he heard a buzzer and the latch to the entry door open.

Jennifer was waiting at her apartment door as Dave approached, but she had not taken off the safety chain. But as Dave approached, she unhooked the chain. She felt very comfortable seeing a good-looking man who resembled Craig but only younger. Her only concern was that he had a gun on each hip.

Jennifer gave Dave a little hug. "Hi, I'm Jennifer Stiles. How did you get here from San Diego?"

"Look, Ms. Stiles, my brother and I don't think you should be in Albuquerque. And my brother sent me here to get you. Do you mind grabbing some things so we can get the hell out of here? I'll explain everything in the car."

Jennifer got the message. "Can you at least tell me where we are going and how long we're going to be gone, so I know what to pack?"

Dave kept on the pressure. "We're going to Craig's house. As for how long, I don't think there's anyone in the country who knows the answer to that question. Just pack bare essentials, and I'll give you just five minutes to put it together!"

Jennifer did it in three, and they were out the door, in the car, and retracing the route at twice the speed.

"You *must* be Craig's brother. You drive as crazy and fast as he does. Do you own a Range Rover? You drive this thing to perfection."

Dave, for the first time, smiled. "No, but let's just say driving in precarious situations is something I have a lot of experience with. Craig wanted me to ask you, why haven't you called him?"

"My cell phone hasn't been working. And I thought he was going to the airport. Are you the only family member that flew in?'

Dave checked his cell phone and noticed he had no connection. "No, everyone in the family's here except Cliff and his family from Houston." Dave paused for a moment. He sure didn't want to start crying in front of his passenger who already seemed a little rattled. So he figured if he said it really fast and drove faster he could maintain his emotions. "Cliff and his family were killed south of Houston. Everyone at the house isn't taking it very well. But Craig's been very worried about you, and I know he will be relieved if I get you back to his house."

"If?" Dave realized his mistake in using that word, "I don't mean to scare you. And I don't know how long you've been locked up in your apartment, but look out the window, young lady."

For the first time, Jennifer quit focusing on Dave and began to peruse the scenery out the large windows of the Range Rover. It looked like a scaled-down version of a disaster movies. Her neighborhood was basically deserted. Same for the strip mall and the shopping centers they were passing. It was rush hour in the middle of the week, and yet everyone was missing. But as they were about to enter the on-ramp to I-40, they came to an abrupt halt. Not only was the on-ramp completely backed up, but also, as they both looked down on I-40, they saw wall-to-wall cars in every direction. It looked like the parking lot for the recent Fleetwood Mac concert.

David slammed his hand down on Craig's steering wheel. "Dammit! And the worst is, both the east- and westbound lanes are completely jammed."

Jennifer thought only for a moment. "Back up. I know some side routes."

So for the next hour, as Jennifer gave Dave one direction after another, they weaved through various residential neighborhoods, all the while moving east. Meantime the two of them struck up a friendly conversation.

"I assume you met my brother at UNM."

"Yes. I often wonder if your brother is really dedicated to his courses, or if he just teaches college because it's such a wonderful opportunity to meet pretty, young college girls."

Dave was thrilled to relax and think of something other than his job, the border, and Anita. Not to mention racing around in his brother's fancy Range Rover was quite a treat. "My brother's always had a way with women. Well, maybe I should correct that. I think my brother has thought he's always had a way with women. I don't know how well you know him, but both of his marriages were total disasters."

Jennifer had just been given an opportunity she'd thought she would never have. Sure, Craig had shared some of the facts about his disastrous marriages, but she knew she had never gotten the whole stories. And here was his brother, who might just be willing to tell all.

For much of the rest of the drive, she picked his brain on Craig's relationships with his two wives. Maybe if she understood all of this better, she could finally get Craig to commit to her.

"That's an amazing story. So that's where he got all his money. So what about you? Let's not just talk about your brother. What's your story?"

Dave was a little embarrassed; he didn't know how to respond. He hadn't been alone with a woman, much less a gorgeous one, save for his wife, for decades. No one at work ever showed any interest in his personal life. Jennifer's backroad directions had worked out brilliantly, so much so that they were only forced to take I-40 for less than half a mile, which Dave had navigated by driving straight down the median. They were on the mountain road to Craig's house when he began to answer Jennifer's question.

"My life is sort of boring when you compare it to my older brother Craig's. Working for the federal government is basically a death sentence. Oh, sure, I love training all the new recruits we've had in the department in the last few years. But working with the people who've been in the department for decades is like working for brain-dead zombies. I don't think they enter into the federal government being such nimrods, but something happens to them after ten years of working for the feds. No motivation, no inspiration, and a void between their ears that makes dealing with them impossible. And especially when they're your superiors. I've hated it since the day I started, and I've been there almost twenty years."

Jennifer was happy to be in the hands of Dave. She observed that Dave was a very confident man, just as confident as Craig. She wondered if it was a Walther thing. He handled the Range Rover as adeptly as Craig, and there was something else he and Craig did that she loved. Jennifer and Craig could carry on a heated conversation in the car, and Craig would never take his eyes off the road. She had learned to appreciate that and became quite cognizant of the fact that, when her friends talked to her while they were driving, instead of watching the road, they would turn and face her. Jennifer realized how dangerous that was and found herself telling her friends that if they couldn't talk and keep their eyes on the road, then she was going to get out of the car. Dave didn't once take his eyes off the road.

"Wow, that's a depressing story. Why didn't you quit? You sound smart. You could've gotten a job in the private sector."

Dave took a big sigh, slumped in his seat a bit, and responded. "I know the past two presidents have laid claim to turning around the US economy, but I gotta tell you, those millions of jobs that they claim to have added—it's just not true. For twenty years, I've sent out various applications but have gotten nothing but rejections. I was just about ready to quit and move when my wife got pregnant. I was approaching twenty years of employment, and I knew I could leave with a pretty good pension. So with a baby on the way, I thought I'd better suck it up and do what's best for my wife and our child."

"Are your wife and child at Craig's house?"

That was all it took. In all of the rush the last few days, no one had asked him about Anita. He didn't know if there just hadn't been time for his family to ask about Anita's death, or they were just trying to be sympathetic. But now somebody had asked him point blank. He swiftly jerked the car off the road onto a wide dirt shoulder. He didn't even bother to put the car in park; he just lay his head down on the steering wheel and started to cry.

Jennifer was smart enough to discern the answer. "I'm sorry, Dave. I didn't know. I'm sorry."

They both just sat there in silence for a long time. Just when Dave thought he had regained his composure, the vision of Anita being attacked and killed and his unborn child dying within her would once again send him back into bawling like a baby, a baby he would never see.

"Hey," Jennifer said. "Why don't you let me drive? We only have a few minutes more, and I've driven this road a hundred times. I know the way perfectly." So they switched seats.

With each minute, Dave's sobbing lessened. He finally sat back up straight again and used the sleeves of his coat to wipe his face dry. And then miraculously, he gave a little laugh.

"Whew, I needed that! Sorry I had to dump on you. Just with so much happening and things moving so fast, I guess I just never have had the time to cry. And I really couldn't cry in front of my family—that's not a Walther thing. It wasn't like crying was forbidden in our house, but even if you fell down and scuffed your knee, if you started to cry in front of our dad or one of my brothers, they'd say, 'Don't be a crybaby,' and tell you to shut up. Even my mom was tough. We all grew up being very rational and practical. Crying just seemed like a stupid waste of time. If you have a problem and have pain, get over it. Be a man. Boy, it's a good thing my parents didn't have any girls."

And then Dave started to laugh, and Jennifer joined in.

Jennifer decided that for the rest of the drive, she was going to do whatever she could to keep the conversation positive. "Well, maybe once this all blows over, you'll have some time to get your life back in order. You've made it pretty clear you don't want to go back to work for the government. You said you are sick and tired of San Diego. And I guess now with your family gone, you sure don't have any commitments to take you back to California. Why don't you stay here?"

"You know, since I've been having a hard time getting a job, I've been thinking I needed to go back to school and get an advanced degree. Isn't that what you're doing?"

"Yes. I already have my masters in psychology, and I'm now working on my PhD. Before you ask, I know you're wondering: why is somebody who's getting a PhD in psychology taking a course from your brother in US-Mexican relations? I'll be honest with you. I took the course to meet your brother. He has quite a reputation around the campus. I just had to meet the man known for being the most eligible bachelor in all of Albuquerque. But hey, why don't you go to UNM? I know your brother could pull some strings, and you probably wouldn't even need to wait a year to get in-state tuition."

How could this be happening to Dave? How could so much wrong be going on in the country and in his personal life, but he was suddenly feeling so good? It was a combination of Jennifer's enthusiasm and warmth and the thought of going back to college and finally getting himself out of the disastrous career he'd been stuck in for so long. It was like a weight had just been lifted from his shoulders.

As they pulled into Craig's compound, Dave turned to Jennifer and said, "You've been a great help. I can't thank you enough."

Jennifer didn't know if it was the right thing to do, but she stretched herself across the console of the Range Rover and gave Dave a little peck on the cheek. When she saw the positive, warm glow on his Dave's face, she knew she made the right decision.

Chapter 105

Was it just going to be impossible for Craig to ever relax? He was glad he had sent Dave after Jennifer, and he was very confident that Dave would find her, and they'd get back. But with that came another challenge: how was he going to have the two women he loved sleep in the same house? After thinking about it for a while, he concluded that when Jennifer showed up, he would take the two of them into his office and have a long conversation. They were all adults. They would understand this wasn't the time for confrontations. They were already going to have enough in the way of confrontations if the Mexicans did, in fact, get to Albuquerque and beyond in the coming days. Craig was confident, and he was glad that he'd come up with a solution.

But things didn't go as planned. Craig had to be on the move, and there was a lot to be done. So Craig took his father and Mark on a survey of the property. Craig had been so busy at work the last couple months that, other than morning and afternoon walks with his dogs, he hadn't been to the perimeter of his thirty-five acres for almost half a year. He felt the three of them should get a good feel for the land; it might be important soon.

They came across a stack of some old six-by-sixes that were eight feet long. His dad suggested that they clean them off and stack them up, and when Dave returned, they could each double up and carry them back to the house. They would be excellent braces for the various entry doors into the house and the other buildings. But because of their distance from the house, Craig didn't hear Dave drive up with Jennifer. His well-thought-out plans were about to be dashed.

As Jennifer and Dave got out of the Range Rover, Dave said, "Go into the house and meet everyone. I'll get your bag. Craig wanted me to park the Range Rover in the garage."

Jennifer opened the kitchen door and didn't find anyone in there, so she strode into the living room. There was Madeleine, playing with little Ricky. Mark and some woman were looking at one of Craig's southwestern Indian-artifact books together.

Katherine glanced up, and as she did, Dave entered the room behind Jennifer. Katherine surmised that this must be some friend of Dave's. But just then Jennifer did two things that proved Katherine wrong. First, Jennifer went over to Craig's wet bar, opened up the refrigerator, and took out a cold bottled water.

Katherine thought, *That's strange. How can this friend of Dave's know the layout of this house so well?*

But what really gave Katherine a clue of who this new young lady was, was when Jennifer took off her baseball cap and coat. As she removed her cap, hair sprang out like it had been dying to be released. As Katherine stared at this beautiful golden hair, it seemed like it would never stop unfurling. Then Katherine got a glimpse of what was under the coat. This was no casual stranger of Dave's. It was a gorgeous, voluptuous young woman, just the kind of woman Craig was known for dating. No, this was no stranger; this was no friend of Dave's. Now standing in front of her looking, gorgeous and threatening, was her rival! *The graduate student.*

After removing her baseball cap and coat and throwing them on the sofa, Jennifer briskly walked to where Katherine and Mark were sitting. She stuck out her hand and said, "Hi, I'm Jennifer Stiles, a friend of Craig's. You must be Mark, and you must be Elizabeth."

Mark was clueless as to the coming confrontation. He stood up as any gentleman would do, shook Jennifer's outstretched hand, and said, "Yes, I am Mark, but my wife, Elizabeth, is in the bedroom straightening up." Mark turned to Katherine and started to say, "This is Ka—"

Katherine interrupted him and stood up put out her hand to shake Jennifer's, and said with a relatively friendly tone, "I am Katherine Lacey"." And then she changed her tone dramatically which was now a bit deep and challenging, "*The*

Professor Katherine Lacey," while giving Jennifer a glare that would melt an entire iceberg.

But Jennifer didn't back down for a minute. She had caught the tone, and even if she hadn't, she sure couldn't have avoided the glare. So this was her rival; this was the famous Professor Katherine Lacey. But Jennifer was pretty smart, even though she was only twenty-three; she decided this was not the place for a fight.

"I've heard nothing but wonderful things about you, Professor Lacey. I can't tell you how thrilled I am, finally getting to meet you."

And while the two of them stood their positions, neither releasing the other's hand, Katherine responded, "The feeling is mutual. Craig often talks about how you are *one* of his favorite *students* at UNM." Katherine tried her best to emphasize the words 'one' and 'students,' trying to put some distance between herself being a *professor* and Jennifer just being *one* of many *students*. But Jennifer was not going to enter into the fight. And realizing they'd been holding each other's hands just a bit too long, she let go and turned to Dave. "Where are the other men?"

Madeleine informed her that the men had gone out to survey the property, and Dave said he was going to try to find them and see if he could help. Katherine drew closer to Jennifer and said, "Would you mind helping me get something out of my car? It's too heavy for me to carry."

Once they were out the kitchen door, Katherine gave Jennifer a wry smile and said, "I knew it was inevitable that one day we would bump into each other, and I often wondered what I would say. But I will have to admit, under the circumstances, I find myself for one of the few times in my life short of words."

"You think I'm too young—go ahead and say it. You think Craig's wasting his time on somebody who's so much younger."

Katherine didn't like Jennifer's tone, "Too young for what, my dear?" Katherine ran a hand through her own long hair, trying to show off that she too was able to keep a long, healthy head of hair, even at her age. "Are we talking about sex or marriage?"

"Let's cut to the chase." Jennifer was feeling her oats. "You know Craig's been sleeping with me, and when it comes down to it, I think it's exactly my youth that he loves."

That cut deep. Katherine knew that her rival was significantly younger. And she knew Craig had a weakness for girls this young and pretty. But Jennifer was much prettier than she'd ever imagined. Katherine had always thought because she'd taken such good care of herself that she could compete at any level for Craig's love. But now standing in front of Katherine was a contender that she had not anticipated. Jennifer was tall and gorgeous, dressed to kill, her makeup perfect—and to make matters worse, she could clearly hold her own in this argument, even if Katherine was a tenured professor.

Katherine loved Craig dearly, and she needed him. And if she had to duke it out verbally with this rival here and now, she was fully prepared. But Katherine hadn't risen to be one of the most respected female professors at UMN and the head of her department without being on top of her game. Just as she was ready to give Jennifer a big verbal salvo, she stopped herself. What if Craig came around the corner and found them in a catfight? Wouldn't she, as the much senior woman in the fight, draw well-deserved condemnation from Craig? How could she allow herself to be drawn into a fight when Craig's brother and family had just been brutally killed? The men were out working on defenses. She couldn't allow herself to be drawn into a fight, even if it was a fight for Craig's love.

So instead she stuck out her hand. "I'm sorry. I mean it. I'm very sorry. I was catty. I know that Craig loves you. And I have the utmost respect for Craig. And if he loves you, you must be something very special."

She stood there with her hand stuck out toward Jennifer, but Jennifer was frozen. Though Jennifer had been around the block a few times, she just wasn't ready for this. She just didn't know how to handle it.

"Look, Jennifer. Do you go by Jennifer? Can I call you Jennifer?

Jennifer was still speechless; all she could do was nod.

"Jennifer, I think the two of us for now need to put our love for Craig on the back burner. This family has already gone through enough strife in the last few days. And what I saw in Albuquerque when I last left, well, we might be in for some of the same in the coming days. I think we would do a great injustice to not only Craig but his entire family if we enter into a feud. Craig and his family have done a wonderful thing by bringing us here. And we both know that it must've been hard for Craig, knowing that the two of us would meet. But I think we need to return Craig's respect. Craig knew that both of us would act like adults. And that's what we need to do."

Finally, Jennifer reached out and grabbed Katherine's extended hand. "What am I supposed to call you?"

Katherine gave her a big, friendly smile. "Katherine works most of the time." Katherine squeezed Jennifer's hand and totally enclosed it with her other hand. "Truce? And I'll make you a deal. When this is all over, how about I take you out for dinner, and we can go at it as long as you'd like?"

Katherine almost considered for a moment of giving Jennifer a hug, but she thought it might come across like she was treating her motherly, and she knew better. So as they turned to walk back into the house, she said, "I know a great Mexican restaurant we can go to, and since you've been dating Craig, I know you know the place."

Chapter 106

Stephanie Jones once again marched into President Denton's office without hesitation. "I got a call from the front gate. John Hardwick is driving into the White House as we speak. Do you want to discuss your game plan with me?"

"No, I don't have a game plan. Now you're starting to sound like that idiot Virginia Wade. If I had a fucking game plan, I wouldn't be calling Hardwick. And what the hell did you find out about Marisa? No one seems to be able to figure out where she is."

"I'm sorry to say that I think this is an incredibly embarrassing day for you and me. We completely misjudged her. Turns out the only person over at the state department who's willing to say anything is that weasel Fran Babicz. Such a nebbish, she would do anything to save her career. She told me that Secretary Lopez two days ago jumped on a plane to Mexico City and seemed to indicate to Fran that she wouldn't be returning soon."

"Crap! It's bad enough that I'm now forced to deal with a collapsing border, but now my entire administration's coming unglued at the seams. Great! I thought the funniest billboard I'd ever see was that one with an oversized Jimmy Carter face and the word 'Thanks.' It didn't need any explanation. At this rate, there's going to be a new billboard with a picture of Obama with the same word. I guess the three of us can vie in history for the worst president this country has ever experienced.

"Okay, get Hardwick in here. I think I'd rather have my fingernails pulled out one by one than have to suck up to a man I just fired."

When Hardwick entered the room, he had the look of a conquering general. Almost everybody in Washington, even some individuals in the Denton administration, was willing to share with Hardwick how things had imploded since he'd left.

And the word had spread like wildfire that the president had just fired Wade. He knew why she'd called.

"Sit down, John. Considering the smirk on your face, I guess I don't need to waste either of our time filling you in on my firing of Secretary Wade and the quagmire I am now in."

Hardwick couldn't imagine that he could enjoy a conversation as much as this one. "Frankly, Madam President, if it was just you personally in that quagmire, to paraphrase Rhett Butler, I couldn't give a damn. But considering you're the president of the United States, and your problems are our country's problems, let me say, yes, I know why I'm here."

For the first time in the last twenty-four hours, Rosemary Denton was actually somewhat relieved. She knew that no matter how much she hated Hardwick, she desperately needed him and was grateful that he would not let the country down.

Denton began, "Now I just don't know how deep your spies go in the White House. So let me clear something up. I fired Wade because I learned working with her was like talking to one of my children. I will admit it. I fucked up. Is that what you wanted to hear? Okay, I admit it. I don't think that woman's capable of leading the campfire girls in singing 'Kumbaya my Lord'. Hell, like everybody in Washington, she would have had so many committees and subcommittees working on this problem, I'd be out of office before she even had a proposal.

"And since we are talking about spies, I know that you and General Grayson have just recently returned from Fort Bliss. It doesn't take a rocket scientist to figure out that the two of you were down there to work on the border problem. And as much as I hate to admit it, I suspect that you already have a plan. Isn't that what you military types spend your days doing, what you call 'war games'? Look, I may be incredibly liberal, but don't think for a minute I'm as stupid as that bozo Obama. He made Howdy Doody look like Albert Einstein."

John Hardwick thought of interrupting, but why? If someone had sold him tickets to this meeting, he would have written a check for $100,000. This was like having front row seats at the Super Bowl, and he was being treated like Tom Brady. God, this was fun.

"Go ahead, I deserve it. I'll eat all the crow you want. If you want to take off your shoes, I'll start munching on one of the soles."

"Remember my last words as I was leaving when you fired me? I pointed out the difference between the two of us. You don't give a shit about this country. You and others like you have never given a shit about this country. Here's what I didn't say: I don't know what I hate most about you, Madam President—that you're a professional politician or that you're a *liberal* professional politician. In my opinion, that puts you just one notch below..." Hardwick paused. "I actually can't think of anything lower.

"One of the most serious things wrong with Washington is that for decades it's been permeated with professional politicians. Thousands of you have never had a real job. You graduate with your law degrees and then go into politics. You never have any clue of what goes on in the real world. You're as bad as your counterparts in the academic world—totally clueless. Everything for you guys is theory. Your mantra is 'If only we had more government, we could solve all the world's problems.' You've never written or drawn a real paycheck, and you've been on the government tit your entire lives. Until the electorate finally wakes up and forces term limits upon Congress and the Senate, you and your cronies will continue to get elected into power and never leave Washington."

Hardwick realized he could probably go on like this for a couple hours. It was almost as enjoyable as when, just a few minutes earlier, the president of the United States had been sucking up to him. For years, the single-most-enjoyable thing he had imagined ever doing in his life was to tell one of these political gods what he really thought of them.

But he was a man of action, and the country didn't have a lot of time.

President Denton nodded. "I knew when I fired Virginia I had a secret weapon. I knew that your love for this country would keep you from refusing my offer to have your old job back."

Hardwick concluded that the time for speech making was over; it was time to get down to business.

"Well, maybe you're a smarter bitch than I gave you credit for. But I know you're out of rope, and lucky for you I'm not going to let you take down the country with your arrogance and inflated ego."

For just a split second, President Denton thought of coming out from behind her desk and shaking Hardwick's hand. She just couldn't do it. Instead, she asked, "So what do you have for me? I know that you and Grayson have probably cooked something up. But before you answer, let's just say I'm going to give you credit for being a great American, instead of making a big stink about you and Grayson flying around the country when you were officially fired."

"You're close. Ever since General Grayson and General Williams and I flew back from Fort Bliss, I have had Grayson working on a proposal. I am meeting with him and the Joint Chiefs of Staff tomorrow, and he's going to give me his plan."

Hardwick could see a bit of relief come across the president's face. "We don't have any time to waste. Get yourself over here immediately afterward and present me with Grayson's plan."

The two of them stood up. There were no smiles and no handshakes. But this time Hardwick's parting shot wasn't going to be given as he was walking out the door. He pressed his legs up against the president's desk and leaned so far forward that he was within inches of the president's face. "No, Madam President, we don't have much time. You and your totally corrupt and inept administration have wasted all the time that America has!"

Chapter 107

Stop them at the border, stop them at the border, we've got to fucking stop these Mexicans from crossing the US border!

This thought had gone through General Grayson's mind something approaching ten thousand times since this entire incident started. But that did not surprise Grayson; that mantra had been repeated almost as many times in the US Congress by conservative Republicans the last couple decades. How could anyone ever address the immigration problem until steps were taken to secure the borders properly? To General Grayson and almost everybody in the Joint Chiefs of Staff at the Pentagon, this prerequisite had been the most obvious priority that Congress had needed to tackle. But under every single administration as long as Grayson had been in Washington, only lip service had been given to the issue of securing the borders. As Grayson liked to say, the only thing ever done to address the problem was to apply short-term Band-Aids.

As politicians so often did, both Democrats and Republicans in the US Congress, the US Senate, and the White House repeatedly took meaningless, short-term steps that were nothing more than drugstore Band-Aids. Instead, what had been needed was a full-blown medical operation. Grayson used this analogy when discussing the issue with his fellow generals. But he and everyone else at the Pentagon knew that what was needed was not a medical operation, but instead a military one.

The reason Grayson had been teaching military tactics at West Point for a number of years was because he was considered one of the premier sources of knowledge of the history of warfare. General Grayson was also equally knowledgeable about the history of bad politics and their effect on military confrontations.

He thought, *A wall or fence between the United States and Mexico* was *never going to work. They've never worked.*

The Great Wall of China had kept out the Mongolian hordes, but eventually they'd found their way around it. And there were the Romans, Emperor Hadrian's wall in England— it was meant to keep out the Scottish raiding tribes. They eventually found their way around that too. Did the French Maginot line protect France from Hitler's invasion? No. And of course there was the wall that most Americans were familiar with, the Berlin wall. The shortest living of all of them. And there had been other walls and barriers: the one between Palestine and Israel, the one along the Strait of Gibraltar and around the Canary Islands. The Spanish had even built a chain of high-tech radar stations to deter immigration from Africa, only to watch illegal immigrant traffic flow to the other sea lanes.

Though Congress every couple of years had okayed additional funding for the hiring of more border-patrol agents and the improving of the fencing and other detection and barrier devices on the US-Mexican border, did these expenditures ever slow down the illegal border crossings? No. No was the answer to all of these questions. And once the walls, gates, and fences had been breached, their value had gone from small to meaningless.

But Grayson couldn't fix history, and he was preparing for a meeting with Secretary of State Hardwick, who had amazingly been rehired by the president. Hardwick had asked General Grayson and his team to prepare a proposal that he could present to the NSC and the president. A proposal on how to *stop them* at the border.

Chapter 108

Craig came down the hallway and found Katherine and Jennifer in some intimate conversation.

"This is a scary notion. Are the two loves of my life now conspiring against me?" he said with a sheepish grin.

"Just girl talk," Katherine said. "But if you must know, we were about to flip a coin to see who gets to sleep with you tonight."

"Having you sleep alone last night just seemed like such a waste," Jennifer said. "And if this mess is going to get serious and one of us might not live, isn't it best that at least somebody gets to go out in style?"

Craig could hardly believe his ears. He had been afraid the two of them were going to be at each other's throats, and now they were joking together about his sex life?

"Nobody is going anywhere. And I think that until this mess is over, celibacy is the best policy." Craig was really uncomfortable with where this conversation was going, but he heard his office phone ringing and quickly moved on down the hall.

An hour later everyone was situated at the dinner table, and Craig shared what he had learned on the phone conversation. "That was Professor Burton from UNM. He said that things have gotten progressively worse the last forty-eight hours in Albuquerque. A large contingency of the Mexicans that crossed the border have moved into town. The only good news was that any attacks or killings have been limited to the all-white northeast neighborhoods, not surprisingly. He repeated the same stories I've been hearing the last couple weeks. The vast majority of all the attacks and confrontations with the Mexicans occur because they're trying to obtain food. Bad news is that, due to lack of food in the stores in town, many of the invaders have moved out into the remote suburbs."

After dinner, Craig corralled everybody in the living room.

"I think from this moment forward, I want every single one of us to be fully prepared for a potential attack. Dave and I have been discussing some strategies, and I'd like him to talk first."

Dave was very proud that both of his older brothers had relinquished some serious responsibilities to him. It was Craig's home, and it was quite a lot of faith that Craig was placing in Dave.

"I don't want to mislead anyone—I'm a US Border Patrol agent, not an Army Ranger or a Navy Seal, but I did go over some of my ideas with Dad, who you all know served some thirty years in the air force." Dave quickly glanced down at his dad sitting on the sofa; his father gave him a big thumbs-up. "We are going to work in shifts. Not including Madeleine or little Ricky, there are six of us. That works out to four-hour rotating shifts. These will be the teams—Craig and Mom, Dad and Jennifer, and, Katherine, I will work with you."

"I'm not a child anymore. I want to help," Madeleine said.

Dave approached Madeleine and gave her a little pat on the shoulder. "I knew you would want to help, and in a situation like this there is always a great need for a backup, what we might call a rover. You will always be there and ready when one of the teams needs additional assistance."

That was all it took for Madeleine; she was now beaming.

"One member of the two-man team is going to take the back door; the other member is going to take the kitchen door," Dave continued. "We are not going to station anyone near the front door. As you clearly observed, there is no glass on or around the front door. Craig built the front door in such a manner that a bulldozer couldn't knock it down, so there's no reason for us to waste any manpower there. Craig and I are going to show each of you exactly where we would like you to position yourself. But before we do, we are going to hand out the guns and ammunition."

As Dave worked with the others, Craig gave a revolver and ammunition to Katherine. Craig was surprised when she said, "I don't want a revolver. If I'm going to have to protect myself, I want an automatic. And don't give me some weenie nine millimeter."

"Where did an illustrious professor learn about guns?"

As Katherine opened and closed the chamber to the Smith & Wesson M&P40 automatic, she looked up at Craig. "There's a lot you have to learn about me. Let's just say that I didn't grow up in a cave."

Next Craig approached Jennifer, who gave him double the shock he had received from Katherine. "I don't want a gun. Please don't require me to take a gun. I hate guns!"

"But, Jennifer, other than Madeleine, I think it's very important each and every one of us has a gun. It's not only for your protection, but it's helping to protect all of us as a team. That's what we're all up here for. That's why I invited my family. There is safety in numbers. There are only six of us, and if you refuse to take a gun and help, there will only be five."

Jennifer was physically shaking. "I can't! To be honest, just to be in the same room with all of you talking and touching guns is making me sick to my stomach."

"Jennifer this is very disappointing to me," Craig said. "I'm counting on you. My family is counting on you. You repeatedly talk about being an adult, but I find your refusing to take a gun is...is...somewhat childish."

Jennifer started to sob. "I'm sorry. I'm sorry to disappoint you and your family." She paused. "In high school, one my very best friends was shot. She was shot by mistake. One of our other closest friends had taken a gun out of her father's drawer and was showing it off. Somehow the gun went off by mistake. I was there. I was there in the bedroom when my friend was shot. Ever since then, I've been totally revolted even by the sight of guns. I close my eyes at movies when people are being shot." She cried a bit more, then trying to stop, she repeated, "I'm sorry, Craig. Please don't make me take a gun, please."

Craig decided not to press the point. As anyone who knew anything about guns was aware, a person who picked up a gun with any intention of using it must not only be totally familiar with the gun, but totally confident in their ability to use it. Clearly Jennifer was not such a person. For Jennifer, having a gun was probably more of a liability than an asset.

"That's fine, Jennifer. I completely understand. It's probably for the best. Why don't you and Madeleine work out a system where you could be of assistance to the rest of us?" He bent down and gave her a small kiss, and she stopped crying.

The next hour, there were numerous discussions between everyone about which particular windows gave the best view of potential attackers and what everyone should do if there was an attack.

Just when the first team was going to take its station, some loud noises sounded in the yard. At first Craig considered turning on his perimeter security lights, but on second thought, he decided it might be best that the intruders not know that the occupants of the house were awake and aware of their presence. Everyone carefully sought out a window to see if they could identify any intruders, but they were unable to. And as the sounds grew louder and more numerous, Craig decided it was finally time to turn on the security lights.

There they were. There appeared to be two groups. One group had arrived in a suburban. It had New Mexico license plates, so it was obviously stolen. There were three or four individuals that appeared to be trying to siphon gas into the suburban from Craig's five-hundred-gallon elevated gas tank. Another group, which appeared to be five to six Mexicans, had some kind of crowbar or lever and was trying to break the lock into Craig's storage shed.

Before anyone noticed, David unlocked the kitchen door, stepped onto the porch, and unloaded three rounds from the twelve-gauge automatic shotgun, shooting over the heads of the group near the gas tank. Both groups immediately scattered into the woods.

For the next hour, everyone stayed on high alert, and Craig left the perimeter security lights on. There was no further activity, no noise, and no sightings of any individuals. Craig put his two Alaskan Malamutes in the back bedroom, so they would be safe.

Mark took the shotgun that Dave had used earlier and announced that he was going to check on the gas tank and see if the lock to the shed was broken. Mark had only been gone a matter of minutes when shots rang out from what seemed like every direction. At exactly the same moment, there was some loud banging on the rear door to the house. Dave and Craig grabbed their guns and went to investigate. A group of Mexicans was trying to batter down the back door. Dave and Craig, using the bedroom windows, got into a gun battle with the attacking Mexicans.

Back in the kitchen, Katherine had been watching Mark's attempt to check out the lock on the shed. She heard another shot and saw Mark drop to the ground. She screamed, "Craig, Dave, Mark's been shot!" But Dave and Craig had a gun battle of their own going on and couldn't hear Katherine screaming.

Bill left his post and rushed to the kitchen. "I can't hear you from the other room, what are you screaming about?"

Without taking her eyes off the window Katherine said, "Mark has been shot. I can see him on the ground by the door of the shed." She reached for the kitchen door and said, "I'm going to go grab him. Lock the kitchen door behind me and open it when I return."

"Katherine, stop. Mark is my son. I was in the military, not you. Let me do this."

Katherine gave Bill Walther a serious look. She knew it would take everything she had to convince Mark's father to not go retrieve his son. "No, Bill, I might be a good twenty-five years younger than you, and I'm pretty fast on my feet. Besides, I have a plan. You're wearing white, and I'm wearing mostly black. Turn off the security lights. I think I can get to Mark without anyone seeing me."

Before Bill could respond she was out the door; Bill immediately turned off the security lights.

The firefight in the back between Craig, Dave, and the Mexicans was still continuing. Though Katherine was worried about the two of them, the noise was a distraction she was glad to have. There was no one in sight, but there still was an occasional shot coming from the forest and the sound of one of Craig's windows breaking.

When she reached Mark, she found that a bullet had penetrated his left thigh and he was bleeding profusely. She started to pull Mark toward the house when she heard something behind her. She spun quickly while she unholstered her automatic and unloaded three rounds into a Mexican who was charging her with what looked like an axe in his hands. She quickly lifted up Mark enough that she could drag him toward the kitchen door but maintain a low profile.

She was less than one hundred feet from the door when three shots rang out. Two of them hit Mark in his back, and what life remained within him was gone. The third grazed Katherine's left forearm. She dropped on top of Mark, not so much to protect him but to ascertain if he was still alive. He was not. She scrambled toward the kitchen door, which Bill opened the second she arrived. Bill and Elsie saw that Katherine was wounded and hurried to her to offer assistance.

"No, leave me alone. I'm fine. It's not that serious. Go back to your station. Don't let anyone rush the house." Katherine was bleeding pretty heavily, and she started looking for something to tie to her arm.

Just then Jennifer entered the kitchen. "Katherine, you've been shot. You're bleeding badly." Jennifer rushed out of the kitchen, yanked the tablecloth off the dining room table, and returned to the kitchen. She started ripping the tablecloth into two long strips and then dropped down by Katherine's side. She ripped back Katherine's shirtsleeve, exposing the wound, and started applying the tourniquet.

Katherine was amazed by Jennifer's efficiency. "I'm impressed."

Jennifer didn't look up. "You might think of me as some sorority girl, but in my younger years I was a Gold Award troop member in my town's Girl Scouts. And if you're not up on your Girl Scout terminology, that's the female version of an Eagle Scout."

Dave and Craig returned from the back of the house to the kitchen. Craig said, "I didn't think we were going to survive that. I think there must've been between twelve and fifteen of them. Thank God Dave is such a crack shot. That twelve-gauge shotgun was a lifesaver, especially considering most of the time I couldn't see what I was shooting at."

Their mom noticed that Dave was bleeding from his forehead. "Son, you've been shot!"

"No, Mom, I'm fine. In all the ruckus, I fell down and hit my head against the wall."

Having finished up with Katherine's bandage, Jennifer turned her attention to Dave's head wound. "Elsie, can you get that medical kit out of the bathroom?"

Madeleine jumped to her feet, "No, that's my job!" And she scampered down the hall.

Elizabeth, who the entire time had remained at her post in one of the side bedrooms, came into the kitchen. "Where's Mark? He's not at his post. With all the shooting, I thought I should stay where I was. But if he's not in the kitchen with everyone else, where is he?"

In the horror that had taken place over the last hour, no one had stopped to think of Elizabeth. The look on everyone's face must've been telling, because Elizabeth gave out a bloodcurdling scream. "Where is Mark??"

Craig now realized his sister-in-law was asking a question that even he didn't know the answer to. But he could tell from the look on Katherine's, Jennifer's, and his parents' faces that they knew. "Where is Mark? I know you know! Tell me now!"

Elsie stepped forward. "I saw the whole thing through the window. When you two were in the back, Mark went out front to see what damage those others had done. Katherine saw him get shot, and she rushed out to save him. She was so brave. She even killed one guy that attacked her. When she was trying to bring Mark back into the house they were both shot."

Elsie and Bill went to the aid of their daughter-in-law, who was crying hysterically.

Katherine looked directly into Craig's eyes. "I'm sorry. I tried. They shot Mark twice in the back as I was dragging him toward the house. I double-checked before I left him. He's dead. I'm sorry."

The room went silent for a long while.

Craig finally broke the silence. "I think there's a good chance that Dave and I got the bulk of them, but I don't think we have the luxury of sitting around and nursing our wounds. I think for now, every one of us needs to man a door or window at least until daybreak."

Craig approached Katherine, who was still sitting on the kitchen floor, and gingerly helped her up. And even though he knew everyone, including Jennifer, was watching, he gave her a long, loving kiss.

"Thank you. Thank you for trying."

He buried his head in her shoulder, and for the third time in just forty-eight hours, he cried. He had lost two of his brothers in just two days.

Chapter 109

It was a special meeting called for the Joint Chiefs of Staff. It was all the regulars: John Hardwick, secretary of defense, and General Kurt Grayson, chairman of the Joint Chiefs of Staff. From the army came Lewis Taylor, secretary of the army, and General Frank Connelly, chief of staff. From the navy was Jeremy Clark, secretary of the navy, and General Nathan Allison, chief of staff. And from the air force were Wayne Baker, secretary of the air force, and General Andrew Williams, chief of staff.

Grayson stood up, banged a water glass to get some attention, and started, "Gentlemen, before John says anything, I just thought I would say that all of us here are both glad and relieved to have you back on the team." He let out a big chuckle. "I'm sure you broke some records in the history books for being fired and rehired. Frankly, you were hardly gone long enough for us to even miss you."

Grayson sat back down, and Hardwick stayed seated and said, "Thanks, John, and all the rest of you. Just for the record, I didn't have time to miss you, either.

"Now, Kurt, I hope you have something good for me because I am having an emergency meeting with the president later today. But first she texted me and asked if I could slip by today's NSC meeting and see, without giving them the details of your plan, if I can at least get them moving in our direction."

"I appreciate your confidence, John, but could you give me an easier assignment, like trying to solve the hundred-year turmoil between the Palestinians and Israel? Or maybe building a four-lane highway across the Atlantic Ocean? We are talking two thousand miles of border! And the geology and demographics couldn't be more opposite. I have hundreds and hundreds of miles of desolate desert to deal with, of course, a few small meaningless border towns, and then some of the largest cities on the border. On the Mexican side is Tijuana on the California coast, and moving east then you have Nogales on the Arizona border and the two-million-plus people living in the metropolis of Juarez, El Paso, and Nuevo Laredo. It concludes on the other coast of the Gulf of Mexico with Matamoros, Mexico. So any strategy I suggest is clearly going to be in two parts: how we handle the vast, unpopulated desert and how to deal with the larger, more populated cities."

General Grayson had stated the obvious. Since these were some of the best military minds in the country, Grayson didn't state anything that everybody was not already not aware of.

"I know you're not going to let me down, Kurt. So what have you come up with?" Secretary Hardwick said in a friendly but pleading tone. Everyone in the room knew that not only were the options limited, but also every day of delay was causing thousands of deaths of both Americans and Mexicans.

"I hate to preface what I'm going to say because I don't think there is a mind in this room that's not fully aware that the United States is confronted with a problem of a magnitude that is unparalleled in our 250-year history. The most recent attack of the United States up until this was the 9/11 attack on New York and Washington, DC, which pales in comparison. Prior to that, it was the Japanese attack on Pearl Harbor, where 2,500 Americans were killed, and the United States was forced to enter World War II. And then you have to go back over one hundred years to when the British attacked both Baltimore and New Orleans in the War of 1812.

"But this attack, as I said, is unparalleled. Already, estimates are that something over four million Mexicans have flooded across the border in the last six weeks. And we now know there are many small communities that have been completely overrun."

Taking a deep breath, Grayson continued. "For now, I'm going to ignore the political ramifications of what I'm going to suggest. Luckily, selling this to Congress and the president is a job for you. And I know it will not be easy, even considering the incredible statistics that are flowing in. There are still many, most of whom are in the current Denton administration, who feel this is not a serious matter. I am not going to launch into another history lesson on how many countries since the beginning of mankind have been decimated or destroyed because of a lack of understanding and commitment by the politicians. But the Roman Empire quickly comes to mind, and we are all far too familiar with the Obama administration's total ineptness when dealing with the initial threats in Syria, ISIS, Russia, etcetera."

He paused. "You gave me an order, John—figure out how to stop them at the border. Every one of us in this room agrees that we cannot address, much less solve, the problem concerning these millions of Mexicans who have already flooded across the border, if we continue to let millions more cross basically unimpaired.

"I have a few more caveats before I present my game plan. You will know that I am not a man that beats around the bush. But since I am very well aware how hard it is going to be to sell this program to Congress and more importantly to this inept, liberal Denton administration, give me just a moment more for a few qualifiers."

Grayson, who had been pacing the room as he talked, sat down at the conference table. "My intent is not to kill Mexicans. My intent is not to kill innocent people. If I could accomplish my goal without killing anyone, I would do so. But my program will kill a good number of Mexicans. The vast majority of them will be those that are at or near the border and have every intention to cross illegally. Yes, there will be some Mexicans who will be killed who just happen to be in the line of fire and who are not intending to cross the border illegally. Those are just casualties of war, like the casualties of every war since the beginning of mankind. Killing individuals is not at the heart of my program—it is only part of my program. There are too many Mexicans involved. We already have estimates from the CIA that, at the rate the Mexicans have been crossing the border the last three to four weeks, within another month, we could have as many as six to eight million *more* Mexicans enter the United States illegally. The numbers just don't work both politically or militarily."

Every single secretary and general in the room was riveted to Grayson's every word—words none of them had ever imagined would need to be spoken in America.

"But the number of Mexicans we kill in this operation is an important factor in the success of the operation. Let me explain. The reason we have an estimated fourteen or eighteen million illegal Mexicans living in our country today, and this does not include those who entered the country in the last two months, is because the United States has never really taken our border with Mexico seriously. There is hardly a Mexican family in Mexico today that doesn't have a family member or relative living in the United States illegally. Anyone living in Mexico who really wanted to enter the United States, either legally or illegally, basically could do so. Our country has been sending the wrong message to Mexicans for decades—'Come on in, no reprisals, no hassles, and we will feed you, pay for your medical, and send you to college for free.' Frankly, it's surprising we don't have tens of millions more illegal Mexicans in America.

"We all know that the Mexican economy is a total shambles. When you combine that with the policy now being put into action by President Denton that the United States is going to legalize millions and millions of illegal Mexicans, it is no surprise to any of us in the room that there is this massive invasion.

"My plan of attack is to completely change the mindset of anyone living in Mexico who is thinking of not only crossing the border with United States but even getting close. My plan of attack is as much psychological as it is physical. I want to, in a matter of days to a maximum of one week, completely shut what has been decades and decades of an open-door invitation to the country of Mexico. Better yet, to slam the door shut!"

Secretary of State John Hardwick, could hardly control himself. "General Grayson, are you sure you're not going to go into politics? I've never seen you pre-sell a proposal so well. Okay, okay I'm already convinced, give us the details!"

"A five-mile-wide demilitarized zone," Grayson continued. "With one very important twist: it's more than demilitarized, it's dehumanized. I call it the NMZ, the No-Mexican Zone. Sort of a spinoff of the DMZ in Korea. And yes, I've already run the math. For the approximately two-thousand-mile border, that's ten thousand square miles.

"Let me go through it step by step. Step one is to get the word out regarding our intentions. We would have every radio station still operating within one hundred miles of the border announce that, starting on a date we work out with the president, the United States is going to heavily bomb and strafe a five-mile-wide band running from Matamoros to Tijuana. We give everybody twenty-four hours to clear the area. In addition to our initial bombing and strafing, we will continue with whatever military force is needed to keep this five-mile band completely devoid of human occupation as long as necessary. Any and all diplomatic and administrative offices that have counterparts in Mexico will communicate to make sure that the message is in as many hands as possible and that there are no negotiations.

"The operation will start at exactly 6:00 a.m. on a designated date. Using army aviation, the air force, and the National Guard aviation from all the US border states, we will drop millions of leaflets in Spanish explaining our intentions and the timetable. We will start immediately to move as many of our air force personnel and planes from around the western part of the United States to the various air force and National Guard bases as close to the border as possible. I took the liberty of already discussing my plan in detail with General Williams."

Air Force Chief of Staff General Andrew Williams had, up to this point in the meeting, been unusually quiet, and now everybody in the room knew why.

Addressing Hardwick, Williams said, "Sir, per General Grayson's instructions, I had to keep this pretty tightlipped. But I have checked with my chief of staff, and we are confident we can be up and ready to start operations by the day after tomorrow. I would like to add something if I may."

Hardwick, who seemed to be as nervous as a cat, nodded. "Go ahead, Andy. You're among friends here. You can speak your mind."

"Everyone on my staff wanted me to convey a message. They've been wondering for weeks what has been taking us so along to make this decision. I don't want you or General Grayson to take this as criticism. I know the both of you have had your hands tied by this screwed-up Denton administration. The reason I bring it up is I want you to know that my staff can guarantee you that every single individual in the air force coast to coast is not only 100 percent supportive but raring to get into action and stop the destruction of property and deaths of innocent Americans."

For the first time in weeks, Hardwick's nervousness eased a bit, and he actually cracked a smile. "Andy, I've never doubted you or your men, and both General Grayson and I have 100 percent confidence in your abilities to carry out this mission. Now you know that both you and your staff are going to come under heavy criticism not only from the liberals in Congress but from those miserable bastards in the liberal press. But you let me worry about that—that is my job. You just tell your boys to do their jobs, and when this is all over, the American people will consider them heroes, and I don't give a goddamn about what anyone else in the press says or does."

"Thank you, sir."

"Okay, Kurt, now give me the difficult part. What are you going to do about the cities? I know you're not thinking of leveling a five-mile-wide swath through some of Mexico's largest cities. If you did that in Juarez, you might kill over half a million people, and even I can't defend that."

"You are correct, sir," Grayson said. "The biggest challenges will be the cities, and of course, our sources tell us that that is where the largest number of crossings have been coming through. My plan is similar but just on a much smaller scale. As opposed to taking out five miles, I'm going to take out five blocks. We conducted significant research, and I'm happy to report that, considering every border city, there are only three buildings we want to avoid bombing. There is a convent in Tijuana, a major hospital in Juarez, and a water-treatment plant in Matamoros. We will just take out everything around those buildings. And we will drop tenfold the number of leaflets in every one of the border cities. Additionally, there are a number of organizations and sympathizers on both sides of the border who have a history of working with the Mexicans, such as Border Angels. We are planning on working with these organizations to make sure they get the word out to evacuate those five blocks."

General Connelly spoke for the first time. "Kurt, if I might just add two things as they relate to the cities. Our research confirms that it is with the two largest border cities that we're going to have the biggest problems: Juarez and Tijuana. As an example of just how bad it's been in the last couple of years, the mayor of Juarez has had to fire four hundred of its own police officers for failing lie-detector tests. My second point is that our research also shows that Americans don't need to be overly concerned about the destruction that will happen in some of these smaller towns and communities that lie in the NMZ. There is story after story about how many, if not most, of these border towns on the Mexican side have been abandoned. There was even a story in the *Wall Street Journal* in 2010 about a town called Miguel Aleman, a town of roughly six thousand people. It had become such a war zone with the drug cartels that the town had basically emptied out."

Hardwick had given up cigars. He had been willing to put up with his wife bitching for years about his smoking, but when the Pentagon finally banned it, he'd decided it was just too much of a hassle. But he pulled one out of his pocket, stuck it in his mouth, and without lighting it, sat quietly for a few moments before he responded. "Well, you all know the first question out of the president's mouth will be, 'What is our estimate of how many Mexicans will be killed?'"

General Williams beat Grayson to the punch. "As many as necessary. As many as it takes so they get the message."

It was the exact answer on the mind of every general in the room. The estimates of Americans killed and injured were multiplying every day. No one had even started to estimate the billions, maybe trillions, in damage to properties and businesses. So, why? Why was the first question that the president was going to ask, "How many Mexicans are going to be killed?"

"John, isn't the real question 'How many American lives are going to be saved by our taking these steps?'"

"Dammit, Andy, you know that's the very question that every one of us in this room has been asking. But we've had to put up with these liberals in this and previous administrations for decades. They always want to ask the wrong questions because they see everything ass backward. Of course, that's how we got here in the first place."

Grayson had been biting his tongue. He knew from past experiences that in a room full of generals and department heads, one had to sit back and allow everyone to blow off a little steam. None of these guys had gotten to be department secretaries and generals by being wallflowers. But it was time to chime in.

"John you know better than anyone that neither I nor Andy can answer that question. There are too many variables: How successful does word of the killing zone get out? After traveling hundreds of miles, how desperate are these Mexicans to get across the border? And ultimately, just how stupid is human nature? I can't give you an estimate of deaths to initially clear the zone, but I can give you and guarantee you the only number that really counts. That after Andy and I have established the NMZ, and I repeat we can have it done in a week tops, 'zero' will be the number of new illegal crossings, with some caveats in the largest cities."

Hardwick reached into his coat pocket and pulled out a naval academy Zippo lighter that he had not used for a long while. He flipped open the lid with a flick of his wrist as if to show everyone he had not lost his touch. He thumbed the flint to ignite the wick, but instead of lighting the cigar, he stared into the blue-green flames while he digested all that he had heard.

"Well, Kurt, I have to congratulate you. I asked if we could stop them at the border, and your plan clearly does exactly that. I agree, we will still have some serious challenges in the larger cities, especially with the metropolis of Juarez, but that is going to be the army's job, or should I say your and Frank's job."

Grayson was caught a bit caught off guard. "My job? I thought you just said earlier this week that you needed me in here in Washington to even up the sides at the NSC."

"I do—God damnit, I do. But I am not going to let this nation's best infantry general rot here in Washington while I am risking thousands of our army's lives. Andy will run the air force's part of this operation and you, as of today, have full command of all land-based operations, working side by side with Frank."

John could tell that Frank was a bit miffed. Even though General Grayson was the top-ranked military individual in the country, historically the chief of staff of each department would be directly responsible for all his soldiers' activities.

About this time one could feel the tension building up in the face of Navy Chief of Staff General Nathan Allison. "I think my Navy Seals have proven their worth as well as anybody the last decade, and I think we deserve an opportunity to be in this fight!'

Hardwick indicated to each of the department secretaries to join him away from the table for a minute. Though each department secretary was in fact in charge of that department and each of the chief of staff generals reported to them, Hardwick knew in this kind of situation it was sometimes best for the civilians to let the generals fight among themselves. He had learned decades ago that military men were used to yelling and being yelled at by fellow uniformed officers. But they seemed to never take criticism as well from somebody in a civilian suit.

Grayson took Hardwick's getting up from the table as a signal. Grayson knew what Hardwick wanted. They had worked on many a battle before, and what Hardwick most wanted now was for Grayson to take control. Hardwick had made it clear he would handle Washington, and Grayson was to handle everything else.

"Now, boys, come on, let's not let this meeting turn into a sorority girls' fight. There was never any intention of leaving anyone out. Matter of fact, I think after we get into the details of my plan, you will find, well, let's just say, that each of you needs to go home, cook some steaks, get drunk, and bang your wives as long as your Viagra will allow because none of you or your staff will be home for at least a month."

Grayson turned to General Nathan Allison and said, "Nathan, Frank and I are going to work as joint commanders answering directly to John. I want you to do the same with Andrew. It just makes sense for the air force and naval air to work together in this project, like you've done in the past. I have already discussed that as soon as you can muster, get as many aircraft carriers within striking range of Matamoros in the Gulf of Mexico, and likewise pull your Pacific fleet in range to support Andy in Tijuana and any other border cities in range. When this meeting is over, Nathan, will you bring your staff into my office? I want to coordinate where it makes the most sense to use the marines versus the army. John, if you don't have anything else, I would like to get to work."

John and the other department secretaries rejoined the table. "Whoa, you don't think I am going to be able to sell this overnight!" Hardwick barked at Grayson.

"Goddammit, John, if we wait on those pussyfooted, bleeding-heart liberals to make up their mind, even Minnesota won't be safe," Grayson said. That was all it took. Secretary of Defense Hardwick stood up and dismissed everyone, telling Grayson to stay behind. Hardwick barely had to look at one of his aides when a bottle of Gentlemen Jack and two glasses with ice were sitting in front of them.

Grayson spoke first, but not until he took a stiff drink. "I am not sure getting drunk is going to soothe my anger over the fact that more American civilians are going to lose their lives and their homes if the president delays any further. If I am reading the cards right, it is going to be my and Frank's job to take on the illegals that have crossed the border after we secure the border. Am I right?"

"Yes, I know the longer the president waits, the harder your job of cleanup is going to be, and more of your boys will be lost. That is painfully obvious. But you and I and just about everyone at the Pentagon have been warning Congress and the president about something like this for decades. And where has it gotten us? Nowhere!

"But look, President Denton is in many ways crazier than that screwball Obama. Don't forget how many secretaries of defense Obama went through in just eight years—Gates, Panetta, Hagel, and Ashton Carter. Now we have to deal with Lady Loony Bird. In less than two weeks, the president has fired and rehired me. Need we say more about her state of mind? Need I remind you of her handling of Algeria?

"She is totally capable, if I don't properly position your idea with her, of firing me once again. I'm not supposed to know this, but the word is she had to fire Virginia Wade, my replacement, because that's exactly what Wade did. President Denton requested Wade come up with an immediate military solution for the border problem, and Wade somewhat refused. I agree, she should've been fired. But right now our country needs your plan. And you, our military, and the American citizens need me to stay in office, so I can convince our crackpot president to let us proceed. I will get it done. I still have a lot of powerful friends in Congress. You have my permission to start preparing, but quietly."

And as those words left Hardwick's lips, he raised his glass and gave Grayson a big wink. "Look, no one other than those in attendance tonight are to know of the ultimate plan of attack. But this country and even those liberal bastards in the press, except for MSNBC, are calling for action. Have Andy get every plane he can in position to attack, and you do the same with the army and the marines. When I get the go-ahead, we may start with less than twelve hours' notice."

With this, one of the aides filled up Hardwick's glass and went to fill up Grayson's; Grayson put his hand over the glass, signaling he had had enough.

"I had better not. I told Nathan I would see him in my office," he said, and he stood up to leave. But Hardwick motioned him to sit back down.

"Well, if you don't mind, I need this second one. I still have to stop by the NSC meeting before I meet with Denton tonight. But I have one final question. I know you too well, Kurt: what was your backup plan? You always have a contingency plan, if for no other reason than because you know I always ask for one."

Kurt leaned forward, took the glass of bourbon out of his boss's hand, took a big gulp, and handed it back. "That is the easiest question because it is something I have run through my mind for decades. A human wall. A fully armed soldier evenly spaced every ten feet. The math? Just over a million men. I think you know the numbers: we have 450 thousand in active duty, over a million if we consider all branches, another 840 thousand in reserves, and if we were to call on the border states and contiguous state's National Guards, it is feasible. But it would never work without first creating the NMZ. Too much loss of American troops, and you would be so thinly spread, you would be jumping from one hot spot to the next.

"But actually, John, it is a plan that I still want to implement. I think internally speaking, we can't just keep flying our planes over a foreign country, bombing the hell out of them, even one that has invaded us. It is going to just be too hard for both Congress and the president to keep it going. And sure, if there are large groups that try to penetrate, then we make discrete, swift strafing runs, but leave the big bombers at home. But then we create the military line—but of course on our side of the border. Only after creation of the No-Mexican Zone can I maintain and support even a thin two-thousand-mile line. And I think with little risk of life."

Grayson got up and walked to the door before he turned and finished with, "And tell those homos at the NSC the best part of our establishing the demilitarized zone: *in comparison to any other available military options, the NMZ will lose dramatically fewer lives!*"

Chapter 110

Hardwick was late, but he didn't give a damn. Those National Security Council (NSC) meetings were always a waste of valuable time, and the biggest waste came at the beginnings of the meetings. In decades past, it had been the previous secretary of defense who tended to have more say-so in the NSC meetings. But starting with the Obama administration, and Obama himself, who everyone knew hated the US military, the secretary of defense had had to kowtow to the national security advisor and the secretary of state. These posts were filled by women for most of the Obama administration and again under President Denton.

It wasn't that Hardwick was a sexist; he was not. But as a general stereotype, liberal women politicians—which Hardwick thought was a redundant phrase—didn't like almost anyone at the Pentagon. Which only made sense. The first thing military officers were taught at any of the military academies—ROTC training or any of the advanced military training schools and courses—was that indecisiveness is unacceptable. In times of war, decisions routinely needed to be made within minutes and sometimes seconds both on and off the battlefield. The enemy did not give the luxury of setting up study committees or holding "group think" sessions one after another.

Hardwick knew quite a few US military officers who had left the military and were now senior executives at major US corporations. They often complained to him how they could hardly stand the waste of time and money by all these government group sessions and committees. They said that no one was willing to ever stick their neck out. They massaged issues for so long that by the time they were done, they forgot what the questions were in the first place. Nowhere was this more evident than in the NSC meetings.

"Take your seat, Secretary Hardwick. I'm glad you decided to join us," National Security Advisor Nancy Wheat condescendingly said to Hardwick as he entered the already-in-progress NSC meeting.

To Hardwick, Nancy Wheat looked like the twin sister of the previous national security advisor, Susan Rice. He didn't know which one he hated worse, Wheat or Rice. Which forced him to chuckle, but luckily no one knew why.

"Well, Ms. Wheat, some of us have more pressing jobs than just sitting on our duffs and contemplating for days on end every potential scenario of every single action by every single individual and every single country—and ultimately doing nothing. But don't let me interrupt you. I'm sure I missed some important academic discussions. I will just do my best to try to catch up and keep up," the last words leaving Hardwick's mouth with as much sarcasm as he could muster.."

Without even looking at Hardwick, Ms. Wheat said, "Actually, Mr. Hardwick, I think it was most beneficial that you weren't here for the initial hour of the meeting. We all know that you and everyone else at the Pentagon think the only solution to this invasion is a military one. I can assure you that everyone here and at the state department couldn't disagree with you more. We have felt from the beginning, and we still feel today, that using the proper diplomatic channels, we will be able to resolve this crisis soon."

"Swell, Ms. Wheat, that's just swell! I can't pull rank on you, but I can assure you I would if you were in the military. But since I have a couple decades on you, let me pull up a little history for you instead. Your diplomatic channels and supposed political solutions haven't worked a damn going back farther than when you were born. And what special insight or experience are you relying on that makes you think they can work now? This horse just isn't out of the barn—it's way down the road and in another county."

Nancy Wheat, still showing her disdain for Hardwick, responded while looking at everyone else in the room but him. Naturally, since the room was basically filled with a bunch of yes-men and yes-women. That's how it worked in

Washington. The president appointed the members of the NSC. President Denton, as with President Obama, surrounded herself with individuals who were willing to agree with everything she did and said, and that's exactly who also got appointed to the NSC.

"That's the problem with you Pentagon types—you act first and think later. You couldn't give a damn about the political ramifications. But the president and I are required to think of the political ramifications of every single action—not only the ramifications here in the country but internationally. We are still the world's leader, and everyone across the globe is watching very closely how we deal with the situation. Pick up a paper, Mr. Hardwick, and you will see that there is many an argument both in and out of this country that the United States deserved this invasion."

That was it. The blood had rushed so forcefully to Hardwick's face that he thought he was going to spew blood out onto the table. It was clear, immediately clear, that there was no way he was going to be presenting Grayson's plan at this meeting. These hacks still weren't going to do a damn thing, and they sure were not going to allow any immediate military retaliation. And since Grayson's plan was anything but politically correct, he wasn't going to waste his breath today. But he was going to get in the last word.

"Oh, I'm sorry Madam Secretary. I just once again forgot to read *the New York Times* today. But of course I'm not shocked that that liberal rag has once again stated an opinion that is completely contrary to the best interests of our country. I do have one question. Do you and the president write these articles and then have someone at the *New York Times* rubber-stamp them for you? Or do they write the articles, and then the two of you use the *Times'* articles to make your decisions?

"But don't respond—I'm not staying. But let me respond quickly to your other criticism. Every morning as I'm staring in the mirror and shaving, I promise myself one thing: I will do everything I can to keep from doing anything that is politically correct. President Denton, you, the Obama administration, and other liberal administrations before you have done nothing on any serious issue without first counting how many votes that action will either gain or lose you. You guys would sacrifice hundreds and even thousands of American lives and spend billions or even trillions of dollars that we don't have to keep from alienating even the smallest number of liberal groups or individuals. You haven't and you still don't today really give a damn about what's best for our country in total. It's only, can you stay in office, and can you get reelected?

"And what makes me absolutely sick to my stomach is that you're willing to allow thousands of Americans to lose their lives and their property because you're afraid of alienating the Mexican vote in the next election. You and I both know that what spearheaded this invasion is the fact that just before he went out of office President Obama said he was going to give American citizenship to some five to ten million Mexicans illegally in this country. In doing so, Obama opened the floodgates."

Chapter 111

When Secretary Hardwick's office called the president to say that he was ready to present his plan, even though it was late in the day, the president told him to come to the White House immediately. As Hardwick entered the Oval Office, he was surprised to see that the president wasn't the only person in the room. Also seated on the sofas were Stephanie Jones, Secretary of Homeland Security, Ronald Smith, Vice President Bob Triden, and National Security Advisor Nancy Wheat, whom he had just sparred with less than an hour ago.

Hardwick did not know Ron Smith well, but what he did know about him he didn't like. Smith was a loser, an ineffective government blob that so permeated the upper echelons of departments in Washington. And as for the vice president, no one in Washington DC, much less the country, ever took any vice president seriously. But Bob Triden took perceptions to a new low. Every time Triden opened his mouth, he made Dan Quayle look good.

The president was being unusually gracious. "Sit down, John. We are all very eager to hear the Pentagon's solution to the border problem. Let me just give a bit of a preface. You know my administration, since the very beginning, has done everything it could to keep this from escalating into a situation that would demand intervention by the military. And frankly, I'm sure you're aware, my advisors here today still feel that way. But I don't, or should I say, I don't any longer. So let me start by giving you a bit of encouragement. When I fired Virginia Wade, I fired her because she was incapable of giving me a military option. If you can convince me that your plan will work with the minimum amount of lives lost, both Mexican and American, I can pretty much assure you we'll have a deal."

"Just so I don't waste my time, or more importantly our country's time, can I get your assurance that maybe, for once, this White House will do what's in the best interest of our country and not what's most politically correct?" Hardwick said.

Rosemary Denton chuckled in response. "Now, John, you've got me in quite a bind. You know I'm already in political quicksand, with what happened in that grade school cafeteria in Las Vegas and the fact that I've seen the recent polls, and surprisingly, even many of my fellow Democrats are calling for military action. So, let's just say I want you to give me an option I can't refuse."

John then began. "I was thinking seriously of bringing General Kurt Grayson with me to better explain the exact details of this plan, since it was mainly he, with the aid of the other Joint Chiefs of Staff, who not only designed this plan, but will be in charge of implementing it. But I know this administration, like past administrations, doesn't have the utmost respect for our military leaders in uniform, so I thought I would handle this myself."

The president didn't like the cheap shot. But to some degree she deserved it; more accurately, she'd inherited it. Sadly, the country had slowly learned that President Obama had a disdain for the military; he saw them all as baby killers. It was why he had been probably the worst commander in chief the country had ever known. Sure, being both a liberal and a woman, Denton would admit to similar thoughts. But she didn't see the military as baby killers. Rather, she thought of them as thick-skulled Neanderthals, boys who wanted to shoot first and ask questions later.

"Go ahead, John. I'm listening. I know you think I deserve whatever you dish out, but let's try to get through this without any more cheap shots."

For the next hour, John Hardwick explained in as much detail as he could General Grayson's plan, even including the extended plan of creating a human wall. He wasn't interrupted once. Interestingly, the president never flinched once, though her advisors strained to keep their faces from contorting out of shape. John didn't know if he got the bigger reaction to the bombing or the human wall.

It was the president who spoke next. "I'm a little embarrassed. I should've thought of that myself. Are you going to offer me any other options or a backup plan?"

Hardwick leaned back on the sofa. "Nope, take it or leave it. But I can assure you that just about everyone over at the Pentagon has tried to come up with some other solution, and every other option we can even think of takes ten times longer and loses probably ten times more lives, on both sides."

"I thought you might say that. Okay, I'll cut you a deal. We will do it, but you have to help me sell it."

Hardwick smiled. "I know you better than you think. I knew you were not going to let me present this and then skip out of Washington to help implement it. I've already told my generals and each of the department secretaries that if we get the go-ahead from you, they're going to have to do this without me. I'm all yours. Where do we go next—Congress or the Senate?"

Now the president was smiling. "I've already checked with all my advisors, not for their approval but for my authority. I will declare war, and then I don't need anybody's approval. I never thought I was going to get to do that as president. I don't mean to make light of it, but I'd be lying if I said there wasn't something thrilling about it. I already have the declaration of war drafted. How soon can the Pentagon put this into action? Let me rephrase that: what would be the absolute soonest that bombs could be dropped?"

Hardwick's expression wasn't exactly a smile. No one who truly understood what war was about and who had just heard that war was about to be declared would be smiling. Americans would die. They died in even the smallest skirmishes. Even in one of the Gulf wars, one of the biggest casualties had occurred when one supply boat turned over. It was just the nature of any major military exercise. The chance of the Mexican Air Force shooting down any US military jet was about zero, but once again, if they flew enough jets in enough sorties, planes were going to crash, and lives were going to be lost.

No, it wasn't a smile on John Hardwick's face, but for the first time in weeks, there was a look of satisfaction that finally his country was going to take action and do the right thing. "I understand that over ten million leaflets are being printed as we speak. Once we get the word out and the leaflets dropped, my people say they can have aircraft in the air between twelve and twenty-four hours from when you give us the order."

For the first time, John noticed that no one else in the room had said a thing. He wondered if the president had warned them not to speak before he'd come in. That was smart on her part. Earlier John hadn't held his tongue for the president, but if one of these government nimrods had opened their mouths in protest, at this stage he would've ripped them a new rear end.

The president stood up quickly, and everyone immediately followed. And for the first time in a long time, President Denton stuck out her hand, took John's, and shook it.

"Oh, you have the order!" she said. "Get your people in gear. And after that, just plan on spending 24-7 on Capitol Hill. But if I understand your plan, and it's one of the things I like about it so much, by the time my liberal constituents can do anything to stop you, you'll be done. Did I understand that correctly?"

"Yes, Madam President, you understood that perfectly."

Chapter 112

There was nothing else like it. It was as if every single individual in every military department in the country—the army, air force, navy, marines, and even the National Guard in each of the border states—was on steroids. Many of these individuals over the last decade had fought overseas in many of America's wars, in Iraq and Afghanistan. It had been painful for them to hear stories the last few weeks about what was going on at the border and in the communities and towns that surrounded it—and to witness their government doing nothing about it. These men and women of the military were more than willing to go overseas and fight for their country; their willingness to defend their very own turf was tenfold. So when the word finally came down to take action, hundreds of thousands of military personnel were like uncaged tigers springing into action.

As General Grayson had indicated, the first phase was to clear the five-mile zone of as many people as possible in as short an amount of time as possible. The Air Force, Army Aviation, Air National Guard, and Naval Air, which were used near the coast, had perfected a coordinated program of dropping millions of leaflets over a five-mile band stretching the entire two-thousand-mile border. The leaflets were simple, and they were in Spanish:

You must leave this area immediately. Within twenty-four hours, a five-mile stretch of land from the US border stretching south into Mexico will be heavily bombed. Anyone remaining in this zone will be killed. There will be no further warnings. Do not go north. Do not go toward the United States. You will be killed if you try to enter this zone again. You will be killed if you try to enter the United States. You must leave now. This area will be called the NMZ or No-Mexican Zone.

Simultaneously, numerous organizations on both sides of the border were doing everything they could do to get the word out. That, too, was working well, but there was one serious problem. Many of the Mexicans who found the leaflets or were told of the bombing program were a very short distance from the US border. Even though human beings can easily walk five miles in twenty-four hours, with much of the border station crossings and fencing broken down over the last couple weeks, it was much easier for many to just quickly move into the United States.

Such a tactic had already been anticipated, and it was decided that for the first couple days of the bombing, no one on the American side was going to try to impede this flow. For decades, millions had crossed illegally. In the last few weeks, many more millions had crossed into America illegally. At that point, a few hundred thousand more wasn't going to make a difference one way or the other. No one, from the lowest-ranking private to both General Grayson and John Hardwick, wanted to kill any more Mexicans than they had to.

Getting the leaflets distributed and getting the word out were even more effective in the cities, which was heartening to the coordinators because of the perception that in the cities, the risk of death was higher. Mexican military personnel were actually going door to door and building to building in the designated five-block segments of each of the border cities, making sure that every single individual vacated the premises.

One of the more ingenious plans was that thought of by one of the marine colonels. He had devised a plan to take approximately three hundred military jeeps along with thousands of gallons of gasoline into Mexico. They would divide the jeeps and fuel up into five groups and present them to the Mexican police and Federales. They were to use them to patrol the southern border of the zone and attempt to keep anyone from entering. Of course, the colonel knew a percentage would just be immediately stolen for other purposes, but the hope was that the majority would be put to good use.

Finally, the word came. General Grayson, who was overseeing the entire operation, received a call from General Williams informing him that his boys had just flown over almost every square mile of the zone, and it was amazingly vacant. Not completely empty by any means, but compared to the masses that had been there just days ago, it was almost like the bombs had already been dropped.

What happened next was not a surprise to a single person on the Joint Chiefs of Staff. Hardwick had already received pressure from many of the more liberal congressmen and senators that if the leaflet-dropping program and other measures were successful in both stopping the flow and clearing the zone, that maybe the need for bombing could be eliminated.

Hardwick hated to make the call, but the president insisted. And when Grayson received a call from Hardwick discussing the option of holding off the bombing, he'd known it was coming.

"John, America has been sending the wrong message to Mexico for decades, and that's how we got into this crap in the first place. Not only have we been sending the wrong message, but we've been sending mixed messages. We give lip service to sealing the border, but we leave gaping holes. We arrest people who come across illegally, and then all we do is release them to have them return the next day. We say it's illegal to enter our country, but instead of jailing them, we set them free. We try to discourage illegal immigration, yet we highly encourage them to come by offering a myriad of free social services and even college. In many border cities, English is barely spoken."

Hardwick said nothing, so Grayson continued. "You can only cry wolf so many times. So far, this program has worked better than I imagined. And I think it worked because deep down inside Mexicans know that Americans are tough. Excluding internal revolutions, the last time Mexico was in a war was in 1916 with the United States. They know America is almost constantly at war. I don't want to repeat my earlier comment, but if I were to put my finger on one thing that has so undermined our border with Mexico, it is that the Mexican people have started to believe that we are soft. At least we are soft when it comes to enforcing our laws relating to the border and immigration. They need to be reminded that we are a strong military nation and that we can only be pushed so far."

Hardwick finally spoke up. "I know, John, you're preaching to the choir. The president just asked me to call."

"I understand the pressure you're under in Washington. Hell, I'd rather be in the NMZ when the bombs go off than have to put up with what you're going through there. But if we show that we were just bluffing, that we never had any intention of bombing the zone, it will be the last hurrah. And we might as well take down what remaining fences are left. In my opinion, the United States has basically been holding up a welcome sign anyway the last couple decades. If you call off the bombing, we might as well give away free baseball caps with every new entry."

Grayson paused for a minute. "John, I hope you're not forgetting one of the key points of this entire operation."

Hardwick sighed and said, "Yes, but you know I haven't told anyone, not even the president, about what we learned about the terrorist bomb. I was saving it. If I got a pushback from the president, I was going to tell her. Thank God I didn't have to. I think she would've come unglued, and this whole thing may have fallen apart. When this thing settles down, you're going to have to help me decide how we're going to present this to the NSC."

"Let me just take a minute more on that subject," Grayson said. "I have some good news for you. I earlier told you about the jeeps we are transporting to have the Mexican authorities patrol the southern border of the zone. I can't take credit for any of this. It was Marine Colonel Bullock. I told all my staff to keep this thing about the bomb just between us, but I guess Colonel Bullock is one of General Allison's chiefs of staff. Bullock came up with the idea of killing two birds with one stone. Using the jeeps to patrol the southern border to keep people out and using them to monitor any suspicious activities or individuals, especially anyone looking Muslim. I wasn't a part of this, but I guess they've offered some million-dollar bonus or award if anyone discovers any suspicious activity. I don't know all the details, and I'm not sure I want to."

Hardwick allowed himself a brief chuckle. "I'd guess Colonel Bullock will find himself on the generals' list this next year. You don't need to say any more about halting the bombing. I didn't want to make this call in the first place, but the president made me promise I would. You have both my authority and the president's. Start as soon as you can."

Jokingly, Hardwick said, "If you hold on a minute, maybe you can hear the bombs before I hang up. Sorry for the jokes, sir. We've all been under a lot of pressure down here. You can let the president know we will commence bombing at 1400 hours."

Chapter 113

General Grayson had decided that instead of staying in Washington, the entire Joint Chiefs of Staff and their staffs would set up their base of operations at Fort Bliss in El Paso, Texas. That had been one of Grayson's reasons for showing up there earlier. He'd wanted to make sure the facilities met his requirements. For so many reasons, El Paso was the perfect location. It was almost dead center of the two-thousand-mile border, being just over eight hundred miles from the easternmost border at the Gulf of Mexico. Second, Juarez, at 1.3 million inhabitants, was the fifth-largest city in Mexico. Juarez was very similar to the other largest Mexican-US border city, Tijuana, which also had roughly 1.3 million inhabitants. These two Mexican border cities were responsible for something like 50 percent of all illegal border crossings and about 75 percent of drug smugglings, drug-related murders, and kidnappings. Grayson felt he would rather be as close to the heart of the problem as possible.

The leaflet-dropping program had gone off exceptionally well. The United States Army's Fourth Aviation had four battalions under the Fourth Infantry Division stationed at Fort Hood, Texas. Fort Hood had one of the largest collections of non– fixed-wing aircraft in the Southwest. The army's helicopters were perfect for distributing the leaflets. California's Air National Guard units throughout the southern part of California also were used in distributing the leaflets to those parts of Mexico closer to California.

It was finally time to start the bombing. Grayson was coordinating the efforts with US Air Force Chief of Staff General Andrew Williams and US Navy Chief of Staff General Nathan Allison, who was coordinating the use of naval air. Working around the clock, they had to make some initial key decisions, the first one being what approach would be the most effective and create the least amount of deaths from the get-go. They decided to work from the center outward. They divided the five-mile-wide zone, the NMZ, into five, one-mile-wide bands. They would bomb the center band first. There was a number of reasons for this. They calculated that even though their warnings and leaflets gave the Mexicans twenty-four hours to vacate the NMZ, there would be those that would move slower than others. The vast majority of those serious about getting out of the NMZ before the bombing should be close to either edge of the zone. The center band also should be the least populated. Additionally, for those who thought the United States was bluffing, bombing down the center would be a strong reminder that the United States meant business.

If anyone in the NMZ hadn't gotten out, they had better do so pretty quickly.

After bombing the entire two-thousand-mile center band, they would commence bombing the two next-closest bands. And after completing that, they would finish with bombing the two external bands, the one bordering the United States and the other, which started four miles into Mexico.

The second-biggest issue the Joint Chiefs of Staff had to decide was exactly *what* they were going to bomb. Though in the last few days, probably the largest concentration of the United States' combined military aircraft had been assembled in the five border states, no one had ever envisioned bombing every square mile of the approximately ten-thousand-square-mile zone. There probably weren't enough bombs in every arsenal in the entire United States to accomplish such a feat. But it wasn't necessary. Some 80 to 90 percent of the land encompassed in this two-thousand-mile-long, five-mile-wide zone was desolate. It was uninhabited desert.

At the outset, this was the strategy for the vast majority of the zone that was unpopulated—everything that wasn't a city, town, or community. Each of the bands was to be treated somewhat differently. Again using the concept of the five bands, the Joint Chiefs of Staff decided that the band closest to the United States would be the least bombed, and each band from there on south would receive more and more destruction.

One of the items that Hardwick and Grayson had discussed over the last twenty-four hours was how the five-mile-wide NMZ was going to end up serving two purposes for the United States. Of course, the most immediate purpose was to stop the hordes that had been moving en masse into the United States during the last month. But there was a second, longer-term objective that would impact the ongoing illegal border crossings. Some 80 percent of illegal drugs that had come into the United States the last couple of decades had come across the very stretch of land defined by the NMZ. And not just illegal border crossings but a laundry list of other illegal activities, from slave labor to kidnappings and other smuggling activities. The NMZ, as long as it was maintained, was finally going to put an end to all of those illegal activities.

It was for this reason that the Joint Chiefs had decided it was best to take out just about every single building in the open areas. It wasn't a big request, since there just wasn't that much. But it was that specific fact—that there wasn't much in the way of buildings—that made each and every one of these buildings, outposts, camps, or way stations so important. Traveling for hundreds of miles in such desolate desert, illegal border crossers heavily relied on each and every one of these remote locations for much-needed food, water, and shelter. Taking them all out would put a serious dent in any future illegal trafficking of humans or drugs.

Grayson and the other generals had a special plan for the southernmost band. Total destruction. The generals had discussed trying to come up with some product they could use to create a line of demarcation at the southernmost edge of the NMZ. They had looked at various dyes and even considered a product that the US forest department used in marking lines when they were fighting forest fires. But none of them were practical for a two-thousand-mile stretch. They devised a plan for a more permanent line of demarcation—scorched earth. Not scorched-earth tactics but actual scorched earth. They would drop, in the heaviest concentration of any bombs they dropped, incendiary bombs. The result would be a band devoid of anything—cactus, yucca, mesquite, and even the rare, dilapidated structures. The ground itself would be blackened, leaving barren gullies, canyons, arroyos, and thousands of miles of dry, desolate desert. Anyone entering the area would immediately recognize this was a true no-man's-land, resembling to some degree the infamous no-man's-land established during World War I between the Allies and the Germans.

There was not a great fear that the fires started from the incendiary bombs would spread far or burn down thousands of acres of forest. There wasn't any forest.

The entire process took three days. It went off flawlessly. There was only one tense moment. On the second day, the Mexican Air Force sent two Swiss-made Pilatus PC-9s and one Pilatus PC-7 to intercept one of the bombing missions south of the Arizona-Mexican border. Though no one took seriously the threat of Mexican retaliation, the Joint Chiefs of Staff took no risk. From the very first day, they had deployed AWACSs that were flying nonstop. The AWACSs quickly picked up the Mexican jets, and within minutes ten Lockheed Martin F-35 Lightning II stealth multirole fighter jets were on the scene. Once the F-35s arrived, within seconds, the three Mexican jets hightailed it south. It wasn't because there was a ratio of ten to three; it was the fact that the Lockheed Martin F-35 Lightning II was considered worldwide to be one of the most sophisticated and powerful aerial-defense jets made. The Swiss-made Pilatus aircrafts were dinosaurs in comparison, and small dinosaurs at that. The Air Force utilized aircraft from the following bases: Cannon Air Force Base, Clovis, New Mexico; Davis-Monthan airbase, Tucson, Arizona; Dyess Air Force Base, Abilene, Texas; Edwards Air Force Base, Edwards, California; Holloman Air Force Base, Alamogordo, New Mexico; Kirkland Air Force Base, Albuquerque, New Mexico; and Luke Air Force Base, Glendale, Arizona. Additional support was obtained from the four border states Air National Guard units: Texas Air National Guard, Kamp Mabry, Austin, Texas; Arizona Air National Guard, Sky Harbor International Airport, Phoenix Arizona; and the 162nd

Wing out of the US base Davis-Monthan in Tucson. The New Mexico Air National Guard, which similarly worked out of the US Kirkland Air Force Base in Albuquerque, New Mexico; the California Air National Guard, March Air Reserve Base, Riverside, California; the Fresno Air National Guard base, Fresno California; and lastly the Channel Islands Air National Guard station, Oxnard, California, also lent their support.

While Chief of Staff General Andrew Williams coordinated all Air Force operations, his counterpart Chief of Staff General Nathan Allison of the United States Navy coordinated all naval air operations. Naval air support operated primarily out of two locations. First, was the Naval Air Station North Island, on the Coronado Peninsula in the San Diego Bay. Also out of the same locale, Navy jets were used off two Navy aircraft carriers stationed at the Naval Base in San Diego. One of the few hang-ups was the shortage of incendiary munitions at the various air force and naval bases that were flying the sorties. The largest nearby stockpile was at the Pine Bluff Arsenal, a US Army installation located in Jefferson County, Arkansas. But Air Force General Williams had anticipated this need early, and had quickly called in various Lockheed C-5 Galaxy aircraft to transport the needed incendiary bombs to the various airstrips.

At the same time the rural bombing was taking place, the more intricate and tricky urban locations were also being bombed.

There was one last precautionary measure taken just before the bombing commenced. Utilizing the jeeps that had been provided, uniformed individuals from various municipal police departments, with some assistance from the Mexican Federales, drove up and down the streets in the designated five-block area utilizing megaphones and barking out one last warning.

There was even an additional step taken to try to contain the destruction as much as possible. All of the various city governments had been put on notice that even though no incendiary bombs would be used within the cities, it was anticipated that fires would break out when natural-gas lines or other flammable materials were struck. The city governments were encouraged to have as many fire trucks as they could muster up running just outside the five-block area, so they could contain any fires from spreading.

Even with all the military's attempt to minimize the loss of Mexican lives and keep the destruction in the cities to the five-block band, there was an equally strict directive—level every single structure, except for those few sensitive humanitarian facilities.

Being the military historian that Grayson was, he had explained the goal using an example from one of the most destructive bombing runs of World War II: Dresden, Germany. In the latter months of World War II, a combined operation of the British Royal Air Force (RAF) and the United States Army Air Forces (USAAF) had dropped over 3,900 tons of bombs on the German city of Dresden. Grayson didn't use the example because so many German lives had been lost; instead, he used the example because almost everybody remembered the photographs of the massive destruction to this once beautiful German city. Each of the Joint Chiefs of Staff was concerned that they had maybe sent conflicting messages to the pilots who would be flying the bombing missions. There was so much talk about protecting this and avoiding that; using the Dresden example would alleviate that mixed message.

In the last-mile band and in the five-block city band, there was to be total obliteration. In a joint communiqué from Air Force General Williams and Navy General Allison, they stated that if reconnaissance revealed any instances where two individual bricks were still held together by mortar, the mission had failed. In a verbal communication with one of his squadron leaders, Allison said, "If a small dog attempts to cross the five-block city band, I want that dog to be visible to the naked eye from a low-flying reconnaissance aircraft. There are to be no structures of any kind remaining. There is to be no place to hide."

In less than twenty-four hours after the last bomb was dropped, step two was implemented, the human wall of US military personnel. This is where Grayson's plan deviated the most from his original thoughts. It wasn't because of any pushback from Hardwick, the president, or anybody in Congress. It was merely the logistics. Commandeering the million men that Grayson had estimated and placing a soldier every ten feet wasn't completely impossible; it was simply a matter of doing it in a timely manner. When the Joint Chiefs of Staff started to crunch the numbers, they calculated that it would take weeks to not only get those men in place, but also to put in the infrastructure to support that many military men stretched out over two thousand miles. Housing and food for not only the soldiers but the tens of thousands of support staff just couldn't be done quickly enough to fulfill the need properly.

Instead, something just over 150 thousand regular army and reservists was utilized. Approximately another forty-five thousand National Guard reservists were called to duty by each of the four border states. It was still somewhat of a logistics nightmare, but as fate would have it, at least immediately following the bombings, the human wall appeared to be unnecessary.

The five-mile band and the five-block city bands had accomplished what they were supposed to, and to a degree that not even Grayson could have predicted. In less than twenty-four hours, the constant reconnaissance that was being flown revealed two amazing facts. Not one, not a single individual, had crossed over the US-Mexican border. And even more amazing, the number of individuals that were spotted in the entire NMZ was minuscule.

Additional steps were being taken that assured even more so that the soldiers now stationed along the US border would not be needed. Both the naval air and the air force remained on full alert. The larger bombers would no longer be needed, but the smaller bombing jets, such as the A-10 Warthog, would do cleanup bombing and strafing, if and when any group of Mexicans entered the zone.

The jets were only scrambled once. It was in the small Mexican town of Allende, situated exactly five miles south of the Mexican border city of Piedreas Negras, a town roughly 127 miles west of Laredo, Texas. A medium-sized cargo truck crossed into the scarred NMZ, which was surprising because the air force had done an excellent job of making almost every highway from Mexico into the United States impassable. But it was a lucky day for the Mexican who was driving his truck. The A-10 Warthog that had been ordered to the scene was already on a reconnaissance mission in the area and was able to intercept the truck just as it was crossing into the band. Though the pilots had been ordered to take out each every individual or vehicle that entered into the band, this particular pilot used his discretion. The pilot observed that the truck was weaving in such a manner that it appeared the driver might be drunk. The air force colonel used the A-10's 30MM cannon to lay down a serious warning precisely one hundred yards in front of the truck. That was all it took. Before the jet had completed its turn, the truck had hightailed it out of the charred NMZ. All that the pilot could think about for the rest of the day was the fact that the truck driver must have completely soiled himself.

Hardwick and Grayson knew this was the easy part. Now came the difficult part: rounding up four million or more Mexicans who had entered the United States since the border had been breached.

Chapter 114

Craig thought it was the longest night of his life. All he could think about was the loss of his two brothers. And what made it ten times more miserable was the fact that the entire night, he stood guard at the kitchen door, where he had a direct view of Mark lying dead in the driveway. For protection, he had decided to leave on the exterior security lights, and one of them shined like a beam from heaven directly on Mark's sprawled body, facedown in the dirt. No fewer than twenty times, Craig had to keep himself from running out and dragging his dead brother back in the house. He didn't stop himself because of the risk to his life; it was that he knew having his dead brother's body in the house would be too much for his mother to bear. He had given both of his parents guard duty at the back of the house, so they would not be able to see Mark's lifeless body prostrate on the driveway.

At the first sign of light, Craig convinced his parents and everybody but his brother Dave to try to get a little shut-eye. But he had another motive for trying to get everyone to go to sleep.

"Dave, now that everyone's gone to bed, I want you to help me bury Mark. I know that with Elizabeth's strong religious beliefs, she's going to want Mark to get a full and proper burial. We just don't have that luxury right now. I don't know how soon we will be able to leave here. If I were to guess, with what all that might be going on in Albuquerque, I suspect every funeral home is booked solid. I want you to help me bury Mark here."

"Sure. What do you want me to do?"

"There's a spot that I have contemplated where someday I might like to be buried. It's a beautiful clearing near one of the largest ponderosas on the entire property. I'd like to bury Mark under that tree. Who knows? Maybe someday I'll be buried next to him. We need to disconnect my blade from my Kubota tractor and attach the backhoe. We can use that to dig the hole and fill it in. But I want to work quickly, because I want to finish completely before Elizabeth or the folks wake up."

After about two hours of work, they completed the burial. Dave made a makeshift cross that he knew Elizabeth would appreciate. When all was complete, they both stood in silence. Dave said, "You know, I make a habit of not going to funerals. There's just something funny about them. I know I must be weird, but it just seems to be...I don't know. Weird. All this big hoopla. A fancy expensive casket. All the big, incredible expense. All those flowers. The person is dead."

"I guess it must be a brother thing. I feel the same way, somewhat. Americans seem to ignore the subject of death. Statistics show that a very high percentage of people don't even make any plans for their demise. I often think it must have something to do with religion. Though the majority of Americans consider themselves Christians, I think it's a much lower percentage that really believe. I think it's this very fact that they are so scared of confronting. They'd like to think that there's a heaven. They'd like to believe that there's something after death. But I think the majority feel like me—when you're gone, you're gone. Dust to dust.

"We're just like that squirrel over there. We may be special, and we may be smarter than that squirrel when we're alive. But when we are dead, and when the squirrel is dead, our ashes will eventually mix. And at that point, we aren't one bit different, and we aren't any better. And that's why I think people try to avoid the subject of death. They don't want to deal with that reality. Mankind wants to think of itself as special because we can read and write, speak, and build tall skyscrapers. We have convinced ourselves we are unique and unlike any other living creature in the universe. I think Voltaire was right, and God is only a being that we have created in our minds to give our lives special meaning and, more importantly, to give ourselves something to look forward to in the afterlife. But most people can't deal with that reality."

"Wow, I never really thought of it that way. But you know, I think that's how I feel, too. I think maybe that's why I feel so funny about funerals. It all seems like a big game."

Craig grabbed his younger brother around the shoulders and pulled him back toward the tractor. "I think we'd better get back to the house. I want to be there when everyone wakes up. I suspect there's going to be a lot of crying and handholding today. And I'm going to need your help."

As they walked along, Dave said, "You know, I could use a little handholding myself. Everything has moved so fast the last two weeks. I really haven't had the time to mourn my dead wife or unborn child." Dave used the sleeves of his coat to wipe the tears from his eyes.

"I'm sorry, Dave. I meant to ask you more about that. There's just been so little time for anything meaningful. I guess our family has shrunk considerably in just the last few weeks. I can only hope the worst is over. But if our family has lost so many, I fear there are thousands of other American families that may have lost even more. Its times like these that I wished I was a religious man. I somehow feel our country needs a god like we've never needed one before. But as I was saying, and as Voltaire did, 'If God did not exist, it would be necessary to invent him.'"

They parked the tractor back in the shed and walked toward the house. Craig said, "How about we cheer things up a bit by changing subjects? Jennifer told me the two of you had a long talk on the way back from Albuquerque. I know you've hated working for the government. I've always thought you were too smart to waste your life away on some bureaucratic job. Jennifer said you are considering going back to school to get an advanced degree. Would you consider going to UNM? It's not Stanford, but at least you'd be getting out of the godforsaken, crazy California, with all those liberal crackpots."

"Yeah, and San Diego has just gotten too big for me. I think I much prefer a city the size of Albuquerque. Any chance my brother could expedite things, so I wouldn't have to wait to get in-state tuition?" Dave asked, giving Craig a much-needed smile.

Just as they were about to open the kitchen door, Craig grabbed his brother and gave him a big bear hug. "Right now, I can't think of anything that would bring more enjoyment into my life than to have you living here. I know when this all settles down, and the deaths of our two brothers sinks in, I'm going to feel a great loss. Funny, maybe it's related to our conversation about funerals and death. My entire life I've never felt close to any of my brothers, but I will have to admit that I do have a special place in my heart for you, the youngest."

Craig paused. "Isn't it sad? But I guess that's just how life works out. I never felt close to my brothers, but now after their deaths, I feel the loss. What was it that John Lennon said? 'Life is what happens to you while you're busy making other plans'? Do me a big favor. I'd like you to give strong consideration to moving to Albuquerque and going to UNM. And if you could make that decision soon, I think it would be a big help to Mom and Dad, with both Cliff and Mark dying. It would make them feel better knowing you're here near me. And I'll make you a trade: you teach me to shoot like Wyatt Earp, and I will teach you to trout fish."

When they entered the kitchen, everyone was shocked to see that the two boys who had just lost their two brothers had big smiles on their faces.

Chapter 115

General Grayson, General Conley, General Allison, and General Williams were each riding in a separate Apache helicopter, all flying over a fifty-mile stretch of the newly created NMZ. The military never took the risk of having so many of the top brass all in one helicopter.

"This is General Grayson. Patch me through to General Tillman."

There was a brief pause. "This is General Tillman. General Grayson, go ahead."

"I have excellent news: the NMZ is working perfectly. We've barely spotted a soul, and we have been out an hour. But I want you to do something for me before I return to the base. When we left Fort Bliss, none of us noticed many of those hordes of Mexicans that we spotted around Fort Bliss when we flew in earlier in the week. It's like they disappeared. Would you send out two or three armed patrols in different directions? You might even think of sending one into downtown El Paso. I don't want to get into some serious confrontation or gun battle, so if they run into any serious problems, have them back off. I should be back on the base by 1200 hours, and I'd like their report waiting when I return."

All of the Joint Chiefs of Staff were in Tillman's office when Colonel Rodriguez entered the room. "All the patrols have reported back. I spoke with each of them, and I have a brief written report."

Grayson barked, "Forget the formalities, Colonel. Just give it to me verbally. What did your men find?"

"Well, General, it's perplexing. It's as if somebody waved a wand. My men could hardly find any large groups of Mexicans who recently entered the country. But there's a problem. And I would like to ask permission to speak frankly."

"Go ahead, Colonel. I've been at this for thirty years, and I'm not going to have my senior officers start mincing their words with me now."

"General, I purposely selected only those soldiers with Mexican heritage and only those who spoke fluent Spanish to go on the patrols. Even though they were in uniform, I thought it best—"

"Good thinking, Colonel. So what are your conclusions?"

"My reasoning for being a little reluctant to speak up is that, you see, a patrol down there is just not that easy a task. Roughly eight-two percent of the residents of El Paso and El Paso County are Hispanic. And during the workweek, during working hours when tens of thousands of day laborers come across the border to work in El Paso, the percentage can often approach ninety percent Hispanic."

Grayson was getting a little anxious. "Is your point, Colonel, that even you, as well as the Hispanic soldiers you took with you on patrol, just can't tell the difference?"

Colonel Rodriguez replied nervously, "That's kind of what I was leading up to. I think all of us in this room expected to find the large groups of Mexicans who recently entered El Paso. That would make it easy. But it seems like they have dispersed. They are not easily identifiable."

While the other generals conversed among themselves, Grayson got up and stared out the window. And then he turned and addressed everyone. "Well, I don't know if it's a solution, but I sure have a secret weapon: Professor Craig Walther." Everyone in the room looked perplexed. "He's my ace in the hole. He's the top expert in the whole country on this entire issue."

Grayson opened his notebook, pulled out a slip of paper, and handed it to one of the orderlies.

"That's his office number, cell number, and home number. If you can get him on the line, patch him in here, and we'll put him on the conference phone."

Within minutes, Professor Craig Walther was on the phone. "Professor Walther, I appreciate your taking my call without any notice. I've got to warn you that sitting in on this conference call are all of the Joint Chiefs of Staff. That should get your attention."

"What, no president of the United States? I'm disappointed." Craig chuckled. "What can I do for you boys?"

"Let me see how up on this stuff you are. What do you know about our bombing mission and the NMZ, what the press is calling the no-man's-land we created extending five miles south of the US-Mexican border?"

Craig paused. "I don't want to burden you with our problems up here in Albuquerque. I'm afraid I haven't had time in the last forty-eight hours to pay as much attention as I would like. But I can say this: if you are planning on running for political office, you can give that notion up. It seems that the liberal press has condemned both you and Secretary of State Hardwick as the modern-day Genghis Khan and Attila the Hun. But I did catch some Fox News, and they say your operation was masterful."

"Thanks. I think. But we've got a bigger problem."

"I know what the problem is, General. Remember, it was one of the last chapters in my book. It's not a new problem; we've been dealing with that problem in America for decades. So let me see if I'm right. The United States now has an additional four million or more illegal Mexicans living in our country, and all of you top brass can't figure out how to round them up."

Grayson gave a quick look around the room to take credit— clearly he had called the right guy. "That's right, Professor, and now our problem is your problem. As I remember your book, though, you didn't have a solution."

"That's because there is no solution. Can any of your people tell the difference between a legal and an illegal Mexican? It's not like they have a stamp on their foreheads. And then there's another problem. What exactly is a legal Mexican? We have so many Mexicans that live in the southern part of New Mexico and Texas, and each of them has a different legal status. We have millions of Mexicans here legally through such things as: passports, a laundry list of Visa programs; ninety day Visa Waiver Program, VSP, both business and tourist, DSP-150 and B-1/B-2 Visa and border crossing cards; and various immigrant employment cards numbering from EB-1 through EB-5.

"And there are even *degrees* of illegal Mexicans. Think of it this way, General, and assume for my scenario that everyone we are talking about is a legal resident of Mexico. So when it comes to those who are here illegally, you first have those who crossed the border legally. They gained entrance by just saying they were going to be here for a day or two, delivering something or seeing a friend, but then they didn't go back. We have those who once had a green card, but now it's expired, and they haven't gone back.

"And, of course, there's what most Americans think of when they think of 'illegal Mexicans,' those who cross the border illegally. We all know there're estimates of somewhere between fifteen to twenty million illegal Mexicans now living in the United States. And it goes without saying that a high percentage of those are concentrated in places like El Paso County, where you are. We can both assume you have no intention, at least at this point, to try to round up illegal Mexicans who have been here for years. Take California. For the last two years, it's been issuing legal driver's licenses to illegal Mexicans. For decades, that was the one distinction we had. If you didn't have a US-issued driver's license, you were probably here illegally. Now in California, they don't even have that aid to identify people properly."

Grayson was pissed. He'd anticipated this. That's why when Hardwick had said it was going to be his job to not only close the border but to deal with the millions of Mexicans who had entered the country, he had been afraid he may have been assigned an impossible job.

Crap, it's like Iraq all over again. Sure, it's always easy for the military to win wars when it's obvious who the enemy is—and especially when you have someone shooting back at you. But Iraq was just a modern version of Vietnam.

Both Desert Storm and the 2003 Iraqi war had been relatively quick, decisive victories. That was what the US military establishment was known for. But just like after

Vietnam, after both of these victories in Iraq, the United States had allowed itself to get bogged down in a protracted, internal, secular war among religious groups. It had been a disaster. The same for Afghanistan. At least that had been on the other side of the world. Suddenly, Grayson was confronted with similar issues in his very own country.

"Boy, what a clusterfuck! Now, Professor, I don't think I have a racist bone in my body. So I want to apologize if this comes out less than politically correct. But are you telling me that it might be impossible to identify these Mexicans who recently stormed across our border because...because..." Grayson, who was never short of words, just couldn't finish the sentence.

Craig Walther appreciated General Grayson's dilemma and tried to come to his aid. "If I can be so bold, General, let me see if I can finish your thought. There are just too many of them. Yes, we've all heard the estimates that over four million Mexicans illegally entered the United States in the last four weeks. But that's not that large a number, when you consider there are already fifteen to twenty million illegal Mexicans residing in the United States. But even that's not the real number. As of the most recent census, 18 percent of the roughly 310 million Americans are Hispanic. That's roughly fifty-five million Americans with Mexican heritage. Now add on the fifteen to twenty illegal Mexicans who are not counted in the census. And then you have to add one last number—the four million who just entered in the last four weeks. That's somewhere around seventy-four to seventy-nine million Mexicans in the United States. And I'm not surprised you are immediately confronted with the situation, considering where you're located. I think the estimates of people with Hispanic heritage in El Paso County is one the highest in the state for such a populated county. I think it ranges between 80 and 85 percent."

There wasn't a face on one of the Joint Chiefs of Staff that didn't look totally dumbfounded. The only one smiling was Colonel Rodriguez. He felt proud that Professor Craig Walther had supported his statement that 82 percent of people in El Paso County were Hispanic.

Craig continued, "I'm not military, but can't you at least round up those massive groups that I have heard are attacking some communities and cities around the Southwest?"

Grayson was a little nervous about giving too much classified information to a civilian. "Now, Professor, can we just say that this phone conversation didn't take place?

"Of course."

"Fine. We have been at the second stage of our operation only for a day. I don't want to put too much weight on what we just learned from our reconnaissance and patrols here in El Paso County. But the immediate reports say there aren't any groups or masses left. They've all dispersed."

There was a pause on the other line, and then Craig responded with a little sigh, "No, General. They haven't dispersed. They've assimilated."

Chapter 116

Sergeant Major Tom Evans of the A&M Corps of Cadets was very nervous, and he had every right to be. He had sent out one of the cadets on motorcycle going west on I-10 from their current location west of Houston, Texas. He had received a number of reports that there was an incredibly large mass of Mexicans moving east on I-10 going toward Houston. That was the very reason that he and another three thousand ROTC cadets, along with thirty players from the A&M football team, had driven from College Station in the first place.

The young cadet had returned and reported that he'd never gotten to see the approaching Mexicans. Instead, he'd flagged down and questioned some people heading west on I-10. They had run into a swarm of Mexicans and turned around.

This verified some reports by drivers that had passed through the cadets' makeshift barrier. Now they estimated that as many as a million hungry, crazed Mexicans were less than an hour away. Sergeant Major Evans was very nervous; he was only twenty-two years old.

Evans was talking to his senior officers about how best to stop a wave of people that was maybe a thousand times larger than his small squadron. A freshman cadet approached and asked him for a word alone.

"What is it, Private? What's on your mind?"

"I'm worried, sir. I'm worried that I'm not going to perform up to my duty. I don't want to let you down, and I don't want to let down the corps. But I'm afraid. I'm afraid I just can't bring myself to shoot another human being." He paused and then regrouped. "I'm excellent with my rifle, and I have one of the best marksmanship records on the rifle range. But there I'm shooting at paper-and-metal targets, not living flesh. I'm not even like a lot of the other cadets who hunt. At least they've killed something living. I've never even shot a squirrel."

Evans thought that talking to this young boy might kill two birds with one stone. Maybe he could help this young kid and at the same time try to get his own hands to stop from shaking. "Private Kenneth, I have complete faith in you. I know when the time comes and the situation calls for it, you will serve your country and A&M proudly. I know this because it is the history of the thousands of cadets who attended and graduated at A&M before you. That's why were called the Fightin' Texas Aggie corp of cadets. The corp was created at Texas A&M in 1876. We may not be West Point, but let me tell you something: the corp of cadets has distinguished itself in every single American war since 1880. Hundreds of A&M cadets served in the army's cavalry wars against the Indians. Amazing, considering that the A&M's military program started in 1876. But that very same year, one of our cadets was killed with General George Custer at the Battle of Little Big Horn. The cadet had enlisted with the cavalry during summer school."

Sergeant Major Evans did a couple knee bends to break the tension he was feeling. "I'm not worried, Private. It's in the blood of every cadet. You will make us all proud."

"But, sir. We aren't really at war."

Evans, for the first time in days, cracked a little smile. "Actually, Private, we are. You must not have gotten word from your superiors. About four or five days ago, the president of the United States declared war against Mexico. The combined air forces bombed a two-thousand-mile-long, five-mile-wide zone of death, now referred to as the NMZ. We are definitely at war. But let me ask you, Private, are you from Houston?"

"Yes, sir. I went to Clear Lake High School. And both my parents and my two sisters still live in Houston," the young cadet said.

"Well, Private, would you risk your life to save those of your parents and your two sisters? Because that's what we're talking about here. What do you think would happen to your family if these Mexicans, these millions of Mexicans, were to converge on Houston?" The sergeant major saluted the young cadet and finished by saying, "You will do just fine. Now get back in position with your platoon."

Sergeant Major Evans went back to conversing with his other officers. The plan was crude but simple. Since they'd learned that the president had declared war, they'd known it was only a matter of time before either the army or the National Guard started taking affirmative action. But the 2.2-million-person metropolis of Houston was less than ten miles behind them, and some of the suburbs were almost within reach of a bullet. He knew with three thousand cadets versus maybe a million Mexicans, they could only accomplish so much. If they could only slow down or delay their advance a day or two, the army would surely come to their rescue.

A corporal approached Evans. "Sir, a car stopped and told us that the Mexicans are just over the hill. They should be here in ten to twenty minutes tops."

Sergeant Major Evans saluted the young corporal and decided it was best to quickly address the men before the battle began. He climbed up on one of the cadets' cars, one of a hundred used to create a barricade across I-10.

"Gentlemen, it is been my honor to serve as your sergeant major my senior year at A&M. Each and every one of you has made me proud to be your commander. And now I know that you will make me, the dean of students, the president of A&M, the secretary of defense, and, yes, our president, your commander in chief, very proud of what you are about to do today. We are severely outnumbered. But from reports we have received, the vast majority of maybe a million Mexicans that are just over that hill are not armed with guns or rifles. That could give us a small advantage, at least at the start. I'm glad to report that each of you has at your side enough ammunition. By 'enough,' I mean—well, let's just say if we somehow were to run out of ammunition, I don't think there would be any Mexicans left. But I will ask each of you to be conservative. If we can somehow persuade this horde of Mexicans to stop their assault on Houston, and if we can do so without killing a lot of civilians, so much the better. But it is clear that we will need to kill quite a few before they get our message that we are serious. Remember what General William Tecumseh Sherman said: 'War is hell.' Now..."

Before he could finish his sentence, what roared across the sky was both an eyeful and an earful. Fifteen Lockheed Martin F-35 Lightning II stealth multirole fighter jets screeched across the sky directly over their heads and barely off the ground. They circled and came back again, this time on a different path. Just at that moment, a couple hundred thousand Mexicans came into view at the top of the hill.

Evans understood what the target of the jets was. The jets flew so low over the front edge of the mass of Mexicans that their tail force alone seemed to knock half the Mexicans to the ground. Or maybe it was the incredible thunder produced by the jet engines. The Mexicans stopped in their tracks, to some degree. But still some were pushed forward by the tens, maybe hundreds, of thousands pushing from behind. The F-35s returned for a third pass, but this time they flew precisely between the approaching Mexicans and the barricade of the cadets—except they flew much higher, and they dropped bombs. Once the smoke cleared, the cadets observed that the Mexicans, for the first time, might be retracing some of their steps.

Almost simultaneously, two other events took place. A very large squadron of army helicopters approached from the south and made somewhat of a barrier in the air between the cadet frontline and the front edge of the Mexicans. They were mainly: Boeing AH-64 Apache Attack helicopters; Sikorsky UH-60

Blackhawks, and Bell UH-1Y Venoms. These Mexicans may not have seen a lot of helicopters in their lives, but having a US Army Apache attack helicopter stare down at them from above was about the scariest sight a human could imagine. It might as well have been the devil himself.

At the same time, roaring up from behind, coming from Houston, was the largest convoy of military trucks Sergeant Major Evans had ever witnessed in person. He hadn't seen such a large collection of military vehicles since he'd watched the movie *Saving Private Ryan.* Within minutes, transport vehicles were unloading fully armed US Army and Marine soldiers by the thousands. A jeep drove up quickly, and a colonel got out. Sergeant Major Evans stood at attention and saluted the colonel.

"Sergeant Major, I am Colonel Carrington. I was sent here at the request of General Kurt Grayson. It looks like we got here just in the nick of time." The colonel looked around for a second and then said, "I have a personal message for you from the entire Joint Chiefs of Staff: 'You, your officers, and all of your cadets are to be congratulated for both your initiative to take matters into your own hands and your clear bravery for being willing to enter into a battle with such lopsided odds.'" The colonel stepped back two feet, snapped to attention, and gave Evans one big, firm salute. "We salute you!"

Then the colonel stepped forward and shook Evans's hand. "I only had girls. But if I'd had a son, I would've wanted him to be like you. You are relieved of your duty. We will take it from here. I think all of you probably have some classes to get back to. Oh, one last thing. I have an additional message from General Grayson. He'd like you to fly out to Washington at the government's expense when this is all over. He said he'd liked to introduce you around to some of the top brass at the Pentagon."

The colonel jumped in his jeep, but just before his driver pulled away, he leaned back looking at Evans and said, "Smart going, kid. You'll have my job in no time!"

Chapter 117

"Kurt, do you feel fairly confident that you're on a safe line?"

"General Tillman assures me that it is. I assume you set up this conference call to get an update?" General Grayson asked Secretary of Defense John Hardwick.

"Well, I'd much rather jump on a plane and come down and see for myself. Anything to get me out of this mess in Washington. I guess you've heard the solution that the president seems hell-bent on announcing. She's going to extend the original Obama executive order, the immigration amnesty plan. That was one of the single biggest problems with Obama's plan in the first place. Just like his Obamacare, it was open ended. So now President Denton feels she has a passkey to not only grant amnesty to all the previous illegal Mexicans living in the United States but to the additional four million that crossed the border in the last month as well."

General Grayson let out a sound of disgust. "Can't the Republicans block her? I remember back in February 2015, a federal court put a damper on Obama's plan for granting them all amnesty. I know the crazy liberals on the Supreme Court eventually gave Obama everything he wanted—that's why we're in this mess in the first place. But can't Congress pass something? This is crazy!"

Hardwick sounded just as disgusted. "Obama set a precedent for just going around the law, Congress, and the Constitution, and he opened a floodgate for President Denton. She's going to repeat what Obama did and put it all in an executive order. But that's not why I called. That's my problem. Actually, it's not *my* problem— it is the country's problem. But I will admit it feels like my problem. After all we had to go through to close the border, it just seems a gross injustice that Denton is going to make them all legal. But I guess if the Republicans are so inept that they can't stop the president and all the liberals, the country gets what it deserves. But I need an update. Anything new on the NMZ? Any attempts at breaching it?"

"John, I've never seen anything go so smoothly. Why we didn't do something like this twenty years ago is beyond me. None of those stupid walls or programs worked before, not even that 'virtual fence,' with its ninety-eight-foot-tall towers and all that radar and camera equipment. I think there was another program called Project Twenty-Eight because they were to make a special, extra-secure twenty-eight-mile stretch somewhere south of Tucson. It, too, was a disaster—only after the government spent about $65 million on it.

"Back to your question, however. We've hardly had a breach, and when there has been a report of a breach, more often than not, it's been innocuous. Ninety percent of the time, it's been somebody who has mistakenly driven into the NMZ at night. We decimated the area, and we turned it black as coal with our incendiary bombs. But frankly, at night it looks like the same desolate place it was before we started the bombing. So some stupid fool just wanders across the border by mistake. But that's been most of it. I've had a couple phone conversations with the director of the DEA. He said we sure made their job easy. The only thing they have to do now is monitor incoming flights. And he said since we still have some jets and helicopters monitoring the NMZ, they haven't had one attempted NARCO flight since we set up the zone. Of course, he said that the drugs already on the street here in America have quadrupled in price because of the lack of supply."

He paused and started again. "We purposely took out almost all the roads and highways leading north. Of course, that's going to become an issue when somebody once again wants to talk about trade. I understand that agricultural land in Southern California has gone up 40 percent in just the last two weeks. It's probably going to be a year before any fruits or vegetables once again are coming from the other side of the border."

"What's your latest on rounding up those roughly 4 million Mexicans that made it across? I've already heard stories that the vast majority of them can't be found. Is that really what's happening?"

"I remember one of the scariest movies I saw as a child was *The Invisible Man*. Maybe we'll have to make a new movie, *The Invisible Masses*. As crazy as it seems, it appears in all four border states, they're having an almost impossible task of not just rounding up the new invaders but even identifying them. I had a conference call with Professor Craig Walther the other day, who is considered the top expert in the whole country on this issue. He said he predicted this over a decade ago. And as I talked to more and more law enforcement departments, this attitude seems to be pervasive. I even talked to Sheriff Joe Arpaio in Phoenix. He laughed when I told him about the problem. He said he could've told us all of this and saved us a lot of time. That is why he is one of the biggest advocates of proper identification. He said that what they're doing in California in issuing driver's licenses to illegals is maybe the most devastating and stupid policy he's ever heard of in his life. Though he chuckled, I think he was half serious when he said that the next thing they'll be doing is changing the laws and allowing illegals to run for president. He added that we've already had a president who was born in Africa, so the requirement that you have to be born in America to be a US president has gone out the window. He said that maybe Arnold Schwarzenegger can now run!"

John interrupted him. "But you were able to round up some large groups in Texas, isn't that correct?"

"Nowhere near as many as everybody was predicting. Let me put that differently. It does appear that about a week before we commenced bombing, there was a group numbering close to five hundred thousand working its way toward Austin and one well over one million moving toward Houston. I know you already heard about the confrontation that very nearly happened between that large group of Mexicans on I-10 and the A&M cadets. We rounded every single one of those illegals up. It turned out to be just under 450 thousand.

"But as for the other millions, somehow in that last week, they have dispersed. I think in Washington we tend to forget just how big Texas is. Flying around down here, I think we could take every Chinaman and drop him or her in the state of Texas, all billion-plus of them, and you'd never know they were here.

The Austin Mexican contingency turned out to be barely over one hundred thousand. We've been transporting them here to Fort Bliss nonstop. As you can imagine, that requires quite a lot of vehicles. I think we will complete it by tomorrow. Luckily, Fort Bliss has a massive amount of acreage that was not being utilized. We are building a tent encampment and are stringing up wire to separate them from the rest of the base."

Hardwick said, "That works for me. Of course, it would make my life a lot easier if you could keep the liberal press off the base. All I can see now is the *New York Times* plastering on its front page some staged photo of some helpless child in your temporary camp. I guess we'll have to wait for the president's press conference to determine exactly what we're going to do with them."

"Well, John, now that you are friendly with the president again..." He stopped to laugh. "Why don't you go over and convince her to do what prior presidents have done? Back during the Great Depression, Herbert Hoover ordered the deportation of all illegal aliens in order to make jobs available to American citizens who desperately needed work. Harry Truman deported over two million illegal aliens after World War II to help create jobs for returning veterans. And I think it was in 1954 that President Eisenhower deported thirteen million illegal Mexicans. It was called Operation Wetback. Like Truman's deportation, it was done to help both the World War II and Korean War veterans have a better chance of finding work. I understand it took him almost two years, but they deported all thirteen million of them."

"You are a history buff, aren't you? I'm not necessarily a fan of Hoover, but I'm not the least bit surprised considering what tough presidents Truman and Eisenhower were. But we're in no such luck. President Denton made it clear when she was elected that she was following through on the Obama amnesty program. Remember, wasn't it your guy Professor Walther who said it was this very policy that instigated this mad rush across the border in the first place? You have anything else for me?"

Grayson stood up and looked around the room; he just wanted to make doubly sure no one could hear. "I have some good news on that terrorist bomb that we suspected had been smuggled by one of the Muslim terrorist organizations into southern Mexico. It's another proud day for the US military. I think you know that the Navy Seals were just itching to get in on this fight. As it turns out, the nuclear device came into Mexico through the Gulf Coast city of Veracruz. It had only gotten as far as Puebla when we tracked it down. The SEALs were flawless. They got in and got out before anyone ever knew they were there. The device has already been transported to one of our naval vessels in the Gulf and has been deactivated.

Grayson couldn't help himself and allowed himself a rare bit of humor. "It sort of reminds me of my favorite 'Jewish-American princess' sex song." Then Grayson sang into the phone to the tune of the theme song for the TV show *Bonanza*, "'Get it up, get it in, get it out, don't mess my hair up.'"

He started to laugh so hard he literally fell out of his chair.

"I gotta get you back to Washington. I think you're cracking up," Hardwick replied, smiling, and hung up.

Chapter 118

"This is the AT&T conference operator. I think we have everybody on the line. That includes California Governor Harry Black, Arizona Governor Jacqueline Brewmeister, New Mexico Governor Judy Rodriguez, and Texas Governor Richard Berry. Please press *zero* if there is any problem."

"This is Governor Black. I just want to say I think it's a wonderful day for America. I got off the phone with the president last night, and I assured her that she has 100 percent of my support in legalizing all those poor Hispanics who have recently entered the country. California, which has a strong Mexican heritage, is more than glad to provide a home to those new Americans."

Governor Brewmeister responded, "Well, Harry, I know none of us on the phone is surprised at your support of the president's anticipated decision. You are one of the few states that supported the initial amnesty program by Obama in the first place. Congratulations, now that you are going to increase California's voting base by another million liberal-voting Mexicans, I'm sure there won't be a Republican elected in California for one hundred years."

Governor Black said, snickering, "Yep, that's exactly how I see it. That's exactly how the president sees it. You Republicans don't have a chance in hell. We get ninety percent of the black vote. We get roughly eighty percent of the Mexican vote, and if I understand the numbers correctly, that just went up by another four million. As I said earlier, it's a great day to be a Democrat in America. Don't be a sore loser."

One of the three Republicans on the phone, Texas Governor Berry, couldn't bite his tongue any longer. "It may be a happy day for the Democratic Party in California, but I can sure you, it's a sad day for the average hard-working California citizen. My state has already started to calculate the enormous cost to our state budget to pick up all the welfare and social services that will be required under the law to provide to all these 'new, wonderful American citizens.' With oil prices down, it's going to put quite a strain on the Texas budget.

"Governor Black, being a liberal Democrat, you run things a little bit differently in California than we do here in Texas. We like to run a balanced budget. California hasn't run a balanced budget in two decades. I guess you reckon you're so bloated with debt, what's another billion here or there? I have a sister in Stockton, California. You know where Stockton is, Governor, or do you ever get out of Sacramento? To remind you, Stockton went bankrupt in 2012. My sister's husband not only lost his job, but even after thirty years of work, he lost his entire pension. My sister now has to bag groceries at Safeway. So, Governor, before you give us any more of your cheery liberal crap, maybe you want to think twice about who you represent. Maybe you should pay more attention to those hard-working individuals who have to do without, so you can put more people on the welfare rolls."

Governor Brewmeister chimed in, "Don't mean to pick on you, Governor Black, but since you threw down the gauntlet at beginning of the phone call, I'd like to second Richard's comments. We subscribe to the same philosophy here in Arizona. Our motto is 'It shouldn't be better at the bottom.' Last year, we conducted a survey in Arizona. What we found was shocking. Arizona's middle-income tier has had both its after-tax income and purchasing power shrink 10 percent over the last decade. But we found the exact the opposite for the lowest-tier residents. Those earning under $20,000 a year or earning nothing, who don't pay any taxes and who live completely off the welfare and entitlement programs, they saw their net incomes go up almost every single year. Hence, 'It shouldn't be better at the bottom.' We don't think we should be taxing and withholding programs that support our hard-working middle-class workers—not only to their detriment but to the benefit of those who don't work."

California Governor Harry Black just laughed. "Well, Californians knew I was a tax-and-spend liberal when they elected me. Umm, let me see...how many times have they elected me as governor? If my math is correct, I've been elected governor almost as many times as all of you added together." He laughed again. "I've heard all you fiscally conservative Republicans. You said when I raised California income tax to the highest of any state in the nation that the corporations and high-paid executives would flee the state. Well, they're all still here. Silicon Valley is as healthy as ever. So eat your heart out. California's municipal bonds, even with our billions of dollars in debt, aren't rated that much worse than the rest of yours."

New Mexico's Judy Rodriguez said, "I think that just proves how corrupt the bond-rating agencies are. Look, I asked you all to join in this conference call, and I was hoping it wouldn't turn into a political debate like our last conference call. I was just hoping that we might share some success stories and discuss how we're all coping with the huge influx of the illegal aliens in the last month. I can only speak for my own state, but our National Guard, state highway patrol, and various municipal law-enforcement departments have gone almost bust in rounding up the new illegal entrants. There have been estimates that as many as three to four hundred thousand Mexicans crossed into the state of New Mexico in the last month. Please remember, we are a very sparsely populated state. We only have two million people in the entire state. If you want to talk about the pressure on social services, think of New Mexico, a poor state. And now I may have the president telling me that she's going to legalize this three to four hundred thousand illegal Mexicans in my state, and we have to provide for them?"

"Wow, Judy!" Governor Brewmeister said. "And I thought we had it bad here. Those are incredible statistics."

Governor Rodriguez continued. "We have been only able to round up around eight thousand of the suspected couple hundred thousand. I've heard every excuse under the sun: they moved to other states, we can't distinguish them from all the Mexicans already here, we don't know which ones are recent or previous illegals—the list goes on and on.

"Though all four of us govern states with a high percentage of Mexican populations, I clearly have the highest percentage. My staff suspects that as these Mexicans entered the United States, a lot of them went to states where they had family or close friends. So what do you think happened when they got there? Their friends and family took them all in. It's the only way we can explain how one day there was tens of thousands of them in the streets, and within a week, they were all gone.

"If they were truly gone, we would be happy. But we all know, legalized or not, they will all be showing up at the welfare counters in the coming months. You all know that I am Mexican, but I am an American first. And as much as I love my fellow Hispanic New Mexicans and even those Mexicans living in Mexico, this is not fair. I for one think it's a sad day for America, and I am very afraid of the precedent set for Americans' futures. I'm not just dealing with illegal Mexicans but all illegal aliens. Europe is currently imploding because of their decades of liberal immigration policies relating to Muslims. This is a horrible precedent."

Governor Black was itching to get in the last word, detesting the crap he had to take from the other governors. "Judy, aren't you being a hypocrite? New Mexico, along with California, filed a brief defending Obama's Mexican amnesty plan."

Everyone heard a click, and Governor Rodriguez was off the call.

Chapter 119

It was 4:00 a.m. and Craig was in the kitchen. He thought the whole family could use something a little special, so he was making his famous apple fritters. He put beer in the batter and liked to make it a couple of hours early so that the batter got all bubbly.

In walked Elizabeth still in her bathrobe. "I smelled the coffee, and I knew that meant that you were up. I was hoping I could catch you before all the others awake. Do you mind if we talk a bit?"

"I've got all the time in the world. I'm all ears."

"I just need to get something off my chest. I know you know how much I loved Mark and how close we were. And so I know you can appreciate how much pain I'm going through from his loss. But there's more. I spent thirty years married to Mark thinking we had a perfect marriage, both here and in heaven. I thought we had a storybook marriage. Our two oldest boys graduated from good schools and have great jobs. And even though Madeleine got pregnant, I think her having little Ricky and living with us may turn out to be the best thing that ever happened to her. And because Mark did so well in his trucking business, we had everything in life anyone could dream of. But I only recently learned just how wrong I was. And the funny thing is, as I now think about my closest friends, I think so many of them are as blind as I was."

Craig turned from his kitchen duties so he could face Elizabeth. "I'm not exactly catching your drift."

Elizabeth sighed. "I lost Mark long before we came here. Sure, we were going through all the motions of a happily married couple. We crossed all our t's and dotted all our i's.

"You know, I always thought that you had such an empty life because even though you'd been married twice, you never had children. I want to apologize to you. I don't mean to imply that I regret in any way that we had three kids. But somewhere along in life, I got misdirected. I know I must not be making any sense."

She paused. It was clear to her that she had not had enough time to think all this out, with so much going on since her conversation at the airport with Mark. But she had lain awake most of the last two nights thinking about nothing else, nothing else but the conversation with her dead husband at the Phoenix airport.

"I lost my husband. I lost my husband because I failed to follow my wedding vows. You know the words—you've been married twice."

Craig could tell this was getting serious. He turned the burner off on the bacon; it could wait. He filled up his coffee and pulled up a chair next to Elizabeth. "It's funny you should say that, because just the other day I was saying how it seems that nobody today takes wedding vows seriously. But how do you mean it?"

"I promised to love and cherish. Don't get me wrong—there was never a moment in our thirty years together that I did not love Mark with all my heart. And I always thought that our love grew with each year we were together. I could never have made it without him. But were we in love? It's hard to look back at the first two years we were married, before we had children, but that's what I've been doing the last couple of days. Our relationship then was passionate, invigorating, stimulating, and all encompassing. I would get goose bumps if Mark would just enter the room. And I'm not being unrealistic. I know with age two people can't be as infatuated with each other as they were when they were dating. I may be a devout Christian, but even some of my friends in Bible study joke a bit on the subject."

She turned toward the living room door; she wanted to make sure no one had woken and begun listening. "The mistake that I only recently learned I've been making is that all that love and cherishing that I promised, on our wedding day, to give to Mark, I transferred to the kids. It just seemed so natural at the time. It just seemed like that's the way all my friends did it. The woman takes care of the children, and the husband goes to work and provides for the family.

"Honestly, I was totally fulfilled. I was getting all the happiness and love I needed. Sure, Mark was there when I needed him, but what I didn't realize is that I was getting most of my love from and giving most of my love to the children. Mark got left out. I was just too busy to notice.

"And now comes the worst part of it. My two oldest boys are gone. Yes, we talk every other week on phone. They have careers and girlfriends, and that's the way it should be. I'm not sure I would be able to go back to an empty home, but luckily since Madeleine and little Ricky are living with me, I have some family to return to. But eventually she too will graduate and move on. And then where will I be?"

Craig started to interrupt, but she stopped him. "But I'm not just saying this because Mark was killed. I've only now realized, even if Mark was here and still alive, it was going to be strange. For almost thirty years, Mark and I have been more like college roommates than lovers. All my love and attention went to the kids. I'm not saying if I could have started all over again that I wouldn't have three children. But I can assure you, I wouldn't throw my husband under the bus again." And she started crying. "And only now as I look back, I realize just how wonderful Mark was to not complain as to what was happening to our love. To his credit, he did on occasion give me hints to his frustration, but frankly I was just so into the kids that I was blind to my actions."

"Elizabeth, I'm speechless. I'm not even sure I'm capable of responding. As you pointed out, children were never a part of either of my marriages. I can only comment on the second part. I know you think I'm a hard man. But I'm no harder on others than I am on myself. And, yes, I have a lot of hobbies and interests, and I have a tendency to totally engross myself in my work. But I love being in love. I love women. I love them for who they are, and I love how they make me feel. Why do you think even after my two horrible divorces, I spend so many my evenings in the company of women? It's because I love having them as a part of my life.

They both grabbed each other's hands and held them tightly. And then Elizabeth said, "I'm going to ask Marcie if she would like to come live with me in Phoenix. I think she has another year of high school. And who knows, maybe she and Madeleine will become good friends, and she will consider going to college at ASU and maybe even living at home with me. That way I can extend my family a few more years."

"That's a fabulous idea. If there's anything I can do to help, let me know. You know, she's staying with my grad-school buddy at LSU in Baton Rouge. I was thinking of flying there and renting a car and driving back to their home in Houston. I don't know if it got damaged in all the recent happenings are not. I know with Cliff being in finance that there is quite an estate and a lot of life insurance. Marcie will be set for the rest of her life. We should stay in close communication to see what, if any, of Cliff's belongings you might want to take. Whatever is left, I'm sure David can use some to set up a new home here in Albuquerque."

Elizabeth look shocked. "Dave's moving to Albuquerque?"

"Yes, I'm ninety percent sure I have convinced him. But if you don't mind, I have someone else I need to talk to before everyone wakes up. But thank you for sharing your intimate feelings with me. I think all of this is going to bring the two of us much closer together in the future."

With that, Craig snuck into one of the bedrooms, where Jennifer was sleeping in one bed and Madeleine and little Ricky were sleeping in the other. He awakened her and asked her to join him in his office. She got up quietly, put on a bathrobe that he had lent her, and followed him into his office.

After a brief hug, he sat down with her on the sofa and spoke very quietly so as to not wake the others. "I think it's time that you and I had another little talk. I haven't slept much the last couple nights, with the death of my two brothers and everything else that's been going on here. Everything is such a blur. But I want you to know it's you I've been thinking about mostly the last couple nights, not my brothers.

"Let me start by saying that you know how much I love you. And you know that I think the world of you. I think you're one of the most wonderful, unique women I've ever met. And though I would love to turn back time and erase all that has taken place in this house, fate is funny. And I think all of us coming together here like this, under so much stress and so much death, has forced me to look at things like I've never looked at them before."

He once again took her in his arms and gave her a big hug. "Though I know we've had a wonderful time together, I want to apologize for some of the pain I caused you. My resentment and mistrust of women was because of how horribly I was treated by my two wives. I know that has caused me to act in a manner and maybe at times say things that were unfair. But I am now ready. I'm ready for a commitment."

Now it was Jennifer who grabbed Craig in a big bear hug.

He pushed her back quickly. "I think you best let me finish. I have been racking my brain for over a decade trying to figure out why my two marriages didn't work. Me, Mr. PhD, Mr. Graduated at the Top of His Class, Mr. Summa Cum Laude, a man who prides himself on trying to always be right. Look." He pointed to the motto pinned to the bulletin board above his desk. "See what it says—'How to win arguments: start by being right.' Mr. Logical, Mr. Rational, Mr. Intellectual. How could I have failed so miserably twice? And maybe it was for that very reason. I was too logical.

"But don't get me wrong. I was madly in love with both of my wives, and I thought they were in love with me. But the old saying 'Love conquers all' is just a flat lie. Love can only get you so far. You know how I am always making lists about everything. Well, before I married either of my wives, I had a list, a list of what I wanted in a woman. And you might think it surprising that they both scored a hundred on my list. I went to the marriage altar twice thinking I would be happily married for the rest of my life. I had perfect women, and they were perfect because they scored so high on my list—smart, witty, attractive, professional, athletic. You know the list—you score perfectly on it also."

For the first time, Jennifer didn't like what she heard. She was smart. Craig had just not only compared her to his two previous failed marriages, he had indicated that she'd scored the same as his ex-wives. That was not a good omen. She scooted back a little farther away on the sofa.

"It's not a list," he continued. "There is no perfect list. Everyone talks about how important it is to have things in common. And those are what fill people's lists. There is a professor I'm friends with that I see every once in a while at the swimming pool, and after a few laps we sometimes share stories in the steam room. He's been divorced for quite a few years, and he spends his time utilizing those matchmaking Internet services. He says the matchmaking is all about the lists required by the dating sites. You fill out list after list. He says his experiences are somewhere between comedy and horror. He can't believe the matches that are made. He wonders if the lists are ever even utilized. He said some of the women he's paired up with couldn't be more opposite."

Craig stood up for a minute and paced a bit. "I'll tell you what it's about. It's wavelength. And you can't put wavelength on a list. It's where your head's at. It's how your brain works."

Craig noticed that Jennifer was looking both confused and exasperated. "Let me try this differently. For most people, Sunday morning is the one time in the entire week that they have absolutely nothing on their schedule. Monday through Friday we all have to work. Saturday we all have to do our errands and clean our homes and mow our yards. Ignoring those religious folks who have to jump out of bed and go to church, for the rest of us, or should I say for most Americans, Sunday morning is the one time in the week when a person could or should be able to do exactly what they want to do."

Jennifer couldn't stand it anymore. "Craig, for somebody who usually makes so much sense, you're making no sense whatsoever. What are you trying to say?"

"I know you hate when I talk about my previous wives, but let me tell you what light bulb has gone off in my head in the last week or so. I finally realized why, at least with one of my wives, we were never going to be happily married. Here was the perfect Sunday morning for my ex: sleep late, cuddle in bed, eat breakfast in bed while reading the Sunday newspaper and one or two girly magazines, cuddle more. All the while still in your pajamas and not even getting out of the bedroom till sometime after noon. You know me, Jennifer. What's the perfect Sunday morning for me? Out of bed by 5:00 a.m., quick cup of coffee and a sweet roll, a quick perusal of the latest international news on my computer, out for a five-mile jog with the dogs. Fix that loose hydraulic hose on the tractor. Quick shower, jogging, tennis and whatever, and it's not even noon. It's a mental thing. It's an attitude thing. It's libido. It's wavelength."

"Okay, Mr. Logical. Where do I fit into all this? Sure, I like to sleep a bit later, and sure I prefer *Cosmopolitan* or the *New Yorker* to your *Wall Street Journal*, and maybe I do like to be lazy on Sunday. But I think I match up perfectly everywhere else."

It was time for Craig to finally drop the bombshell. "Two things have happened over the last couple days, neither of which was planned or purposeful. Quite the opposite. First of all, I've had more intimate contact with my family in the last four days than I've had in the last twenty-five years. It affected me. It made me feel older. It made me feel more vulnerable. And it created some fear, some fear of being alone.

"You've heard me say before that I don't think anyone can be happy with anyone else if they can't be happy alone, alone with themselves. But I'm almost sixty, and before you know it I'm going to be seventy, then I'm going to be eighty. I don't have any children. I don't want any children. But I don't want to be alone when I'm seventy and eighty. I want to be married again, but this time I want to make sure it lasts, as the vows say, 'till death do us part.'"

Jennifer didn't know how to react. She was getting such mixed signals, she figured she just better be quiet.

"And now for the second thing I learned. I'm going to ask Katherine Lacey to marry me."

He stopped, mainly because he was shocked. He had been expecting a bloodcurdling scream or some hysterical crying, but Jennifer offered neither. She just sat and stared.

"Please believe me when I say I never planned this, but having the both of you under the same roof for the last few days has given me the opportunity to do some comparative analysis," he said. "But before you get your dander up, let me repeat what I said at the beginning. I love you, I love you still, and I still think you're one of the most amazing women I've ever met. And I know we could continue to have lots of wonderful times together in the future.

"But I want to settle down. I want to settle down permanently. I don't want any more open questions, and more importantly, I don't want to and I'm not willing to take any more risk. Katherine Lacey is more like me than you are. And I'm not going to be able to explain that to you now or ever. But more importantly, I think it's best that I don't. I want us to part with you remembering that I think you are as close to perfect as a woman can be. It's just that Katherine is more...my wavelength. Inasmuch as I know this fact will upset you, it may be for no other reason than the fact that she is my age. You may think that's unfair, an unfair comparison. Well, let me assure you, she thinks the fact that you are thirty years younger than her is likewise an unfair comparison. As much as she tries, she can't compete with you in that area. Mother Nature is unfair in that way. But she has thirty years of experiences you don't have, and a lot of her past experiences are similar to mine. She has grown into the woman she is because of those trials and tribulations. And lucky for me, she is now a woman with a mindset, an attitude, an opinion, and a persona that are very close to my own. And if she will have me, I want to ask her to spend the rest of her life with me."

Jennifer stood up and stopped Craig in his tracks. "Do you wonder why I'm not crying? You're not going to get an argument from me. You know how you're always complimenting me on how perceptive you think I am. Well, don't you think I saw the look on your face as you observed

Katherine and how well she's gotten along with your family? She took over in the kitchen and was such help to your mother. And most of all, how she risked her life trying to save Mark? I saw the disappointment in your face when I was unable and unwilling to take that gun.

"I'll let you in on a little secret, Professor. I would have been shocked and maybe, just maybe, a little disappointed in you if you hadn't made this decision. I knew, with our almost thirty years' difference, that as the decades passed, the differences were going to be accentuated. And I let my love for you blind me. But I love you more than you will ever know. And I love you so much that I would rather lose you than have you lose someone like Katherine. Oh, yes, it's probably the better match. And I want to thank you. Because of you, I think I will not make the mistakes that so many people make in trying to find a partner. Love is a must. Sex is wonderful. But you have taught me there is more—there is so much more."

They stood and kissed liked they'd never kissed before, and it was Jennifer who was in control.

She finally pushed him back just a bit and said, "But you know, Professor, you've ruined me. I might be single for a very long time. How can I settle for anything less when I now know how great it can be?"

Chapter 120

"Professor Walther, can you hear me okay? This is Senator Ted Boone."

"I hear you loud and clear, Senator."

"Craig, since you and I know each other, let me introduce everybody else here in the conference room. But first, let me thank you for agreeing to speak to all of us on such short notice. I know you've been up to your armpits with all the problems there in Albuquerque. And I want to thank you for once again being willing to help me and this distinguished group of congressmen and senators I have compiled here today. And, of course, to help our nation that is in such disarray on this border issue.

"We have with us Representative Steve King from Iowa, Senator Jeff Sessions from Alabama, and Bob Goodlate, Representative from Virginia. Now I've told everyone here in the room about our previous discussions, and I've shown them your books on America's historical relationship with Mexico and the border itself. Other than being probably the most knowledgeable guy in the country, you really garnered credibility with them when I told them that you had predicted this entire blowup on the border years ago. Now, we don't have any set agenda today. But I will tell you why this conference call is so incredibly important.

"There is a strong indication that President Denton is going to announce maybe as soon as this week that she is going to make every single illegal Mexican alien living in this country an immediate American citizen with all rights. There is a large group of us, both from Congress and from the Senate, that is going to move for impeachment if she takes that step. If we have time, we can talk about that a bit later. I don't expect you to comment much on that, as it's pretty much up to us politicians. But between her administration's total mishandling of the recent border invasion and the fact that she's going to go against the Constitution and do an end run around Congress to make all these Mexicans immediate American citizens, we feel strongly she's committed impeachable offenses.

"Now, with that little introduction, why don't you take over and kindly give us an overview of where you see things right now?"

Steve King jumped in first. "I just want to say, Professor Walther, that when I heard we were going to be having this conference call, I speed-read both of your more recent books. All I can say is it was a sad day for America when you decided to leave Washington, DC. Maybe if you had remained and opened more eyes here in Washington to the real problems, maybe we would've accomplished something, as opposed to having it blow up in our faces."

"Thank you, sir, and why don't we drop the formalities and everyone can just call me Craig? I wish I could be as optimistic as you in thinking if I had stayed in Washington, I could've made a difference. It was for that very fact that I left Washington in the first place. After twenty years in Washington, I found our nation's capital is maybe the world's most perfect example of legislative procrastination. It was too frustrating a place for an action-oriented individual like me. But that's a subject for another day."

Craig took a drink of water. "In my twenty years on Capitol Hill and eight years at Georgetown, I feel I received an excellent working knowledge of the myriad of federal agencies and departments. And that would include their management, operation, and effectiveness. It is my educated opinion that our government's handling of the US-Mexican border and the entire immigration issue relating to Mexico is somewhere between a comedy of errors and a complete atrocity. For the last forty years, every administration has dealt with the border issue with either lip service or chest beating, depending on the election cycle.

"I appreciate that all of you on the phone are Republicans. I am a registered Republican, but I prefer to call myself a fiscal conservative. I agree with you wholeheartedly that the Obama administration and now the Denton administration have totally exacerbated the problem. But the Republicans are not blameless. Your party has held Congress, the Senate, and the White House and failed, just as the Democrats have failed, in ever taking any meaningful steps. I don't need to tell you that. But let's not fool ourselves. It has been this volleyball politicizing of significant national issues that ultimately caused the complete breakdown at the border. And I agree with you, it only adds insult to injury for the president to just now wave a magic wand and make them all American citizens."

Jeff Sessions spoke up. "I for one will apologize—for myself, for my colleagues, and even for our previous elected officials. We have failed the American public completely. But if you visit my website and read some of my proposed legislation, I hope you will think kindly of me. I am trying. We are trying. That's why we need your help. And we are running out of time."

Craig said, "I appreciate that, Senator. I know that, and it is why I agreed to this conference call. There is no way I'm going to be able to list all the problems and challenges. They are so incredibly monumental, and that's what the purpose of my books was. Let me see if I can encapsulate what I see as some of the most pressing issues today.

"Let me start at the end and work backward. I believe the entire problem can be summed up in one sentence: America for decades has presented to the country of Mexico an open invitation. Of course, the recent No Mexicans Zone, the NMZ, is a major change. We will talk about that later. But let's talk about how we got here. Because I'm afraid, and I'm very serious about this, that we are going to go back to where we were.

"Why do I say it has been an open invitation? For those who cross into the country illegally, the chance of being apprehended is somewhere between 25 to 30 percent. Then the chance that you will be released, and I mean released here in the United States, runs around 50 percent. The 50 percent that are sent back to Mexico are released to a government that doesn't want them back. Something around 40 percent of all the Mexicans caught entering this country illegally and returned to Mexico come right back into the United States, many of them repeatedly. Eventually, it is a win-win game for those who enter the country illegally. Even if they fail at first, persistence will reward them.

"And now let's look at the other side of the equation, maybe the single most important part of the equation."

Craig caught his breath. "There was an excellent book I read in college entitled *Crime Pays*. It was a book on white-collar crime in the United States. It outlined that the financial rewards for perpetrating financial crime are so incredibly high in proportion to the chance of being caught that it is worth the risk. In other words, crime pays. The author argued that the main reason white-collar crime has been ever increasing in this country is because it's a smart business decision.

"This is an excellent analogy for those Mexicans entering this country illegally: it's a very smart business decision. I already pointed out that the risk of being caught is low, and worst case, you're just sent back. But now let's look at the rewards. If you have a copy of one of my books available, look at some of the most recent charts. In almost every comparison, the United States is ten times the country that Mexico is. None of us is surprised by that fact. But do you think for a second, with American television and movies playing 24-7 in every Mexican home, Mexicans don't realize the disparity?

"It's not just that this is a much more wonderful place to live—on just about every single creature-feature comparison you can think of—it's that we have morphed into a socialist society. Between the welfare and other entitlement programs in this country, a Mexican family can move to this country, never work another day in their lives, and live like kings and queens.

"You know the numbers. Before the additional four million Mexicans flooded across the border, we already had somewhere between twelve to eighteen million Mexicans living here illegally. And we've had at least one million coming across the border illegally every year. And that doesn't even include the roughly half-million people who come here legally and then never leave.

"But I would put this question to you, for the reasons I just gave and the fact that crossing into United States has been a cakewalk for the last thirty years: why aren't the numbers even higher?"

Ted Boone spoke up for the first time. "Those are depressing statistics, Craig, and I've even heard that the numbers are worse. And I saw a CIA report the other day that said that revolutionary General Zapatista is continually gaining strength. And that is just one more factor putting pressure on people wanting to leave Mexico."

Sessions butted in. "Another one of my pet peeves is what they call 'labor dumping.' I don't know if any of you saw an article back in 2007 in *Forbes* by Steve Hanke, a professor of economics at John Hopkins and a senior fellow at the Cato Institute here in Washington. He said that Mexico is the world's largest labor dumper, that being the practice of countries sweeping their unemployed and less-productive individuals into other countries. He wrote that, more than those of any other country, the forty-seven Mexican consulates in the United States facilitated this sweeping by issuing passports and offering assistance when Mexican immigrants ran into trouble. He wrote that as far back as 2007, roughly 30 percent of Mexico's labor force was working in the United States and sending back home roughly $23 billion, which equals 12 percent of Mexico's exports."

Senator Boone said, "Since we are voicing our peeves, what the hell are we doing giving almost a billion dollars to Mexico in foreign aid? My God, in 2013 we gave $971 million in aid to a country that is shoving their unwanted into our country and costing us billions. I think we should tell Presidente Nieto he either gets serious about controlling the border from his side, or we cut him off totally from any aid whatsoever.

"Here's a story that shows you just how upside down things are. In early 2015, the state legislatures from the Mexican state of Sonora traveled to Tucson to complain about Arizona's new employer crackdown on illegals from Mexico.

It seems that many Mexican illegals who are returning to their hometowns in Sonora, consisting of mostly small towns, cannot handle the demand for housing, jobs, and schools because of the returning illegals.

Ted Boone continued, "I don't mean to steal your thunder, Professor Walther, but while I have the floor, I'd like to read a couple sections from a Special Report on immigration by the Heritage Foundation written on November 3, 2014 by a David Inserra. 'As the Heritage Foundation has outlined, the 'President cannot effectively amend a law by exempting entire categories of law breakers from the application of that law, particularly if done for political or policy reasons.' The Administration's current non-enforcement of US immigration laws damages the US's commitment to these principles of the rule of law...furthermore, not enforcing the law encourages more law breaking. As with amnesty, lax enforcement of US immigration laws sends a signal to would-be illegal immigrants that illegally entering or remaining in the US is an offense not likely to be punished by the US government. As a result, more unlawful immigration is encouraged, and more calls for lax enforcement and amnesty arise in this vicious cycle of nullification and lawlessness.'

"On page 6 of this report it says that 'In 2013, ICE released approximately 104,000 criminal aliens, many of whom were illegal immigrants. Of these 104,000 criminal aliens, 36,007 convicted aliens were freed from ICE custody during deportation proceedings, or even after they were over. These 36,007 criminal aliens accounted for 87,818 convictions, including at least 193 homicides, 426 sexual assaults, 2,510 burglaries, just over 5,000 cases of assault or battery, and just over 16,000 DUIs. While it is not certain how many of these individuals were here illegally, most of these individuals were in deportation proceedings and should have been detained or at least more closely supervised and monitored until their deportation order was finalized and executed.'

"I've read that piece and I'm very familiar with it," Craig said. "It is one of the more powerful reports on this issue in my library. Prior to the NMZ, any and all attempts at securing the border have been a joke, a complete joke. You have hundreds and hundreds of miles where there is no fence, barrier, or obstacle whatsoever. In much of Texas, there's nothing but the mere Rio Grande. Where do you think the term 'wetbacks' came from? I would sure swim across a small river for all the benefits we have in America.

"And let's talk about our recently constructed fences. I hope you've all seen the photos. You had a brand-new, expensive, twenty-foot metal fence that just ended. All one needed to do was walk around it. And let me comment on that. You may think these are stupid Mexicans. They are anything but stupid. The message that our country has been sending to them for decades is one of incompetency, a message of complacency. Do you think anyone in Mexico, from the president down to the lowest dirt farmer, thinks our country is really serious about deterring illegal entry? For something around seven hundred miles, we had no barriers at all. And the barriers we had just terminated in the middle of a field. We looked like fools. I repeat again, it was an open invitation."

Senator Sessions said, "I was one of the major supporters of the 2006 Secure Fence Act. It authorized the building of seven hundred miles of fencing. I wish I could explain why we only built thirty-six of the seven hundred miles."

Craig didn't give the senator a chance. "And let's look at some statistics. There's the DACA program that Washington passed. In 2014 alone, 66,127 children came to this country from Mexico and were allowed to enter legally. There was a 412 percent increase in families coming into this country under that program, legally. And though both presidents promised those families weren't necessarily going to be made US citizens, that was a lie.

"And I love the statistics that the Department of Homeland Security keeps putting out. Again in 2014 they stated that something around half a million Mexicans entered the country illegally. Don't you just want to laugh when you hear that number? You first have to ask yourself, if they are entering illegally, how does anyone know the number? But more important is that this figure is woefully short. Most knowledgeable people estimate the number that enters each year illegally is something closer to three to four times that."

Craig was on a roll. "And here is a separate point. There was an article in July 2013 in the *Weekly Standard* by Fred Barnes. He pointed out that nearly two-thirds of immigrant visas go to relatives of existing residents, under an expansive definition of 'family preference' that includes not just spouses and minor children but parents, siblings, and unmarried adult children. There was a similar article in the *Wall Street Journal* in January 2015 discussing presidential candidate Jeb Bush's liberal policies toward immigration. It pointed out that since the 1970s, America has become the only nation whose immigration system is primarily based not on work and skills but on family preferences. It pointed out the same statistic, that nearly two-thirds of the million legal immigrants each year come through some kind of 'family preference' program and that hundreds of thousands safely arrive, thanks to the expanded definition of 'family' in the current immigration laws. That only leaves 13 percent of visas that are available for those wanting to come and work here and bring valuable skills.

"But what do you expect when the *New York Times* ran an editorial that urged that 'American immigration policy should give priority to the world's neediest refugees'? You have in both the past Obama administration and the current Denton administration politicians who want to give American jobs to illegal and legal aliens for Democratic votes. Let me quote an article titled 'Amnesty for Unamerica.' It said, 'The immigration system is broken because it was reformed so many times that it makes as much sense as an outhouse on a space shuttle. Its main function now is to bring millions of people without jobs to a country where millions are out of work.'"

Bob Goodlate injected, "I have a question on the drug trafficking. I have three teenagers, and this is one of my biggest concerns for America's youth. What is your opinion on the progress we're making there?"

"The numbers are not good, Congressman. This year alone, the DEA estimates a record number of pounds of marijuana being imported to the United States from Mexico, seventeen million. I can't even begin to address all the problems we have concerning the drug traffic from Mexico. But let me make a point you might not have heard of. The drug cartels in Mexico are also tied directly to the traffic of illegals into this country. It is a side business for them, and it is very lucrative. But the drug cartels have a secondary motive of both encouraging and helping the illegal traffic of Mexicans across our border. For those US counties on the border, the cost on not only the various federal agencies but on the various state agencies and the law-enforcement and sheriff departments is overwhelming. So much of their resources are expended fighting the human trade that there's little leftover to fight the drug trade.

"And let me make an additional comment on this last point. Ever since the Obama administration's policy, which has been continued by the Denton administration, of the federal government refusing to enforce the immigration laws, an incredible burden has been placed on the local law-enforcement agencies in the four border states."

Ted Boone said, "I can personally attest to that, being a senator from Texas. I don't think a week goes by that I don't have a police department or a sheriff's office call my office and complain that they have to do the federal government's job, and they just don't have the resources."

"I understand, Ted. Again it's back to what I said earlier—the incentives are just too great. This country has got to take the incentives away from entering this country illegally. Those of you on the Judiciary Committee will appreciate this. The first thing our nation needs to recognize is that each and every single man, woman, and child—and I repeat, *child*—who crosses that border without proper documentation is entering the country illegally. They are breaking the law. It is a felony.

"Recent statistics show that a decent percentage of criminal activity conducted in the United States is being done so by those living in this country illegally. As the Heritage

Foundation Report that was read pointed out. I think it's one of the most alarming statistics. But sadly, it's not surprising. Once a person breaks the law, breaking the law the second time is just not that big a deal. I know they refer to it in the criminal justice system as the 'recidivism rate,' or they refer to the people as 'repeat offenders.' It's not just that they cross the border illegally, but each and every day they stay here, they are well aware that they are breaking the law. So what's the big deal of breaking one more law? And what will happen if they are caught? We'll just send them back to Mexico, and then they will just come back here.

"By not enforcing our laws about illegal immigration in this country, we send a strong message to those millions of Mexicans who continue to come here illegally that the United States is not a country of laws. Or put another way, we are a country of laws that we don't enforce. Here in America, we refer to Mexico as a lawless society. To the Mexicans coming here illegally and even legally, America now feels like the same lawless country they left."

Senator Sessions interrupted again. "I agree with you, Craig. I am appalled by this entire criminal element issue. But President Denton, like Obama, just brushes it all under the rug. I have statistics from the FBI that sixty-eight thousand illegal Mexican aliens living in the United States with multiple criminal violations have been released back into our society. It's bad enough that the Mexican government encourages their sick and poor to emigrate to the United States—that gets a lot of hungry mouths off their hands. But the worst part is they are pushing their criminal elements across the border.

"Sure, they give us lip service and swear they are not participating in that activity. But we have tens of thousands, maybe hundreds of thousands, of examples of quite the opposite. And even if the Mexican government was willing to help us identify those Mexicans who enter our country both legally and illegally with criminal records, it still wouldn't fix the problem. Some 80 percent of the Mexicans who enter this country illegally come with no identification at all. That problem is exacerbated when you have states like California that are issuing legal driver's licenses to known illegal aliens with no identification at all."

If Craig could only have seen the rapt attention those in the conference room were giving him.

"I hope you're all aware that a very large percentage of the Mexicans living in this country illegally didn't originally cross the border illegally," Craig continued. "They crossed into the country through one of the various legal programs or visas. Yet the immigration department admits that over 40 percent of the Mexicans who enter this country legally overstay their visas. And because our immigration department is somewhere between incompetent and inept, these illegals go undetected, much less apprehended and deported.

"But back on the incentives. You guys have got to keep it in perspective. Let's take the border between the United States and Canada—it's 3,987 miles, not including the 1,538 mile border between Canada and Alaska. That's double the length of the border with Mexico. Ask yourself, why are there hardly any fences at all between the United States and Canada? It is because, for the vast majority of Canadians, they have no interest in emigrating to the United States. Their standard of living in many cases is higher than here in the United States."

Representative Goodlate said, "I never really thought of it that way. But so many of the liberals in Congress incite their liberal base that we should let the Mexicans in for humanitarian reasons. They even try to pull the heartstrings by quoting the plaque on the Statue of Liberty. You know: 'Give me your tired, your poor...' But there are seven billion people in the world today. Just think of the living standards in such places as India, Central America, and worst of all, Africa. I don't care how humanitarian you want to be—we are not boundless. The liberals forget we haven't had a balanced budget in a decade. Every extra dollar we spend, we either print or borrow, and eventually both are going to bite us in the butt. And I'm not making excuses for our lack of ever putting together a meaningful program to stop the illegal entries, but when we have to fight the liberal press, liberal politicians, and the let's-feed-the-world California crazies, it's an uphill battle and has been for decades."

As a round of "we agree" between the representatives and senators could be heard, Craig started back in. "I wish I could take credit for the famous quote, 'A nation without borders is not a nation,' but I have to give that credit to Ronald Reagan. It's so dead on, I quote him in both my books. Not having a meaningful, secure border demeans the very fabric of our country. And the list of benefits of having a secure border alone would fill an entire book.

"As I'm sure you are all aware, in 2015, federal judge Hanen at first struck down Obama's attempt to legalize so many Mexicans. I've probably quoted some words from his ruling one hundred times that, 'the DHS should enforce the laws of the United States – not break them.'

"Let's talk about another one here: OTMs, or Other Than Mexicans. The US customs department estimates that an ever-increasing percentage of those individuals crossing into the United States across the Mexican border are not Mexicans. Many of these OTMs are coming from countries that the state department qualifies as 'countries not particularly friendly to the best interest of the United States,' such as Honduras, Syria, and Venezuela. It is a long list. "And though we can debate for hours on end whether Mexico is a third-world country or not, there is no doubt these OTMs definitely are coming from third-world countries whose healthcare systems are somewhat Neanderthal. These illegal aliens are bringing all kinds of infectious diseases with them across the border. It is only a matter of time before there's a serious outbreak in the United States brought in from one of these illegal aliens, who by definition come in completely undetected, much less tested. Look what happened just in the last couple of years when there was the outbreak of Ebola in Guinea and Liberia. The liberal Obama administration refused to block flights from those countries."

"I was as mad as a hornet over that," Senator Goodlate interrupted. "But what else would we expect, when our past president was in fact from Africa?"

King said, "The CIA reports may be the worst news on the subject of the OTMs. A larger and larger percent are Muslims. Though no one will go on record from Homeland Security, numerous high-ranking officials have told me behind closed doors that they received specific directives from Obama to do whatever it takes to allow more Muslims into this country. And it appears that directive is still taking place under President Denton. But again, why should we be surprised? In Barack Hussein Obama's book, *The Audacity of Hope*—hell, I even can remember the page number. On page 261, Obama wrote, 'I will stand with the Muslims should the political winds shift in an ugly direction.' Not to mention his regularly quoting the Quran and saying that he thinks the Azan, the Islamic call to worship, is the most beautiful sound on earth."

Sessions got into the fray. "I can fully understand why Mexicans don't try to enter this country legally when it is just so much easier to waltz across the border. Or, as you pointed out, to just come to the country legally on one of the various visa programs and then just never leave. But I guess the most frustrating to those of us, like yourself, who consider ourselves fiscal conservatives and want to see our nation reestablish itself as the greatest, most prosperous nation in the world, is our backward immigration policy of favoring the sick, tired, poor, and homeless. It seems we do everything we can to keep out the intellectuals, the academics, the scientists, and the wealthy industrialists and entrepreneurs. It's probably the single most destructive policy, other than our policies on the border itself, that we currently have in this country. But ever since the Obama administration attempted to instill in this country that the successful and wealthy are evil, greedy capitalists, until we get a conservative in the White House and replace all these bleeding-heart liberals in each and every department of the federal government, we're stuck with this system."

"You're right about that, Jeff," said King. "My bill, the English Language Unity Act, was killed by the liberal Democrats before it even got to the floor. There are millions of

Americans who believe, as I do, that there is no more unifying force in the world than a common form of communication. Every sovereign nation state including the Vatican has at minimum an official language. My English Language Unity Act would provide consistency among Americans by requiring all official functions of the United States to be conducted in English, establishes a uniform language requirement for naturalization, and places an obligation on the federal government to encourage individuals to both learn and speak English. We never had this language problem going back to the immigrants in the late 1800s and early 1900s. It's only been over the last couple of decades that we have had large blocks of immigrants who basically refuse to assimilate. And we all know, watching what's been happening in Europe, that the Muslims are the worst."

Craig was able to get back in. "Gentlemen, I applaud all of you. There's only one problem—there's not enough legislators in Washington who feel like you do."

Senator Sessions said, "Professor Walther, that may be the most depressing part of all of it. You are right—there are not enough logical conservatives in Washington. But poll after poll shows that the American people are behind the conservative opinions on all of the subjects we have been discussing here today. Let me share some statistics with everyone. I purposely pulled these polls from when Obama was president to show that the American people have opposed not just what President Denton is doing now, but even what President Obama was doing then." Senator Sessions then read off the results of compelling polls and public opinions on immigration and the US-Mexican border issue.[1]

Senator Sessions continued. "The American people are clearly behind those of us in Congress who want to solve this problem. But it's sort of like Obamacare. President Obama and his liberal administration jammed it down the American throats even when they didn't want it. But I can tell you, ever since the border was breached a month ago, my office has received thousands of phone calls from patriotic Americans all across the nation wanting to help. They were so mad that those of us in Washington ad not called out the military and the National Guard that they wanted to form an army of their own to go down and help the border states.

"You know, it's kind of funny. One guy from Wyoming called me because he's aware of my being the ranking member on immigration policy. He said that the citizens of Wyoming have the highest rate of gun ownership in the country, at 59 percent. Then he gave me another statistic I didn't know. He said if you took the number of gun owners in just a few states, such as Michigan, South Dakota, Oklahoma, and a few others, it would be one of the largest armed militaries in the world. He was proposing they march on the border.

"Guess who else I got a call from. Ted Nugent. I guess a number of people from all over the country had been calling him, asking him to form a group to come to the aid of their fellow Americans in the border states. I even got a call from Phil Robinson from the TV show *Duck Dynasty*. I guess he was getting the same calls Ted Nugent was. They were all Americans who were mad at the inaction of the Denton administration and thought it was time that Americans came to the aid of fellow Americans in the border states. I have to tell you, I found it quite moving."

There was a lull and Craig interjected, "Gentlemen, if you don't mind, I have one more key point I'd like to talk about for a moment. I know you may think I'm picking on Washington, and maybe I am. God knows they deserve it. It's the issue of NAFTA, the North America Free Trade Agreement. Some of your previous legislators thought it would be an agreement that would solve many of the problems we have today. Frankly, in my opinion and in the opinion of many other academics and professionals, it has been to a large degree a disaster, depending exactly on whose frame of reference you are considering. In 2014, it had its twenty-year anniversary—it was enacted in 1994 between United States and Mexico.

"Since this call is about Mexico, let me start there. Since NAFTA was enacted, the per-capita growth in Mexico has averaged 1.2 percent over the last twenty years—that's the lowest in the entire hemisphere. Wage growth is down, and unemployment is up in Mexico. Some 25 percent of the people in Mexico don't have access to basic food needs, and malnutrition is rampant. NAFTA restricted Mexico from the tariffs they had been putting on the American grains that we ship to Mexico. The Mexican farmer has been greatly disadvantaged because the United States subsidizes American farmers, and I'm speaking most specifically about corn. Corn is the main staple in Mexico, being the main ingredient in tortillas. To the average Mexican, tortillas are what bread is to Americans and Europeans. Almost 1.5 million farm jobs have been lost due to NAFTA.

"Now let's talk about the disadvantages of NAFTA in the United States. To some degree, NAFTA has been a boon for American manufacturers, but it has been the opposite for American workers. Hundreds of thousands of jobs have been shifted just across the border by American manufacturers. It is estimated that between 1994 and 2010, around 682,900 jobs shifted from the United States to Mexico. Eighty percent of those jobs were in manufacturing, mostly from the border states, though New York and Michigan also contributed. A large percentage of those jobs were in motorized vehicles, textiles, computers, and electronic appliances. Where American manufacturers didn't shift work to Mexico, they used the threat of shifting jobs to Mexico to negotiate lower wages here in the states.

"Both President Obama and President Denton have been wrangling to pass the TPP, the Trans-Pacific Partnership. It is stylized much like NAFTA, and many argue it will also be disadvantageous to the American worker. Interesting, when you consider that the Democrats try to present themselves as friendly to American workers and unions."

"Now, there's something really close to my heart," Steve King burst in. "I'm not sure if you're aware of this, Craig, but I proposed legislation called the New IDEA, or Illegal Deduction Elimination Act, which would help protect American workers. New IDEA would make wages and benefits paid to illegal immigrants nondeductible for federal tax purposes. I have felt for years that one of the major ways to put a dent in illegal immigration is to take the incentives away from those US employers who purposely and knowingly hire illegal aliens, to the detriment of American workers. The Democrats and their liberal constituents always try to argue that Mexicans and other low-wage immigrants just take jobs that Americans refuse to take. I think that's always been a contradiction. But I can assure you, since unemployment the last decade has been much higher than previously, most Americans I know would prefer to work, even in low-skilled jobs.

"But I have some statistics that counter the liberals' argument that Mexicans don't come here to steal Americans jobs. If that were true, why during the 2008-through-2010 economic debacle in the United States, when unemployment shot through the roof, why did the number of Mexicans coming here both legally and illegally slow to its lowest level in decades?"

King continued. "And I've never agreed with this whole baby thing. It's been a complete con, and I don't know who's guiltier of this scam being played on Americans—the Mexican government or the bleeding-heart liberals here in America. Our laws say that anyone born here in the United States is automatically an American citizen with full rights, and that even includes when both parents are aliens. And worse, and a complete travesty, is when both those parents are not only aliens but also illegal aliens. Again, I agree with Professor Craig—it's an open invitation. We've got millions of Mexicans coming here illegally, just to have a child. Now they have a child who under the law is an American citizen with full rights. Then the parents apply to be citizens so they can stay here and support their American child. It's a mockery."

"Let me give you a statistic that makes it even worse," Craig responded. "Some 80 to 90 percent of the Mexicans who come to America are Catholic. They don't believe in birth control. But the statistics are that Mexican families living in America are having babies at a 50 percent higher rate than white American citizens. So the problem you were just talking about, Congressman, is exacerbated by these birth-rate numbers. If you add up all the Mexicans living here legally and illegally, which is estimated to be around eighty million, and then you pile on top of that their birth rate, you are looking at explosive numbers. When you consider that a vast majority of these people will be on welfare, you boys in Washington— let me rephrase that—*we Americans* are in deep trouble."

"I know, I know," chimed in Goodlate. "And we've heard testimony that illegal Mexicans living in this country are collecting tax refunds. Can you believe that? Tax refunds going to people who've never paid a dime in taxes and who aren't even legal citizens! And for those Mexicans entering the country who are seniors? Our liberal Social Security programs are even making Social Security payments to these illegal citizens. We tax Social Security payments from fourth- and fifth-generation Americans who've worked forty or fifty years helping build our nation, and yet we hand out free Social Security to illegal senior Mexicans who have never worked a day in their lives in this country and never will. It is completely out of control."

Representative Steve King said, "Oh, it's out of control, all right. President Obama, the one most responsible for the border invasion due to his amnesty program, was unbelievably contemplating in December 2014 sanctioning our most precious ally Israel over some minor violation. The guy was a nut, but worst of all he was a nut who thought he was king. And to follow his lead, President Denton may be planning on announcing with this across-the-board legalization that she is going to make Martínez DeCastro the head of the National Council of La Raza, a left-wing Hispanic advocacy group, as the latest czar.

"I think we should let Professor Walther go, and we need to talk about impeaching President Denton if she fulfills her threats immediately to legalize every single Mexican living in the country."

"That's fine with me, gentlemen. I really only had one last comment," said Craig. "And it's on the NMZ."

But before Craig could get started, Representative King butted in. "I might mention that, because of my background in construction, I proposed an amendment to build a massive concrete wall the entire two thousand miles. Of course, it went nowhere in Congress. But I will say this: I studied the five-mile NMZ that the US Air Force and US Army have now created, and I think it's brilliant, absolutely brilliant.

"Yes, Congressman, I agree with you 1,000 percent. This country should have done something like this decades ago. But here's something you need to think very, very seriously about. I am afraid that Washington, once again, is going to slip back into its malaise. If President Denton is elected for a second term, you can rest assured that your efforts to keep the border sealed will be almost impossible with the liberal onslaught. You must absolutely maintain the NMZ, whatever it takes. Because if, in fact, President Denton does legalize the tens of millions of Mexicans who are now living in this country illegally, I will repeat my opening line: you are sending an open invitation to Mexico. If you let the border once again become meaningless, this is my new prediction: the Mexicans who once again flood to our country illegally will increase tenfold."

1. "A Gallup poll recently found that 65 percent of Americans disapprove of Barack Obama's handling of immigration, while 68 percent opposed Obama's handling of illegal immigration in an Associated Press-GfK poll."

    "A recent Reuters poll found that 70 percent of Americans believe illegal immigrants 'threaten traditional US beliefs and customs,' while 63 percent felt that 'immigrants place a burden on the economy."

    "A Polling Company poll found that a majority of Americans wanted fewer immigrants and also that 90 percent of likely voters feel that 'US-born workers and legal immigrants already here should get first preference for jobs."

    "A majority of Americans opposed Obama's amnesty decree and support GOP efforts to defund it."

    "Paragon Insights found that 58 percent of registered voters opposed Obama's executive actions, compared to 36 percent in support. Fifty-three percent said they support

'Republicans in Congress taking away federal funding for this executive order,' with just 36 percent opposed."

"Americans in general, by a fifty-point margin, wanted tougher rules against hiring illegal immigrants, and that included a majority of Hispanics—56 percent to 37 percent."

"Sixty-two percent of US voters opposed Obama's plan to mainstream illegal immigrants via executive action. Only 24 percent now say Obama has the legal authority to change immigration policy without agreement from Congress. Just 26 percent are in favor of Obama's plan."

"Seventy-five percent of voters answering exit polls in the 2014 midterm elections reject Obama's executive decree amnesty plans, and 80 percent did not want foreign workers taking jobs from Americans."

"Ninety percent of Americans believe illegal immigration is a serious problem, and most want expedited deportations! This JUST WHEN YOU THOUGHT IT WAS SAFE 647 poll found that 67 percent of respondents felt that illegal immigration was an 'extremely serious' or 'very serious' problem. Another 22 percent felt it was a 'somewhat serious' problem, while only 10 percent said it was 'not too serious' or 'not at all serious.'"

"A majority of respondents said that illegal immigrant juveniles fleeing violence should not be given refugee status and feel the law should be changed so those not from Mexico and Canada can be more quickly deported."

"Seventy-one percent of Americans, including a majority of Democrats, say that illegal immigrant newcomers should NOT receive government benefits! Only 16 percent think 'they are entitled to government aid,' while 13 percent are undecided. A strong majority, 68 percent, also 'say the new illegal immigrants should not have the same legal rights and protections that US citizens have,' and that includes a plurality—and a near majority—of Democrats, 49 percent. The poll found that '89 percent of GOP voters and 70 percent of unaffiliated think illegals should not have the same legal rights and protections that US citizens have!'"

back

Chapter 121

It had been a long, arduous journey for Fernando and his wife, Carla. But Fernando never once felt sorry for the two of them. How could he? The entire time he was surrounded by tens of thousands of his countrymen. He now understood the phrase "misery loves company."

But Fernando was not happy that he was traveling to the United States with so many of his countrymen. It made him nervous. Sure, the current and previous presidents of the United States had promised that they were going to make millions of Mexicans legal citizens. But he suspected that American presidents weren't much different from those in Mexico; their promises were worth the paper they were written on. So the entire trip, Fernando had been constantly thinking, *How can I separate myself from the masses?*

By the time he crossed the border near Laredo, Texas, he had devised a plan. And he had one other distinct advantage over many of his compadres—he had over $1,000 hidden in his underwear. Of that, $500 was in US dollars, and the rest was in pesos. He had used it sparingly on the month-long trip, only drawing on it when they were close to starving. And he was always careful to make sure no one ever saw more than a few pesos at one time. It was not that Fernando didn't trust his fellow Mexicans, but he knew a man who was hungry would do things he otherwise would not.

The first part of his plan was to get as far away from the border as possible. There were just too many of his fellow countrymen. He needed to separate himself from them. He had seen killings along the way, and he knew there would probably be reprisals. Houston, Texas, was his destination. It was the perfect city for him and his wife for so many reasons. It was not only one of the largest cities in the entire Southwest; it was the oil capital of the world.

In the last month that Fernando had worked for PEMEX in Mexico City, he had been recognized by his superiors as being one of the smartest new employees. He had been transferred to the trading desk, trading oil futures. It was a natural fit for him. He found trading commodities no different from the stocks and options he'd been trading on the Mexican Stock Exchange for decades.

The other thing his superiors had been impressed with was that not only did Fernando have a college degree, in the early years when he was working at the Bolsa Mexicana de Valores, Fernando had gone back to night school and had gotten a master's degree in finance.

His plan now was simple. If Houston was the oil capital of the world, he could clearly score an excellent job, probably even a high-paying job.

Fernando realized he had one other major challenge for his plan to come to fruition. He needed identification. He did not want to wait and hope that the current president would make him a US citizen. Things could easily change, with the huge flood of his fellow countrymen into the United States. No, he wanted to secure a job now, but to do that he would need either a false birth certificate or a US driver's license. He had heard from some of his fellow travelers that California was issuing legal driver's licenses to Mexicans who had entered the state illegally. For that reason alone, many of his countrymen were going to California. But Fernando had his heart set on a job in the oil industry, hopefully trading oil futures in Houston.

Various schemes were going through his head. Could he steal a wallet from a Hispanic US citizen? No, that would not work, as the Hispanic would report it stolen. If he killed someone, someone who looked somewhat like him, then the victim couldn't report it stolen. But Fernando could not make himself even think of such a horrible act.

But an opportunity came to him that solved his problem. One night, he and about fifty of his countrymen had bedded down for the night in a small gully just west of Laredo. Three pickup trucks drove up, and a bunch of Mexicans got out. At first he and some of his fellow travelers thought they were individuals like themselves who had recently crossed illegally into the United States and had stolen some trucks. They had witnessed this over the last week. But instead they turned out to be US citizens; they just happen to be of Mexican heritage. They had come to rob Fernando and the rest of the Mexicans sleeping in the gulley.

But what the twelve attackers didn't realize, because it was dark, was that there were fifty Mexicans in the gulley. And the other thing the attackers hadn't anticipated was that about a third of the Mexicans had guns that they had stolen from a gun store.

The entire incident didn't last long. Within a matter of minutes, all twelve of the robbers were dead. But before the last shot was even fired, Fernando immediately realized he had just been given the opportunity he so badly needed. He spotted one of the attackers that most resembled himself, and when that man was shot, Fernando immediately searched his jacket and pants for a wallet. Bingo! A Texas driver's license, about $200 in cash, and something called a Social Security card, which he would later learn was invaluable.

Then a fight broke out among the travelers as to who was going to take the three pickup trucks. Even if they crammed them full, including the beds, at most they could maybe take thirty people. Fernando did not have a gun, as some of the others did, so he did not have a strong negotiating point. As everybody was deciding who got to go in the pickup trucks, Fernando decided it was maybe best if he and Carla didn't go at all. Someone might have seen that he took the wallet. For weeks, he had witnessed attacks and stabbings among his fellow Mexican travelers. These were desperate times. There was a good chance that once the trucks had driven off, those with the guns would rob the others and throw them out. So they stayed behind.

The next day Fernando and Carla came to a small truck stop. They hung around the coffee shop. Fernando was looking for a special individual. But he was still nervous; he had heard of more killings and was concerned that the authorities might start making arrests. He watched the trucks that rolled in to find one that had Mexico license plates. Fernando calculated that anyone with Mexico license plates was probably driving produce from Mexico into the United States. He knew this was one of the biggest areas of trade between Mexico and the United States. The reason Fernando wanted to find a truck driver from Mexico is because that driver would obviously be returning to Mexico and could utilize Fernando's pesos. Pesos would be worthless to Fernando in Houston; they were worthless to him now.

He was now talking to the fourth truck driver that he had approached that morning, a Mexican truck driver who was going as far as Victoria, Texas. This was excellent because that was more than half the distance to Houston. Fernando had purchased a map, so now he knew what cities were between him and Houston. The truck driver drove a hard bargain, and Fernando had to part with almost all of his pesos. But the cab was clean, and the truck driver said he would allow both Fernando and his wife to ride in the cab with him. He was delivering onions.

Eventually, Fernando and Carla made it to Houston. Now it was time to put in the next phase of his plan. He found a small, dumpy, flea-bitten hotel on the edge of town and was able to negotiate $150 for a week. But before he could go on job interviews, he needed a suit. Fernando was happy he was going to get the full benefit of having learned English in high school.

He left Carla at the hotel, and after hitching a ride, he finally caught a bus to downtown Houston, where he thought it would be easy to find a man's clothing store. He was surprised by the lack of people he saw on the sidewalks. Sure, Houston was nowhere as big as Mexico City, but he understood it was one of the largest cities in the United States with a couple of million people. As he was contemplating this, he came upon a newsstand and spotted a *Houston Chronicle*. The headline read, "Houstonians Slowly Returning to the City". He read a bit of the article and learned that tens of thousands of Houstonians had fled in fear of a Mexican invasion.

As he was walking along Louisiana Street, he passed a bus kiosk that had ads plastered on all sides: MEN'S WAREHOUSE SALE—GET THREE SUITS FOR THE PRICE OF ONE—$150.

Fernando looked up at the sky and did the sign of the cross on his chest. "Thank you, Jesus. I know I'm going to love America." It'd been a year or so since Fernando had last purchased a suit, but $150 for three! When Fernando left the downtown Houston's Men's Warehouse, he had two dress shirts, three ties, several T-shirts, some stockings, a pair of dress shoes, and a beautiful suit, and he had only spent $235.

As Fernando rode the bus back to the hotel, he was so excited he could hardly sit still. Countless times over the last couple of weeks, he had thought that he and his wife would either be murdered or that they would starve to death. Even with the $1,000 in his underwear, they had gone for days when there had been no food at all, no matter how much he was willing to pay for it. Now he was in America. He was finally in America. He thought *finally* because there was a story that he had not even shared with his wife.

When Fernando had lost his job at the BMV, he'd decided that, with his college degree, advanced degree, and his incrediblly successful experience trading stocks on the Mexican Stock Exchange, he could easily find a job in America. But what he had found still shocked him to this very day.

The United States Citizenship and Immigration Services wouldn't grant him citizenship. The more he read and the more people he talked to, the more he learned that the United States' immigration policy was completely turned upside down. And this crazy policy wasn't just limited to people trying to enter the United States from Mexico; it was across the board. What he learned was people had a ten-times better—no, one-hundred-times better—chance of being granted citizenship in the United States if they were poor and uneducated.

It drove Fernando crazy. The most successful industrialized country in the world? Didn't the United States have the need to put to use those individuals in the world with the highest levels of education, experience, and knowledge? It wasn't like he was trying to become a citizen of Paraguay. Could it be that the United States had too many educated, intelligent individuals? No, that couldn't be. The only excuse that some of Fernando's better-educated friends could give him was that the department in the United States that determined the immigration policies was run by a bunch of liberals who weren't interested in making America more successful. Who were not interested in improving the standard of living in America. These liberals must have felt it was their job to take in the world's hungry and needy.

The US immigration department's unspoken motto was, "What's best for the individual applying for citizenship, not what's best for our country." As a once very successful businessman with a master's in finance, Fernando thought it was the stupidest policy he'd ever heard of. But who was he to argue with the most powerful nation in the country?

So here was Fernando, less than a year later, in America illegally. Because of America's crazy immigration policies, he had to break the law. But Fernando was not going to allow himself to be like the millions of Mexicans that had illegally crossed the border into America. He did not want the free handouts that so many millions had come for. He was smart and motivated, and for decades he had provided well for his family. He could do it again, and he wanted to do it again. He was excited to be in America and to have the opportunity. He had come to America to better himself, not to be a leech like so many of his countrymen.

When he arrived at the hotel that night, Carla had good news for him. She had been worried that he would not be able to get a job soon enough, and she knew that, with the money he had had to spend on new clothes, they only had a limited amount left. She had found a job as a waitress in a small Mexican restaurant that she could walk to. It was not much money, but it would at least pay for the hotel. Fernando was proud of her. He knew they would make it.

The next morning, he rose early and put on his new clothes, but not before he gave himself a haircut and a shave, which he had not had for almost a month. There was only one small, cracked mirror over the sink in the tiny bathroom. He took a look at himself stepped back and said loudly so Carla could hear, *"Guapo! Guapo!" Handsome, handsome!*

He was out the door, but this time he knew the bus lines and was able to catch a bus fairly close by. He did not want to scuff his new shoes. It did not take him long to find a library in downtown Houston, and shortly after that, he had the addresses for ten of the largest oil companies that had offices in Houston. His experience at PEMEX had taught him who all the major oil companies were in the United States.

For most of the rest of the day, he went to every one of the ten offices. But it was the same story at every office. In every single employment or human-resources department, he was told the same, sad story. Every single oil company, regardless of its specialty, was not only not hiring, they were laying people off. The plunge in oil prices in the last year was putting serious financial constraints on the entire oil industry.

Fernando was devastated. His dream and plans had seemed so perfect. What was he going to do now? What was he going to tell Carla? What were they going to do for food? Was he going to have to take a menial labor job—wait tables, or worse, dig ditches? It was almost four o'clock, and he was just wandering around downtown Houston in a state of depression.

He was almost afraid to go back to the hotel. The last month had been very hard on Carla, and he thought the bad news might just put her over the edge. He sat down on a small bench. Just when he thought he might break down and cry, he noticed a group of very smartly dressed young men leaving a tall office building that was directly across from where he was sitting.

Don't they look rich and successful? I wonder where they work, he thought.

Fernando looked up and saw the answer on the side of the building: MORGAN STANLEY.

He jumped to his feet like a lightning bolt had hit him. *The Morgan Stanley? The New York Stock Exchange Morgan Stanley?* Why hadn't he thought of this earlier? *This is even more perfect than working in the oil industry. I only worked in the oil industry a few months—I worked on the stock market for over twenty years!* he thought, smiling.

He strode across the street, found the floor for Morgan Stanley, straightened his tie, and walked in.

An hour later, he was back on the street, an employee of Morgan Stanley. As it turned out, Merrill Lynch had just made a raid on the Morgan Stanley office, and they had three empty offices. Just that very day they had started to interview for new brokers. They loved the fact that Fernando was fluent in Spanish. The Morgan Stanley Houston office was constantly trying to acquire more Mexican clients. It was a match made in heaven.

Even though Fernando was very experienced, they would require him to go through a month-long training program. He was hired on the contingency that he would pass the FINRA Series 7 exam. Then he would become a licensed, registered representative of Morgan Stanley. The job was commission only, but for the first six months, which would include the month of training, he would receive a draw against his future commissions of $5,000 a month.

What Fernando would never know was that in this very Morgan Stanley office, there was one additional empty office—it was that of Cliff Walther.

Chapter 122

Things could not have worked out better for the Morales family; their new life in Chicago was better than they had even imagined. Of course, their high-rise condominium couldn't compare to their spacious compound in Monterrey, but the restaurant and entertainment options in Monterrey paled in comparison to Chicago's. Alberto's wife, Maria, was finding shopping in Chicago to be an aphrodisiac. Their daughter, Gabrielle, and their son, Raul, had already made a good group of friends.

Alberto's successful brewery business in Mexico had made him a rich man. And though there was no need for him to work again, it was in his blood. He did not want to be compared in any way to those millions of Mexicans who had flooded into the United States the last couple of decades to suckle off the government's tit. He also didn't feel that simply driving brand-new Jaguars was enough of a separation. He wanted to be seen as a successful businessman.

Alberto had done some research, and it had become pretty obvious that even though he had decades of experience in the brewery business, the competition was fierce. The microbrew business in the United States had exploded in the last couple of decades, and downtown Chicago was littered with independent microbreweries. Alberto had stumbled on another opportunity, though—Mexican-style chocolate. He'd learned that Americans, especially those living in the cities, loved sweets, candies, and especially chocolate. But American-made and European-made chocolate was dramatically different from the chocolate made in Mexico. Mexican-style chocolate was stone ground; it was earthier, spicier, and made with less sugar, and thus less sweet and less creamy. Alberto had already found and purchased an old confectionery company and was feeling very confident that within the coming months he would once again be a successful businessman—but now an American businessman.

It was Saturday, and Maria and the kids had gone to the movies. It was a beautiful afternoon, and Alberto was on his second microbrew, which he was learning to love. He was sitting out on the porch overlooking Lake Michigan from their twentieth-floor penthouse. He had spent a lot of time the last couple weeks talking with their new friends and other business owners about the entire issue surrounding the US-Mexican border. He had now formed some of his own conclusions as to why for so many decades so many of his fellow countrymen had emigrated to the United States both legally and illegally. He saw the problem as threefold.

Though Americans complained that the rich had it too well, they had no concept of a true wealth-poverty disparity, when the United States and Mexico were compared. In Mexico, the concentration of wealth at the top was one of the highest in the world. Ten of the largest industries were controlled by just a few families. It was more like America in the days of the robber barons—Carnegie, Rockefeller, Mellon, Vanderbilt, and DuPont. Things had changed dramatically in the last hundred years in the United States, whereas they hadn't in Mexico. In Mexico, there was a proportionally small middle class, despite the fact that in the last couple of decades, the middle class had grown by leaps and bounds. The trickle-down theory had never worked as well in Mexico as it had in America. In Mexico, there was the well to do, and there was the poor.

Alberto thought to himself, *Mexico is a member of the G20 and ranks eleventh or twelfth in the world in gross domestic product. Why then do we still have so many poor—and no large middle class like the United States?*

He then remembered something else his friends had told him. Americans didn't think of Mexico when they thought of countries famous for what they produced—Germany and Japan for high-quality cars, France for cheese and wine, Japan and Korea for electronics, for example. When they thought of

Mexico, they thought of tequila, Kahlua, and beaches. Of course, Mexico's second-largest export was tourism.

And that created the second problem. There was a huge disparity between the poor in Mexico and the poor in the country that bordered it for two thousand miles, the United States. Alberto's friends quoted numerous studies that had compared the supposedly poor in the United States with the poor in countries around the world. In comparison, American's poor, defined as those at the lowest end of the economic scale, lived like kings. Even the poorest of the poor in America had the latest cell phones, owned cars and often homes—not to mention that they ate well and got free education ranked as some of the best in the world.

And then there was the third part of the problem: the huge social-welfare system in the United States. It was almost shocking, what percentage of the United States' budget was spent on social-service programs, welfare, and other entitlement programs. Compared to not just Mexico but many countries of the world, America was now considered a socialist country.

With the border that America has never taken seriously, how can anyone be shocked that over one million people every year cross into the United States illegally? Alberto thought.

The catapult, though, had been the decision of two presidents who'd made anyone from Mexico who was residing in the United States a legal citizen. That had opened the floodgates.

Alberto thought that he and his family were living proof. Alberto, a rich, successful industrialist, had left Mexico for America. If even a filthy-rich Mexican like himself was willing to break the law, it would make ten times more sense for some of his poorest fellow Mexican countrymen to do the same.

As Alberto was finishing his third beer, he found himself staring at a sailing yacht streaming by.

Wow, America is such a wonderful place. I think I'll buy myself one of those yachts.

Chapter 123

Fran Babicz marched into the presidential conference room in her typical, dykish fashion. As hard as she tried, and boy did she try, all those bright clothes and massive jewelry weren't going to hide the fact that God had not been kind to her at her birth. But that was no surprise; President Denton had a history of surrounding herself with women who were as unfortunate as she was. In fact, some rumored that President Denton was so portly that her suits and dresses were custom made by Bruno the Tent Maker. In comparison to President Denton, Fran Babicz was a goddess.

Babicz had a history of running presidential press conferences with an iron fist, but today she knew she would have to come out with both barrels loaded. Everyone in Washington already knew what the announcement was going to be, and as she looked out onto the Washington press corps, even the normally friendly, supportive faces of the liberal press wore a bit of disapproval.

"As I'm sure all of you can well imagine and appreciate, President Denton tried to do everything in her power to speak to you today herself. But as you can well imagine, with the events the last couple of weeks relating to the Mexican border, she is putting in eighteen-hour days doing everything physically possible to make sure that all Americans are safe."

Fran heard a few snickers from the audience.

"We're still compiling the statistics, and I think it will take us months if not longer to get the actual figures. And so I do not want to speculate today. But we now know that at least somewhere between four hundred thousand and eight hundred thousand Mexicans crossed the border illegally in the last month. The causes of this were plummeting prices of petroleum products in Mexico and, on a temporary basis, some challenging financial circumstances in Mexico. Both the Department of State and our president have been in close

605

communication with Presidente Nieto, and he assures us that both he and his government have taken emergency steps to reverse these temporary financial challenges completely.

"Today, President Denton announced that she is using her presidential powers to grant an immediate $100 billion in aid to Mexico, which will be in addition to our annual financial aid for Mexico. President Denton is completely confident that the financial challenges in Mexico will be so quickly reversed that the need for Mexicans to seek refuge in the United States will be completely exhausted."

There was more snickering, whereupon Babicz shot the entire audience a look that could kill. As many of the individuals of the Washington press corps had experienced, Fran's glare could make a person lose her lunch. But Babicz was elated. She had given them the totally false range of four hundred thousand to eight hundred thousand without anyone questioning her, much less laughing.

"President Denton feels that this entire border situation has brought to the forefront an issue that was originally the legacy of the Obama administration, an issue that President Denton has been trying to finalize during her first two years in office. You all know I'm speaking of the Obama presidential order to establish the Immigration Reform and Amnesty Bill. Tomorrow, President Denton will make history. She will issue an executive order that makes every individual residing in the United States an American citizen.

"We are confident, with last month's vacancy on the Supreme Court and President Denton's new appointment of Carmen Fernandez, that her order will be upheld. There will be only one limitation. Any individual of Mexican nationality or heritage that has a criminal record at a level-one felony, instead of being granted automatic amnesty, will go before a review board."

This time instead of snickering, there was dead silence. The word had already gotten out. Everyone in Washington knew that President Denton was going to take the levels of amnesty even beyond those of Obama. But no one had envisioned this broad, totally encompassing amnesty. Even though most of the liberal Washington press corps supported this move, they were still shocked by it.

"Before I conclude, I'd like to resolve a couple of issues. A number of times over the last couple weeks, some of you here today questioned the president's handling of the border issue, especially those of you from Fox News. I want to put those concerns to bed. At all times, the president and her staff were fully aware of even the minutest detail of what was taking place at the border. And though some of you accused the president of being dilatory or of procrastinating, I can assure you it was quite the opposite. Because of national security, I can't give you all the details. But working hand in hand with Presidente Nieto, the president handled this in an exemplary fashion, as I'm sure you will discover. President Denton has accomplished an incredible feat. We are confident that she, like President Obama, will be awarded the Nobel Peace Prize. Pressures and problems that have existed on the border for decades have all been resolved in just a month's time. Our country has fulfilled an obligation we have had since its birth. We have taken in hundreds of thousands of poor. That is our history. The president is proud of that history. I am proud of that history.

"With the legalization of all Mexicans now living in America, the president is going to use her authority to dismantle the US Immigration and Customs Enforcement agency, or ICE, which, as you all know, is the enforcement arm of the Department of Homeland Security, the entity responsible for rounding up illegal aliens working in this country. There will be a huge savings, since this department is no longer needed."

For the next forty minutes, members of the liberal press corps did everything they could to only ask questions that supported the president's position. It was easy. Babicz had provided them with the questions, as usual.

But there was that pesky Ed Henry. President Denton had specifically told Babicz to not answer any questions from anybody from Fox News. But this time, Fox News had arrived in power—there was not only Ed Henry, but also Mara Liasson, A.B. Stoddard, and Jonah Goldberg. They must've arrived early, because the four of them were shoulder to shoulder on the front row.

Every TV station in the country was represented. The cameras were rolling, and it was becoming painfully obvious that Babicz was avoiding the four of them. She finally decided that if she had to take one, she would take the safest route. She pointed at Mara Liasson.

Mara went right for the heart. "You said that the president's across-the-board amnesty was going to only exclude only one small, limited segment of the millions of illegal Mexicans now living in the country. You said that segment was those with a level-one felony record. Fox News has learned that the Mexican government is completely thrilled that so many Mexicans will be made citizens, specifically including thousands of felons. Mexico has issued a statement that all of their criminal records were recently destroyed by a raid from Zapatista. Therefore, the country will be unable to provide evidence of any criminal records whatsoever."

Babicz was an artist. She had been defending political leaders who were loose with the truth for a decade. It was an easy salvo to return.

"The president categorically denies such allegations."

Chapter 124

Elsie yelled at everyone in the driveway, "You all can finish packing the cars later. I have lunch ready."

The entire Walther family piled into the kitchen, grabbed a sandwich, some chips, carrots and a soft drink, and found a seat at the dining room table.

"Craig, I hope you appreciate my decision. I can't take you up on your offer to start now at UNM, or your wonderful offer to allow me to stay with you until I find a place. After twenty years at the border patrol, with Buck gone, I just feel I owe them something. I know it's going to be a real quagmire cleaning up after this mess. And as I know you can appreciate, all I need to do is stay there four months, and I will get my full twenty-year retirement and pension. I will give my notice as soon as I get back, and I should be able to start next fall at UNM."

"Frankly, I'm proud of your decision, Dave. It's just too bad that too many Americans don't take their jobs more seriously and feel more commitment to their work, even jobs they hate. UNM will still be here when you get back. And I did some reading last night, and with you being an immediate family member, I can get you in with in-state tuition on your first day."

Craig then turned his attention to his folks. "Are you sure you won't let me fly down and pick up Marcie? That's a long drive for you."

Bill Walther said, "Nope, we're committed. And as it turns out with all the mess, the Phoenix school district and ASU are going to shut school down for another two weeks. When we get home, Elizabeth is going to check on her house, and we're going to go and check on ours. Once we get everything secured and locked up, Elsie and I, Elizabeth, Madeleine, and little Ricky will have a wonderful little vacation, driving over to Baton Rouge to pick up Marcie. On the way back, we will stop in Houston and see what we need to do about funeral arrangements, shutting down the house, and a slew of things. I know I will have some questions, but I will give you a call from Houston."

After lunch, they all finished packing up the cars. Dave approached Craig. "Hey big brother, I hope it won't hurt your feelings. Jennifer offered to drive me to the airport in her car. And your car was so crowded on the way in."

For a split second, Dave was reminded that one of the reasons the car wouldn't be so crowded on the way back was because their brother Mark won't be making a return trip. But before he could get too choked up, he quickly changed the subject and pulled Craig slightly to the side so no one would hear.

"You don't mind... Would it bother you if I were to communicate with Jennifer when I'm in San Diego? She has been so wonderful, and she offered again to help me in selecting some classes.

Craig gave his younger brother a little hug. "No, quite the opposite. I'll explain it to you later. You would really be doing me a big favor, a very big favor."

Craig walked over to Katherine, who was helping Bill and Elsie load their suitcases in the back of the Range Rover. "I hope you don't mind that I asked you to wait to pack your car. I just wanted to get everyone else loaded up first—they've got a plane to catch. And even though I've heard everything has completely calmed down in Albuquerque..." He chuckled. "Can you believe it? No one can find the supposed couple hundred thousand Mexicans who recently entered the state. I guess I'll be writing a sequel to my book!"

Everyone continued to pack up while others were cleaning up the kitchen and making the beds. Craig heard a car honking and went back out into the yard. Jennifer and Dave were packed up, and both were in the front seats, about to drive away. He gave his brother a hearty handshake through the window and crossed around to the other side. He leaned in and gave Jennifer a big kiss. "You two kids be careful."

Craig went back into the house and found his father. "Dad, could you help packing up Madeleine's and little Ricky's things? I need to talk to Katherine for a second before driving you to the airport."

Katherine was in one of the bedrooms, removing all of the dirty linens and throwing them in the washing machine.

"Katherine, can you step on the back porch for a moment and let Madeleine finish that up?"

As they stepped outside Katherine said, "I'm about finished helping everyone else. It will only take me a few minutes. I'll get my things packed up, so we can all leave at the same time."

"That's what I wanted to talk to about. I thought maybe I could talk you into skipping packing up."

"You want me to stay the night?"

"I had something else in mind."

"What exactly did you have in mind?"

"I thought you might stay a bit longer."

Katherine came closer and put her arms around Craig, and she pulled his head down toward her shoulders. "I know this all must've been horrible for you. I never had any siblings, but I know you must be going through a lot of pain, losing two brothers in the same week. Sure, honey, I understand. I can stay longer."

Craig was nervous. No, Craig was scared. He was afraid he was not going to be able to say the words. "It's not just that. It's not just my brothers. Matter of fact, that's not it at all. I was thinking maybe...I was thinking maybe...Maybe you could stay *a lot longer*."

Katherine had never seen Craig short for words, much less acting insecure. This was a side of Craig she'd rarely seen. But she could tell he needed help. Craig wasn't a warm and fuzzy guy, but she liked where the conversation was going. "Well, Professor Walther, just how long did you have in mind?"

"Is 'a very long time' a sufficient answer?"

Katherine was about two steps ahead of Craig. She was going to play along with the game, and play it coy. "'Very long' is relative. What might be 'very long' for one person might not be 'very long' at all to another. Are we talking about to the end of the week? The end of the month? Are we potentially talking about till the end of the semester?"

This was making Craig feel very uncomfortable, and he did not like being uncomfortable. "Katherine, I can't play this game. First of all, I'm not very good at it, and secondly, I have to take my parents to the airport. Can I get you to agree that you will be here when I get back?"

Katherine relished the conversation, and she was not going to let Craig escape by running to the airport. "No. You started this conversation, not me. I want you to tell me exactly how long you meant when you said 'a long time.'"

The words just exploded out of Craig's mouth. "Forever! I want you to stay forever!"

Katherine knew the game was over, and she had won, but there was one last issue to clear up. "Is that your manly way of proposing to me? Because I might have once moved in without a proposal of marriage. But that day is gone. We don't need any more experimenting. No more trial and error. I'm ready. I've been ready for a long time. And I know you're ready. I want you to know that I know that. If I thought there was any true reluctance in your heart, I wouldn't push. I might even be willing to move in on a trial basis. But I know we are right for each other, and it's clear that you finally know that too. So let me make it easy on you. Yes, I will marry you, and I plan on living here for a very, very long time."

Chapter 125

The Old Ebbitt Grill located on Fifteenth Street in downtown Washington, DC, was the oldest bar and restaurant in the city, being originally established in 1856. It was a favorite haunt of both General Grayson and Secretary Hardwick, which was not surprising, since it had been a favorite bar for the powerful and famous of Washington for over a century. Hardwick loved it because he could get lost in one of the back booths away from peering and prying eyes. Grayson loved it because of the beautiful bar and the strong drinks. He and others from the Pentagon found if they showed up in uniform with a lot of brass and ribbons, they never seemed to pay for drinks.

This evening, the two of them specifically found a booth where there was no way they could see any television. They were both sick and tired of the president's announcement that she'd legalized every single Mexican living in the United States.

"I'm glad you called this meeting, Kurt. It's much needed. I've got a kitchen pass for the entire evening. Matter of fact, I'm planning on getting rip-roaring drunk, and I've already booked a room at the Hay Adams because I'm not planning on driving home tonight. I would suggest you do the same."

"John, I am a step ahead of you. I already booked a room at the Hay Adams! I figured we could have breakfast together before we drove home with our horrible hangovers. We can talk about anything you want, but I'm sick and tired of talking about the president legalizing the Mexicans. Let's see if we can stay away from at least that one subject."

"It's going to be hard. That was maybe the single stupidest decision ever made by our federal government, and it's going to affect just about anything and everything in this country. But I'll try.

"You know, I've been thinking about the NMZ we created. I think it's the smartest thing you've ever come up with. If you were dead, I'd nominate you for the Congressional Medal of Honor. One of the best things about the five-mile zone is that it stops all that nonsense about the wall."

Hardwick was interrupted by a waiter. They both barely looked up and just said, "We'll both have the usual."

The waiter responded with, "Let me see if I have that right, gentlemen. That's a Bombay Sapphire dry martini, straight up with two olives for the secretary and a double Gentlemen Jack whiskey sour for the general?"

Grayson finally looked at the waiter. "Tonight's on me, and I want you to just keep them coming. If my cocktail ever gets less than a third full, and there is not a backup waiting on the table...Well, let's just say, don't let it happen.

With that, the waiter scurried off.

"No, walls don't work," Hardwick continued. "But our NMZ is brilliant. But I guess that's not too surprising— the Korean demilitarized zone has worked perfectly since 1953 when it was constructed. It's half as wide as the one we just did in Mexico at only two and a half miles. But unlike our NMZ, the DMZ is only 160 miles long. And that's what scares me. I don't know if the liberals in Washington will do what it takes to maintain the NMZ. If they don't maintain it and, importantly, enforce it, it will do more harm than good. Currently the Korean DMZ is the heaviest militarized border in the world. I don't think we need anything like that on the southern edge of our new zone. We're talking about Mexico, not those crazy North Koreans. General Allison has proposed we completely eliminate the use of the air force from here forward. He suggested we use what the border patrol in Arizona is effectively using. It's the MQ-9 Predator-B Drone. Now somebody's just got to get Congress off their asses and get them to okay the funds. I think using the Predator drones will make the NMZ every bit as effective as the DMZ, as long as they use hundreds, if not thousands, of drones.

Grayson responded, "I can tell you this: if you leave it up to the citizens of the four border states, they'll do everything they can to keep the NMZ effective. After the invasion of those four states, I don't think there's going to be a citizen in the Southwest that's not going to lock every single door to his or her house for decades to come. You know, John, I've been thinking that Denton's refusal during this whole debacle to admit there was a problem at the border is synonymous with President Obama's refusal to admit that ISIS was a threat. That buffoon Obama stuck his foot in his mouth more times than even Jimmy Carter. Remember when Obama referred to ISIS as the junior varsity team, and just a couple months after his comment, they threatened the entire Middle East? My God, we've had some stupid people in the White House. But what would you expect when you elect a Muslim president?"

Hardwick said, "That narcissistic, self-centered socialist was more than I could take. The statistics show that he was on television something like five times more than any other president. Hell, someone could fart in South Dakota, and if he could turn it into a racial issue and run it up the flagpole, he would have a national press conference the very next day. You know the sad thing? His other famous statistic is that he and his family took more vacations than the previous three presidents had, combined. Ironically, if he had just stayed on the golf course 24-7, our country would've been a whole lot better off."

Hardwick took a hit on his drink. "I know you're the history guy, so I know you'll remember this story. I think most historians say that one of the biggest political blunders ever made by a politician was when Neville Chamberlain flew to Germany to meet with Hitler after he invaded Poland. Chamberlain came back and told the world that Hitler was no longer a threat and that he had no more aggressive intentions. But I think that, between Obama and President Denton and their complete refusal to admit the seriousness of the Muslim terrorists and the threats from the Mexican border, Mr. Chamberlain is probably smiling in his grave."

"You know, John, that 9/11 commission found that the hijackers who drove those planes into the World Trade Center towers and the Pentagon circumvented the immigration department. We've got to throw out every one of those morons over there and start over. I agree, if this country doesn't maintain the NMZ, the Mexicans will just go back to what they've been doing for decades—one million or more a year crossing the border. The sad reality is if Mexicans started voting for Republicans, the Democrats would run out and build a fifty-foot wall themselves!"

He slammed his hand on the table and chuckled. He lifted up his double whiskey sour and downed it. Just as he was thinking the waiter had let them down, the waiter arrived with new cocktails for both of them.

"Would you gentlemen like to look at a menu?"

Hardwick looked at the waiter. "We're just getting limbered up, my friend. By the time you bring me the menu, I want my eye sockets filled to the top with gin."

He downed his martini, grabbed his second one, ate one of the olives, and while he was still taking a drink, started talking again.

"I'm starting to feel good, and I haven't felt good since this crap at the border started. Frankly, I haven't felt good about my position in this country since that nimrod Obama got elected, and Rosemary Denton has just added insult to injury. But let's make a pact. I'd like to try to enjoy this evening to the max. Let's not bring either of their goddamn names up again. My wife is pleading with me, now that you and I have fixed the border problem, to resign. And I'm thinking very seriously about it. Denton is such a loose cannon, she's probably going to fire me again anyway. But isn't that how it always works? You're the history buff. Don't you agree with me?"

"Well, I probably wouldn't be much behind you, in terms of leaving. But I don't think President Denton can break Obama's record. In his first five years in office, Obama fired 197 senior military commanders." Grayson swirled his drink. "I maybe think the worst example ever of someone being thrown under the bus is when England voted Winston Churchill out of office just months after the Germans surrendered. My God, Winston Churchill? The man is credited as single-handedly saving England from complete annihilation by Hitler. It was he and Eisenhower who saved all of Europe. And it was Churchill who from the very beginning saw that Stalin was almost as big a threat as Hitler. And yet the country threw him out of office. How's that for a big, 'Thank you very fucking much!'"

Grayson finished the next drink but without worry, as he had already taken note of the backup sitting on the table. "And what about General Patton and General MacArthur? In my opinion, if you add those two to Winston Churchill and President Roosevelt, the four of them are probably eighty percent responsible for winning the entire war. And look what our country did to Patton and MacArthur. Truman threw them to the lions because they wouldn't kowtow to his political agenda. If Patton had been let loose with his third army, we may never have had a Berlin wall. And of course, if Washington had given in to MacArthur's demands to drive the Chinese back over the Yellow River, there may have never been any Korean War—or for that matter, any Vietnam War. Ultimately, the politicians always throw the military under the bus."

Grayson was now gnawing on the stem of the maraschino cherry out of his whiskey sour. "I didn't listen to the presidential press conference or the president's speech. I knew it would just make me throw up. But those who watched it at the Pentagon said you would think that the president and her staff had personally marched down to the Mexican border and closed it themselves. Not once was the air force, the US Army, or anybody at the Pentagon given one ounce of credit for the success we had in creating the NMZ. I'm sick and tired of it. Thirty years I've given my life to this country. You know, if you quit, I think I'll go with you."

The waiter arrived with another round of drinks and some menus. Hardwick brushed them off with his hands. "Don't give me those damn menus. I'm just getting the buzz, which means I couldn't focus if I had to. But we don't need them anyway. We will both take your thickest prime rib, medium rare, baked potatoes loaded to the top. And bring us both a Caesar salad to start." He looked over to Grayson to see if there was any argument.

"You got that perfect. Only one addition. Bring us some raw horseradish for the prime rib, and don't bring us any of that horseradish mixed with cream. That's for women and little girls." He turned to Hardwick and said, "There's nothing that'll clean out your sinuses faster than real, raw horseradish."

Hardwick slumped back into the booth and let out a long, exasperated sigh. "Kurt, I'm going to tell you something I've never told anybody. I've never told my wife, and frankly this might be the first time I've admitted it to myself. And maybe it's because I know I'm coming to the end of my service to this country and my work with fine officers like yourself."

A look came over John's face that in their decades of friendship Kurt had never seen. He thought for a second that John was going to tear up. But that was not his style. Grayson just took another hit on his drink, dug into the Caesar salad that had been served, and waited.

Hardwick took a couple bites of his salad and then began. "I'm tired. No, I'm sick and tired. And if it was just for myself, I could go to my grave a happy man. But I'm tired and frustrated for all those brave men that are buried right here in Arlington Cemetery. For all those brave men buried in those graveyards in Normandy, France. For all our soldiers, all fifty thousand of them, that are listed on the wall here in Washington at the Vietnam Memorial. And, of course, for all our brave military men who fought so bravely in Afghanistan and Iraq.

"I'm tired of the United States being the world's policeman. I should ask you—you're the military historian. I thought after both World Wars that not just the world but more specifically Europe would've learned their lessons. We both know that in both World Wars, if not for the will of the American people, the billions of dollars we spent, and the hundreds of thousands of American military lives we lost, everyone in Europe would be speaking German today. But they didn't learn a damn thing.

"Why was America forced to go into Korea? Were America's borders being threatened? Same question for Vietnam. I know, I know—it was to fight the spread of communism. But it's the same mantra the last twenty years in the Middle East. Except this time, as opposed to communism, it's radical Muslim terrorists. Don't get me wrong—I've supported every one of those wars. But what I'm sick and tired of is the United States basically having to go it alone every single fucking time."

Hardwick was starting to feel the booze, but his mind was a sharp as a tack. He only wished the waiter would bring the more substantial parts of the meal. Caesar salad did a shitty job of soaking up alcohol. But that was a funny thought; he was still drinking. That was one of the problems of drinking heavily as an intellectual. He ran into all kind of personal debates with himself.

"Let me ask you a question. Do you remember that skirmish we had with Gaddafi in Libya?"

Grayson was feeling his booze himself. He was so astonished by his boss's pronouncements that they were having a sobering effect. "Sure, John, I remember. And since I'm getting the drift of where you're going, let me be so bold as to finish your thoughts."

It was perfect timing. The waiter brought enough food to feed five people. The smile on Hardwick's face showed that, at least for the moment, he'd rather eat than talk, so Grayson continued.

"The United States decided to run airstrikes on Libya and try to take out Gaddafi. It was 1986 and the name of the operation was El Dorado Canyon. Muammar Gaddafi had gotten out of hand. His ties to Russia were getting more serious, and there were indications that he was making moves to create nuclear weaponry. It was one of Ronald Reagan's finest hours, and we both know he had many. Reports proved that Gaddafi and his terrorist organization were responsible for the attack in Berlin that injured 229 people. It was the last straw.

"Reagan ordered an airstrike. It was F-111s out of England. But the route the air force wanted to take had them fly over France. France refused to allow the United States to fly over its country to attack Gaddafi. It was a sad day for the world. The very country whose asses we'd saved, both in World War I and World War II, and they wouldn't allow us to fly over their country to take out one of the worst Muslim terrorists in the world.

"And since we're getting down and dirty, let me tell you what my opinion was when France made that announcement. Luckily, I wasn't the Chairman of the Joint Chiefs of Staff, or I might've rewritten history. Personally, I wanted to have our jets fly over France, and 'Oops, some bombs mistakenly dropped off our F-11's. Sorry about that, France. Sorry, no more Eiffel Tower— sorry, no more Arc de Triomphe, no more Notre Dame.' And yet, here we are thirty years later and still making kissy kissy with France.

"Which reminds me of the best quote of General Patton's, and he made a lot of them. He said, 'I'd rather have a German division in front of me than a French one behind me.'

"John, you know as well as I do in the last thirty years of the world's skirmishes and wars, that in almost every single one of them, America's pocketbook and our military personnel have had to carry ninety percent of the action. Hell, we both know the problem, and there's nowhere it's more obvious than in Europe. Those countries spend at best five percent of what we spend annually on our military budget. And who can blame them? They go around making lovey dovey with characters like Vladimir Putin and Bashar al-Assad, knowing all along if things get out of hand, once again the United States will come to their rescue. I couldn't agree with you more."

Hardwick looked up from his attempt to devour one very large prime rib to give Grayson a thumbs-up. His mouth was too full to respond. Finally, there were a few moments of respite.

While Hardwick was unable to speak, Grayson said, "I won't bore you, since I know it's your and my favorite quote about how we go out of our way to try to do everything we can to be anything but politically correct. But I think it's that very issue that is becoming the downfall of our country. I find myself these days referring to it as the 'Kumbaya American.' And since I've been using the term so much lately, I took the time the other night to look it up on the Internet. Now of course, skipping the definition that it is a song from the '60s sung by Girl Scouts and Campfire Girls, 'Kumbaya' is defined as 'a blandly pious and naïvely optimistic view of the future.' Another definition was 'a hippie-like, starry-eyed, mindless belief that all is good. Free love, an unrealistic goal to save the world.' And there was another definition: 'artificially covering up deep-seated disagreements. We "join hands and sing 'Kumbaya'" or "it's all 'Kumbaya'" means we pretend to agree, for the sake of appearances or social expediency.' It's the same mentality of that stupid Coca-Cola advertisement. I can't remember if it was from the '60s or '70s. You know, it was that scene of some hundred people from every nationality they could find all singing the song..."

Grayson was feeling the liquor. He actually started singing the song, but with a sarcastic sneer on his face. "'I'd like to sing a song in perfect harmony...'It's the same liberal, socialist crap that gets us in trouble and forces the military to come to the world's aid. 'Let's all be one big, happy family.' It's like the liberals never took any history courses. Ninety percent of all the college professors admit to being liberals, but what they really need to admit to is that they are socialists. I suspect anyone coming out of high school and college today doesn't know the truth. They probably think that Genghis Khan, Attila the Hun, and Hitler were just misunderstood, and with proper psychoanalysis, they could all have been great leaders. Remember how Obama kept trusting Putin, and then almost on a weekly basis Putin proved what a trusting fool Obama was? Frankly, most of us over at the Pentagon were enjoying watching Putin make a fool of our president."

Grayson decided it was time to cut into his prime rib before it got cold. He dipped his fork into the raw horseradish and then speared a big hunk of prime rib. It was only in his mouth a second before his eyes teared up. He felt like he was having lighter fluid flushed through his nasal passages. It took him almost a minute to regain his composure, and he let out a big gratifying, "Wow, that's great horseradish!"

Hardwick was still munching away, so Grayson continued. "I know, it's more than anybody can take. The liberals and metrosexuals have convinced everyone that you and I are dinosaurs and not to be trusted. Anyone over the age of sixty, anyone white, male, successful, or wealthy is an outcast. Just something like thirty or forty years ago, the American Psychiatric Association labeled homosexuals as deviants. Yet under pressure from liberals, now they label those very same individuals as engaging in a 'lifestyle choice.' You know, with this trend the courts will find that people sleeping with sheep and marrying them is equally okay—it's just a lifestyle choice. It's the same thing that drives our entitlement programs. 'People shouldn't be disadvantaged or have any less because they're too lazy to work—it's a lifestyle choice.'"

He paused. "I haven't thought of that 'Kumbaya' song since I was in Cub Scouts. But I think we've hit the nail the head. It is a complete change in America's mentality. Anything goes. If it makes you feel good, it must be okay. We've got legalized gambling in most of the states in the country. More and more states are legalizing the use of marijuana, and I suspect if this trend continues, Las Vegas will not be the only places where prostitution is legal. It's a very slippery slope that we're going down."

Hardwick was doing his best to finish his baked potato. But there was only so much room, and no upright, substantial American went to the old Ebbitt's Grill without saving room for the chocolate-chip bread pudding with bourbon sauce.

"The political system in America is broken," he said. "Barely fifty percent of Americans vote, and most of those don't even know who they're voting for. The problem is we put too much power in the hands of the president. And therein lies the problem—every four years America elects another god. And then the voters go back to what they do best, nothing. It's funny you mentioned sheep earlier. That's exactly what the American voters have become, blind sheep being led to the slaughter by the politicians."

What had been a wonderfully enjoyable evening was becoming a bit morose. What was supposed to be an evening celebrating their success on the Mexican border was slowly evolving into a bout of depression. It was depressing for two great Americans to see so many decades of their hard work, and that of thousands of great Americans before them, get flushed down the toilet. So they both ordered the chocolate-chip bread pudding and a couple of glasses of port, trying to finish the evening on a positive note.

With bourbon sauce dripping off his chin, John Hardwick said, "You know it's sad that roughly 2,500 years ago, Plato wrote out the perfect formula for government. That was one smart Greek philosopher. It was around 400 BC that he wrote his famous treatise, *The Republic*. In it he wrote out the model for a perfect democratic government. He called those individuals who would govern, 'Guardians of the State.' What a great phrase, what a great title. Isn't that what it really should be about? Our elected officials should be all about protecting the state and its citizens.

"Plato even recognized 2,500 years ago that you couldn't leave the decision of who would rule the country up to either the people or the individual himself. The people, the masses, didn't have the wherewithal to decide what the best qualifications were for the country's leaders. And Plato recognized that you sure couldn't leave it up to the powerful politicians, just as it is today. They only care about power and money. So in the republic Plato laid out, not just anybody could run for office. This is opposite in our country today; we only have two criteria for running for president. Isn't that amazing? The most powerful position in the entire world, and there's only two criteria: you have to be a natural-born citizen and you have to be over the age of thirty-five. That's it, that's fucking it!

"But Plato was smarter than that. He said that a person must go through a regimented study program and indoctrination into the history and philosophy of governing people. Only after decades of study and testing would a person even be a potential candidate to serve as one of the country's Guardians of the State. He even addressed the issue of conflicts of interest, requiring that all elected candidates would have their entire estate put into trust so there could be no conflicts of interest. Yet here we are, 2,500 years later, and the process we go through to elect our leaders is a complete joke. Patrick Henry was right, and he was right to boycott the 1787 Continental Convention. One of the greatest American patriots refused to participate. Patrick Henry sensed the problem we now have today—too much power in Washington, too much power in our elected officials."

At this point Hardwick was beyond commenting. But he was so thoroughly enjoying the history lesson from his best friend, Kurt Grayson, that he sank even further into the cushy cushions at the back of the booth, only keeping himself upright enough to keep from spilling the second glass of port.

Grayson was on a roll, the sugary, buttery bourbon sauce having given him a sugar high. "It's amazing. Most every time I find myself having a couple of drinks and worrying relentlessly about the future of our country, it seems that I always find myself quoting Thomas Jefferson. Basically Jefferson said that a true democracy will never work in America, because a true democracy is based on two premises: one, that the electorate is intelligent and, two, that the electorate is fully informed.

"But after this much drinking, I don't think it's best I rely on my memory." Grayson reached into his left breast pocket but mistakenly pulled out his wallet. He put it back and reached into his right breast pocket and pulled out a smallish, worn leather notepad. "I keep this book of quotes handy for when I unluckily find myself stuck in a conversation with some liberal. Let me give you a sampling. The first few are by Jefferson:

"'An educated citizenry is a vital requisite for our survival as a free people.'

"'The man who reads nothing at all is better educated than the man who reads nothing but newspapers.'

"'The cornerstone of democracy rests on the foundation of an educated electorate.'

""'No nation is permitted to live in ignorance with impunity.'"

Grayson took a deep drink. "Now let me finish with two from one of my favorite, more contemporary writers, George Bernard Shaw:

"'Democracy substitutes election by the incompetent many for the appointment by the corrupt few.'

"'Democracy is a device that ensures we shall be governed no better than we deserve.'"

Grayson continued, "I think that pretty well sums up my original interpretation of Jefferson. We have a voting public that is anything but intelligent. And even if they were intelligent, they don't care. Surveys have shown that the vast majority of Americans, regardless of who is in the White House, can't even name the vice president. And when it comes to being informed, even though today we are bombarded with news 24-7, instead of being fully informed, we are misinformed because the liberal press has an agenda that doesn't include the truth."

Secretary of Defense John Hardwick propped himself up, leaned completely across the table, and held forth his last sip of port as a measure to toast the chairman of the Joint Chiefs of Staff, Kurt Grayson.

"I think you may be missing the most appropriate quote of all. And to the best of my recollection, it was from somewhere around 1970, in the cartoon strip *Pogo*: 'We have met the enemy and he is us.'"

I designed this cartoon in 2008
amazingly, my prediction came true.

Mr. Schulz brings a powerful and distinctive resume to the world of fiction. At age 62 he has had a string of fascinating and successful careers, with an emphasis on finance, criminology, and litigation. His first book, ***Brokerage Fraud: What Wall Street Doesn't Want You to Know***, was an acclaimed study of the underbelly of Wall Street.

Mr. Schulz's credentials and lifetime experiences have given him special insight into the myriad of issues surrounding not only the US-Mexico border, but the Country of Mexico itself. Mr. Schulz is a fiscal conservative, which we hear too little from in our country today. He is referred to by those who know him well as a modern day Ayn Rand. His first political thriller, Just When You Thought It Was Safe, is likened to Atlas Shrugged; where Ms. Rand was successful in thoroughly entertaining the reader while at the same time instilling a unique perspective on what is right and wrong with America.

Discover more about Mr. Schulz
at
http://douglasschulz.net